THE MARTYR'S BLADE

Joel Manners

The Martyr's Blade

By Joel Manners

This book is available in print and electronic format at most online retailers.

Cover art and map by Joel Manners

ISBN 978-0-9972594-0-7

Colquhoun Books
2704 Pruett St.
Austin, TX. 78703

www.JoelManners.com

For

Christie.

Who encouraged

and supported

and allowed

and read

and read

and read

and read

and read

and read

and read

and read some more

and even explained about prepositions

and was mad when he died

and let me type in bed

and

shared

this

journey

with

me.

Part One

PART TWO

N
High
Ironback Mountains
Sliabh Log
Twin Pines
Kuray
Dún
Caomhnóir
Rathad an Chuaidh
Abhainn Albyn
Irongate
Glen Walden
Greywater River

Mountains
Highward Tor
Mt. Dorn
Nóinín Cnoc
Dolich
Blockley
Toireadh Cnoc
Newbridge
Lough Laith
Bandirma
Littleford
Greymouth
Rathad an Siar
Abhainn Albyn
Abhainn Fuar
Inner Sea

Part One

Sliabh Mór

A deep Voice stirred in the vast space of the room. "I am glad to see you safely returned."

"The journey was… harder… than I expected," the Lady spoke softly, her gaze lost far beyond the fire. "I had forgotten how long it was. Are we too late?"

The Priest shifted his heavy robes as he turned to allow the warmth of the fire to seep in, and the cloth steamed gently in the heat. A kind smile crossed his face as the firelight made a glowing halo of his wispy, grey hair. "You are in time, never fear. But what was mere caution when you departed has become a much more urgent need."

The fire popped and a log settled amongst a shower of sparks while the Priest gathered his thoughts. Usually he found great comfort in the massive stone walls and pillars of this room. A sturdiness surrounded the chairs, rugs and tables arranged around the fireplace for the honored guests of the Mountain. But tonight, the shadows of the room felt deathly cold, and stretched eerily from somewhere far beyond the walls.

He re-adjusted his robes against a chill that would not lift, no matter how close to the fire he stood.

"There has been violence in the north, near a town named Dolieb. Farms burned and temples razed. Many are dead," the Priest sighed dejectedly, turned to the fire, and held his hands outwards to warm them. "And Lord Lucious sends word that he cannot bring the marauders to justice."

"Lucious is an irritating and useless lordling, but he should be able to defend his people against bandits or the like." The Lord was not pleased with Lucious. The Priest saw that the Lady also looked concerned, but her expression held more compassion for the victims than anger at those who let it happen. Her gaze remained on the Priest as she waited for the rest of the story, for she knew that no hinterlands raid could be cause for their urgent summons to the Mountain tonight.

Only the Knight seemed unaffected by the news. His face was hidden deep in shadow, although the Priest knew it would be unreadable even if it were bathed in midday sunlight. The Priest wondered if the Knight already knew what was about to be revealed. The Knight usually did.

"We sent someone to see what she could discover." The Priest turned and let the heat of the fire play across his back.

The Lord's boots scraped against the stone floor as he shifted, his hands at rest on the pommel of the massive steel hammer he carried at his side. His deep voice brought echoes from the stones that vaulted the chamber. "Not bandits."

"No, unfortunately not," the Priest glanced up to meet the furrowed gaze of the Lord. "The temples were not just ransacked. They were desecrated. The people not just killed. Sacrificed."

The Lady sat forward. "Sacrificed? In what way?"

The Priest picked up an iron to poke at the logs in the wide fireplace before answering. Sparks swirled in the flames with each jab. His gaze was lost in the blaze, and when he spoke his voice was cautious, and quiet.

"Ancient ways. I am told that in the archives there are mentions of rituals like these from long ago."

"Some cult perhaps? Could they have revived these rituals?" The Lord's armor creaked as he thoughtfully stroked the thick braid of his black beard.

The gesture brought a fond smile to the Priest's face as he suddenly saw once again a young knight, who even then towered over his peers, but thin and gawky instead of the broad and powerful man before him now. Even as a youth, the Lord boasted the same bristling beard. He now tamed it with dozens of leather ties, but the smoothing gesture remained the same. The Priest had seen it on battlefields, as the Lord stood amongst smoke and fire, on riverbanks as the Lord waited for a tug on his fishing line, and on farms as the Lord readied to pull a stump from the ground.

"It could be worse than that," the Priest's smile faded as he continued. "There is an ancient, dark thought that clings to my mind like a forgotten shadow. It has grown stronger as the months have passed."

The Voice spoke again, a rumbling noise that echoed in the vast stone room. "I have seen it. An abyss of darkness. Eyes that search from its depths."

The Priest nodded his head, still looking at the fire. "Yes."

The Lady rested her gaze on the long bundle on the table in front of her. "So you sent me to retrieve this."

"Yes." The Priest paused as he waited for guidance from beyond the great stone doors in the far wall of the chamber, but the Voice remained silent for now. The Priest absently ran his fingers over the small silver medallion that hung around his neck. With a deeper breath the Priest straightened and met the eyes of each of the other three before continuing. "I am afraid that this is not some cult, but rather something much more ancient, returned from story and nightmare."

"You mean the Crunorix?" the Lord asked. "I thought them wiped out centuries ago. Did not Ruric kill the Nameless King?"

"Yes," the Lady answered, "and Ruric's knights sealed the Nameless King's magi inside the Black Grave, and a watch was placed over the site. At least, that is what my Old Nan used to tell me."

The Lord laughed, a booming bellow that filled the stone vault above them. "As did mine."

The Lady smiled, teeth white against her dark skin, and she extended a long leg clad in soft riding leathers to bounce an unseen child on her lap. "I can see it now," she teased in her rich accent that always made the Priest think of cinnamon, "do not fear, little lord, King Ruric triumphed in the end, evil is gone."

"My nanny always favored the Martyr but yes, that is what we are told," the Priest said. "And yet, I am also told that these rituals are mentioned in Beledain's *Codex Necronix*, and it is claimed that Beledain journeyed to Fellgate Castle and had access to its archives before the Fellgate was buried."

The Lord's face grew somber. "So it really is fuil crunor."

"But where would they have learned such rituals? And who are they? And why use them to desecrate temples in the north?" asked the Lady.

"They search," rumbled the Voice. "They sense the power that I hold. They seek it."

"And they must not find it." The Priest's voice was strong, defiant. It flashed around the circle. "They will not find it."

The Priest moved to the table and rested his hand on the bundle the Lady had placed there, peeling back a corner of the blanket that wrapped its long shape, until his fingertips touched the metal beneath. Then, as if addressing the heavy bundle before him, he spoke to the others.

"My lady, I am afraid that you cannot give up your burden just yet. If the Crunorix have truly returned, we may need its power to defeat them once again."

The Lady nodded agreement, rose from the chair, and smoothed the soft fabric of her long coat before answering. "I shall do it gladly." She laid a gentle hand over his where it rested on the bundle.

"And what of me?" The Knight spoke from the shadows of the room.

The Priest turned to look at the Knight. Most of him was hidden in the vast shadow cast by the Lord. All the Priest could see was a pair of long legs, clad in simple, threadbare leggings still splashed with mud from his recent journey.

"You must discover who resurrected the fuil crunor rituals." The Priest's voice grew sad and hushed. The dark void in his thoughts loomed ever-present, a coldness that felt like… nothing. An absence. He had never felt the like before, and it unnerved him. If the emptiness was linked to those who were resurrecting these fuil crunor rituals, then he was asking these three to place themselves in great danger.

"Give me a day or two," the Knight said wryly.

"You are getting slow in your old age. It's just all of the hinterlands." The Lord hooked his thumbs into his belt and grinned ferociously, and the Priest was once again thankful for the friendship that had bound this group together for so long.

The deep Voice rumbled into booming laughter that filled the room. A smile flashed across the Lady's face at the sound, for she had not heard it in this room for too long. The Priest watched her and saw her weariness melt, leaving behind a stunning beauty of raven hair and golden eyes, and his sadness lifted as well.

As the cavernous laughter faded, the Voice spoke again. "It is pleasing to have my faith in you rewarded so often."

A smile played across the Priest's round face. "Now your speed must be put to the test."

Torbhin

The small town crouched in the foothills astride a stream that flowed so swiftly into the valley below that it never froze, even in the bitter depths of harsh winter. The dense forest pressed on all sides, but the thick fir trees did nothing to stop the winds that flowed from the stark High Fell mountains. Snow poured onto the buildings and streets where it piled into enormous drifts, or was churned to a thick, icy mud by the boots and hooves of the town's denizens.

A single road led to the town, a steep, winding track barely wide enough for the carts that creaked and slid their way along it, heavy with the pelts and gold dust that kept the town alive.

It was named Dolieb, although who or what a "Dolieb" had been… no one now knew. A sturdy palisade surrounded the town, its rough, wooden stakes driven into the frozen earth, capped with spikes and watch platforms. Like all towns in Albyn, the Queen's treasury provided for a town guard and the maintenance of the crude fortifications. Here in the north, those defenses stood a constant vigil against the creatures who dwelt in the forest and the mountains above it.

This winter, Dolieb was crowded with men. The inns were packed with them, small groups shoulder to shoulder around the tables, dressed in thick wool cloaks and heavy boots. The locals stayed away from them, for they looked dangerous, armed with broad-bladed swords and accompanied by the heavy clink of steel shifting underneath their tunics when they walked. Newcomers to the town were traditionally victims of the locals, fresh money that begged to be taken, but as the taverns and alleys of Dolieb filled with these new visitors, even the hardest of the locals learned to cross the street and get out of the way.

As dusk fell on another grey day and snow began once again to cascade from the sky, one of the newcomers hurried down the main road and into the sea of icy mud and dirty snow that was the town square. On the other side of the open area he spotted a low-slung building made of cut timber. Above its door hung a sign that featured a faded painting of a large bird in flight, carrying an arrow in its beak. Apparently the sign's painter had only second-hand knowledge of what a duck looked like, but under the painting the words "The Lucky Duck" were carved into the wooden board.

Torbhin entered the tavern and shook the snow from his cloak. The room was crowded, thick with the smell of a bubbling brown stew and hazy smoke from the fire, but damp as well, and the walls glistened with chill moisture that the blaze in the center of the room could never quite reach. A low rumble of conversation welled and waned, and a slap followed by a quick peal of good-natured laughter tumbled through the crowd as one of the men at the tables was rejected by the tavern-keeper's daughter. And yet, the room was quiet for being so crowded. The men here were not drunk or boisterous. They were serious, and the few locals left in the place took their cue from the visitors and kept quietly to themselves in a small cluster at one end of the room.

Torbhin picked his way between the crowded benches to the back of the room, where the man he was to meet waited.

Neither man said anything as Torbhin gratefully slid onto the bench and sipped the still-steaming drink that waited for him. Torbhin had not seen his companion in years, and although he looked travel weary, Torbhin realized that he had not changed at all. He was not a huge or powerful man. He was tall, but lean, and his face was weathered and thin, with a sharp nose and lines etched from years of wind and sun. He was unshaven, and Torbhin saw that the few days' worth of whiskers he bore were streaked with grey, and his shaggy hair was more iron than brown. But for all the wear his companion bore, he had a steely strength in his long legs and shoulders that belied his thin frame and threadbare clothes. Torbhin's companion had just completed an arduous journey through the winter wilderness, yet looked, if anything, more at ease than Torbhin did.

His companion watched Torbhin from across the table. Leaning against the wall, he indicated the crowded room. "I see you got my message. How many men have arrived so far?"

Torbhin pushed back his hood and brushed the last of the snow from his leggings as he answered. "Almost three hundred, and that again expected within days. I emptied every temple between here and Kuray."

"Good. Did anyone make a fuss?"

"No sir, not really. A few of the priests complained about leaving their temple unguarded, but most of the soldiers were happy to take the field, despite the weather," Torbhin answered. "It was mostly just grumbling, and your letter took care of that."

The two men were silent for a moment as Torbhin watched his companion let his gaze wander amongst the murmur and rumble of the packed room.

"Does this have anything to do with the murders?" Torbhin asked after a moment. "The ones at Crevan Combe farm, and the temple at Tapa Beck?"

His companion gave Torbhin a questioning glance. "You know of the murders?"

Torbhin nodded silently and suppressed a smile, trying to remain as calm as the older man. "Of course," was all Torbhin said, but he was secretly pleased to have surprised him.

"What have you heard?"

"Only that everyone was killed, so no one really knows what happened," Torbhin admitted. "But the rumors tell of Korrigans, or the victims consumed by some terrible beast."

"Do you think any of that is credible?" Torbhin's companion leaned forward and swirled the wine in his cup as he watched Torbhin's face.

"No, of course not."

"What good would an army be for finding a murderer, in any case?"

"Very little, I would think," Torbhin ventured. "I could track him with no problem…"

"There you are then."

Torbhin sipped from his cup to stop himself from blurting out more questions. Experience had given him the patience of a stone, and he knew he would learn nothing more this night. Years of Torbhin asking questions had never convinced his old tutor to divulge information prematurely.

"Tell me, have the others I mentioned in my message arrived?" his companion asked.

"No, only the men I have summoned here."

"If they do not arrive tonight, I need you to go south in the morning to search for them. I am heading north. Follow with the rest of the men as soon as you can."

Torbhin finished his drink in a long swallow and the remaining heat and the alcohol warmed his throat on its descent. Torbhin stood and replaced his hood, and his face vanished once more into the comfortable shadows. "Then, Sir Killock, I will see you in the mountains."

***

Torbhin waited on the road for the party to draw near. All around him the deep forest stood silently under the thick blanket of snow. He pulled his cloak tightly around him, thankful for its warm wool and thick fleece lining. This far into the north, the winter air was cold even to an Albainn like him.

At daybreak he had ridden south along the winding track to search for the two travelers mentioned in Killock's message. He spotted the group as it made its slow way from the valley below him. He caught only glimpses of them through the thick trees, but the thud of their horses' hooves and the jingle of their harness carried clearly through the frigid air.

He stamped his boots to keep his feet warm as he waited. The black wool and brown leather of his cloak and clothing, which usually allowed him to blend so easily into the wilderness, contrasted harshly with the snow-whitened forest.

Still, he considered, *better not to surprise a Templar if you can help it.*

Torbhin had ample time to think as he waited, for the party's progress up the hill was slow as they struggled to follow the trail under the fresh pack of snow. It was strange to meet one Templar in the wilderness, but at least Sir Killock belonged here in the wild, far more at home than at any court or temple. But two? If Lord Bradon was in the approaching party, as Killock's message had indicated, two of the Temple's most powerful guardians were as far into the wilderness as you could get and still be able to call it Albyn.

And as instructed, Torbhin had emptied every temple in northern Albyn of its knights and soldiers and sent them all to Dolieb. *It makes no sense.*

So Torbhin waited patiently on the forest road as the group drew near.

The party was not as large as Torbhin expected. Killock's message read "Lord Bradon will be escorting the Lady Danielle d'Lavandou" and Torbhin assumed that a Templar traveling with a noble lady would command a fearsome escort of knights. But the group approaching numbered only a dozen or so horsemen.

Perhaps a Templar is escort enough, Torbhin decided. The group was certainly well-enough armed. Torbhin could see that the horsemen carried broad swords and heavy axes, and the steel of their helms and armor was obvious despite their thick coats and cloaks. Torbhin saw the massive shape of Lord Bradon as he rode at the head of the small column. The Templar's powerful form dwarfed both the horse he was riding and the smaller rider next to him.

As they moved within bowshot, two of the riders spurred forward at a trot, their horses blowing and snorting clouds of steam as they stamped through the snow. Torbhin flipped back the corner of his cloak to show the steel medallion of the Temple that he wore as a brooch and raised his hand in greeting.

"Who are you, friend?" challenged the rider, glancing at the brooch on Torbhin's chest. The rider bore a crescent of tattooed dots around his left eye, and a long sword with an elegantly engraved pommel in the likeness of the Queen's arms, a stag's head with an emblazoned shield of silver and black. Torbhin was surprised to see that the rider was young, hardly older than himself, for the sword was a weapon Torbhin expected to be in the hands of a knight of the Queen's guard, and the tattoos to be on the face of a seasoned veteran of the western frontier.

"My name is Torbhin. I have been sent to find Lord Bradon and act as his guide."

The rider turned slightly and called down the road, never letting his eyes leave Torbhin. "M'lord, this man says that he has been sent to find you."

Snow flew from the hooves of his horse as Bradon spurred forward to join the two soldiers. He eyed Torbhin from under shaggy brows, his black beard streaked white with snow.

"Sent by whom?" Lord Bradon's voice was harsh, and Torbhin realized that the entire group was on edge. There was something more going on here, for no party such as this should have been so wary of a single man on the road, even this far into the wilderness.

"Sir Killock."

"Killock? You have seen him recently?"

"Yes, m'lord, last night, in the town that lies up this valley. He asked me to find your party and guide you to him."

Bradon frowned at Torbhin and leaned back in his saddle, which creaked dangerously. The Templar regarded the ranger and thoughtfully stroked his braided beard as thick puffs of breath wisped into the morning air. Then he came to a decision and leaned forward to tower over Torbhin.

"Fine, lead on."

Torbhin bowed his head briefly, collected his horse, and retraced his path up the valley.

Bradon moved next to him, and the two rode together without speaking. Torbhin was patient in his silence, and submerged himself in the world around him. He had no real desire to speak with Lord Bradon, and although Torbhin could feel questions attempting to boil out of the Templar, they both knew he could answer few of them, if any.

As they approached the town, Lord Bradon returned to the riders and Torbhin heard the rumble of his voice as he talked with the small rider Torbhin had seen earlier. Torbhin assumed she must be the Lady Danielle, and he was very curious to see her. He had heard her name several years ago while training in Bandirma with another ranger, who swore that Lady Danielle was the epitome of nobility and beauty. Torbhin risked a short glance backwards, but there was little to tell from the figure huddled in her thick cloak at the front of the group, her face masked by the ermine lining of her hood. Torbhin saw she rode her horse easily and in the Albainn fashion, not side-saddle as he had seen noble ladies do, and she breathed air as a mortal would, sending small puffs of vapor into the chill air around her hood.

Once through the gates, Bradon remained close to his guide as they wound through the narrow, winding streets of the town. The wooden buildings pressed on all sides, their upper floors looming over the street, often leaning against the buildings on the other side. The streets passed through and around the buildings and created a bewildering maze, especially now that the roads and passageways were tangled with the soldiers and supplies that Torbhin had mustered here.

But the crowd moved aside as Lord Bradon shouldered his way forward, his jutting beard and shaggy hair towering above all but the largest of the warriors who waited in the town. The locals retreated as well, quickly imitating the gestures of respect that these fierce strangers gave to the Templar.

Torbhin led them to a suite of rooms in the center of town that had attached stables and a common room spacious enough to house Bradon's entire escort. The soldiers tended to the horses and carried the packs inside, while Torbhin patiently watched Bradon appraise the rough lodgings. The rooms were simple, but the walls were well-caulked against the cold, and the furniture looked solid enough to sit on. Rare luxuries this far from civilization.

Bradon appeared satisfied. Soon, a roaring fire blazed in the main room, and servants scurried with buckets of hot coals to warm the other rooms. As Torbhin slowly unwrapped his cloak and settled his bow against the wall, Lady Danielle emerged from the room she had chosen.

"Is that wine I can smell simmering?" Lady Danielle asked hopefully, her accent rich and exotic to Torbhin's ear. "Maker, please let it be wine."

Torbhin found it challenging not to stare. Although Lady Danielle was dressed plainly in leather leggings and tunic, a mail jacket of steel rings and a fur-lined cloak, she still radiated a noble grace and beauty. Her movements were long and supple and made him think of silk, not steel and stiff leather. She was long-legged and full-breasted, and her noble blood showed in her dark skin and in her smooth raven hair, which reflected a dark glow from the firelight despite being swept back into a peasant's simple braid.

"It is indeed wine," Lord Bradon answered, and Lady Danielle took a cup of the steaming drink from him with a grateful smile. "I believe the girl said that it was full of spices. Which ones, I am not so sure. Perhaps all of them, judging from the taste."

"It tastes wonderful," Lady Danielle assured him. "And it is warm. And the aroma is… striking."

Bradon's bellowing chortle filled the room. "I am glad you are so forgiving. Welcome to the hinterlands."

"Not at all," Lady Danielle chided the Templar. "Everyone has been very kind and welcoming. They even left an ice pick next to the water jug in my room. Very thoughtful."

Torbhin glanced beside him as the Captain of the Lady's escort moved next to him. With a smile the Captain tilted his head to indicate Lady Danielle. "It has not been so terrible an assignment."

***

On the morning of the second day after the arrival of Lord Bradon and Lady Danielle, the column of Temple soldiers departed the village and followed Sir Killock's marked trail into the hills to the northwest. The small bag of silver coins that Killock had given to Torbhin was sadly empty, but it had pried enough food, supplies and pack horses from the villagers to serve the Temple's requirements.

As the company rode through the north gate of Dolieb and across the small ford, the townsfolk gathered to watch them go, crowding the alleys and rooftops as they passed. From a small hill on the other side of the ford, Torbhin looked along the long line of soldiers as they wound their way across the narrow valley. In the end almost five hundred had joined them, soldiers and knights from every temple within a week's travel.

Torbhin rode at the fore of the column, as his trained eye could most easily distinguish the familiar signs Killock used to mark their path. Behind him rode Lord Bradon astride his black warhorse. Bradon wore a shirt of heavy steel scales and a thick black bear pelt as a cloak, having won it the night before from a local trapper who dared challenge Bradon to a contest of strength. From his belt hung his mighty steel hammer, and Bradon rested his hand upon it like a talisman as he rode.

Next to Bradon rode Lady Danielle, garbed in a jacket of fine steel rings under her hooded cloak, upon whose saddle was fastened a long, broad-bladed sword. The sword was sheathed in a plain scabbard and its hilt was wrapped in rough cloth, and Torbhin wondered if it concealed precious stones or rare metals from prying eyes. It was a strange sword to bring on such a journey, for it was nearly as long as a great cavalry sword, and would be awkward for her to wield.

Behind the Lady rode Alistair, the Captain of Lady Danielle's guard, hand-picked by Lord Bradon. Captain Alistair had traveled with Bradon to Dolieb, and looked every bit the soldier. Powerful through the chest and arms, Alistair nevertheless moved easily and with a grace normally not seen in large men. Even his face was muscular. He had a square jaw, a nose with a prominent ridge, strong cheek bones and a heavy brow, and his eyes watched everything. Alistair was clean-shaven, and his dark hair was cropped brutally short under his helm. Under his winter cloak he wore a breastplate made of bands of steel over a tunic of steel rings and rigid leather, but the Captain bore it with ease and seemed more at home in it than if it were a cloth tunic.

Torbhin knew that the Captain had served for many years in the west, for he had adopted some of the customs of the clans of the Ironback mountains. A spiral of dots was tattooed around his left eye, each one representing an honorable foe defeated in single combat, and both of his arms bore a tattoo of a dragon circling from his shoulder to the back of the hand where the dragon's head lay, jaws agape.

Torbhin knew that the dragons represented a reward from the mountain gods for overcoming some extraordinary challenge or trial, and supposedly gave the bearer mystical strength and savagery in combat. Only a shaman could tattoo them on a warrior, in a ritual that lasted several days. To wear two such dragons would be exceedingly rare, even amongst the men of the clans. For one of their sworn enemies to have earned them… Torbhin had never heard of such a thing.

Each of Alistair's hand-picked men had also served in the west and proved themselves in battle, and many also bore dots around their eyes or markings on their arms or faces to tell the story of their triumphs and their honorable friends and foes. A group with a grim history, but for all the savagery the tattoos implied, they bore themselves easily, with many a quiet joke and knowing look passed among them as they rode.

Killock

At first light the knight rose and moved to the edge of the trees, where he crouched to watch the country to the west. Grey slowly seeped across the land and revealed rolling hills that rippled into the icy mist.

Everything was barren, stark. Colorless under an icy rind. Killock remained motionless, huddled in his cloak, blanket and furs, patient. His grey eyes searched the land before him, looking for movement or color. Behind him the forest stood utterly silent, its life in hibernation. In front, the open land lay equally lifeless, low hills covered in a crust of snow, stark figures of bare trees scattered like grey sentinels in the mist.

The temple sat alone atop a rocky hill that squatted in the center of the valley. A low wall made of piled stones surrounded the small building, its narrow line sunk into the sparse tufts of dead grass and patches of ice that covered the hill. Behind the wall, the temple hunched low on the hilltop, its pale stone walls blending into the icy clouds that smothered the sky. Thin streams of ash-grey smoke drifted into the white mist from the slit windows cut into the temple walls. Otherwise, neither movement nor sound disturbed the valley.

Killock knew this temple well. It was called Nóinín Cnoc in the old northern tongue, and its pastor, Reverend Ezekiel, was a tiny, ancient man with near limitless energy. Reverend Ezekiel could frequently be found in the fields or the cow pen, his robes filthy as he joyfully helped the tenant farmers who worked the temple's small fields and tended its herd of cows. Ezekiel had spent many years in Bandirma as the Temple Archivist before deciding his true calling was in the hinterlands, and he had not left all of his scholarly ways in Bandirma. The cellar under Nóinín Cnoc was packed with books and scrolls. He had brought an over-filled wagon with him when he came to the temple over twenty years ago, and every visitor knew to bring a choice volume with them to add to the collection. Killock had found maps here, drawn centuries ago, which showed paths in the mountains not marked on any map found in the archives in Bandirma.

Ezekiel valued Nóinín Cnoc for its isolation and claimed it did more for his scholarship than proximity to any library, but Killock suspected that Ezekiel found the life of a parish priest far more rewarding than that of an archivist. The temple served three villages, each about a day's ride away, and Ezekiel would visit each one in turn.

But isolation also carried perils. The priest, his two acolytes, and the two tenant families who lived in the stone houses at the base of the hill comprised the entire population of the temple proper. If trouble arrived, they could only bar the doors to the temple and hope it went away. This strategy sufficed when wolves or trolls appeared. Those unwelcome visitors would be satisfied with a dinner of a cow or two at the worst, but if the trouble wore armor and wielded swords, little could be done to stop them.

Killock saw no sign of any of Nóinín Cnoc's residents now. The farmhouses were dark, and no smoke from a morning fire rose from them. Nor could he see any movement around the barn, and Killock heard the lowing of distressed cattle drifting faintly to him through the mist.

Killock slowly stood, wiped his nose on the back of his glove and stamped feeling into his feet. He carefully packed his small bag, eased himself from the dark, twisted shadows of his hide, and crept across the valley towards the temple, bent double to avoid any watching eyes as he moved.

Killock reached the low stone wall and crouched against it as his breath steamed into the bitter air. The temple slumped, a dark mass that slept in front of him, and from this close he could smell the damp ash and cold smoke that congealed around the hill. He paused to rearrange his cloak so that he could easily get to his weapons, and carefully rocked his sword in its scabbard to make sure it had not frozen in place. The broad steel blade would be the best choice if he had to fight within the dark, cramped space inside the small temple, and no sound or light would reveal his presence to any unseen watchers.

He slipped through a gap in the wall like a shadow. The ground around the temple building was ice and stone and made for slippery footing, but Killock moved silently across the open area to the walls of the temple. The smell of ash and smoke grew stronger, and was joined by a new scent that hung in the still air, stale and bloody.

Killock ignored the door, hanging askew on its hinges, and slid up and over a window sill into the darkness inside, where he dropped silently to the cold, stone floor.

Dim shafts of light made small slashes of grey across the ruined floor of the temple. Parts of the roof had collapsed and made a pile of broken beams and shattered debris in the center of the room. Snow fell through the hole in the roof and hissed slightly as it landed on the pile, which smoldered even now. Otherwise the temple lay in silence.

Killock knew she was nearby, but he could see no sign of her. The wreckage of the temple was undisturbed, and no sound or movement revealed her hiding place. Only the slender tracks that he had followed here told him he was not alone.

Killock's voice growled into the darkness, pitched low to carry no farther than necessary.

"Alright, Wyn. Where are you?"

There was a soft sigh of leather against smooth stone as she uncurled from a patch of shadow where ruined wall met shattered roof, and then the slightest whisper of air as she dropped to the floor.

Killock saw she was exceedingly pleased with herself. Her boots padded soundlessly amongst the stones, shattered wood, and ice as she moved across the room. Her woolen coat was black, as were her leather leggings, and her boots, and she wore a thick cloak made of black wool. Her face was smudged with ash, and she had tied her blonde hair back and hidden it under her hood. In the dim light of the ruined building, all Killock saw was a lithe shadow gliding towards him. Only the faintest gleam from her eyes as they reflected the light marked her as something more tangible.

Wyn slid into the shadow against the wall next to Killock. "Good to see you, Sir Wolf."

He nodded in return. He was glad to have finally joined Wyn. She had been alone out here, acting as his eyes and ears, for far too long. "And you, Lady Shadow. Is this their handiwork?"

"Yes," she replied, "two days ago I think."

She looked down and spent a moment wrapping her cloak more securely around her shoulders, and then she gazed from the gaping window to the valley outside. She met his eye for a heartbeat as she glanced up, but quickly looked away, awkwardly.

"And where is Lord Lucious?"

"That one?" Wyn wrinkled her nose in disgust. "Last I saw, he was a half-day south, heading the wrong way in a hurry. I don't know what he's chasing, but it doesn't have anything to do with this. Useless."

"Has he been to the sites of any of the rituals?"

"He went to the first one, the first temple. And to the first farm as well, but not since then. Since then it's been 'charge across the forest and wave my shiny stick at nothing,' then charge back again."

"And what you found here. Is it like the other places that were attacked?"

"The bodies are the same as the others were. The markings as well." She glanced towards the back of the temple, concealed behind the pile of debris from the collapsed roof. "They're back there if you want to see."

"I do."

She nodded. "I'll keep watch."

Killock hesitated a moment, watching her face. Underneath the ash and grime was the face of the pretty girl he had first seen two years ago through a set of heavy iron bars. Wide eyes, slightly turned upwards at the edges, high cheekbones and a pointed chin.

Wyn had become an exceptional thief over a career that started at the age of nine and ended eight years later in an attempt to break into the Queen's apartments that landed her in the dungeons of Kuray.

Killock was not sure which of the two of them was more fortunate that he had been in Kuray at the time. Wyn would never have survived the dungeons if he had not recruited her out of them, but she had repaid that decision ten-fold in the years since, becoming one of Killock's best students, and then one of his best agents.

He had brought her to Bandirma for training after securing her release, and it had taken her only months to master the skills that usually took his students years to learn, if they ever did. And she did it with a joy and exuberance that made him wish she could have gone a little bit slower, if only to extend the lessons. Her gift was astounding.

Still, for all of her skill in concealing her body, Wyn had always been terrible at concealing her mind. Killock could read every thought and emotion that passed across her face, although he rarely needed to as the thoughts usually became words with little filter in between. Whether she was joyous or angry, he knew promptly what Wyn was thinking.

And now she would not meet his gaze, and instead stared resolutely from the hole in the wall as if she expected pursuers to appear in the valley at any moment. She did not want to think about what was in the back of the temple, let alone see it again, and she was ashamed of that fact.

Which means she is afraid of whatever is back there.

Killock rose and followed the wall of the room until he could see past the collapsed roof into the shadows beyond. There he crouched, careful not to move any farther.

The bodies had been laid on their backs in a pattern across the stone floor, arms and legs spread wide, fingertips touching in a parody of gentle comfort.

Nine comprised a circle, their skin covered in dense black markings that squirmed in the grey light when Killock tried to focus on them. Under the bodies, black slashes spiraled outwards across the floor into a ring that surrounded the corpses.

In the center lay the remnants of a tenth body, pieces of flesh and streaks of blood smeared on the stones. Killock found his eyes fixated on a foot, somehow standing in the middle of the tableau as if its owner had simply walked off without it, like a discarded shoe.

But the bodies did not look like they had been lying there for a few days. They looked like they had been there for decades. The corpses had become dried husks, emaciated and desiccated as if they had been sealed in a tomb for years. Dried skin stretched over clearly visible skeletons. Lips, eyes and noses withered away leaving behind blackened flesh and a few clumps of ragged, straw-like hair.

A rank smell filled the air, sharp and sticky at the same time, wet and rotten, frozen into permanence.

Killock shivered. It felt colder here, as if the cold came from lightless depths instead of from wind and snow and ice. He clenched his fingers into fists and tried to blow some warmth into them, but all comfort vanished in the silence of the dark room.

The outer ring of black markings squirmed on the floor in front of him. They were unlike any letters or runes he had seen before; jagged, harsh and scrawled, and Killock thought they looked thicker, more congealed, than ink.

Carefully he poked at the markings closest to him with a long splinter of wood. The stick broke the surface free and smeared the markings, and Killock realized that the ink was indeed blood. The black markings on the bodies were bloody gashes, and the once-fresh blood was the paint used to stain the floor.

Killock stood and walked around the circle. His boots softly crunched splinters and stone into the crust of snow and ice as he forced himself to examine the ring from every angle.

Nine bodies. Six men and three women. Some fat, some thin. One with ink stains on his fingertips. Some old, some young. One very young.

No rings or necklaces. No weapons. No clothing.

Killock paused after completing the circle and knelt. His leather buckles creaked slightly and the hem of his cloak brushed the stone floor with a sigh. A cold feeling grew deep within him, twisted and wrong, but he knew he could not rush from this horror. He had to absorb what he could, understand what he could. He let his gaze linger on the markings, let them wash over him in the hope that some long-forgotten piece of lore might resurface in his memory.

But no understanding came.

He rose and returned to Wyn, who still determinedly watched over the valley.

She waited for him to sit against the wall before she spoke. "There's something black in that room. You can feel it."

"Yes, I felt it."

"They were all like this," she said, and Killock saw a fierce frown appear on her face. "Always ten, always in a circle, always all shriveled and horrible. Always something dark left over."

Killock glanced at her profile. "Why do you say it was left over?"

"Because it feels that way, doesn't it? Like a stain or an old scar."

Killock turned to the window. *No, that isn't right.* It did not feel like a stain or a scar, the mark of something that had happened and then passed away.

It felt like an echo, still pulsing, still alive, even if it was fainter and farther away than it had been.

Something was still out there.

"There was no sign of whoever did this? At any of the sites?"

"Not that anyone told me," Wyn shrugged. "Course, it was mostly blubbing into their ale, 'oh Maker be good', and 'I'll not ever forget their eyes staring back at me' and such rubbish. But whichever bastard did the deed, he was gone by the time I ever got there, that's certain."

Killock nodded and scratched absently at his ear. *It was never likely that anyone who saw the actual rituals, and not just their remains, would escape to tell. But it would have been helpful to know something, anything, about those we are here to find.*

"They may have run, but they will have left signs." Killock rose and pulled his hood over his head firmly.

Wyn followed him around the muddy yard and quietly watched the knight comb the ground for tracks. The ice and frozen mud showed dozens of trails, to and from the temple, the barn, the pasture gate, and the farmer's houses at the bottom of the hill. But few strayed beyond those well-worn paths, and it did not take long for Killock to find tracks that did not belong. The hoof prints of three horses, shod for riding, and heavy boot prints that strode from the horses to the doors of the temple.

There was also a churn of tracks moving together from the farm houses up to the temple, but these were less clear. What was certain was that the only tracks that left the temple were those of the heavy boots, which returned to the horses and rode down the hill.

Killock squatted in the lane and gently traced the outline of a hoof print with his finger. The horses had turned northwest, away from Lord Bradon and the approaching Temple army, and away even from Lord Lucious, off somewhere to the south.

"Shall we go after them then, before we freeze?" Wyn scuffed a stone loose from the mud with the toe of her boot.

"These men are on horseback," Killock indicated the tracks with a sweep of his hand, "and they have several days' head start on us." Killock glanced skyward at the heavy, grey clouds. "Right now the trail is clear, but that could change soon. I will need to travel very quickly or risk losing their tracks."

"Let's go then." Wyn's faint eyebrows made a small furrow between them. "You're not telling me to stay behind, are you? I'll keep up, you'll see. Sir," she added hopefully.

"Wyn, I wish you could come with me, but I need you to find Lord Bradon and bring him as fast as you can," said Killock.

"Oh yes?" Wyn's fists went to her hips defiantly.

"Bradon has horses, and scouts. If he is quick about it, he could catch up..."

"Then let's go find Lord Binkie together," Wyn interrupted eagerly. "Besides, he won't know who I am, even if I do find him. 'A girl to see you, m'lord, says to hop a horse right quick and bugger off west.' Doesn't sound too hopeful, does it?"

"Which is why I told him all about you," Killock reassured her. "We finally have a trail, Wyn. I can find these bastards and lead Bradon to them. I know you want to come with me, but it is more important that you go for help, because we cannot let them perform another one of these rituals."

"I know that, it's just, I thought… well I just thought we'd be the ones to get them, together." Wyn glared at her boots for a moment before trying a different tactic. "Anyway, who cares about armies and high muckity Templars? Three tracks you said, and that means one, two, three riders, right? We'd need to have a race to see who got to knife the last one in the face, but we don't need a stupid Templar, nor a humongous army. Just us."

"You already have a Templar, so there is no avoiding that."

"What? Oh, you mean you," Wyn gave Killock a wry smile. "You know what I mean."

"I do." Killock was quiet as he deliberated how much to reveal to Wyn. *We have kept our trepidations a secret, for fear of spreading unfounded rumors, but surely that caution is no longer necessary. Now that I have seen the ritual, I am certain this is the work of the Crunorix, and the more Wyn knows, the more she will be able to help.* But certainty was not fact, no matter how much he wished it to be.

"It could be much worse than three men committing murder," Killock explained. "The last time such rituals were uncovered, they were a precursor to an assault that was defeated only by years of warfare, and thousands of lives lost. Our hope is to stop those who are performing the rituals before that can happen again, but if we are too late, or we cannot, our army will be here, and ready. Perhaps that will prevent the enemy from gaining their full power, but I would rather not put that to the test."

Wyn kept his gaze for a moment, a bemused smile twitching at the corner of her mouth, and then she threw up her hands in surrender. "Fine, I'll go find Lord Muckity Bradon like a good little girl, but if I'm eaten by a troll, or if you kill those bastards without me, I'll not be pleased." Wyn crossed her arms and glared at Killock. "Not pleased at all."

"That is more than fair," Killock smiled in acknowledgement. "I know being sent as a messenger seems like a poor reward, not just for finding these ritual sites, alone and in danger of stumbling across God knows what if you arrived at the wrong time. But for everything you have accomplished since you left last summer."

"It wasn't that hard, was it?" Wyn said happily. "Nick Sir Jellybum's keys, read Lord Whatshisnose's letters, find Sir Ploppy's little hidey-stash. Hardly a real caper among 'em. Plus, I learned how to dance! Did I tell you?"

"You did not. You have done very well." Killock glanced at Wyn, and was rewarded with the quick flash of a pleased smile. "Perhaps after this is over you would like to return to Kuray for a while? There's always work to be done in Kuray."

"That sounds lovely, and the least I deserve," Wyn sighed dramatically. "Although I may not survive this 'be a messenger' assignment. It sounds very difficult."

"I could draw you a map."

"Oh, he's gone from heartless to insulting," Wyn rolled her eyes. "I'm sure I can remember a few directions."

"If you are sure," Killock agreed gravely.

"Wait, what about the poor poddies in the barn?" Wyn objected. "You're not thinking we'll just leave them? They'll die, the poor creatures."

"We can give them some feed and they will be fine until the army gets here."

"Give them some feed, he says. Do I look like a milkmaid to you? What do they eat besides grass?"

"No, I cannot imagine you as a milkmaid," Killock chuckled. "Come on then, and you can learn how to feed a cow, because you clearly know very little about milkmaids."

“Pfft, I do too,” Wyn giggled. “I know they have very soft hands, and they know a lot about teats.”

“I’m sure the cows appreciate that,” Killock mused.

They walked across the frost-brittle pasture to the barn, and Killock heard Wyn softly humming under her breath as they went. The barn had fortunately been untouched by the fire that had damaged the temple itself, and the small herd of cows was healthy, if hungry. Killock methodically explained the concept of hay to Wyn until she resorted to threats to get him to stop, and they filled the pens with enough feed to hopefully last the cows until the Temple army arrived. Killock knew there would be plenty of farmers, drovers, and perhaps a milkmaid or two amongst the soldiers of the army, and the cows would be well-tended while the army was there.

Then he took his farewells from Wyn. She listened quietly as he described the landmarks to follow along his trail, and waved away any more details with an impatient hand.

“Alright then, I’m off. But remember,” Wyn raised a warning finger. “No killing them without me.”

Then she was gone with a skip and a laugh, and Killock watched her hop over the pasture wall and hurry across the fields eastward, a small black shape who turned at the forest edge to give a merry wave, and then disappeared under the trees.

Killock took a deep breath and readied himself for the long chase ahead of him. There was a scent of more snow in the chill air now, from the north, and Killock knew a storm was pushing towards him from the High Fells. He started down the road after the tracks of the horsemen, easily falling into a loping stride that would devour the distance. The mist slowly absorbed Nóinín Cnoc and the ruined temple, until finally there was no trace of its ominous bulk, and the winding road stretched into grey nothingness behind him.

Wyn

Wyn hated the woods. Endless trees and rocks and the track kept disappearing, sometimes for thousands of paces, and she had to guess where it might appear again. And no place to hide except up a tree. *Useless. That's the first place anyone would look.*

Wading through the thick, wet snow under the trees exhausted her. No matter how diligently she tried, Wyn left a ridiculous trail behind her, one even a child could follow, and she soon gave up trying to hide her tracks. It was too cold, too wet, too tiring, too useless.

What this forest could really use, Wyn decided, *is a tavern.*

Killock had promised that Bradon would not be far. The Lord and the Temple soldiers with him were following the trail Killock marked for them leading from Dolieb, and should be less than a day behind. But dusk had fallen on the first day with no sign of the Temple army, and Wyn had spent a miserable night wrapped in her bedroll next to a fire that gave off more smoke than heat, and it was already noon of the second day and still no sign.

Since she and Killock had parted ways at Nóinín Cnoc she had already climbed two trees, once because the stupid trail had disappeared *again* and she needed a better view, and once because she had clearly heard the chuffing of some kind of troll in the distance. *Which you rarely heard,* she thought angrily, *in a tavern.*

Wyn knew she could not keep pace with Killock, but she wished they could have traveled together. She felt very alone in the wilderness, with no alleys to duck into and no crowded streets in which to get lost.

So Wyn trudged eastward to find Lord Bradon. This close to the High Fells the land rippled as it was forced upward to meet the massive peaks to the north. Steep, forested ridges became basalt and granite cliffs as the land rose up to the knees of the imposing mountains. In the forests, towering fir trees bent and scraped against each other in the winds that flowed down the mountains, creaking and groaning and cracking as they moved.

The few small settlements in the hinterlands were found in the valleys, with small fields hacked from the forest over generations of backbreaking effort. None of the settlements were larger than a few dozen families, people as unbreakable as the mountains that loomed over them. Most farmed in the summer, trapped in the winter, and sent their furs down the glacier-fed rivers or sold them in Dolieb to the merchants who flocked there in the spring. A few dared to hunt even farther from home, and climbed the mountains to where trees no longer grew and the world was rock and ice. Those harsh peaks were where the stone trolls lived, giants who towered over their smaller forest-dwelling cousins. Their skin was as impenetrable as their granite home, and they could tear a man in half, but if they could be brought down, their bones, teeth, and blood would make a man rich.

A few roads in the valleys connected the farmsteads, but none crossed the hills. The iron ground and thick forests would not allow them to be carved. Not by the efforts of a few farmers. It would take an army, and years of labor. Travel from village to village happened along the rivers, with portages around the numerous falls and unnavigable rapids. Each river formed its own community as the villages upstream or down were much more important and accessible than those across a ridgeline.

So Wyn had no path or road to follow, only a few landmarks from Killock to lead her to Lord Bradon. And what, to Killock, must have appeared as a unique rock formation or brook appeared to Wyn the same as every other stone or stream. During the summer she had toured the hinterlands with a group of bards who traveled with the fur buyers and their guards. They journeyed from village to village to purchase directly from the hunters and promise coin for the next season. Wyn had juggled and danced and smiled invitingly, and had cut purses and stolen secrets in every holdfast they had visited. So Wyn knew where Dolieb lay, and generally how to get there, and she knew she could not be far from the right path.

Wyn paused for a moment to catch her breath. Wind sighed through the tall firs around her and snow slid from the upper branches with a hiss and burst into showers of tiny flakes intent on settling into every gap in her cloak and on every mote of exposed skin.

Wyn decided she needed another look-around. She was not lost, she judged, but the track she had thought was the trail led impossibly into a steep rock face above her.

Wyn grabbed one of the lower branches of the tallest tree she could find and ascended. Aside from the sticky sap and prickly needles, a tree was an easy climb and she fairly flew through its branches. Near the top she found a good perch, wrapped her legs securely around a branch, and lay along it as far as it would support her body.

Looking north, Wyn could see the ridgeline she was crossing climbing higher and higher into the clouds. Jagged rock escarpments reared from the forest less than a league away, stacked one on top of the other with sheer faces of grey stone capped by streaks of ice. From the top of each cliff snow streamed into the air, ripped from the ground by the winds coming down the side of the mountain. Above the cliffs she could sense the true bulk of the mountain behind the clouds, a half-felt shadowy mass that pressed the clouds downwards. Every now and then the wind would tear a hole in the clouds and Wyn saw black rock that reached ever higher, but the topmost peaks never revealed themselves.

Eastwards from her vantage point, she looked into the valley as if from a tall tower, and she saw patches of black trees, snow-covered meadows, and a long column of men trudging towards her across the valley.

Thank the Martyr, she thought, *maybe they'll have wine. And blankets. And maybe even a horse for me so I can get out of the snow before I freeze.*

Wyn laid her face against the rough wood of the tree, closed her eyes, and enjoyed the sensation of the branch swaying in the wind for a moment. She always loved being high in the air. Tucked into the corner of a roof, or high on a tower ledge, she felt remote and hidden. Even in broad daylight, few people bothered to look up and she felt free to move and watch and hide at will. Most of all being high above the ground made her feel safe. No one could surprise her when she was perched on top of a church steeple, and she had never met anyone who could out-climb her if she needed to escape.

Being in a tree was not as good. She felt more trapped in a tree. Stuck, if anyone should happen to spot her. The swaying was, however, fantastic. Wyn loved to feel the flex and bounce of the wood underneath her. The constant joy of keeping perfect balance during the tree's fluid motion felt like a supple dance, flowing with the wind. If towers could sway she would never set foot on the ground.

However, trees were colder than towers or roofs, although she admitted the icy air might have something to do with the High Fells, which towered across the northern sky. Soon she could not ignore the chill that settled into her legs, and her fingers were numb. With a sigh she uncurled from the branch and flowed to the ground.

She took a single step down the slope and stopped, still as ice, as she realized that the forest around her had changed. A presence she could not pin down, but she was certain it was near. A noise, a scent, a shadow? She was not sure but she knew to trust her instincts, and they screamed that she was not alone.

For a moment she considered making a run for safety. The soldiers she spotted were not too far, and it was downhill. But she did not actually know if they were friendly, and the thought of trying to outrun someone through deep snow and thick forest did not appeal to her.

Alright then, next best thing. Time to disappear.

Wyn whirled around the tree behind her and dove between two moss- and ice-covered rocks, putting them between her and whatever lurked in the woods. She rolled to her feet, dashed across a gap in the trees, and leapt gracefully over a fallen tree. Landing silently on the other side, she curled into the shadows underneath the trunk and slid as far back as possible until she could tuck her legs all the way underneath her and watch from her shallow hide, knife held firmly in her hand.

For a moment the forest was still, as if shocked by her sudden disappearance.

"That was incredible," a voice called from down the slope. "Where did you go?"

Ha! thought Wyn. *How stupid is this idiot? At least now I know it's a man, not a troll. A man I can kill.*

She listened to the soft sounds of the snow-laden forest and waited for the Idiot to make some noise, but there was nothing.

"If your name is Wyn, then Sir Killock told us to look for you," the voice called out again, this time from somewhere to her left, along the slope. "You match his description pretty well I'd say."

What did Killock tell him? Look for a girl in black perched in a tree? Wyn was pretty sure that Idiot was with the Temple… people in the wilderness did not just happen to blurt out both her name and Killock's in the same sentence… but that did not mean that she would give him the satisfaction of sneaking up on her again.

"All right, I'm heading down to tell Lord Bradon that I've found you. You can follow me if you want to. I'll whistle so you know where I am," Idiot called, now from the slope below her.

Wyn heard Idiot move off then, stomping and whistling as he went. She waited for the sounds to fade, then uncurled from her hide and moved down the hill after him, slipping silently from shadow to shadow. She hugged the ground as much as possible, used her hands and feet to flow over boulders and tree stumps, and slid under low tree branches. A quick climb down a basalt outcrop and she was ahead of Idiot. A slight gully with some dense bushes made a perfect ambush site.

Sure enough, Idiot passed close by, his face all puckered up to whistle. He was wrapped in a brown and green cloak with a deep, fleece-lined hood, and Wyn saw thick wool leggings and fleece-lined boots. He was thin, with Killock's leggy wiriness, had a few days' growth of a blonde beard, and eyes so light they looked like ice. He was younger than she had thought from his voice, maybe just a few years older than she.

With his hood up, the assault she planned was going to be a bit more challenging, so Wyn attacked as soon as he was in range and smacked him right in the pucker with a nasty, icy, dirty snowball.

***

Idiot was still scooping snow from his tunic long after Lord Bradon arrived and Wyn had related her report, although it turned out that Idiot was actually named Torbhin. Wyn felt a bit sorry for Torbhin, not because of the snow down his tunic which he deserved, but because he was so serious about it, solemnly scooping bits of ice and snow from the neck of his hood without the slightest smile, or laugh, or bluster, or curse.

Lord Bradon was accompanied by a soldier with the most amazing shoulders packed into his armor, and dragon tattoos on his arms that coiled and rippled from his coat sleeves as he stood and listened with arms crossed. *I wonder where their tails get to?*

"Do they have names?" she asked. Torbhin stopped rummaging in his tunic for a moment, glancing between Wyn and Bradon, and Wyn realized that Bradon had been asking her something Terribly Important, because everything Lord Bradon said was apparently Terribly Important.

"Sorry," she said to Bradon, and flashed her best innocent-girl smile, the one with wide, shining eyes and lots of eagerness, the one that usually got men to stumble and stammer just when they were getting all serious and angry.

Bradon simply stroked his beard, but Wyn saw that Torbhin was staring.

"Quite alright," rumbled Bradon. "Where does Killock want us in such a hurry?"

"Nóinín Cnoc, the temple where the last ritual was," Wyn said. "That's where he found the tracks, so if we hurry we can follow and catch up."

"And you said the trail went northwest. But Lord Lucious has gone south?"

"Lord Lush-ous?" Wyn shook her head. "He was about a half-day south of here last I saw, and headed more south."

"Were there any attacks to the south?" Bradon asked.

"Not that I've heard," replied Wyn. "All were north of here, or west a bit."

"Lucious, what are you up to?" Bradon turned and stared southward as if he could see through the hills and trees and mist simply by willing it. *He seems nice enough*, Wyn reflected, *though I bet he can get scary angry if he wanted to. And that's one serious beard. But I wish he were a bit faster.*

"Killock said it was important we got there as soon as we could, yeah?" Wyn said. "I bet Lord Lush-ous can answer all your questions better than those trees."

Bradon turned to look at her, an eyebrow raised in surprise. Wyn made sure not to blink as she stared back, hands on hips, balanced on both feet just in case she had to move. *I guess people don't talk back to him much.*

Bradon laughed then, a booming sound that rolled over the group. "I will wager you are right."

He turned to Torbhin. "How quickly could you find Lord Lucious?"

Torbhin thought for a moment, another serious expression on his face. "I should be able to pick up his trail very quickly.

Depends on how far I have to go after that, but heading south is very easy riding compared to the terrain to the west or north."

"Very good," said Bradon. "Tell Lucious to bring whatever men he has to this Nóinín Cnoc temple Bronwyn was telling us about."

"It's Wyn," said Wyn.

"Your pardon," Bradon corrected himself. "To the temple Wyn told us about. Then join us as quickly as you can."

"Yes, m'lord," Torbhin replied. "And where will you be?"

"We will ride ahead of the army and get started chasing down Killock and these people he is following. Alistair," Bradon continued. "We will need horses and a spare for Killock when we catch him. Light supplies, and please tell Lady Danielle we will be leaving as soon as the horses are ready. You will command the army. Get them to Nóinín Cnoc and await our return." *At least Shoulders has a name, even if his dragons don't.*

"Of course, m'lord." Alistair's voice was as smooth and hard as his shoulders, and made Wyn blink in astonishment. "Except I'm sure you meant that Sir Lochlan should take the army to Nóinín Cnoc, as he is a very capable field commander, while my men and I were brought all the way from Irongate because, and I believe I remember my orders from you, m'lord, because we are 'the elite, and I want unrivaled soldiers with me for running down and eliminating these murderous villains'. And of course, that I was to guard Lady Danielle personally."

"Did I really call you 'elite'?" Bradon stroked his beard thoughtfully. "That doesn't sound credible at all. Or perhaps I sent you the wrong message. In either case, I don't have time to argue, so you and your men may come too. Send a scout patrol ahead to Nóinín Cnoc as fast as they can to secure it. And tell them to find these tracks that Killock followed so that we don't have to mess about in the dirt when we get there."

"Yes, m'lord," Alistair replied, and hurried to the column of soldiers.

"You can ride?" Bradon asked Wyn.

Wyn loved riding, although she had not ridden often. She rarely needed to in a town or city, and a big, noisy horse was not much help in staying quiet or hidden. But the few times she had ridden had been exhilarating. The rush of speed and the beautiful smooth rhythm of an all-out gallop were intoxicating. Plus, horses were nice, with soft noses and kind eyes, and they liked to laugh at people, snorting and stamping and whickering with amusement as folks tried to push them around.

Most important right now was that horses were warm, and taller than the snow banks.

"Yes, please," she replied.

Torbhin

As darkness deepened across the valley, the assault on the old tower reached its end.

Fire glowed against the walls of the tower, and black smoke created a thick pall under low, icy clouds as it rose from the humble buildings at the tower's base. At a distance the attack was strangely hushed, as if the cold air had frozen any sound long before it reached the far side of the valley.

Torbhin crouched in the shadow of an ancient hedgerow that bordered an abandoned farm. From there he had an unimpeded view of the doomed village. Occasionally he would flex his hands or adjust his hood and scarf to better cover his face and head from the cold, but otherwise he remained motionless as he watched carefully.

After he left Lord Bradon, Torbhin had quickly travelled southwards over forested hills and along valley trails. He had traversed the frosted meadows and dark woods with nothing but the rhythmic thud of his horse's hooves on the icy mud to interrupt the silence of the frozen landscape.

By midafternoon he had reached a crossroads at the foot of a tall, bare hill. A leafless tree stood at the junction, a massive oak with deep roots and gnarled limbs that splayed black across the misty sky. Its branches were home to dozens of ravens who croaked contemptuously at the ranger as he moved underneath them.

The crossroads showed signs of recent use. The road from the east was trampled into deep mud by the passage of hundreds of heavy boots and several wagons. They turned at the crossroads and took the south road, and Torbhin found tracks of two horses that stood beside the roadway and watched the column of men pass.

Torbhin had pursued them. Their tracks stuck rigidly to the path, and Torbhin saw no signs of scouts or outriders. *A confident army traveling without concern of any attack.*

Torbhin had discovered their camp from the night before, set in a small meadow close to a frozen stream. The signs of tents and cooking fires were obvious, but no evidence of pickets or defenses had been left. They appeared to have left that morning, and Torbhin knew that he was rapidly overtaking them.

He had seen the first signs of the battle a short time later. Black smoke rose over a small ridge of trees that curved into the valley. Torbhin had concealed his horse and crept to the edge of the woods, where he saw across black fields a small village perched on the edge of the stream. A thick stub of a tower made of grey stone sat hunched on the bank of the stream, and around its foot clustered a few dozen buildings with dark, wooden walls and a mixture of grey shingle and thatched roofs. A small mill was the only building of any size. Its short stone tower poked out of the village from a long, low, wooden building along the stream bank.

The fighting had already begun. Several of the buildings blazed redly, and thick black smoke poured from their thatched roofs. Torbhin could distinguish soldiers as they moved between the buildings, but from the woods he could not tell more.

Torbhin had used the short winter evening to slowly move toward the village. He had avoided the open farmlands and stayed in the muddy bottoms of the fields where low rock walls and hedgerows provided small cover. The attackers were wholly focused on the assault, but the ranger could not chance being spotted by an alert sentry, so he had settled to watch the end, invisible amongst the black, twisted shadows underneath a hedgerow.

Flashes that lit the valley like lightning bursts suddenly bathed the town. The brightness etched into the ranger's vision a black-and-white negative of the lonely trees scattered across the valley. Torbhin softly counted to five before the dull thuds of the explosions rolled through him. He watched the flashes dim to an ugly red cloud of fire and smoke that roiled like a scab into the air above the tower. The ranger peered forward intently. The attack had started as a simple, brutal, physical assault. Now, a much more powerful Weapon was being used.

As the fireball cleared, the ranger saw that the tower's gate had been obliterated, and an ugly hole with glowing edges gaped where the portal had been. Attackers rushed through the breach as a few desperate defenders fired arrows upon them.

A faint red line shimmered through the billowing smoke from the top of a dark hill behind the village and touched the face of the tower. A momentary pulse of dark red throbbed against the tower's stone wall, gone almost as quickly as it was glimpsed, and then another flash of lightning lit up the valley as the front of the tower boiled into fire and smoke.

The attackers were offered no more resistance after that as they finished their work. Heavy figures smashed in doors, set fire to buildings, and broke what could be broken.

Later, in the darkest part of the night when the fighting had ended and the victors' celebrations had begun, Torbhin threaded his way across the valley and climbed the thickly forested slope above the attacker's camp. Under the trees the snow piled deeply, and hidden roots and stones made for poor footing, but Torbhin made little sound as he climbed, save for the soft scrunching of thick snow underfoot, quieter than the sigh of wind through the trees.

A huge wind-bent fir tree stood at the top of the slope, its thick branches almost brushing the ground. Torbhin eased underneath and sat against its trunk, grateful for the bed of fallen needles between him and the icy ground, and thoughtfully chewed a piece of dried venison from his small pack as the black night slowly turned grey.

Icy mist seeped through the trees and hung in the valley, feebly lit by a vague, cold glow from somewhere beyond the low clouds to the east.

Torbhin peered through the mist to the village and its ruined tower. His gaze came to rest on a large pavilion that stood in the center of the attacker's camp upon a small hill. Torbhin saw a long banner raised in front of the pavilion on a spear thrust into the ground. The banner boasted three red swords crossed against a white background.

The arms of Lord Lucious.

Torbhin did not wait any longer. He slipped away under the deep shadows of the trees until he was concealed from the village by a low ridgeline, then collected his horse and turned northwards again. The ranger urged his tired horse into its distance-devouring gallop as he raced to catch Lord Bradon.

Killock

When Killock reached the ridgeline he paused for a moment to catch his breath and let the sounds and scents of the forest seep into him. The tall pines rustled warily as the wind gusted, and a vast chorus of creaking limbs washed along the ridge with its passage. Snow swirled between the trees and filled the nooks and divots of their roots. The flakes had started to fall at dusk as Killock began his scramble up the steep hill, and now that he was at the top the snow was a steady flow.

There's more coming. Much more.

He could smell it on the northern wind, and sense it in the movement of the trees. The wind had come from the High Fells, chill air driven by a massive weight of ice and snow as it plummeted towards the lowlands.

The storm was nearly upon him, and it was here a day too early.

Killock had chased the horsemen for a day and a night and then another day, loping northwards along the valley trails at first, then following the tracks as they plunged into the forest. The trail had been easy to read, and Killock had pursued with as much speed as he could manage, only stopping for the briefest of rests before continuing.

The animal trail that Killock had followed to the ridge twisted into the dark shadows ahead of him. He knew that the horsemen had started up the hill using the same path, as they had left a trail of hoof prints and broken branches easy to read. But even such blatant signs had disappeared as the wind, snow, and darkness grew. So Killock held himself still and let the forest flow through him as he searched for a trace that did not belong.

When it came it was faint. The scent of ashes, cold and thin.

Enough, though, to follow, waiting patiently as the wind tore through the trees, then proceeding once the scent returned between gusts.

It led Killock down the hill northward, toward a rugged, narrow valley that lay pinched between the hill and its twin to the north as if it were the gap between the out-flung fingers of a spread hand.

Killock found the campsite in a hollow between three ancient elm trees. The trees groaned continually as the wind roared through their branches, the gusts that had stirred the forest just a short time ago now combined into a constant gale. Killock crouched in the deep shadow beneath a bush and wrapped his ragged cloak about his shoulders as he watched the hollow. It was dark and deserted, no sign of any shelter or fire, but Killock knew better than to take that at face value.

He watched, and listened, and let the smell of the cold ash swirl around him. Killock would have preferred to wait all night and use the false light of the pre-dawn sky to approach the campsite, but he had no time to spend the night watching. Long before the middle of the night Killock slipped from his hide and made his way to the hollow, a grey shadow amongst the driven snow.

The hollow had been used as a campsite several times in the last few months, most recently just the night before. A poorly buried fire pit still contained traces of heat at its heart, and there were fresh tracks in the mud and dirt, although they were disappearing fast under the snowfall.

But how many men had sheltered in the hollow on that night, and which direction they had departed in, Killock could not discern. There were two paths leading out, one moving along the hillside, the other heading down the hill towards the valley, and Killock knew that he could tell which path displayed the freshest tracks in an instant… *if only there was no snow, or no wind, or some light.*

The most ferocious blast of wind yet ripped through the forest in reply to his thought. Killock squinted as snow lashed against his face and sliced through the wool of his coat as if it were a summer tunic.

Killock did not ponder his choice for long. The valley trail promised easier passage, and although that meant little to the Templar he hoped that it would matter more to the horsemen he was chasing.

By the time Killock reached the valley floor sheets of snow drove horizontally out of the darkness, limiting Killock's world to less than a stone's throw of thrashing branches, huddled shapes, and the swaying trunks of trees. Ice crusted in his eyebrows and on the stubble on his cheeks, and his ragged grey cloak tore free from his grasp and fluttered uselessly from his shoulders.

The trail crossed a small frozen stream, and on the far side a rough wooden gate in a low fence suddenly loomed into view. The gate hung open, dragging its stake through the frozen ground as the wind streamed past. Beyond the gate Killock saw a rough dirt path that cut through a meadow, but both disappeared behind the howling wind and snow.

Killock hurried along the fence line, bent low as he stayed close to the wind-whipped bushes and scrub trees that lined the meadow.

A low building with a small enclosure appeared out of the gloom, and Killock scurried into the darkness against its wall. A quick glance around the corner into the enclosure showed him that the building was a pig sty. The long, pale shapes of its residents lay in the dark mud of the enclosure, a half-dozen lumps slowly being buried by the snow.

The Templar slipped over the enclosure's rail and sank into the deep blackness under the sty's low eaves, where the rough boards afforded a small shelter from the wind's assault.

Killock unpacked a small wallet, slowly and carefully unrolling the soft leather onto crushed straw and mud. Inside were a dozen metal hoops that varied in size from the diameter of a wine glass to one the width of his thumb nail. Each was elegantly crafted from multiple strands of spun metal, precisely twisted and bound with inscribed metal studs. Killock fitted three of the hoops together so that they overlapped each other.

Then he carefully considered his Word.

He let it flow through his mind and into the three hoops held in his hand, then whispered his Word to give it form. Precisely uttered, precisely focused, so that only the most skilled and powerful watchers would have a chance to detect it.

Within the hoops, bindings clicked open in response to his Word, and the intricate geometric patterns channeled the pulse through the twined threads until the empty space within the metal rings began to twist and bend. Killock raised the hoops and peered through them.

Buildings loomed suddenly into view through the falling snow, pale misshapen mounds obscured by the drifts piled against them. Holes gaped where windows and doorways opened into darkened rooms. Killock slowly moved the Device back and forth across the farmstead, carefully taking in every detail. A small farmhouse made of cut timber, and a long bunkhouse near it, showed him where the farmers lived, and behind them a large barn, its doors open wide to the gale.

There were no signs of life anywhere in the farmstead. Shutters swung wildly in the wind, banging forlornly against their frames, but no hand reached to secure them, and no warm light spilled forth as they opened.

Killock flexed his fingers to try and get warmth into them and wiped the crusted snow from his eyebrows. He repacked the delicate hoops of his Device, and arranged his cloak so that the hilt of his sword was easy to hand.

Killock slipped from the sty and crossed to the bunkhouse, through the sheets of driving snow. A gaping window offered itself and he slid into the black interior of the building with only the slightest of creaks from the sill, lost in the roar of the storm.

The bunkhouse was one long room, with a heavy stone fireplace and rough trestle table in the center, and beds filling the remainder of the space. Snow swirled through the room and settled on every surface, rapidly smothering the contents under a smooth, concealing shroud. But even so Killock could see the signs of a normal day, interrupted without warning.

The table still carried the remnants of an evening meal, with mugs and trenchers scattered across its top. One of the benches was tipped on its side, and there was a chaos of dropped bowls and cups on the floor around it. Four beds in the corner surrounded the remains of a game of dice, left with the last roll standing amidst a few scattered coins. Thick winter cloaks hung from pegs about the walls, flapping in the wind, and Killock saw heavy work boots in a line by the door, ready for the next morning.

Killock prowled silently forward, carefully stepping around the beds. There was no heat in the ashes of the cooking fire, nor in the heavy iron cauldron of congealed stew that hung above it, but Killock had not expected it. The pigs had died of starvation and exposure, telling the ranger that whatever had happened here had occurred many days ago.

Killock ignored the door and crept to the far end of the room, where a window the twin of the one he had used to enter the bunkhouse allowed him to ease into the storm. The main farmhouse was now visible through the driving snow, a sturdy building of cut timber and river stones built to survive the northern winters. A wide porch graced the front of the farmhouse, with a hand-carved railing that must have been an evening hobby for many a night. A kitchen garden lay against the side of the house, bare for the winter months and now thick with snow.

But now the farmhouse stood dark and empty, just as the bunkhouse had, and here also shutters had torn free and now swung wide in the gale. Killock passed through the kitchen door, and once again found rooms filled with signs of normalcy. Needles and thread attached to a half-darned woolen sock, hand-carved knights and soldiers scattered across the floor, a pipe resting in its holder next to a chair.

Outside the front door Killock found the first sign of the fate of the farmstead's inhabitants. A body lay on the open ground at the foot of the porch steps, contorted under the layer of snow as if he had died in terrible agony. A large man, young and strong, but now twisted and cold. Killock paused long enough to see that no wounds marked the corpse, then hurried across the open space to the barn.

Snow blocked the open doorway, and spilled into the dark space beyond, but the barn was deep enough that it had not reached the back where Killock discovered the frozen remains of the same ritual he had found in the ruined temple on Nóinín Cnoc. But this time the stains of blood shaped into twisted markings framed nothing… nine empty spaces where the corpses had lain in the temple.

Killock circled the ritual slowly. There had been corpses here too. The impression of their bodies could clearly be seen in the patterns of the blood writing, and in the scrape of the packed dirt floor. There were tracks across the writing, scuffs and smears that did not care what they stepped on.

Killock paused next to one print that stood out beyond all of the others. It was long, much longer than any of the other tracks, and heavy. The hard-packed dirt of the floor bore deep scrapes where the foot had pressed down, as if talons had clawed across the ground as whatever had left the track stepped forward.

Killock became motionless, and pushed his senses into the dark building around him. Beneath the icy wet scent of the snow there were still the expected aromas of the barn, faint, but still there. The dry, musty smell of hay, the warm scent of a horse, the oiled fragrance of leather. The odor of corruption also lurked, frozen now, and indistinct.

The barn groaned in the wind, timbers shifting and bowing under the strain. Metal clinked in the dark recesses where the shapes of tools and gear shifted and swung from their hooks.

No other sound, no other scent. No movement save for the swirling snow.

The Templar crept to the door and peered outside, looking now beyond the barn to the far end of the farm from where he had arrived. Any chance of finding more tracks had been obliterated by the storm, but huddled shapes on the ground at the far end of the farmstead, at the very limits of sight, drew his attention.

Killock crept towards the shapes cautiously, ignoring the fresh fury of the blizzard as it whipped stinging snow into his face.

Four bodies lay on the path just inside the clearing. Killock knelt and cleared the snow from them. They were dressed in simple clothes, sturdy and warm. Two were older, with grey in their thick beards and deep lines across their faces, but still sturdy, with the lean arms and shoulders of those well-used to hard labor. The other two were younger, with smooth cheeks and wide shoulders.

All four had weapons. An axe, a dagger, a cudgel. But none had been drawn, and still rested in sheaths or hung from belts.

They had been brutally torn apart. Deep wounds ran across torsos, ripping and eviscerating and shattering bone. Blood stained the homespun cloaks and coats. And something had feasted upon them, tearing enormous chunks of flesh free from the corpses, and strewn the remains haphazardly across the ground.

What has happened here? Killock glanced around the small sphere of swirling snow that his world had been reduced to by the storm. *A ritual, such as the one in Nóinín Cnoc, carried out on the farmers, that much is clear. Many days ago to judge from the body by the farmhouse, and the pigs. But these four bodies. A day ago, perhaps, two at the most.*

But where have the corpses from the ritual gone? What made the clawed tracks? And what killed these four? Farmers from their look, perhaps from a holding down the valley, come to check on a neighbor. All four slaughtered before they could run, or even draw their weapons. Killock pulled his gaze from the wall of snow and re-examined the bodies at his feet. *Consumed, but not as a wolf would eat. Great chunks ripped from the chest and stomach, but the arms and legs and neck ignored, and all four ravaged equally.*

Killock rose to his feet and stared at the path in front of him. Then he turned his back on the path and began to run. He passed the farm buildings, and the empty sty, and crossed the clearing to the gate and the frozen stream beyond it. He flashed through the snow, leapt the stream in a long bound, and scrambled up the steep hillside beyond without breaking stride.

We thought the ritual had ended in Nóinín Cnoc, Killock realized. *But it hadn't. This is what the end of the ritual looks like. The corpses somehow vanished, and something summoned, a creature with taloned feet able to kill four men so quickly that they had no chance to defend themselves. A creature that feasted on their flesh.*

This is how the ritual at Nóinín Cnoc will also end, Killock thought. *And I have sent my friends there.*

Killock ran faster with every step, a grey shadow that streaked southward between trees that trembled and swayed as the blizzard unleashed its full fury upon them.

Bradon

"So, you're a Templar?" asked Wyn.

Bradon nodded. "That is correct."

"And that means you're a priest, right?" she continued.

"I have been anointed, yes," replied Bradon. "Which is why people call me 'Reverend' sometimes. But, no, I have never been a priest as you would think of one, with a temple and a parish. Books and chanting and robes do not suit me." He chuckled but Wyn's face remained serious.

Wyn was quiet for a moment as they rode next to each other and Bradon hoped for a clue as to what might be on her mind.

"But, you've talked to God, right?" Wyn asked.

Bradon smiled, thinking of the chamber deep in the Mountain and the booming Voice laughing in the vastness of the room. "Oh yes, many times."

"So He's real?"

"Indeed."

"I knew it!" Wyn grinned in triumph. "I knew it. Mellon owes me coin."

"Mellon?" asked Bradon, confused.

"A guy I know in Kuray," said Wyn. "You probably don't know him. He said the Temple was just having us on. That the priests were all making it up."

"But, as you just mentioned, I am a priest too. Perhaps I am making it up as well."

"You're not a real priest, you just said. And anyway," Wyn continued, squinting at Bradon, "you know that if you lie to me I'll cut your beard off while you sleep."

Bradon stroked his braids defensively. "A dire threat."

"That's not a threat, it's a… well, yes it is, I guess."

Bradon laughed. "I swear by my beard then, God is real."

"What's He like?"

"He is kind," said Bradon, "and strong and fierce as well. But most of all He is difficult to explain. All I can say is that He cares very deeply for us. Have you not talked with Killock about this? He is your mentor, and a Templar as well."

"Asked Killock?" Wyn was incredulous. "You can get more answers from asking a stone. It's always 'what do you think?' and 'it's what is inside of you that matters' and useless stuff like that. But I knew you would tell me straight."

"Of course. But Killock is right," Bradon said. "It is your spirit, the desire in your heart that is your true strength, the true power that is inside of you. That is what matters."

Wyn snorted in laughter. "Yeah, of course it is."

They rode in silence again. Bradon felt he had somehow failed, although exactly how he was not sure. It was so clear to him in his heart and in his mind, and the words to express it came so easily to Reverend Benno. Bradon had heard him speak of it many times, each time as clear and inspiring as the first time. *I have even heard it from God Himself, yet my own words always fail to impress. I suppose there is a reason I am a Templar, not a priest.*

"Very well then," Bradon sighed as if in defeat. "I will tell you the secret of life, but only because I swore on my beard."

"On your beard, that's right."

"Well, God has told us that long ago the Maker created all things. Trees, rocks…"

"Gold?"

"Yes. Gold, silver, iron. And…"

"Fishes?"

Bradon cleared his throat. "Yes, even fishes. And…"

"Beards?"

Bradon glanced down and met Wyn's wide, innocent eyes staring at him.

"Of course beards. Beards were first," Bradon continued quickly as Wyn drew breath. "And the Maker also created people. Now, as it has been explained to me, the Maker made people differently from the rest of all of that. The Maker gave us a spirit, a spark that lives within us." Bradon paused to remember how Benno had described it to him. "That spark is part of the Maker. That is the Maker's gift to us."

"So there's a little Maker inside of me?"

"No, it's the Maker's blessing. It's what makes *you*, your desire, your spirit. And it's not just a myth. It is a very real power, something that you can use to do amazing things."

"You're telling me we all have that?" Wyn scoffed. "Because I've seen some pretty unspectacular people before, and I've never had some lightning bolt come out of my bottom, I would have noticed."

"*That's* the secret, Wyn," said Bradon, his deep voice rolling with the intensity of his words. "Some people waste their power, while others wield it easily. And some people become so adept that they can do miracles."

"Like how?"

"Think of a blacksmith who can forge a perfect steel blade, or a farmer whose crops are always strong. Why is their work so much better than others? It is because they have learned to use their gift. Or consider a warrior," Bradon indicated himself, "who can turn the spark into speed and strength, or who always knows what his opponent is thinking. Or think of exceptional minds," Bradon nodded towards Danielle, "who can understand the most complex mysteries, and control the most powerful magics simply by thought."

"And anyone can do this?"

"Some do it instinctively, but it can be taught if the person has the aptitude for understanding, and that is what the great schools of the Temple do. This is what God revealed to us, the truth that we had forgotten."

"Even me?"

"Yes of course," agreed Bradon. "I would guess especially you. Killock would never have brought you to the Temple if he hadn't been very certain."

"Well it hasn't shown up yet, that's for sure," Wyn laughed. "And anyway, why keep this a big secret? People should know."

"We don't keep it a secret," Bradon chuckled. "Every priest and priestess in every temple preaches it and we teach it to every acolyte and every squire in our schools. You might have heard it before if you had ever actually gone into a temple."

"It may have been a while, true," laughed Wyn.

A comfortable silence covered them then, with only the soft noises of the horses plodding on the trail and the creak and jingle of their gear. Wyn was lost deep in thought, a small frown furrowing her brow as she gazed unseeingly at her hands on the reins. A snowflake settled on Wyn's cheek and she brushed it off, but it jogged her from her reverie.

"What do you talk to Him about?" she asked.

"You, mostly."

Her eyes blinked wide and her mouth made a perfect 'O' in surprise, then a wry smile washed it away. "Ha ha, very good. 'Lord Bradon is a funny man' is what I'll tell them when they ask. Really what did you talk about?"

Bradon laughed again, a deep rumbling noise. "About many things. But those are for Him and me."

That seemed to satisfy Wyn for she nodded and again rode silently, lost in her own thoughts.

***

The storm descended on them in the early hours of the morning, a gale that shrieked down the mountains, tore tents from their stakes, and drove chaos through the camp. Men rushed to secure the horses and salvage what gear they could, shouting to be heard by those standing next to them. Bradon moved easily through the tempest, leapt to corral a runaway tent, hauled those that stumbled to their feet, and bellowed orders and laughter with equal measure. The horses were saddled as the storm unleashed snow to join the wind, and the forest around them disappeared behind a wall of slashing flakes.

Dawn found them still struggling through the rugged hills, their progress reduced to a crawl by the storm. Each time they reached a crest, the wind seemed to double in its fury as it skimmed snow and ice off the ground and flung it into Bradon's face, scoured his cheeks red and crusted his beard white. His huge bear cloak thrashed around his shoulders as he rode.

About time we got a proper blizzard, he thought. *Should blow out the cobwebs.*

Most of his companions did not seem as happy. All he could see of the girl, Wyn, was the tip of a red nose poking out miserably from her lowered hood as she sat hunched on her horse, her long legs pulled under her tightly wrapped cloak. Bradon could hear snatches of a continuous stream of curses coming from her between gusts, directed at him, Killock, the mountains, her boots, the Maker, the wind gods, and most of all the forest. Bradon committed to memory the ones he had not heard before.

Danielle should have been more miserable than anyone. Bradon had traveled with her to her family estates in the south of Venaissin, where her home sprawled across high cliffs above the shore of the Inner Sea, nestled amongst fruit orchards, cypress trees and fields of beautiful purple flowers. It was the daily custom to bathe in the gentle sea at the height of the day's heat, and to bless the sea air when it drifted in to cool off the land. Not exactly seasoning for a blizzard in the far north.

But she rode without complaint, and smiled gamely at Bradon through lips blue with cold when she saw his questioning glance.

"Are you alright, my lady?" Bradon shouted through the wind. "You look cold."

"Not at all," Danielle replied through chattering teeth. "I am a hardened northerner now."

"After four years I would hope so," laughed Bradon.

Only Alistair enjoyed the blizzard as much as Bradon. Snow clung to the stubble on his cheeks and crusted his eyebrows, but he met the wind with a fierce smile and let it flow over him, his cloak snapping and writhing behind him.

This is my place too, Bradon thought, *this is where I came from, my ancestry*. Bradon felt it in his bones, a deep tie to the highest mountains and the harshest cold. His family had long called the western borders of Albyn home, where the Ironback Mountains marked the boundary between civilization and the barbarian clans of the west. Different mountains than these High Fells, but some of the Ironbacks were just as high and their storms could be just as deadly.

The clans that lived in the Ironbacks were as savage as the mountains. Few in number, but immense in size, strength and brutality, their summer raids on the frontier resulted in a state of almost constant fighting around Albyn's western settlements. Bradon had seen single clansmen fight off entire squads of armed soldiers, using heavy iron axes, iron-shod clubs and sheer strength to overwhelm armor, steel, swords and training.

Bradon's family traced its origins to Otho, the greatest of the ancient barbarian kings, a warrior who had conquered dozens of the surrounding clans and forged them into a force that had ruled over their mountain valleys and passes for decades. As the story went, the King of Albyn agreed to grant Otho the mountain fortress of Irongate Castle and all of the towns and villages in its domain in return for Otho's fealty.

Bradon knew that the stories were true. He could feel the power of the western clans coursing through him when he went into battle, an energy that filled his muscles and sinews with strength, speed and fury. And he could feel it in the heart of the coldest winters. He held a deep satisfaction and knowledge that snow, ice and cold at the top of the world were *right*.

Bradon pushed his hood back and let his long black hair stream into the wind. He yanked the ties off his beard, spread his arms wide, and roared an ancient battle cry that joined the wind's howl. The wind drove fiery fingers down his throat and neck and wrapped around inside his chest. Alistair joined him. A deep bellow of joy rose above the wind, and Bradon grinned savagely and roared again, and again, until the two warriors finally succumbed to laughter as they rode together through the gale.

But the laughter died away when dusk approached and the grim mass of Nóinín Cnoc and the shapes of the dark buildings huddled on its top finally loomed out of the snow ahead of them. Bradon could see the jagged holes in the temple's stone walls staring blackly at him when the wind tore a gap in the shrouds of snow, and Bradon felt that the dark holes watched him as they drew near.

He shook the feeling from him with a shower of snow and guided his horse through a gap in the low rock wall that surrounded the temple's fields. Too often he had seen black entrances waiting for him, with the threat of death watching from within, to be unnerved by a foreboding façade. The Ironbacks were rotten with caves and tunnels, and the clans used them whenever they were threatened, lurking in their depths, watching for any enemy foolish enough to try to follow them into the black roots of the mountains.

But where his foe went, Bradon followed, no matter if it be a black cave or a green field, and he was well-used to the grim challenge those dark holes encompassed.

Besides, this is no cave, and there are no fierce warriors awaiting us, Bradon chided himself. *It merely appears ominous because I know what lies within.*

A faint light flickered from one of the temple windows, a torch guttering in the wind. Bradon's horse snorted and stamped as it found its way up the slope, slipping on the icy mud hidden under the fresh snow. Bradon urged it upwards, and the horse leapt gamely forward.

The wind moaned around the ruined temple as they dismounted in front of its sagging door. A faint glow on the side of the doorframe was the only sign of whomever was within, and Bradon hesitated. The patrol he had sent ahead from the army encampment should have set a guard, but there was no one to challenge the riders. Again Bradon felt a twinge of unease, and he realized that more drove the feeling than instinct.

Something is wrong about this place. Wyn said it and she was right. There's an echo here. Of something.

Bradon turned to Alistair. The Captain had unstrapped his war axe from across his back and was absently polishing imagined rust from its immaculate edge as he watched the temple. He too was unsettled, and when Bradon caught his eye a simple nod was enough to know the two warriors were ready if there was danger lurking within the temple.

"Lord Bradon!" A shout carried through the wind.

A soldier had dismounted a short distance from the others near a low rock wall, one of the twins, Cormac, Bradon could tell from the round shield slung across his back. Cormac crouched next to a deep drift of snow that had piled against the wall, and Bradon joined him in a half-dozen quick strides.

It took Bradon a moment to understand what he was seeing. The grey light did little to reveal the dark shapes lying on the rocks and mud, and the snow concealed more. It was a body, that much was certain immediately. A soldier, his ringed mail visible under his cloak, and a steel blade in the mud next to his out-flung hand. Blood stained the mud and snow around him and formed a broad pool under his body, and Bradon realized that it still glistened wetly despite the freezing air.

But there was much that made no sense. The soldier lay face-up and Bradon saw that his coat had been ripped open and his armor torn apart down the middle of his chest. A terrible wound crossed his torso, the flesh rent in a long track from ribs to navel. Bones were shattered, flesh ripped, his bowls eviscerated. Bradon had seen many wounds, but this one looked more like the remains of a deer ravaged by wolves than any mark a weapon could leave.

"Only a short time ago, m'lord." Cormac carefully moved across the snow towards the buildings, bent low. "He came from the temple."

"And his pursuers?"

"I'm not sure, m'lord." Cormac stopped and squatted to peer at the ground. "There's a track here, heavy, but I am not sure…" The soldier's voice trailed off as he considered the marks on the ground.

Cormac stood after a moment. "A troll. Perhaps."

"You don't sound certain," Bradon rumbled.

"No, m'lord." Cormac shook his head as he frowned intently at the snow at his feet.

Bradon nodded to himself silently, then rejoined the others where they waited near the temple.

"What is it?" Danielle drew her cloak tightly about her shoulders as the wind whipped past.

"One of our soldiers, killed but a short time ago," Bradon stroked his beard as he considered. The dead soldier was clearly from the scout patrol he had sent ahead of them, and there were no signs of the rest of the group.

"Ready yourselves," Bradon told them, and slipped his giant hammer from its loop on his belt. "Whatever killed that soldier may wait for us within."

"He'll wish he hadn't," Wyn grinned fiercely as she produced two long, curved knives from behind her back with a flourish. But Bradon could see that the girl's face was pale within her black hood, and her mouth was set in a thin line. *The lass is fearful, despite her bravado*, Bradon realized. *But she does not hesitate.*

Bradon returned her smile and joined Alistair at the door. At a nod the two warriors moved through it into the temple, weapons ready.

The front of the temple was filled with deep shadows. A faint orange glow flickered from beyond the mountainous pile of debris that filled the center of the room where the roof had collapsed, and the dull evening light did little but create pale grey shapes where the windows gaped open on the blizzard outside. The room reeked of death, an old, dry odor of the tomb lying underneath the fresh, wet stink of violence and blood.

Bradon moved past the shattered remains of the roof. The light came from a single torch, lying on the stone floor beyond the tumbled beams and stones from the collapse. Its wan flame sputtered and wavered as it fought against the snow that swirled through the roof to land on it.

But the torch was bright enough to see the fresh slaughter that lay next to it. Three soldiers had died here, victims of a brutal assault. They lay near each other, as if they had fought back-to-back until their dying moment. Great wounds crossed their bodies, their steel armor ripped, the flesh shredded underneath. Blood soaked the floor in a deep pool and long rivulets stained the wall near where they sprawled.

Beyond the soldiers spread the ghastly ritual, far more ominous than he could have imagined.

The withered remains of the sacrificed lay as Wyn had described them, in a circle around the center of the room, undisturbed by the violence nearby. Blood from the soldiers had spread across the stones and pooled under the nearest of the sacrificed bodies, obscuring the black markings of the ritual circle.

Wind howled across the gaps in the wall and roof. Snow danced and shimmered in the torchlight before settling in an even, white layer over the floor, debris, and corpses.

A few footprints in the snow made tracks around the back wall of the temple, but the area around the ritual was pristine. Clearly, no one had approached the ritual circle, at least since the snow had fallen.

Bradon moved forward to the edge of the circle, the thick black markings still evident under the thin layer of snow. He examined the bodies, one hand gripping the haft of his hammer, the other stroking his wind-blown beard, now a wild mass of tangles and ice.

"Search for tracks," he told Alistair, and he glanced up to catch the Captain's eye. "Find whoever did this."

Alistair nodded and left the temple, calling his men with him. Bradon could hear shouted orders receding into the hissing wind as they moved down the hill.

"My lady, I need you to take a look at this," Bradon rumbled.

Danielle pushed back her hood and stepped lightly around the collapsed roof to stand next to him. From a pack worn against the small of her back she took a carefully wrapped object.

She pulled one glove off with her teeth, letting it drop to the floor as she untied the object and let the leather wrappings fall away from the small metal amulet within.

Bradon bent and retrieved the glove, small and soft in his armored gauntlet, and he gently held it for her as she concentrated on the amulet. The amulet unfolded gracefully as her long fingers moved smoothly and assuredly over its intricate shapes, and threads of silver and gold around its edge formed themselves into a delicate braid at her touch. She closed her eyes briefly, and Bradon felt the slight tug of her Word as she whispered it.

Energy rippled across Danielle's amulet, and when her eyes opened Bradon saw that her golden irises had turned completely black as her gaze reached far beyond any mortal eye.

"Has someone returned and performed another ritual?" Bradon asked.

"I am not sure," Danielle replied quietly. "I do not believe so."

"We should burn them," Wyn whispered. "Right now."

Bradon had not heard the girl move behind him. She stood a couple of paces back, and met his gaze defiantly as he turned to her.

"Not until Danielle has a chance to discern what is happening here," Bradon said as gently as he could. "We have nothing to fear from a few old corpses."

"I'm not afraid of corpses," Wyn hissed at him. "It's what they're doing. Something's happening and they're doing it. Can't you feel it?"

Bradon nodded. *I can indeed. The 'dark emptiness' Wyn called it. It's colder than that, and it's not empty. It's hungry.*

"This will not take long," Danielle said, her gaze still locked on unseen distances.

"That's nice. Burn them," Wyn seethed.

Bradon tapped the haft of his hammer. *It's growing stronger, fast now. Closer.*

"My lady, Danielle, I think Wyn is right. Please hurry."

"I am," Danielle murmured. "There is magic here. I can see it, but it is unlike anything I have seen before. There is something…"

The wind moaned across the open gaps in the temple and snow glittered as the torch flickered. Bradon frowned. *There is something there…*

"That is strange," whispered Danielle from far away.

A shape watched them from the dark recesses of the room, a shadow still amongst the swirling snow. Then it stirred, and black eyes within the shadow locked on Bradon's, and he saw pale skin, and black claws on the ends of long fingers.

"Protect Danielle," Bradon barked to Wyn, and he swung his hammer from his belt and lunged towards the figure.

It waited for him. A few enormous strides and Bradon was upon it, and his hammer swung down to crush whatever stood there. But the shadow met it with a sword as pale as its flesh, and the weapons screeched as if in pain.

The shock of the impact ran up Bradon's arm like a dagger strike, but he ignored the pain and let the swing carry on, bringing his hammer back around for another blow. But the shadow struck first and freezing claws wrapped themselves around Bradon's neck with strength like steel. Bradon grabbed the arm by its wrist and pulled, but could not break its grasp. He brought his hammer down upon the arm, but the shadow met it with its blade and caught it, holding it above their heads.

But it was not a shadow any longer. Bradon could see a figure shaped like a man but taller, with white skin stretched over ropes of sinew and muscle. Lethal black talons tore at Bradon's steel gorget. The creature's face was shaped like a man's, but sharp fangs ripped from black gums and black eyes stared coldly at Bradon.

Bradon felt freezing cold encircle his throat, probing downwards into his chest as if searching for his heart. He roared and let rage fill his limbs with fire. With renewed strength, he fought against the creature's cold grasp. He drove the thing backwards, pushing with the power of his legs against its steely strength. He felt its clawed feet gouge the stone floor until he slammed it into the wall. The creature twisted its blade free and struck at Bradon, but he blocked it with his hammer, and brought the massive steel head down onto the arm holding him, wrenching and twisting with all of his strength. The creature bent, ever so slightly, and Bradon felt its talons scrape across the steel of his armor as its grasp slid loose.

Free of its choking hold, Bradon breathed deeply and bellowed again. The creature howled in reply, a shriek of inhuman fury that rasped across the chamber and seemed to reverberate and grow instead of fading away.

Bradon raised his hammer high and struck down and across and down again. The creature stood against him, meeting each crushing blow with its own sword and unnatural strength, turning the hammer aside so that it blasted stones from the wall and cracked the floor instead of smashing its enemy.

But Bradon felt it give ground, and the cold was receding from his chest. He doubled his assault, gripped the hammer with both hands and attacked with unrelenting fury.

He heard Wyn's cry of warning just in time, and he leapt away as something rigid clutched at his boot. The withered husks on the floor were crawling towards him, staggering to their feet. Bradon lashed out with his hammer at the one that had tried to grab him and he felt bones splinter as the blow connected, knocking the husk backwards.

In the next instant, cold fire cut across his back as the white creature slashed its sword across him. The blade scored across steel plates with a screech and tore through chain mail at the joint under his left arm. Bradon twisted away from the following attack as numbing cold spread from the wound like ice across the surface of a well.

The thing attacked again, and again, its pale sword ripping through the air to carom off Bradon's hammer as the Templar fought to regain his balance.

Danielle's Word exploded into the room, a concussion of force felt by the spirit rather than the body. The temple was bathed in light as emerald fire ran from a silver medallion held in her outstretched hand, raced across the floor to engulf three of the corpse husks as they stood, and raged into a tornado of flame that wrapped itself around Bradon's opponent. Bradon saw its pale flesh blacken and split open under the fire, and its mouth gaped open in a silent scream.

It turned from Bradon and with swift strides moved across the circle towards Danielle, and as it charged, the flames surrounding it blew into nothingness, their power expended. The husks also turned towards her, reaching with skeletal fingers as they advanced.

Danielle retreated two quick steps. She raised the medallion as she tried to race through her Word a second time. But the Device, potent though it was, was not crafted for the speed of battle. It was powerful and elegant, and its Word was correspondingly elaborate. Danielle's eyes closed in concentration and she stood tall with both hands wrapped around the Device, and Bradon saw her enter the state of trance-like focus required to activate such a Word.

She'll never make it. Danielle was one of the most skilled adepts Bradon had ever met, capable of mastering Words of awesome power and intricacy, but they took time no matter how skilled the user. Bradon surged towards her, fighting the cold numbness that engulfed his left side and arm, but the white creature already loomed over Danielle as the husks surrounded her, reaching towards her as she stood unflinchingly against them.

Then Wyn darted in front of Danielle, slipping between two of the husks. Two long, curved knives flashed and the husks staggered as the blades cut deep gashes through their necks. The girl moved like a shadow, her black cloak whirling as she dove beneath the white creature and lashed out with a spinning kick that should have swept its legs away. But it was too strong. The kick might as well have been delivered to a tree, and Wyn dived and rolled to avoid the creature's sword as it swung at her.

Bradon reached Danielle, and his hammer whirled to sweep aside a husk. He shouted her name and she blinked as her eyes focused on him.

"There is no time for magic," he begged her. "There are too many… use your blade, find safety before you try again."

Then the husks were on him and he fiercely returned to the battle. He wrenched cold, clutching fingers from his arm and flung the husk into its neighbor. From the corner of his eye he caught sight of Danielle, short blade in hand, hacking at the back of a husk as she leapt for the pile of debris in the center of the room.

Then Alistair vaulted from an opening in the wall, his axe a silver blur as it cleaved through the husks around Bradon. Left and the right the axe swept through the air as the soldier weaved and spun, and the husks fell like grain under a scythe.

Bradon turned towards Wyn, still locked in a dance with the white-skinned demon. She ducked low under a vicious swing of its sword, her knives dragging sparks from the stone floor, then she dove under its reverse swing, and the sword's blade ripped only air where she had crouched a moment before. She rolled out of her dive behind it, knives flashing as she whirled away, cutting twin gashes across its back.

The creature was not slowed though. It twisted like a snake and struck after the spinning girl. Fabric ripped as the point of the blade tore through her woolen coat and the slim black tunic she wore underneath, and Wyn was forced to desperately leap away, again on the defensive.

Bradon bellowed a challenge and stepped forward with his hammer high. The white creature turned to face him, its fangs bared in fury. Bradon's hammer arced through the air and when it fell it struck with the impact of a tremendous siege engine against a castle gate.

The creature recoiled from the blow, and its steel-strong skin split open. Before it could recover, Bradon struck again and his hammer smashed it backwards. A primal cry welled from the depths of his chest as the hammer fell faster and faster. Once again stones shattered and the walls trembled as the creature knocked the hammer aside, its unnatural strength seemingly limitless. But Bradon could feel each attack plunging deeper, each parry coming later and rebounding less. And then the hammer struck home again, smashing aside the sword to land heavily on the creature's shoulder. It staggered under the blow and Bradon struck again, and again.

The temple throbbed as Danielle's Word pulsed again, and green fire roared around the creature, raced across its skin and poured into the cracks and fissures. The creature writhed and lashed out but the fire consumed it, blistering its skin until it burst, and then there was nothing left but a pale shadow that drifted into smoke.

Bradon turned to the others, ready to attack the corpse husks, but that fight was over, too. Alistair drove his axe into the last of them, pinning it to a wooden beam so immense was the strength of the blow, while the other husks lay on the floor around him with terrible cuts across their desiccated bodies.

Danielle stood on the collapsed roof debris. Her arm dropped to her side and the last flickers of emerald flame fluttered between her fingers.

Wyn rested on the floor, her back against a beam from the ceiling, her arms draped over her knees. Her hood was pushed back and her blonde hair had come free from its tie to hang wearily over her face. *Knives still ready*, Bradon thought, noting the two long, thin, steel blades held to either side of her legs, *that one will fight to the end. Good to know.*

He knelt beside Wyn, concerned that she might have taken a wound from the cold blade of the white-skinned creature.

"No problems here." She glanced up through the hair falling across her face, a wry smile on the corner of her lips. "Hasn't yet been a horrible death thing summoned that can catch me. Although this one came close, I guess," she continued ruefully, investigating the tear in her tunic. The rough wool shirt was slashed for almost the length of Bradon's hand, and he saw a faint red line traced on her skin from her hip all the way to her ribs through the gap.

"I can't say the same for you," Alistair said to Bradon. Bradon had to agree. Now that he knew the others were safe, the pain from his wound was finally starting to break through the battle fury that had sustained him. It was a strange pain, burning cold and numb at the same time, and the weakness on that side continued to grow.

He tried to rise from his knee, but swayed and went down again.

"Lady Danielle, he needs you. Hurry," Alistair urged.

She quickly moved to his side and unbuckled his breastplate, letting it clatter to the stones beside him. He could feel fingers pressed to his side near the wound, but the touch felt strangely numb to him, as if it were on the other side of a thick pad.

"Hold still now," Danielle said as she pulled another Device from her pack.

Bradon laughed softly. "I'm not going anywhere, don't worry."

"Captain," Danielle instructed Alistair, "in my saddlebags, my kit is in a small wooden box." The soldier hurried from the temple. She donned a thin silver circlet that glimmered as it nestled in her dark hair, focused for the space of a dozen breaths, and spoke its Word. Danielle examined the wound with confidence then, the circlet guiding her and filling her with knowledge.

"The wound is deep, but the cut was sharp, and the blood is clean," Danielle frowned. "But the flesh turns pale."

"It is cold," Bradon murmured. "Numb."

Alistair returned with the small mahogany box from Danielle's bags, and she took a flask of boiled wine and quickly washed the wound out. "There is a splinter," she announced.

Danielle took a pair of steel scalpels from her kit and bent close to the wound. A deft cut and Danielle raised a thin shard of pale metal from the wound, held between the blades as she examined it. Bradon felt the searing cold melt away, replaced by a fiery pain that outlined the gash in his side.

"Now it hurts," he grumbled, but the pain felt like any other wound he had suffered, and he settled back, well-versed in what came next.

"I can put it back," suggested Danielle as she prepared a short steel needle with a sturdy thread. Bradon held a cloth against the wound to slow the bleeding while Danielle stitched, her fingers sure and quick as they worked. Danielle pressed a fresh cloth over the wound and wrapped bandages around his torso to hold it in place.

"There," Danielle said, and Bradon felt the pulse as she released the circlet's power. Danielle drew a breath and removed the Device, and rested gentle fingers on the bandage. "You will live I think. You need to learn to duck better."

"You say that every time," he laughed.

Danielle laughed as well, and rose to her feet with a long stretch of her back. "You will never listen. I will just keep mending you, it is easier."

She extended a hand and he held it gently it as he climbed to his feet. He tested his side with his hand, and winced. "Good as new, my lady. My thanks."

"I have an idea," said Wyn from the ground at his feet. She looked at the three of them, chin resting on the palm of her hand. "I think we should burn them."

Torbhin

It was long past the middle of the night when Torbhin spied a flickering yellow light far ahead of him through the blinding snow. It faded from view almost instantly, but Torbhin had fixed its location in his mind, and pressed on towards it through the gale.

The ranger's horse plodded heavily through snow that piled up to its knees, and stumbled frequently as it stepped on rocks and divots hidden under the smooth surface. Torbhin knew it did not have much more left to give. *Neither do I*, he shivered and beat his arms together to try and restore some feeling in his numb fingers. He had long ago given up hope for his feet, blocks of ice wedged into his stirrups, but he needed his hands to clutch the edges of his cloak together and hold his hood in place. *It must be a light on Nóinín Cnoc. It must be, or else I am completely lost.* But he had told himself that twice already this endless night, when he had encountered hills rearing out of the floor of the valley he was following. And each time he had labored to the top, only to realize there was no temple.

This time there's a light, he persuaded himself. *So there must be something there. If it's not, I must have passed it, and I need to turn around.*

The ride should have taken a day at most, but the wind had started almost the moment he had begun his ride the dawn before, and the snow had arrived less than an hour later, turning a grey morning into a world filled with flying white. Torbhin had counted his horse's steps as well as he could, but there had been so many stumbles, and so much backtracking, that he had long ago given that up.

The ground began to rise ahead of him, and a low, stone wall spitefully appeared to block his path. He guided the horse along it until he found a gap, unwilling to risk a jump with a horse already pushed to its limits.

The light appeared again, now hovering above him, weak and transient in the storm. But Torbhin could tell that it was much closer. He urged his horse upwards with a steady stream of encouraging words, until at last they reached another wall, and an open gate with the black lumps of buildings looming at him from the snow.

Torbhin dismounted and staggered on his numb feet. The light came from the rear of the compound, a swinging lantern hung above the doors of a barn. He led his horse towards it, but had not gone ten steps before a voice came to him through the wind.

"Torbhin? Maker, is that you?"

The ranger gratefully let strong hands urge him through the barn doors. He caught a glimpse of a friendly smile behind a red beard crusted with snow, and recognized one of the soldiers that traveled with Bradon. Someone took the reins from his frozen fingers and led his horse deeper into the barn.

They had lit a campfire in the center of the barn's packed dirt floor, and set bedrolls around it to stay close to the warmth. Torbhin saw huddled shapes wrapped in blankets, and heard a chorus of snores that competed with the shrieking wind and the groaning timbers of the barn's roof.

Seated near the fire, deep in conversation, were Lord Bradon, Captain Alistair, and Lady Danielle, but all three quickly climbed to their feet when he stepped into the light. Torbhin wished that they had not. He very much wanted to sit.

Lady Danielle wrapped blankets around Torbhin's shoulders, and called for food, a steaming broth in a dented tin mug that he gratefully wrapped his fingers around.

"Torbhin, lad, where did you come from?" Bradon's voice rumbled in astonishment.

"From Lord Lucious," Torbhin managed to keep his voice from shaking as he shivered. "At least, I found where he was, m'lord."

"You did? Well done, lad," Bradon clenched Torbhin's shoulder in a huge hand and squeezed it reassuringly. "Is he coming? How many men does he bring?"

"None, m'lord." Torbhin shook his head and felt snow slide down his neck. "I didn't speak with him, as his army was attacking a village when I found him, and I kept my distance."

"What's this?" Bradon's eyes narrowed and his voice rose in disbelief. "Attacking a village? Are you certain?"

"Yes, m'lord." Torbhin held his gaze. "They had set fire to the buildings, and I saw Lord Lucious' men storm the tower. They used a Weapon to destroy the tower gate."

Bradon straightened to his full height and quietly stroked the wild tangle of his beard, his face suddenly closed and dangerous.

"When was this?" Alistair's voice was steel.

"Last night." Torbhin had to think for a moment to confirm that was true. It seemed ludicrous that something so long ago could in fact have been just a night before. "I left at first light, but I was delayed by the storm."

"Of course you were," Lady Danielle consoled him. "I am amazed you made it through at all."

"You saw Lord Lucious?" Alistair pressed him.

"No, sir. But I saw his sigil. Three red swords, crossed."

"Is that Lucious?" Alistair asked Bradon, and the Lord silently nodded his head.

"Why would he do such a thing?" Lady Danielle frowned in confusion and anger. "Is it not enough that there are killings, and dark magic, and even terrible storms? Now he adds slaughter to the list?"

"Whatever the reason, we shall put an end to it at first light," Bradon stated quietly.

"And the other ritual sites?" Lady Danielle pressed. "If what happened here has also happened there…"

"This is exactly why we brought an army," Bradon reassured her. "Alistair, in the morning, send word to Sir Lochlan. Ask him to send patrols to each of the other ritual sites we know of, as soon as he can, and make sure he understands to send them ready to fight. And tell him to hurry up and get here with the rest of the army. We've got girls and southerners here who made the trip already, so no excuses."

"Southern girls, even," Lady Danielle pointed out. "And what is your plan for Lord Lucious and the village he attacked?"

"I get to deal with Lucious," Bradon smiled humorlessly. "I need something to do instead of just waiting for the snow to stop so that we can find Killock's little paw prints." Bradon turned to Torbhin. "Unless you think you can find his tracks under all of this snow?"

"No, m'lord, I'm sorry," Torbhin answered. "But the snow may be a blessing once it stops falling. Any tracks they made after it stops snowing will be as clear as smoke from a fire. If Sir Killock was at all successful at tracking them before the storm hit, we should be able to pick up their trail right away."

"So we just have to keep busy until the storm passes, is that it?" Bradon shifted his grip on the pommel of his hammer. "A perfect excuse to pay Lucious a visit in person."

"The storm passes, m'lord, and Sir Killock returns to tell us where he tracked them to."

"Very well," Lord Bradon said with finality, and raised his voice to fill the barn. "Then at first light we ride south, so anyone who didn't enjoy the little flurries we rode through to get here had best pray to Ddraighnall for some better weather."

"Ddraighnall wouldn't listen to this lot," Alistair sadly shook his head. "Not a true warrior among them."

"Thank you, Captain," a voice called from near the campfire, and there was a murmur of chuckles and agreement that interrupted the snores for a moment.

Lord Bradon chortled to himself under his breath as he watched the smoky room with a smile. He glanced at Torbhin and continued in a quieter voice.

"Grab yourself some kip, lad. You did well to make it through to us."

"Thank you, m'lord," Torbhin nodded his head and carried his mug to the back of the barn, away from the good-natured grousing and laughter, to find a quiet spot to sleep. There were stalls and a small manger, and Torbhin was surprised to find that the animals were not alone. Wyn was busy explaining straw to one of the soldiers, the one with the silver sword and blonde hair.

"As long as they have plenty of straw, they'll be fine until the army arrives," Wyn stated matter-of-factly. "Oh, hello," she added cheerily as Torbhin entered the stall. "Come to help feed the poddies? When did you get here? Missed the fight, you did. Oh, this is Corlath, I think, might be his brother, not sure. And this is Torbhin, although he likes to be called Snowball."

"I know Torbhin very well," Corlath replied with a slight smile. "He is my oldest friend in the north."

"Funny old world, that's a fact," said Wyn, uninterested, but Torbhin nodded to Corlath in appreciation. *I hope Snowball doesn't stick. I wonder if it would be better to say something or ignore it? Neither seem to have much hope*, he decided morosely.

"There are six cows, and a couple of goats," Wyn spun in a circle to make sure of her count. "An old plow horse. And there's a lovely orange cat somewhere, although he's not one for company."

Torbhin tried to think of something interesting to say, but his tired mind was not up for it. He took refuge in his mug, then good-naturedly agreed to help Corlath fill the stalls with hay from the bales in the back of the barn.

When they returned they discovered that Lady Danielle had joined Wyn and was brushing down one of the cows as if it were a horse.

"They are so wooly!" Lady Danielle objected with a laugh as the brush got tangled in the cow's shaggy coat. "Are all cows like this in Albyn?"

"I suppose so," Wyn twisted her mouth in concentration. "I mean, they're just cows, aren't they? How else should they be?"

"With short hair. Go on with you now," Lady Danielle chided the cow she was brushing, which insisted on leaning towards her, and gave it a firm push. "Like a horse's I suppose, and different colors than brown or black. I am not sure, to tell the truth. I have never been so close to a cow before."

"Their long hair keeps them warm," Torbhin ventured, suddenly tongue-tied. "The dark colors too," he concluded lamely.

"What sort of colors are they where you come from, then?" asked Wyn.

"Brown as well, but also blonde, and some are white with black spots," Lady Danielle replied.

"Spots and short hair?" Wyn giggled. "Sounds like a boy I bedded once in Glen Walden. He was even named Bull. Not for the reason I thought he was though, there's the shame of it. Which is why… once."

"His name was truly Bull?" Lady Danielle asked, and shook her head, astonished. "I would never have dared speak to a man named Bull."

"It wasn't really Bull, that's just what we called him. I don't know what his real name was," Wyn shrugged him away.

"What does 'noeenynock' mean?" Danielle asked, to Torbhin's relief.

"What does what mean?" asked Wyn.

"This temple. Is it not called 'Noeenynock'?"

"You say it 'Noineen Cnoc'," laughed Wyn.

"That is what I said," insisted Danielle.

"Well, it's the Old Language, innit?" Wyn said. "It means 'Daisy Hill' or something like that."

"Is that all?" Danielle sounded disappointed. "It sounds so lovely."

"It does, that's a fact. It's a shame really," mused Wyn.

"What is a shame?"

"That we had to change all our words just so that you lot could talk to us."

"You mean so that you could be understood," Danielle laughed. "Although half of you are still impossible to understand, even after hundreds of years of speaking a proper language."

"Do you use Common in the south also?"

"We do, although it is spoken far less in Venaissin than here in Albyn. For many Venaissine, Common is their second language, especially amongst the nobles," Danielle replied. "I did not learn Common until I was seven, and my mother insisted."

"Why don't you lot learn Common then?"

"I have heard it said that Venaissine is such an ancient and elegant language that it cannot be replaced by Common, but I believe it is truly because we are extremely pretentious." Danielle glanced at Wyn. "But it is true that Venaissine is a very beautiful tongue, like yours. Would you like to learn it?"

"Oh, I couldn't do something like that." Wyn shook her head ruefully. "It would be like trying to get a pig to dance. Really all I was thinking was that if folks used Common in the south, then if I ever visited or something, traveled there, it would be easier. Oh, it's stupid, I'm not going to travel anywhere except horrible little towns in the ass-end of nowhere."

"I think you would enjoy it in Venaissin," Danielle said. "There are more towns and cities, and not so many trees."

"That does sound nice," Wyn agreed. "I think you've made a friend there, by the way."

"I know, she is impossible." Lady Danielle pushed uselessly on the cow again. "Far too pushy, it will never do. Did all of the animals survive?"

"Not the chickens." Wyn shook her head and smiled slyly. "There's a cat around here somewhere, and I think he ate all the chickens, the devil. He told me his name was Ranga."

"But none killed by those who performed the ritual, they sacrificed only people," Lady Danielle said thoughtfully. "Nor by the white creature, who feasted on men but left the animals alone. It reminds me of something..." her voice trailed off for a moment. "When Sir Lochlan arrives I will have to send a bird to Bandirma. I think I may know what the white creature is."

"The white creature?" Torbhin asked, perplexed.

"Oooo, he was terrible!" Wyn's green eyes grew wide and stared intently into Torbhin's. "Came at us out of the dark, with claws and fangs and such. Killed four soldiers before we had him. Horrible thing. Her Ladyship did him in, but it was a might close there for a while."

"It was hardly me that defeated it," Lady Danielle objected. "Bradon hit it with his hammer so hard I thought the roof might collapse, and you…" she closed her eyes and gently shook her head, a soft smile on her lips. "Well, you were amazing, Wyn, with your knives, and whirling around it." She opened her eyes and blinked away her vision. "I cannot even begin to describe it."

"I call it 'running for my life'," Wyn grinned, thoroughly pleased. "Oh, and Shoulders was there too. But don't listen to her Ladyship. It was her that set the thing on fire, and just by waving her fingers about. It was something to see, that was."

Torbhin looked to Corlath for help, more confused now than he had been before the women had explained it to him. But the soldier merely shook his head.

"Don't ask me," he smiled wryly. "I was wandering around the hill in a blizzard. I missed all the fun."

"You can have the next one," Wyn assured him, laughing.

"There are more?" Torbhin asked.

"Unfortunately, I think that is very likely," Lady Danielle replied. "It was almost certainly summoned by the ritual, which means there could be one at every one of the sites. That is why Lord Bradon is so anxious to send troops to them. I cannot bear to think of the slaughter several of these creatures could inflict on the farms and villages nearby if they are not destroyed."

They finished feeding and watering the animals in a subdued mood after that, and retired to their bedrolls, fighting off yawns as they went.

Torbhin drifted off to sleep with his mind filled with images of clawed, white-skinned creatures that menaced a beautiful girl with long, golden hair, and dreamed of her smile and bright green eyes once he had saved her by felling the creatures with deadly shots from his bow.

***

By dusk the gale had blown itself out. Snow poured from the sky, huge powdery flakes that piled up in drifts across the ruined village and the encampment of Lord Lucious. As daylight faltered the soldiers dug a communal grave in the frozen dirt. Black smoke from the burning tower and the small village at its base stained the falling snow a dull, dark grey. Pale banners drooped from spears lodged in the ground, their crossed red swords a twisted blot in the heavy folds.

Villagers who survived the attack carried scorched bodies through the piled snow and icy mud to the pit, laid them in rows, gently covered them with what could be spared, and then waited numbly until the pit grew large enough to hold them all. The soldiers methodically hacked at the unyielding soil, and paused only to adjust a hood or scarf, or to wipe wind-bitten tears and soot from their eyes.

Torches were being lit when a dozen horsemen arrived. The muffled thud of hoof beats along the snow-choked lane rose in volume until it could be heard over the short, sharp noises of axes and shovels hitting the earth. Soldiers huddled in their cloaks and warily watched the riders pass through the camp. Tall black shapes wrapped in leather, metal gear, and flowing cloaks rode on horses that blew hot clouds of steam into the frozen air.

The camp was not inspiring. The tents were set up in orderly rows around the supply wagons, paths between them had been shoveled though the deep snow, and guards stood watch on the fields. But no scouts or exterior pickets watched for enemies on the approach, and Lucious' men were clearly intent on settling here for several days. They were even digging latrines.

Are we not meant to be pursuing our enemies? Torbhin wondered. He knew it was what drove Bradon and the Temple forces. He had his doubts about Lord Lucious.

Lord Bradon led the riders through a gap in the gnarled hedgerow that bordered the track and towards the low mass of a large pavilion that overlooked the ruined village.

Torches hissed yellow in front of the tent's entrance and illuminated more soldiers who wore Lord Lucious' arms. A long pennant fluttered weakly from the peak of the pavilion, and its tip dragged heavily across the tent's fabric as it shifted in the chill, snow-filled air.

The horsemen reined to a stop and dismounted. Torbhin handed the reins of his horse to one of the guards and followed Lord Bradon to the pavilion.

Bradon exchanged a few words with the soldiers standing guard. One entered the tent and Torbhin heard a brief, muttered question and response through the canvas before the guard returned and invited them inside. Bradon entered first, sweeping aside the heavy fur that covered the opening. Torbhin held the flap aside for Danielle, who smiled her thanks as she passed, followed by Wyn, who rolled her eyes.

Inside, lanterns hung from tent poles and illuminated the pavilion with a weak glow. A small iron stove hissed and gave off damp warmth that could only be felt when standing directly next to it. Furs and tapestries slinked across every wall, clung to the roof, and crawled across the ground.

Lord Bradon's bulk filled the tent. One hand rested on the hilt of his war hammer, the other stroked his tangled beard as he glanced about the interior. Torbhin stepped to the side and feigned interest in an open chest filled with silver plates and goblets, and made note of the fact that the crest stamped on them was not three crossed swords.

Of the two men waiting for them in the pavilion it was obvious which one was Lord Lucious. He was a tall man, and young, which surprised Torbhin. His tall, velvet collar framed a face with a thin beard that was trimmed to a point, and his dark hair was short and swept back from a high forehead and long nose. He wore a sable cloak against the chill, and at his waist hung a long Weapon, sheathed, with an engraved hilt on which he casually rested his hand. He stood at ease by the stove, but Torbhin could see that Lucious was nervous.

The other man waiting for them in the tent was a knight, perhaps Lucious' master-at-arms. Torbhin felt that he had the look of a soldier long removed from actual soldiering. Older and with a strong build, but going to fat now. He had a thick mustache and chin beard, eyes that stared from slits, and a frown that rested in deep wrinkles.

Bradon stood in silence and regarded the pair in front of him, his face neutral. Danielle moved to stand beside Bradon, while Wyn remained by the entrance and leaned against a tent pole. Her eyes roamed the tent and a frown of distaste crept across her face.

"Lord Bradon," Lucious ventured, and he took a hesitant half-step forward to greet the Templar. "I am so very pleased to meet you, but I must admit I am surprised. What brings you so far into my very humble slice of the hinterlands?"

"I thought I was here for the same reasons as you, Lucious." Bradon's voice rumbled through the tent. "Burnt farms, destroyed temples."

"Murdered people," added Wyn.

"Aye, and also murder." Bradon agreed solemnly. "Are you surprised that this concerns the Temple as well?"

"No, of course not," Lucious answered quickly. "'Tis of concern to all of us. That is why I have been running down the bastards responsible. And with great success, might I add! Just two nights ago I destroyed a stronghold that provided them with shelter in this very village. A mighty blow against them."

"Glad news then," said Lady Danielle. "And you are sure the enemy was sheltering here?"

"Of course, my lady." Lucious paused, clearly uncomfortable. "My lady, I am grieved to say that I don't believe we have met before, so I do not know how to address you."

"That is true," Lady Danielle agreed, and she turned to Torbhin. "What was the name of this village?"

"Blockley, m'lady, named for the brook that runs through it," answered Torbhin. He had been to Blockley many times over the years. It was the last village of any size before the true wilderness began, and Torbhin used it as a starting spot for many of his rangings as he roamed the hinterlands. A small mill by the brook had a room that the owners would rent to travelers, as the village was far too remote to support any size of inn. Torbhin had noticed the smoldering ruins of the mill as they crossed the ford on their way into the camp.

"And who rules Blockley? Whose keep gave shelter to our enemies?" Danielle's voice sounded merely curious, but Torbhin saw that the questions made Lucious more and more nervous. The young lord wanted to say something, but nothing came out.

"Sir Harrigan ruled here," Torbhin answered. Torbhin had never met Sir Harrigan, but he had seen him many times— a fat man with a red face and unkempt beard who came to the village every market day, and liked to ride from farm to farm around the valley with only a steward and a cask of beer as his escort.

"Yes, Sir Harrigan," agreed Lord Lucious. "We tracked the raiders here and confronted Sir Harrigan. He refused to open his gates and turn over his allies to us." Lucious turned to his master-at-arms for agreement. "But we made short work of them in the end, didn't we, Sir Robert?"

"Yes, m'lord."

Bradon pointed to the Weapon at Lucious' side. "And is that the Weapon that made such short work of them?"

Lucious lifted his chin proudly. "That is correct, my lord. This is my family's Weapon, the Silver Fang, Bane of Giants, whose light carries death to all who stand against it."

"Oooo, is it really?" asked Wyn. "How many giants have you baned with it?"

"Well, none of course," Lucious said, taken aback. "There are no more giants. But legend has it that my ancestor Lord Belamy Lucious hunted down and killed a giant with it many years ago. Thus its epithet." Lucious looked down his nose at Wyn. "Its name, that means."

"Does it." Wyn looked like she had more to say, but Bradon spoke first.

"I believe that I knew Sir Harrigan."

Lucious' eyes darted to meet Bradon's, but he quickly dropped his gaze. "Is that right, my lord?"

"Yes." Bradon took a step forward and held out his hands to the steaming heat of the stove. Lucious stepped back to give the Templar more room and bumped against a camp chair behind him. "I met him years ago. There was a land dispute between him and your father, over this village and its tower, I recall. Duke Thornton himself had to mediate, and I represented the Temple in the proceedings. The Duke gave this village to Sir Harrigan."

Bradon glanced at Lucious. "It angered your father immensely."

Lucious licked his lips before he summoned up his next words. "I do not think I care for what you are implying, my lord."

"What I am implying?" Bradon's voice rose to a bellow. "Your lands are being overrun by murder, dark rituals and sacrifices, and you decide it's time to settle an old land dispute and destroy a village instead of going after the real enemy."

Lucious shrank from the Templar. "No, my lord, I swear on my life…"

"Oh be careful now, boy, be careful what you swear on. I might just collect on that," Bradon growled.

"We tracked them here. Harrigan wouldn't open his gates!"

"Wouldn't he? To armed men and Lord Lucious with his Silver Spoon demanding his head? Tell me how many men were in that keep? Show me the bodies of those who desecrated your farms and my temples. It had best be more than a handful of men-at-arms wearing Harrigan's livery if you are going to swear on your life and expect to keep it."

"Some may have gotten away before we got here," stammered Lucious.

"Damn you and your lies, I've heard enough," Bradon turned to face the lord.

Torbhin saw Lucious grab for the hilt of Silver Fang, but Bradon moved faster. He delivered a blow from his fist to Lucious' face that sent him staggering backwards over the chair to the ground.

Sir Robert managed to draw his sword, but before he could make a move a long, curved knife was pressed against his throat, and Wyn whispered in his ear, "Don't you dare." Torbhin had not seen her move from her place by the door.

Bradon strode forward and grabbed Lucious by the collar of his cloak, but the lord simply sagged from his grasp, unconscious.

Bradon dropped him to the floor and turned to Sir Robert, still frozen in Wyn's grasp.

"Are you his man?" Bradon pointed at Lucious on the floor.

Sir Robert's eyes narrowed. "Not unless you say I am, m'lord. He was a right prick he was, and a shame on his family's name."

Torbhin slowly exhaled and lowered his bow. It did not look like he was going to have to shoot Sir Robert just now, but he kept the arrows he had drawn held ready just in case.

Lady Danielle stepped in front of Sir Robert and held his gaze. "Then you can help make this right. How many men do you have?"

"Just over one hundred, m'lady."

"Leave twenty of them here with your best healers to tend to the hurt and to rebuild what the survivors need, and you will march the rest north to join our men."

"Yes, m'lady. We will head out at first light."

"And if you have not arrived by dusk tomorrow, we will return to find you. You understand that Lord Bradon here will not be forgiving if we have to do that?"

"Yes, m'lady. M'lord."

"Wyn, you can let him go now. He is leaving."

Wyn angled her knife slightly and Sir Robert flinched as a small red drop appeared at the tip of her blade. She whispered, "I'll be the one to come and find you," and then slid away.

Sir Robert hurried from the tent.

Bradon removed Silver Fang from its sheath on Lord Lucious' belt. Torbhin saw that it was a beautifully crafted Weapon. Above the elegant hilt, three thin engraved shafts twined about each other as they ascended, each one made of a polished metal that shone in the lantern light. The shafts were inlaid with silver that formed ornate runes and markings, and Torbhin saw that they were hollow with numerous carefully shaped openings along their length. At the tip the three shafts came together into one narrow point.

Bradon handed it to Danielle. "What do you think of this?"

Danielle held it lightly in her right hand and rested the tip of the scepter in her left as she examined the engravings. "It is actually exquisite work, and is likely as old as he claimed. In the hands of an adept, it might be extremely powerful."

She glanced at Lucious' crumpled form on the floor. "Clearly he was not such an adept. From what Torbhin described of its use against Sir Harrigan's tower during the attack, I would guess he could barely activate it, let alone unleash its full potential. We should send it to Bandirma. Perhaps they can determine its true Word and unlock it."

"What will we do with him?" Torbhin asked, pointing at Lucious with an arrow.

"I hate to lose the men to take care of this garbage," grumbled Bradon. "But there's no help for it. We send him and an escort to Kuray for the Queen to deal with him. And we send the Silver Spoon here to Bandirma with another escort."

"I can find a better home for it than that," Wyn laughed. "I know some people who value a Weapon, even without its Word."

Bradon frowned, but it was Danielle who answered. "I do not think it is a good idea to have this one unaccounted for, no matter how profitable it might be."

"Probably right," Wyn sighed regretfully. "Shame though."

Bradon turned to Torbhin. "I think it is time to let Alistair know we are done in here."

Torbhin nodded and shouldered his way through the tent flap. Outside the pavilion Captain Alistair stood beside the horses, waiting patiently as he watched over the two soldiers who guarded the pavilion. Under the Captain's gaze, neither had budged from their position beside the tent flap, and they stared rigidly ahead as if they could not possibly have heard the commotion that had just taken place on the other side of the pavilion's thin canvas walls.

"Any trouble inside?" Alistair asked.

"None whatsoever," said Torbhin.

Danielle

The Temple army encampment spread across the meadows to the north of Nóinín Cnoc, tents grouped in orderly circles around blazing fires that made hazy, glowing spheres in the pouring snow. Soldiers filled the nearby forest to chop enough wood to keep the fires well fed, shoveled snow to keep the passages between tents open, and settled in under blankets and tents whenever possible to watch the world shrink smaller and smaller as the air filled with snow.

Despite the conditions, Bradon had left that morning with as many scouts as he could muster to search for any sign of Sir Killock, anxious for his return. Danielle had watched the horsemen disappear into the snow in ones and twos as they spread across the hills and forest to the northwest of the valley.

Danielle walked quickly through the center of the encampment towards Nóinín Cnoc, followed closely by two soldiers who carried between them a small chest made of polished wood. All of her belongings had arrived with the army, and she had spent the morning carefully unpacking the myriad bundles that the soldiers had set up in her tent, searching for just the right items to fill the little wooden chest. *And finding a warmer pair of boots.*

They began the long climb up the hill, following the crude path the soldiers had marked to stop people from wandering into the storm. Snowflakes somehow managed to drift under Danielle's deep, ermine-lined hood and sting her cheeks, but the wind's absence made the day seem almost pleasant.

They were met at the small rock wall that encircled the temple buildings by one of Alistair's men, a massive warrior with a bristling black beard and a bald head that seemed immune to the heavy snow.

"M'lady," he greeted Danielle with a booming voice. "I think the lads have finished setting up in the temple like you told 'em to. Captain Alistair would like to speak with you first, if you don't mind. He's in the barn."

"Of course," Danielle agreed.

The bearded warrior slung Danielle's chest onto his shoulder and led the way to the barn, disdaining any help from the two soldiers who had carried it up the hill. "Ha! My girls could carry this tiny thing by themselves, and my youngest is barely walking yet. Those two can go and chop wood or whatever duty they thought they were going to get out of."

Inside the barn, the small campfire had been built up and was now contained by a proper ring of stones, and Danielle saw that the soldiers had turned the barn into an outpost of sorts, with the small tents they carried in their saddlebags pitched around the fire on the barn's dirt floor. Wyn and Alistair stood next to the fire as Danielle entered, and Wyn's cheerful, bright laughter filled the barn at some comment of the Captain's.

"… but then where would the tail go?" Wyn asked Alistair mischievously, and laughed again. "Hello, your Ladyship. Captain Alistair was telling me all about his lovely tattoos. But he says I can't have a dragon, which is stupid because wouldn't it look wonderful?"

"The dragons are beautiful," Danielle agreed, "but the Captain had to earn them, you cannot just decide you want one."

"I could earn one myself, that's no trouble," Wyn waved away the concern with a flip of a hand. "No, the problem is, well look." Wyn held her arm alongside Alistair's. "I mean, it wouldn't fit on my arm, would it?" Wyn frowned seriously. "It would have to wrap around all over the place."

"I am sure it would not mind," Danielle said.

"Exactly," agreed Wyn. "So, how far do they go under there?" Wyn stared intently at Alistair's breastplate. "A long way? Can I see? Are they doing something rude?"

"They go a very long way," Alistair said mysteriously. "As for what they are doing, do you not know the story of the dragons and how the world was made?"

"No, go on," Wyn said eagerly.

"I'm afraid I can't," Alistair said gravely. "People have been known to grow faint, and swoon. I cannot risk it."

"What? We won't swoon, I promise," Wyn insisted. "Will we, your Ladyship?"

"It is not you or her Ladyship I am concerned about," Alistair raised his voice to carry through the barn. "It's these tender hearts here."

"You're not telling the dragon story again?" one of the soldiers near the fire replied. "Look alive lads, we'd best make ourselves scarce, or else there'll be tears."

"I'm not having you lot sobbing on my shoulder again," the tall, bearded warrior holding Danielle's chest shook his head. "Have mercy, Captain, I've just got my cloak dry!"

Laughter chorused around the campfire as the men gathered around the bearded warrior and begged for comforting, with Alistair smiling fondly at the commotion.

Danielle laughed to herself as she watched, and then on impulse leaned in close to Wyn.

"I know the story," Danielle whispered.

"Did it make you swoon?" Wyn sounded skeptical.

"Mmmm, a bit," Danielle revealed quietly. "I can tell you later if you would like."

"Oooo, yes please!" Wyn smiled and flashed her green eyes wide. "Aren't you full of surprises."

Danielle agreed. *I wonder why I said that? Hopefully I can get through it without blushing or embarrassing myself.*

"I am surprised to see you still here on the hill," Danielle hurried on.

"Oh, no, your Ladyship, this is the best up here," Wyn told Danielle eagerly. "Four walls and a roof, and a fire. I'd stay even if I had a tent. Which I don't, but even if. And lots of lads about just in case they're, you know, needed. It's a bit smelly, I'll grant you, but the cows don't seem to mind, and Captain Alistair promised the boys will wash eventually."

"Are you certain? Is it not hard to sleep, being this close to the temple?"

"It's alright now that they've burnt all of those nasty corpses. Made a big pyre and they burned up right quick."

"As long as you are not alone," Danielle insisted.

"I've got Ranga!" Wyn said brightly, and then frowned at the soldiers around her. "Oh, and this lot too."

***

Alistair's soldiers had prepared the temple for her, exactly as she had asked. They had placed bright lanterns on iron stands and stretched a tent canvass across the gaping hole in the roof to keep the worst of the snow out of the temple. Danielle's chest was carefully placed on the ground next to the ring of ritual markings, and blankets were laid out for her to kneel on. Alistair set five of his men to stand guard nearby, and positioned himself so that he could reach Danielle in a couple of quick steps while still staying quietly out of the way.

Danielle was barely aware of the soldiers. She surrounded the blanket with candles to cast a bright light, and then opened the chest and from it took myriad Devices that she arranged on the rough wool in front of her.

And then she began her work. For hours, Danielle used the Devices to probe the mystery of the fuil crunor ritual that had taken place in the ruined temple. The elaborate Words and intense focus needed to channel and direct these precise Devices exhausted her, but she barely noticed as she lost herself in the puzzle.

It is as if it were ink written on flowing water, she thought. *The power is there. It lies black and thick in the clear stream. But the shape of it, the purpose, ripples and changes even as it is seen. There seems to be no foci, no structure. And yet it clearly has powerful effect.*

Danielle wished she could have been here days ago, while the fuil crunor spell was fresh. Even the few moments she had seen before the attack had been more illuminating than everything she had discovered since the battle. At that moment the flow of the magic had been unfiltered and potent. Now all she felt was a faint echo.

With a sigh, Danielle sat back on her feet and from the neck of her tunic drew a small, plain ring threaded on a simple, silver chain. She held it to her lips briefly, and absent-mindedly twisted it between her fingers as she straightened her back, bowed her head and closed her eyes, remaining still and silent as she relaxed.

"Not going well?" asked Wyn.

Danielle opened her eyes and looked up. Wyn was nestled against the wall a few steps away, completely wrapped in her cloak with her knees drawn up to her chin, only her head and two black boots showing. Danielle had not heard her come in. She was not sure there had been any sound to hear.

"No, not well," agreed Danielle, and she tucked the ring away inside her shirt where she could feel its cool weight against her chest. "I am trying to discover the source or the nature of the ritual we discovered. If I can do that, perhaps we could uncover those responsible for it, or learn how to counter it next time."

Wyn nodded her head slightly, and poked a hand out of her cloak to point at the blanket in front of Danielle. "Is that what your knick-knacks are for then? Looking for magic?"

"Yes," Danielle smiled. Spread in front of her were the works of some of the most respected and powerful artificers in the Guild, treasures acquired by the Temple decades or even centuries ago, unique and irreplaceable. *Yes, my knick-knacks.*

Wyn pushed her hair from her face and tucked it behind an ear, from which it immediately escaped to hang back across her eyes. "What is that one for?"

Wyn pointed at a Device carefully set aside from the others, very different in size and shape. The Weapon was beautifully crafted, a short, thin shaft much like the blade of a stiletto attached to a wide bell and a grip crafted to fit perfectly in Danielle's hand. The blade was not sharp like a knife, however. It was a tube never wider than the tip of Danielle's little finger, the length of it engraved with ornate patterns of geometric shapes, lines, and elegant runes. It was inlaid with a silver metal that was stronger than steel, wound in long threads around the blade to form a solid band that encircled the tip. A small hole at the very end, no larger than the quill of a feather, showed that the blade was hollow.

Where the blade was a work of elegant simplicity, the bell shield was a piece of art. Polished metal curved around the grip in long, twisting wings, each one carved with exotic shapes and covered with ornate runes. Danielle thought they looked like flowing waves that wrapped around her hand when she held it, like the surge of water that leapt from the prow of a fast-moving ship, frozen in silver.

The Weapon was no ancient artifact. It had been crafted especially for Danielle at considerable cost. A fleet of trading ships, a silver mine in the hills above Vordoux, and a wide swath of land had been sold to pay the Guild's fee, an extravagance that still sent quivers of guilt through Danielle whenever she thought of it.

"That is my lance," Danielle replied, and she picked it up and let it rest lightly across the fingertips of both hands. "Would you like to hold it?"

"Is it alright? I won't ruin it or set fire to something?" asked Wyn as excitement and nervousness combined and erupted into a small giggle.

"Yes, of course you can," smiled Danielle.

"Well, maybe just a touch," Wyn knelt next to Danielle, removed her glove, and leaned close to the lance. She tucked her hair behind her ear again, but otherwise kept her hands firmly in her lap. A smile played across her lips as she examined the Weapon, and her eyes shone as she glanced up to receive a smile of encouragement from Danielle. Wyn reached out and stroked the blade lightly with the fingers of one tentative hand as she traced the patterns slowly from base to tip. "It's beautiful," she whispered.

"Yes it is," agreed Danielle as she watched Wyn's deft fingers move delicately on the blade.

"Does it have a name?" Wyn wondered.

"Not yet."

A moment more of silence and then Wyn straightened again and replaced her glove. "What does it do?"

"It destroys," replied Danielle softly.

Danielle returned the lance to the blanket at her side. She had been caught unprepared for the fight in the ruined temple, her only real weapon the medallion named Shape of Fire. It was a potent Device in its own way, but unwieldly as a weapon, its power an enormous burst that took time to collect and was difficult to refine. It was only luck that she had even the amulet with her. She had slipped it into her pack on a whim when she left the army for Nóinín Cnoc, thinking only that it might be welcome on a cold, winter night.

The Weapon she had needed, her lance, had been nowhere at hand, as it was still safe and protected in the small chest, carried with the rest of her possessions by the soldiers who had set up the camp.

Danielle shook her head slightly at the thought. *It will not happen again. It stays with me.*

"So are your other knick-knacks not working then?" asked Wyn.

I wish that were true, Danielle thought, *if the Devices were not powerful enough or precise enough. But they are working perfectly. I simply cannot understand what they are showing me.*

"I do not know," she replied. "Whatever was here, whatever the ritual was, it fades away like smoke."

"That's good," said Wyn. "Gives me the shivers thinking about it. Not the good kind."

"I am not so sure," Danielle wondered softly. Wyn arched an eyebrow and held Danielle's gaze, a smile creeping across her lips until Danielle realized what she had said.

"Not about the shivers, no. I agree, not the good kind," Danielle laughed. "I meant it is not good that I cannot unravel the ritual magic. Yes, it is good that it is gone, but it came from somewhere. Someone performed this magic over and over again in all of the places you found, and did it for some purpose, and I fear what will happen if we cannot discover that purpose."

"So it's no good when it's here and happening and making nasty dead things attack us, and it's no good when it's gone because it's off doing something worse somewhere else?" Wyn scowled and tucked her hand into her cloak, drawing it closer around her shoulders. "So what are you going to do?"

That is a good question, Danielle reflected. *The fuil crunor ritual is not gone, not entirely. There are still echoes, but they are like nothing I have ever seen before. I cannot unravel them here.*

"I must try something different," Danielle answered. "I saw something when we first arrived here, just before we were attacked. Power was being pulled from the bodies. Their energy was somehow bound into the ritual as it drained them. It was drawn somewhere, and I caught just a glimpse…"

The memory was still there, or perhaps better to call it the feeling of a memory. A gaping pit of darkness with blood flowing into it through a rift. Something was in the pit, a thicker texture in the empty abyss. Danielle could remember its presence, an emptiness in the darkness that consumed the blood and used it to grow.

"I think I saw where the power was going," Danielle said.

"What, to that creature, the thing with the black eyes?" asked Wyn.

"They used to call them wights."

"Who did?" Wyn frowned.

"Ruric's knights. At least, a creature much like it is described in the histories and is named a wight. A revenant of shadow with black eyes that feasts on the living, a corpse given unnatural life through fuil crunor," answered Danielle.

Wyn stared at her. "High King Ruric's knights? From the stories?"

"Yes."

Wyn laughed, a sharp sound with no humor in it. "That's wonderful, that is."

Danielle agreed with that. She had spent most of her sixth year unable to venture from her bed after dark, convinced that wights were lurking in the shadows of her room after Old Nan had told her the story of Ruric's knight Sir Corvicus and his rescue of Lady Elizabeth from the Black Grave.

"The power was not going to the wight, it was merely a servant, summoned by the ritual," said Danielle. "The power went to something else, somewhere dark. That is what I glimpsed. If I could find that place again, perhaps I could lead us to it."

Wyn considered that idea as she watched Danielle. "That would be fine with me. Then we'll see how much magic he can use while he has a knife stuck in his face. So how do you find it again?"

"I search for it."

"That doesn't sound too bad," said Wyn, her face lighting up with a smile.

"No, it does not," Danielle replied, smiling in return. But the smile was a mask just for Wyn. *Unfortunately, the truth is that this could be very bad indeed.*

"Well then," said Wyn, her eyes shining with excitement, and she peered closely at the arcane Devices spread out before her through a thick fall of blonde hair. "So, which one do we use first?"

Danielle felt the tension melt from her smile as it became real. *Perhaps it is that easy,* she thought, *merely ask, 'what is first?' and then do it.*

"Thank you, Wyn," she said.

Wyn glanced at Danielle, a slight half-grin on her lips. "What? What did I do?"

"You have helped me remember that a challenge must be attacked with excitement and anticipation, not trepidation and fear."

Wyn smiled in confusion, "Well, that's sweet, but I have no idea what you're talking about."

Danielle laughed. "No, I am being very cryptic, aren't I? I just mean 'thank you' and never mind the rest. Now, which is first, you ask? This one I think."

She picked up a small box from the blanket in front of her. It was made of a dull grey metal, with small, stumpy feet, a metal clasp that was bent and hung undone, and a simple spiral circle engraved on the lid. Danielle ran a fingertip along the circle and felt the bindings inside. With a whisper she released them and the box clicked open.

Inside was another Device. This one was not a Temple relic like the others. This one came from her family. One of their most precious heirlooms, kept safe for generations in the vaults buried deep beneath their sprawling estate.

It appeared to be a simple pendant hung from a chain of small, steel links. The setting was plain, and somewhat scratched and nicked. In the setting was a diamond. It was rough and unfinished, and looked more like a chunk of glass or quartz with a deep flaw in it. But it was far more precious than any gemstone.

"What is that?" asked Wyn.

"It is a Wardpact, one of the great Devices of protection crafted by the guild long ago."

"Oh," said Wyn softly, then she giggled and sat back on her heels. "That gave me some good shivers that did."

Me as well, Danielle thought, looking closely at the small flaw in the pendant. A vast power was poised inside the simple gem, and its familiarity gave her a warm flush of confidence and excitement.

Danielle took in a deep breath and cleared her mind. She focused on the pendant's Word, bringing her will to bear on it. The Word was a powerful one, and hideously complex, but she carefully held its shape in her mind and let it flow from her into the pendant. Deep within the stone the Device stirred and power ignited. She settled the pendant around her neck.

"I am going to try something that perhaps I should have done at the very beginning instead of poking around the edges," Danielle told Wyn. "It might be very dangerous. The Wardpact should protect me if something goes wrong, but if anything else happens, you and Captain Alistair should be ready."

"Anything else?" Wyn's eyes narrowed. "What are you going to do?"

"All day I have searched the remnants of the ritual for traces, anything that could tell me where the power went, or what it was feeding," Danielle breathed in deeply and let the breath run smoothly out through slightly pursed lips, and calm settled deep within her. "But I found nothing doing that. So now I am going to try to follow the power. If it works, I should be able to find out much more."

"Alright, but why is that so dangerous?"

"Because I must travel there to do it. I must enter the dragon's lair and try not to step on its tail."

"Oh." Wyn nodded her head and determination settled on her features. "That I understand."

Danielle picked up one of the Devices lying on the blanket in front of her, a Diviner in the shape of a thin length of shining metal held in a small loop by a simple clasp. Again she settled her thoughts as best she could. The Word had to be so precisely focused that no one could possibly hear it, no matter how strenuously they were listening.

She pushed her weariness aside, gathered her thought and shaped it into the Word. It flowed easily into the loop, the bindings aligned, and power filled the metal.

Danielle pinched the loop of wire in one hand, and turned it with the other hand until the entire length had passed between her finger and thumb. As she did, the loop grew, expanding wider and wider until it was the size of a plate, then a shield.

Only then did she look up. In the air in front of her hung the echo of the fuil crunor ritual. Through the metal loop she saw it clearly, writhing in the air like slowly roiling smoke or thick ink dropped in water. Tendrils of shadow still marked the spots where the corpse husks had lain, slowly rising to join the center like faintly smoking embers. Danielle could tell that the scars the ritual had left on the world would take a long time to heal.

Danielle reached with her hand and carefully touched the stain, dragging her fingertips through it. It felt ice-cold, and oily, and it curled around her fingertips in a way that sent a chill down her back. *A bad shiver*, she thought, trying to summon courage.

She kept her fingers in the inky shadow. She could feel it move past her as it flowed and curled in different directions. *But to where?* The shadow crept up her hand and coiled around her wrist like a snake, but she ignored it as much as possible and kept her senses focused on the feel of the stream.

And then she felt it, a slight flow from a different direction, an eddy in the thick, oily stream. She pursued it, letting her fingers run smoothly through the current.

Shadow coiled around her shoulders, and flowed slowly across her chest. Her skin cramped painfully under its touch, and fiery needles of cold made her shiver.

She could feel the current's source. It flowed from a darker void that was hazy and indistinct. She knew she needed to focus on that emptiness without touching it. She needed to know its surroundings without it ever sensing that she was there.

The shadow wrapped around her back, and slid across her stomach, over her hips and coiled around her thigh as it descended. She had only a moment before she would be completely submerged. Her body shook uncontrollably now, but she kept her mind still as ice, making no ripples in the stream to betray her.

Slowly the world around the empty void emerged. Underground, cold and black. Crudely carved ancient passageways through deep rock. An altar. Above it, a fortress with a tall tower, covered in thick ice and surrounded by clouds.

Suddenly a vast pressure swelled and pressed on her, as if some leviathan of the deep rose under her as she swam in the ocean, and she realized the shadow was aware. She tried to pull back, but the void engulfed her, and she felt its hunger as it rushed towards her from the abyss.

Her pendant shattered as if it were crystal hit by a hammer. The ruined temple snapped into focus, and Danielle caught herself with a hand on the floor as vertigo made the world dance around her.

Wyn kneeled next to her, peering into her face as she asked if she was hurt.

Danielle smiled weakly back, and lay on the blanket, too dizzy to sit upright. The pendant had worked. It protected her and snapped the spell, and itself in the process.

My Wardpact gone, and for what? A cave, an underground altar. An old tall tower in the clouds? It means nothing to me!

Wyn knelt by her side and held a flask of cold water to her lips. She drank gratefully, for her mouth was dry, but she wanted something hot. Her body was still wracked with shivers, and where the shadow had crept she could feel bands of numbness spiral around her. She shivered violently. The feeling went deeper than mere cold. She had been naked under that oily, dead touch, vulnerable, open and defenseless.

"What should I do?" Wyn leaned over her, concerned.

Danielle reached up and gently tucked Wyn's hair behind her ear for her. "Some warm wine, I think. And a few moments down here on this blanket, please."

Captain Alistair brought the wine while the rest stood around the two of them, unsure what to do. Wyn helped Danielle to sit against the wall, and she gratefully sipped the wine, feeling its warmth spread a pleasant glow as it went down.

"So," said Wyn. "Did it work?"

"I think so," Danielle answered. "An ancient fortress, very high in the clouds. And underneath it, caves, tunnels and an altar. That is where it is."

"Well, I hope Killock knows where that might be," said Wyn.

Danielle nodded her head wearily. *As do I.*

Benno

Officially named the Tower of Tithius in memory of the Bishop who had commissioned it over five hundred years ago, most people in Bandirma called it the Bird Tower. It soared above the outer wall where the Abhainn Fuar flowed alongside it, rushing past in its carved channel with a roar that never ceased as the waters of wide Loughliath drained into it.

The tower was the tallest on the walls and rose higher than even the massive Tùr Abhainn, but it was thin, and stood like a talon pointed at the sky. It needed no battlements as it was built on a section of wall that was unapproachable with the rushing river at its base, and on its roof nested the colossal beacon fire in its sheltered cage, forever ready to be lit in time of need. The beacon, and the thousands of birds Bandirma used to communicate with its far-flung temples across the north. Bird Tower was filled with long cotes packed with carrier pigeons cooing incessantly while they awaited their next errand. Dozens of acolytes tended the birds and dozens more wrote and received the messages they bore.

Benno disliked coming to the tower, and avoided it whenever possible. Beacon duty was called Bird Shit duty for a reason by the soldiers who drew the short straw. The entire tower stank, and the smell rose as quickly as the spiraling staircase. The open windows, designed to allow the birds easy access on their flights, made the interior impossible to heat during the day. The floors were frequently damp from rain or snow that blew in with the wind. Only at night, when the windows were shuttered, did the rooms lose their chill, and then the suffocating smell became even more potent.

Benno had no idea why Tithius had thought that the birds would need to perch half-way to the sky, but his predecessor had been obsessed with making the tower as tall as possible. *Which is absurd*, he thought as he puffed up the endless stairs, *birds live quite happily at ground level in all the other temples and castles I have ever seen.*

Benno paused on the next landing to catch his breath. He was nearly at the top now, and he would not give Reverend Sebastian the pleasure of seeing him winded. Benno adjusted his robes so that they fell about him in proper majesty and smoothed down the wispy halo of grey hair that wafted in all directions in the cold breeze. Then, once his heart returned to a more natural rate, he climbed the remaining stairs to Reverend Sebastian's nest.

Sebastian's quarters took up most of the top two levels of the tower. Ancient and broken furniture filled the cramped rooms, most of it splattered with bird droppings. *Which actually is a good description for Sebastian, too*, Benno realized, and he had to suppress a smile as he moved to greet the other priest.

It was true though. Sebastian had been a tall man, but now he was bent and he shuffled carefully as he walked. It had been years since he had left the tower, and Benno doubted that Sebastian could make it back up the stairs if he ever did leave. Sebastian's robes were ragged at the hems and the elbows were patches on top of patches, and stains from his charges usually adorned the shoulders and sleeves.

But Benno had to concede that Sebastian's mind was still sharp. The same biting wit that had scoured Benno as an acolyte many years ago was still present.

"Your Grace," Sebastian croaked, and indicated a dilapidated chair with a stained yellow cushion on it for Benno to take. Benno half-heartedly brushed at it before he took a seat, perched uncomfortably on the edge so as to touch as little of it as possible.

Usually he would change into simple clothes before coming to see Sebastian, but this time he had been conducting a ritual in the inner temple when the message had come, leaving him dressed in much nicer robes, and he regretted it immensely.

Sebastian ran a sharp eye over him as he settled. "A cup of wine for the Bishop," he called. "He looks weary from his climb."

"I am fine, Sebastian," replied Benno, trying to wave off the acolyte bringing the wine.

"Nonsense," Sebastian said. "You look quite flushed. Take the wine before you expire."

Benno nodded his thanks and drank gratefully, for he was actually quite thirsty after his climb despite his protestations. Sebastian quietly regarded him as he did. Years ago the joke had been that Sebastian looked like one of his hawks, with his long nose and unblinking eyes that watched your every move. *Now he looks like a ragged old crow*, Benno reflected, *although I feel sure that I look more like one of his pigeons. One of his more plump ones probably.* Sebastian had a low, beetled brow crowned by long, wiry eyebrows, a nose as sharp as a beak, and a pale, gaunt face with cheeks covered by patches of grey stubble.

"Thank you, Sebastian," Benno said, and he placed the cup carefully on a stack of books that perched on top of the small, shit-spattered table. "Now then, your runner said that there was a message for me."

"Indeed. I would have sent it down to you, but it is one of your special ones," replied Sebastian testily. Benno sighed inwardly. Sebastian would never forgive him the fact that there were some messages that only the Bishop himself could open. Sebastian felt it was a grave insult to him personally, despite the fact that the tradition had held for generations and generations, long before Sebastian was made Master of Birds, or Benno the Bishop of Bandirma.

"Excellent," Benno ignored Sebastian's tone. "May I see it?"

The same acolyte who had brought the wine entered once more, this time holding a carrier pigeon gently in her hands. The bird sat quietly, its black eyes blinking as it watched the humans. Secured to its leg was a thin, metal cylinder, fastened and sealed with an engraved clasp. The acolyte brought the bird to Benno's side, and he carefully pressed his ring to the message container. A Word passed through his mind and the container clicked open and dropped several thin pieces of parchment into his outstretched hand.

Benno instantly recognized Lady Danielle's tiny and elegant handwriting that filled each piece of parchment. But his eyes were drawn to the figures she had sketched, a series of harsh markings, slashes jabbed on the parchment.

"News from the north?" asked Sebastian. His eyes flickered over the parchment in Benno's hand.

"Yes," replied Benno absently as he absorbed the message. *The rituals confirmed, strange markings of unknown purpose, and an attack by some kind of creature… does she really mean to say it was actually a wight, or perhaps something that was similar to one? There is too much uncertainty here.* Benno slowly leafed through the thin sheaves of parchment and then sat back, lost in thought, until Reverend Sebastian returned him to the small room by noisily clearing his throat.

"Your Grace?" Sebastian prompted, impatient.

"Thank you for the wine, Sebastian, but I must take this to the archives immediately. I will let you know once I have a message to send in return." Benno rose, took his leave and hurried down the steps that he had so recently labored up, abandoning the Master of Birds to croak indignantly behind him. Benno would pay for that perceived rudeness sometime in the near future, he knew, but right now he had no time for Sebastian's petulance.

By the time he reached the tower door he was out of breath again. The outer bailey was a hubbub of noise and motion, as always. Bandirma was home to over one hundred priests and nearly one thousand acolytes, as well as fifty temple knights and another thousand soldiers, in addition to the many thousands of stewards who managed the magnificent temple, making Bandirma easily the largest settlement in eastern Albyn. Everything that entered or left the temple came through the River Gate, an imposing series of doors and portcullises carved through the bulk of the Tùr Abhainn. The Tùr Abhainn connected with the township of Bandirma on the opposite bank of the Abhainn Fuar over a stone bridge that arced across its carved channel.

Once through the River Gate, visitors emerged into the outer bailey, a huge, open courtyard spread between the soaring river walls and the looming bulk of the temple of Bandirma. Around the edges of the bailey were all the things needed by a bustling town and castle. Stables, workshops, guest quarters, barracks, taverns, vast storage sheds, a smithy, and even a temple, whose existence always amused Benno, built so that those who lived in the outer precincts would not have to make the long trek into the Cathedral to worship.

On the far side of the bailey rose the hill into which the temple of Bandirma was carved. The hill was a massive plug of ancient rock that rose high above the river valley, the petrified core of a fiery eruption from the dawn of the world. The unyielding stone stood impervious to the eons of erosion that had carved away the land, leaving sheer cliffs of grey stone on every side of the hill. The top of the hill was an island over two thousand paces across, completely inaccessible save by the most adventurous of climbers.

Or at least it had been until the Temple had made Bandirma its home centuries ago. Armies of workers and craftsmen armed with the most powerful Devices the Temple possessed had descended on the hill and carved a network of hallways and grand rooms into its heart. Wide steps and immense doors had been crafted facing westward towards the Abhainn Fuar, while workers channeled the thundering river into a new course and built outer walls and towers alongside the channel.

In all the time since the founding, the work of building had never ceased. Battlements and balconies appeared high on the cliff walls, and engineers dug new chambers deep into the stone. Passageways were carved to emerge at the top of the hill, and soon it was covered in farms and gardens.

Benno hurried across the bailey to the temple doors. Chill drizzle covered him almost immediately, coating him in a layer of damp droplets that clung to the fabric of his robes and dribbled down his neck. It was cold enough that snow was likely before too long, and Benno feared how bad the weather would be in the foothills of the High Fells if it was already this cold in Bandirma.

The main entrance of the temple faced the River Gate, a wide series of steps that made a grand dais almost thirty paces across. Majestic pillars of stone surrounded the dais and supported the overhang of rock that soared above it. At the foot of the cliff two enormous stone doors stood open, allowing passage into the temple.

Benno circumnavigated a herd of cattle being driven from the River Gate to the pens at the back of the courtyard, and a train of wagons unloading sacks of grain into the storehouses. Once clear of the courtyard he joined the flow of acolytes and soldiers moving through the temple doors, returning greetings as best he could without slowing down.

Inside the doors was the grand Atrium, a wide hall that led directly into the hill. Polished marble laid in ornate patterns of different colors covered its floor, and wide pillars rose high to its curved stone ceiling. Polished metal inlaid into the ceiling reflected the bright light of hundreds of lanterns hung from chandeliers.

Along the length of the Atrium were shrines dedicated to the illustrious figures of the Temple, each one memorialized with a likeness carved of white marble, more than three times Benno's height, framed to tell their tale. One stood with a fearsome sword above a curved bridge of stone; another held a tremendous iron chain, broken; the third bore twelve ornate scrolls; the fourth carried a book in one hand and a sword in the other; the fifth received a scepter from a mighty king; and the last held her sword defiantly above her, sheltering a fallen figure who lay beneath her feet.

As an acolyte, Benno had found himself drawn to Reverend Fionn, he of the book and sword. Behind Fionn's tall, patrician figure were carved reliefs of dozens of hooded priests and armored knights arrayed in ranks as they marched from two buildings that stood on opposite sides of his shrine, while a resplendent sun shone above him. Under his boots lay five laurel wreaths, a not-so-subtle representation of the five kings that

Fionn had defied when he established the great Temple schools of the Order of Priests and the Order of Knights. Benno loved each of the five stories that made up Fionn's tale as he cajoled, tricked, threatened, allied, out-maneuvered, and finally triumphed over each of the kings in turn, until the two schools as they existed today were established, open to the most humble and the most mighty, equally, if they demonstrated the gift and the dedication.

But today, Benno paused only at the shrine of the sixth and final figure. She was tall and elegant, with a serene face that somehow radiated hope and strength at the same time. She was garbed in ornate armor, beautifully engraved. At her feet a mighty warrior lay wounded and helpless, a crown with seven peerless gems upon his brow. Her sword was raised above her head, defending against some unseen threat. Benno spent a moment in silent reflection as he gazed at the statue and her blade, then resumed his journey into the hill.

At the inner end of the Atrium stood Taliesin's Sanctuary, a grand circular space with a soaring domed ceiling. A high balcony encircled the Sanctuary far above the floor, lined with elegant railings and statues of revered priests and knights from the Temple's long history. Lanterns hung from a magnificent chandelier in the center, filling the space with light so bright that many visitors believed that windows covered the ceiling.

In the center of the floor a towering statue rose on a tall column- the legendary Saint Taliesin himself, founder of the Temple and the man to whom God first revealed Himself. This Taliesin was depicted in the ornate robes of a High Priest with a serene expression on his noble face and a comforting hand outstretched to greet visitors. Benno had always enjoyed looking at this statue, mostly for its utter disregard for any attempt at accuracy. The Taliesin that appeared in historical sources, although few in number now, painted a far different picture, one of a vagabond adventurer with a very suspect past whose desperate journey to discover a mythical Isle of Magic had, fortunately for him, led him instead to God.

Wide hallways radiated from the Sanctuary and the stone walls echoed with the murmur of a hundred low conversations.

Benno passed across the floor and took the passageway that led directly into the hill towards the Inner Temple. More statues stood in the alcoves between the pillars, and Benno found himself passing beneath the withering gaze of dozens of his predecessors, each one more stern and unforgiving than the last. He supposed his own statue would one day stand somewhere in the temple. Not in this hallway, for it had filled long ago. Benno hoped it would be tucked away somewhere quiet, or perhaps near the kitchens, and with any luck not look so horribly serious.

At the end of the passageway Benno reached the entrance to the Inner Temple. Two temple knights guarded wooden doors, elegantly carved and banded with polished steel. Only priests and those granted ecclesiastic permission were allowed through these doors.

The knights bowed low and pulled the doors open on their massive hinges, and Benno passed into the Inner Temple.

As busy and loud as the Outer Temple had been, the Inner Temple was the opposite, hushed and restrained. Books, scrolls and scribbling priests filled the scriptoriums, flanked by dormitories and apartments for the clergy and their most respected guests. In the center reigned the Cathedral, a vast chamber of soaring pillars and elegant altars that could seat hundreds in its tiered pews. A few acolytes passed quietly, but otherwise the hallways were empty.

Benno turned northward and entered the archives, two vast reading rooms separated by a balcony and a wide staircase. Tall windows spread across the far wall, offering a view from high up the side of the hill, northward across the wide, grey waters of Loughliath to the dark shapes of distant mountains. The windows were closed on this misty, cold day, but in the summer they stood open, allowing access to a curved balcony that jutted from the side of the cliff. Benno loved that balcony and regretted the chill drizzle that soaked it today.

Dozens of acolytes served the many archivists who knew, or knew how to find, every piece of information kept in the archives. They spent their lives reading, learning, and discussing, and yet their knowledge could only contain a fraction of what was stored in the stacks.

The commander of this scholarly army was Reverend Whitebrooke, who assumed the title of Temple Archivist when Reverend Ezekiel left two decades ago. Benno heard Whitebrooke's voice the moment he entered the reading room. Its deep rumble rolled across the murmuring whispers of the other occupants, and Benno descended the stairs to the main floor to join him.

Whitebrooke stood in deep discussion with several of the archivists. Tall and powerfully built, Whitebrooke looked like a giant under siege from an army of scarecrows. He stood with feet apart and thick thumbs hooked into his belt while he listened intently to the clamor of his flock.

The priests surrounding him were tiny in comparison. Archivists in general were not the most physically imposing bunch, but Benno felt this group laughably pushed the stereotype to its extreme. Wrinkled bald heads and boney arms poked from robes that hung as if from sticks. Thin young faces with earnest expressions and pallid skin impatiently waited for Reverend Whitebrooke's attentions.

He recognized some of the faces, both old and young, but some he did not, which upset him. *I should know every priest in Bandirma, at least by face if not by name. I have let myself become too distracted by my duties. But there is nothing to be done about it until this crisis has passed.*

Whitebrooke glanced up, met Benno's gaze over the heads of the archivists and put an end to their discussion with an abrupt gesture.

"Your Grace," Whitebrooke greeted Benno expectantly.

"Good afternoon, everyone." Benno smiled at the silent group around the Archivist.

"We say 'Good afternoon, your Grace' when the Bishop comes to visit," Whitebrooke admonished, his bushy eyebrows furrowed in annoyance.

Most of the younger priests and acolytes had the good grace to look embarrassed and mumble their greetings.

"He said what?" a harsh croak of a voice demanded from the back of the group, and Benno groaned inwardly.

"Good afternoon, Reverend Turlough, you are looking very well," Benno ventured hopefully.

"What on earth for?" asked Turlough, peering at Benno. Benno felt that Turlough had grown even more odious since the last time he had seen the ancient gnome, with his shrinking mouth, long, beaked nose, and deep bags under his cloudy, watering eyes.

"I said 'you are looking very well'," repeated Benno more loudly.

"Never mind that, someone said the Bishop was here."

Benno looked to Whitebrooke for help.

"This *is* the Bishop," Whitebrooke stated.

"That can't be the Bishop. The Bishop is a young man," complained Reverend Turlough to the amusement of several of the younger priests.

"Don't be an ass, Turlough," Whitebrooke's voice boomed out and silenced the chuckles, and his thick, brown beard bristled. "I'm sure the Bishop has something important to ask us. If you can't help with that you can return to bed and leave the matter to us."

Reverend Turlough's face reddened and he spluttered with rage, but he did as he was told. *Maybe I should threaten more people with being sent to bed like naughty children. I never thought of that,* reflected Benno. He could not wait to try it on Reverend Sebastian and see what the Master of Birds made of it.

"Lady Danielle has sent us a message," Benno began. "She has been to the site of one of the rituals."

"What did she discover?" Whitebrooke asked. "I hope it was more than this thief of Killock's did."

"Yes, although it seems that the description of the ritual was accurate. Killock's scout is reliable." Benno uncurled the sheaf of parchments from the message and handed them to Whitebrooke. "Danielle sent us a description of the ritual, plus these markings from the ritual site."

Whitebrooke took the parchments in his massive hands, carefully unrolling them and holding them to the light. He traced his finger across Danielle's drawings, then let the parchment curl into its roll and offered it to a young priestess who stood beside Turlough. "Meara, what do you make of this?"

Benno felt sorry for the lass if she were Turlough's assistant. Meara was likely no more than eighteen, and small for her age, with a shock of dark hair over a round face. She carefully examined the parchment, and respectfully held it for Turlough to read.

"Oh, very interesting, yes, now let me see," the ancient priest muttered, but Benno noticed that Meara paid no attention to him and instead replied directly to Whitebrooke.

"These are of the same provenance as the ones described by Beledain in the *Codex Necronix*. A different arrangement, but definitely fuil crunor."

"Can you tell what the purpose of the ritual might be?" Benno asked her.

"No, your Grace, I'm sorry. Beledain describes the Crunorix and goes into considerable detail on how to recognize their works, but since all representations of the fuil crunor rituals were destroyed by royal decree, he does not include specific depictions of the rituals themselves," said Meara in a tone of sad disbelief that anyone could order the destruction of a book.

"Oh yes, all destroyed, every last one of them what a shame," chuckled Turlough to himself.

"All right, that's enough for now," Whitebrooke interceded before Benno could say anything in response. "It just means we have more research to do, so back at it."

The Bishop and the Archivist walked together to the sweeping windows. The grey mist obscured all but the near shore of Loughliath, and beaded raindrops on the panes of glass blurred the image even more.

"I did not wish to mention it before. Danielle found the markings in Nóinín Cnoc." Benno paused, but Whitebrooke remained silent. "They have not found Ezekiel, but Danielle fears he was killed. I am very sorry."

"Thank you." Whitebrooke examined the scarred knuckles of one huge hand. "I haven't seen Ezekiel in over ten years, strange to think."

Benno paused for a moment to consider his next words, unwilling to open yet another old hurt.

"Is Meara correct in her interpretation of Beledain?" Benno eventually asked.

"Yes, for the most part," Whitebrooke mused. "She knows what she is doing."

"I am glad to hear it." Benno hesitated again. "I know you spent many years studying Beledain, and uncovered many more of his works than the *Codex Necronix*. I thought perhaps there might be more than what Meara could discover so quickly."

"'Studying' is it?" Whitebrooke chuckled to himself, then drew in a long breath. "I seem to remember the word you used then was 'obsession'."

"I apologize for mentioning it." Benno glanced at the Archivist. "I know it was a painful time for you."

"It was." Whitebrooke kept his gaze on the beaded glass, and absent-mindedly rubbed the bridge of his crooked nose, broken so often it resembled a staircase. "But Meara has the right of it. Beledain never described any ritual. We will need to look elsewhere."

"Good," said Benno, and he dropped his gaze and turned to the window as well. "With all speed. God is concerned. More concerned than I have seen Him."

"Is He now?" Whitebrooke turned from the window and glanced at Benno, but Benno remained facing outwards, absently running his fingers over the small silver medallion that hung around his neck. "What has He said to you about this?"

"Only that the power seems familiar, and that it searches," Benno replied quietly.

Whitebrooke waited for more, but Benno had nothing more to give him. It was frustrating, but Benno knew that He was not being cryptic just for the sake of letting Benno discover his own path, as was so often the case in the past. This time there was nothing for Him to tell Benno. Whatever was out there was hidden, even from Him.

"We will get started with the search then," said Whitebrooke. "If there is anything in the archives that sheds light on the purpose of these rituals, we will find it eventually. Ask Him if He has any hints as to where to look the next time you chat."

"Chat? Yes." Benno smiled to himself. "I will do so."

Killock

A trail, rutted by boulders and roots, overgrown and forgotten, wound its way through the dense forest. Wet snow smothered the path in a thick blanket and left only vague lumps and hollows to show where the floor of the forest had once been.

A dark shape glided along the trail during the night. The shape padded swiftly and tirelessly through the forest, its thick, black fur marked only by streaks of grey around the muzzle. Occasionally the wolf stopped, sniffed the air, and searched the eastern sky for a sign of dawn. It panted hot breath into clouds of steam as it watched and listened. Then it was off again, silently slipping along the trail.

***

The tracks were deep, visible from far up the slope as they cut through the pristine snow that covered the forest floor. Killock took his time examining the tracks from a distance before leaving any tracks of his own by approaching.

There had not been any real snowfall since before dawn, just a few flakes fluttering to the ground as the trees shifted under the weight of fresh powder draped over their limbs. Killock saw that the tracks were fresh enough that they must have been made after the snow had stopped.

Four or five horsemen, riding in a single line, although whether they did that to conceal their numbers, or because the path is narrow, there's no way to tell, Killock thought. *But whoever they were, I wish they were here now.*

The horsemen had come from the south, following a game trail through the dense woods as it wound its way from the valley. Killock rose wearily and slid down the hillside from his perch until he reached the trail, his steps heavy in the deep snow.

He had been on the move now for so long that the days had blurred together, battling his way through the height of the blizzard as he struggled southward through the forest and over hills toward Nóinín Cnoc. Killock had been forced to navigate purely on instinct, unable to see more than a stone's throw through the snow, relying on half-glimpsed trees and walls that loomed from the white limits of his world as his only landmarks.

And all the while heavy, wet snow streamed down in endless, thick curtains and piled into deep drifts that smothered every hollow and enveloped every tree and rock.

By the time he found the horsemen's tracks Killock's iron will was starting to lose its grasp on his body, losing its struggle against the exhausting weight of long travel and cold futility, and he was willing to put aside caution to chance a friendly encounter with someone who could provide him with a horse.

Killock had realized that he was far too late to warn Bradon of the dangers that lay in wait in the ruins of Nóinín Cnoc before he had even turned southward. But there was always a chance. A chance that Bradon had been delayed as much by the weather as Killock had, or that Wyn had not found Bradon as quickly as he feared she must have. And as long as there was a chance that he could somehow return to Nóinín Cnoc before anyone arrived, unaware that the ruins were no longer empty, Killock would continue to drive himself southwards.

Killock decided to use the tracks as the horses had ploughed a reasonable furrow through the deep snow. Hidden roots and divots caught at his boots and made him stumble and clutch at nearby branches for support, but at least he was not wading through thigh-deep snow any more.

The trail led the way down the side of the hill and into the open valley beyond, where it cut across the snow-covered meadows. Killock followed it, his heavy feet scuffing rhythmically on the trampled path.

A small mound beside the trail caught Killock's eye as he slowly passed, and he stopped to examine it. He brushed snow from it with numb fingers and found a small cairn of grey stones concealed under the thick drift, a road marker to help travelers find the path. Killock glanced around at the soft shapes that were all the snow had left of the world. *I must be on a road*, he realized, his tired mind slowly making sense of his discovery. *Now if only I knew which road, or how far south I have come.*

Killock stumbled into motion, but he had not gone more than a dozen steps before he stopped again, listening intently. A sound carried to him, faint but clear in the chill air. The thud of hoof beats, and the jingle of a harness. The sound was coming from behind him, so he stopped and sat heavily in the middle of the trail and waited.

Soon the rider appeared, left the forest in the same spot Killock had, and followed the same path across the valley. Killock watched the rider for a moment, then stood and waved his hand above his head. The rider broke into a steady canter and quickly covered the distance between them.

The rider reined to a stop a step away, and pulled a scarf from his face to reveal a wide smile.

"I thought the tracks might belong to you." Torbhin extended a hand to haul Killock onto the horse.

Killock gratefully struggled onto the horse behind Torbhin. "I'm glad you were right. We must hurry though. How far are we from Nóinín Cnoc?"

Torbhin urged his horse south along the trail. "Not far at all. A league at most. You were almost there."

"And are there others there? Have they searched the temple?"

"Yes to both questions," Torbhin replied. "Lord Bradon and Lady Danielle rode ahead to the temple as soon as we received your message from Wyn, and the rest of the army arrived last night."

"They went to the temple?"

"They did, and found a creature that had killed several of Lord Bradon's scouts. They destroyed it, although not before a fierce battle." Torbhin glanced behind him. "You knew?"

"I feared it," Killock muttered. "You say the scouts were killed? Was anyone in Lord Bradon's party injured?"

"No, although it sounds as if it was a close-fought battle. At least, according to Wyn. I haven't spoken to Lord Bradon about it."

"Thank the Maker." Killock allowed himself to close his eyes for what seemed like the first time in days.

"Lord Bradon will be pleased you have returned," Torbhin continued. "He ordered out every man with a horse to look for you."

"For me?" Killock tried to picture a worried Bradon, wringing his hands as he fretted over a missing comrade. Then Killock smiled wryly to himself. *Of course not. He is impatient to pursue his enemy, that is all.*

"He may be disappointed then. I did not catch my prey before the storm arrived, although I was very close. One day more before the storm and I would have found them."

"I did tell Lord Bradon that the fresh snow would aid our search," Torbhin ventured, and Killock smiled to himself as he heard the note of concern in Torbhin's voice.

"Good," Killock assured the young ranger. "I am sure it was a comfort for him as he waited."

"I don't think so," Torbhin said solemnly. "As soon as I have taken you to Nóinín Cnoc I will ride and let Lord Bradon know you are returned."

"You don't have to ride too fast," Killock stifled a yawn. "A bit of a rest would do me good."

***

Killock left Torbhin at the outer picket guard and walked the rest of the way into the camp, his hood drawn low over his face, and avoided the camp's inhabitants as much as possible. He slipped into the back of the massive tent the quartermaster had rigged to cover the food supplies, and found a small corner hidden behind sacks of potatoes to curl up in his blanket and fall asleep, hopeful that his precautions would delay the news of his return for as long as possible.

It was near dusk when he finally awoke to the bustle of the cooks as they prepared the evening meal. Killock sat up and leaned against a sack as he collected himself.

"Sir Killock, I thought that might be you," Captain Alistair's voice preceded him around the pile of sacks. "Although I wasn't sure if you were dead or not."

Alistair stood above the Templar and casually inspected a potato as he waited for Killock to climb to his feet.

"Dead, I think," Killock ventured thoughtfully. "How did you know I was here?"

"As soon as the guard changed they reported your arrival. But I had already heard through the rumor mill. It *is* an army camp, after all."

Killock nodded in defeat. "I appreciate the nap."

"Well, it's not as if I had any other duties save for waiting on you to get your beauty sleep." Alistair replaced the potato and hooked his thumbs in the straps of his breastplate. "But I do feel like I should have your report before Lord Bradon returns. He can be a bit fussy about such things. You sent young Torbhin to find him?"

"I did. Torbhin said that Bradon was getting anxious." Killock rubbed his face vigorously and gestured for Alistair to follow him out of the busy tent. "I thought it might be best to put the old bear out of his misery."

"Lord Bradon was no worse than when he's waiting for the passes to thaw every spring," Alistair frowned as he considered the comparison. "Weeks of pacing, grumbling, and riding up and down a mountain each day to check, all condensed into a few days."

"He even headed into a blizzard again," mused Killock. "Do you remember the year Bradon decided we would campaign early, to catch Redaxe and his warband in their village before they left to raid? I scouted for you all that spring."

"I had forgotten Redaxe," Alistair shook his head, "but I do remember the storm we rode into. Yes, very similar to that. Only this time without old Redaxe to come and save us."

"What did happen at the temple?"

Alistair walked a few paces in silence before answering. Killock watched the Captain as Alistair worked through his thoughts. A deep frown settled on the warrior's face.

"I am not sure what happened," Alistair said. "There's some magic in that place, something I've never seen. Or felt. It's bad, Killock, worse than anything the shamans ever threw at us."

"The shamans worship spirits, and devils," Killock pointed at the white dragon wrapped around Alistair's arm. "And dragons. Dangerous, to be sure, but all part of this world. What happened in that temple, fuil crunor, that is not natural. It's wrong."

"That's it, Killock, that's exactly it. It was wrong, you could feel it." Alistair scowled and twisted the hilt of the long knife he wore on his belt. "We arrived here at dusk, in the middle of that blizzard. We'd sent a patrol on ahead, and we found them, all dead."

"Were the bodies despoiled?" Killock asked, and Alistair nodded in return. "I saw the same, at another ritual site."

"Lord Bradon sent us to patrol the hill, to see if whatever had killed them was still about," Alistair resumed his slow walk along the narrow track of dirty snow that the soldiers had cleared between the tents. "But it wasn't long before there was an almighty flash of light from the temple. You could feel the Word from half-way down the hill. By the time I got back, there were all of these husks, the corpses that were there, all up and attacking Lady Danielle and Lord Bradon. And your girl, Wyn, her as well. But worst of all was this white creature that was going after them.

Tough as stone, with a sword made from a pale metal. Black eyes, and claws. We finally got the best of it, or should I say Lady Danielle and Lord Bradon got the best of it, but it wasn't easy."

"This creature, it had taloned feet?"

"You think I took the time to examine its toes?" Alistair grinned fiercely at the Templar. "Well, you're right. Yes, it did have talons. How did you know?"

"I saw tracks like that, at the other ritual site," Killock said quietly.

They stopped on a small rise in the middle of the camp and looked at the dull mass of Nóinín Cnoc looming above the glowing fires of the camp. Small lights shone from the ruined buildings at its peak, wan stars against the dark clouds.

"Your girl did well," Alistair said quietly. "She fought valiantly. You should be proud of her."

"I am," Killock agreed. He waited patiently for whatever Alistair was working his way to telling him. He had known the warrior for ten years now, off and on, and it was clear that Alistair was waiting for the right moment to say something. *He will do it when we get to that part of his plan*, Killock was confident.

"Anyway, weren't you supposed to be giving me a report?" Alistair laughed.

"If you wish," Killock shrugged. "I discovered another ritual site, and found tracks that must belong to another of the white creatures you encountered. And I know where the trail of the men who did the rituals is, so we should be able to find them very easily now that it's finally stopped snowing."

"That's it?" Alistair snorted.

"That's the important parts," Killock nodded. "I know where they are, and we can go and get them."

"Lord Bradon will be happy to hear it." Alistair flattened a clump of mud in the trail with his boot.

"That's why I did it, of course," Killock said dryly. "I'm going to go and speak with Lady Danielle. Will you come as well?"

"I think I'll wait for Lord Bradon." Alistair stomped another clump of mud flat. "He'll want a report right away."

"As you wish," Killock agreed, and turned to leave.

"One last thing," Alistair ventured, and Killock paused. "About Lady Danielle. She did something up there in the temple, I'm not sure what it was. She said she was researching the ritual. But I think something happened, something very dangerous. She wouldn't say what it was though."

"You would like me to speak to her about it?" Killock asked. "I will, but she won't listen to me either, you know that."

"Perhaps not," Alistair laughed again, and clapped Killock heavily on the shoulder. "Mostly I wanted you to tell Lord Bradon that there was nothing I could do to stop her."

Alistair left then, and Killock watched him stride away between the tents, exchanging greetings with the groups of soldiers gathered around the fires as he went. Then Killock wrapped his cloak around his shoulders and strolled slowly in the opposite direction until he saw his destination, a larger tent set a short distance from the others. Its flap was closed against the cold but Killock saw a faint, golden glow escaping from a crack across the bottom edge of the entrance. The wet snow had been carefully brushed off its roof and shoveled from the walls, leaving a small open area around it. Killock knew that it would have been easy to find volunteers for the duty, each one hoping for a chance to catch a glimpse of the tent's occupant.

Killock slowly walked the last few steps to the tent and scratched on the tent flap.

"Come in," Danielle's voice called out, happy and welcoming.

Killock eased through the entrance. Danielle was settled on a small camp chair pulled close to an iron brazier piled with glowing coals, wrapped in a thick blanket. She turned towards him, a lovely smile of pleasure on her lips.

"Ready for a story about dragons?" asked Danielle, and then stopped as she saw who it was. Her expression instantly changed to one of welcome as she leapt to her feet to usher him into the tent, but clearly she had been expecting someone else. *That first smile was not for me.*

"Quickly, you are letting in the cold," she chided him, although the interior of the tent was only marginally warmer than the outside. The colors of the tent were cheery and warm enough… lanterns and candles brightened flowing shapes of twined emerald green and gold that adorned rugs and tapestries, thick fleeces, fur-covered camp chairs and a cot. But Killock could not feel the warmth of the braziers if he stood more than a few steps away from them.

"For a moment, I thought you were Wyn." Danielle draped her blankets across the chair she had been sitting in and smoothed them into place, then turned to an engraved silver flask that steamed on the tent's small stove. "You look as if a cup of wine might be welcome."

Killock nodded his thanks and watched as she gently stirred the flask and prepared the spices. She had changed from her heavy traveling clothes and now stood in a long, warm dress of deep blue with sleeves that draped from her arms, heavy with red and gold embroidery. She wore a belt of silver loops, and a rich quilted shawl of red and gold that was folded around her shoulders and hung gracefully from the crook of her arm to trail on the floor. Her long fingers were covered by fur-lined gloves of soft doe-skin dyed a deep grey that matched her boots.

A simple golden pendant hung in the hollow of her long neck in the gap of the dress' high collar, and she had brushed out her hair to descend in waves of deep black fire down her back.

"You look beautiful," Killock told her as he gratefully accepted the cup of wine and savored its spicy warmth as it settled in his gut.

Danielle smiled, a white flash between red lips as the lanterns turned the soft curve of her cheek the color of deep, golden honey. "I was so pleased to get out of that heavy coat. I do not know how you and Bradon wear armor all of the time, it is never comfortable. And I suspect those pants could walk on their own by now."

"Armor?" Killock regarded the stiff leather guards he wore on his arms and shoulder. "I believe Bradon would consider these nightclothes."

"Well, none of it is comfortable," Danielle replied. Then her expression became somber. "Did you find them? Did you find the Crunorix?"

"I did, or at least, I know where their trail lies." Killock shook his head and felt a cold finger of ice shift and melt down his collar. "In the morning, we should be able to ride in pursuit. I found another ritual site, this one missing its corpses, and with the tracks of a deadly creature. But I hear from Alistair that you have already encountered it much more closely."

"A wight," Danielle said it defiantly. "I know it sounds absurd, but I am convinced that is what it was."

"I believe you," Killock nodded to himself. "The same thought had occurred to me."

Silence spread through the tent as they stood lost in their thoughts, with only the small pops from the braziers and the low murmur of voices through the tent's canvas to break the spell.

"It is horrifying," Danielle took a deep breath and returned from her thoughts. "And you say that you saw another? Its tracks?"

"Yes, at the ritual site I found. And the husks, the corpses, they were gone. They may well be creating an army, just as we had feared." Killock pondered the surface of his wine for a moment. "Alistair also said that you had discovered more from the ritual itself?"

"Yes, I think so," said Danielle. "Much of the fuil crunor ritual was incomprehensible to me, but we were able to make a very important discovery nonetheless."

"We?"

"Wyn kept me company," said Danielle, a faint echo of the smile he had first seen when he entered the tent traced on the corner of her lips.

"She has never shown much interest in magic before," Killock's eyebrows arched in surprise.

Danielle lowered her eyes and gently swished her wine. "Not at all, she was very helpful, kind and concerned. She is such an interesting girl, is she not? She seems such a cheerful spirit, but she grew so fierce when Lucious dared to play the lord with her." Danielle smiled at the memory.

"She is very fierce, and very joyful as well," Killock agreed.

"I do not know why, but I expected her to be, well, callous and cruel," Danielle shook her head. "When you said that she was a thief who grew up on the streets, I suppose."

"That life can make some people very cruel," agreed Killock, "and Wyn had her family and home taken from her long ago. Wyn won't speak of it, but I was able to discover that her father abandoned them when she was very young, and her mother died a few years later. Enough to harden anyone's heart, but with her, it had the opposite effect. She has tremendous compassion for others, from seeing and living their struggles first hand, and is more protective of those who need help than many of the knights who swear oaths to do the same."

"And how she fights!" Danielle shook her head in amazement. "She moved like a blade dancer, although in earnest of course. It was beautiful."

"I asked her once who had trained her, and she laughed at the idea." Killock smiled softly. "It's part of her gift I think." Killock paused and glanced at the entrance. "As is eavesdropping. Hello, Wyn."

"How did you...?" complained Wyn as she pushed through the flap. "I don't believe it! When did you get here? Did you find them? You didn't kill them all without me did you? Plus, guess who else I just saw in the camp? Plus, stew is on its way."

"I will guess that you saw Lord Bradon," said Killock. "How long were you there? I only just now sensed you."

"This is exactly why people say you are no fun," said Wyn, and she did a slow, graceful pirouette on one pointed toe. "Yes it was Lord Bradon, and it was only a moment, which is what makes it so frustrating. You said I laughed at you, which is not very surprising, and that I was gifted, also not surprising."

"I did not find you in the temple," Killock pointed out, "when you were actually trying instead of playing."

"True," agreed Wyn, mollified, and she turned to Danielle with a gleeful grin on her face. "Have you told him what you found yet?"

"No, not yet. Perhaps I should wait for Bradon so that I only tell it once?"

"I am sure he will be excited to hear it," said Killock.

***

"Now here is a shameful sight." Lord Bradon filled the entrance to the tent, his thumbs hooked firmly in his belt. "A knight, a Templar no less, sipping wine in the company of beautiful ladies, surrounded by luxury, while his comrades scour the countryside looking for him. Disgraceful, but I expected no less."

Bradon crossed the tent in two strides and engulfed Killock in a bear hug that made Killock's armor creak. "Making us wait about for you," Bradon chided fondly.

"The wine *is* very good," Killock pointed out once Bradon released him and he could breathe again. "Shall I pour you some?"

"Please." Bradon pulled his heavy gloves off and took the cup Killock offered him. "Torbhin tells me that you were able to track the Crunorix from here all the way to another ritual site? And that you will be able to find their trail again very quickly now that the snow has stopped?"

"Both are true," Killock nodded. "I was no more than a day behind them when the storm began."

"Then at dawn we shall begin the chase," Bradon quaffed deeply from his cup and brushed drops from his tangled beard. "At last."

"Alistair tells me that you have kept quite busy while you waited," Killock reminded Bradon.

"Too right we did," Wyn said. "We got to punch Lord Lushous in the face. Well, Lord Bradon got to punch him, but it was a laugh to see. And we had a huge fight against this nasty creature that Danielle killed by shooting flames out of her fingers! And also we fought some corpses, but not dead ones. And then Danielle found out where the horrible baddies came from with her magical whatsits."

There was a moment of silence as Bradon blinked at Wyn, and then he cast a questioning look at Lady Danielle. "She did what?"

"She found the nasty what's its name, with her knick-knacks," Wyn answered hesitantly, glancing between the Lord and the Lady. Danielle took a deep breath and visibly steeled herself as Bradon's face darkened into a deep frown. "Shit, I've mucked it up somehow, haven't I? Was I not to tell?"

"No, Wyn, of course not, I was about to explain." Lady Danielle carefully set her wine cup on the table and met Bradon's gaze. "While you were busy searching for Sir Killock, I took another look at the ritual, with my best Diviners. And Wyn is correct. I was able to follow the traces of the ritual, and saw a powerful presence in a deep chamber under a ruined fortress. The presence was feeding off the power of the ritual… I believe it must be the magus."

"Magus! That's what you said," Wyn said excitedly. "I'll remember that this time, I will."

There was silence in the tent for a moment.

"Danielle, that's…" Killock struggled to find the right word. "Astonishing."

"Astonishing?" Bradon gripped the haft of his war hammer tightly and looked at the noblewoman fiercely. "Foolhardy is more like it. You Divined a magus? What were you thinking?"

"I did not know that it was a magus…" Danielle started reasonably, but Bradon continued unabated, rage billowing from him like storm clouds.

"I made a solemn vow to keep you from harm, yet the moment I leave the camp you cast aside all reason and expose yourself to the greatest peril," he boomed.

"That is quite ridiculous," Danielle swept his argument aside with the flip of a hand. She stood with her arms folded and chin raised as she confronted Bradon, her golden eyes flashing dangerously as she glared at him. "It had to be done, and it had to be done by me. Whether or not you were in camp would have made no difference."

"No difference?" asked Bradon, stunned. Killock felt sorry for Bradon, so clearly at a loss and yet so clearly convinced that he had to do something right. *Poor blustering bear,* thought Killock, *you simply have no chance here.*

Bradon strode in a wide circle, red spots appearing on his cheeks as he paced. "What if another creature had appeared?"

"Then Alistair and the men you left here to protect me would have attended to it," Danielle said, exasperated. "You said they were your best men when you left, if I remember correctly." Danielle dropped her voice as low as she could, and tried to adopt Bradon's rumble. "'These men will guard you with their lives, my lady, you have nothing to fear' you said." Her rich Venaissine accent made it perhaps the worst impression Killock had ever heard.

Wyn giggled quietly from her corner. Bradon spluttered, fingers helplessly twisting his tangled beard as he tried to think of something to say.

"Oh Martyr's tears, will you please let me tie that for you again?" asked Danielle, and she stepped to Bradon, a graceful figure dwarfed by the Lord, reached up to his beard, and started to quickly weave it into an elaborate braid. The lantern light made rich shadows across her smooth cheek and long neck as she worked.

"I am alright," she said softly. "I am fine and it needed to be done."

Killock let the silence rest for a moment, watching Danielle's long fingers twist and tuck and weave. Food arrived and stewards placed the trays on the small table—steaming bowls of brown stew, thick with chunks of venison and slices of potatoes, and crusty black bread waiting to soak it up. Killock carefully picked up one of the wooden bowls and blew across the broth, savoring the rich smell and the heat that radiated through his fingers.

"So!" announced Wyn. "What *is* a magus? You lot obviously know, and it's evil and nasty, right? Is it like the white creature, a wight you said that was, *not* the most original name that, by the way."

"My lady," Bradon mused. "Are you certain it was a wight? Or a magus? Ouch!"

"Do not talk while I am dealing with this tangled mess of a beard. Yes, I am certain," answered Danielle.

"It's written," Wyn added solemnly, "in Ruric's books. Is that where magus come from too?"

"It does," Killock answered. "Or rather, they do. You know of the Crunorix, the followers of the Nameless King, and the great war that High King Ruric waged against them a thousand years ago?"

"Course I do," Wyn scoffed. "Nameless had a bunch of baddies, but Ruric killed him off. That's when the Martyr saved Ruric, so he could kill old Nameless."

"That's right," agreed Killock. "The magi were the high priests of the Crunorix, the most powerful of the Nameless King's followers. If I remember my Beledain correctly, the priest had to perform a ritual that would transform him into a magus. If successful, they claimed it gave them eternal life and power over death. They became a lich, a creature trapped between life and death. If they failed, they were consumed."

"Sounds like a real charmer," Wyn curled her lip, disgusted. "And there's a bunch of them you say? Splendid. But if that's what's crawling around out here murdering all of these people, you'd think someone would have noticed. I mean, an evil undead high priest seems a bit, noticeable."

"And it was very far away," Lady Danielle added.

"No one knows how many magi there were, but less than a dozen are mentioned by name in the *Codex Necronix*. And I don't think the magus itself would be the one performing these rituals," Killock said. "The magi were the high priests, but there were thousands of lower priests, men and women who perverted themselves in their search for the power over death that fuil crunor promised. That is whom I believe we are pursuing, a slave desperate to feed power to his master."

"Lovely," Wyn laughed bitterly. "Some little worm crawling around murdering so that his horrible magus will give him a little reward. But then what's a wight? Where does that come from?"

"Beledain believed that the wights were undead creatures, created by fuil crunor rituals that imbued a corpse with terrible power and hunger to consume the living. It was a foul mockery of immortality." Killock knew the stories well. When Ruric faced the Nameless King and his magi, the most feared creatures in the enemy's army had been the dreaded wights. *The Black Grave is full of them*, Killock remembered the story, *trapped centuries ago along with the magi when the gates were sealed.*

"Was that the purpose of the rituals we discovered?" Bradon asked carefully. "To create the wight?"

"I do not think so," Danielle answered. "The power of the ritual, the lives that it drained, did not flow into the wight. It flowed to the dark presence I found, the magus."

"Then I would guess that the ritual merely summoned the wight, from wherever the magus is," Killock shook his head. "But there is no way to know, unless we find the one responsible for the ritual."

"And you said that you had found him, or that you were close to tracking him down?" Danielle asked. "When you found the ritual site at the farm?"

"Yes," Killock replied quietly. Killock could hear the soft scrunch of snow as the guards made their patrol around the camp, the crackle of the bonfire in front of the tent, the thick thump of ice-heavy canvas stirring against a pole, and the murmured voices of the men as they took their supper outside. So it only felt like the world had gone as silent as that farm. Killock forced himself to ignore the memories. "But the ritual was empty. The blood markings were still on the ground, but there was no sign of any of the corpses. They had vanished."

"The patrols we sent to the other sites are reporting the same thing," Bradon added.

"So they're just wandering around out there? A whole pack of them?" Wyn asked.

Killock nodded. "I fear so." He gulped a spoonful of the broth, scalding his tongue, and had to wipe a lovely trickle of grease from his mouth with the back of his hand.

Wyn groaned in exasperation. "Why didn't I just set fire to the lot of them when I first saw them?"

"There was no way to know," said Killock. "Setting fire to them may have made things worse."

"How could it be worse?" asked Wyn, incredulous.

"It could have drawn the wight," answered Danielle. "With you there, alone."

"Worse. Got it," muttered Wyn.

"Could there truly be a magus, after all these years?" asked Bradon.

"The stories say that the magi claimed that fuil crunor made them immortal," answered Danielle. "However, the stories also say that when Ruric slayed the Nameless King, their power was broken, so fuil crunor should not exist anymore."

"So much for that part of the legend," said Wyn.

Killock nodded his head slightly, but something had stirred in the back of his mind. *She's right about the stories. No one knows which ones are real and which ones are not, and many contradict each other. No one has had access to any of the books or writings for over six hundred years. But that doesn't mean that the stories are useless.*

"Danielle," Killock said, "could you describe the fortress you saw through your Diviner?"

"Very tall," she replied, "and very ruined. I saw clouds passing around it, and ice and snow all over it, but on the bare patches I saw that the stone was covered in moss and lichen. One enormous gate passed all the way through it and out the other side. It looked very old and very abandoned."

"Think about how high it must be!" Wyn laughed at the thought. "I'd climb that and you would never get me down."

"It matters not," said Bradon. "No one can build a tower tall enough to touch the clouds."

"You can if you build it high in the mountains," said Killock. "Danielle, do you remember if the fortress was built on the edge of a cliff?"

"It was, I believe."

"And were there eight huge statues in front, four on either side of its gate?"

Danielle held still and closed her eyes as she thought back. "Yes, I think so. They were tumbled and broken on the ground, but yes."

"Killock, do you know this place?" Bradon asked.

"I believe so," replied Killock. "As we spoke of Ruric, my thoughts were drawn to the story of his passage through the Fellgate as he led his army to do battle with the Nameless King. Do you remember how it goes?"

"I do," replied Bradon. "Once the way north was revealed to the High King he gathered his army and passed over the High Fells through the Fellgate. It took them months to get across because they had to build the High Road as they went. That road had to be strong and wide to convey an army with horses, wagons and siege engines."

"Not just the High Road," added Killock. "Ruric feared what would come to pass if they were defeated now that there was a way through the High Fells. So near the summit of the Fellgate he built a powerful fortress to defend the pass. Highward Tor was its name."

"I remember!" Danielle said excitedly. "And after the war, they built statues to watch over the pass, Ruric, the Martyr, and the other honored knights who died."

"Eight statues," agreed Killock, slurping another spoonful of broth.

"The Fellgate and the High Road were buried centuries ago in the Cataclysm," Bradon frowned. "Nothing lies to the north now but the High Fells themselves, and with the Fellgate gone, they are impassible."

"The Fellgate was indeed buried," replied Killock. "And the High Road destroyed in the Cataclysm as well. Few know where its ruins lie. But other paths are available."

"You have heard where to find these paths?"

"I have walked them," replied Killock. "Many years ago I searched for a way to cross the High Fells. I never found one, but I learned that, although the Fellgate was closed and the High Road ruined, not all was lost. Much of what Ruric built is still there. Some of the grand viaducts that crossed the crevasses still stand.

Many of the old waystations and some of the small patrol towers are also still there. Highward Tor could still stand."

Wyn grinned hugely. "Good thing her Ladyship did the magic thing then, isn't it, because now we know where old magus is."

"Yes, it was a good thing," said Danielle, and she finished tying Bradon's braid, laid it against his chest and gently smoothed it flat. "Now you look worthy to protect me, not like a wild bear that has found some armor to wear."

Bradon ran his fingers down the length of his braid. "Thank you, my lady." He turned to Killock.

"You can find these paths again? In the middle of winter? We cannot wander the mountains for weeks, not when we are needed here."

"Yes," replied Killock. "I can find them again, although one thing has not changed since Ruric's time. The mountains are no place for an army."

The tent was silent as Bradon pondered what he had been told. Killock heard a challenge and response from the guard, then a distant chorus of laughter from some campfire. He slowly wiped his bowl with a hunk of bread, keeping expressionless as he waited on Bradon's decision. *The magus is the real threat… killing one of its priests will do little to harm it.*

But Killock knew this decision was not his to make. Three of them had been sent, because all three would be needed. He had to acknowledge that truth. Killock had some tricks up his sleeve, but none were likely to be useful if he found the Tor occupied by a magus.

Bradon walked to the table, unrolled a map, and weighed it with cups and Killock's empty bowl. "Show me where," he asked.

Killock examined the map. The northern hinterlands of Albyn spread across it. Countless valleys wound their way into the mountains, carved by long fingers of rivers that twisted and merged as they tumbled southwards towards the lower plains. The barrier peaks were marked on the map, the closer ones detailed with ridgelines, faces, and cliffs. But behind those details the map was vague. A few massive peaks were shown as landmarks, visible from afar, but what lay between them and the first ranks of mountains was unknown. In the middle of the unknown, written in faint ink, as if the cartographer were ashamed of its imprecision, a single name. Tír an Síoraí.

"Here is the start of the High Road," Killock said, pointing. "To the north of us. From there the path leads along the valley carved by the Carrock Beck as it descends from Ice Fall. After that, it heads north, where remnants of the old High Road can be used all the way to the Léim Mhór, which is here." Killock pointed to a spot where the map's ink faded to blank parchment.

"How far from there to Highward Tor?" Bradon asked.

"I don't know," Killock admitted. "I have never gone farther than the Léim Mhór."

"And all this way, from the Carrock Beck to the Léim Mhór, into the High Fells… can horses follow this path?"

"No, we would need to leave them at the base."

"Killock, this is a month's journey, in good weather, even with a small group that could carry their own supplies," Bradon pondered. "Then who knows how much farther after that. And all that time, the rituals will continue?"

"I believe so," replied Danielle. "Whoever performed the rituals and sacrificed those people is still out there, and the power they served did not seem satisfied."

"That should be our goal then." Lord Bradon straightened from the table. "We must track down and stop those who are performing these atrocities."

Bradon would not be argued with, Killock knew, but he also knew Bradon was wrong. *The rituals are terrible, but the real threat is what the rituals serve. Destroying that threat should be our goal. If people die to achieve that, then so be it, whether they be soldiers, villagers, nobles, or Templars. I could be at the Léim Mhór within a week, if the weather is kind. And I go alone.*

"Bradon, are you sure?" Killock began. "We know the magus is out there. It will grow more powerful every day that we fail to stop it. Surely we should find it and destroy it as quickly as possible?"

"We cannot leave the people here undefended while we search the mountains," Bradon shook his head.

"That's right we can't," said Wyn fiercely, and she uncurled from her chair and rose to her feet as if ready to depart that instant.

"Bradon, we don't know what terrible purpose all of this serves. If we give the magus under Highward Tor time to complete its work, the result could be far worse. Is saving a few more lives now, any lives, more important than stopping that?"

"Even one life, yes," said Bradon. "One life that I knew I could save versus many who may never be in danger, yes."

"That is why we brought an army," Killock pointed out. "We feared that exactly what is happening would occur. Wights and husks raised and gathered somewhere as the Crunorix gain strength. Send our soldiers to protect the villages and farms. Send them to find the priests and stop the rituals, while we search for Highward Tor."

"We do not have enough soldiers to defend every settlement or farmstead in the hinterlands," replied Bradon. "We need to track these bastard Crunorix priests down and make certain they do not escape." Bradon leaned heavily on the table with both fists and Killock feared it would break as the legs trembled. "And *then* we will find this magus that is feeding off the rituals, and we will destroy it." Mugs rattled as Bradon thumped the table with each statement.

Killock nodded his head slightly. "It will be more powerful the longer we wait to challenge it."

"That will make it more interesting," Bradon boomed, a smile flashing from behind his beard.

"True," Killock smiled in return. He could not even say he disagreed with the decision. He felt again the empty cold of Nóinín Cnoc and the silence of the farm lying dead under its covering of snow. It must not happen again.

But for all that, Bradon is wrong. Alistair and Sir Lochlan are more than capable of tracking down the priests and putting an end to them. And if the Crunorix are gathering an army as it seems they are, we have no more potent weapon than the five hundred men we have assembled for combating exactly that threat. Bradon and Danielle and I should leave those tasks to them, and do what they cannot… track down and put an end to the magus. Remaining here with the army is the wrong decision.

"Then my path leads to the mountains to search for Highward Tor," Killock announced. "With any luck by the time you have caught the Crunorix priests responsible for the rituals, I will have found the Tor and can lead you directly there."

"You're going already?" Wyn asked quickly, and an anxious frown crossed her face. "But you just got here."

"Do not worry," said Killock. "Torbhin can track the Crunorix as well as I can."

"Agreed then." Bradon glanced around the group. "Make your preparations tonight, for we ride at dawn."

Bradon caught Killock's eye, and motioned for the knight to follow him from the tent. They walked quietly together for a while, content to watch the life of the camp. Bradon knew someone at every campfire, and exchanged jokes and stories for a few moments before moving on. Eventually they reached the horse line and they stopped so that Bradon could brush down his massive warhorse.

"You are right that you must search for Highward Tor," Bradon finally spoke his mind. "But you will be sorely missed."

"I am sure you will survive my absence," Killock observed wryly.

"You think I speak of myself?" Bradon frowned at him. "I am counting the moments until I can be rid of you."

"I suppose not," Killock replied, at a loss.

"You are remarkably unobservant for a ranger." Bradon shook his head sadly.

"Many agree with you, I am sure," Killock frowned, puzzled.

Bradon sighed in exasperation. "Did you not see the look on young Wyn's face when you made your announcement? She was crushed."

"Bradon, you couldn't be more wrong," Killock laughed at the thought. "I assure you that I am nothing but a teacher for Wyn, and likely not a favorite teacher at that. She is young enough to be my daughter."

"Remarkably stupid for a ranger, as well," Bradon mused.

Torbhin

The sky was merely a pale patch of grey above the black lumps of the tents as Torbhin quietly made his way through the encampment and into the meadows beyond. The only sounds were the soft scrunch of his boots in the pristine snow and the faint rustle of an occasional breeze through the dry grass that poked through the white surface.

Torbhin knew that the silence would not last long. Orders had been given that the army would decamp as soon as the morning meal had completed, and already smoke rose from the commissary tents as the cooks prepared the food. But Torbhin would not be there to see it happen, for he was to depart with Lord Bradon, and the Lord was not in the mood to wait past dawn to ride.

So Torbhin enjoyed the tranquility while it lasted.

At the far side of the meadow a small copse of trees stood as scouts for the dark mass of the forest that lurked at the edge of the valley. Torbhin selected a low-hanging branch, scooped twenty snowballs and arranged them along it. Then he carefully paced out fifty strides and unlimbered his bow.

The bow thrummed and the first snowball exploded silently. Torbhin stepped back two paces and took aim again. A second thrum, and the second snowball disappeared in a small puff of flakes.

Torbhin worked his way backwards across the meadow, one shot at a time. His firing was methodical, each motion the same whether it was the first easy shot at fifty paces, or the last at ninety.

After the final snowball had vanished Torbhin returned to the branch, crafted another twenty targets, and then returned to the spot of his last shot and began again. Once past one hundred paces his motion changed, a longer pause as he adjusted to the intermittent breeze and the slight pulse of his own heartbeat.

The tenth arrow passed through the side of its target and did not demolish it. The eighteenth struck the branch just beneath its target with a hollow thunk and shook the branch with the impact. Torbhin continued to fire as the branch wobbled, using only four arrows to hit the last three snowballs despite the movement.

"Very nice," Corlath said from behind Torbhin.

Torbhin finished securing the covers on the quivers of practice arrows he had brought to the meadow before greeting the twins. Cormac held out a bowl of porridge for the ranger, and Torbhin accepted it with a nod of thanks.

"I haven't seen anyone shoot like that in years," Corlath said thoughtfully.

"Not since Kuray?" Cormac asked his brother.

"Not since Kuray," answered Corlath.

"The tourney," added Cormac. "Have you ever been to Kuray?"

Torbhin realized the question was directed at him. "Only once. What tourney?"

"The Queen's tourney," Cormac replied. "Every year, at midsummer. Feats of skill and strength, and the best in the land crowned at the end."

"And you have been? Did you compete?"

"Four times," Cormac smiled wistfully. "In the melee. But that was before we joined up with the Captain. Now we spend our summers in the Ironbacks."

"You think I could compete?" Torbhin wondered. "Surely there are others far more skilled."

"You could," Corlath told him. "Not sure if you would win. That would depend on how well you can shoot under pressure, and if you can shoot your best every time. Cormac here has fought dozens of men in real battles and never lost, or else he wouldn't be standing here. But in the melee he gets careless."

"True." Cormac did not seem to mind the critique.

"At midsummer?" Torbhin asked. He suddenly very much wanted to go, although he had hated Kuray the time he had gone. It had all of the things he disliked about any town, but multiplied dozens of times. Crowded streets, tall walls, and filled with people that seemed not to care in the slightest what was going on around them. But something about the idea of the tourney reminded him of the stories he had loved as a child, of knights and fair maidens. And a chance to prove himself. *It would be nice to be able to say 'I did that, I stood next to the best in Albyn', even if I don't win.*

He had never really minded his anonymity before. The life of a ranger would be a hard one if he craved recognition, and he knew that he was good at his trade. It was not hard to realize why the chance of proving himself was suddenly appealing. *There are those that don't know me, don't know who I am or what I can do, and they are worthy people. I would like their respect in return.*

The twins, with their easy confidence. Captain Alistair, the consummate warrior. Lord Bradon. *And I could finally prove to Wyn that I wasn't useless.* But that was a selfish, unworthy reason. One of posturing and bragging, and he did not want to think that he could be motivated by such a thought.

"Midsummer," confirmed Cormac.

"For a whole week," added Corlath. "The final competitions are on midsummer day."

"And the feast is midsummer night," continued Cormac.

"Will you go this year?" Torbhin asked.

"Perhaps," laughed Cormac. "But we'll likely be up a mountain somewhere, fighting whichever clan has decided they are hungry enough to try raiding. Besides, I've had my fair share of chances. I know I'm not going to win."

"What about you?" Torbhin asked Corlath. "Have you ever competed in the Tourney?"

"Once." Corlath smiled faintly, and he absently rubbed a speck from the polished silver pommel of his beautiful sword. "Once was enough."

The twins shared a look and a grin at that.

"Perhaps I will go this year then," Torbhin said quietly as they began the walk to the encampment.

"You should, unless you are busy," Cormac nodded.

"Busy? Well, a ranger never stops traveling, and scouting. But I am sure a week in Kuray would be acceptable."

"I'm sure," Cormac replied.

"Except, I heard his lordship and the Captain talking about you," Corlath added. "If you keep on doing as well as you have been, I think you might find yourself up in the Ironbacks with us, come midsummer."

Torbhin barely noticed the rest of the walk to the encampment as his thoughts churned with the possibilities his future might hold. A chance to join this group of warriors, to call them his comrades. But at the same time, to leave the solitude of the wilderness that he craved and exchange it for long months of hardship. His thoughts swirled back and forth, and could come to no resolution, not even when he reminded himself that there was no offer, merely an overheard remark, and the days ahead would carry the chance to prove himself, or let the opportunity slip through his fingers if he could not.

The horses of the party were being readied when Torbhin and the twins returned, and Torbhin quickly gathered the pack he had prepared before heading to the meadow and secured it to his saddle.

Captain Alistair moved quietly amongst his men, exchanging a word or two with each of them as he passed. None of the ten soldiers needed encouragement or instructions, and the Captain did not offer such, but joked easily or simply shared a nod.

Lady Danielle and Wyn stood slightly apart from the soldiers. Danielle had once again donned her traveling clothes and mail, and spoke soft words to her horse as she fed it an apple from her gloved hand. Torbhin ventured close to Wyn to say good morning. She stood motionless with her head resting against her horse's neck, and she merely blinked sleepily at him from under her hood until he trailed into silence.

Lord Bradon's voice rolled across the group as he arrived, Sir Killock walking quietly at his side. The knight joined Torbhin while Lord Bradon conferred with Alistair.

"My lady," Killock greeted Danielle. "Wyn, I see that you are ready to go."

"Sleepy," Wyn mumbled. "Cold."

"Torbhin, you know your path?" Killock asked. Torbhin nodded quietly. The knight had given him clear landmarks to follow all the way to the farmstead where he had found the empty ritual. Torbhin was confident that he could find it easily, as well as the small hollow where the Crunorix priests had sheltered nearby. *After that, it will be up to me to find their trail.*

"Good." Killock stood silently for a moment before continuing. "I am glad you are the one to guide them."

Torbhin felt a flash of warmth pass through him, but he kept his expression as stoic as his mentor's. "Thank you," was all he said.

"If I have not returned by the time Lord Bradon has finished with the priests, it will be up to you to follow my trail into the High Fells," Killock continued. "Look for my signs."

"I will, you can count on it." Torbhin's voice was quiet but it carried an edge of the intense pride he felt.

Killock nodded his approval, and then Lord Bradon arrived.

"Killock, will you please stop pestering your man and let him lead us out of here?" Bradon chided them. "Your Ladyship, might we depart, or is your steed's breakfast incomplete? Wyn, lass, you are on the wrong side of your horse. You ride on top."

Bradon gently plucked Wyn off her feet and placed her firmly in her saddle, then knelt and offered his cupped hands for Lady Danielle's boot as she swung into hers. Torbhin scrambled onto his horse before Bradon could turn to him.

Then they were winding their way through the awakening camp, past groups of soldiers gathered around their fires as they awaited the stewards with the morning meal, past the sentries and the outer pickets and on to the north.

***

It took Torbhin less than a day to find the trail of the Crunorix priests, just north of the farm where Killock had abandoned his pursuit. The priests had weathered the storm in a small camp hidden deep in the forest, and had left a clear trail in the fresh snow when they finally departed, but Torbhin did not need something as obvious as footprints to track someone. A gate carelessly left open in a field, snapped branches where someone had moved through the trees off the game trails, the remains of a meal left under a tree. And in such cold weather, there were campfires. Hidden and buried made no difference to Torbhin. The signs of burying were as obvious as a fire pit itself.

The tracks showed Torbhin that he was following three men, all on horseback and traveling light. They knew where they were going, too. Their trail moved easily through the woods, passing over the hills where the ridge was gentle, crossing streams where the banks were low. Torbhin quickly surmised their destination, which made following the trail even easier.

But it took time to cross the rugged terrain, and Lord Bradon seethed at every hour, driven to catch the ones responsible for the ritual at Nóinín Cnoc before they could perform it again somewhere else. The Templar drove the group hard, rousing them long before dawn and refusing to make camp until long after dusk, and Torbhin sank wearily into his bedroll each night as their small campfire flickered on the branches over their heads and low voices chuckled and murmured around him.

Their efforts were rewarded by steady signs that they were catching up to their quarry, until Torbhin could say with certainty that they were less than two days behind.

But Torbhin was concerned. The trail had led them north into the foothills of the High Fells, far beyond any farm or village or temple. There was only one place that Torbhin knew of that could possibly be their destination, and the trail had led directly towards it. Torbhin had hoped that they could close the gap and catch their prey before they reached it, but as dusk approached and Torbhin crept forward through the thick trees, he knew he was arriving two days after the Crunorix, and he feared what they had done with that time.

The settlement ahead of him was small, a score of cabins and a scattering of tents strewn through the woods alongside a frozen stream called the Gylden Beck, but the settlement itself had no official name. Some of the settlers called it Twin Pines, after the two massive trees towering prominently on the ridge above it. If a farmer from the valley below were asked, he would name the camp Squatters' Creek.

In summer, the inhabitants sought their fortune in the stream bed by panning for gold. Every year a few small nuggets were found, carried down the stream from some richer vein lodged high in the inaccessible mountains. And with the gold, hope returned, pulling the residents into the stream to scavenge in the chill waters for the mountain's cast-offs. In winter, the camp served as home to trappers, often the same people who spent the summer panning for gold, with a livelihood to carry them through the cold months. Farmers from the valley who had not done well enough in the harvest to last through the winter joined them in the forest.

Torbhin guessed that perhaps thirty families lived in the camp. Smoke from cooking fires rose from the cabins and most of the tents nestled under the surrounding trees and created a thin haze in the grey evening light. The recent storm had left thick snow on the roofs of the cabins, but from the ridge overlooking the camp Torbhin saw that paths had already been shoveled between the cabins and down to the stream, where axes had broken the ice into chunks small enough to be carried to the camp. The light dimmed under the thick trees, and through the cracks of several cabin walls Torbhin noticed warm candlelight spilling onto the new-fallen snow, and the tents glowed a hazy gold underneath dark fir boughs.

As he watched, Wyn slid smoothly to the ground next to him to peek over the ridge. Torbhin had asked her to stay back while he scouted the camp, but he was not surprised to be ignored. Not that he was disappointed.

"Looks nice and quiet, don't it?" Wyn asked softly. "You sure you were following the right trail?"

Torbhin nodded his head. He found himself watching her face, only an arm's length from his, as she peered into the camp below, her eyes bright as they caught reflections from the lights in the camp.

"Do you think they'll have something hot cooking?" she smiled. "And enough to share?" She caught his gaze on her, and her eyebrows furrowed in puzzlement. "What? Do I have something on my face or something?" Wyn brushed off her cheek and wiped at her nose with gloved hands, then broke into a grin. "Tell me… do I have something horrid frozen in my nose?"

"No, you look fine," he mumbled, and cursed himself for proving once again that he was absolutely the idiot she thought he was. *Another chance to be funny or friendly or witty, or in any way interesting, wasted.* Torbhin sighed despondently. He had made such a fool of himself with the whistling and the snowball. *The start of a pattern.*

Torbhin knew he needed to be sharp now. Something was amiss in the hushed tableau before him. Cooking fires and candle light be damned, the camp was far too quiet. There was not a single soul moving outside, not even to go to the privy or to collect ice from the stream for water. And something tall stood in a small, cleared space in the center of the camp. Torbhin could not quite see through the gloom, but the shape had not lurked there the last time he had visited Twin Pines, and an ominous feeling emanated from its dark bulk standing so still amongst the cabins.

Wyn shifted in the snow beside him, impatient. "Shall I go down and ask someone if they've seen anything? Before the stream thaws?" she whispered fiercely.

"Wyn, can you see what that is in the center of the camp?" he asked by way of reply.

"Looks like a tree stump or something," she said. "Is that what we're waiting on? The scary tree stump to go away?"

"I don't think it's a stump," he began, but just then a cabin door opened and torchlight streamed across the snow. Several figures bundled in ragged coats trudged into the night air. Two carried torches, and Torbhin discerned a man, a woman, and three children, two older boys and a toddler who instantly demanded to be carried. More doors opened around the camp, and more families trudged into the snow bearing torches, as if the first had been a signal.

The light of the torches revealed the dark shape to be a thick post, twice Torbhin's height, with smooth sides and a rounded top. Iron chains with manacles attached to the ends were nailed into the post half-way up. Torbhin noticed a grey stone slab on the ground underneath the manacles, and he recalled that there had been a Temple shrine in that spot, a small pedestal used when the priest came through on his rounds. The rest of the shrine was missing but the stone base remained. The post seemed to have been positioned so that whomever was bound to it would have to stand directly on the slab.

More and more of the camp's inhabitants gathered near the post. They clustered in small family groups, and kept their distance from the stake and its chains.

"Damn," Wyn exhaled in a long sigh.

Torbhin nodded slightly to himself. "We need to get closer so we can hear."

"No going back to Bradon for orders?" Wyn raised a questioning eyebrow.

Torbhin thought he probably should. Lord Bradon and the other riders were only a half-hour or so away, waiting for the ranger's report, but Torbhin was not sure yet what he would tell them. The camp might have recently caught a criminal and was about to mete out some hinterland justice. Torbhin did not believe that was true, but he did not actually know.

Most of all, Wyn's question goaded him, even though he did not want to admit it. He had survived out here on the edge of the world for years without having to run to a Templar every time he saw something a little mysterious, and yet Wyn was convinced he was nothing more than a glorified trail guide.

"You can if you want," he replied. "But I thought Lord Bradon was clear. Find out what's going on here, then report back." Torbhin risked a glance at Wyn. She was watching him, a slight smile on her lips. "So that's what I'm going to do. Not a problem is it?"

Wyn giggled softly and pulled her hood down low, hiding her face in shadow except for the flash of a smile. "No problem. Sounds like fun to me."

Torbhin was not sure if he had made a fool of himself, again. *Probably.*

The two crawled from their spot on the ridge and slipped through the shadowy woods to the stream. Torbhin was in his element now, keeping out of sight, never rising above the low undergrowth, and staying at all times downwind of his target. The snow was thick and concealed loose rocks and dry branches, but Torbhin could tell where they must lay and stepped smoothly over them with only a quiet scrunching of snow to reveal his approach.

Wyn followed him, quieter than his own shadow. Torbhin had to check to make sure she was still there, each time reassured to see she was right behind him, a dark patch in the night with a grin.

Once among the shadows of the cabins Torbhin paused, unsure of where to go. People with torches milled around in the center of the camp, and more emerged to join them. But Wyn knew what to do. With a light step she used a window ledge to leap to the roof of a cabin, and extended a hand to help him up. They lay prone, and the pair quietly snaked their way to the front of the roof, careful not to disturb the layer of snow. The center of the camp lay directly in front of them. At least fifty people stood hushed in small, isolated groups, waiting.

What little noise the crowd was making stopped. Silence spread from the far end of camp, each group turned mute in its wake, until no one uttered a word and the only sound was the crackling of torches and the sighing of wind through the tall trees. Then Torbhin heard it. Slow hoof beats of several horses approached. Orange torchlight appeared through the trees, less than a bow-shot from the ring of settlers.

Three horsemen appeared from the darkness, leading a fourth, riderless horse. Two of the men carried torches that flared and cracked in the chill air. They followed the first rider into the ring of settlers, who drew away and let them pass.

The lead rider slowly approached the post and walked his horse around it once, staring into the ring of people as he passed, and none in the crowd could meet his gaze. The two other riders dismounted, placed their torches in sconces on either side of the post, and waited for the leader.

He completed his circle and then dismounted. He was tall, and dressed in thick robes that fell to the ground and swept the snow as he moved. His head was shaved, and his face gaunt, with deep shadows across his cheeks and a sharp beak of a nose between two sunken eyes. A crude tattoo slashed across the bridge of his nose, spiraled over his head and disappeared down his neck into the collar of his robes.

As he turned, torchlight flashed from something around his neck, and Torbhin felt a surge of rage as he recognized the Temple symbol on a small silver amulet. The man had the sign of a Temple priest, and, Torbhin realized, the robes as well. The priest began to pace the circle again, staring at each of the settlers in turn as he passed while the other two riders waited. One of the two was a huge man dressed in simple clothes, with matted hair and a thick neck. The other was younger, nearly the same age as Torbhin, dressed in a warm sheepskin coat, thick leather gloves and boots. The younger rider was clean-shaven with long, dark hair, and he stood aloof, never glancing at the people gathered around him as he toyed with the lining of his gloves. Both were armed, the brute with a heavy hammer that looked as if it had been taken from a smithy, and the younger rider with a long steel sword sheathed at his side.

The emaciated priest completed his circle on foot and stood in front of the post. He stood in silence for a moment with closed eyes and arms raised to either side, then he opened his eyes and pointed into the crowd, each time uttering a name. Five times he pointed, and each time the crowd moaned and gasped, and uttered cries of despair that were quickly stifled.

Each of those named stepped forward. Torbhin saw their steps falter and their knees buckle even from a distance. The last of the five was a slender young girl, perhaps twelve or thirteen years of age. She had been standing with an older man, her father, Torbhin decided, the two of them alone in the crowd. When her name was called the girl had to pull her hand free of his, sobbing, to move forward.

The girl reached her place with the other chosen four, stumbled, sank to her knees in the mud, and seemed unable to rise again. Those to either side of her made no move to help and she stayed on her knees facing the robed priest and the stake behind him.

Torbhin heard a slight hiss of metal on leather beside him as Wyn drew her blades, their steel blackened by charcoal. Her eyes gleamed in the torchlight, and her lips compressed into a severe line as she drew her legs up, ready to leap. But Torbhin held up a hand and motioned for her to wait. He wanted to learn as much as he could, although he carefully slid his bow free and notched an arrow, ready to strike as soon as was necessary. He did not need to learn at the cost of a life.

The tattooed priest faced the five selected settlers and watched them, but Torbhin thought the man's gaze never left the young girl in the muck before him. When the priest raised his arm and pointed one last time, Torbhin was not surprised that the finger was aimed at her.

A moan passed through the crowd, shocked and dismayed. Whispers hissed into the night air, and Torbhin heard a woman directly beneath him gasp "Not again… he can't pick them again!" before her husband desperately hushed her.

THE MARTYR'S BLADE

The other four people who had been pulled from the crowd now scampered away from the post, leaving the girl alone on her knees. The large rider moved forward, grabbed the girl by her arm and dragged her to the post. He clamped the manacles roughly to her wrists and left her hanging from them, her toes barely touching the stone slab beneath her.

Then the tattooed priest approached her, and Torbhin saw the gleam of metal as he pulled a short curved dagger from within his robes. Torbhin rose to his knees, drew back his bow to its full extent and readied to let fly. The shot would be an easy one, less than a stone's throw and the target illuminated brightly by the torches surrounding him. Torbhin knew he could plant three arrows in the priest's back before he hit the ground.

But the priest did not raise the hand with the knife, and Torbhin held his shot. Instead, the priest leaned forward to the girl and placed his mouth next to her ear. He remained there for several moments, whispering, but Torbhin could see no reaction from the girl hanging from the iron fetters. Then the priest passed the knife slowly down the back of each of her arms, and Torbhin saw a long, thin, red line open and a slow drip of blood splash to the dirty snow beneath her feet. The girl cried out in pain as the priest left her and re-mounted his horse. He turned once more to the crowd, and singled out the girl's father, still on his knees. The priest slowly drew a finger along the side of his blade, then wiped a red smear across each cheek as he stared down his nose at the father.

"You know what the punishment is for freeing her," the priest rasped, his voice cruel and sharp in the frozen night air. "And you know the punishment if you are late."

Then he wheeled his horse and rode into the night, back the way he had come, the other two riders following in his wake.

A sigh swept through the crowd, and the people returned quietly to their homes. Many passed the father kneeling in the frozen mud, and Torbhin saw hands gently touching his shoulders and head as they passed, and there were whispered words of comfort, but the man did not hear, and only stared at his daughter where she hung from the post.

Soon the ring was deserted again, and dark. All that was left were the girl, her father, and the horse tethered to the post, and the only sound was the girl's exhausted sobs.

"Fuck me," hissed Wyn. "Tell me we can cut her down now."

"I don't know," whispered Torbhin miserably. "The priest said there would be punishment. What if he kills someone else?"

"Why are we even talking about this?" Wyn held up a gloved finger, counting. "We free her." Another finger. "We kill that bastard." A third. "Everyone is happy."

"I'm not sure," Torbhin said softly. His stomach knotted as he tried to think. It would be so simple to leap down and free the girl. He wanted to save her from her fear and misery, and Wyn wanted him to do it. *And it's a chance to actually do something impressive for Wyn, well, not for her but where she could see it. Although of course that isn't the reason to do it. Mostly.*

He was pretty sure Bradon would do it. *'Even one life' and all that.* But Killock would not. Killock would make sure that saving one life would not jeopardize dozens more.

There's more going on here than just rescuing one girl. Bradon trusted me to do this right. Not an hour ago I was dreading Bradon rushing in without thinking, and now I am about to do the same thing.

"Wyn, listen," Torbhin whispered. "She's not in danger right now."

Wyn drew breath to disagree, her green eyes dangerously fierce.

"Scared and miserable, yes," he added quickly. "But not actually in any danger. Look down there, Wyn, what do you see? Where's the ritual? Think about it. There must be others, other people the priest took somewhere, who are out there right now about to be sacrificed. We have to find them, we have to stop that ritual. That's more important."

Wyn stared at him, not letting him blink or drop his gaze. He could feel his heart beating so loudly that he feared the family in the cabin below would hear it vibrating through the roof. Torbhin was not sure if Wyn was about to knife him and leave him bleeding to death, or whether he had just ruined any chance of her ever thinking fondly of him. But at that moment it did not matter. He simply gazed back.

Wyn finally relented and turned to face the scene below. Torbhin allowed himself to watch her profile a heartbeat longer. She had not killed him, and she had not called him an idiot and leapt down and freed the girl, so perhaps she agreed with him. It was difficult to tell.

"So let's go find that ritual and put an end to all of this shite," she whispered. "And quickly, right? I've got something to say to that priest prick."

"Agreed," Torbhin said. "You find someone here in the camp who can tell us what's been going on. Quietly. Who knows what ears the priest has here, magic or otherwise. I'll get Lord Bradon and Captain Alistair and Lady Danielle," Torbhin continued. "I should be back within the hour."

"And while you're off I'll make sure no one makes trouble for that girl," stated Wyn.

Torbhin knew there would be no arguing with that. He wanted to say something to her, something heroic, or, failing that, at least something to let her know… what? *That I'm not an idiot?*

He sighed, disheartened. Another chance lost. "I will see you in an hour then," was all he said.

***

In the end it took less than three-quarters of an hour for Torbhin to return to Twin Pines with Lord Bradon, Lady Danielle, Captain Alistair and his ten soldiers. Bradon had chosen speed over stealth and they had ridden hard, following the twisted path of the Gylden Beck whenever possible, veering onto game trails when the stream's channel became too steep. Alistair and his veteran soldiers knew how to move quickly through harsh terrain and what to do when they caught their enemy.

The party left their horses concealed downstream from the camp and crept forward on foot as a small concession to stealth. Torbhin led them to where the stream wound from the camp, paused, and waited to see some sign from Wyn. The camp appeared unchanged from when he had left. Torches still flickered next to the post, and the girl and her father remained alone in the center of the camp. The girl hung limply in her manacles, quiet in her despair. The cabins and tents were dark and only a few gleams of light showed where some inhabitant remained awake.

The shadows on the embankment stirred and Wyn materialized beside the group.

"About time," she whispered, a wisp of steam escaping from her hood as she spoke. "Did you stop for dinner or something?" A smile flashed in the darkness as she knelt next to Bradon.

"Indeed," Bradon pitched his voice low. "And yet I find that I crave something more to satisfy my hunger this night. What have you learned about our upcoming feast?"

"Enough," Wyn replied. She nodded up the embankment towards the settlement. "C'mon. I want you to meet a new friend of mine."

Wyn led the way through the outskirts of the camp, weaving through the shadows between the tents until they reached one of the larger cabins, set back in the trees above the rest. Wyn tapped softly on the cabin's door, and it opened just wide enough to let a small shape slip out in response. A boy, perhaps fourteen years of age, with a mop of dark hair that sheltered wide, nervous eyes. But he did not flinch, and apart from glancing at Wyn for reassurance every few moments, he stayed composed.

"This is Colin," Wyn whispered. "He lives here. We had a nice chat when he came out to get wood for the fire."

"Hello Colin, my name is Danielle," said Danielle softly, pulling back her hood so that the boy could see her face. She gave him a friendly smile and the boy nodded his head in return, and attempted an awkward bow.

"M'lady," Colin managed.

Danielle indicated the others. "These men are Bradon, and Torbhin, and you can see Captain Alistair and his soldiers over there. We are here because we are worried that something bad is happening here. Can you tell us anything about that?"

"Yes, m'lady," Colin whispered in reply. "He's been taking people every night, ever since he had us tear down the shrine and put that pole up." Torbhin could see the boy was fiercely angry. His words tripped over each other in his haste, and his hands clenched into tight fists as he spoke.

"Who has? The man in the robes?" Danielle asked, and Colin nodded. "Who is he?"

"That's Reverend Crassus. He's a priest, though he usually only comes in the summer. He made us put up the pole and then he chooses them that have to go."

"Where do they go?" asked Danielle softly.

Colin shook his head. "I don't know, m'lady. Someone from the family has to take them up the mountain, but I don't know where. But them that's chosen never come back."

"Tell her about Meghan's family," Wyn whispered.

Colin nodded, and his expression grew grim. "Meghan, she's the one he chose tonight. The one chained up right now. Reverend Crassus chose from her family five times in a row now. When he was here last it was her sister Meadow, then her mum, and then Myrna her other sister. And then last night Lyall her brother. Her da will be the only one left now, once he takes her up the hill." Colin angrily wiped at his eyes with the back of his hand, smearing tears across dirty cheeks.

"Do you know Meghan and her family well?" Danielle asked gently.

Colin nodded and furiously wiped his cheeks again. "Pa and her da are friends. We built our cabins together. I was goin' to marry Meghan next summer, Pa said."

"Do not worry Colin, we will help Meghan. But tell me, how long has Reverend Crassus been doing this?"

"All winter," said Colin miserably. "Since before the first snow. He leaves sometimes, for a week or so, but he always comes back, and he's sent dozens and dozens of us up there."

"Has anyone ever tried to stop him?"

"Yes'm, m'lady, of course," Colin said. "First time he told us to hang someone from that post two of them bear trappers, Ryland and Thorley, told him damn if they would, and Thorley, he once killed a bear all by himself." Colin shivered and glanced around. "But Reverend Crassus just killed 'em both right there. He says 'damned is right' and then they was screaming and on the ground and blood everywhere, and then just dead."

"Then, the first time he left, one o' them farmers from the valley, Yorik, he pulled down the post," continued Colin. "But when Reverend Crassus came back he made us put it back up, and he picked Yorik that night, and since then no one's said nothin'."

Colin glanced fiercely around the group. "But it's not right, is it? We should have stopped him, shouldn't we?"

Danielle took Colin's hand in hers and shook her head. "No, Colin, you did as much as anyone could. Thank you for telling us. Now Lord Bradon and his soldiers can do the rest."

"Good," said Colin softly. "I don't want Meghan or no one else to go up that mountain."

"They won't," said Wyn.

"Do you know where up the mountain they go?" Torbhin asked.

"Not for sure," said Colin. "Some hunters went once while Reverend Crassus wasn't here, but they came back pretty quick, too scared to go all the way up I'd say. And them that take their kin up the hill won't say neither. But Pa says it must be up to the high meadow. They used to say there was a gate in the high meadow, a magic one that led to treasure in the hollow mountain if you could find it, but Pa says now we know it weren't no treasure it leads to."

"Alright Colin, that is all we need for now. Go back inside, stay warm and quiet, and we will take care of Reverend Crassus," said Danielle. Colin hesitated, clearly wanting to stay, and glanced at Wyn for support.

"Go on with you," said Wyn with a comforting smile. "But don't forget to make sure Meghan is alright tomorrow."

Colin's mouth opened and closed a few times, and he stared at his feet as he stammered something about "Mayhaps I could" before he retreated into the cabin.

Wyn giggled to herself, and turned to Bradon. "Time to rescue a girl?"

Bradon nodded. In the short time that Torbhin had known the Templar he had not seen Lord Bradon look quite as dangerous as he did now. Bradon had not said a word since entering the settlement, and a deep scowl of rage had settled on him as he listened to Colin's story.

"Danielle, you should speak to Meghan's father. If what Colin says is true he will not want us to interfere until he knows they will be safe. Wyn will free young Meghan," Bradon growled, his jaw clenched. "Alistair, go with them to make sure no one interferes. Torbhin, with me." And with that Bradon walked towards the northern edge of the settlement.

"Come on, Shoulders, let's go be heroes," said Wyn cheerfully.

***

On the north side of Twin Pines, Bradon stopped and looked towards the mountains. They were not visible, of course, but Torbhin felt them looming over him, a massive presence of cold cliffs and chill ice pushing up the ground at his feet.

Snow fell lightly, drifting between the trees to settle on hoods and cloaks. Torbhin waited quietly, listening to the soft sounds of the trees shifting in the wind.

"The boy mentioned a magic gate into a hollow mountain," pondered Bradon. "Have you ever heard of such a thing in your ranging?"

Torbhin had heard of many magical gates. Every village had its own legend of secret caverns, or Elvhen ruins, or Korrigan lairs. Although he had spoken to countless shepherds and hunters who had 'seen them with mine own eyes,' none had ever been found by any Temple ranger or scout. Torbhin once asked Killock if the Templar believed that Elvhes still lived in the world. Killock simply asked in reply if Torbhin had ever seen one himself. *Which of course I haven't. Every 'Korrigan' lair I've ever tracked down has turned out to be a troll den, or just an empty cave with some wind moaning through it. Not exactly the stuff of legends.*

"Not this particular gate, m'lord," Torbhin replied. "But every place has its own myth."

"Perhaps there is more to this legend than the others," said Bradon.

Torbhin nodded silently. *He wants Killock to be standing here, not me.* Torbhin tried to imagine what the knight would do. *Probably ask just the right question to show Lord Bradon the answer.* But Torbhin did not know what that question would be.

"The priest, Crassus," Torbhin began hesitantly, as he struggled to force uncertain thoughts and instincts into a clear vision. "What he's doing here, m'lord. It's very different from the other places where he did the rituals. At Nóinín Cnoc and all the other ritual sites he forced everyone into the ritual, killed those that resisted, then sacrificed all the rest, right away."

"Yes, the same thought had occurred to me," Bradon agreed. "What do you make of that?"

"I'm not sure, m'lord, but it must be important." Torbhin was certain about that, even if nothing else was clear. "They said Crassus comes back here over and over. And he makes the victims suffer before they go, hanging all night on that pole, and with their family to take them and all. I don't know what it all means, but I do know it's important to Crassus, which makes this place special."

"A place of consequence," Bradon growled, and his hand dropped from his beard and rested easily on the hilt of his hammer.

"Yes, m'lord."

"Then he will not lightly walk away from it," Bradon grinned fiercely. "He is forced to defend what he cannot replace, and when we take it from him he will suffer."

"Yes, m'lord," Torbhin repeated, and patiently waited for the Templar.

"As Wyn would remind me, there is little sense in asking the trees, not when the man we wish to question is but a short distance away." Bradon shifted his weight and turned slightly to face the ranger. "Go and find him for me. Carefully. He must not know we are coming."

Torbhin nodded, and slipped away.

***

The trail was very easy to follow. The denizens of Twin Pines had obviously used it for years, perhaps decades, on their trips from the camp. It wound through the forest alongside the Gylden Beck, then cut up to a ridge through a series of switchbacks. Torbhin had no trouble following it, even in the dark, and the fact that several horses had recently used it made it laughably easy.

Torbhin moved slowly nonetheless. Following the trail might be easy, but staying hidden on such a well-worn path required caution. Once he reached the high meadow, however, it became much more difficult to remain concealed. The priest's trail led directly towards the middle of the plateau, but the only cover was the giant boulders that littered the meadow. Torbhin moved cautiously from shadow to shadow and hoped the trio had stopped somewhere close ahead, or else he would take all night to catch them. The wind hissed across the crusted snow, and stung his face where it was not covered by his hood or scarf.

He crossed a slight ridge and felt the ground slope gently away. Far ahead he saw the dim, flickering light of a fire. Torbhin quickly ducked against a nearby boulder and peered through the swirling snow.

Torbhin shivered and wrapped his cloak more tightly around himself, and tucked his hands into his cloak to get some warmth into his fingers. The heat he had generated from his scramble up the trail was rapidly dissipating into the boulder's shadow. He tugged his hood lower over his head and wiped his nose on the back of his glove miserably. The orange light winked at him faintly, taunting him.

No one is watching, he decided. *It's too cold. They will be by the fire.* Torbhin was not sure how much of that idea was driven by the cold and how much by sense. *Either way, I need to get closer.*

Torbhin began stalking his prey across the meadow. He moved patiently, finding small covering ridges in the ground when possible, and used the deep shadows underneath the boulders to pause and survey his route. Gusts of wind carried the smell of cold, damp smoke mixed with the sharp ice from the mountains, and Torbhin instinctively moved to keep the smoke blowing towards him as much as possible. His scent would not reveal him to the priest or his companions, but wind carried sound as well as smell.

The fire grew more distinct as Torbhin slowly crept towards it. A winking star, a steady beacon, then several distinct flames, until finally, a large central campfire with several smaller torches that guttered around it. The bright firelight painted flickering orange light onto the large boulders that surrounded the camp.

Torbhin disappeared into a boulder's long shadow and crouched as low as possible. Some savage freeze had long ago split the rock, leaving a deep fissure that gaped blackly in front of him. He slipped into it, feeling his way until he reached a spot high enough to look into the camp. He settled into the rock as comfortably as possible and wedged his boots into small cracks.

Below him blazed the campfire, cracking and popping and sending showers of sparks dancing into the chill air. It had been banked steeply and stacked with wood, a fire built for heat and light. Next to it were the two men Torbhin had last seen with the priest in the village. The larger of the two sat on a small rock, poking the fire with a branch pulled from a nearby pile of cut wood. The other paced back and forth, stamping his feet, beating his arms, and rubbing his hands under his cloak.

Around the fire stood six torches on poles, creating a circle a stone's throw across. The torches flickered and swayed with the gusting wind.

Of the priest there was no sign.

The big man jabbed his branch into the fire, sending a cloud of sparks into the snow-filled air, and then chucked it into the blaze. He glared at the fire. "I'm freezing," he muttered through clenched teeth.

The other man did not respond, merely stamped his feet as he continued to pace back and forth.

"I said, I'm freezing!" the big man repeated angrily.

"I heard you," the younger one replied.

The big man glowered at him behind his back, and yanked another branch from the pile beside him and began poking the fire again, stirring more flames from the blaze.

"We need more wood for a good fire," he muttered sullenly.

The young man glanced over his shoulder. "Then go and get some."

"I'm not going out there." His companion shook his head and hunched closer to the fire.

"No, I didn't think so," the young man laughed.

"Fuck you," the big man shot back. "I don't see you fucking going out there neither."

The young man laughed again, but then stopped with his hand out, listening. Torbhin had heard it too, a susurration from the darkness beyond the ring of torches.

"Quiet!" the young man said, and at his tone the big man scrambled to his feet, suddenly wary.

For a moment there was no sound except the cracking of the fire and the faint whisper of wind over the frozen crust of the packed snow. Then Torbhin heard the crunch of footsteps approaching, and on the far side of the torches the priest strode out of the night. His hood was thrown back, and he was oblivious to the freezing air that caused his robes to billow around him.

"It is done," the priest announced. "Bring the girl and her father to me when they arrive."

"Yes, Reverend," the young man replied, bowing his head.

The priest turned abruptly and disappeared into the darkness, and the sound of his footsteps quickly faded. But the other noises did not fade. Torbhin could hear faint sounds drifting in the night air. Something was moving out there. Many somethings.

Below him the young man checked on the torches, packed more stones around their base and stamped them down, while the big man stood next to the fire and watched him.

A soft whisper of skin on stone behind Torbhin made him slowly turn his head to look. The roaring fire had spoiled his night vision, and at first he could see nothing. But then a pale shape moved past the mouth of his hiding place. Pale, and covered in black markings. Torbhin froze against the stone, motionless, still as ice. The shape paused beneath him and Torbhin held his breath for what felt like an eternity. Then it moved, disappearing from view.

Torbhin felt a bubble of panic rise within him, a pressure on his chest that sucked the breath from his body and narrowed his vision. His hiding place had suddenly turned into a trap. His arms and legs trembled with the urge to run, and he feared he would lose his perch and tumble to lie helpless and revealed.

But Torbhin did not let the panic wash him away. *I am the hunter,* he told himself, and with that thought came purpose and an icy clarity that burned out the panic. Torbhin did not like his chances in an escape across open terrain, in the dark, chased by however many of the husk creatures hunted in the snow.

Instead, he moved forward, scrambled over the lip of the boulder and dropped softly to the ground beneath. He knew one place where other men thought they were safe and that is where Torbhin wanted to be.

The two men had not noticed Torbhin's drop from the boulder. In ten steps, Torbhin crossed the distance between the stone and the imagined boundary between two of the torches. He dropped to a knee in the snow and unlimbered his bow. He bent the bow and strung it in one smooth movement before they saw him. The big man shouted a warning and grabbed his hammer.

Torbhin's fingers pulled apart the ties on his quiver, and he grabbed a fistful of shafts and drove them into the ground at his knee as the big man swung his hammer above his head and lurched into a charge. Torbhin fired twice before the big man reached him and buried barbed, steel-tipped shafts into the big man's shoulder and chest.

Then the big man was on him, choking out a roar of rage and pain as he swung his hammer down. Torbhin rolled smoothly under the hammer swing and rammed his last arrow into the big man's leg behind his knee as he passed.

Torbhin came to his feet and then the younger man was on him. His sword hissed through the air and sliced through Torbhin's cloak, sending him stumbling backwards to regain his balance. The man pursued, keeping his sword held high, ready to strike. Torbhin drew back his empty bow and fired, and the man ducked backwards from the imagined arrow. Torbhin scrambled to his readied arrows. Two came into his hand and he turned, drew and fired the first arrow in one rapid movement. The shot flew with more speed than accuracy, but that was Torbhin's intent. His shot forced the target to jump sideways and Torbhin's second shot, held and aimed precisely, caught him before he could recover and dodge again.

The man collapsed with the arrow buried deeply in his chest, and bright red blood frothed thickly from his mouth as he choked out his last breath.

The big man cursed and struggled to rise. Blood streamed from his wounds and he took only a single step before he collapsed again. Torbhin pulled one last arrow from the ground at his feet and calmly released the big man from his pain, as he would for any wounded animal.

Torbhin quickly picked up his quiver and replaced the few arrows that had spilled when he dropped it. He kept a wary eye on the shifting darkness beyond the torches. Pale shapes moved there, drifting in and out of view.

He moved to the fire and circled it, facing outwards, his bow at the ready. Standing silhouetted against a fire was not a ranger's first choice for cover, but against this enemy, he knew his only real defense was the fire, its ring of torches, and his hope that two dead men's faith in its protection was well-founded.

Pale corpses came to the ring, and watched him with dead eyes. Withered faces bore dried skin stretched rigid over bone. A few rotten wisps of hair lingered where a beard or a cascade of curls formerly grew. None wore clothing, and all were covered in jagged black markings, the same as the ones he had seen at Nóinín Cnoc.

They did not stay for long, drifting into the night after staring for a few heartbeats, but more appeared; a large one with the remains of a beard, a small one that must have been a child.

None stepped past the torches. Torbhin did not know if they formed a magical barrier or if something was controlling the husks and stopping them, and he did not care. He had to warn the others.

Danielle

Alistair ordered his men to collect the horses, then he and Danielle followed Wyn between the tents and cabins toward the center of Twin Pines. Wyn fairly skipped along as they went, and Danielle caught pieces of a happy tune Wyn was singing under her breath.

Danielle felt she might join her. *At last we can help, not just chase after horror and pain. 'Let us be heroes', Wyn said, and it is truly that simple.* "Is it not lovely to see such joy?" Danielle asked Alistair.

"I know how she feels," Alistair smiled in return.

"It does not fade, even after you have been the savior so many times?"

"Not at all. Nor does it hurt less when we are too late."

"When have you been too late?" Danielle laughed. "I do not believe it. I have never seen such a thing."

"Perhaps you have not, m'lady, but it has not always been so." A brief scowl passed across Alistair's face.

Danielle had no answer, and was content to walk quietly in Alistair's shadow for a moment, enjoying the comfort of the soldier's easy strength.

"Have you fought along with the boys then, your Ladyship?" Wyn asked.

"I have, but only the last three summers, since I came to Albyn. And I have done little enough compared with what the Captain and his men have accomplished," Danielle replied. She had seen the aftermath of the brutal fighting the soldiers endured over and over in the caves and villages of the Ironback clans, and still found it hard to believe that any could survive it. Yet after each battle the same faces had cheerfully gathered around the campfires. All the soldiers bore wounds and an assortment of bandages, but those had no effect on their bearers. At least, not until there was time to grouse about them.

"Don't you believe her," Alistair chuckled. "Until her Ladyship joined us their shamans gave us a terrible time. Now they hide as far up the mountain as they can."

"I bet they do!" Wyn waved her hands dramatically in the air. "Whoosh! Eek! They must look awful silly with their britches on fire."

"I suppose they would," mused Alistair. "If they wore britches."

"Why, what do they wear?"

"Blue paint," Danielle answered. "And some bones."

"They never! In the freezing cold? With their dingles all dangly?" Wyn cackled with glee. "That must make for a very un-heroic sight."

"They don't all do it," Alistair explained. "The shamans do, and the berserks. They say the runes they paint on their bodies protect them."

"Yes, but… doesn't it just flap around?" Wyn burst into more giggles. "I don't think I could fight, I'd be trying so hard not to pee my pants."

"It does sound ridiculous," Danielle admitted with a smile. "But when they come screaming down the mountain at you, with their axes and their spirits and devils, it is quite astonishing. Especially their women."

"The girls do it too? Paint their ditties and run about in the snow? No wonder you lads are so eager to head back up there every summer."

"As her Ladyship said, you don't have time to, ah, appreciate, anything," Alistair shook his head. "You'd be dead the moment you think of anything except the strength and speed of your opponent. They are too fierce, too strong, to think of them in any other way."

Wyn watched Alistair's face for a moment. "You like them, don't you? With all your dragons and such."

"I do, very much," Alistair nodded. "And I respect them. But I also know they are very dangerous, and will raid our villages and slaughter our people if we do not stop them."

"It is a shame," Danielle said softly. "They are a beautiful people. They care so much for their family, for their clan. They die for one another, they care for one another's children. And they have such stature, tall and golden-haired. You may have some ancestor from the clans, Wyn, for your hair is the same beautiful color."

"A skinny little boney one, maybe," Wyn flashed a smile. "But I'm not painting my boobs and going starkers. I'm cold enough as it is."

"Much too cold, I agree," Danielle laughed as she felt warmth rush to her cheeks.

"I would miss my armor," Alistair said thoughtfully. "I like the way it stops sharp things from killing me."

"Are you sure?" Wyn said, and she gazed at Alistair with wide, innocent eyes. "I mean, how can you know until you try?"

"What makes you think I haven't tried?" asked Alistair.

"No chance," Wyn scoffed. "I don't think that armor actually comes off. Now, her Ladyship I'm not so certain of. She's blushing quite a bit now, although she's trying to hide it. Don't you run about naked in the south? I think I heard that once."

"Not at all," Danielle objected, trying to will the blood from her cheeks. "It is true that we wear lighter clothes because of the warmth, but we are certainly not naked. Just for swimming, but that does not count."

"Anyway, if there were two people who should run into battle naked, it's you two," Wyn declared. "There'd not be a soul who wouldn't be distracted by that. You could take your time whacking them and setting them on fire."

"Hmmm, perhaps," Alistair refused to say more, and Danielle remained silent, caught as she imagined dragons curling around her body, fire leaping from their painted lips. *In a place where it is warm, or else I would be a small, shivering lump.*

Danielle forced her thoughts away from fire and splendor and back to the frozen night and darkened settlement. They had reached the small, open area that served as the center of Twin Pines. It was as Wyn had described it. The torches flickered in their sconces on either side of the tall, dark post, their light cold and thin in the chill air. Meghan still hung from her manacles, too exhausted now to stand or raise her head, and her father still knelt silently on the frozen ground in front of her. He ignored their approach, his gaze locked on the grey stone slab under his daughter's feet.

Wyn strode past him and knelt at Meghan's side. "Meghan? Meghan, we're here to help you, don't worry."

Meghan flinched away from Wyn and stared down in fear.

"No!" Meghan cried out, and her father looked up, startled, and stared at the newcomers in confusion.

"We're here to help," Wyn said brightly.

Alistair caught Danielle's glance. "Shall I get rid of that thing?" He patted the haft of his axe.

"Yes, please," Danielle replied. She was shocked by the feeling of dread and despair that emanated from the dark wood of the post, and she could not wait for it to be gone.

Doors opened in the cabins surrounding the clearing as the settlers came to investigate the voices and Meghan's cries. The light from their torches cast dozens of long shadows from the pole, wavering and pulsing on the ground at Danielle's feet.

"Don't worry, lass, I'll take care of those chains for you." Alistair hefted his axe in both hands and tapped it lightly against the wood above the iron spike that held the manacles to the post, leaving a small bright mark in the dark wood. Then he raised the axe to strike.

"No! Please!" Meghan wailed, and she pulled as far away as the manacles would allow.

"It's alright, sweetheart," Wyn said softly. "He looks a bit terrifying, but we'll not do anything to hurt you."

"Please tell him not to break the chains," Meghan sobbed.

"No?" Wyn blinked in surprise. "Are they not horribly uncomfortable? There's no need to worry, we'll have you out in a shake."

"Please no, he'll kill me if you do, and Da, and six others he said."

"He'll kill us all, m'lady," her father begged. Shouts of agreement echoed from the small crowd of settlers. Alistair looked to Danielle for guidance, and she gestured for him to hold.

"He will not, I promise you," Danielle assured Meghan's father. "We are here to make sure Reverend Crassus does not harm anyone, ever again. We have soldiers, and knights. We will keep you safe."

"But, m'lady, you don't understand." A trapper as shaggy and unkempt as the bearskin coat he wore stepped forward. "He'll know. When Yorik took down the post, Reverend Crassus knew."

"What does it matter if he does?" demanded another voice from the crowd, a young woman with a serene infant balanced on her hip. "Let him come and complain about his damn post when we've got soldiers here. I'd like to see that."

"Have you forgotten what happened to Thorley?" the trapper insisted. "What good are soldiers against that?"

"More use than you, that's certain," the woman scoffed, and Danielle agreed. But many in the crowd did not, and there were angry cries and shouts. More settlers arrived with every passing moment, and Danielle had to raise her voice to be heard.

"You have endured a nightmare beyond imagining," Danielle began, and the crowd quieted expectantly. "And you are not alone. Other good people, in farms and temples across the north, have suffered as well at the hands of this Crassus. But it will end now, before any more of your sons and daughters, your husbands and wives, are taken from you."

A murmur of agreement ran through the crowd, and a shout of "Hear her!" carried to them, but more voices raised up in protest.

"M'lady, you say it true when you call it a nightmare," the trapper stood in the center of a dozen settlers who muttered grim defiance and shouted support for their spokesman. "But you can't stop a nightmare with swords and soldiers. We've seen it, right there where you're standing, your Ladyship, and we know what'll happen if we try again. Maker bless you and I pray you do kill him, but until you do it's best we do as he says."

The woman with the infant spat on the ground at the trapper's feet. "That's easy for you to say, all alone in your little tent, no family to care for. But you'll sing a different tune when it's your turn, and no one speaks for you. You'll show your true stripe then."

This is absurd. Danielle gazed about the ring of settlers as a storm of shouts filled the circle. Arguments had begun throughout the crowd as neighbors shoved angry fingers into each other's faces and hurled insults. Alistair caught her eye and patted the grip of his long war axe, but Danielle shook her head. *We must be able to end this peacefully. There is so much fear here that force might well lead to bloodshed, and they have suffered enough.*

Wyn still knelt next to Meghan and spoke softly to her. Tears washed down the girl's face, but she was listening to Wyn and nodding her head to whatever Wyn was saying to her.

"You cannot mean that you will send this poor girl up the mountain tonight?" Danielle challenged the trapper. "That is madness. It will all be over long before she could make the trip. Why force her to endure this ordeal any longer?"

The trapper began an angry reply, but a new voice spoke up and he stopped in mid-word. The voice came from near Danielle's feet, and was so quiet that it may have been speaking for some time. Slowly the shouting died down as more and more in the crowd quieted to listen.

Meghan's father was still on his knees. "It's for the best," he muttered, and he rocked slightly back and forth and wrung his hands together. "It's for the best."

"Let him decide," the trapper hissed triumphantly. "She's his daughter."

Danielle felt sure that a slap across the father's face would stop the cursed muttering, but already a chorus of agreement was sweeping through the settlers standing around the trapper.

"Is that what you told your wife, when you took your children up the mountain? Is that what you told yourself, when you took your wife?" Danielle snapped at him, but the words made no impression, and she wondered if he had even heard her.

Then a child's wail cut through the noise of the crowd, hopeless and afraid. It silenced the circle instantly, and even Meghan's father ceased his mindless chant.

"Please, Da," Meghan begged him. "I don't want to go. Please take me home, Da, please!"

"It's for the best," he replied softly.

"No it fucking isn't!" Wyn's voice snapped across the silent circle like a whip. She stood in front of Meghan with her hands on her hips and glared with icy hatred at the man kneeling before her. "You coward," she sneered in disgust. "You shit-stained, son of a bitch coward." Meghan's father jerked as if he had been slapped and he stared, baffled, at the furious girl that loomed over him.

Wyn turned to include the trapper and his gang. "All of you, pissing your pants, sending a little girl to be killed just so that you can save your own skins." Wyn shook her head. Before anyone could recover, Wyn turned to the shackles and with a few quick twists popped them open with a raspy, metallic clunk.

"There, it's done," Wyn stared down the startled settlers. "So stop bleating on about it like a flock of sheep. Martyr's tears!"

***

Danielle's horse shifted and stamped a hoof, and she bent to stroke the chestnut mare's neck and whisper comfort. Danielle could hear the murmur and clink of the rest of the party as it waited on the trail around her, the soldiers of Alistair's squad in their leather and steel mail, and Wyn next to her, perched on her saddle with her legs tucked under her cloak, as balanced as if she were seated on a boulder instead of on the back of a horse busy tearing at a clump of snowflower that grew beside the trail.

Biting cold stung every scrap of exposed skin and seeped into the thickest gloves and boots. The night was more than three-quarters finished, and save for the cold, Danielle felt that she could easily fall asleep in her saddle and let her horse find its own way.

"Something's happened, or he would've returned by now." Though he spoke softly, Captain Alistair's gruff voice carried through the darkness from where he stood next to Lord Bradon a short distance up the trail.

"Perhaps," Bradon rumbled in reply, but Danielle saw concern written clearly in his rigid stance. Bradon stood in the shadow of a towering fir tree and glared at the trail as if he could force it to reveal some sign of Torbhin's return.

For the ranger was long overdue. Torbhin had been gone for most of the night, and although it had taken the party much longer than Danielle had expected to free Meghan and leave Twin Pines, still they had been waiting for his return for what seemed like hours.

The memory made Danielle smile, and she glanced over at the small shadow that was Wyn perched atop her horse. *So much fire, so much passion to do what she thinks is right, and so little care for the consequences. Such a beautiful spirit.*

"You were wonderful," Danielle said to Wyn, who turned at the sound of Danielle's voice. Danielle could not see Wyn's eyes under the deep shadow of her hood, but she could feel the questioning gaze. "In the camp. You showed them the right thing to do, and you had the courage to do it for them when they wavered. They would be chaining that poor girl to the post again right now if I had asked Captain Alistair to free Meghan, which was all I could think of to do."

"They were just being stupid," Wyn's voice was quiet. "Plus, I didn't even know what I was saying until I said it. That happens quite a bit."

"It was perfect," said Danielle.

"I like 'perfect'," Wyn laughed softly. "That's better than 'loud and rude'. Still, it probably would've ended up a sad story if Shoulders hadn't been there to stop things going sideways."

"Perhaps," said Danielle. "He forced them to listen, true, but it was you who changed their minds."

Wyn giggled. "Well now I'm blushing, so I'm glad it's dark. Anyhow, you're not so bad yourself, your Ladyship. Most high-muckities I've met were too good to wipe the rest of us off their pretty little boots. But you're almost like a real person, even though you have scary magic and fine ways about you."

"I will accept that as a marvelous compliment," laughed Danielle. "Thank you."

A comfortable hush fell about them. Trees sighed sporadically in the cold wind that gusted down the mountains. Danielle tucked her hands deep within her coat to try to restore feeling to her long fingers, and listened to the soft creak of leather and the occasional muffled thump of a horse's hoof.

"Do you think Torbhin is coming?" asked Wyn after a while.

"I do not know. Lord Bradon is worried," replied Danielle.

"Worried? Him? How can you tell?"

"I have known him for a long time," Danielle said softly. "When things are not right, he becomes still. When he is certain, he is a bear."

"I've seen the bear part," agreed Wyn. She was silent for a moment, and then continued in a whisper. "So, are you and he... together?"

"I love him with all my heart, but no, we are not lovers," replied Danielle, just as softly. *Why am I telling her this, a girl that I have known only a few days?* But it felt good to do so, perhaps most of all because of the fact that Wyn did not know who she was, or who her family was. Danielle realized that even if Wyn knew her heritage, she would not care in the slightest.

"Why not?" Wyn continued. "I mean, Maker's breath, look at you! Plus, you seem nice and all. And he's really big and gruff but he seems nice, too, in the right ways, yeah?"

"Yes, he is nice in the right ways, but it is complicated," said Danielle sadly. *And he has never asked. Never asked, thank the Maker, because I would say no, and it would wound him terribly.* Danielle wondered if Bradon somehow knew what she would say, and why, and that was why he had never asked for more. She hoped that was true.

"Alright," replied Wyn, but she was clearly unsatisfied with Danielle's answer. "I'm not very good with talking about deep stuff or whatever. Sorry I'm being such a nosey bitch."

"You are not. Well, perhaps a little nosey," chided Danielle softly. "But I do not mind. So few people ask me direct questions, they would prefer to just assume what they want. I like this better."

"Well, all I'm saying is, I wouldn't care how complicated something was. If I wanted it, I'd just say so. Otherwise you might never get it, right? And life's too short for that."

Danielle felt her breath catch for a moment. *I know that is true, and I wish that I had her clarity, but I have always been tangled in complications. My whole life they have been around me. That is not so simple to change.*

"Perhaps you can help me with that," Danielle said. "With some things, it is very difficult for me to ask for what I want."

"My pleasure, your Ladyship."

Danielle resisted the urge to reach out and take Wyn's hand. Danielle feared that such forwardness would confuse her, so instead she let the urge remain yet another desire she never satisfied because it was complicated. A mocking laugh echoed in her thoughts at her own instant reversion to form, but she pushed it down for later. Now was not the time to rebel against herself.

Instead she watched Wyn. Wyn pushed back her hood and gazed into the trees. Her blonde hair curled around her long neck, and her breath wisped into the night air. A pale, dim light filtered through the tree canopy, tracing the curve of her cheek and giving a gleam to her eyes. A small smile crept to the corners of her lips as her gaze settled on something high in the trees and ahead of them. She rose high in her saddle and peered eagerly ahead.

There was a soft hiss and a thump as a tree branch dropped its load of heavy, wet snow onto Bradon and Alistair.

Wyn giggled gleefully and turned to Danielle, teeth flashing in a smile, eyes wide with excitement and delight. Danielle felt something stir deep within her breast, and her heart beat more heavily. It took her aback with its sudden, intense pressure. *What is this?* Danielle wondered. She breathed deeply, but the feeling did not subside.

"Did you see?" grinned Wyn. "Couldn't have planned it any better! I knew trees had to have something good about them."

"I did, it was perfect," replied Danielle as she tried to concentrate on sounding normal. "Although now he will be very grumpy, I am sure." The strange feeling surged again as Wyn smiled at her in reply.

Wyn laughed softly, then snuggled into her cloak. "Well, grumpy isn't exactly a big change."

Danielle pulled the silver ring on its chain from her tunic and held it to her lips as she tried to calm her heart. Deep breaths of the chill night air did nothing to help. *It will pass.* She found herself focused on Wyn's face, although all Danielle could see of Wyn with her hood pulled so low was Wyn's chin, the tip of her nose, and her smiling mouth. Wyn's upper lip was thin and delicately bowed, her lower soft and generous, and Danielle wondered what it would be like to kiss her. It was not a new thought. Danielle had let her mind wander to such things at times as they rode or sat near the campfire together, or late in the warmth of her bedroll, and she would imagine Wyn's lithe body free of its heavy winter clothing, or picture her laughing green eyes.

But this time the thought did more than just make her ache pleasantly. Now it made the strange feeling grow stronger and her heart pound, and filled her with a longing that came from her heart, not her body.

She is a beautiful spirit, Danielle soothed herself. *Perhaps that is why I am so moved. No more than that.* But the pull in her heart and the catch in her throat felt like much more than that.

I should think of other things, Danielle insisted to herself. But it did no good. She noticed that Wyn's blonde hair had once again escaped from its simple tie to hang in her face, and Danielle longed to reach out and brush it back for her. Even as the idea crossed her mind, Wyn tucked the hair behind her ear with a long-practiced gesture, and she smiled at some unvoiced thought.

Danielle had noticed other things about Wyn as the days had passed. Wyn had a laughing smile for when she was joyful, a sly grin for when she teased, and a fierce smile for when she was angry. Her eyes danced as she laughed and shone like ice when she raged, and when she was cheerful and content she quietly sang to herself. And when she fought… it was as if she were dancing, all speed and lithe, flowing movement, strong and deadly.

But the vision Danielle treasured the most was of Wyn seated by the campfire at night as she smiled at Danielle and laughed in joy. The fire's flickering light cast warm shadows across her cheek and flashed in her golden hair. In Danielle's dreams it was her words, not Bradon's, which made Wyn laugh with such happiness.

It is strange, she felt. Wyn was pretty to look at, and would have caught her eye in any crowd, but Danielle knew she had seen other girls as fair. The thing that captivated her was Wyn's quick joy and sharp wit and carefree spirit. It was a fire Danielle had rarely seen.

Excellent job thinking of other things, she chided herself.

She searched for a distraction, and watched Bradon and Alistair for a moment as they morosely scooped snow from their tunics. She smiled to herself at the sight, and slowly the pang in her chest subsided as the world crept back around her.

She tucked away her ring and called out softly to Lord Bradon. "Is there still no sign of Torbhin?"

Bradon moved down the trail and stood next to Danielle's horse.

"No sign," he replied. "And Alistair is right, it has been too long. Something has happened."

Danielle waited quietly as Bradon made his decision.

"We will proceed on our own. The trail, so far, has been easy to follow, and perhaps it will remain that way." Bradon brushed a hand along her horse's neck, as if the chestnut mare was the one in need of comfort. "I am sure the lad is fine. But we have little choice. There are but a few hours of darkness remaining, and the priest will soon be wondering where Meghan and her father are."

"On foot?"

"No, we may need the horses."

Lord Bradon and Captain Alistair mounted their horses, and the party headed up the trail.

They emerged from the trees at the foot of a vast outcrop of rock that loomed over the valley. It reared high above them, and Danielle saw that the sides were sheer. But the trail continued to rise as it skirted the base of the cliff until it climbed to reach the same level as the plateau above.

The way ahead was terribly exposed. A few boulders littered the ground where they had tumbled from the cliffs, but there was little concealment otherwise. The trail was a broken black line where hooves had churned the snow and exposed the rock beneath. Away from the trail, the snow was white and unbroken, a pure surface to betray those who crossed it.

They could do little to minimize their vulnerability to any watchers lurking on the cliffs. Alistair rode first and moved a furlong up the trail before the others followed, in case of ambush. Then Lord Bradon and two of Alistair's men followed.

It was Danielle's turn. She took a deep breath and tapped her horse with her heels to urge it up the path. The skin across her back itched in anticipation of an arrow strike from above, and she felt the gaze of a hundred imagined eyes watching from the ridge. The cold, black stone loomed above, and a trickle of stones made her press against her horse's back, and grip the mare tightly with arms and legs to steady herself against her pounding heart. An eternity passed with only the quick clomp of hooves in the snow and the rustle of the wind in the trees below her.

She reached the top of the trail and took shelter amongst the ruins of a massive boulder. Ahead of Danielle lay the high meadow, a wide plateau along the back side of the ridge, bounded on the north and east by ramparts of rock that rose into the dark clouds, and on the south and west by the sheer cliffs of the escarpment under which she had just passed.

Wind from the mountains gusted down the face of the cliffs and sent snow swirling into strange patterns and shapes. Enormous boulders littered the plateau, as if she had discovered the place where giants played games of bowls. A frozen stream twined amongst the boulders, passing a stone's throw from Danielle. A series of frozen waterfalls marked the stream's path into the forest far below.

As the rest of the party arrived, Bradon moved next to Danielle, towering above her on his stallion. She answered his questioning glance with a quick nod of her head: she was alright. Bradon reached down and checked the straps on the great sword sheathed on Danielle's saddle, making sure it was still secure. It was, she knew, having checked it herself a dozen times a day as she rode. It was never far from her thoughts, or her hand. She even slept with her hand resting on it.

"Keep this ready," said Bradon. "You may need it tonight."

"I hope that is not the case," she replied.

Bradon nodded his head in acknowledgement. "I do as well, but He would not have asked you to bear it unless He thought it would be necessary. Just keep it ready."

"I will."

Bradon turned to Wyn next. "Are you prepared?"

"Of course I am," she snorted disdainfully. "What's the plan?"

"We will have to search the plateau. It should not take long with as many riders as we have."

"Let's go."

Alistair's voice carried low from where he watched over the plateau. "Something's coming."

Danielle turned to look. At first, she saw nothing but darkness and the windblown snow. But as the snow eddied and thinned, Danielle saw a faint glimmer of orange light that flickered far off towards the center of the plateau. It came and went with the wind, but after she watched it for several heartbeats, Danielle could tell that the source of the light was drawing nearer.

"What is it?" she asked.

"A torch, perhaps," said Bradon.

"It's a torch," replied Alistair. "Someone's carrying it. Running."

Danielle strained to see. The light bobbed and weaved as if its bearer was executing a very complicated dance, but she could not see the carrier. Only the orange light was visible. As it drew nearer, she saw that Alistair was correct. A figure became discernible, clearer with every passing moment. He was certainly running, but along a strange zig-zag route. First he headed hard to the left, then he cut to the right, and every now and then he disappeared from view behind one of the huge boulders that lay in the meadow.

"It's Torbhin," announced Alistair.

"Thank God," rumbled Bradon. "Let us go and join him."

But Alistair held up a hand. "He's shouting something."

Danielle held her breath as she listened to the soft hiss and moan of the wind. There was something there, small fragments ripped apart by the wind, but yes, they were words.

"What is he saying?" Bradon asked.

Alistair listened intently for the length of several heartbeats, and slowly drew his axe.

"'They're coming'..."

Killock

Dawn turned the night into a palette of a thousand grays and whites as the high valley slowly became visible. Ice-rimmed stones littered the valley floor, dark lumps of gray amidst the patches of icy snow that accumulated in the gaps and hollows. A frozen stream, the Carrock Beck, spread across the glacial scree.

Killock emerged from his shelter, pitched against one of the larger boulders, and wrapped his scarf and cloak tightly around himself. He scooped snow over the small fire he had made and buried it, then smoothed the snow so that no trace of his presence remained.

He stood, stretched, and thoughtfully chewed on the last mouthful of stiff, dried venison that had been breakfast as he surveyed the massive Ice Fall glacier and the head of the valley above him.

To the north lay the vast bulk of Mt. Horn, towering high over the surrounding mountains. On a clear day the peak of Mt. Horn was visible to the south for as far as a man could travel in a week as it reared majestically above the clouds scattered around its base.

Today it was completely obscured by the snow-laden clouds that covered the valley, but Killock could feel its colossal presence nonetheless. Mt. Horn's tremendous weight crushed the northern wall of the valley. Fractured faces of stone cracked and readied to sheer away under the pressure of the bulk behind them.

Beyond Mt. Horn lay the Fellgate, the high pass that once had climbed the flanks of Mt. Horn and crossed the barrier peaks, finally descending into the deep valley of Tír an Síoraí to the north.

Killock longed to see Tír an Síoraí, the legendary setting of Ruric's war against the Nameless King, sealed away over six hundred years ago by the Cataclysm that destroyed the High Road and buried the Fellgate. But years of searching for a path had been fruitless.

But I did discover the old High Road, what is left of it.

For centuries this valley had been the gateway to the High Road, one of the great constructs of the old kingdom. The remains of an ancient archway marked where the road began its ascent, and enormous embankments crisscrossed the valley floor where the way had been leveled to bear the road, although the surface itself had long-since disappeared under rock and snow and ice.

It must have been magnificent. The ruins revealed to Killock what had been lost. Buttresses that had soared high into the air were now only jagged stumps. Wide ramparts that had gracefully curved across the high cliffs were now piles of rubble far below. Elegantly carved statues and smoothed paving stones were smashed into debris indistinguishable from the raw stone from which they had been lovingly sculpted.

At the head of the valley Killock made out the black stump of a waystation tower where the road crested above the high glacial field. The waystation towers were built a day's journey apart for a laden wagon team, assuming they had a well-maintained road to travel on. Killock thought he could reach the second tower in one day, but after that he would face a much more challenging path.

And then the Léim Mhór. As far as I have ever journeyed on the High Road. The Léim Mhór, an immense viaduct that had arched gracefully across a gorge so deep it appeared bottomless. The remains of the span now perched on either edge of the chasm, shattered stumps of fitted stone slowly crumbling into the depths.

But it was possible to cross. Killock had seen it years ago while searching for a route north. Thick cables had been slung between the Léim Mhór's towers and wooden planks had been attached to them, forming a swaying bridge that would have supported only a few people on foot. Killock thought the simple span must have been built by those who had survived the Cataclysm, desperate to re-establish a passage to Tír an Síoraí.

It certainly looked six hundred years old the last time I saw it. Most of the old wooden planks had rotted away, and the cables hung limply, frayed and twisted after centuries of mountain storms.

Years ago, Killock had decided not to chance a passage and instead looked for another path which never appeared. He harbored a deep regret that he had not made the attempt to cross when he had the chance.

But now I will. I must.

Killock settled his pack more comfortably on his wiry shoulders and adjusted his hood lower over his head. *Time to move.*

***

The Léim Mhór was far worse than he remembered.

Only one ancient, frayed cable still spanned the chasm, whipping and tugging in the fierce winds that screamed through the narrow defile. Threads of tattered rope streamed from it like ghostly hair, and nearer the towers a few shattered pieces of rotted wood still twisted forlornly in the thin air, or dangled down the cliff face at the ends of other strands of unraveling rope.

Killock stood on the massive stone foot of the Léim Mhór near its jagged edge, where the smooth, fitted stones of the bridge abruptly terminated in a sheer drop into endless space. Behind him stood the weathered remains of a waystation tower. Half-way up, it had broken and sheared from the cliff, and the empty shell now stood above mounds of fallen stones and rubble.

The knight kicked a small stone off the ledge in front of him and watched it fall silently into the darkness of the ravine. Then he sighed wearily and stared across the gorge at the remains of the Léim Mhór on the other side, so far away.

"Shit," he muttered.

It might hold me. Maybe. But there's no chance all of the others could make it across. Killock smiled to himself as he pictured Lord Bradon trying to crawl along the cable in full armor. *No chance.*

He had some rope in his pack, a small coil of finely spun cord that would be useful for climbing or hunting, or countless other needs in the wilderness. But not for building bridges. It was far too short, and far too thin.

Killock had already searched the ruins behind him. There was nothing left on the surface, and the storerooms were buried beneath tons of fallen stone. It would take days to shift enough of the rubble to gain access, and Maker only knew what would be left in there.

My only hope is that there is something on the other side I could use. A slim hope, he conceded, but possible. The remains of the old guard post could still be seen on the other side of the ravine, low stone buildings built to house the soldiers posted to the Léim Mhór. They looked to be fairly intact. *That's where I would have stored any building supplies. Not on this side, where you could always bring up more. But there is no way to know without going over there. Time to give up or get on with it.*

Killock turned from the gap and began to make his preparations. He carefully cut a short length of rope from his supply and fashioned a tether and slip knot so that he could pull his pack along the bridge cable after him. He had briefly considered leaving the pack and his weapons behind to lessen the weight, but he decided he could not risk needing them when he arrived on the other side, or worse, being separated from them if something went wrong. *And I somehow survived it.*

He stuffed his cloak and coat into the pack along with his thick gloves, and he fastened his sword to it as well. He considered using the rest of the rope to fashion a safety line, but abandoned that idea. The rope would not stretch across the gorge, so he would need to somehow release the harness half-way across while dangling from the cable and proceed without it anyway. He would have to rely on the tether to hold him if he slipped, and if the bridge cable broke… that would be that.

Then there was nothing more to prepare.

Killock walked to the edge and blew warmth into his fingers. He took a firm grasp on the cable. It was wound around the thick stone pillar that marked the start of the bridge proper, an anchor Killock felt was unlikely to shift under his added weight. The wind sucked over the jagged edge at his feet as if it were hungry for him.

He yanked and pulled on the cable as vigorously as he could, but produced no more than a few creaking noises from the ancient rope. It was far too heavy to pull in any slack. He tied the pack and its tether to the cable, and made sure the end was securely attached to his belt.

With a grunt he climbed under the cable, and hooked his legs firmly in place. By tilting his head as far back as possible, he could see the cable dropping as it arched across the gorge, but he quickly re-focused on his hands as they gripped the thick cable right in front of his face.

Then hand over hand he crawled over the chasm, sliding his legs along the cable after each pull.

It was frayed and rough and damp with ice caught in its cords, and the faint vibration he felt in it near the base grew into an unpredictable sway as the wind rushed past him. Loose threads snapped at his face and hands, and caught on the pack's tether as it tried to slide past. A fire began to blaze across his back and shoulders while perversely his fingers burned with numbing cold. Several times he passed over sections of cable that were mere threads, the final remains after centuries of storms, but he did not let that deter him.

Then it got worse. The far side was slightly higher than the near, making the incline longer and steeper. The rope swayed and bounced in the streaming wind as if it were alive, and now his exhausted arms had to drag his weight up the slick rope, steeper and steeper as he progressed.

A quick break with his elbows hooked over the cable allowed him to flex some feeling into his hands and then he pulled onwards. He forced his awareness away from his body and its pain and fatigue. Hand over hand it slowly moved along the rope as Killock watched dispassionately, as if someone else's body dangled with exhaustion, pain and cold over endless emptiness.

Slowly the far side became the near side, then there was only a short distance left, and finally he dropped, thankfully, to the solid stones of the bridge.

Killock rested on his back, staring at the underside of the clouds scudding past, but only long enough to catch his breath. His arms screamed in protest as he slowly rolled over and pushed himself to his feet, gratefully retrieved his gloves and cloak from his pack and buckled his sword at his side.

The guard post was larger than he had expected. One long, low, stone building might be the remains of a barracks, and there was a larger building behind it that must have been stables. The slate roof of the barracks was still intact, although the wooden door and shutters had long ago been torn from their hinges by the wind that sliced past the buildings and dragged ice across the stones.

Killock carefully crossed the open area between the Léim Mhór and the barracks, keeping an eye on the black hollows that were the door and windows of the building. He had not heard or smelled anything beyond old stone, ice, and wind, but any type of shelter in these desolate lands was valuable, and therefore likely to have been claimed by whatever was strongest.

In the High Fells the strongest creatures were stone trolls, the much larger, much tougher cousins of the forest trolls found in the hinterlands. *Although I might get really unlucky and run into a proper mountain troll.*

A quick glance inside the barracks showed that it was cold and empty, although dried troll spoor was scattered around the main room. A wide stone hearth stood, blackened by soot, against the far wall, empty and cold. Broken tables, cots and other smashed wooden furniture were shoved against the walls, making piles of debris.

At the back of the room a doorway gaped in the wall. Killock's cloak whispered softly across the floor as he glided forward, careful to step around the bits of wood and stone that littered the floor. The wind moaned through a hole in the roof and sent ice grains skittering across the floor, but otherwise no sound reached Killock's ears.

He halted with his back against the wall next to the doorway. A rank scent seeped through the opening, thick and feral. It was dark enough inside that he could not discern any details, so he waited patiently for his eyes to adjust to the dim interior light as he learned the sounds of the building around him. The old timbers of the roof creaked and shifted in the wind. A broken shutter bumped against the sill. A long rasping breath was the wind across the stone shingles.

Soon the dim light inside the back room revealed piled, jagged shapes. Wooden racks had been pushed over, spilling baskets and casks to the floor. Crates had been torn apart, their planks scattered.

All of this had happened long ago. Snow had drifted into the room over the years to fill most of it with deep, crusted drifts smoothing over the destruction. But there had been more recent visitors. Deep tracks marred the dirty snow, and the remains of what had been a mountain goat were scattered across the floor, no more than a few days old.

Judging from the tracks, he was likely standing in the den of at least four stone trolls, although it had been days since they were last here. Trolls would sometimes stay in the same den for months at a time. Or they would leave for months at a time. It all depended on the nearby hunting. He had been fortunate to arrive while the trolls were gone, but he had no idea how long he might remain alone. He had to move quickly.

Killock entered the storeroom, ignoring the smashed containers near the door. Anything torn apart was likely to have contained food and would have attracted whatever pack had done the damage. What Killock was searching for would have been stored in the back, out of the way, and would not have smelled interesting to a troll, or bear, or even a goat.

The Templar picked his way over the piles of debris near the door, careful not to lose his footing on the uneven shapes under the snow's crust. A twisted ankle would be bad enough, but accidentally pulling a rack down upon himself would likely be fatal. Ancient snow crunched under his boots, and ancient wood creaked dangerously as it shifted, but disaster was held at bay.

Killock began pulling lids off the baskets lined against the back wall. Blankets, nails, tool handles. Then exactly what he had hoped for. A tall basket filled with carefully coiled lengths of rope.

A few quick trips back and forth and Killock soon had several furlongs of rope coiled on the floor of the barracks. It was rough and stiff, crude stuff that likely would not last more than one winter in the elements, but right now it was exactly what he needed.

Killock formed most of the rope into a tight bundle and tied it off securely. He left out enough rope to stretch across the gorge twice. One length he would secure to this side, the other he tied to the large bundle. This way he could bring a length across with him to create a second secure line, then pull the bundle of rope across to repeat the process coming back. He would repeat the process one last time on his return journey, leaving him with three fresh lines strung across the ravine, plus the old cable. *Even Bradon should be able to cross with all of that in place.*

Killock paused and listened. A faint sound caught his attention, different from the sounds of the ruined building. He quietly stood in the shadows and peered through the open windows. Soon he heard it again, a deep cough, carried faintly on the wind, but louder now. The sound came from beyond the stable, and was certainly a troll of some kind. There was no mistaking the low, guttural chuff.

Then he saw it, a grey, hunched shape half-seen through the swirling clouds on the far side of the stable. At first it looked like a boulder glimpsed through breaks in the mist, but it moved with a plodding gait, using one forearm and its hind legs while it clutched something to its chest with the other arm. As it became clearer, Killock saw that it was a stone troll. It was characteristically dull grey, its skin covered with a tough, wiry pelt. Curved tusks sprouted from a massive out-thrust jaw, and a thick neck topped mountainous shoulders. Long arms, thick as the knight's thigh, sprouted from a barrel chest, and ended in wide hands with long, white claws.

It was relatively small for a stone troll, perhaps thrice Killock's weight and no taller than his shoulders, and Killock guessed it was a female or perhaps a young immature male. Either way, it would not be out here alone. The only trolls that lived alone were rogue males that had been pushed from the pack by the alpha.

Killock crouched and hurried across the room. He did not have much time before the troll caught his scent. Stone trolls could detect a scent as easily as a dog, and Killock knew that it was only luck that the wind was gusting towards him. Soon that would not matter though. If the troll got close enough it would smell him no matter which direction the wind blew.

He donned his pack, slung the free length of rope over his shoulder, gathered the bundle of rope, and slipped out a window on the far side of the barracks. The bundle of rope was unwieldy and heavy, causing him to stagger as his boot slipped on the icy rocks beneath the window. Killock kept going, keeping the barracks between himself and the troll, and moved towards the bridgehead.

At the edge of the ravine he paused and looked back. The troll was clearly visible from here. It had approached the barracks and paused outside, sniffing the air with gaping nostrils and slapping the ground with its free hand, clearly agitated by the scent of man emanating from the building.

The troll was no more than a stone's throw away, and Killock kept still. If it would go inside the barracks he could secure the rope and perhaps be gone before any other trolls arrived. But it would not go in.

He could not wait any longer. Killock gently put down the bundle of rope. Never taking his eyes from the troll he quickly uncoiled the length of rope looped around his shoulder and fastened one end to a jagged stump of stone. The tether that would bear the weight of his pack hung where he had left it, and he reached to snag it.

The cable creaked as the wind gusted around it, and suddenly Killock found himself staring into the eyes of the troll as it turned to the sound. It glared at him for a heartbeat, then reared back and bellowed a challenge, its mouth gaping wide.

Killock cursed. His sword leapt from its scabbard in a long sigh of steel against leather and he charged the troll, screaming his own challenge at the top of his lungs. He knew that forest trolls could be intimidated by such a tactic.

He covered half the distance to the troll before it charged. Huge fists pounded the ground and it sprang forward into a run, with a feral roar to challenge Killock's war cry. Two mighty bounds and it was on him, with claws and fangs bared.

Killock ducked under the wide-sweeping attack and lashed out with his sword as he passed the enraged troll. The blade struck heavily across the troll's ribs but barely cut through the tough skin, and left only a long, shallow slice. The troll's flailing claws snagged in Killock's cloak as it streamed behind him. He was yanked brutally off his feet and spun around, and would have been dragged into the troll's crushing embrace if the cloak had not ripped with a long, rending tear, sending the knight sprawling to the stones instead.

Killock scrambled to his feet as the troll bellowed in rage and struck out with sweeping blows of its mighty fists. Killock leapt backwards and dodged to the side as the troll's fist slammed into the ground a hand's breadth behind him.

The troll pursued, but Killock had regained his balance. He planted both feet firmly and lunged at full extension, a perfect thrust with the full weight of his body behind it, and the blade sank deeply into the troll's neck underneath the jaw. Thick blood sprayed from the point of impact, steaming hotly in the frigid air.

And then the troll's monstrous arm swept across and smashed through Killock, wrenched the sword from his grasp and sent him staggering. A second blow glanced off his left shoulder and numbed his arm from the impact. He bounced off a stone wall behind him and sprawled heavily on the ground.

Blood filled his mouth and the world threatened to recede to a blurry dot as darkness pushed in from the edges of Killock's vision, but he shook off the shock and pushed himself onto his hands and knees. An immense shadow and a gurgling roar loomed over him, and he rolled away from it as claws raked across the stones where he had lain.

His knife came into his hand as he turned to face the troll. Blood coursed down its shoulder from its neck, and sprayed from its mouth with each bellow, but it had not noticed the wound yet. Killock gave the monster the time it needed and danced out of reach, slashing at the thick arms with his knife as he went. The troll spat and bellowed, enormous sprays of blood drenching its front. It was definitely slowing, and Killock stayed back. Its next lunge made it stumble to the side, and the one after made it sink to the ground, panting. Killock backed to his sword on the ground and picked it up, returning the knife to its sheath.

The troll lumbered to its feet. It barked and choked at him and pounded its chest, but Killock merely hung back, his sword raised and ready. The charge still almost took him by surprise. The troll lunged forward, brutal, clawed hands reaching to shred the knight. Killock barely avoided its reach and brought the sword down onto its skull in a vicious overhand that landed with an impact that felt like he had chopped into a boulder. The blade bounced and a bolt of fire ran up his arm. The troll merely snarled its anger and turned on him, completely unfazed by the gash that now ran from its torn ear across the side of its head.

Killock waited for its next attack, another flailing explosion of claws and fangs and spraying blood. He leapt to the side, and sprinted for the barracks as the troll slipped in its own blood. Surprise gave him a ten-step head start, all he needed. He reached the building and vaulted to the roof in one smooth movement, using an empty window sill as a step. The troll tried to follow, grabbing and tearing at the edge of the roof, but it broke off in the creature's hands and sent it staggering to the ground.

The troll pounded the dirt and bellowed in rage, but could not get onto the roof. The building shook as it slammed into the stone walls, but Killock stayed firmly put.

The troll's roars grew weaker, and it began to cough and gurgle and moan, clawing and slapping at the fearsome wound in its neck. Killock knew the end was nearing.

Then a tremendous bellow roared out and echoed from the cliffs around, and a chorus of deep, barking chuffs rose up amidst the echoes. Killock's heart fell as he saw a half-dozen more trolls lumber into the guard post. In their center was a monstrous troll, easily twice the size of the one he had been fighting, with a spiked ridge of black hair raised along its back. It looked as if the troll could simply reach onto the roof and pluck him off, so long were its forearms, and it bellowed in rage as it spotted the Templar perched on the roof above his blood-soaked adversary.

Killock leapt from the roof and landed running, his worn boots pounding across the smooth stone roadway. The huge troll roared, but Killock did not look back. Ahead was the bridgehead and the length of rope with one end wrapped around the pillar. Killock slid to a stop and grabbed the free end of the rope. The ground shook as the alpha troll lumbered after him, each enormous stride eating the distance between them. Killock did not have time to do anything but shove the end of the rope through his belt and grab the cable, frantically swinging hand over hand over the chasm.

The troll stomped to a stop at the edge of the shattered bridge and raged at the knight. Savage claws swept out at him but he was past their reach and moving farther away with each moment. The troll slammed its fists into the ground in fury, and large stones broke free and cascaded down the cliff to shatter far below.

Then, to Killock's horror, the troll reached out and grasped the cable in one massive fist. Killock barely had time to wrap his legs and arms around the cable before the troll shook it violently, yanking it back and forth. Killock hung on desperately, and he felt deep twangs within the cable as strands parted under the strain.

Killock waited for his chance, then scrambled a few arm lengths down the cable when the troll paused in its shaking, and clung to the cable again while the beast roared and re-doubled its effort.

Then the shaking stopped. Killock glanced back. The troll grasped the cable and slowly drew it down, then reached as far as it could and grasped the cable with its other hand as well. Killock realized what the troll was about to do in the heartbeat before it happened. He fumbled with the rope at his belt as the troll slowly lowered its weight onto the cable and swung towards Killock. Killock felt strands snapping inside the ancient cable as the troll approached hand over hand. The cable held for a moment, then with a deep shock it parted somewhere past Killock, over the ravine.

Killock felt the cable go slack and let go immediately. He twisted the rope at his waist around his hand and braced for the shock he knew was coming. The rope roared over the edge of the cliff, snapped to a quivering halt, and brutally wrenched Killock towards the face of the cliff. Above him the troll bellowed and flailed, still holding on to the severed bridge cable. The cable parted again where it pulled tight over the edge, and the troll dropped into the chasm, screaming its rage.

Killock had no time to watch it fly past him. The cold, grey mass of the ravine wall rushed towards him as he twisted desperately at the end of the rope. Killock hit heavily, his shoulder and back taking the brunt of the impact, then his head slammed into the rock and the world exploded into bright lights, and darkness.

Bradon

The Templar urged his horse through the snow towards Torbhin. The scout's legs labored through the snow and his torch waved in wild circles around his head as he ran to meet Bradon. When Bradon finally reined in next to Torbhin the scout could barely speak, gasping out words between deep, sucking breaths.

"They're coming, m'lord, the husks. They're right behind me."

Bradon glanced around the darkened plateau, but nothing appeared.

"How many?" Bradon asked.

"I don't know. I counted twenty-seven different ones, but there might be many more."

"And the priest?"

"He was there, but he left heading north about an hour ago. He said 'it is done' whatever that means. I took care of the other two."

"Did you, indeed?" Bradon smiled broadly. *I see why Killock likes this young ranger so much. Sent alone on a scouting mission and he returns having killed two of the enemy, and calmly run past twenty-seven undead creatures to report back*. "Well done, lad. Now hop up and we will go and get the others."

Bradon took Torbhin's hand and hauled him onto his horse, then thundered back to the party at the trailhead.

"Torbhin here says that there is a pack of undead horrors headed our way, and we know the priest is not far ahead. We no longer have to be concerned with the priest's henchmen, thanks to Torbhin," Bradon answered before they could ask.

"How soon until they get here?" Danielle asked.

"Very soon, m'lady." Torbhin shifted and glanced towards the meadow. "They were moving very fast. I had to run to overtake them."

"How far?" Alistair asked.

"One thousand paces, no more."

"How did you know we were here?" the Captain asked.

"I guessed," Torbhin replied simply. "All of a sudden the husks around me headed this way. I decided there was only one reason they would do that."

"What do you think?" Bradon asked the Captain.

"One thousand paces is not so bad, so long as we keep moving and stay together. No archers, just a mob. If we're lucky."

Bradon nodded. *If we're lucky and it's just the husks.* They had been relentless when he had fought them in the desecrated temple, and tougher to kill than a normal man, but they were mindless and no challenge for a trained soldier. *The wight, on the other hand…*

"Are we planning on going before the undead army arrives?" asked Wyn pointedly. "He said they were almost here."

"Indeed." Bradon slipped his hammer free from his belt. The long haft made it a superb weapon to use from horseback, and he allowed himself to enjoy the feeling of its weight for a moment before continuing.

"We will ride in column. Alistair, you and Torbhin here will blaze the trail. Get up behind him, lad, and show him where to go. Then three protecting the rear, and the rest on either side of the ladies."

The soldiers nodded. Helms were tightened and weapons freed, and Alistair wheeled his horse and moved off at a trot, Torbhin holding on tight behind him.

Bradon gave them no more than three deep breaths before urging the rest after them. The horses snorted and stamped high in the thick snow. Bradon rode easily between Alistair and the main party, his horse responding eagerly to the smallest guidance of pressed knee or shifted weight, horse and rider practiced with each other's every habit.

The wind gusted and slid across the snow's crust, and then Alistair shouted and gestured to the left with his axe. Pale shapes emerged from the dark, and Bradon was surprised by how quickly they crossed the snow towards them. He remembered the husks in the temple as being slow and shambling, but these were loping towards them with a strange, uneven gait that made Bradon think of a marionette on strings. *How did Torbhin stay ahead of these things for so far?*

"Captain, traverse right and canter!" he bellowed, and the column shifted, each rider angling to the right, away from the approaching husks. The horses responded, pushing into a fast smooth gait that sent snow flying into the air.

Bradon let himself drift farther to the right. The entire column was moving diagonally into the darkness, and he felt a warrior's distrust of his blind side.

With a command he pulled the three soldiers riding rearguard to him and they spurred forward as fast as the horses could break through the thick snow. They swung to the right of the column in a wide scythe, weaving around boulders as they loomed from the swirling snow.

One of the soldiers shouted a warning and then pale shapes emerged from the darkness in front of them, jerking and twisting as they plunged through the snow.

Bradon rose up in his stirrups, loosed a roar, and let his mount surge forward. His hammer swung down to the right and a husk exploded into a shower of pale, desiccated flesh. Another reached towards him and was trampled by the soldier to his left. A new group appeared in front of them, and amongst them

Bradon saw several that carried weapons, a new twist. Axes and spears for the most part, but at least one carried a heavy, broad-bladed sword.

Bradon bared his teeth into a fierce smile and let the momentum of the charge carry them onto the husks. His hammer rose and plunged to the left and right in a smooth arc, spinning and smashing enemies under its heavy impact. He felt blows against his legs and chest as he passed, but shrugged them off.

And then they were through the horde and they curved to the left, away from more pale shapes emerging from the darkness.

A quick check showed that his troop was intact, and he reined to a slower canter, the horses blowing thick clouds of steam as they labored towards the rest of the column. Bradon was surprised by how quickly they reached the others. *This meadow is getting very small. We are almost out of maneuvering room.*

Bradon swung his horse next to Alistair's.

"We are flanked, we need to ride straight through!" Bradon commanded, and the Captain nodded and turned his mount to the left, his face set with purpose.

Now they pushed forward grimly. The horses labored in the thick snow and stumbled over hidden rocks and divots. His own mount began to favor a leg, and a quick glance down showed Bradon a deep gash across its shoulder that was bleeding freely.

Lights loomed ahead of them, and suddenly they were ringed by torches. Two bodies lay sprawled near a flickering campfire, and pools of thick blood stained the dirty snow around them. Alistair and Torbhin disappeared into the night on the other side, the scout pointing ahead to show which way the priest had gone.

Bradon checked on the others as they passed the torches. All ten soldiers rode easily, weapons at the ready, although he saw that several of the men who had gone with him bore minor wounds.

In the center of the column Danielle rode with a look of fierce determination on her face, urging her mare with encouraging words. Beside her, Wyn rode with her hood thrown back. Her black cloak and blonde hair streamed behind and her wild grin gleamed in the torchlight.

And then they plunged between the last two torches and into the night.

For perhaps ten heartbeats they rode with no sounds but the thud of their horses and the rush of the wind around them. Suddenly, Bradon heard Alistair shout, and the impact of steel on flesh as the pale shapes of husks surrounded them. Scores emerged from the shadows or lurched into view from the snow-filled night.

"We must keep going!" roared Bradon. "Full charge!"

The column surged forward as the weary horses drove ahead with renewed strength. Shouts of defiance filled the night air as soldiers raised their weapons. And then they were amongst the husks, pale shapes that darted in from all sides, eerily silent as they reached and grabbed and slashed at the riders. Blades rose and fell as the column tried to break through the horde.

A horse fell on the left, screaming as a spear ripped into its throat. A huge explosion of snow and twisted limbs enveloped the riders. The rearguard instantly swerved and hewed at the pale husks that swarmed the fallen horse. One soldier jumped to the ground and Bradon saw him trying to pull his fallen comrade from under his mount's thrashing weight. The husks turned on him, and he leapt to his feet to defend himself with a short infantry sword. The wide blade sliced brutally through flesh and bone. One of the rearguard pulled close and extended a hand and he scrambled up, but the horse reared to avoid an axe blow and both men were thrown.

And then they were gone.

A vast, dark shape loomed in front of Bradon. Massive rocks reared from the plateau, black and jagged, forming a sheer cliff wall. Shattered boulders lay strewn across the ground at its base. Bradon swerved to his right and reined in strongly, and the column milled in disarray around him. The husks descended on them once more, and the night air rang with songs of steel on steel and flesh, and cries of warning and rage.

Bradon knew he had only a few moments before they were overwhelmed. *Which way had Alistair gone?* He had lost the Captain in the chaos of their arrival.

Then he heard Alistair's bellow from nearby, "To me! To me!"

Bradon wheeled his horse in that direction.

A pale shape fell upon him from the nearby cliff face. Bradon twisted in his saddle and whipped his left arm upwards, but the impact was too quick and the weight of the husk tore him from his horse to crash to the ground below.

Bradon rolled quickly to his feet. Husks hewed at his horse, and it reared and kicked out at them. To his right, he saw another soldier go down under a husk plummeting from the cliff. Behind, he saw Wyn, her horse rearing in panic. The girl vaulted gracefully from the horse to land, knives drawn, in the middle of a swarm of pale shapes that descended upon her.

Bradon lashed out with his hammer and crushed the husks around him as he searched for Danielle. The noblewoman was nearby, still mounted. Her horse reared and lashed out at the husks around her but she controlled it with ease, shying it away from the enemy, then slipping forward through a gap to rejoin a group of still-mounted soldiers.

"This way!" he roared, and plunged through the snow towards Wyn. Bradon's hammer whirled around him as he charged forward, never ceasing its crushing spin. Husks crumpled and tore apart under its impact, and flew backwards from the heavy blows. He reached Wyn in a dozen steps, the girl still ducking and weaving amongst a swarm of enemies who could not touch her. His hammer swept them aside and he continued to press forward. Now there were soldiers with him, too. Several still mounted, several more on foot. Staying close, they formed a defensive ring.

But the husks kept coming. A soldier was dragged to the ground with three clinging to his arms and legs while a fourth hacked at him with an axe. Another fell when a spear lodged in his calf, fighting from one knee until overwhelmed. Then a horse went down screaming in pain and trapped its rider underneath. Bradon paused to heave the thrashing horse off the soldier, but he had been broken by the animal's death throes. Weakly, he coughed blood as he writhed in the reddening snow. Bradon swiftly released him with a merciful thrust of his knife, then whirled to his feet to defend against the constant rush of enemies.

A riderless horse plunged from the darkness, blood streaming from a dozen wounds as it fled in panic, and Bradon recognized Alistair's long cavalry sword in the sheath on its saddle.

Danielle was now on foot as well, her short blade ready in one hand, the long sword she carried now strapped across her back. Three of the ten soldiers were left, none mounted. Bradon commanded them against the cliff and formed them into a perimeter, a semi-circle of axes and swords ready for the foe. Taking advantage of the momentary safety inside the ring, Bradon focused on his hammer, calling forth its Word.

It was not a thing of elegant beauty such as the Devices that Danielle carried. His hammer had been crafted by one of the greatest artificers in the history of the Guild specifically for being used in the thick of battle, a simple, powerful, and brutal Weapon. It took only heartbeats for him to focus on the hidden bindings deep within his hammer and release them with its Word. The bindings opened and poured forth their power in a gout of energy. A fiery emerald glow surged around the hammer, brighter than any lantern or fire.

Bradon took his place as the keystone in the arc. The hammer blasted left and right, an unstoppable force that threw his opponents back into the night. Bradon planted his feet wide and roared his defiance as he swung, a trail of fire from the hammer whirling around him.

Yet the enemy kept coming, and Bradon saw the ring collapsing on either side of him. Only his presence kept it from being completely washed away by the tide of husks coming against them, and he knew that soon he would not be able to protect everyone.

"Bradon!" Danielle's shout cut through the haze of battle rage, insistent.

Bradon risked a quick glance over his shoulder and caught a glimpse of the noblewoman, a small, glowing light held in her hand, gesturing for him to follow.

"This way! Quickly!" she shouted, and she ran along the cliff face in the direction from whence they had come.

A quick command and the defensive circle moved with her, guarding them as they moved. As if shocked by their sudden reversal of direction, the assault paused, allowing them to move quickly.

Danielle's glowing light pulsed and she stopped and faced the cliff. A dark, shadowy cleft split the sheer face, and Danielle scrambled into it. Bradon urged the others to follow, then took the last position, backing in to provide the rearguard.

With each step he expected to reach the end of the small gap, but it continued. His boots touched stone and he trod upon rough-hewn steps that twisted upwards. The wind moaned as it passed over the narrow gap, and the sound of scuffling leather and the clink of metal on stone filled the ravine as they pushed up the stairs, each twist taking them higher and higher.

After the fourth turn, Bradon called a halt. The soldiers took a knee, breathing strenuously, while Wyn bent over with hands on her knees, head drooping. Danielle leaned against the stone wall, face turned upwards and eyes closed. Bradon doused his hammer, letting the blazing, emerald light dim until the only light in the chasm was the small glow in Danielle's hand.

Bradon crouched next to her. She opened her eyes wearily and gave him a tired smile, then opened her hand to reveal a small Device held there. He stroked his beard as he examined it. It was no more than the size of a duck's egg, made of a heavy, dark metal. Concentric bands encircled it, each one engraved with tiny symbols that pulsed and throbbed with a faint light. Bradon saw that each of the rings could be twisted and slid forwards and backwards into intricate patterns, but other than that he could discern little about its function.

It doesn't matter, it's leading us.

"I will go first," Bradon said to the group. "Keep a careful watch behind. God only knows how long it will take the husks to pursue us up the stairs, but surely they will, eventually."

They clambered to their feet, and headed up the stairs. The steps seemed endless, twisting to and fro behind the cliff face, but eventually Bradon felt wind knifing past him and saw an opening above. One final twist and the steps led onto a high shelf far above the meadow. Ancient pillars stood on either side of the steps. Weathered and cracked, the dark shapes were unidentifiable. A torch stood in a bracket affixed to one of the pillars. It wavered in the wind that howled across the shelf and drove stinging ice into Bradon's face.

The shelf was no more than a bow-shot across, and leaned precariously over the plateau. At first, it appeared completely featureless, and Bradon paused, unsure of which way to go.

Not empty… there's something there.

There was a shape, a gap in the driven snow that loomed over them. Then it was gone.

Bradon took one cautious step, then another, until he passed between the ancient pillars. He could see the shape more clearly, and with each step it changed. It grew and became a thick shadow that wavered on the edge of visibility, then a black shape that reared from the shelf. Then towers appeared, drifting in and out of the thick snow, and tall, thin spikes stabbed the dark clouds. Ahead, a massive, black iron gate materialized, flanked on both sides by black stone buttresses that arced from the tower to the cliff. The gate was carved deeply into the base of the tower and torches flared on either side through the streaming snow. It stood more than twice Bradon's height, and appeared to be made of dull, black metal engraved with runes and symbols similar to the markings they had seen on the husks and the desecrated temple floor.

Bradon approached warily, searching for any signs of guards or watchers in the high tower. But the stone face had no windows, the tower no ramparts. The spires looked like some natural formation, a twisted horn perhaps, or thorns on the crown of a plant. The spires twisted around each other and tapered into unexpected protrusions, each sharper and more vicious than the last.

In front of the gate, four wide steps had been carved. They were covered in brittle ice that crunched loudly under Bradon's heavy boots as he climbed them. He held his hammer in two hands over one shoulder, ready to strike at anything that might come through the gate.

It remained shut. The torches on either side flared and roared in the wind, snow hissed across the stone, and icy needles burned on his cheek and ear, but the tower itself was eerily still. There was no more sense of impermanence about it. The stone glistened wetly under an icy sheen, and the tower stood blackly against the dark sky. Despite its height it stood no more than a stone's throw across… enough to dominate the ledge, but hardly the massive fortress that Danielle had described from her vision.

A few heartbeats passed, and then a few more, and still Bradon held his guard. Finally, he relaxed his stance and gestured for the party to join him. They hurried across the exposed shelf, and Bradon saw them glancing at the tower as they came.

"If this is the way the priest came, then he must be inside," Danielle spoke loudly to be heard over the moaning wind. Bradon nodded his agreement.

He looked around the group. He saw that all were weary, with dull eyes and blank expressions. Danielle's hair had escaped from its ties and the wind whipped it into her face and tugged her cloak sideways, and she hugged her arms miserably across her chest as she stamped her feet for warmth. Wyn huddled against the tower wall with hood drawn low and held against the wind with one hand, her cloak clutched tightly around her with the other. As he met her eyes she gave him a wan smile, but he could see that her shoulders were shaking. The soldiers forced themselves to stand with weapons ready. All were suffering in the bitter cold, and all were wounded in some way or another.

Brok was the largest of them, a barrel of a man with a thick black beard that rivaled Bradon's, a shaved head, and arms like a blacksmith's. He still carried his long, single-bladed axe over his shoulder, but he had taken a spear thrust to the ribs, and a red stain spread down his tunic and onto his leggings.

Cormac, who fought with small shield and a short, broad-bladed sword, had fallen heavily from his horse. The side of his face was a mass of swollen flesh and torn skin, and his left shoulder hung at an awkward angle. His twin brother Corlath stood beside him, identical except that he wore his shaggy blonde hair cropped instead of long. He had lost the elegant longsword that he had won in the melee at the tourney to celebrate the Queen's ascension to the throne. Its empty scabbard hung at his waist and a crude iron axe, better suited for chopping wood, was his only weapon. His leg had been brutally slashed across the thigh, and the jagged wound gleamed wetly in the torchlight.

"Very well, let's get this door open and see if they have anything to drink in there," Bradon rumbled, and a few tired grins answered his feeble humor.

Under close examination the gate appeared to be two imposing doors which joined in the middle under a peaked arch of stone. Bradon placed one hand on each door and pushed. The hinges groaned as the doors scraped open across the stone floor.

Inside was a small, semi-circular room which followed the outer curve of the tower wall. The floor was the same black stone, unadorned and roughly carved. On the curved walls, torches had been placed in black iron braziers and they wavered in the gust of air let in by the open doors. On the far side of the room a stone railing cut across the floor, and on the other side, darkness.

The party entered and Bradon quickly closed the heavy iron doors, shutting out the howling wind. They closed with a bang that sent echoes reverberating through the tower, each one fainter until at long last they died away. There were no bars or locks on the inside to secure the doors, and only their weight kept the wind from blowing them open.

With the doors closed, the only sound was a nearby trickle of water.

Danielle did what she could for the wounded soldiers, but many of her Devices were still in her saddlebags, somewhere on the plateau. Bradon looked for Wyn and spotted her leaning nonchalantly over the stone railing on the far side of the room.

Bradon took one of the torches and joined her, then instantly grabbed Wyn by the arm as he saw what was on the other side. A pit gaped before him, a stone's throw across, and deep enough to disappear completely into the darkness below. A staircase hung precariously around the pit and spiraled downwards, completing a full circle around the pit at wide intervals. The stairs were made of stone and were held by crumbling braces anchored into the wall. Bradon counted two landings going down before it was too dark to see.

"You might want to hold on to something else besides my arm," Wyn giggled. "'Cause I don't think I could hold you if you tipped over."

Bradon released his grip, placed his hand firmly on the railing, and held the torch over the edge as far as he could. "I feared you might fall."

"Don't worry about me. I'm not going anywhere," she smiled. "Just seeing how deep this thing goes." And with that she pursed her lips and spat a thick blob of saliva into the pit. They watched it fall, spinning, into the darkness, but there was no sound of a splat from below.

"That's a serious hole," Wyn laughed.

Bradon glanced sideways at her. The girl looked exhausted. Her hair fell wearily about her face as she leaned forward, and there was a smear of blood across her cheek, likely from one of the wounded soldiers. Bradon saw tracks of tears from the corner of her eye through the grime, and her lips were almost blue with cold. But despite all of that her eyes shone as she peered downwards, and her breath made puffs of steam as she breathed out in excitement. And she could still laugh and make jokes, which lifted his heart.

"Thank you, lass," he said, and he smiled as she turned questioningly to him. "For the laughter."

She nodded and held his gaze for a moment before she turned to regard the pit.

Bradon realized that the stairs joined their floor on the far left side, starting the clockwise spiral downwards.

"No lights," said Wyn. "Reverend Asses must have taken his torch with him."

"I must have misheard young Colin. I thought the priest's name was something else."

"Pretty sure."

Bradon watched for a few moments more, but the view remained unchanged. He was dismayed by how far their path stretched ahead. When he had seen the tower he had thought that they had caught the priest, that there was nowhere left to run. A few rooms to search, and it would be over, one way or another. But what lay below them could take hours to search, maybe more, and they were tired, wounded, and had only the supplies that had not been lost with their saddlebags.

With a grunt he hauled himself upright. Handing the torch to Wyn, he turned to the group by the gate, but before he could walk away Wyn called out softly to him.

"Do you think the others made it? Alistair, Torbhin?"

"I do not think it likely, alone and on foot," Bradon shook his head slightly. "But there is some hope, still, for all that. Alistair has fought his way out of terrible places before, and we know Torbhin has already traversed the plateau twice tonight, alone and unaided."

Wyn nodded quietly, and returned her thoughts and gaze to the empty pit.

Bradon left Wyn and returned to the others. Danielle knelt beside Corlath, wrapping a bandage around his wounded thigh. Brok helped Cormac sit against the wall. His face was very pale, but his shoulder looked to be back in place. Danielle rose as Bradon approached, wiping her hands on a small piece of cloth.

"How are we?" Bradon asked.

"Brok put Cormac's shoulder back in, and I do not believe there is anything broken in his head. He seems to know where he is."

"That makes a first," Brok growled.

Cormac raised his right hand. "This one still works fine, m'lord." His speech was thick, barely understandable through smashed mouth and swollen tongue.

"What of him?" Bradon asked, pointing his hammer at Brok.

The bald warrior laughed. "I'm fine, m'lord, just a poke. I've gotten worse playing with my girls."

"He will not let me examine him," said Danielle, her hands on her hips.

"He needs you more," said Brok, and he pointed at Corlath.

Bradon agreed with that. Corlath lay on his back, his face pale, breathing in short, panting breaths that made small wisps of steam in the frozen air. The bandages that Danielle had just wrapped around his leg were already soaked through.

"Danielle, do you not have anything to help him?"

"No, I have nothing, because instead of taking my bags from my horse I grabbed that," she seethed, pointing to the great sword propped against the wall nearby. "I have no supplies save for what is in my pack, and I do not have my circlet. Bradon, that circlet contains the knowledge and skill of all the physicians and surgeons who have used it. Without it I am useless. Every soldier knows more about first aid than I do."

Before Bradon could say a word she continued, furious. "All I could think of was to make sure I did not lose that sword. He said it was important and I had to take care of it. So I did, I took care of it, and now we have a useless sword instead of something to heal Corlath. Almost all of my Devices were in those saddlebags. Food, as well," she laughed bitterly. "Even my spare stockings."

"I am sorry, my lady," said Bradon. "But we may have a greater need of that sword than any of the things that were lost in your saddlebags."

"We have other Weapons," Danielle pointed to the hammer in Bradon's hand.

"We do, but none like that," Bradon held up his hands to fend off Danielle's retort. "None like that, my lady. We can find food, and we can heal, and I have faith that you will remember far more of what the circlet showed you than you fear."

"I pray you are right," Danielle replied, unmollified.

"And once we are finished here I swear we will return and find your bags. Small consolation I know, but your Devices will not be lost forever."

Bradon turned to the wounded soldier on the floor nearby.

"Well, Corlath, I am afraid you will just have to manage the same as the rest of us."

"No problem, m'lord. Mayhap we could do it quickly though."

"Then there's no time to lose. Gather your weapons, we have a walk ahead of us."

Alistair

The sound of falling water filled the open pit at the center of the black tower, echoes of a thousand heavy raindrops as curtains of water dripped and glistened on the walls in the flickering torchlight. On the flat landings it splashed and plopped into wide puddles lined with a scum of slippery, black moss. On the stairs it gurgled as it poured over each lip and made small waterfalls that flowed to the next landing, or off the edge into space.

The water was ice cold to the touch, barely above freezing, and the air cold enough that their breath created huge clouds of steam as they descended the stairs.

Captain Alistair was not pleased. The constant chatter of the water drowned all other sounds, leaving the veteran soldier feeling vulnerable to ambush. The torches they carried hissed and steamed as drips landed on them. If the torches failed, they would be in utter darkness, stranded on a narrow, crumbling staircase, reduced to crawling on hands and knees to avoid the fatal plunge. Ice water dripped onto him, pinging as it hit his steel breastplate, and slid between the metal bands to soak through his tunic in numbing paths traced across his skin.

"Anything?" Alistair asked quietly.

"No, Captain, I'm sorry," Torbhin shook his head. "There's no sign they came this way."

"Torbhin, there's no other way they could have gone," Alistair reminded the young ranger. "You said Lord Bradon and the others came into the tower, so they must have passed this way."

"Yes, Captain," Torbhin agreed miserably. "They did. Their tracks definitely entered the tower. Wyn, Lord Bradon, Lady Danielle, and three others. But I haven't seen a trace since the gate."

Alistair glared at the wet stairs. He believed the ranger, which made the captain extremely uneasy. *How can six people simply disappear?* Several times as they had descended the stairs he thought he heard voices, far off and echoing, but each time when he stopped and listened, all he heard was the God-damned water dripping. Torbhin had heard the voices as well, but again, not when they had stopped to listen.

Alistair was tempted to do some shouting the next time he heard anything. It was not as if their presence could possibly be a secret. Their torches were the only light on the stairs, and their footsteps echoed in the open shaft. Anyone waiting in the tower would have plenty of forewarning of their approach.

We're damn lucky to be here at all.

When his horse had collapsed under the rusted blades of the horde on the plateau, it had been a miracle that neither he nor Torbhin had been seriously hurt. Alistair had even kept his broad-bladed axe in his hand, and climbed to his feet ready to strike before any of the husks made it to them.

Standing in front of the ranger, their backs to the cliff, they had fought off the husks. Alistair smashed them backwards with heavy swings of his axe while Torbhin peppered them with a stream of arrows. The steel-tipped shafts would knock the husks backwards, and the axe would finish them.

The pair had soon realized that no one was coming to their aid. Alistair was not sure what had happened to the rest of the soldiers, but he had long ago learned that waiting for rescue was a sure way to get overrun. *If they do not come to you, you go to them.*

Two soldiers had appeared from the swirling snow, fighting back-to-back against the foe. One of the soldiers fell to their hacking blades even as Alistair had called to them, but the second soldier, Ormand, was still with them, and guarded their rear.

But even with three skilled warriors, they could not reach Lord Bradon and the others. They had been driven against the cliff wall, where he and Ormand had carved an arc of bodies around them. It had not been fighting. It was butchery, plain and simple. Their weapons had hewn and torn the bodies of the husks, axe and spear rising and falling constantly with no more skill or tactics than if they had been chopping wood or slaughtering cows.

But far too many of them pressed forward, and the two soldiers were tiring fast when Torbhin called out that he had found a way up the cliff. They wedged themselves into a narrow crack, pushed upwards as it turned into a small chimney, and had finally dragged themselves up to a small ridge, exhausted and bleeding.

They had only rested a few moments before Torbhin had spotted a faint glow which flickered on and off through the swirling snow. Alistair could not see it, but he trusted the ranger's eyes. They made their careful way along the ridge to the west until all three of them could see the small light bob and weave ahead of them.

It was Torbhin who had first realized the dark figures clustered around the light were Lord Bradon and the rest of the party. They bellowed and shouted and even threw rocks, but they were too far away and Bradon had not heard them, and the figures soon moved from sight around the corner of the cliff face.

It took them nearly a half-hour to reach the spot where they had seen Lord Bradon's group, and from there it had been easy to follow their tracks to the eerie, black tower.

But there had been no sign of the Templar or his group when Alistair pushed open the imposing outer doors, nor any tracks of them visible on the stairs leading down. There was no other path to follow, so they had taken two of the torches and proceeded into the dark, empty shaft.

"They're in here somewhere," Alistair said. "We will just have to find them, even if they've decided to disappear on us."

Torbhin nodded, but he was clearly unconvinced, and concern was etched across his face.

"Don't worry, lad," Alistair reassured him. "Lord Bradon and the boys have the ladies to protect them. They'll be fine until we show up."

"I wish the ladies were here with us," Ormand grumbled softly behind Torbhin. "I could do with a bit of protecting from her Ladyship and your sweetheart, lad. I'd feel much safer than with you two."

"Wyn isn't my sweetheart," Torbhin objected quickly. "She thinks I'm an idiot."

"Is she not? That's a shame, what with those legs she's got. Have you not told her you fancy her, then?" Ormand grinned at the ranger. "Never mind, it's probably for the best. A wildfire like her… you'd not survive her, lad."

"If the two of you don't mind," Alistair interrupted. "Can we gossip about girls later?"

"Yes, Captain," Torbhin said, embarrassed. Ormand added something under his breath that sounded suspiciously like 'Shoulders' but Alistair let it pass.

They had not gone farther than one hundred steps when Torbhin suddenly stopped and called out softly. Alistair stared across the shaft to where Torbhin was pointing.

"A door," Torbhin whispered.

Alistair could not see it in the dim light of the torches. But he knew it would be there all the same.

"Good," he said gruffly, his voice a low growl. "Anything that isn't another flight of God-damned stairs."

Ormand chuckled. "That's a shame, because I was hoping for more God-damned stairs."

"I'll make sure you pull Bird Shit duty when we get back to Bandirma to make it up to you."

"Thanks Cap'n," Ormand's bushy red beard split into a wicked smile. "I knew all those awful things they say about you couldn't be true."

"Not a one," grunted Alistair. "Alright, let's see what this door is all about."

Alistair hefted his axe in his hand, comforted by its weight. The massive, double-bladed weapon had seen him through countless battles and could cut through armor and bone with ease.

He walked carefully, boots barely splashing as he eased through the puddles. Mist brushed against his face as he passed across a landing, water fell and splattered into the air as it landed on the stone railing. He could see the doorway, one flight below where he stood. It was featureless, with heavy, wooden planks bound by black iron in a simple, stone frame. A single iron ring stood on the right side of the door, perhaps attached to a latch on the other side.

They reached the door, and Alistair stationed Ormand on the other side, motioning for Torbhin to stand back.

Alistair placed his left hand on the door, and gently pushed. The door remained motionless, clearly latched in place. Alistair grasped the iron ring in his hand, and felt it turn slightly.

The tattoo of Ddraighnall, the white leviathan of the mountains, coiled about his left hand where it rested on the iron ring. The dragon's red eyes seemed to be staring at the door, its jaws gaping wide to swallow the iron ring under his hand. *Ddraighnall should be well at home here in the dark, as similar as it must be to his home deep under the Ironback mountains.* Alistair hoped that the beast would see fit to visit him here, under these northern peaks.

Tiernarnon, on his right arm, would be more likely to aid him. The black dragon stretched long talons down Alistair's wrist and across the back of his hand, ready to strike at any moment. She understood the need for vengeance, and Alistair could imagine the roar of triumph she would give as her poison boiled Reverend Crassus' blood in his veins. The men, women, and children sacrificed in Crassus' rituals were not the dragon's own offspring, but surely she would find justice in the slaying of their murderer.

As Alistair tensed to turn the ring, a loud splash sounded on the stairs behind them.

Alistair spun, axe held high, Tiernarnon's talons wrapped around the haft on top of his own fingers. Ormand raised his spear and crouched, ready, and Torbhin quickly raised his bow, barbed arrow nocked.

But the stairs were empty. Dark water glistened as it ran towards the three men, making the stone dance in the torchlight, but clearly nothing stood in the dark. Alistair felt his hackles rise and kept his axe raised high as he listened intently.

Water trickled and dripped, but nothing else stirred.

"A puddle overflowing all at once?" ventured Ormand, but Alistair could tell the red-haired soldier did not believe that either. It had not sounded like water pouring from a puddle, it had sounded like something heavy falling into a puddle.

Alistair shook his head slightly, waiting, but nothing changed. He lowered his axe, and turned to Torbhin.

"You keep a good watch behind us."

The ranger nodded silently, an intent look on his face.

Alistair returned his attention to the door, and caught Ormand's eye. The soldier nodded his readiness, and Alistair carefully twisted the ring until he felt the latch come free, then pushed the door open.

It creaked on its metal hinges as it swung, stiff under his push. On the other side was a narrow passageway made of rough brick that reminded Alistair of a dungeon or a sewer. The torches flickered in the freezing air that flowed from the passageway, and Alistair could smell something thick, congealed, and rank.

Alistair knew his axe would be useless in the cramped passageway. He had fought in such conditions before, close-quarter struggles against the Ironback clansmen in their caves and burrows, a nightmare of violence with neither foe able to retreat and the victor forced to climb over the defeated to reach the next enemy.

He hung the axe across his back and drew the long, bone-handled knife he used for such fights, pried from the hand of a clansman who had used it to leave a long scar on Alistair's right calf in the deep dark under the Ironback mountains. Alistair touched the bone hilt to the spiral of black dots around his left eye, where that enemy now lived, took the torch from Ormand, and carefully moved into the passageway.

Ormand followed behind him, checking the left and right turns with his spear. The shaft had been broken in the fight on the plateau, making it the perfect length for close-quarters work. Its broad-bladed tip flowed smoothly around each corner in front of its wielder, always ready to strike. Torbhin came last and held the other torch as he watched behind.

Alistair moved toward the flowing air. He cautiously stooped under an arch, and the torch roared and spat as its flame licked the low ceiling. On the far side of the arch a small chamber abutted the passageway. Alistair thrust the torch through the open doorway.

A corpse lay on its back on the ground, naked on the cold stone floor. The body looked as if it had melted, slowly spreading across the floor. Alistair had seen such corruption before, bodies that had been left to rot and liquefy, causing the flesh to collapse and drain away, but this one was covered in a network of livid red welts, crossing and re-crossing the trunk and limbs.

The smell coming from it was rank, a combination of festering flesh and a sharp, dry odor Alistair could not identify.

"Maker's breath," Ormand cursed quietly.

"I hope not," Alistair grimaced. Dreading what he would find, he moved to the next opening and held the torch to light the chamber on the other side. It was nearly identical, save that there were two melted corpses on the floor.

"Come on, before they decide to start moving," Alistair growled. He carefully crept forward, lighting his way with the torch. They passed room after room, each one a nightmare of scabrous flesh covered in red welts.

One last turn and the passageway opened into a much larger space, a wide, circular room with steps on one side between two towering pillars. Tall, stone walls loomed at the edge of the torchlight, covered with carved figures that could barely be discerned in the dim light. The room echoed slightly, and the scuff of a boot or the creak of a strap returned cold and empty.

Alistair held the torch high, but the shadows around the edge of its light stayed impenetrable.

He handed the torch to Ormand and sheathed his knife. The axe returned to his hand, heavy and reassuring.

Alistair moved towards the steps, motioning Ormand to his left. Pillars emerged into the torchlight, carved to resemble robed figures with long, clawed hands. Ornate cowls hid their faces in deep shadow, and their arms stretched to support the weight of the ceiling far above. On either side of the pillars, Alistair noticed small balconies, high on the walls, which reminded him of pulpits in a temple.

Alistair took a step forward, and then stopped, suddenly wary.

Something watches us.

Alistair was not sure how he knew. The room was too still, or perhaps too quiet. But he knew.

Ormand caught his eye with a questioning look. The bearded soldier did not feel it, but he stayed ready as Alistair raised his hand in warning and motioned for Ormand to hold. Alistair risked a glance back at Torbhin. The ranger's senses were sharp, sharper than his, and Torbhin was scanning the room intently, probing into every corner with a hawk's gaze. He found nothing, and turned to Alistair with a slight shake of his head.

Alistair waited and listened. Nothing but the steady trickle of water over stone, the patter of drops hitting his armor.

The Captain ascended the wide stone stairs, each step slow and careful, anticipating an attack as he climbed. A deep, dark space waited for him at the top, as tall and empty as the one below.

Still no sound or movement betrayed the watcher. It would wait for him to reach the top of the steps, he felt it. Behind the towering pillars where the torchlight could not reach.

He curled both hands around the haft of his axe, his body and mind singing with the anticipation of battle. His boot came to rest on the landing, and his heavy armor creaked as he stepped forward.

Nothing. Water dripped and trickled down his neck, but nothing else.

Then a wet, crunching noise grated through the room, and the rending scream of metal torn apart. Alistair whirled to the noise, down the steps. Ormand choked out a gurgling cough and stared at something long and black and barbed that gleamed wetly as it emerged from his chest, tearing through the bands of his steel breastplate, spraying blood across Torbhin's face. Ormand's spear clattered to the floor as he grasped at his chest, struggling to free himself.

Three colossal strides took Alistair to the bottom of the stairs. Ormand staggered as the black thing ripped out of him and he went to his knees, blood staining his beard as he choked a last rattling breath. Black skin and hooked thorns and spikes that gleamed wetly moved in the darkness behind him.

Alistair did not hesitate. His axe sliced through the air as it arced towards the half-seen thing in the darkness, then again as it slid away from his first blow. The axe blurred a third time, left to right in a horizontal arc that would have felled a tree, but again the thing slid backwards, and suddenly forwards as the swing passed. A blur of hooked spikes tore through Alistair's steel breastplate as if it were parchment.

Pain flared and Alistair staggered from the blow. Another attack glanced off his raised axe head, then another slashed across his chest and wrenched one of the steel bands of his breastplate free as Alistair threw himself backwards. This thing was fast, and inhumanly strong. Skill and training would win this, not simple strength and savagery.

Alistair moved to his left, jabbing with his axe to keep the thing at bay. The spiked tip of the axe bit deeply and a harrowing screech echoed in the chamber. Razor-sharp limbs beat against the haft of the axe and gouged long splinters from the hard wood.

The light shifted as Torbhin dropped his torch, raised his bow and circled the other direction. Torbhin's bow thrummed twice and Alistair heard the arrows rip the air as they impacted in the nightmare of limbs and gleaming black skin.

Then the monster disappeared with a rasping echo and a half-glimpsed blur of movement into the deep shadows. Alistair ran to Ormand but the man-at-arms was already dead. A gaping wound split him from back to chest, piercing his heart.

A long scream of rage leaked into the room, and a scraping sound echoed from nearby.

Pain leaked down the Captain's side from the long wound across his ribs. He rose, axe ready.

"Come on," Alistair barked. "We need to go before it returns."

Torbhin nodded mutely, stopping only to grab the torch from where it lay. They ran up the steps together, boots pounding across the stone floor. Black shadows danced amongst the carved figures as they raced to the far wall.

Two massive doors loomed from the shadows as they approached with the torch. Thick wooden beams bound by riveted metal rose to more than twice Alistair's height under a stone arch thick with carved images that perched in the shadows. Alistair ran to the door, pushed on it, then slammed into it with his shoulder. The door shook but did not budge, and Alistair realized it must be barred on the other side. With enough time he could hew his way through the wood.

A shriek echoed through the chamber, long and grating like a knife across bone.

"The balconies!" Torbhin pointed upwards.

Alistair nodded. He did not know where the openings behind the balconies led, but it was better than here. In a few quick strides he crossed the floor to stand underneath the closest of the balconies.

Alistair cupped his hands, crouched, and heaved Torbhin upward. The ranger grabbed a carved spike and scrambled higher. Another scream echoed in the chamber, a long hiss, closer still. Alistair planted a boot on a half-seen jut of stone and pushed, grabbing handholds of wet stone as his boots slipped and scrambled for purchase. Hand over hand he hauled himself up, the dragons on his powerful arms coiling and uncoiling as he reached and pulled. He reached the balcony and threw a leg over the stone railing. A quick glance showed him that the opening in the wall led to a passageway. He leaned over the railing, extended a hand to Torbhin and grasped him by the wrist.

Alistair pulled Torbhin to the railing and the ranger grabbed it with his other hand. Then suddenly Torbhin was yanked downwards and a terrible weight pulled Alistair to the railing with a crash. Alistair braced and held Torbhin's wrist. He pulled with all of his immense strength, feet spread wide, both hands wrapped around Torbhin's wrist. The boy yelled and thrashed against whatever held him and Alistair felt him rise. The Captain reached forward quickly and grasped Torbhin around his arm and pulled again.

Torbhin shouted and grabbed the railing with his free hand, but then his yell turned to a scream as a black spike slid through his shoulder. Alistair pulled desperately as Torbhin thrashed, grabbing at the railing and at the spike that pierced him. His screams rose piteously as another spike erupted from his chest, and long, black talons wrapped around his face.

Alistair bellowed defiance and managed to pull Torbhin to the balcony railing. The young ranger coughed out a choking scream, and blood sprayed over Alistair as the cruel, barbed spikes ripped out. Alistair fell back, dragging Torbhin's body over the railing with him. The boy's hand clutched at him weakly, and he took one shallow, choking breath before Alistair felt him go limp.

Alistair struggled to his feet, and grabbed his axe from his back. A rush of writhing blackness poured over the stone railing of the balcony. Alistair stabbed with his axe, rolling as he took the thing's weight and threw it into the passageway beyond him.

It landed violently in an explosion of writhing limbs. Alistair came to his feet smoothly and fell on his enemy with a flurry of blows from his axe, using his speed and strength to catch the thing before it could recover. Sparks arced from the walls as the axe caught stone on its way to fall on barely glimpsed black skin, and the steel blade struck torso and limbs as they flailed.

Again and again Alistair hurled heavy blows against his opponent, the vicious steel axe biting deep, driving it into the wall. It shrieked defiance and lashed out, razor-sharp claws slicing through steel and gashing flesh. Alistair roared and brought the axe down with both hands and buried the head deep into gleaming, black flesh. The impact drove it to the ground, but the axe stuck fast, and was wrenched from his hands as the creature reared up, filling the passageway with slashing limbs and quivering barbs.

It descended on the Captain, razor limbs seeking him in the darkness. Alistair lunged forward to meet it, and his powerful hands locked in a death grip on ridges of chitinous armor as he lifted and then twisted to drive it to the ground beneath him. Knife-edged limbs slashed his arms and shoulders, and serrated teeth scraped across his steel-plated back. His fingers scrabbled for the hilt of his long knife and he pulled it free. He roared in fury and wrenched with all of his strength on the edge of the armored plate, and it twisted with a wet, tearing sound. Alistair slammed the knife into the soft flesh beneath, driving it in and up until the tip grated against something hard deep within. The nightmare shrieked and thrashed, desperate to escape, but Alistair was relentless and drove the knife over and over again, twisting it and pulling it free, heedless of the blows that tore through him.

It was weakening fast. Alistair plunged the knife in once, twice more, and pushed the thing away. It quivered where it lay, sharp talons scratching feebly on the stone floor. Alistair crawled to the far side of the passageway and slumped against the wall. Blood streamed from a dozen deep wounds and pooled underneath him. His arms felt too heavy to move, and his legs were turning numb. A cruel thirst made him fumble for his canteen. He drained it in several deep swallows, but it did not seem to help.

A rasping hiss sounded from across the passageway.

"Fuck you," he answered, and threw his empty canteen, striking the black mass.

The pain was receding rapidly, a comfortable numbness replacing it. *Not good.*

Alistair was surprised by how little he feared what was coming next. He had seen so many men die, and he had been curious how he would act when it was his turn, for there was no predicting it. Some of the bravest men had spent their last moments in terror. Some of the meekest had gone with serenity.

Alistair felt peace. He had always known that he would die bloody, and he had hoped that he would give a good accounting of himself, no coward to the end. *Turns out today is the day. Too bad no one will know of this, it would have made for a grand story.* But there was no helping that now.

Just a few more moments, he reckoned. He hoped the Maker was watching, or perhaps Ddraighnall in his stone hall, surrounded by all of the legendary heroes of the Ironback clans. Alistair gripped his knife carefully in both hands and held it to his breast. His dragons watched him and he gazed back, tracing their coils, re-examining every detail one last time until darkness fell.

Benno

The Bishop sheltered from the rain in the long tunnel of the Tùr Abhainn as he waited. The honor guard was not so lucky, standing drenched in disciplined ranks across the courtyard, drops pinging off their helms and breastplates. Water trickled amongst the stone cobbles and made dark puddles that reflected the dull, gray sky.

Benno smoothed down the wisps of hair floating freely in the cold draft that blew through the tunnel and settled his robes around himself more tightly. *It will snow again tonight*, he guessed, *it is close to freezing*, but right now it was mist and rain and mud.

Nasty weather for a surprise visit. A messenger at first light had brought word of the impending arrival before Benno had a chance to have his morning cup of hot tea, and the day had been a rush of preparation ever since.

Best robes, best armor, get everyone out of the Sanctuary, light all the candles, stoke the fireplaces until they were glowing with welcoming flames. And now, the waiting.

Benno tucked his hands into his robes and stamped his feet. He wondered if it would be acceptable if he ducked into the guard room for just a moment to warm his hands at the stove. *It would set a poor example*, he decided morosely.

At the far end of the tunnel and across the bridge a crowd had gathered. Townsfolk lined the road from the west and milled around the town square. Wagons on the road had been moved off to the side, and the carters stood on the backs of their loads for a better view.

With a shout from the tower, the honor guard came to attention, spears held rigidly upright, shields raised into place. Benno hurried to his spot in the center of the courtyard where two acolytes waited with an awning on poles for him to take cover from the rain. It felt a bit silly to stand in the middle of all of the soldiers with his dainty rain cover, but Benno was not about to tell the acolytes to take it away.

Benno smoothed his robes into place for the umpteenth time and adjusted the small, silver amulet so that it hung just so. He heard cheers from the crowd across the bridge, and the heavy thunder of many hooves on the cobblestone road. Horses crossed the town square and the stone arch of the bridge. Two knights in steel armor led the way, soaked pennants heavy on their spears. Behind them appeared a small group of riders in thick cloaks, fine mail, and winter clothes splashed with the mud of the road. They were led by a small rider on a beautiful chestnut mare, followed closely by two others, one seated easily on a bay stallion, the other bouncing awkwardly on a skinny grey pony.

At the rear of the column rode a group of twenty soldiers in heavy, grey armor and thick, black cloaks.

The two knights clattered to a halt in front of the Bishop and carefully turned their mounts to stand on either side of him. Benno recognized the craggy face of Sir Ceredor under his hawk-shaped helm, and nodded to him when he caught the knight's eye. He did not know the other knight, a younger woman with short, black hair and watchful eyes who barely acknowledged the Bishop's presence.

The three riders trotted to a halt in front of Benno, and the Bishop went to a knee, head bowed. Around him the Temple soldiers stamped their spears in unison with a clash that shook water from their cloaks.

"Your Majesty," said Benno. "Welcome to Bandirma."

Long, cream-colored riding boots splashed to the ground in front of him, and a small, gloved hand extended to him. He took her fingers gently in his and let his lips brush briefly against her knuckles, then rose as she urged him to his feet.

The Queen looked into his face with a smile. "Thank you, your Grace. Shall we get out of the rain before your poor soldiers wash away?"

Benno nodded and stepped aside, but the Queen held on to his hand and indicated that he should walk next to her. They crossed the courtyard to the wide Temple doors together, and Benno's acolytes dutifully kept the awning over their heads as they walked.

Benno glanced at the Queen as they crossed into the Sanctuary. *She really has not changed much since I last saw her, almost two years ago. At the funeral.* Benno had worried that the weight of that time might have lain heavily on her, but she looked radiant, even mud-stained and soaked as she was now. Older, yes, but the time had merely served to melt the last of the girlishness from her and bring the sophistication of a young woman to the surface.

If the funeral had been two years ago, she would be twenty-one or twenty-two now. Two years of reign could mature someone quickly, even in prosperous times such as they now enjoyed. Endless squabbles amongst the proud noble families, the protection of her people, and the entreaties of thousands of supplicants weighed on her shoulders every day. *Not to mention the unrelenting machinations of those who feel they are better suited to rule than the foreign widow of a childless king.* Benno felt that he had aged five years for every one since ascending to the Bishopric, and he had the advantage of having spent his entire life in the Temple. It was his home. The Queen, on the other hand, still spoke with the rich accent of Venaissin even after five years of living in the north. One look at her and it was obvious Albyn was not her home.

Under her ermine hood, raven-black hair swept back in long waves from a simple, silver circlet. Her dark, honey-colored skin glowed even in the dull, northern winter light. Lips the color of wine graced a delighted smile as she gazed around the Sanctuary and took in the statue of Saint Taliesin gleaming under the light of a thousand candles.

She looks so much like her sister.

Of course the people of Albyn loved her. They loved her as the exotic beauty from the south whom their newly-crowned king had brought home as a bride, a young love that conquered immense distance. They loved her as their new Queen, a kind heart who had fallen in love with their cold, misty land.

Who would not love such a fairy-tale? And yet when the fairy-tale had ended two years ago in such a tragic manner, the adoration of their new monarch had only deepened as they shared her grief, and they mourned the loss of a beloved king and a husband together.

The monarchs of Albyn were usually referred to as "Silver". Silver for snow, ice, and steel. But this Queen they called the Summer Queen.

As the Queen and the Bishop entered the Sanctuary, the crowd of priests and acolytes sank to their knees as one, and a majestic ripple of cloth shushed through the cavernous room. A soft murmur rose as they quietly greeted the Queen as she passed, and Benno was pleased that everything appeared very proper and decorous.

Three of the Council waited here, dressed in ornate robes as befitted their lofty status. Benno introduced them to the Queen. Reverend Ail, Reverend Hayley, and Reverend Liadán all made very good impressions, Benno thought, so he frequently called upon them to be front and center when a good impression needed to be made. The high priest and the two high priestesses were old, but not decrepit. They struck a balance of grey hair, soft wrinkles, sharp minds and strong opinions.

Reverend Liadán in particular shone today, her dark red hair carefully braided and her robes immaculate. Liadán knew the court well, having served as the pastor of the cathedral in Kuray for more than ten years, and she had known both the Queen's husband and his father well. The Queen took Liadán's hand in hers, and the two women conversed in the old Venaissine language of the Queen's home, too fast for Benno to catch more than a word or two. From the earnest smiles and comforting tone he surmised that care, friendship, and support were being offered and returned.

After courtesies had been exchanged, Benno led the group past the doors to the Inner Temple, arriving at last at the vast apartments that were traditionally used by monarchs when they visited Bandirma. A fire roared and snapped in the main room, and Benno gratefully felt warmth begin to creep into his fingers and toes again.

The two knights inspected the Queen's chambers while Benno heard the stewards settling the Queen's escort in the dormitory across the hallway.

The Queen gratefully removed her cloak and revealed an elegantly embroidered coat the color of her hair, made of soft wool and lined with fur, worn over soft leather riding pants that matched her boots. Long gloves of the same cream color were carefully pulled off and tossed onto her cloak as she warmed her hands at the fire and accepted a glass of mulled wine.

The Queen's two companions joined them at the fire.

Benno exchanged a nod with the first of them, a tall man with iron-colored, close-cropped hair. Benno had met General Boone many times over the years, the illustrious Albainn general having served as commander of the royal army for even longer than Benno had been Bishop of Bandirma. The general looked as fit as any of his soldiers, strong and lean, and he had a penetrating gaze. He had grown a chin-beard and mustache since the last time Benno had seen him, the same iron grey as his hair. Benno decided it made the general look even more fierce than usual, somehow accenting the imposing, aquiline nose and stern mouth.

Boone was dressed in a long, leather coat over steel scale armor that creaked heavily as he stood. A broad-bladed infantry sword hung from a simple leather scabbard at his waist. Benno saw that the general's tunic and armor were unadorned, although exquisitely crafted.

The other man Benno preferred not to greet. In fact, he preferred not to acknowledge his existence.

Short and gnarled, Karsha Hali looked like the offspring of a spider mated with a shrubbery. An old, diseased shrubbery. He wrapped his gaunt frame in multiple layers of old black wool, one threadbare robe over another threadbare robe over another, each one more ragged and worn than the last. A wrinkled, bald head the color of a walnut poked from the mass of robes. His long face bore pronounced cheekbones, a crooked nose, and massive ears with pendulous earlobes that had long, ivory spikes driven through them. Blue tattoos covered every piece of visible skin, swirls, slashes and stars alongside strange runes and arcane symbols that Benno had never seen except on Karsha's skin. Tiny, hunched, and ancient, the man huddled far in the back of a deep armchair, and his small, bare feet hung out of the bottom of the robes.

Benno had hoped that Karsha Hali would fall from favor when the king had died, but apparently the Queen valued his counsel as much as her husband had, and his father, the king, before him. *And his grandfather, the Grand Duke,* if Benno remembered correctly, although that was over forty years ago and Benno had not paid as much attention to the royal court back then as he did now.

Karsha Hali had been a fixture at the court for as long as Benno could remember, and the rumor was that the King's grandfather, the Grand Duke, had brought him from the far south when he returned from one of his famed explorations.

Karsha has not changed at all, and he looked ancient the first time I saw him, more than forty years ago. Benno felt sure that was because a human being could not look any older than Karsha Hali did, no matter how old he grew.

"Your Majesty," Benno began. "I hope your travels were not too horribly wet and cold?"

"Please, Reverend, my name is Gabrielle, I wish you would use it," the Queen smiled. "There is no need for formality when we are not on stage."

"As you say, my lady." A frown appeared on the Queen's face, a pretty furrow between her brows. "My Lady Gabrielle." He finished.

"Much better," she smiled, and drank deeply from the glass, her eyes closed a moment to savor the flavor.

"It is good to see you too, my lord," Benno turned to Boone. "It has been years since we received such visitors here in Bandirma."

"Eight," agreed the general, placing his glass on a side table. "King Conall and I came to discuss the summer campaign against the Ironback clans with you and Lord Bradon."

"Was that eight years ago?" Benno wondered.

Karsha Hali laughed, and his robes tinkled and chimed as the dozens of charms that dangled from it bounced. "The years fly by as you reach the end, don't they Reverend?" he croaked.

"I wouldn't know," Benno replied, patting his stomach. "I feel certain that I am in my prime."

Karsha Hali laughed again at that, a harsh sound that reminded Benno of ravens squabbling over food, and raised his glass to the priest. "I like that… prime indeed! And how is your god? Still in his prime too?"

Benno felt himself tense. *Three sentences! The wretched man. Three sentences and already he starts to mock.*

"Of course," Benno answered, trying to keep his tone light. "He does not waver in His attention and concern for us."

"I am glad to hear it," Karsha replied, and gulped greedily at his glass, spilling some wine onto his robes in his haste. "Shit, what a mess." He dabbed uselessly at his robes with his sleeve.

The Queen laughed, a light, sparkling sound. "You are terrible, Karsha. Stop teasing the Bishop. He has not done anything to deserve it."

"As you say, nothing at all," he skewered Benno with a one-eyed squint as he continued mopping his robes.

Benno sipped his wine, comfortable to wait and enjoy the fire. He did not know why these fine visitors had appeared at his doorstep, but there was no chance it was a social visit. It was a long journey from Kuray to Bandirma. Even if the visit was an impulsive thought of the Queen's there would have been plenty of time to send a message ahead. But there had been no bird.

Silence settled over the room. Benno listened to the snap of the logs in the fire, the soft jingle of Karsha Hali, and waited.

The Queen was the first to break the silence.

"Reverend, where is my sister?"

Queens are bad at waiting, Benno reflected, taking another sip of wine to collect his thoughts.

"I am sorry, your Majesty, she is not in Bandirma right now."

"I was worried that might be the case when she was not with you to greet me." The Queen's tone was light, but Benno heard a slight edge of impatience. *Queens are very bad at waiting.*

"Ah. Indeed, of course you were," Benno agreed pleasantly.

The fire popped and crackled merrily as they waited for more, but Benno said nothing.

"You haven't answered the Queen," the General's voice cut through the silence.

"Haven't I?" Benno wondered. "I apologize."

Again he let them wait. Benno was now very curious to discover what these three knew. *Even if she somehow heard that her sister was here, would that have sent the Queen racing through the winter to Bandirma? No, this visit portends something else.*

Karsha Hali croaked a deep, hacking laugh that made him jingle again. "I think the Bishop likes playing this game. So maybe you should try just asking him."

Benno watched as the Queen glanced from Karsha to Boone and receive a curt nod from the General as she did.

She turned to Benno and gazed at his face for a moment more before speaking.

"Very well. Reverend Benno, we know that my sister recently returned from visiting our home. Danielle sent me a bird when she arrived here. And we also know that she brought something with her. Something that belongs to my family."

Benno took a slow sip from his glass to try to cover his surprise. *There is no way they could know that. It was Veiled, and I do not believe Lady Danielle would have told anyone. Not even the Queen. And that is an interesting way to put it… 'belongs to my family'.*

"She may well have, your Majesty," Benno answered. "I am sure we can ask her when she returns."

"You know that she did," Boone's tone was matter-of-fact. "Where is it now?"

"Lady Danielle is on Temple business, I'm afraid," Benno chose to answer the easier question. "I am not sure when she will return."

"Maybe in the northern hinterlands?" Karsha asked. "Many Temple people there now."

"As I said, I am not sure when she will return."

"My lord Bishop, the Weapon my sister brought with her belongs to my family, not the Temple," the Queen smiled reasonably, but Benno decided she was likely near the end of being reasonable. "Whatever business she is undertaking for you, the Weapon is not for the Temple to use."

"I am sure that is true, your Majesty. And yet, is it not also true that Lady Danielle is the Marquessa? She is two years older than you, and I feel sure that she inherited the title when your mother passed, my goodness, was it really fifteen years ago now?"

"Yes, that is right," the Queen answered sharply. "What of it?"

"It seems to me the family treasures are at Lady Danielle's disposal, as she is prima."

"You are speaking to the Queen," Boone reminded him sharply. "It doesn't matter who the head of the house is. If the Queen commands, it will be done."

"An amusing thought, my lord, since Lady Danielle is not one of the Queen's subjects. I believe the archon of her house owes fealty only to the High King, if there ever were another High King. Is that not right, your Majesty? In any case the point is moot, as Lady Danielle has long been a Paragon of the Temple, and is therefore beholden to no kingdom. As I am sure you recall, my lord."

"We are not here to discuss political niceties, Benno," Boone said pointedly. "That sword is needed by the Queen, and not for some Temple crusade. If you have sent it into peril…"

No more 'my lord Bishop', Benno noted sadly to himself. *The game is nearly over.*

"And why does your Majesty need this sword of which you speak so desperately? Surely you have many swords in your arsenals?"

Karsha Hali cackled at that. "You know why. Why else would you send Lady Danielle for it? Or do you think you are the only one who can read the signs?"

Benno sighed inwardly. *I really hate that man. How does he know these things? He has not been to the ritual sites, he doesn't have access to our archives. Yet he seems to know as much as we do. Maybe more.*

"Reverend Benno, there is no need for this," the Queen's voice was gentle, conciliatory. Benno was glad he was dealing with her, not her father-in-law. This Queen was reasonable and open, not cold and unyielding. Benno regretted he could not help her.

"Give us the sword," Boone's voice, on the other hand, was steel. "Order Lady Danielle to bring it to us."

Benno finished his wine, relishing its spicy taste, and placed the glass carefully on the side table. He bowed to the Queen, and then moved to the door, pausing with his hand on the latch.

"I am sorry, your Majesty. God says 'No'."

Then he left.

Wyn

Wyn glided down the stairs silently and gracefully, taking each step with the delicate tip of her toes first. No puddle splashed, no scuff of a heel on stone gave her away, a dark patch in a shadow against a black wall.

The others were a half-turn back, directly across the yawning hole. They tried to be quiet, but the chasm echoed with their movement. Heavy boots splashed in water, armor and weapons clinked on stone, and low voices murmured constantly. The light from their torches flickered and flared, illuminating thousands of sparkling drops of water as they fell down the vast central hole.

Ahead of her the stairs had crumbled away and left only a narrow shelf of stone against the wall. *An excellent place to stop and wait for the others, especially since half-way across the hole is as far away as I care to be in this horrible place.*

She sat with her back against the wall, drew her legs under her and huddled in her cloak to try and stay warm, but the cold seeped through her threadbare clothes and made her shiver.

A loud splash from somewhere below startled her, and she froze in place. She listened intently, but it did not repeat. She snuggled deeper into her cloak and watched the others approach.

Poor old Corlath. I feel so bad for him. The wounded soldier was trying his best, but each step was clearly agony, and he hung heavily from his brother, Cormac, and the other soldier, Brok. Wyn liked the twins. They were quiet, but enjoyed a good story or a bad joke in their own way. She could not understand why they insisted on cutting their hair differently, since it limited the opportunities for mischief, but when she had confronted them about that they had merely nodded and smiled, and Wyn had known that there was a secret there. *I like that.*

Brok, on the other hand, she was not so sure about. Big and gruff and strong, he was exactly the type of soldier she usually tried to avoid at all costs, one who had seen most everything before, and could rarely be fooled.

Wyn's stomach rumbled softly and reminded her that she was starving. She took a piece of biscuit from the small pack she wore against the small of her back and nibbled on it, trying to make it last. The vile, tough biscuit somehow managed to be dry and pasty at the same time, but it was all she had left. She had not eaten a proper meal since before she and Torbhin had left for Twin Pines. Luckily they had been able to fill their canteens with melted snow, so they at least were full. She did not want to try the water that ran down the sides of the big hole. The black moss that grew in the puddles was not encouraging.

I wonder where Alistair and Torbhin are now? Wyn thought as she chewed the biscuit. She had not believed Lord Bradon for a moment when he had said he did not think it likely that the soldier and the ranger had survived. *There's no way Shoulders was offed by a bunch of withered nasties. But they should have caught up with us by now, what with Corlath limping down the stairs. I suppose they didn't find the tower. What kind of a ranger is Snowball anyway, can't find a tower? I bet they're back in Twin Pines by now, having a lovely bowl of whatever's cooking.*

Comforted by the image, Wyn brushed crumbs from her lap and moved on to being cross.

Really, it's pathetic, if I'm honest. Snowball should be here, taking a turn or two in front instead of just me. I hope Shoulders got all grumpy with him when he couldn't find our trail. But Wyn found it difficult to stay angry. It felt wrong somehow, as if she might jinx the two missing companions if she thought ill of them, and she tried to conjure up the image of them slurping stew in a cabin again.

The others finally drew near so she stood up and rubbed some feeling into her frozen butt.

Lord Bradon and Lady Danielle led the way, Bradon with one of the torches held aloft as he towered over the woman beside him, Danielle with the great sword still strapped across her back.

Torchlight fell across Danielle's face and made her dark skin glow the color of amber held before a summer sun. Wyn wished that she looked like the noblewoman, so beautiful and graceful. She watched Danielle as she walked, each long leg stepping with a languid sway as she moved, the curves of thigh and hip and waist so sensual it made Wyn want to trace her fingers along them just to feel the smooth arc. She had proper breasts too, that pulled her tunic taut and hinted at the softness underneath. Her hair swirled as she tilted her head to speak with Bradon, a raven-black cascade that flowed down her back.

But it was her face that most amazed Wyn. The soft curve of her cheek, her long, elegant neck, her golden eyes with their heavy lashes, her exquisite lips and dazzling, white smile, even now directed at Wyn as they made eye contact. So lovely, Wyn felt herself smile in return without thinking about it.

But instead I get to be me. Skinny girl with small boobs and hair like straw. Good enough for a quick tumble or a squeeze or two in the barn, but not someone anyone would look twice at. Although my butt is pretty amazing, if I say so myself. Wyn giggled softly. *Self, your butt is amazing. Why thank you, Self, I agree.*

A deep grumble from Lord Bradon interrupted her reverie. Wyn suddenly realized that she had been gazing at Danielle unabashedly, although from her friendly smile Danielle did not seem to have taken offense. *I guess she's used to being stared at, or else she's used to me being rude,* Wyn decided.

Bradon stood at the broken stairs and stroked his beard as he frowned furiously at the gap. Wyn hurried to his side while the other soldiers helped Corlath to sit and rest. Cormac's swollen face was turning a dark purple now, and blood oozed from cracks across his lip and cheek.

Danielle moved next to Wyn and placed a gentle hand on her shoulder as she held the torch high to shine light across the gap in the stairs.

Danielle frowned in exasperation. "Another broken stair? This is absurd."

Wyn pointed at the stub of stone left attached to the wall. "There are still steps, your Ladyship, look. Just like the last one. I can get across no worries."

"Yes, but the last one terrified me, as did the one before. You are like a deer, or no, a mountain lion. I am … I am not sure. Perhaps a duck?"

Wyn laughed. "A swan, more like. They're graceful creatures, but maybe not the best climbers."

"A swan then, although truth be told I feel more like a little brown duck."

"Not likely," Wyn snorted in disbelief. "Tell her she looks like a beautiful swan, your Lordliness."

"Indeed, my lady, most elegant," Bradon said from far away, still staring at the gap in the stairs.

Useless, thought Wyn, although Danielle was smiling now, just a bit, so maybe Bradon's feeble attempt had been enough.

"So, do I go across with a rope like last time?" she asked.

Bradon turned to her, a frown still buried deeply on his face.

"Wyn, when you say it is like the last time, how much like the last time?"

Wyn glanced at the broken stone steps.

"Pretty much the same."

"Pretty much, or exactly the same?" the Templar asked, his deep voice a low rumble.

Wyn looked more closely. *Three jagged steps, then a nice flat one just begging to be landed on. Then a wobbly one ready to trick you.*

"Um, maybe exactly the same?" Wyn was confused now.

"That was my thought as well," Bradon agreed.

"But that was a half an hour ago," protested Danielle.

"Yes, and that again to the first gap," Bradon planted his hands on the pommel of his hammer, "and in all of that time, the shaft has otherwise been completely empty. Where did the priest go? He cannot have clambered up and down hours of broken stairs every time."

"We're going round in circles?" asked Wyn. "But we've been going down the whole time. Round and round this stupid hole."

"True," nodded Bradon. "And yet I fear we are indeed in some type of maze, one we cannot see. This shaft is too deep, too featureless, these gaps too identical."

"Ohhh!" Wyn groaned in exasperation. "Wonderful."

"Are you sure?" Danielle asked softly as she retrieved the small, glowing Diviner she carried from her pack. "This has never wavered. Downwards."

"Perhaps it is correct, but mayhap we are not actually travelling downwards. I only know what my eyes tell me, and right now they are telling me that we have been here before."

"Then what do we do?" asked Danielle.

"I believe we must try a different direction," said Bradon.

"What, go back up?" Wyn wrinkled her nose in disgust.

"Nay, there is no gain in returning to the entrance, even if we could. I meant downwards, but in a different manner," said Bradon, and he glanced at the gap in the stairs.

Wyn laughed. "You want me to climb down into that hole? Did a horse kick you in the head?"

"You would use the rope, of course, and I would pull you up if needed. If you stayed close to the wall of the shaft, surely…"

"I'll do it," interrupted Wyn. "But it's crazy. My kind of crazy, which should worry you. And it's a hole, not a shaft. I know the difference."

Bradon frowned in confusion. "Yes, certainly, a hole if you prefer."

"Don't get me wrong," Wyn smiled mischievously. "I like a good shaft as much as the next girl. It's just that there's something to be said for a really nice hole too."

There was a moment of silence that pleased Wyn deeply, then Brok snorted in laughter and Danielle blushed beautifully, a deep flush that rose up her neck as she stared with wide eyes at Wyn. Wyn felt heat rise into her face under Danielle's gaze, so she quickly turned away. *Where did that come from? Am I embarrassed? I don't feel embarrassed. I feel nervous or something. Butterflies. Why?*

"I…" started Bradon, but the Lord ran out of words at that point, and he glanced at Danielle for help. The Lady could not meet his eye, so he simply floundered to a stop.

Wyn smiled at them all, her brightest, most innocent-girl smile. *Ha! Got him. Speechless, finally!*

***

The black stone walls glistened in the torchlight as they slowly rose past Wyn. Ahead of her the hole gaped into pitch darkness as she descended face first, using her legs to walk slowly down the wall as she kept pace with Bradon letting out the rope above her. One hand held the torch attached to a lanyard clear to the side, while the other reached behind her to hold the rope for balance.

Wyn had removed her thick cloak and coat for the descent, not wanting anything loose to potentially snag or entangle, and now thc chill air cut right through her thin woolen tunic and black leather leggings. She had even discarded her supple leather boots and padded bare foot along the wet stone walls. Thin as her boots were, there were cracks she could use with bare feet that boots would never find. Right now that made no matter, dangling as she was from a nice, firm rope, but Wyn knew not to count on that carefree state to continue for long.

Not that my boots were keeping my feet warm anyhow. Maybe I can wear Danielle's extra stockings when we get her saddlebags.

Step after step she lowered. Wet stone slid under her toes, chill water dripped onto her back and then trickled across her ribs and stomach. She shivered, goose-bumps prickling her skin.

And still, the darkness stretched unbroken before her.

Which makes no kind of sense. The landings were no more than a knife's throw apart, I saw them.

"Wyn, what do you see?" called Danielle, concern in her voice.

"Nothing," she called back, and then softer to herself, "dark as the Black Grave."

She cursed herself for that. *Why think about that? Martyr's tears, that's all I need right now.*

Wyn said a quick prayer to the Martyr, begging her for no more bottomless black holes or wights with dead eyes. Wyn rarely thought about her namesake, other than to curse, but in her deepest heart the Martyr gave her comfort. Wyn had seen a statue of her in the royal chapel in Kuray once. Like most representations of the Martyr, this one had depicted her with sword raised, shielding the fallen High King, head held high in defiance as she stared at her foe, absent, of course, from the carving. But she had looked so very real. Her face was young and beautiful, but not like an angel, like a real person, and she looked brave and angry, not serene and unnatural like the other statues Wyn had seen. She had beautifully braided hair, and it made Wyn wonder who had tied it for her.

Wyn had traced her fingertips over the name carved into the plinth at the base of the statue and lingered on each letter. *Bronwyn.* She had never felt proud of her name, embarrassed by false piety, but at that moment in the moonlit chapel she had felt a fierce pride, and it had lasted deep in her heart ever since.

She knew from the stories that Bronwyn the Martyr had died just a few years older than she was now, and it made her feel sad to think of it. It was all very well to bluster about how Bronwyn had defended Ruric from the Nameless King when he had fallen, and how she had wounded the foe, and driven him back while Ruric recovered from the blow that had felled him, but in the end she had died under the Nameless King's blade, and Ruric as well, so what was the point really? The Nameless King had been defeated because of her sacrifice, but the victory felt hollow to Wyn.

Something caught Wyn's attention, a flutter of light in the corner of her eye that swam into view and then was gone before she could focus on it. It was far below, and around the edge of the hole. Wyn let her feet drop away from the wall, hung with her full weight on the rope, and watched it.

Again the glow appeared, faint and yellow and hazy, and again it disappeared in an instant.

Gotcha.

Wyn extinguished her torch on the wet stones, then let it drop to hang from its lanyard. She twisted and let her toes rub gently across the wall until they found a nice jutting brick. She eased her weight onto it and felt the rope go loose.

Wyn clung to the wall and let her fingertips and toes sink into it. The stone was cold and wet, slippery, and the cracks no more than the width of a fingertip. Wyn let her weight press her into it, her clothes soaked through in an instant, the black stone pressed against her cheek, her breasts, her stomach.

Then, satisfied with her grip, she sank lower and her weight pulled downwards on her fingers instead of outwards. The stones were wet, but they were unevenly shaped and gave her good choices for finger- and toe-holds. She edged sideways across the wall towards the intermittent light. As she moved closer it wavered in and out of visibility, as if it were seen through dark water or thick glass. It made Wyn uncomfortable to watch it, but she pushed the feeling down and concentrated on the cold stone instead.

A few steps, then a few more, and Wyn felt the weight of the rope start to pull on her harness.

The light became a flickering glow, and there were two of them, spaced a little way apart. Wyn saw they were two torches set in black metal sconces on either side of a door. At their base Wyn could discern a stone floor and a railing that stretched out until the torchlight could no longer touch it on either side.

The door was closed, and there was no sign of life on the landing.

Wyn stayed still and watched and listened. The pit echoed with the sound of trickling water, but otherwise was silent.

Time to get on with it.

Wyn slowly leaned into her harness until the rope took up the slack, then as her weight carried her away from the wall she ran with the motion and she was carried in a long arc across the wall. At the top of the swing she turned to face the other direction and ran down the wall, faster now and farther, until she flew across the wet stone.

She was close to the landing with the torches now, but not close enough. Again she scampered across the wall in an enormous arc as Bradon paid out even more rope through the belay. On the return she pushed powerfully with her legs and leapt across the wall in tremendous bounds. The landing came nearer and nearer, and then she was over it. She twisted in mid-air like a cat and knifed to grab the stone railing before she could drop past it.

A quick scramble and she landed, crouched on the platform. The stone was cold and unyielding under her bare feet, and her breath steamed in the chill air, real and solid. She had half-feared she would drop right through, so ghostly the torches had seemed from afar. But here they were, snapping and flaring in their sconces, with thick streams of smoke that twisted into the dark.

To her surprise Wyn saw that the platform extended across the wall to connect to stairs on either side. She was certain that had not been the case as she hung above it, but the stairs were clearly visible now.

Wyn quickly untied her harness, looped the rope around the stone railing, pushed her hair from her eyes, and padded to the door. She crouched next to the door and pressed against it with her fingers and an ear to listen. There was a noise from the other side, a murmur or rumble, too faint to identify. She shivered, her wet clothes clinging to her skin, but forced herself to wait. The sound continued, fading in and out. Wyn decided it was a voice chanting from far away.

A heavy splash sounded on the landing behind her, and Wyn twisted from the door, poised to move. The landing was empty, but something was disturbed, as if there was a momentary gap in the falling water, or a ripple in the puddles. Wyn froze. Her senses strained to find the cause, but there was no telltale sound or hint of movement to reveal it.

But Wyn knew something was there. Something watched her. If she were asked to explain it she could not, but she knew when she was safely concealed and when she was the prey. She cursed as she hesitated, unsure of which direction to move. The end of the rope tied to the railing called to her from across the wide-open landing, but so did the dark shadows along the wall beyond the torches. She knew the worst mistake was to wait and leave herself vulnerable, but there was no sign to lead her.

Then she caught it. The softest of clicks, almost completely hidden by the sounds of water. Then a rasp of something hard against crumbling stone, just as quiet, but long enough that she could tell it came from above her. Slowly Wyn raised her eyes and peered through the falling drops of water.

A slight movement stirred above her in the dim mist beyond the torchlight.

Martyr defend me.

The faint torchlight gleamed on long black shapes, rigid and sharp, a mass that writhed and shifted as she watched. Wyn could see quivering spikes and serrated teeth but the jumbled shapes made no sense to her.

Her toes curled against the stone floor and then she jumped, quick as lightning. She flew across the landing and her hair streamed behind her as her feet pounded against the stone floor. She heard a heavy splash as something landed close to her, and a hiss as something sliced through the air behind her, but she did not stop to look. With a leap she hurdled the stone railing and pushed off with her hand as she flew over, then twisted and extended to her full reach, toes pointed and back arched, to grab the drooping rope as it flashed by.

She let her momentum swing her high above the wet rope, and then she twisted and landed on it with both hands and both feet, fingers and toes gripping it firmly. Then she was off, scrambling up the rope. A dozen steps and she stopped suddenly and twisted to face her pursuer, feet balanced deftly on the shifting rope, both knives held ready in her hands. Whatever was chasing her, Wyn was determined that she would send it plummeting into the pit before she was knocked from the rope.

But there was nothing behind her. The rope swayed and bounced, empty, the torches flickered on an empty landing.

Wyn stood easily on the rope and let it move under her feet as she scanned the murky pit around her. Nothing moved, and there was no sound save for her heavy breathing and the omnipresent drip and trickle of the water chasing down the stone walls.

Slowly her breathing settled, and she became aware once again of her soaked clothes clinging to her body, and the deep chill of the air. *Fine. If you're not coming, I'm not waiting.*

Wyn sheathed her knives and climbed, hands and feet on the rope until it neared the wall, then a scramble up the wall with her feet while her arms pulled on the rope. Bradon's massive hand reached for her and she gratefully grasped it and let the Templar easily swing her up and over the edge.

Danielle quickly wrapped Wyn's cloak around her, and rubbed warmth into her back and shoulders and arms. Wyn shivered uncontrollably, overwhelmed by cold and tension and fear and relief all at the same time.

"Are you all right, lass?" Bradon's voice rumbled reassuringly.

Wyn nodded. "Just cold."

Bradon hesitated, unconvinced, but she made sure to meet his concerned eyes and not look away until he had to accept that as truth.

"Very well then," said Bradon. "And what did you discover while freezing yourself near to death?"

"Well, first off you were right, there's a door down there with torches and everything. Sounded like someone's on the other side too, chanting or praying or some such, I'd say," said Wyn. "And some stairs, too."

She paused, suddenly reluctant to talk about the half-glimpsed presence in the shadows. It already felt more like a nightmare than something real, and she was not even sure what to say to the others about it. *I saw something really scary that made me run away? There was a spooky sound behind me?* Even as she thought about it she felt a lump of panic starting to press on her chest that made it difficult to breathe. *How can I explain this in a way that doesn't make me sound like a scared little child?*

But they were all waiting on her to say something, and Danielle's hand on her back felt reassuring. *Might as well get it over with, and if anyone laughs I can just shave their beards off while they're asleep.*

"There was something else," she ventured. "Something guarding the door I think."

"You think?" asked Brok.

"That's what I said, right?" Wyn glared at the soldier, daring him to take it further. "Something hiding in the shadows, but it was there all right, and fast. I didn't get a good look, and I wasn't going to wait and see if it was friendly or not."

"No, of course not," agreed Bradon, and Wyn felt absurdly grateful for his immediate acceptance. "Would we all be able to make it to the landing?"

Wyn nodded eagerly. "No problem, your Beardyness. I tied the rope to the railing, so we can just shimmy down, easy as wishing."

Bradon laughed deeply. "Well, we will see how easy it is for some of us." He turned to the three soldiers and issued orders to prepare to descend to the platform below.

A deep chill shook Wyn again, and her teeth chattered loudly. Now that Bradon was talking to the rest of the group there was nothing to take her mind off how frozen she was.

Danielle collected her boots and coat and brought them while Wyn huddled in her cloak and tried to control her shivering.

"Those do not look like nice shivers," said Danielle with a concerned smile. "Do you have any dry clothes at all?"

"Not a stitch." Wyn shook her head. "What I have, I'm wearing."

"Here, hold on to me then, at least until your clothes warm up a bit," said Danielle, and she wrapped her cloak around them both and held Wyn tightly against her.

"I don't want to get you all wet too." Wyn curled into the embrace gratefully.

"I am not concerned about a little extra damp," Danielle rested her cheek against Wyn's hair, "but you are soaked."

Wyn nodded her head and felt the shivering start to subside as she relaxed into the gentle rhythm of Danielle's breathing against her.

"I hate wet clothes," Danielle said sympathetically. "Horrid cold, clinging things."

Wyn sighed ruefully. "Revealed my girlish charms to everyone, did they? Wonderful."

Danielle held her close and gently rubbed her shoulders until Wyn felt a low warmth start to spread from where their bodies touched. Her shivers calmed, and as the cold receded, Wyn felt a dull ache build in her throat, and her eyes stung.

She suddenly realized that she was going to cry as exhaustion, fear and desperation conspired to overwhelm her. Whatever she had seen on the landing terrified her in a way that nothing else had ever done, even as a half-glimpsed memory that she questioned more with every passing moment.

Wyn wiped furiously at her eyes with the edge of the cloak. She did not think anyone would see in the dim light, although Danielle could probably tell because the noblewoman held her close as she shook. Danielle felt warm and soft and her hair smelled like sunshine, so Wyn gratefully let herself huddle in Danielle's arms until she could wipe away the tears and gulp down her stupid sobs.

"Are you alright?" Danielle whispered softly as she gently tucked Wyn's hair up away from her face.

Wyn nodded and smiled at Danielle. "I haven't boo-hoo'd like that since I was ten. I feel ridiculous. Do you think they noticed?"

"I doubt it," said Danielle. "Men miss almost everything around them."

Wyn knew Danielle was trying to make her feel better, but it felt good to hear it.

"Thank you, your Ladyship," Wyn sighed forlornly. "I bet I look like a drowned cat."

Danielle laughed. "A bit bedraggled, but you look beautiful. Strong and brave."

Wyn was not sure what to say. *Beautiful?* It seemed unlikely, with her ragged hair and broken nails. Still, it felt good to hear Danielle say it. If someone as exotic as the noblewoman could think it, it might be true. Wyn made a mental note to find an inn with a mirror the next chance she got. Maybe something had changed in the years since the last time she had seen herself.

Bradon returned with a creak of leather and stood with one hand on his hammer, the other stroking his beard as he waited. Wyn let him wait.

"My Lady, Wyn, if I might," Bradon cleared his throat. "We are ready to go if you are."

"Nope, I'm good here," Wyn smiled at him over Danielle's shoulder.

"Perhaps in a moment then, when you are finished," said Bradon.

"A moment?" Wyn asked, and her smile changed to a grin in an instant. "Takes longer than a moment to finish if you're doing it right. Someone should show you some day. Anyway, not likely with you lot gawking at us."

Wyn felt Danielle laugh softly against her as Bradon chuckled.

"I am sure you are right," the Lord replied. "So perhaps instead I might offer you an evening of glorious deeds and mighty struggle against a foe who well-deserves a bloody end."

"The glorious deeds part sounds the same, either way, but yeah I would quite like an evening of knifing that Reverend Asses. In the face."

"Good." Bradon gave his beard one last pat, then gestured towards the edge of the ragged hole in the staircase, where Brok stood with a coil of rope in his hands. "Brok and I will descend to the platform below and make sure it is safe. Then you will string another line and help the rest to cross."

Wyn eased from Danielle's embrace with a grateful smile, stretched her shoulders loose and settled her knives against her back.

"Let's go then," said Wyn.

Killock

Something shifted in the darkness nearby, a vague movement that sent small fragments of awareness darting across his vision like fireflies.

Killock could tell that something was very wrong with the world, but it remained unknowable as he slipped into and out of consciousness. Focusing on it made no difference. The world swam and swayed and drifted just out of reach, then retreated far away again and became empty blackness.

***

Killock jerked as something moved near him. He was awake now, but still nothing made sense. Stones coated with ice swam woozily in front of his face, swaying backwards and forwards, and when he tried to move, his legs and arms waved uselessly. One arm at least. His left arm would not move at all, and seemed anchored in place.

He bumped into the stones. They were solid enough, although it appeared as if he were floating above them.

The noise happened again. A scuffling and a small trickle of stones falling. Killock twisted towards the noise and found himself face to face with a confused-looking goat perched sideways on a rock jutting from the floor. The goat bleated and leapt away, and suddenly the world snapped into sense. Killock realized that he was not floating above the ground, but dangling next to a cliff.

He kicked and thrashed until his boots found purchase against the stones, then dragged himself onto a small ledge. His left arm was tangled in the rope from which he had been hanging, and he had trouble freeing it. The arm was completely numb, and trying to move it sent stabs of agony through his shoulder. He gingerly unwound the rope and gritted his teeth as he gently lowered his arm. It hung awkwardly, the shoulder dislocated at least, and Killock did not like the look of the grey skin of his fingers when he peeled back his glove to inspect them.

Probably a good thing it's numb. Don't want to pass out again when I put this back in place.

His perch was precarious, a small ledge on the side of the sheer cliff underneath the ruined Léim Mhór. Wind whipped past, tugging on his cloak and moaning over the rocks as it went, and he wedged his boots a bit more securely into gaps in the ledge.

It was still day, so he had not been hanging there for too many hours, but as the goat proved, clearly long enough for the trolls to grow bored and wander off. *Hopefully they went farther than the barracks.*

The goat watched him from a safely distant perch. Killock could spot the series of small ledges the animal had used to escape. Small, but usable.

If I had two arms. He gritted his teeth. *Best to get this over with.*

Killock tucked his knees up and carefully laced his fingers together over his left knee. His numb hand was useless, but he gripped it firmly with his right, keeping it in place. Then he leaned backwards, stretching gingerly. Red flares of pain burst across his chest and back but he maintained the steady pressure, slowly pulling farther back moment by moment.

Suddenly there was a slick pop and a stab of agony that wrenched his stomach and made Killock groan through his teeth, and the arm hung normally again.

Still numb though, and I'll lose those fingers soon if I don't get them warmed up.

Killock groaned again as he levered himself from his seat. He tucked his left hand inside his jacket, a cold, dead thing against his stomach, both to warm it and to support the shoulder. The path the goat had taken was not that challenging, he decided, and he began to carefully make his way across the cliff.

The goat watched, perplexed, occasionally ripping at the tough grass and lichen that grew among the rocks. Killock drew slowly nearer, bracing tired legs on every step, straining with weary back, cradling his aching shoulder. When he was within a stone's throw of the goat it decided it had seen enough and leapt away again, finding another path across the cliff. *Not a bad guide*, Killock decided.

Killock continued to follow the goat as best as he could, scrambling and lunging and clinging with his good hand. The goat continued to keep its distance, eventually leading the knight all the way to the top of the cliff before giving up and racing away for good.

A quick glance around showed Killock that the trolls had indeed departed, leaving him the spoils of the deserted buildings. Darkness had fallen by the time he had shoved enough discarded tables and beds to block the windows and doors, shutting out howling winds that shook the broken shutters and made the roof groan. Killock stacked broken furniture high in the fireplace and managed to light it one-handed, and soon a roaring fire thawed the room for the first time in centuries.

Killock sat in front of the fire, carefully presenting first one side of his hand and then the other to the blaze. To his relief, terrible pain trickled its way into the hand, starting from the elbow and slowly making its way to the fingertips. When all five fingers were singing with agony, he tucked it inside his shirt again and fell deeply asleep.

***

The winds turned to blow strongly from the north, streaming snow from the knife-edged peaks and howling through the valleys between. Heavy clouds raced along with the wind, poured amongst the mountains and filled the air with snow that stung skin as it whipped past.

The wolf loped quickly through the storm as it followed a wide ledge high up the side of a bleak mountain cliff. Snow caked the wolf's heavy, black coat and turned to ice around its grey muzzle, but it pressed on. The faint tracks of a small herd of goats caught its attention for a moment, and spoor from a pack of trolls made the wolf stop and sniff furiously before it kicked snow over them and continued on.

A stone shape loomed from the gale, a low wall of fitted stones along the outer edge of the ledge where it crumbled into the gulf below. The wolf ignored it, uninterested. The wall was ancient and smelled simply of stone and ice, as much a part of the mountain as the steep cliff face that rose on the other side of the ledge.

More shapes appeared as the wolf continued; the stumps of two colossal stone feet, one on either side of the ledge; a crumbling pile of weathered blocks that used to be a tower; huge buttresses that stood alone in the swirling sky, arching into nothing.

As the wolf followed the ledge around a sharp ridgeline it stopped to sniff the air. A scent of death and corruption flowed towards the wolf, carried by the gale. The wolf moved forward cautiously. The blood was interesting, but the wolf sensed something that felt wrong, and dangerous. The odor, or perhaps some sort of vibration carried through the stone? The wolf whined and shied away from it.

A dark shape appeared in the snow ahead. A tower slowly emerged from the storm, so tall that it disappeared into the clouds, and so massive that it completely blocked the ledge ahead of the wolf. Its ancient stones rose into the sky, sheer and uninterrupted, as it perched on its ledge far above the valley below. Eight magnificent statues lay ruined in front of it, toppled to the ground or smashed by falling stones. All had weathered into shapeless anonymity.

A dark tunnel through the tower stood open, its gate a rotten mass slumped to the side, the iron bars of its portcullis twisted and bent behind it.

The wolf approached the fallen statue nearest the gate. Once as tall as a tree, the statue lay on its face in the snow, one leg still standing alone on the plinth behind it, one arm shattered and missing, just a stump now. It had once been a representation of a beautiful woman with a long sword raised above her head to meet across the center of the gate with the statue on the other side, but long centuries of winter had erased most of this dramatic scene. The stone was pitted and cracked, worn smooth by wind and rain and cold. The sword was long gone, along with the missing arm.

Sniffing and shying away repeatedly, the wolf crept to the statue and along its base until it reached the ancient plinth on which the statue once stood. The wolf could feel the wrongness more clearly now. It was coming from somewhere beyond the far end of the tunnel. The wolf growled, its head low to the ground, its bushy tail tucked underneath it.

The wolf retreated to the ledge and settled on its haunches. The day passed slowly as the wolf watched patiently, eventually finding a shallow depression in the ledge where it could curl up against the wind and still see the ruined tower. Every now and then the wolf would raise its head and perk its ears, or sniff the air, but soon it would lie down again to watch.

***

Highward Tor was designed by the High King's engineers to be a fortress, built to guard the High Road against an invading army. The only passage through the immense outer towers were the two long tunnels that pierced them, each one defended by heavy, reinforced doors and portcullises made of thick iron bars.

The heart of Highward Tor had also not been neglected. The engineers had tunneled directly into the sheer cliff wall between the towers and created a labyrinth of rooms and tunnels defended by solid stone thicker than any wall. Temples and barracks and armories were also excavated, everything a defending force could want, hundreds of rooms deep beneath the cliff.

Only one way existed to enter the cliff. The heavy Inner Gate stood behind tall pillars, carved directly into the cliff face. Thick steel braces held the gate's mighty wooden beams, and the door was set in a stone frame as thick as a man's shoulders, with a series of steel latches that slid neatly into slots in the stone.

Killock stood at the end of the tunnel and gazed across the ruins of Highward Tor. The way to the Inner Gate was blocked, the courtyard choked with ruined buildings shattered by slabs of stone that had sheared from the high towers, obliterating anything beneath them when they fell.

From where the knight stood he could easily picture what the fortress must have looked like in its heyday, and he paused at the end of the tunnel to take in the vision. Imposing towers that pierced the streaming clouds, and walls that stood massive and impossible to breach, covered in siege engines ready to hurl death upon any approaching foe. *I wish Bradon were here to see this.* Killock had seen Bradon lose himself for days as he examined a fortification, scampering giddily from rampart to rampart, carefully examining every stone, gate, buttress, choke point, and field of fire. *I fear we should never get him to leave once he got here. He would spend a week investigating the interlocking stone facing of the walls.* The effort that had been required to build the fortress, to drag the giant stone slabs into place, to raise the mighty towers, here at the highest, most remote point on the High Road, was unimaginable.

But what caught Killock's eye was the evidence of the colossal power that had destroyed the fortress. The immense towers had twisted with such force that stones thicker than a man's reach had shattered with enough strength to spray shards across the courtyard, and buttresses built to support the weight of thousands of stones had cracked clean through. Killock could see where mighty waves had lifted walls and raised ridges across the solid stone of the courtyard, fracturing it into a jagged chaos. A vast section of the tower had slid from its perch and destroyed the rear of the courtyard, burying it in chunks of rubble bigger than a house.

The Cataclysm, Killock thought reverently. *I can see its touch so clearly here, as if I could simply close my eyes and be swept away in its destruction. It must have been far worse than I had ever imagined.*

Killock picked his way around the mountains of debris, close to the crumbling edge of the outer cliff where it plummeted into the clouds below. The wind howled across the ruins and snapped his ragged cloak as if it were a pennant on a lance, and grains of ice and snow stung his face despite his best efforts to hold his hood in place.

The remains of a long building perched on the edge of the cliff blocked his path. One end of it had fallen into the abyss, and only a few forlorn stones clung to the edge to show where it had rested. But the main bulk of it still stood, thick walls pierced by wide doorways and capped by a sturdy, slate roof.

A wide space showed that the building had once been open. In the center stood a sleek shape, crouched and dangerous. The dim light glinted softly on its metal skin and traced its curved lines. Long wings swept elegantly around it as if it were an eagle shielding itself from the cold, and there was a gleam off the metal feathers of its wings. The knight saw the curved scimitar of its nose and the dark glitter of its windows, shaped like the sharp eyes of a hawk. Most of it was made from a dark metal, almost black, but when Killock approached it he saw elegant carvings of gold tracing the talons and beak, and outlining the crest that ran down its back.

Killock ran a hand along the graceful line of the wing and felt the steely feathers. Dirt and grime came away on his glove and revealed the smooth, polished metal beneath, each feather carefully molded of hundreds of delicate, metal vanes that brushed softly into place under the pressure of his fingers. He had heard of such Devices before, but only in books, and only as the stuff of long-departed legends. Metal creatures that could bear their masters into battle, their armored skin and immense strength made them an unstoppable force. *Into battle, or through the sky.*

He wondered what storied lord had commanded such a Device, and what grandmaster artificer had constructed it. A sigil was engraved on the flank of the flyer, a golden falcon on an onyx field, but it meant nothing to Killock. He searched for the hatch, hoping for a glimpse of the interior, but it was constructed so cunningly that it could not be found, and Killock knew in his heart that it would not open for him without its Word.

Killock stood back and gazed at the flyer. He regretted its lonely fate, trapped in a dim ruin that crumbled around it. He gazed a moment longer to commit the lethal shape to memory, then turned his back on it.

Killock crouched behind the wall of the building to shelter from the worst of the weather and chewed thoughtfully on his last piece of dried meat. He would have to hunt on his return journey.

No goats though, he reminded himself.

Food was not going to be the only worry facing him on his journey back. The rope bridge across the Léim Mhór was a hopeless ruin. Tangled ropes hung forlornly as they bumped and knocked against the cliff face, but nothing connected the two sides. Killock felt he could eventually find his way to the lowlands, but he knew the journey would take weeks, especially in the winter. *And what good would it do us? We would still need to return to Highward Tor, more weeks and weeks of travel, assuming whatever path I find could even be used by Bradon and the others, a very faint hope.*

For Killock was utterly convinced that Highward Tor was the place Lady Danielle had seen in her vision. *A fortress with a tall tower, very high in the clouds. And underneath it caves and tunnels and an altar.*

He had felt the truth of her vision as he approached the towers, a dark presence akin to the one at Nóinín Cnoc so many days ago, but much stronger. If Nóinín Cnoc had been the bitter echo of a faraway pulse, Highward Tor was the corrupted heart. The stone walls reeked of wrongness, and the air carried its oily touch.

Killock sighed in exasperation and hugged his cloak tightly about himself, but the threadbare cloth did nothing to defend against the shadow that lurked under the stones. He feared that nothing could.

This was an exceptionally bad plan. Still, he was here now, and he was not going to give up and leave. Killock stood and brushed snow crystals from the wrinkles in his cloak and tunic, then clambered through the ruined fortress towards the sheer cliff wall that reared behind the debris.

The shattered stones shifted and slipped beneath his weight as he scrambled over them, and rotten ice made every perch precarious. Killock was forced to backtrack repeatedly, until he feared that he had become trapped in some cursed maze of endless teetering rocks and howling wind.

He dared to scurry across a wide section of leaning wall that twisted and crumbled as he leapt from its end. He shook his head as he looked back upon it. *That won't last a second crossing.*

He hoped he would not need it. Killock was very close to the cliff wall now, and just ahead he saw the tall pillars which flanked the entrance. Killock pushed between two shattered boulders and found himself in front of the massive Inner Gate.

The wide terrace offered no shelter. The wind swirled and blew from all directions as it writhed around the huge stone pillars, but lost none of its intensity.

The knight quickly moved to the towering doors. They stood closed, ancient wood and steel warped and twisted.

Killock threw his weight into the door. His shoulder and chest throbbed murderously from the effort, but he did not relent. With a violent groan the door shifted and shook on its rusted hinges, and shuddered across the stones to leave a small space wide enough to squeeze through.

Killock wormed his way through the gap, knife in hand, and pulled his pack through after him. He eased into the shadows and waited for his eyes to adjust to the dim light.

Perhaps because it was dug into a cliff, or perhaps because of its legendary origins, Killock expected the interior of Highward Tor to resemble Bandirma, with wide hallways and soaring open spaces. But it looked nothing like the grand temple. The hallway was less than five paces across, and had a low ceiling supported by fat pillars and thick stone arches. Instead of the carved stone of Bandirma, the arches, ceiling, and walls were lined with stone bricks, and the floor was tiled with bare rock.

Many of the bricks had come loose from the ceiling and fallen to shatter on the floor and create piles of broken rock. Heaped mounds of rotten wood had once been tables and chairs. Ragged tapestries hung from the walls, ravaged by mold to such an extent that whatever images they had borne were lost forever.

Old brass lanterns hung from sconces in the hallway, but Killock hesitated to fuel one to see if the wick would still draw. Highward Tor was lightless. Killock could see the area immediately around the Inner Gate by virtue of the pale light that seeped through the gap he had opened, but the hallway quickly disappeared into darkness. Killock could not think of a better way of announcing his presence than by carrying a brightly lit lantern with him.

However, I do have another option.

Killock took the small wallet that contained his Diviner and carefully unrolled the soft leather on the stone floor. A small adjustment on the metal studs brought the geometric designs covering the hoops precisely into line, and exactly centered the hoops on each other.

Then he sat back and prepared his Word. He could take no risks with this one. It had to be perfectly uttered and perfectly controlled, or its echo would certainly be heard by those nearby who had a sensitivity for Words. Killock could sense their works seeping from the depths, so there was no reason to doubt that they would be able to sense his Word echoing from the upper floors.

He cleared his mind and blocked out physical sensations as he focused on the small Device and the bindings within it. He released his exhaustion and the pain in his back and hands. He released the brush of burning cold across his skin. Slowly, gratefully, he released the deep ache from his shoulder. Each release brought him closer to the Device and its bindings. He could sense them buried in the labyrinthine geometric patterns that adorned the hoops, each one connected in an intricate web, ready to shape and guide the power they held. When he was ready he let the Word flow from him into the Diviner, and whispered it to give it form. The threads of the Device pulsed with power released by the bindings and channeled it precisely to fill the hoops with energy. It swirled and shifted, each layer working in concert with all the others, until Killock could peer through the focused hoops to see the passageway in front of him as clear as if it were broad daylight.

Killock sat back with a satisfied sigh. He rarely had cause to activate all of the hoops, but it was certainly worth the risk. Now he could stay in darkness as he scouted the heart of the Tor.

The Templar returned the empty wallet to his pack and carefully walked down the hall, using the Diviner to find his way in the dark. The hallway ended in an open area. Broad stairs descended on both sides of a central stairwell from which a remorseless chill seeped, carrying a scent of decay. The stairs spiraled downwards until they ended abruptly in a jagged edge where they had collapsed. A tall statue stood on the lower floor in the center of the stairwell, some colossal figure that Killock could not identify from his vantage point.

The knight descended the stairs cautiously. Half-way down the flight, he reached the statue's head, an armored lord with the crest of a lion rampant on his helm. Killock had no idea who he was supposed to have been, or why he had been placed in this darkened stairwell.

Not legendary enough to guard the gate, I suppose. Well, don't feel too badly. I doubt I will be trusted to guard a stairwell. I could hope for a small shrine in a hinterlands temple.

Killock dropped the final distance from the shattered edge of the last step to the stone floor.

He landed in a wide-open area. Statues stood in alcoves around the walls, each one a nameless hero who might have been a companion to the one in the stairwell, so similar were their armaments and stature. Several of the statues had tipped over long ago and lay shattered on the wide floor. A thick iron chandelier had come free from the ceiling to lie twisted and ruined amongst their remains.

Several passageways yawned along the wall of the room, as if it were the hub of a vast wagon wheel. He crouched and listened intently. A small trickle of water ran across the stone floor and flowed into one of the passageways, and a sigh of air came from that direction, ancient and dank. Then, soft and distant, an intermittent murmur of voices emanated from a second passageway.

The voices came again, and faded just as quickly, dancing on the edge of his hearing. Killock moved in that direction until he came to a sturdy, wooden door. Killock carefully slipped the latch and winced as the old iron grated against the frame. On the other side stood a cavernous room lined with thick pillars, with a vaulted ceiling, barrels stacked in the corners, and racks of dust-covered weapons and shields along the walls.

On the far side stood a scarred, wooden table, sturdy and crude, and several cots piled up against the wall. A lantern was placed on the table, free of dust and cobwebs. Behind the table was a door made of heavy iron bars, and Killock guessed that he was looking at a guard room or armory of some sort.

The voices were clear and came from behind the iron-barred gate. To Killock's surprise he could tell that the speakers were two young girls, conversing with hushed voices in the pitch blackness.

One was comforting the other, trying to be reassuring as she recounted a summer festival not long past and promised the other that they would both be home when the next festival arrived.

"It will be a special one," she whispered. "Since we'll both be old enough to go to the summer dance this year."

"We're never going home," the other responded, her voice a thin wisp.

"We will, you'll see," the first girl whispered back, but Killock could hear the desperation in her voice, a catch as she suppressed a sob.

Bradon, why aren't you here? Killock sighed to himself. Bradon could always be counted on to be good with children. He knew instinctively what to do to get them to laugh, to play, and most of all to do what he asked them to do. Killock had no illusions as to his own ability. *I scare them. No matter what I do.*

Killock had often joined Bradon in Irongate. Bradon's family castle was a grim pile of stone on a spire of rock perched on the western edge of the city. It was over one thousand years old, and showed every one of its winters in its weathered stone and cracked walls.

The castle always felt warm and full of life, despite its bleak outer shell. Bradon had never married and had no children of his own, but the place was filled with his cousins and the children of his retainers, a huge family that laughed and roared and bellowed merrily.

Bradon always claimed that his life in the field commanding the Temple's forces made him unsuitable for a marriage, let alone children, but Killock knew that was not the truth. *He would be an excellent husband and father, but he will never find another woman who could possibly shine bright enough to catch his eye.*

Killock wished everyone's favorite uncle was with him now. The knight did not want two scared girls in tow as he explored Highward Tor, but he could not leave them here, terrified and alone in the dark.

With any luck I can get them to the surface quickly, and hopefully convince them to find a place to hide in the ruins while I search. Although he was not sure how he was going to get them to the lowlands after that. *One problem at a time.*

Killock padded through the ruins of the guardroom to the table. He would need light, another unfortunate consequence of the rescue. The lantern was freshly fueled and it lit on the first try. Killock lowered the glass into place and turned the flow to the minimum, then approached the barred gate.

A key rested in the gate's lock, and scrape marks marred the rust surrounding it.

He carefully turned the key in the lock and the latch fell back with a resonating clunk. The girls stopped talking at the sound, and Killock could hear hushed gasps and half-suppressed sobs. He pocketed the key and crept down the short passageway. Small wooden doors stood in a row along both walls, spaced only an arm's length apart, each one secured with a heavy iron lock. The dust and dirt on the floor showed Killock that many feet had traveled it recently, and the doors had swept dusty arches on the floor from recent use.

Killock kept his voice pitched as low as possible as he called out softly at the doors.

"I am here to help you, don't worry. I am a knight of the Temple."

A small voice answered him from behind one of the doors.

"How did you find us?"

Killock fitted the key to the door's lock. It turned reluctantly and the door swung out with a groan.

"Fate," he answered as he looked inside.

The cell was a bare stone box, small enough that Killock could easily touch both walls, and only slightly longer. Ancient iron manacles hung from the far wall, but otherwise it was featureless. The prisoner stood against the back wall, pressed against it as she peered wide-eyed at the doorway to see her rescuer. She was young, fourteen at the oldest, and wore a peasant's dress and blouse, stained and torn. Tracks of tears lined the dirt smeared on her face, and her hair was a tangle of brown curls. She held a hand against the soft glow from the lantern.

"What's your name, lass?" he asked gently.

"Mairi," she replied.

"My name is Killock." He reached out and took her hand. "Come, let's get you and your friend out of here."

Mairi nodded mutely and followed him from the cell.

Killock moved to the next door. It opened to reveal an identical cell beyond. A younger girl, perhaps ten years old, huddled against the back wall on the floor. When she heard the door open she gave out a quick gasp of fear.

"It's all right, Aileen, he's helping us," Mairi whispered. Killock approached the second girl and gently took her hand. She rose uncertainly and followed him through the door.

"Is anyone else in here?" Killock indicated the other cells in the hallway.

Mairi shook her head slightly. "Not anymore," she whispered.

Killock pondered for a moment, then nodded.

"You girls wait right there while I check. Take the lantern."

He opened the other cell doors one by one. Each cell was empty, but showed signs of recent occupants.

Satisfied that he was leaving no one behind, Killock rejoined the girls. They huddled in their threadbare clothes, holding on to each other for warmth as much as support as they shivered in the chill air. Killock took his blanket from his pack and wrapped it around them, then opened the gate and led them into the guardroom.

"It's not far to the surface, but we need to search for something warmer for you to wear," Killock told them. *And they will need some sort of shoes,* he reflected with a glance at their small, bare feet as they followed him across the guardroom. *I doubt we will find anything that has a chance of fitting them. Perhaps some cloth to wrap them?* Escape through the mountains seemed less and less likely.

Half-way across the guardroom Killock suddenly stopped. *Something has changed.*

The room was hushed and full of shadows, quiet, save for the small breaths of the girls who stood behind him. The soft glow from the lantern sent black shadows across the room from each of the squat pillars. Vague shapes clustered in the dimness beyond the reach of the light, the racks and crates Killock expected to be there. Nothing moved, yet something in the chill air touched the hackles on the back of his neck.

Killock slowly drew his broad-bladed sword from its scabbard with a quiet rasp of metal on leather. The worn grip nestled snugly in his grasp, the unadorned steel blade as comfortable a weight as his own hand.

One of the girls stifled a gasp.

Killock waited and scoured the room with his senses. The uneasy feeling changed into a certainty of something wrong. It was twisted, unnatural, corrupt. A dry, cold, and ancient scent wafted into the room, the stench of a tomb. Killock felt watched, as if something waited for him in the shadows just beyond sight.

Killock handed the lantern to the older girl, Mairi. "Hold tight to that, and be ready to run when I say." The girl nodded, eyes bright with fear.

Killock drew a deep breath and the ache of bruised flesh and sinew threaded across his shoulder and chest. He pushed down the pain, made it a fact to consider, no more, a tactical weakness to shield. Then he moved towards the deep shadows by the door.

A shape waited for him, pale in the gloom. With each step the shape became clearer. Black eyes gazed unblinking at the knight, white skin as smooth as marble pulled away from a nightmare of razor-sharp fangs, and a cruel, pale blade was held in black claws.

The two girls shrieked in terror as the wight moved forward and raised its sword to meet the Templar's. Steel screamed as the blades ground together. The wight's strength was immense, and the shock of its blow traveled up Killock's arm as sizzling stabs of lightning. Killock stepped aside from the second attack and let the wight's sword rip the air as it passed. Then he counter-attacked, his sword a streak of silver in the lantern's light as he struck right, then left, then right again. The razor edge of his blade sliced long gashes across the wight's skin but could not penetrate farther, and the steel grated as if it cut stone.

The wight struck with blazing speed, its sword a pale blur. Killock met it with both hands wrapped around the hilt of his sword and still the blow drove him backwards, his sword wailing under the impact. The knight side-stepped and glided backwards to recover, and the wight's next attack whipped past Killock to blast stones from one of the pillars.

Killock's sword struck twice in a flash, a blow across the creature's sword arm, followed by a long thrust into its chest. Then his cloak pulled murderously tight around his neck as black claws yanked it and fangs sought his exposed throat.

Killock twisted like an eel and left his cloak to the wight as he spun free of the powerful grip. His sword blurred through a long arc and connected with the wight's head to open a gash along the side of its skull. The steel blade rebounded before it could do more damage, and the wight's counter came fast as a snake's strike. Killock could not get both hands up in time and took the parry one-handed. The shock of the impact twisted the sword cruelly and ripped it from his hand to clatter on the floor.

Killock rolled and came to his feet at a full run. He searched for one of the racks of weapons that lined the room. A brace of infantry spears with bladed tips stood at the ready. Killock pulled one free of the cobwebs that adorned it and turned to face his assailant.

The wight was close behind him. Its heavy footsteps crunched on the stone and broken wood that littered the floor. Killock whirled the spear two-handed, the bladed tip slicing through the air with lethal speed. The creature did not hesitate and plunged forward with sword raised. Killock let the spear flash at full extension and tore the wight from shoulder to ribs, then let the momentum of the strike spin him away.

The wight's sword collided with the floor where Killock had stood moments before, and cracked the stone with a rending shriek. Killock thrust the spear at the thing's face and jammed the point into its hollow cheek with a lunge that had his full weight behind it. The spear bent as it took the wight's weight, lifted it off its feet, and drove it into a stack of barrels that cascaded onto it with a thunderous crash.

Killock did not waste a heartbeat before his foe recovered. He ran to his sword and called to the girls. "Run to the door and wait for me there. Run!"

Mairi grabbed the younger girl by the hand as Killock sheathed his blade and turned to face the wight.

Barrels creaked and groaned as the creature stood. A terrible wound gaped across its face where the spear had driven through its cheek, and a long shriek of rage leaked through its bared fangs. Killock spun the spear again, preferring its reach to that of his sword. He backed slowly towards the door, careful to stay between the wight and the girls as he stepped around the pillars and crates that littered the room.

Talons scraped on the stone floor as the wight came at him in a rush. Killock stepped to the side and let the spear's blade slice across the thing's leg. Then he turned and brought the spear down across the back of the wight's neck. The blow landed heavily and the spear rebounded, momentarily still. In that instant, the wight grabbed the spear by the shaft and pulled savagely. Killock staggered forwards as the wight lunged to meet him with its blade. The point flashed as it sought his chest. Killock twisted desperately to the side and the blade tore through his coat. The fabric rent in a long slash as Killock sprawled to the ground at the wight's feet. One of the girls shrieked in terror.

The wight plunged its sword down and Killock released the spear to roll to the side. The pale blade cracked the stone behind him, then raised and struck down again. Killock reversed his roll and the blow missed. The wight lunged forward to grab at Killock with its black claws, and its mouth gaped open as it screamed.

Killock planted both boots on the wight's chest, rolling backwards as he took the thing's weight. Claws ripped at his legs and fangs snapped at his face as he pushed. He felt its weight shift and the wight tumbled over him to land with a crash on the floor that shook dust from the cracks in the ancient ceiling.

Killock scrambled to his feet and winced as he felt cold fire spread from the gashes in his leg. He snatched a round, wooden shield from a pile, and turned just in time as the wight fell upon him. The creature's pale sword made a sound like ripping parchment as it arced towards him. Killock raised the shield and braced. The shield shattered explosively under the blow. Splinters of wood sprayed in all directions. Killock let out a gasp of pain as his injured shoulder took the impact and he slammed into the stone pillar behind him.

He stumbled to the ground and scrambled away from the wight, his left arm numb and useless, his mouth full of blood.

"Get back!" he barked at the girls. "Down the hall, quickly!"

They fled through the door, Killock close behind with sword in hand. He could hear the heavy tread of the wight in pursuit, and he turned to face it as the girls ran. *Just slow it down, then run.*

It loomed at him, fangs bared in a rictus grin. Killock swiped at its face, then danced out of reach. The creature attacked relentlessly, and its sword struck sparks from the walls of the passage as it came. Killock ran through the doorway into the wide circular room with its ring of silent stone statues, and slammed the door with a boom that echoed throughout the cavernous space.

Killock kicked the latch heavily and bent the iron bar in its socket. It would not hold for long, but Killock needed every instant he could buy.

He glanced around the room. The two girls stood terrified in the center of the room, their eyes wide as they waited for him to tell them what to do. Behind them Killock saw the broken stairs. A short scramble up the stairs and they would be on their way to the surface.

But how could he get both the girls up there? Already the wight assaulted the door behind them, and the latch shook and pulled from the ancient wood. He could not throw the girls onto the stairs, nor did he have time to retrieve a rope from his pack to haul them behind him.

One of the other passageways? Killock chose the closest passage, the one that the small stream of water trickled into after it fell from the balcony. The girls hurried with the lantern as he pointed the way. Killock followed and turned to face the opening as he heard the door give way. The wight entered the passageway behind them, and Killock saw its cold black eyes glint in the lantern light as it pursued them deeper into the earth.

Bradon

The rope creaked perilously as Bradon settled his weight into his harness. It twisted and groaned and cut brutally into his thighs as he dangled over the yawning pit. He gripped his tether firmly in one hand and clung to the crumbling stone of the platform with the other.

"I think that might actually hold you," Brok sounded surprised.

"Let's see how funny you think it is when you are out here," Bradon growled in response.

Bradon twisted slowly until he could grab the guide rope that Wyn had strung between their landing and the balcony below. It vanished beyond the range of their torches, but Wyn promised that the other end was securely fastened.

Bradon forced himself to let go of the stone, pulled slowly on the guide rope, and waited while Brok hooked his harness to the tether. Wyn checked his ropes, and whispered something to Danielle. The two women laughed, and Danielle smiled joyfully as she rested a graceful hand on Wyn's arm.

I haven't seen Danielle smile like that in a long time, Bradon thought. *Not since we were at her home in Venaissin.* Bradon was glad that Danielle was finding pleasure in Wyn's company. An energy and a joy grew whenever she was around the young thief that was strong enough to push back the weight of her cares.

Their trip south together to Venaissin had been a pleasure for Bradon. Their ship had enjoyed fair weather that grew warmer every day, and he had spent the time with Danielle, promenading her around the deck, listening to her discourse on her family, on politics, on the court. She grew more excited the closer they came to their destination, and on the day they sighted the tall cliffs and the endless sprawling manor atop them, Danielle was ready to dance and sing.

Danielle had led him on a grand tour as soon as possible. She pointed out sites of ancient events, portraits and statues of mighty legends, and showed him banners and shields from exotic lands, every one unknown to Bradon. Much more to his liking were the places Danielle remembered from her childhood. Her favorite place to read a book, the place she and her sister would hide from their Nan, the garden where they played.

She had even persuaded him to swim with her in the wide bay at the foot of the cliffs. The terrifyingly deep water was clear, and strange shapes swam amongst the rocks and coral at the bottom. But he could not stay in the boat, not when all the children from the household were leaping and splashing like porpoises. Not when Danielle laughed and dove into the waves herself, and he watched her graceful form move effortlessly through the water, deeper and deeper, until she drifted amongst the coral like a mermaid.

It was a day he would always remember with exceptional fondness, and Danielle's happy laughter and glowing smile were the heart of it.

The day after their swim marked the end of that blissful time. They had journeyed to Danielle's home for a reason, and that heavy burden had been retrieved from the vaults the very next day. And the return to Albyn and its cold environs was much harder than the warm sail to Venaissin. The wind fought against them, and they suffered through storms as the air grew colder. Messages found them when they docked in towns for supplies, urging them to greater haste, and the weight of the responsibility she bore continued to grow heavier on her shoulders. And Danielle's laughter faded and disappeared. *It is good to hear it again, especially here in this dismaying place.*

Bradon extended his hand to pull himself farther along the guide rope. *A little bit closer, thank the Maker.*

Torchlight from the stairs above revealed a maze of glistening cuts and scratches on the rough-hewn bricks in the wall beside him. Water pattered off his helm and breastplate in a steady rain, soaked his chest and ribs, and matted his beard into bedraggled rattails. The sound of it echoed all around the pit, an endless cacophony of trickling, splashing, and dripping. Bradon secured the guide rope with one hand, and stretched carefully with the other to pull another arm's length closer to his destination.

"So," said Wyn. "That part about you and Brok going down to the door. When does that happen? Soon is it?"

Bradon glanced towards the girl's voice. Brok hung a short distance above the Templar, awkward as he dangled with weapons and armor in disarray. Beyond the soldier Wyn twirled at the end of her tether with toes pointed and head arched backwards as if she were on a swing under a tree, not suspended over a black, bottomless pit.

"Very soon we will leap into motion," rumbled Bradon. "You will see. I will float across the gap like a feather."

Wyn snorted in amusement. "Good, because I was beginning to worry that I might die of starvation."

"You could give us a push," muttered Brok as water beaded on the top of his shaved head. "Instead of just moaning."

"It'd be like watching a kitten try to push an ox," laughed Wyn.

Brok squinted up through the rain. "An ox, am I? I'll have you know even my youngest daughter can move an ox, and she's not yet out of nappies."

"Takes after her mum then, does she?" Wyn grinned. "Lucky thing."

"Alright the two of you, quiet," admonished Bradon. "I cannot concentrate on floating like a feather with you two jabbering."

The ropes creaked again as Bradon pulled in another arm's length of guide rope, then another. *Very heroic, very brave indeed.*

Bradon guessed that he must be half-way. The balcony beckoned as the guide rope sagged towards it. Save for the door, it looked identical to every other landing they had passed. Unadorned, covered in puddles where the uneven surface funneled the steady flow of water, the balcony precariously perched on top of crumbling supports. The door was a simple, wooden portal with a peaked top, bound in thick, black iron.

There was still no sign of the guardian that Wyn had encountered, and Bradon was grateful. *One archer, and this climb will become a lot less amusing.*

Another arm's length, then another. Freezing water ran freely down his arms and soaked the few parts of him that were not already wet.

A few more pulls and he would be there. The balcony appeared completely empty, the two torches smoking as they illuminated it with a wan glow. Bradon drew a knife, careful to keep it far from his harness, and gripped it in his teeth. He pulled himself over the railing and dropped to the balcony in a crouch, ready to defend himself.

Bradon searched for sounds other than the steady trickle and splatter of the water, the splutter and pop of the torches. *Nothing.* He quickly tugged his harness free and gave Brok a hand onto the balcony.

Wyn slipped over the railing as well and quietly crouched as she waited for the two men to ready themselves. Bradon passed her the two harnesses.

"Back in two shakes." A smile flashed and she was gone, a blur in the darkness.

Bradon sheathed the knife and readied his hammer while Brok unlimbered his long axe. The two warriors slipped across the balcony to take positions on either side of the door. At a nod from Bradon, Brok pushed the door open and Bradon stepped through.

He descended a short staircase, the stone steps slick with running water and so worn that they slumped in the center. The stairs opened onto a high balcony that overlooked a large room. A man's voice wavering in a strange singsong chant and an occasional clatter of metal against stone echoed in the space.

Bradon stared in revulsion at the center of the room. A dread altar had been raised on a dais. On top of it lay a young girl, no more than thirteen, spread-eagled on her back and dressed only in a coarse, woolen slip. She lay perfectly still, staring at the ceiling with unblinking eyes, and at first Bradon feared she was dead. After a long heartbeat he realized he could see a small movement as her chest slowly rose and fell with each breath.

A man dressed in the simple winter clothes of a peasant, a ragged coat and threadbare cloak, crouched at her head. In his hand he gripped a long iron dagger with a twisted blade that he held to the girl's throat and rested the tip against her skin. His head was lowered, and he slumped against the altar as if he were weakened in some way.

But the third person in the room made Bradon's face fill with fury and his hands grip his hammer until the wooden haft creaked.

A man stood next to the altar, his arms raised above the girl. He was bare-chested, his emaciated body covered in harsh tattoos that twitched and jerked as he moved. His voice cracked as he screamed twisted words from a foul tongue, and writhing, black marks on the floor pulsed and jumped to the sound. A silver Temple pendant hung against his withered chest and bounced on the end of its chain as his bald head swung back and forth in rhythm with his chant.

Bradon heard a sharp intake of breath as Brok joined him on the balcony. The soldier's face was pale with rage and he started as if to leap over the railing to the stone floor. Bradon grabbed his arm and stayed him momentarily. He had seen what Brok had not--curved stairs that descended to the floor of the circular room below.

Bradon motioned for Brok to follow him, and headed for the stairs. He kept behind the railing as much as possible. He wished Torbhin were here with his bow. It did not seem possible that he could cover the distance to the altar before the man with the dagger could kill the girl, or at least threaten to, and a quick shot from the balcony would have taken care of that problem.

They reached the bottom of the stairs without being noticed, but now they stood in full view of the priest if he merely glanced their way. The stone floor was bare save for a pattern of deep channels that radiated from the center of the dais to form a ring of entangled markings that squirmed and writhed around its outer edge. Around the outer wall statues lurked, strange shapes with unnatural proportions that made Bradon uneasy. Rough-hewn and unadorned, with their faces hidden by long cowls and their sharp, clawed hands twisted towards the ceiling, but none stood close enough to the altar to provide Bradon any advantage.

But the priest was entranced, his eyes closed in rapture as he wailed his twisted chant, and Bradon did not hesitate. The warriors closed the distance in a quiet rush, Brok moving left, Bradon right as they approached the altar.

Bradon's eyes were locked onto the dagger and the hand that held it as he drew near. The man holding it was not large and appeared to be unarmored and unarmed save for the dagger. His arm shook violently, and small drops of blood beaded on the girl's skin under the dagger's tip.

Bradon saw that the scratches on her neck were not the only wounds on the girl's body. Long slits were cut from her wrists all the way up her arms into her armpits, and her shift was stained from two parallel gashes on either side of her stomach that reached from her hips to her ribcage. Large areas of her face and torso had been covered with the strange markings, scrawled in her own blood.

Blood had run from the four cuts on the girl's body to pool into channels carved into the top of the altar, circular patterns centered under her torso, hips, and hands.

Bradon was almost close enough to grab the man with the dagger, and still the priest had not seen them. A strange subdued noise came from the hunched form in front of him, and Bradon realized that the man holding the dagger was sobbing laboriously enough that his shoulders shook.

No time for puzzles. Bradon grabbed the man's arm by the wrist and pulled back mightily. He wrenched the man from his knees and dragged him bodily into the air. A terrified face with a thin brown beard stared wild-eyed back at Bradon as the man struggled in Bradon's grasp, then the Templar brought down the haft of his hammer onto the man's skull, snapped his head back and knocked him to the floor in a heap.

A shrill scream echoed in the room as the priest opened his eyes and stared at Bradon looming at the head of the altar. The priest shouted in an unknown tongue as he leapt backward and stumbled to the floor.

Brok did not hesitate. He bellowed in rage and swung his axe as if he were chopping wood. The axe impacted heavily into the priest's neck and shoulder. The curved blade sank deep, cut through skin and flesh and bone, and lodged in the priest's chest. Blood sprayed forth from the tremendous impact and drenched Brok and the girl as the priest crumpled to the floor, limbs twitching and scraping across the wet stone.

Brok wrenched the axe free with another cry of rage and hewed the corpse again, then a third time, before finally he ceased.

Silence descended on the room, broken only by the deep breathing of the two warriors and the drip of blood onto the stone floor. The girl stayed inert and stared at the ceiling, oblivious to the carnage around her. *A small blessing.*

"Tie him up," Bradon told Brok, indicating the unconscious man on the floor, but Brok did not seem to hear him. The soldier stood poised above the red ruins that had been the priest and held his axe ready with both hands as if prepared to continue the fight.

"Brok!" Bradon's voice was strong yet not harsh. Brok slowly turned to meet his eye. "Tie him up please."

Brok became aware of his axe in his hand, and let it fall into a resting position. He nodded and moved to the unconscious man, pulling a length of rope from his pack as he went.

Bradon approached the girl on the altar. She lay on her back as the priest had left her, arms held out to her sides palms up, staring at the ceiling. The left side of her body was liberally sprayed with the priest's blood, and Bradon spent a moment wiping her face as best as he could with the rough edge of his cloak, then spread the cloak over her and tucked it under her chin as if she were asleep in her own bed. The cuts on her arms and stomach worried him, but there was not that much blood, and her color was not too pale, all things considered. He did not dare do any more until Danielle arrived, as he feared moving her might aggravate her injuries.

Then he turned to Brok.

The soldier had expertly trussed the unconscious man and left him curled on the floor with his hands and feet tied behind his back to a rope knotted around his neck. If he struggled he would strangle himself long before he could work his way free.

Brok sat on the floor next to him, slowly rotating his axe as he watched the lantern light catch the drops of blood that still covered it.

"Brok, are you alright?" Bradon asked.

The veteran soldier slowly nodded his head, his eyes never leaving his axe.

"Yes, m'lord, I'll be fine." He shook his head slightly. "I'm sorry about that. Likely we could have found out something important from him, I suppose. I just couldn't stop myself, m'lord."

Bradon understood. He had fought beside Brok for more than ten years, and he knew the man almost as well as he knew his own family, perhaps better in some ways. *His daughter Aneira was only a year older than this poor girl when it happened. She would have been sixteen I believe. Such a tragedy. It must have been more than anyone could bear, and seeing this, another helpless girl… I understand completely. I hope never to be in his position, but if I were, I know I would have done the same.*

Bradon tried to make his voice nonchalant. "He likely would have told us nothing, and he more than deserved his fate. You acted justly."

"Thank you, m'lord," Brok nodded.

A slight movement caught Bradon's eye, and he looked up to see Wyn descend the curved stairs into the room, knives held ready.

"Where is Danielle?" asked Bradon quickly.

Wyn moved closer and peered past Bradon at the remains of the priest on the floor. "She's right behind me with the twins," she answered absently. "I said I would scout ahead. What happened to him? Is that the priest?"

"I was hoping you would tell me," answered Bradon. "You are the only one here who has seen him before."

"I think so." Wyn tilted her head, tapped one knife against her leg, and chewed her lip in concentration. "It's tough to tell, he's just slops now, ain't he. Shame, because I really wanted to…"

Wyn trailed off as her eye caught sight of the girl on the altar.

"Meghan?" Wyn was shocked. "Meghan what are you doing here? What's happened to her?" She turned on Bradon, eyes fierce with anger.

"The priest was performing a ritual… but we stopped him," Bradon answered, confused. "Is this the girl from the camp? How did she get here?"

"What kind of ritual?" Wyn demanded, her eyes darting between the crumpled form of the priest and the inert girl on the altar. "Why isn't she moving?"

"I don't know. We need Danielle quickly, and we can ask the priest's lackey when he awakens. He was helping with the ritual, so perhaps he can tell us what they were doing."

Wyn glanced towards the unconscious man, and the Templar saw her eyes go wide with anger and heard her breath hiss in surprise.

"That's her father," she said softly.

Bradon turned in confusion to the man on the floor.

"Meghan's father?" he asked.

Then Wyn was past him in a blur, and she launched herself onto the prone man with fists flying.

"What did you do, you bastard! What did you do!" she screamed, the words rising into a primal shriek as she bludgeoned the man. Bradon heard bone crunch under the assault, but he could not move, so utter was his surprise.

Blood sprayed and the man came awake with a start, choking and screaming as blood filled his mouth from torn lips and smashed teeth. He struggled against the ropes but could not move. Wyn did not pause in her assault, and her scream rose into one long wail of rage as her fists fell over and over.

Bradon finally moved, and with two quick strides he was there. He wrapped Wyn in his arms and pulled her off the broken man. She thrashed against Bradon and twisted and screamed in rage, and cursed and spat on the bloody body on the ground in front of them. It was all Bradon could do to hold on to her without hurting her.

Then Brok stood above the prostrate figure.

"That's her father?" Brok demanded of Wyn, his face a hideous mask of the priest's blood.

"Brok, no!" Bradon shouted.

"Yes!" Wyn screamed.

Brok took a deep breath, and raised his axe.

"Brok! Stop!" Bradon reached for him with one hand as he tried to disengage from Wyn.

"Do it Brok!" Wyn shouted.

Brok brought the axe down. The blade fell heavily onto the man's neck and severed it completely.

Brok rested the axe on his shoulder, and turned to Bradon.

"Justice, m'lord," said Brok simply.

Bradon let Wyn go, and the girl pushed savagely away. She stepped to the severed head and spat on the upturned face.

"Bastard!"

Bradon felt tired. There was no pity in him for the dead man. He had held a dagger to his daughter's throat, and he could think of no more hideous crime.

But he knew that this death was not justice, and a deep weariness flowed from that knowledge. He could not blame Brok. What could be worse for the soldier to confront than a young girl in danger and a father who allowed it instead of protecting her?

Bradon knew that Brok would gladly give his life for a chance to go back in time to protect Aneira when she needed him the most.

And who knew what demons lurked in Wyn's past? Bradon knew little about her life before she had joined Killock, only that she had been orphaned at a very young age and had spent her life on the street. Bradon despaired to think of the daily horrors she must have confronted and endured.

Although he could not blame them, he knew that killing Meghan's father was wrong. What he had just seen was revenge, plain and simple. A bound man, helpless, killed in rage without a chance to speak for himself? Murder.

Bradon feared what it would do to them.

***

Meghan sat quietly and stared disinterestedly at the far wall of the room as Danielle examined her. The girl had not said a word to anyone, and sat or lay passively until she was moved to a new position. Her face held no expression, just dull eyes that would not focus as she slumped with her head slightly bowed, loose hair hanging down the sides of her face.

Danielle cleaned and dressed Meghan's wounds, wiped the priest's blood off her, and wrapped the girl in a blanket. Wyn hovered nearby, anxiously keeping watch over Meghan.

Bradon caught Danielle's eye but the noblewoman gave a slight shake of her head and moved instead to Brok.

The soldier stood impatiently near the wall of the room, occasionally scratching at his arms or scalp where blood from the priest and Meghan's father still coated his skin. His axe stood on the floor in front of him and the veteran rested his hands on the pommel.

Danielle approached him and he smiled viciously, a grisly split in his blood-soaked beard.

"I'm unhurt," he said flatly.

"Let me clean you up and check," Danielle said gently and the solder acquiesced with a brief nod. Danielle carefully wiped the soldier's face and head with a corner of cloth ripped from a blanket, the rough wool smearing more than absorbing the blood. Brok flinched as she worked, and Bradon saw Danielle concentrate carefully on one spot. As gentle as she was, the Templar saw Brok wince again.

Danielle stopped and poured a small amount of water from her flask over the side of Brok's head and dabbed with the cloth. Then pulled back.

"Does it hurt?" she asked.

"A bit. What did I do? I don't remember getting hit."

"I am not sure. It is like a burn, not a cut."

Brok shrugged. "It doesn't hurt much. Just itches."

Danielle nodded and handed the soldier the cloth. "Water will help soothe it."

Brok laughed, a sharp sound with no humor, but he did as he was told and gingerly wiped at this head and arms, taking far more care than Bradon had ever seen him show for much more serious wounds.

Danielle moved to Bradon, carefully removing her gloves, which had become bloody as she tended to the others.

"Is the girl alright?" Bradon asked. Meghan still sat motionless, staring at the floor from under her drooping hair.

Danielle spoke softly. "I am worried, Bradon. They need better help than water and a poultice."

"What is the matter with Brok? He was not wounded in the fight."

Danielle looked at Bradon. "When I examined Meghan I noticed that her skin was turning red in long welts, as if she had been struck by a switch. But it was everywhere, dozens of lines appearing all over. It was the places that she had been splattered with blood. I checked Brok, and he is the same. Long red welts, all over his face and arms. And he is hot to the touch, as if he were fevered. I fear that they may need a magical cure for whatever malady afflicts them."

Danielle sighed sorrowfully and looked towards Meghan.

"Of course some welts on the skin are not the worst thing that has happened to Meghan. Her wounds are very serious, especially the ones on her abdomen. They are deep and long…" Danielle paused, and her voice was uncertain when she continued. "But the wounds are not bleeding, or at least, not bleeding very much. I do not understand. A cut like that should be fatal… and yet, just a trickle. I packed the wounds with some herbs and covered them as best as I could, but they need to be properly cleansed, and then sewn. I can do neither here, and if they do start bleeding, she could easily die."

Bradon stroked his beard as he considered her words. They had come here to find the priest and stop the rituals, and they seemed to have succeeded. *Some sort of ritual anyway, even if it was not the same as the ones we have seen before. Clearly fuil crunor. But does that mean the power of this place is broken?* The catacombs felt just as threatening as they ever had, as if the walls could sense their presence. *And can we leave even if we wanted to? Will the stairs still be ensorcelled, trapping us to wander without progress, or is their power gone now? My heart tells me that there is more to this place. But we are wounded and without supplies, and I have an army that can search this place from top to bottom.*

Bradon turned to Danielle, waiting patiently at his side as he pondered. "Let us find a place where we can rest and tend to our wounds, then we will discover a way to leave as quickly as possible."

"Not in here." Danielle gave a small shudder. "It reeks of death and perversion."

"No, not in here."

***

Bradon expected to find a place where they could stop for a moment to catch their breath much sooner.

He would not return through the endless pit. They had escaped its strange magic once and he was hesitant to risk it a second time. Instead they followed one of the low passageways that led from the ritual room, and took with them the lanterns the priest had used to light it.

The passageway wound interminably through the darkness. Bradon worried about Brok. As they walked, the soldier suffered more and more. His face was flushed, and the red welts that covered it became swollen and irritated. He discarded his cloak, and then his coat, and let the icy water fall onto his skin to gain some relief. He staggered, and used his hand to steady himself against the wall.

Danielle and Wyn took turns guiding Meghan. She followed meekly, moving forward without question when they pulled her hand, stopping patiently when they held her back. Like Brok, the red welts on her face and side became irritated and grew more pronounced, but in her profound shock she did not react to them.

Cormac and Corlath brought up the rear, Cormac half-carrying his twin as Corlath struggled to keep pace on his wounded leg. Bradon was concerned that, if it came to a fight, Corlath would barely be able to stand, much less swing his axe.

They passed stone figures that stood in the alcoves between the pillars. All were cowled, with long hands that jutted from robes that hung strangely from their forms, as if the shape underneath were twisted and inhuman. Often the figure's hands would be posed aloft as if it reached for something beyond the ceiling. Bradon hated them, but they did serve as markers in an otherwise featureless path, and for that, he gave thanks.

He overheard Wyn mutter something as they passed one of the figures, and he realized that the girl was naming them. They passed Desmond and Fergus, and then Mellon, which made Wyn laugh softly as she said it. When they reached Quinn, whose long fingers were thrust through his own abdomen, Bradon felt a stir in the air from ahead. The passageway emptied into a foyer where many passageways came together before a wide opening that led into darkness filled with the roar of falling water.

Bradon sent Cormac to check two smaller doors to the side while he stepped across the floor to the wide opening.

On the other side lay a balcony suspended over a vast natural cavern filled with the rush and trickle of water. A strong breeze blew through the opening, and a fine mist coated Bradon's beard with freezing droplets. Bradon held the lantern high so that its light could shine as far as possible.

Stalactites loomed above him, slick in the light from the lantern. Beyond them a frothing motion blurred in the darkness, the rush of a waterfall that plunged far beyond the reach of his lantern and thundered on unseen rocks in the depths. Bradon searched for any platform or bridge that might allow them to cross this chasm, but the way appeared impassible. He shrugged his huge cloak more tightly about his shoulders and returned to the others.

Cormac had already returned from his search, and Bradon let him speak first.

"There's a room back there, not too large but big enough for us to fit in. Only one way in, and it's about as dry as I've seen down here."

"Good. We can sleep in shifts while the others stand guard. Only an hour I'm afraid, then we must be moving again. We will need to scout these other passageways, as there is nothing ahead but a vast natural cave, and there is no way to cross that. We will have to locate some way around."

The party stacked their packs in the small room, and Danielle laid out a blanket for Meghan. Cormac set a lantern near the door and turned it down low to conserve the oil.

Bradon dropped his pack on the floor and then paused. A slight change in the sound caught his attention, something faint and far away. He moved to the center of the foyer to wait for the sound to repeat. The roar of the waterfall echoed in the room, but nothing else. Bradon moved to the open balcony and stood, hand on the wet railing, and waited.

A faint shimmer far off across the cavern caught his eye. A glow slowly formed a long arc that grew brighter with every heartbeat. While he watched, he realized he was seeing the rim of another opening on the far side of the cavern lit by something in the space beyond it, something drawing closer.

The faint echo came again, and this time Bradon was sure that it was someone shouting, yet so far away that it almost was not a sound at all. And he recognized a sharper sound, metal on metal.

Then a scream, thin and terrified.

Bradon hurried to the room.

"There is someone out there," he announced. "On the far side of the cavern."

"You saw them, m'lord?" Cormac asked.

"I heard them, and I saw their light. I think they are fighting. At least, I heard a scream, so someone is in trouble."

Bradon considered for a moment as he surveyed the party. Then he spoke decisively, his voice booming in the small room.

"Cormac, you are coming with me. Danielle, too, we may need your skills to locate them. The rest of you stay here. Brok, guard them well until our return."

"What?" Wyn's voice was indignant. "You want me to stay here?"

"Yes, Wyn, you and Brok are staying here to look after Corlath and Meghan." Bradon's deep voice was firm, but not harsh. "Get some rest, we will be back soon."

Wyn spluttered indignantly, but before she could find words, Bradon turned and strode through the door, followed by Cormac. He was not going to waste time in an argument with Wyn, and he needed those two to have a chance to think about what they had done and hopefully regain themselves before they were needed again. Bradon was not sure that he could depend on Brok, as the soldier was clearly wounded in some fashion that he did not understand.

I'll figure it out when we get back. They need to cool off and get some rest, then they will be fine.

He chose the passageway that he thought was most likely to lead around the chasm and plunged into it.

Killock

Killock had never been so desperately weary in his life.

His boots splashed heavily in the endless puddles as he trudged along the passageway at a lumbering jog, the fastest he could run. He could not stop catching his toes on the rough stone slabs, and his feet tripped and scuffed instead of taking easy steps, but he did not have the strength to raise his waterlogged boots high enough. They were just too heavy.

Killock gulped the dank, chill air as his chest heaved like bellows. His sword arm ached with a deep fire that extended from wrist to neck, and his sword felt like it had tripled in weight. His left arm had regained some feeling, although he wished it had not. His elbow raged with a deep throbbing pain, and every step flooded shards of agony through his shoulder. He did not think it was dislocated again, but there was damage deep within the tissue.

He continued to plod forward as he chased the light that bobbed and danced ahead of him, always just out of reach. The girls clutched each other as they ran, helping each other as their bare feet splashed and skidded on the wet stones. But they kept going, and Mairi held the lantern as she led their way through twists and turns and intersections. Killock had no idea how she chose their path, and he did not care as long as they kept going.

Behind him a shriek rasped and echoed from the shadows beyond the reach of the light, much closer now, and the heavy sound of pursuing footsteps. The wight grew near again.

Three times Killock had turned to face his pursuer to delay it while the girls fled. Three times he had barely escaped, and the delays were becoming shorter and shorter.

How many more do I have in me? He wondered. *Two? One?* He cursed himself for not finishing it back in the guardroom, one way or another. He would never have a better chance.

The wight was close now, perhaps one turn back, maybe less. Several times they had gained ground by slipping down side passageways and dousing the light, then moving on once the heavy footsteps had faded, but the safety never lasted. Either the wight could track them, or the lantern light revealed them. Killock did not know, and it did not matter. He knew that their only chance of escape was to destroy the thing.

Ahead of him, Mairi turned and led them down yet another passageway. The lantern light gleamed off the wet stone walls and caused deep shadows to dance as they passed another stone figure. The statues in the passageway were much different from the ones Killock had seen when he first entered the Tor. Instead of colossal, armored knights, these figures appeared to be hooded priests or cloaked creatures carved into strange, twisted poses.

The footsteps were closer now.

"Mairi," he gasped. The girl glanced back but continued to stumble forward. "Find me somewhere open, I can't fight it in here."

She nodded to save her breath, and pushed forward faster, using her last strength to buy a few more moments.

Another twist and another turn, and just as Killock thought he was going to have to make his stand in the cramped passageway, Mairi led them into an open space.

The lantern revealed a ceiling of natural stone that ascended in graceful, undulating waves that reached beyond the light. Towering columns and curtains of smooth stone gleamed wetly as they descended towards the floor. The floor itself was also natural stone, smooth and polished, and led to a wide pool of water, still and black. Stalagmites rose up and met their cousins to create miniature ranges of mountains and tall towers made of pale stone, and monstrous shadows reared and shifted behind them as the lantern moved.

A tremendous rush of water roared dimly from far away, and Killock felt a touch of mist in the small movement of air against his face.

Deep recesses had been carved into the walls along their length as they curved from the light. Shapes lay in the recesses, withered bodies by the dozens, an ancient crypt.

It will have to do.

"Mairi, I need the lantern," Killock panted, his hands on his knees. "I am going to try to burn it. Take my pack. There's oil in a small flask. Try to make a torch. We're going to need the light."

Mairi nodded, her eyes wide with fear as she gave Killock the lantern. Killock held it in his left hand, then gripped his sword firmly in his right as he turned to face the entrance.

The footsteps neared, then stopped. Killock raised the lantern higher to catch a glimpse of his foe, but the light did not penetrate the passageway far enough. Then a shape stirred in that darkness and Killock saw the black eyes gleam in the shadow. The thing moved forward quickly, a rush of pale limbs and black claws that charged from the passageway, fangs bared.

Killock stepped to the side and deflected the pale sword with a screech of tortured steel. He swung the lantern at the creature's head, a clumsy attack with his ruined arm that missed badly. But the wight stepped back from the fire, the first time Killock had seen it retreat, even momentarily.

The wight recovered like lightning and attacked again. Killock knew he had not the strength to block the attacks directly, so he forced his exhausted legs to skip backwards as his sword flickered out and struck the wight's pale weapon to the side, and the steel blade screamed with each impact.

Another clumsy swipe with the lantern bought him a moment to regain his footing on the uneven floor, and he backed up a few more steps to buy more time and distance.

The wight followed and attacked with heavy swings of its sword. Killock parried and retreated and watched for any sign of anticipation in its movements. But there were none. The creature was as methodical and unyielding as a mill wheel grinding grain.

Another parry and this time it was Killock who staggered as his feet dragged across a slight rise in the floor. The wight clutched at him. Its long claws ripped through his tunic and scored deep gashes across his chest. Killock desperately thrust the lantern at the creature's face and forced it to pull back for an instant as the knight fled. He circled around one of the large stalagmites, careful to keep the glistening stone between himself and the wight. It pursued relentlessly, and Killock found himself once again on the defensive, as he parried blows to the left and right while he scrambled back. He lunged with the lantern to buy some time but the wight seemed to have tired of that game and brushed it aside. The wight barely missed Killock with a slash that ripped the air as the Templar threw himself backwards. He stumbled once again on the uneven floor and landed heavily on one knee.

Then a small burst of light from the side, orange and flickering. The wight turned with fangs bared to stare at the two girls who knelt on either side of a small clump of burning rags as they blew furiously to save the flame.

Killock lunged to his feet and swung the lantern into the side of the wight's head and neck. Glass shattered, brass twisted, and flaming oil sprayed onto its skin. The wight reared back and its mouth gaped wide. Killock staggered away as long fingers of burning oil spread rapidly down the wight's torso. He saw the creature's pale skin blacken and split open under the fierce blaze, and smoke poured from the wounds.

The wight whirled one way, then the other, and tried to tear the flames from its body with its claws. Suddenly it rushed across the floor towards the deep, dark pool of water. Killock was taken by surprise. He had not expected it to show that kind of reasoning, it had been so mindless in its pursuit of them. Killock lurched after it and forced his weary legs to pound across the floor towards the wight to cut it off. He dove desperately at its feet as it passed by and clutched at its legs to bring it down. The wight stumbled and collapsed to the ground in a thrashing nightmare of flaming limbs.

Killock crawled away and eased into a sitting position to watch the end. The flames covered most of the creature now. Its skin cracked and popped and burst under the intense heat, and a foul smoke filled the air. It still tried to drag itself across the stone floor toward the water, but it would never make it, Killock could see that. The distance was too far, the creature too slow.

Then a scream, high and despairing. Killock whirled and scrambled to his feet. Around the girls loomed withered shapes with long, skeletal fingers that reached for them. Killock began to run as Mairi desperately thrust her makeshift torch at them. Aileen's terrified wail echoed from the ceiling as dead fingers clutched at her and cruelly tore at her hair and legs as Mairi clung to her hand.

His legs seemed to be mired in deep mud as he strove forward. His boots pounded heavily on the stone floor yet the girls only slowly drew nearer.

A husk raised a bent dagger as it pulled on Aileen's leg, and Killock knew that he was too late. But Mairi plunged her torch into the husk's face and the yellowed skin blackened and curled in the fire. Flame licked across tufts of dried hair and suddenly the husk was ablaze. It released its hold on Aileen and Mairi dragged her away. The remaining husks retreated from the fire for a moment, then pressed in towards the girls again as Mairi swung her torch in wide arcs in front of her.

Killock's blade whirled right and then left as he leapt in front of Mairi, and the husks were hewn and hurled back from the girls.

Then a dry rustle swept through the room.

Killock rose to his feet and turned in an arc. The torch light cast wavering shadows that jumped and played across the dark recesses in the wall, but Killock saw that it was not just the shadows that moved. Withered shapes stirred and shifted, and metal rasped across stone.

Aileen screamed, a hopeless wail of terror. Killock scooped the small girl into his arm and she clung to him as he followed Mairi past the puddle of flaming oil that had been the wight, past the dark pool. Husks loomed at him from the darkness and his blade sang out and tore through them and drove them back. Sparks flashed in the dim light as the steel caught metal, rusted swords and axes turned aside and knocked from their wielder's skeletal grip.

But there were more of them, and Killock's blows slowed and weakened as his last reserves of strength dwindled.

A dark opening loomed ahead and they plunged into it, uncaring of where it led. Two more husks barred their path and Killock struck them down with heavy thrusts and drove them backwards into the stone wall of the passageway. They fled again as the torch roared and spat against the low ceiling.

The passageway opened into another wide, natural cavern filled with the deep roar of rushing water. A bottomless gulf yawned blackly at the far end, and Killock saw a wide torrent of water that streamed from somewhere far above to pour into the chasm, tumbling and echoing as it fell.

At the other end of the cave a set of doors was carved into the natural rock wall. Wide steps led up to it and twisted markings were engraved into the door's surface.

On either side of the door dark recesses lined the rock walls, and each one disgorged a husk that immediately moved towards the knight and the girls. More husks emerged from the passageway behind them, dozens of them that spread out across the uneven floor.

Killock led them to the wall, lowered Aileen to the floor, gave Mairi's hand a gentle squeeze and then released it.

"Hold the torch high, sweetheart," Killock said softly, and the girl bravely raised it above her head with both hands as tears silently flowed down her cheeks.

There was no more time to talk. Killock guarded warily as Mairi and Aileen stood with their backs pressed to the wall, and his blade drove back reaching hands and weapons and struck heavily into withered flesh. More and more of the husks pressed in and Killock could no longer carefully measure his strikes. He heaved the blade in wide arcs to the left and right and it hewed flesh and bone as his arm grew numb and the sword twisted in his grasp as his fingers weakened.

A bent spear sliced across his ribs, and a hand clutched his arm long enough for a rusted axe to catch his shoulder. Killock whirled away and knocked them back for a moment, but they pressed forward again as more and more husks moved in. A wide sweep of his sword struck down another three, yet more simply took their place. Killock took one step back, then another, as his circle of defense collapsed under their relentless assault. Aileen screamed as a husk fell to the ground a handbreadth from her, its limbs still feebly beating on the stone floor.

A Word filled the room, a deep concussion that resonated in his chest. A bright golden ray scythed through the husks in an arc and cut them down as if they were dead grass. His eyes sought the source and found a figure bathed in golden light on the far side of the room near the deep chasm. Another Word pulsed forth, and a small, thin object held in the figure's hand erupted with the blazing light of the sun as another golden ray seared forth and felled every husk it touched.

Danielle? The figure shone too brightly to see, but he knew that it was somehow, impossibly, her.

A war cry filled the room, a mighty bellow that drowned the roar of the waterfall, and Lord Bradon was there, hammer whirling in devastating arcs through the husks. The bodies tumbled away from the impacts like wooden pins.

The remaining husks turned to face the new threat and Killock sank against the wall, exhausted. Mairi placed a small hand on his shoulder and he reached to gently hold it as the room filled with the sound of destruction.

***

Killock remained seated on the floor with his back against the wall as Bradon, Danielle, and a warrior whom he remembered was named Cormac approached. The trio had dispatched the army of husks, and left behind carnage the likes of which Killock had rarely seen. Bodies lay strewn across the floor, piled two or even three deep, dozens and dozens and dozens of them.

A massive grin dominated Bradon's face as he neared. He extended a hand, hauled Killock protesting from the floor, and gave the knight a bear hug that made his ribs groan as he hung in the embrace. Bradon dropped him to his feet, then bent and offered his hands to Mairi and Aileen.

"Hello, young ladies," his deep voice rumbled pleasantly.

"Mairi, Aileen, this is Lord Bradon."

Aileen stared wide-eyed and uncertain. Mairi dropped an awkward curtsey, made more difficult by the fact that she still held her torch, then realized that Bradon's hand was still extended. Hesitantly she reached for it. Bradon gently took her hand and kissed it lightly. Emboldened by Mairi's survival at the hands of the imposing Templar, Aileen extended her own small hand, and Bradon graced the younger girl with a friendly smile and a courtly kiss on the knuckles before he straightened to his full height and turned to Killock.

"Thank you for looking after this one, Mairi. I would have missed him if something had happened to him."

"Yes, m'lord."

"Now, lass, this is Lady Danielle. She is going to have a look at you two to make sure you are all right, and I'm going to borrow Sir Killock here for just a moment," Bradon continued.

"It's alright, Mairi, I will be right over there," Killock reassured her, for the girl looked quite overwhelmed. "You did so very well. Thank you."

Mairi nodded her head and lowered the torch. She drew a deep breath and turned to Aileen. "Would you like to carry this now? It's very important but you can do it." Aileen nodded her head and clutched the torch with both hands.

The two Templars moved aside and spoke in lowered voices.

"Thank God you came when you did, Bradon," said Killock, and he shook his head in disbelief. "I could not have held out much longer."

"It was more luck than anything else," Bradon's voice dropped as he considered it. "Pure chance that I heard you and saw your light. If I'd stayed inside the room, well, best not to think on it."

"I'll try not to," said Killock softly.

"Tell me then," Bradon's eyes sparkled with humor, and he hooked his thumbs into his belt, as he always did when he thought he was about to say something incredibly funny, "what was worse for you, dealing with the husks, or dealing with two young girls?"

Killock smiled tiredly. "I may have wished to trade places with you when I first found the girls. But truth be told I am very proud of them both, especially Mairi."

"I always knew there was space in your heart for a couple of pups," Bradon beamed.

"I'm not sure about that," Killock shook his head, then continued, puzzled. "But, Bradon, how on earth did you get here? How did you cross the Léim Mhór?"

"Léim Mhór?" Bradon hesitated, confused. "We didn't go anywhere near it. We followed the trail from Nóinín Cnoc up to a gold-panning camp on a little stream called the Gylden Beck. A priest named Crassus has been up there all winter, performing rituals on the people in the camp, so we followed him here. We fought our way in through the front door once we found the place. But, Killock, I was going to ask you the same thing. I did not expect you for weeks. Was the High Road blocked? How did you catch us so quickly? Did you locate Highward Tor?"

"I did, yes," Killock's voice trailed off as he realized what they were saying. His tired mind tried to work through it, but the fog of exhaustion made it difficult. *There's no way that they could be here. Even if they had chased after me the moment I left them they could never have crossed the Léim Mhór.* Then another thought crossed his mind and he glanced over to where Mairi was talking with Danielle. *And I was so caught up trying to determine how to get Mairi and Aileen down the mountain that I never stopped to consider how on earth they had gotten up the mountain in the first place. Where did they come from? There were no signs of anyone else on the High Road, let alone two young girls.*

Killock glanced around the cavern. "Sliabh Log… the hollow mountain."

"We heard about that myth at the camp." Bradon was surprised. "You know of this tale?"

"They tell everyone," replied Killock. "Always in strictest confidence. That's where they say all of the gold in the beck comes from. The treasure rooms in the Sliabh Log."

Killock returned to where Danielle spoke softly with the girls. The knight crouched next to them and caught Danielle's eye, and the noblewoman paused and waited for Killock.

"Mairi, what village are you from?" asked Killock.

"Da works a farm for Sir Harrigan, but we stay winters in Twin Pines and Da goes trapping. Rabbits and mink and such."

"Is that the camp on the Gylden Beck?"

"Yes, sir, it is. Do you know it?"

Killock smiled. "Yes, I have been there before, but not for many years. Not since before you were born I'll warrant." Killock rose and turned to Bradon who stood nearby, stroking his beard as he listened.

"You found an entrance to this place in the hills above the Gylden Beck?" he asked, although he knew the answer.

"Yes, a black tower on a high ledge," Bradon answered.

"I found an entrance in Highward Tor," said Killock, and he paused for a moment until he saw understanding flood Bradon's face. "That is where I came from."

Bradon's brow furrowed furiously. "There cannot be tunnels linking the two so far under the mountains. That is impossible."

"No, that's not what I think. I think that they have been joined magically somehow. Perhaps that is what the rituals are for. Power to cross between."

"We found the priest performing some kind of ritual in a chamber here in the catacombs. A different one from the ones he performed at Nóinín Cnoc and the farms," Bradon's voice grew somber, and Killock realized that Bradon looked weary and there was a dullness to his gaze. He too had obviously endured hardships to reach this point, and not all of them had been physical.

"We stopped him," Bradon concluded brusquely. "Perhaps that put an end to it?"

Killock was certain that was wrong, but he could not quite put the feeling into words. *I'm far too tired and it's too difficult to think right now to sort out ancient Crunorix bullshit.*

"We shall see, I suppose," said Killock. "But we know that there was something far more powerful that lurked underneath the Tor. Danielle saw it. The magus, she named it, and now more than ever I know she must be right. I fear that this Crassus was no more than a lowly slave, tasked with providing it power."

"Aye, I had the same thought, though it gives me no pleasure to voice it," rumbled Bradon.

Killock laughed. "Since I believed that I was going to have to take on a magus on my own until just a few moments ago, I have to say that I am actually feeling a lot better about what may be next for us."

"What was your plan, poke it with your sword? Or perhaps bite it to death?" Bradon's laugh boomed through the room.

"I hadn't worked that out yet."

"Don't be too hard on yourself. That's our plan right now too." Bradon laughed again, pleased with himself, then his face brightened even further as Danielle moved to join them.

"I am glad the two of you find our situation so amusing," she chided, her face lit by a fond smile as she regarded the two Templars.

"I was just telling Killock that he was a natural with those two girls." Bradon was just as pleased with his joke a second time. "I think he's ready for his own pack."

"You are such a cruel man," Danielle teased Bradon. "Why would you doubt that he would?"

"I wasn't sure that he actually knew what a child was, to tell the truth," Bradon beamed.

"They are the annoying things that look like little people, I believe," Killock defended himself.

"I recant all of the nice things I was going to say about either of you," Danielle admonished them. "Now, will one of you please tell me what is going on?"

"I hope you will think it amusing as well," said Bradon, and he explained all that Killock had told him. Killock tried to stay focused, but his mind kept clouding with weariness, and after a while he found that he had little idea what Bradon and Danielle were saying.

His gaze wandered around the cavern. Cormac spoke with Aileen and Mairi as he showed them a trick with a coin that made the girls smile. But Killock found that the sight did not relieve a sense of unease that began to stir within him. *Something is amiss, more than the catacombs around us and the threat ahead of us. But what?*

"I agree," Danielle was saying to Bradon, and Killock tried to concentrate on her words. "Crassus was no more than a slave, a priest tasked with feeding his master power from the rituals. But there is still so much we do not know. The ritual Crassus was performing on Meghan, in a special chamber in the heart of these dark catacombs. It was very different from the ones he performed to give the magus power. What was its purpose? Something even more dreadful? And where did he learn such rituals in the first place? The boy, Colin, told us that Crassus was no more than a parish priest, traveling from village to village. Where would one with such a calling have possibly come across knowledge that even the archivists in Bandirma cannot unearth?"

"Could not the magus have shown him?" Bradon asked.

"But that is the wrong way around," Danielle shook her head in frustration. "How could Crassus have first discovered the magus, if he needed the magus to teach him the rituals? Unless he found it simply by chance."

"There is no way of knowing." Bradon shook off his frown of displeasure and replaced it with a wide smile. "As Wyn would remind us, there is no use asking these stones. We can ask the magus when we find it, if we want to."

Then Killock realized what was bothering him.

"Where are the others?" he interrupted Bradon. "Wyn, and Torbhin, and Alistair?"

"Wyn is back at our camp," answered Danielle as Bradon hesitated. "She is just fine, and she is not alone. We left her with two of our soldiers and Meghan, the girl we rescued from the ritual. But Torbhin," Danielle paused, and pain filled her eyes. "I am so sorry, but we have not seen him or Alistair since the fight in the High Meadow."

"They were together," Bradon added flatly, but Killock could hear the doubt in his voice. "I am sure if anyone could have escaped it would be the two of them."

Killock nodded silently. He felt a numb disbelief, despite the dread certainty in Bradon's and Danielle's faces. *I cannot believe Torbhin fell, not while in the company of Alistair.* A skirmish in a lonely valley was not where Torbhin or Alistair could possibly be fated to die, and the chaos of battle could make any doubt grow to dire proportions. Yet Bradon knew that as well as any man, and stood painfully certain of the worst tidings. *He cares so much, and these catacombs weigh ominously on all our hearts. That is all.*

Killock forced his thoughts away from Torbhin and Alistair, and turned them instead to the relief of hearing that Wyn was well, and nearby.

"We should summon Wyn and the others. There's no telling if this place is at all safe, or if we will ever return this way."

"Indeed, I hope that we never shall," agreed Bradon, and he strode across the cavern to the far side where it opened into the larger waterfall cave. There he cupped his hands and bellowed a mighty "HO THERE!" that echoed over the roar of the water.

The echoes faded with no response and Bradon frowned.

"No light and no reply," he grumbled. "Did they not post a guard outside? What is Brok thinking?"

Bradon took a torch and waved it back and forth, but there was still no response. The far side of the chasm remained dark and still.

"We should return, m'lord," said Cormac. The soldier stood pensively, clearly not at ease.

"Your brother?" Bradon asked.

"I don't know, m'lord. I'm not sure."

Bradon nodded. "Then we shall return to them at once."

"Perhaps Killock should stay while I make sure he is alright," Danielle said. "You look as if you could use some rest."

"He looks like a mangy old dog that doesn't know to stay away from behind a horse, is what he looks like," chuckled Bradon. "But I agree. Cormac and I will return as quickly as possible. If anything happens, head towards us."

"We will," said Danielle. "And we will be alright until you return. I have my lance if anything happens."

Killock did not wait to be told again and eased against the wall as Bradon and Cormac hurried from the cavern. Danielle knelt beside him and examined his many hurts.

"Maker, what happened to your shoulder," she gasped. "It is black from neck to elbow!"

"A wight," he replied. "Oh, and a troll. And a cliff. Pretty much everything I met, actually."

"You should have a sling to support it so that it can heal."

"That sounds wonderful," agreed Killock, and Danielle started to fashion one from strips torn from a blanket. Killock fought off a yawn as he listened to the gentle sounds around him. The rush of the waterfall, the tiny clink of the coin as Mairi practiced the magic trick, the rustle of Danielle's clothes, the sound of her humming.

Something about Danielle…

He opened his eyes and watched her work for a moment. He could not see anything different, but when she leaned in close to tie the sling around his neck he realized what he was sensing.

He smiled and relaxed against the wall.

I wonder if she's told Wyn.

Wyn

Wyn awoke with a start and peered around the dimly lit room. The small lantern was still on the table, turned so low that it provided only the softest of glows. The others' packs were still slung against the wall, and Meghan lay quietly on her blanket next to them, staring at the ceiling with vacant eyes. The room was otherwise empty.

The silence was broken only by the eternal trickle of water, but Wyn sensed a gap behind it, an echo where there had been noise an instant before.

Then boots scuffed the floor and a shadow moved in the doorway. Wyn leapt to her feet, and her hands flew to the knives kept sheathed at her back before Brok stepped forward and the lantern revealed his face.

"Damn it, Brok! I just about peed myself. Don't sneak up on people like that."

The bearded soldier regarded her silently. His eyes roamed openly across her face and body and lingered on her legs, her stomach, her chest. Wyn crossed her arms defensively as her skin crawled, the thin wool of her tunic suddenly feeling as translucent as air. *What is wrong with him?*

"Just came to check on you," Brok replied.

"Where are the others?" Wyn's eyes darted around the room.

"Corlath's on watch, out by the cavern," Brok replied, his voice low and strained. "So I thought it would be the perfect time to make sure you had what you needed."

He stepped forward and Wyn fought the urge to move away from him. He did not smell of liquor but he seemed drunk, his voice slow, deliberate and awkward. His eyes darted to and fro as he looked at her, and the red welts across his face and arms pulsed swollen and infected.

"I'm fine." She cursed her voice for sounding so small and cleared her throat. "You can go."

"You don't look fine," Brok murmured. He placed his hand over her wrists and pushed her arms down. Her shoulders hunched forward as he stared unashamedly at her breasts under her tunic.

"That's better," he said to himself.

Wyn snatched her hands free of his. "You can piss off. I hope you got a good look because that's as close as you're going to get."

"No, I don't think so," Brok replied, and he raised a hand to stroke her cheek.

Wyn flinched and glared at the soldier. His eyes narrowed and a sneer flickered across his lips.

"What's the matter, girl? Don't you want a good shaft?"

"Touch me and I'll cut it off, you asshole."

Brok scowled and his mouth twitched as he glared back at her. Then he reached out and deliberately stroked the curve of her breast.

Wyn hit him hard in the mouth and split his lip open, then grabbed for her knives.

His fist struck under her ribs like a thunder bolt, drove the air from her lungs and bent her double in helpless agony. Her knees buckled and she staggered to stay upright, one hand raised vainly in defense. The second blow smashed into her cheek and spun her to the ground. Her head bounced cruelly off the stone floor, and sparks of light flashed across her vision as blood rushed into her mouth.

Wyn fought to draw breath but could not, her diaphragm locked in agony. Blood dripped from her mouth to the floor under her face. Her feet scrabbled for purchase as she tried to rise.

A boot crashed into her stomach, a massive impact that lifted her and spun her over onto her back.

Then a crushing weight landed on her. His hand slammed under her chin, gripped her throat with the strength of iron, and cut off any chance of a breath. His knee drove into her stomach and hip and pinned her on her back.

Wyn twisted and thrashed underneath him, but could not strike with any strength. She lashed out at his face, and tore at his arm and the hand around her throat. She heard him hiss in pain, then his weight shifted as he struck downwards again, a vicious blow that connected with the side of her head in an explosion of pain and jagged blackness.

Wyn lay stunned, her hands held weakly in front of her face as he regained his grip on her throat. One small gasp of air shuddered into her lungs before his hand clamped shut around her neck again.

Pain and desperation stabbed through the thick wall of confusion that dimmed her thoughts as she pushed uselessly against his wrist and shoulder. Blood oozed from between her clenched teeth as her hand scrabbled frantically for her knives. Her fingertips brushed against the hilt and she awkwardly pulled it free, but he was ready for it. His free hand grasped her wrist and twisted it so that it was pinned helplessly. Pain screamed down her arm and her hand opened reflexively, and the knife dropped to the floor with a clang.

"No you don't, you little bitch." Brok's face twisted with rage, his eyes locked onto Wyn's.

Wyn could not answer, her throat closed by the relentless strength of Brok's grip. Darkness loomed from the edges of her vision, but she fought with all of her strength against his arm, trying to tear it free as she stared back at him, defiant. Her back arched, and her legs pushed and strained against his weight.

But he was too strong and too heavy. His hand around her neck squeezed and twisted, then Brok's other hand released her wrist and drove up between her legs.

"Let's see how ripe this peach is," he leered as he probed painfully with his fingers.

Tears of rage squeezed from her eyes as she pulled uselessly on his powerful wrist. She had to loosen his grasp, somehow, or she would suffocate within a few more heartbeats. Desperately she forced herself to lie still, then moved against the hand between her legs and arched her back against him.

His eyes narrowed as he leaned close to her, and she closed hers to slits, terrified that he would see the murder in them. Again she moved against his hand, slowly and purposefully, and she let the tip of her tongue run briefly across her upper lip.

His hold on her throat relaxed, ever so slightly, and Wyn pulled a gasp of air into her lungs.

Brok gripped her between her legs again, and Wyn pushed back and let out a small moan. *Not too much, not too soon. Don't blow it now he still has you.*

She let one hand drop from his wrist and rest on his belt. She pulled at it, fingers scrabbling across his breeches as she felt hardness stir underneath her fingertips. She forced another moan past his choking grip and ground against the hand clamped between her legs.

"I knew it," Brok whispered. He spat in her face, a bloody gob of saliva that landed on her cheek and ran down her face and neck behind her ear. "You whore."

"Brok, God's sake man, what are you doing?" a voice cut across them. *Bradon? Oh Maker, please…* But the voice was not the Templar's deep rumble. *Corlath!*

She tried to find him in the darkened room, her eyes desperate and pleading.

"Just getting some of what she's been promising," Brok answered. He removed his hand and forced her legs apart with his knee. His hand tugged on the laces of her leggings and ripped the knots loose. "Why don't you fuck off?"

"Get off her, Brok! Are you out of your mind?" Corlath limped a step closer, his voice pitched low. "Martyr's tears, what have you done to her?"

Brok shifted as he turned slightly to confront the younger soldier.

"You can either fuck off, or wait your turn," Brok growled, his face contorted by a twisted smile. "Oh yes, I've seen you, boy, you want it too. But I'm having her first, so shut up."

Wyn tried to catch Corlath's eye, frantic for help, but she could not see him behind Brok. And Brok would not let go of her throat, and kept her head pinned to the floor as he yanked at her leggings. She could only see Meghan, lying quietly on her blanket, still staring at the ceiling.

Corlath stayed silent and there was no sound save for the dry rustle of cloth as Brok pulled the last of the knots free.

Then the scrape of a boot as Corlath stepped forward.

"Get off her." His voice was dead and flat.

Brok froze, and Wyn felt his weight shift slightly on top of her as he leaned back off his knees.

"Alright, Corlath, if you're sure," Brok's voice was dangerous, a snarl in the darkness.

"I said get off her, you bastard."

Brok twisted and rose in one smooth movement. There was a crack of fist against bone as his uppercut took Corlath in the face. Blood burst from Corlath's shattered nose as he reeled backwards.

Wyn dragged a frantic, shuddering breath into her lungs as her body instinctively curled into a ball. Behind her, the two men struggled and smashed into the wall as they twisted and struck out at each other.

Get up get up! she screamed at herself, but her body would not respond. Her legs would not straighten and the floor swayed from side to side, as if it were riding the peak of a towering, gale-wracked wave. A second breath shuddered through her, and then a wracking cough sprayed blood onto the floor.

A blow echoed across the room, and then another, and Wyn heard Brok grunt in pain as Corlath lashed out and scored. A crash shattered across the room as Brok closed with the younger soldier.

Wyn forced herself to roll to her hands and knees and drew deep breaths, her body shaking with effort as her mind screamed for her to rise to her feet.

Corlath wrapped one arm around Brok's head and trapped it against his side as he rained blows against the larger man's unprotected ribs and flank. He struck heavily again and again as Brok fought against his grip. Brok lifted Corlath and smashed him into the wall. His shoulder drove into the younger man's midriff with such force that Corlath cried out. Corlath staggered to the side as his wounded leg collapsed underneath him, but he did not release his grip and dragged both of them to the ground.

He needs my help. Get up you stupid bitch! Wyn got one shaky foot under her, and pushed, only to sag against the wall as the room swam.

With a roar Brok reared and slammed on top of Corlath. Corlath clamped his other arm around Brok's neck and pulled. His back strained as he levered Brok's head backwards. Brok drove a massive hand under Corlath's jaw and pushed. Wyn heard Corlath's breath hiss through clenched teeth as his head was driven backwards. His arms slipped from Brok's neck.

Brok moved like a snake. He twisted as he wrapped his legs around Corlath's chest and then heaved backwards on his right arm. Corlath screamed as his elbow locked, then shattered with a terrible crack.

Brok released Corlath and stood up, his breath heavy as he towered over his opponent, red welts raw across his skin. Corlath writhed in agony, his legs convulsing uselessly on the stone floor. His left hand drew his knife, but Brok stood on his wrist and ground it under his boot until Corlath's hand opened and the knife dropped to the floor. Brok scooped it up, and knelt heavily on Corlath's neck. He paused for a moment. His chest and shoulders rose and fell deeply. Then with a quick movement he bent and sliced Corlath's throat with the knife. Blood sprayed across the floor from the long, deep cut, and Corlath choked out a gasp that bubbled in his throat.

Then Brok rose to his feet and turned to Wyn.

Blood had soaked his chest and arm, and Wyn saw that one side of his mouth was twisted where it had been smashed. Blood poured from his ear and created a slick, wet sheen into his beard and down his neck. He slapped Corlath's knife casually against his thigh as he stared at Wyn.

Wyn drew her remaining knife.

Brok smiled hideously, lips stretched over bloody teeth. "You want to play, too?" His voice was strangled and harsh. "I'll fuck you to death if you do."

"Come and get me," Wyn seethed through bared teeth, and spat blood on the floor in front of him. "We'll see who gets fucked."

Brok came at her with no hesitation. The knife flew at her face in a vicious lunge, the blade a shadowy blur as it flashed towards her.

Wyn dodged to the side and did not let the powerful soldier close with her. The world pitched and swam as she moved and shards of pain sliced through her head, but she forced herself to ignore them. Energy surged through her limbs as rage gave her the strength to fight and survive.

Brok lashed out again and again. A wide cut sailed over her head as she ducked low, then a quick jab turned into a feint as he followed with a thunderous punch that caught her on the shoulder as she twisted away, and sent her tumbling to the floor.

She rolled and came to her feet, then whirled to her left as Brok lunged forward with his knife. Her blade scythed out as she moved and left a long, red slice along his arm and sprayed blood in an arc across the wall.

Blood frothed around his mouth as Brok roared like a beast and lashed out again. Wyn felt fire trace across her face as the knife flashed in front of her eye and the point scored her from eyebrow to cheek.

Brok followed savagely with knife and fist. Wyn scrambled to the side, swept a blanket from the floor and flung it in his face.

Brok threw it aside, but Wyn's blade was right behind it. Her knife ripped a gash across his forehead, and Brok stabbed at her blindly as he clawed frantically to clear the cascading blood from his eyes. She guided his lunge to the side and let it pass close over her shoulder, and then she stabbed upwards under his extended arm. Her blade bit twice before he could pull away from her.

Wyn pursued him relentlessly. She passed him low and to the side. Her blade laid open his thigh as she went, then she leaped onto his back and wrapped her legs around his shoulders as he staggered to the ground. She landed on top of him, drove her knife into his neck and felt it grate against bone as it sank in deeply.

She screamed rage and death as she plunged the knife into his throat and ripped it out again. She felt him twist beneath her but he was wild, his strength wasted as he thrashed and beat against the floor.

She stabbed again, and again. The thrashing stopped, became twitches, then nothing. She screamed and drove her knife over and over and carved the meat that lay under her until she had not the strength to lift her arms.

The room spun around her and the wound across her face blazed like fire. She retched heavily, hunched on hands and knees, until there was nothing left inside. Shivers wracked her body, and her fingers sought out the blanket that Brok had hurled to the ground, in need of its protection once again.

She pulled the blanket tight around her as she huddled, knees held to her chest, against the cold, wet wall.

Benno

"Well, your Grace, we have discovered a few things, but there appears to be something much more interesting that we haven't found," Reverend Whitebrooke's voice rumbled and echoed off the stone walls in the empty passageway.

"What on earth does that mean?" asked Benno as he hurried to keep pace with the Archivist's long strides.

"We may have some very important items missing from the archives," declared Whitebrooke as he swept through the wide doors into the archives, sucking Benno in his wake. "At least, Reverend Turlough believes we have."

Benno came to a halt in the middle of the room. Whitebrooke continued walking for a moment, then stopped and faced the Bishop.

"Reverend Turlough believes?" Benno asked. "And you think this is more than just dementia?"

Whitebrooke pondered the question longer than Benno would have guessed necessary before answering. "It's true he has more bad days than good. I'm not sure how much of his mind is left at this point." Whitebrooke resumed his journey across the reading rooms. "He seems very sure about this, though."

Benno sucked in a deep breath. *Maker, please give me the patience to deal with an old fool.* Benno reflected that it may not have been the most charitable of prayers, and followed Whitebrooke.

Whitebrooke led the Bishop to a smaller room set aside for the use of the archivists. Whitebrooke opened the door and stood aside to allow Benno to enter first.

Inside the room the archivists stood and sat amidst a shambles of haphazardly placed books, stacks of scrolls, piles of parchments, and rolls of tapestries. Broad, sturdy tables supported the piles, but no scrap of free surface could be seen. Lanterns dotted the room and cast a bright light over the mess.

The archivists had been talking loudly when the door opened, but silence doused the conversation in the musty room as Benno walked through the door, giving him some small satisfaction. Whitebrooke pushed into the room and completely filled what little space remained as he glanced around at his charges.

"Martyr's tears, is it that difficult to remember?" demanded Whitebrooke.

Benno smiled inwardly as a chastised chorus of "Good afternoon, your Grace" floated around the room.

"Now then," Whitebrooke continued. "Turlough, tell the Bishop what you told me."

The old archivist huddled in a thick blanket in the corner of the room with Meara at his side. He blinked in surprise as he heard his name and stared around the room with confused eyes.

"What did he say?" he asked Meara.

"Tell the Bishop about your book," Meara prompted.

"Very well," muttered Turlough. "The *Sanguinarium* is missing."

Benno waited for more, but Reverend Turlough sat quietly and munched his gums, pleased with himself, and ventured nothing else. Benno turned helplessly to Whitebrooke.

"It's an ancient tome," Whitebrooke explained. "Reverend Meara, tell the Bishop what you have discovered."

"We scoured the archives to uncover any record of actual Crunorix rituals," Meara spoke clearly and with certainty. "But because of the destruction of all depictions of fuil crunor rituals ordered at the Conclave, most of the surviving records provide only vague descriptions and unhelpful guesses."

"Except for the *Sanguinarium*," Turlough croaked devotedly.

"Which is?" Benno prompted.

"Well, your Grace," Meara's voice grew hushed, as if she were in the presence of a hallowed relic of a revered saint. "The *Sanguinarium* was a tome of fuil crunor rituals written by the Crunorix magi themselves, brought from the Black Grave before Ruric's knights sealed it."

"And when you say it is missing?"

"That's right, missing!" Turlough choked in fury. "The vault empty. I have looked everywhere for it, but it is gone!"

"You don't mean…" Benno looked around the room, stunned. "It was here?" All of the archivists looked immensely proud, but the idea that such a thing had been stored underneath Bandirma all these years made Benno's flesh crawl. Representations of fuil crunor rituals had been ordered destroyed for a reason, and now it was revealed that the worst of the lot had been in his cellar the whole time. "How on earth did such a thing come to be here? And why didn't I know about this?"

"It isn't actually the real thing," explained Whitebrooke. "As Reverend Meara described it to me, even without the lich priests to command it the *Sanguinarium* was too powerful to contain. So King Ruric's sages made two copies and then destroyed the original."

"One kept in Fellgate Castle, the other brought here," mumbled Reverend Turlough.

"And, as for why you didn't know, I did not know, myself," grumbled Reverend Whitebrooke. "It appears that Reverend Turlough was the only one who did know, and he kept that knowledge to himself."

"Of course I did," snapped Turlough. "It was to be kept secret until it was needed. I haven't told a soul since Reverend Ezekiel revealed it to me."

"And you are positive you remember the place it was kept?" Benno could not keep the doubt from his voice.

"Of course I'm sure," said Turlough peevishly. "Ezekiel showed it to me before he left, and we warded it and veiled it and I haven't opened it since."

"When Ezekiel left?" asked Benno. "Twenty years ago? That was the last time you saw this book?"

"Don't be ridiculous," snapped Turlough. "I just told you it was when Reverend Ezekiel left."

Benno stifled his response. *Patience!*

"Thank you, Reverend Turlough, Reverend Meara," Whitebrooke said firmly, ending the conversation.

Benno and Whitebrooke closed the door solidly behind them and left the archivists to pour over their books and scrolls. The two priests slowly walked across the reading room floor, Benno deep in thought, Whitebrooke comfortable to wait in silence.

They reached the broad windows before Benno turned to Whitebrooke.

"Is he demented? Is he confusing some ancient legend with reality? Surely there wasn't really a treatise on fuil crunor sitting in our archives since before the Cataclysm?"

"It does seem unlikely," agreed Whitebrooke. "It's a shame we can't ask Ezekiel."

"It is," Benno agreed. "And why would he have told Turlough and not you? I know you were close before he left, and it seems like something an Archivist would tell his successor."

"If Turlough is right, and there was such a book here, then I can only guess that Ezekiel was trying to protect me by hiding its existence." Whitebrooke sighed deeply. "After Aislin died… well, Ezekiel was probably right that I would not have behaved well, if I had known."

"You were not yourself. How could you have been, after such a loss?" *To lose her to such simple mischance was unfair beyond enduring, and for a time it seemed her death would take both of them. But that was long ago, and there is no need to linger now.* "Even if it were true that the book was in the archives, how could someone make off with it? No one even knew it was there, and the archives are guarded and warded."

"True," Whitebrooke nodded his head. "Except Ezekiel… he knew it was there. I have heard that he took a great many books with him when he left the archives and stored them under that temple of his."

"That is true," pondered Benno. "Bradon's report said that Nóinín Cnoc was set on fire after the ritual was performed. I wonder if its storeroom was destroyed too."

"If not, this book may still be there."

"I will send a message to Bradon and Danielle," Benno nodded his head. "They may be able to find it, if it is there. While we wait to hear from them, you should investigate to see who might have known, or suspected, its existence. Turlough claims he told no one, but I cannot believe that. He could not keep a choice piece of knowledge like that from others for long. How else would they know how smart he was?"

Whitebrooke laughed, a booming sound that startled the room. "True enough. At least we can determine if this is a recent dementia, or if he has believed it for longer."

Benno nodded his head and left the Archives, his head bowed in thought as he went. Whitebrooke watched him go, then strode purposefully to his work.

Benno paused briefly at a scriptorium to scribble a message to Danielle, and hurried through the Atrium and across the bailey.

He took a deep breath as he readied himself to climb the Tower of Tithius again. *If I can think of some reason the tower needs to be used for something else, I could move Sebastian and his flock somewhere less vertical. Perhaps a little cottage on the hilltop. Downwind of the gardens, of course.*

Benno sighed despondently and started up the stairs. *It wouldn't be so bad*, he told himself, *save that this must be the fifth time I have had to make this climb in the last three days.*

Since the Queen had arrived, there had been no end of special messages that needed to be sent or received. Trying to locate Danielle and Bradon had suddenly become very difficult. Urgent messages to the Temple forces in the hinterlands came back unopened or were answered by Sir Lochlan, who could only report that Bradon and Danielle had taken a small force and left

Nóinín Cnoc, leaving orders that the army should split apart to occupy strategic positions in the area.

The birds he sent to Danielle had elicited no response at all. The last message he had received from her was now over a week old and spoke of tracking those responsible for the desecration of Nóinín Cnoc into the hinterlands. Benno was frustrated, but he knew that there was little he could do from Bandirma but wait.

Unfortunately, the Queen was not so patient. Every day Benno received a request to meet with the Queen and her advisors, and every day they pressed him for news of Danielle, and failing that, for his acquiescence in granting the Queen the sword. Benno feared that soon the Queen would lose patience and begin her own search, and Benno knew that he would have little chance of controlling the situation after that. What he needed was some real information about Bradon, Danielle and Killock. He could present a fait accompli to the Queen and bypass the sticky issue of the sword altogether.

Benno's boots thumped up the stairs rhythmically. He started counting the stairs at the bottom, but as always, his mind wandered to more interesting thoughts and he lost count somewhere after fifty.

He reached the landing below Sebastian's apartments where he would normally stop to regain his breath and his dignity, but he could not be bothered this time. He pushed his way up the last flight of stairs and into the ramshackle room before he realized the room was occupied. Two men sat at ease and conversed over cups of Sebastian's ghastly, weak tea. Benno fought an urge to flee down the stairs at the sight. *Perfect…*

Karsha Hali grinned at Benno from his nest in the stained, yellow chair, the tattoos on his cheeks contorted into strange new patterns with his gap-toothed smile. Sebastian peered at him somberly, his frown of disapproval etched deeply into the lines of his face.

"My goodness, Bishop, you look quite over-exerted. I believe you are perspiring! Are you quite well?" Sebastian smirked.

Benno mopped his face with a handkerchief. "Just the climb, Sebastian," he panted. "Invigorating."

"I see," said Sebastian. "Would you care for some tea? We have just brewed a pot for our guest here."

"No," Benno said quickly. "No thank you, I won't stay. I can see that I am interrupting your conversation."

"We talk about the birds," said Karsha Hali morosely. "There is so much I did not know."

Sebastian nodded serenely in agreement, but Benno could not fail to note the gleam of mischief in Karsha's eye as he mocked the priest. Benno stifled a smile as Sebastian continued. "What brings you here, your Grace? An important message?"

"Of course." Benno looked around the room for a place to sit to catch his breath. With the stained yellow chair claimed, the Bishop was left to perch on the edge of Reverend Sebastian's table. Benno decided he would simply stand rather than risk the ignominy of upsetting the table with his weight. He moved to the window and breathed in the chill, outside air. It made him shiver as it touched his sweat-beaded skin, but it smelled infinitely better than the rank odor of the room.

"My legs are too weary to carry me down the stairs, yet," Karsha continued, oblivious. "I will sit here and contemplate mortality while you send your message."

"Ah, Temple business though, you see." Reverend Sebastian peered down his nose at his visitor.

Karsha scratched absent-mindedly at his ear. "Of course."

"It's all right," Benno stayed the Bird Master's response. "I am sure it will not matter one way or the other if our guest is here."

A slight smile played across Karsha's thin lips.

Reverend Sebastian looked aghast. "Your Grace, you cannot possibly…"

"Right away please." Benno held out the small metal tube that contained the message.

Sebastian spluttered helplessly, but his acolyte scurried away without hesitation and brought back a carrier pigeon held gently in her hands. Benno watched her secure the tube to the bird's foot, and Benno sealed it with his ring.

The acolyte carried the bird to the roof of the tower while Benno returned to the window and looked over the rushing river to the township on the other side. A light dusting of snow crusted the rooftops and the distant hills, but the day was not cold enough and the layer too thin for the snow to stick to the ground. Despite the cold air, the town was bustling. Several stalls sold wares in the square; converted wagons filled with winter produce, handmade knits, candles, and other cold-weather necessities. Benno saw one with a load of winter squash and another that sold furs. Several wagons slowly crossed the bridge, loaded with coal for the hundreds of fires and furnaces Bandirma required to keep warm.

Benno stifled a yawn as Sebastian prattled about the proper construction of dovecotes. A barge launched from the lake dock, and Benno watched the bargemen use long poles to maneuver the heavy vessel around the squat fishing boats to the mouth of the Abhainn Fuar. No large boat could pass from Loughliath into the river due to the low arches of the Bandirma bridge, so cargoes were hauled through the town to the river dock if a river boat was waiting, or were transferred to one of the long, low barges that could clear the bridge. This barge had a massive pile of crates lashed to it that weighed it very low in the water. Benno was curious if it would clear the rapids below the bridge. The bargemen pushed nimbly and launched themselves into the strong current. The barge sped precisely between two of the bridge's pillars and shot into the wash below. The barge seemed to dip perilously several times but always emerged, the bargemen nonchalantly tapping their poles against the stone slabs of the waterway to guide their craft.

With a frantic flurry of wings, a pigeon swooped past the window. It arced over the town and flew diligently to the northwest.

"Faithful creature," said Karsha. "Stupid though."

Benno had not heard Karsha move next to him at the window. The smaller man appeared to be a strange creature from some fantastical story. He had so many robes and cloaks wrapped around him that he looked almost spherical, a mass of ragged cloth, patches and fur. His wrinkled head poked from the top and his two scrawny feet poked from the bottom.

"Stupid?" scoffed Sebastian. "They are among the fastest and most reliable of messengers. Ridiculous to suggest otherwise."

"Oh, yes. Fast," agreed Karsha. "Pitiful to try so strenuously when all know the gods laugh at them and curse them to serve men. No, they are only fit for a pie." He croaked horribly and Benno grew concerned until he realized the tiny man was laughing.

"Would you prefer then to consign your messages to a horseman?" Sebastian shook his head sadly. "Slow, and far less trustworthy."

"No. Here is your answer and my reward for waiting so patiently," and Karsha indicated the windowsill.

Benno turned to the window as a bird landed on the sill. It was a huge raven, glossy and black. It spread its wings, shook itself, and settled to preening its feathers into place. Benno guessed the visitor was tall enough to reach his knees if it were standing next to him, and its black eyes carefully watched Benno from its perch.

"Ah, Bran, good to see you," crooned Karsha as he stepped to the raven.

The southerner extended his hand to the bird, who peered at him for a moment before it carefully dropped a small bone cylinder onto Karsha's outstretched palm. Karsha's hand disappeared into his robe instantly, and reappeared with a small cob of corn stolen from the kitchen. The raven cawed loudly, snatched the corn, and settled on the sill to tear it to bits.

"But," said Reverend Sebastian, stunned. "Ravens are not trained to carry messages. And even if one was, how could it know to come here?"

"True, they cannot be trained, all know this," agreed Karsha good-naturedly. "They watch and listen for the gods, so how could they also serve men? No, they do it because it pleases them. They wish to see what people are doing and they want to know their secrets. If you ask them nicely and let them in on the secret, they will gladly join in the conspiracy. Of course, they tell the gods everything they hear, so you must be careful. As to how he knew to come here, I told him," Karsha shrugged. "How else?"

The raven cawed loudly at this, and Benno felt that it sounded like laughter.

"Bran says he could have found me even if I did not tell him where I would be," chuckled Karsha.

Benno had to smile. It certainly did sound as if the raven was mocking Karsha, and for that the Bishop decided he liked the bird. He watched it greedily gulp the last of the corn, caw harshly again and launch from the window. It flew down to the lake docks, most likely to terrorize the fishermen.

Benno was about to turn his back on the window when three riders on the bridge caught his attention.

They reached an easy gallop as they crossed the center point of the bridge. Foot traffic huddled against the railing as they passed. All three riders were armored in heavy steel, and the two at the back bore shields and lances. The lead rider wore a black cloak over grey scale armor, and rode a magnificent chestnut stallion. His head was bare and Benno could clearly see the iron color of his close-cropped hair as he rode.

"Where is General Boone going?" asked Benno.

"The General returns to Kuray," Karsha shrugged. "A lord is accused of murdering another lord. A man named Lucious. Boone goes to render judgment since the Queen is occupied with her visit here. I feel this will be unwelcome news for Lord Lucious."

"Mmmm," agreed Benno.

Karsha wagged a finger at the Bishop. "I have been told of your modesty, but Gabrielle knows she has you to thank for bringing this rogue to justice. In fact, Lucious blames Lord Bradon by name."

Gabrielle? Does she really allow such familiarity?

Benno thrust his hands deep into his robes for warmth. It was difficult to decide whether the chill air from the window or the foul smell in the room was the worse alternative.

"Joyous news, of course," Benno replied, and he started toward the stairs. "If you will excuse me…"

"I will walk with you." Karsha hurried across the room and joined the Bishop. "That way if I fall and die someone besides the gods will hear my last words."

The two men descended the stairs in silence for several landings before Karsha spoke again.

"It was good fortune that brought Lord Bradon to the hinterlands."

"Fortune? I am not sure I would call it that," answered Benno carefully. "As I am sure you know, a temple was attacked and destroyed, and the priest and the families who lived there slaughtered. It seemed appropriate to send aid."

"Yes, terrible deeds. And such evil cannot be left unchecked. It offends the spirits of the world," said Karsha. "That is why the Queen ordered Lord Lucious to bring justice to those responsible."

"It is heartwarming to see a monarch so concerned for her people."

"All think so." Karsha sighed contentedly, then extracted a currant bun from his pocket and nibbled on it as he walked. "Mmmm. Your bakers are very good. I like these currants. Small, brown, and shriveled, yet so sweet on the inside."

Benno laughed despite himself. As frustrating as Karsha was, Benno could not help but appreciate his nature.

The two men walked in silence again as they slowly descended to the base of the Tower of Tithius. Karsha was unaffected by the endless stairs. He hopped and scrambled down the steps with his awkward gait, then waited for Benno to join him. Benno moved at a more leisurely pace, slow and steady.

They reached the bottom of the stairs and stood in the doorway that led to the outer bailey. As always, all was ordered chaos between the River Gate and the temple doors, and Benno was content to watch it for a time. *Perhaps Karsha will grow bored and wander off?*

"So many people to worship just one god," wondered Karsha. "He must be very mighty to need so many people to sing his praises. Does he listen to them all, or just to you, I wonder?"

"He listens. The praises are for us. They remind us of what we owe Him."

"I have something to speak to you about, something more important than birds, or even raisins." Karsha paused to brush crumbs from his robes.

"Yes?" asked Benno. *That didn't take too long to get to, thank the Maker. I was afraid he was going to chase me all the way to my chambers.*

"I must ask you slowly, because the gods like to hear a story. Also because you play this game very well, and I do not want to be the pigeon," Karsha grinned. "So, we begin. The Queen wishes me to ask if Lord Bradon has caught the ones who destroyed your temple and her farms. Since Lord Bradon has arrested Lord Lucious and taken his men, she hopes that he has also taken up his task?"

"She need not be concerned. Lord Bradon will take care of it."

"I see. I will then tell her that she need not be concerned about five hundred soldiers moving about her lands, deposing her lords, commandeering her sworn men."

"I am sure you have lived here in the north long enough to know that the Temple and its forces, both the priesthood and the order of the Temple knights, owe allegiance only to the High King and are granted rights to bear arms and protect the Temple regardless of which kingdom those temples are in." Benno felt he had sounded nicely pompous giving that little speech. *It would be difficult to hear that and not be annoyed.*

But Karsha was unaffected.

"The High King, yes I have heard of him. He was in a story I think? A great man who did great things a great long time ago. The gods enjoyed watching him, but now? Now there is no such a thing as a High King, not for many hundreds of years. And the Queen feels that assembling your temple garrisons and occupying her lands is beyond what the High King envisioned when he granted the Temple those rights."

Benno dismissed the idea with a wave of his hand. "How so? A temple was destroyed, the Queen's vassal was unable to prevent it, was unable even to prevent similar attacks on the villages which were his to protect. I cannot conceive of a clearer call to action."

Karsha cackled like an old crone. "The Queen disagrees."

"Then perhaps you, as her loyal counselor, should advise her. The Queen is young and has such compassion for her people. It is understandable that she should wish for some tangible success from her lords. And from her counselors." Benno stepped from the doorway into the bailey and turned to face the southerner. "But in the absence of any kind of said success, the Temple will exercise its right, granted by the High King, to defend itself and its people. If the Queen wishes to see the Temple forces return to their garrisons, she should ask her counselors why they had to leave in the first place."

Karsha stared at Benno with amusement. "You will be pleased then when I tell you that I agree with you, and so does the Queen. That is why General Boone will take the northern army into the hinterlands as soon as he has finished hanging Lord Lucious. Ha! I must say *judging* him, not *hanging*, for a bit longer. When the General arrives, your army may go home to its temples and sing praises to your god again."

"When we think our temples and the people of the hinterlands are safe again, then, yes, I will gladly order my knights to return to the temples. But not before then."

"You doubt that the General will be successful? How is that possible? He has won more battles than I have had farts. Unless you fear the challenge he faces? A few raiders, I think?"

"Do you?" Benno asked.

Karsha ignored the question.

"Now it is time for me to ask you my next question. Are you ready?" Karsha grinned again.

"Of course, it is my privilege to satisfy the Queen's curiosity," replied Benno easily.

"Good. We have already talked about the Weapon that Lady Danielle, the Queen's sister, took from their home at your orders."

"Lady Danielle uses her Weapon as she sees fit. It is not mine to order, nor is it the Queen's."

"Yes, you have said so," Karsha bobbed his head. "But you have not said where the Queen's sister is, or the Weapon. The Queen would like to speak to her sister, so she would like me to ask you again where she is. But before you answer, it is fair to tell you that I know she is with Lord Bradon. So, if you are ready. Where is Lady Danielle, your Grace?"

"Why do you think she is with Bradon?"

"Because Lord Lucious has told us she was there. 'A woman of extraordinary beauty, with raven hair and dark skin, from the south by her accent'."

"If that's true, then why ask me where she is?"

"Because that was many days ago, and we would like to know where she is now."

"So that you can take the Weapon from her."

"Of course not. The Queen wishes to ask her to give it to us."

"I will let her know the next time I talk with her. Now then, is that all?"

Karsha looked surprised. "No, not all. But be untroubled, because now is the time for me to tell you something. Something very important. And I tell you this because I have one more thing to ask you, and I want you to know this important thing before I ask you."

"You want to tell me something important, right here?" Benno glanced around the busy courtyard.

"No, but you stopped walking."

"I suppose I did," laughed Benno. "Alright then, where shall we go to speak?"

Karsha scratched one of his pendulous earlobes, then motioned for the Bishop to follow him. "Come with me. I have something to show you that is part of this story."

Benno followed Karsha through the temple to the apartments that had been given to the Queen and her entourage. Karsha had chosen a cramped room on the outer wall, usually given to a squire or some other functionary. The window had been left open and gusts of chill air had blown chaos into the stacks of parchment left lying about in the room, scattering them into every corner. Luckily the fire had been allowed to go out and the hearth was cold, or else Benno feared that the room might have caught fire from blowing sheets of burning parchment.

"What a mess," Karsha fussed. He gathered up a few sheets of parchment and held them dejectedly as he looked for where they might go. "Wind is a spiteful spirit. It repays me with this vandalism for not telling it a story today."

Benno held out a piece of parchment helpfully. "You said you wished to show me something."

"Yes," said Karsha, and he dropped the parchments and rummaged in the pockets of an old pack that had been left on the floor. "While I find it, let me tell you the story I promised."

"Far to the south lies a vast jungle. The gods of the sky there are quarrelsome brothers who cannot agree on anything, so in this land it rains every day and also the sun shines every day. Because of this, the jungle is very large and filled with the greatest plants and creatures in the world." Karsha pulled a small, wooden box from the pack and carefully held it in both hands.

"In this jungle live terrible creatures called harimau. They are many times the size of a wolf, larger even than a bear, and they hunt everything that lives. They can hide in the shadows, they can swim the fastest rivers, they can climb the highest trees. Only the greatest or foolhardiest warriors will hunt them.

"The god of the harimau is named Nharghrod. He is a spirit that all other spirits fear, as all other creatures fear the harimau that worship him. He can only be seen if he wishes it, his claws can rip the strongest armor or scales as if they were parchment, and his fangs are as long as your arm. And Nharghrod is cunning."

Karsha paused to hop into a chair by the window and he wrapped an enormous bear-skin blanket around himself before he continued.

"One day, many years ago, a young wizard traveled to the jungle. He wished to capture the fearsome Nharghrod and make him his servant. The gods laugh at such pride, so the wizard knew they would not help him, but he also knew that the gods would watch to see such a thing.

"The wizard searched the jungle and asked all of the creatures and spirits 'do you know where Nharghrod lives?' but none would help him. They feared what Nharghrod would do to them if he found out they had helped the wizard. Word reached Nharghrod that a wizard was seeking him, so he decided to stalk this wizard and kill him.

"Of course, the wizard did not know that Nharghrod hunted him, but many other spirits served him. One of his servants, Bran the Raven, came to him and told him that he had seen Nharghrod approaching through the jungle, for no secret can be kept from Bran.

"The wizard prepared himself for the struggle to come and waited. Soon Nharghrod approached. The wizard could not see him or hear him, but he could feel the power of the spirit draw closer. Cruel eyes watched the wizard from the darkness. Savage rage and hunger yearned for him. It was the most terrible thing the wizard had ever felt, and he knew that he would likely die that day.

"It is a good story I think. Nharghrod is a terrible spirit for he is implacable, unrelenting. He hunts and kills. But like all spirits he is also part of this world. A scary part, yes? But still a part."

Karsha paused and brought the small box from inside the bear-skin blanket. He held it in his lap and stared at it intently.

"But now there is another watcher who is more terrifying than Nharghrod. I have seen it. There are eyes that search from inside a terrible darkness. They are cold and are not part of this world. And those eyes hunger for more than Nharghrod ever did." Karsha raised his glance to the Bishop. "I know you have seen them too."

Benno nodded slowly. There was no point in denying it.

"Yes, so now I think that it is time for us to stop playing," Karsha continued. "This shadow is more powerful than any spirit I have seen, and it grows stronger. And yet we keep secrets and squabble as if we were pigeons who fight over crumbs when we should be harimau who hunt our prey. So now it is time for me to ask my last question. Bishop, shall we help each other?"

Benno went to the window and looked out. It was placed high up the southern side of the immense hill, far above the rolling farmlands that covered the eastern shore of the Abhainn Fuar. He saw smoke from a dozen farm house chimneys as it rose into the grey clouds above.

"Snow tonight, I think," he said softly.

Then he turned to face the little wizard.

"You are right, Karsha, I have seen the eyes you are talking about, and so has He. For months we have seen them. But since we are no longer playing the game, I can tell you that the reason we have not told you about it is that we are not sure who we can trust. This power has servants who have enabled it to grow and spread into our land. Why would I risk telling one of them what we know and what we are planning?"

"When someone comes asking for one of our most powerful Weapons, and wants to know where we have sent it and what we are doing, I am suspicious. Even if you are not a servant of the watching eyes you could reveal our efforts to one who is."

"So I will not give you the Weapon, and I will not tell you our secrets. But if Boone is going to take the royal army into the hinterlands, and if you truly want to join in the fight against this black watcher, then prove you are our ally with your actions. Join us and help. Stop trying to weaken us."

Karsha nodded thoughtfully. "Now we sound like true allies, bickering and arguing but speaking openly. I like this."

"And what will you tell the Queen?"

"I will tell her that we can be allies against this foe." Karsha gave a sly grin. "She will be very pleased. She got what she wanted."

Benno straightened his robes and turned to the room. He spotted another chair, concealed under a pile of books that he suspected were meant to be in the Bandirma archives. He carefully moved the books to the floor and sat heavily in the chair.

"What is in the box?" Benno asked, indicating the object still held in Karsha's lap. It was fashioned of some strange wood that was so dark it appeared to be black, fastened with bronze hinges and clasps sculpted into the shape of whirling flames.

Karsha held the box up to his eye level and slowly turned it back and forth as the light played across its polished surface.

"Nharghrod, of course."

Danielle

Danielle had never seen Bradon look so grim, so thunderous and dark that she feared violence might erupt from him at any moment, although at what target she could not tell. Bradon's hands were clenched into fists as he returned to the cavern, one wrapped in a choke hold around the haft of his hammer.

Wyn was shattered and pale as if grievously ill. Fresh blood smeared her face, stark against her pallid skin. Her eyes darted from face to face but did not linger, as if she could not stand to meet the gaze of those in the cavern, and they were glassy as if feverish.

When Wyn saw Killock her hands flew to cover her mouth. The knight stepped forward and reached out to her, but she turned away and hid her face from him, and Killock's arms hung empty for a moment before they dropped to his sides.

Cormac was the worst of all. His face had completely closed, as if he had donned an expressionless mask. Except his eyes, which burned with a deep rage.

All were broken in some way. Meghan remained vacant and followed the trio from the passageway in the mindless daze that had stifled her since they had found her in the ritual chamber.

Bradon related the grim story to Danielle and Killock in a low, strained voice, like boulders grinding together. Danielle listened as the details built to their terrible conclusion, far worse than she had feared, and she found her hands had clamped themselves over her mouth in horror.

Killock was stone and iron as he listened, but Danielle could feel the strain of helplessness and anger as he stood perfectly still next to her.

Wyn lingered in the shadows against the wall and listened but did not join the group. Danielle extended her hand to Wyn, not sure what to do or say but knowing that Wyn needed her now. But Wyn remained apart.

"I blame myself," Bradon concluded angrily. "I knew that Brok was not himself. Danielle, you told me he was not well, and I could see it. I thought it the burden of battle, no more, but clearly he was afflicted by this cursed place."

"What?" Wyn stepped forward and confronted the Templar. "The caves made him do it, is that it?"

"Something about this place, yes," agreed Bradon. Danielle saw Wyn's eyes narrow as they suddenly became sharp and focused again.

"Because it was different for him than the rest of us?" The words tumbled from Wyn faster than she could control them. "Or are we all about to start murdering and raping each other?"

"Something about this place was preying on Brok, I don't understand how," said Bradon shortly.

"He tried to rape me! He tried to murder me! He murdered Corlath!" Wyn's voice sliced through the air. "He was a murdering rapist shit stain, and I'm glad I cut his God damn heart out! How can you defend him?"

Wyn brushed angrily at her eyes as she glared at Bradon. Danielle wanted so desperately to say something, anything, to help. But she knew that Wyn needed to speak, to shout, to rage, and that right now silence was the best comfort she could give.

"Wyn, I am not defending him." Bradon sounded gruff and affronted. "I am saying that something must have made him, something must have forced him against his will."

"You *are* defending him! It wasn't his fault? Something made him? Something like a girl flashing him one smile too many, maybe that got him going, or something like his friend telling him to stop?"

"That is not possible," Bradon said abruptly. "You don't know what he has been through. His daughter Aneira was assaulted and killed four years ago. The pain he went through as he lived every day with the knowledge that those responsible are still out there. That is why I say it isn't possible."

"Yeah?" Wyn spat back. "Or maybe I just killed the one responsible."

Bradon's cheeks turned bright red above his beard, and his chest swelled, but Danielle spoke before he could.

"Bradon!" Danielle's voice snapped like a whip. "That is enough."

A moment of silence settled briefly, and Bradon deflated with a deep sigh that made his shoulders sag and his face grow ten years older, weary and sad.

"You are right." Bradon turned to Cormac, who stood still and silent. "I know this will give you no comfort, but there is no doubt in my mind that your brother was one of the noblest, bravest men I have had the honor of knowing. He sacrificed everything to help a comrade in need, and did not hesitate, despite knowing that it most likely meant his death."

Bradon turned to Wyn next. She stood with arms crossed and chin defiantly raised as she glared at Bradon.

"Wyn, I am sorry," Bradon said quietly. "I failed you. I should have protected you, and I thank God for your strength that saved you when I could not. I hope you can forgive me."

He turned then and walked towards the roaring waterfall.

Wyn watched him go, hands gripping her arms tightly. As Danielle watched, Wyn slowly released her anger, her back and shoulders relaxing, eyes unlocking from Bradon's back until finally she found Cormac. Wyn hugged the soldier tightly around his shoulders, squeezing with all of her strength.

"Oh, Cormac, I am so sorry," she said softly, then leaned back and looked him in the eye, her expression miserable. "He was so brave, he fought so hard."

"Thank you, Wyn," Cormac nodded. Deep lines of pain etched his face and his voice cracked with grief.

"For what?" Wyn asked.

"For justice. For avenging him. I can tell our parents that Corlath died to save a comrade, and that the man responsible was brought to justice."

Wyn nodded silently as her eyes brimmed with tears, and a gleaming drop escaped the well to trace across her cheek.

Killock hugged her awkwardly, arms around her shoulders, and Wyn rested her cheek against his chest, her hand clutching at the straps of his pack.

"Wyn, I'm so sorry." Killock stroked her back softly. Wyn gave a small nod, and Danielle saw Wyn's eyes close in misery as she tried to hold in her emotions. "You did everything you could. None of this is your fault, you know that."

"Yes, sir," Wyn whispered.

"Good." Killock gently held Wyn away so that he could see her face, and Wyn gave him a forlorn smile, her lip trembling.

"Don't worry about me." Wyn took in a deep breath and tried another strained smile.

"I don't." Killock brushed a tear from her cheek, let her go, and crossed the cave to join Bradon.

Danielle's heart ached with the need to take Wyn into her arms and comfort her. Wyn was so lost and hurt and alone as fresh tears left trails down her face.

"Wyn?" Danielle whispered her name. Wyn's green eyes flooded with gratitude, then her façade broke and she crumpled into Danielle's arms as misery and fear became too much to bear. They sank to their knees and Danielle held her and felt her own heart break as Wyn's soundless wail shuddered through them.

Danielle did not know how long they held each other, only that eventually Wyn's breathing became easier. Wyn stirred, sat up, met Danielle's eyes, and nodded her thanks with a sad smile.

They helped each other to stand and Wyn wiped her eyes uselessly, smearing dirt and blood and tears. She stamped her foot in frustration. "Damn it," she said in exasperation, and shook her head as she tried to fight off a fresh surge of tears and emotion.

"Let me help you with that cut," Danielle said. The slice started above the eyebrow on the left side of Wyn's face, and continued from her cheekbone to her jaw line. Blood oozed from it and ran down her neck. Danielle decided it was a healthy flow that should have washed out the cut.

Danielle cleaned the wound with fresh water from her canteen, then carefully applied a paste of gold leaf oil mixed with littlefeather from her dwindling supplies, gently applying it along the cut until the bleeding stopped.

"Is it hideous?" Wyn asked quietly. "It hurts like crazy."

"No, it is fine," appraised Danielle. "I wish I had some thread to stitch it above your eyebrow where it is deepest, but the cheek will heal on its own. We just need to keep it clean. I doubt there will be much of a scar on your cheek. Your eyebrow may not be so lucky, I am afraid."

Wyn nodded and wiped at her nose with the back of her hand, then rolled her eyes in frustration as more tears came forth.

"I'm sorry," she said. "It won't stop."

"Do not worry, tears do not scare me," comforted Danielle. The pain in Wyn's eyes stabbed Danielle cruelly, but at least Wyn was angry and sad. *Not broken like poor Meghan.* "Let me see where else you are hurt."

Wyn drew a deep breath, then slowly pulled back the cloak from her neck and looked away from Danielle in embarrassment. Danielle sucked in her breath at the sight. Deep, red contusions twisted around Wyn's slender neck, bloody and purple. The skin had torn under the assault to leave long abrasions that circled her throat like a morbid torc.

Danielle carefully washed the skin as gently as she could, but Wyn winced at the touch. Then she took a poultice laced with lamb's blossom, wrapped it in place, and rearranged Wyn's cloak to cover it.

She smoothed the cloth and glanced at Wyn's face. Wyn was looking at her with a puzzled expression in her blood-shot eyes.

"You're crying," Wyn said softly.

Danielle nodded, letting the tears spill. "So much pain."

Wyn smiled feebly. "Yeah, I really hate this place. I think I'm ready to be done and go find a good tavern."

"That sounds nice," agreed Danielle. "I think I will come too."

"Good," Wyn's laugh was a half-sob, and she wiped her nose again, "because I'm broke."

"Come with me," Danielle held out a hand. "I want you to meet someone."

Wyn followed, confused, as Danielle led her across the cavern to Mairi and Aileen. The girls scrambled to their feet as they approached.

"Mairi, Aileen, this is Wyn," Danielle introduced them. "Sir Killock found the girls in the catacombs. They are from Twin Pines."

Wyn crouched to bring her face lower. "Hi Aileen, hi Mairi. I'm not usually so loud and scary. Well, that's not true, but I usually wait until people get a chance to meet me first, so sorry about that."

"That's alright," Mairi replied, and glanced at Danielle. "Did someone die?"

"Yes, I am afraid so. A friend of ours, Cormac's brother," Danielle replied.

"Some of my friends died too," said Mairi softly.

Danielle and Wyn exchanged looks.

"You're from Twin Pines?" Wyn asked, and Mairi nodded. "I was there last night, or maybe the night before. Not sure what day it is. I met a nice boy named Colin, do you know him?"

Mairi nodded again. "He likes Meghan."

"That's him," agreed Wyn.

"Is that Meghan?" Mairi asked and she risked a glance across the cavern. "It looks like her… a bit."

"Yes, that's her," said Wyn. "Would you like to say hi?"

Mairi nodded hesitantly. "Is there something the matter with her? She looks strange."

"I think she is very sad, and it has made it difficult for her to think," answered Danielle. "But maybe seeing a friend will help."

"What do you say?" Wyn asked brightly.

"Alright," said Mairi tentatively. Wyn took her and Aileen by the hands and led them across the room.

Danielle sighed with relief. Wyn had appeared ready to collapse, her strength a frayed thread, and Danielle feared to think how devastating it would be for the fiery young woman to have her spirit fail her. *But nothing is better for helping yourself than helping someone else.*

The three men had gathered at the steps and were engaged in deep conversation beneath the still-unopened doors which dominated the other side of the cavern.

"Please tell me that we have a plan to leave here?" Danielle asked as she joined them.

"We think so," said Bradon, his voice still strained and hoarse. "Right now our task is to find the one behind the fuil crunor rituals, the magus. I had hoped that Crassus' death would break the power of the Crunorix, but Killock tells me the thought was foolish."

"I would say that Killock is right," agreed Danielle. "Crassus must have been taught the rituals somewhere, but clearly he was not the recipient of the power. He was a tool, and whatever was built with his efforts will still exist."

"That is what Killock said as well, and when it is put plainly, it seems naïve to think otherwise," Bradon acknowledged. "If we do uncover the magus, can you kill it?" Bradon asked Danielle.

"I do not think so," said Danielle. "It crushed my Wardpact in the blink of an eye, and that was my most powerful Device. All I have left are my guide and my lance, plus a few other Diviners suited only for gathering knowledge. My lance could perhaps kill it, but only if I had enough time."

"I think what Lord Bradon meant was, could you kill it with that," said Killock, and he pointed over her shoulder.

It took Danielle a moment to realize what he was referring to, as she had become so used to its awkward weight that she had forgotten her burden. But once remembered, it hung heavily from her shoulder again, and she could feel it press against her back. *The Blade, of course.*

"That is no easy question to answer," she replied. "If the rumors of its provenance are true, then no servant of the Nameless King, no matter how powerful, should be able to stand against it."

"If they are true," repeated Killock.

"Yes," answered Danielle, and she drew in a deep breath before she continued. "Bishop Benno and I believe that this sword is the Martyr's Blade, the Weapon Bronwyn used to defend Ruric after he fell, when she stood alone against the Nameless King. It is possible that the Blade was entrusted to my centuries-gone ancestor Marquessa Augustine to carry home from the battlefield."

"We do not know whether this legend is true or not," Danielle sighed in exasperation. "Some texts mention that Augustine was granted the Martyr's Blade to safeguard, but other tales disagree. And as to whether she decided to keep it hidden in her home, only my family's private papers tell such a tale. I do not even know if the Word I was taught is the right Word."

"I hope that you and Benno are right," Bradon's voice was low and grim. "But we must face the magus nonetheless."

"With three young girls," Killock pointed out. "We must bring them with us. They cannot stay here."

"Are you sure?" Danielle questioned Bradon. "Not an hour ago you spoke of leaving the catacombs and letting the army search through their depths."

"That was when we thought that this was merely an isolated stronghold, and Reverend Crassus its keeper," said Brandon purposefully. "Now we know otherwise."

"Very well," Danielle replied. She reached into the small pack she wore under her cloak and retrieved her guide. Its dark metal reflected the torches dully as she held it close to examine the concentric circles of symbols that wrapped around it. The guide's Word came easily into her mind and she let it flow into the Diviner. The symbols that surrounded it glowed faintly and appeared to lift off the surface as energy pulsed through it. Danielle carefully moved the rings, sliding them over each other and around the Device until she had the exact sequence she wanted. She held the guide outwards and watched the symbols react until she knew which way to go.

"Through the doors," Danielle said.

***

The guide led them deeper into the caverns, through vast amphitheaters of natural stone where their torchlight could not reach the ceiling, past still pools of black water, through tunnels gnawed from the rock over countless eons, and across rushing rivers that plunged into darkness far below. Always downwards.

The walls were honeycombed with dark niches that held the withered remains of countless men, entombed with arms and armor at hand. None stirred as the party passed by, but their hands stayed ready on weapons, as surely the time would come when these dead would walk again.

Danielle held the guide steady with one hand while she grasped her lance with the other, a Weapon that, if wielded by an adept, could carve through metal and stone as if they were freshly churned butter. Danielle was such an adept.

Killock led the way into the deepest roots of the mountain with surety and calm purpose, a tonic for nerves frayed by recent horror and the knowledge of the nightmare from legend that lurked ahead of them.

Bradon came next, with so heavy a tread that he sent ripples through the small pools of water as they passed. He held his hammer ready in two hands, and his beard bristled as he sought his enemy. Bradon had been deathly silent since they began the last leg of their trek, and Danielle sensed the strain and anguish that surrounded him. His eyes, deep-set under a furrowed brow, were lined with red from unshed tears.

Danielle came next, and the light from her guide shifted and played in the darkness as she whispered guidance to the Templars.

Wyn and Cormac came behind Danielle, and helped the girls traverse the dark path. Mairi clutched a small dagger in both hands as she walked, sheathing it only to help Aileen or Meghan across difficult patches of floor. Aileen carried her flickering torch, carefully holding it to dispel each shadow as she passed. Meghan continued to walk as if in a dream. She followed when guided and stood still when left alone.

The passageway opened ahead onto a wide, curved shelf above a narrow pool of still water. Twisted statues stalked the shadows along the shelf. Beyond the statues, the ground fell steeply, a near vertical fall into the pool. Black lichen grew up the sides of the cliff and wrapped around the statues, giving them a leprous look.

The path descended around the outer wall until it reached the level of the pool on the far side of the room. Beyond the water stood a massive stone door under a heavy lintel carved into the wall. Wide steps rose from the pool to a portico surrounded by more twisted statues with long, gaunt hands extended as if they pointed towards the statues on the ledge far above.

The guide pointed straight to the doorway. Danielle gripped her lance tighter. The air in this cave was bitterly cold, far below freezing, and it penetrated unnaturally through cloaks and fur and tunics. Her breath steamed in the torchlight and crystals of ice reflected from the cracks in the walls and floor as the cold reached black fingers deep into her limbs until her bones ached.

The party made its way along the ledge towards the pool. With every step Danielle could feel a presence growing nearer, a deep and ravenous hunger beyond the foreboding stone seal. The cold flowed from the hunger and did its bidding, sapping heat and life to feed into the abyss. Danielle heard a soft curse and a whispered prayer behind her as they approached the black pool and echoed both.

Killock reached the water and hesitated as he peered into its depths, but the torchlight would not penetrate the liquid. He carefully stepped off the path into the water, first one foot then the next. Small ripples spread out but were quickly absorbed. The liquid seemed thicker than water. The surface broke around Killock's leg unwillingly, and it sucked and stretched as he moved.

Killock pushed through the muck and reached the steps that led to the stone door, and he pulled his boots from the pool with disgust. One by one the party followed him. When it was Danielle's turn she stepped in very slowly and searched for the bottom with her toes. The water felt resistant and pushed around her foot like mud. It quickly seeped into her boots and numbed her toes. The bottom of the pool felt slippery, like algae-covered stones in a lake. Danielle stepped carefully, not relishing a fall into the pool. When she reached the far side she rushed her last steps to regain sure footing on the stone slabs.

The door loomed ahead. Frost shimmered across the surface of the stones and gave them an ethereal look, as if they were shifting backwards and forwards like smoke. Killock pressed his palm against the door as he searched for any clue as to what lay beyond, and turned abruptly as a scream ripped through the chamber behind Danielle.

It was Aileen's voice, a terrified wail that tore from her throat as she stood in the pool. Mairi held on to her hand and pulled her towards the steps, and Danielle took a step towards her before realizing that the girl's screams were not for herself.

Meghan stood in the pool, her tunic drenched in blood, terrible swathes of it flowing from the two long gashes across her stomach. Her arms glistened wetly as more blood flowed from the cuts that ran along them. She suddenly staggered and went to her knees in the ink-black water. Meghan's hands scrabbled on the wet rock wall, and her legs collapsed under her. As she sank, her blood stained the water as it slowly spread across the thick surface.

Cormac reached her an instant later and plunged his arms under the surface. Endless heartbeats passed before he hauled her into the air. Meghan lay passively in his grasp as blood poured from her wounds. Cormac carried her towards the steps as Aileen screamed again, terror making her cry shrill and piercing. Danielle and Bradon raced towards Cormac to help the soldier.

Cormac lost his balance and fell to a knee as he approached the first step, but Bradon reached out and pulled Meghan onto the stone. Danielle pressed frantically on Meghan's stomach with a blanket torn from her pack, but it was instantly soaked with blood. More blood streamed across the stone steps and into the black pool. The girl's breathing grew shallow and the blood flowed less freely. Danielle knew there was nothing she could do. The wounds were mortal.

The group was quiet now save for Aileen's sobs and the soft comforting words Mairi whispered to her. Meghan lay still as the blood slowed to a last, gentle pulse. Danielle still held her hand, although she knew that Meghan was far beyond knowing. It did not matter.

Then a low hiss sighed through the room, as if a strong wind no one could feel blew past them. A surge rippled through the black water of the pool, emanating from the stain of blood spread across its surface. Shapes writhed under the water, pale and ephemeral.

"Back! Away from the water!" Bradon thundered, and Danielle leapt to her feet.

Then another noise filled the room, stone grinding upon stone, that drowned all other sound. Behind them, the doors began to open.

"There!" Killock shouted, his outstretched arm pointed to the pool. A pale head rose from the water, black eyes gleamed in the torch light, and a lipless mouth stretched across black gums and bared fangs. The wight rose slowly, water oozing from its head and shoulders. Then the water was broken a second time, then a third.

Danielle readied her lance as the wights waded through the black pool. Bradon shouted instructions, but his voice became indistinct as Danielle brought the Word into focus. Her mind stroked the lance and carefully adjusted it as its energy swelled. She let it flow around and back on itself over and over as it built like a colossal ocean wave. The Word coursed through the lance as she released its bindings in a precise sequence until it thrummed with power almost beyond containing.

She looked up and the room was strange and distant. Figures flashed past her, jumbled and half-glimpsed in the wavering torchlight. Bradon's hammer pulsed as he released its Word and emerald fire blazed forth. He whirled the fire into a deadly arc as he unleashed it against his enemy. Silver flashed to the side where

Killock's sword met the pale blade of a wight in beautiful, endless arcs as the knight clashed and danced away and clashed again, his sword never still. Wyn flashed behind Killock's foe and her knives scythed across pale flesh, then she was gone before Danielle realized that she was there.

The third wight attacked Cormac. The soldier deflected its savage blows to the side with his small shield, and unleashed a counter-strike with his short broad-bladed sword.

But the wights were undeterred. Blades sliced their skin and their weapons were turned aside with a grinding screech, but the wights pressed forward without hesitation. Only Bradon's hammer gave them pause.

Then another cry of warning from Killock, and Danielle saw that more were coming from the pool, black eyes and pale swords rising from the depths.

She whispered the Word and released the lance. A beam of light blazed forth, golden, pure, and bright like the fire from the heart of a great forge. It carved across the back of the wight fighting Killock, and its skin burst and boiled away under the touch. It twisted towards her, mouth gaping in a silent scream, but she held the lance on it and golden tendrils of energy coursed across its smoking skin, then black smoke erupted and a huge gout of flame engulfed the creature.

Danielle did not hesitate. She let the energy in the lance circle and amplify, then unleashed a second bolt of golden light across the chest of the wight menacing Cormac. The creature writhed away from its touch but Danielle held the lance on the wight until it, too, was engulfed in flames.

The remaining wights strode from the pool towards her, their long fangs gleaming wetly against black gums as they came. Danielle unleashed the lance a third time, but it was hurried. She had not given the lance enough time. Its beam caused the wight's skin to blacken and split, but lacked the power to immolate its target as it had the first two.

Then Bradon stepped between Danielle and the wight. His hammer crushed the foul creature to the ground as the Templar bellowed loathing and rage at it.

Danielle heard Killock shouting, but it was difficult to focus on her Word and the world around her at the same time, and she was not sure what the knight was saying.

Then Wyn's face flashed in front of her. Wyn held her by the shoulders and stared intently at her as she repeated her name, and Danielle turned to see what she was pointing at.

The massive stone doors were open. As Danielle watched, they sank into the walls with a thud that reverberated through the floor into her feet. The markings carved into the doorframe were alive, cold, black, writhing things that were painful to look upon. Beyond the doorway, a wide room with twisted pillars led to a high altar and a hideous throne.

A dark figure sat on the throne. Eyes the color of blood stared from lidless sockets. Skin so burned and corrupted that it had turned pitch black stretched like leather over jagged bones and pulled away from gums and nose. A grotesque, black iron crown rested on the figure's head, capped with twisted spikes that rose high above it. The figure was garbed in black armor, heavy and ornate, and its long fingers clutched the hilt of a dread sword that it held unsheathed across its lap.

The magus. Danielle knew it was true, although she had only heard rumors of the Crunorix magi from legends and myths.

Danielle felt each labored pulse of her heart as she stared at the creature. Its coldness wrapped around her to suck at her heart, slowing and stifling it with every beat.

She brought her lance to bear. She could feel its energy swell as it coursed through her Word's structure over and over. It was near its limit, a seething cauldron of fire ready to be unleashed.

She set it free. Golden light bathed stone walls, a flare so bright that it seemed the sun shone through a crack in the mountain. Power dripped from its finger-thin beam as it crackled through the air. It touched the magus and the air boiled. Shining drops sprayed from the impact to spark and smoke as they danced on the cold stone floor. A shriek filled the air as black armor melted and flowed away from the lance's touch as it passed over the magus, leaving behind a glowing trail.

But a shell of cold and darkness resisted the lance's power. Danielle could feel the shell blister and writhe, but nevertheless it remained intact, impenetrable. Danielle let the energy flow, holding back no reserves. The golden light surged and pulsed, and power to melt stone poured forth across the ancient room and unleashed itself onto the corrupted creature sitting on the throne.

Then the magus pushed back. Danielle felt a vast pressure as cold hunger engulfed her. The beam of light from the lance suddenly wavered, tracing destruction across the altar and the rows of twisted statues as Danielle staggered under the impact. Her senses dimmed and a vast abyss yawned beneath her feet. She was dimly aware of emerald fire that glimmered somewhere far away, but it was impossibly remote.

Then with a rush, the pressure released her. The concussion wrenched her from her feet, sent her spinning through the air and dashed her brutally against the massive stone slabs of the doorframe. The world twisted around her, then slammed into her arms and chest.

Danielle lay stunned on the floor. Pain and shock overwhelmed her senses completely. Chaos reigned around her—shouts and cries, the clash of steel, and the ground trembled, but it was all distant and muffled. Her hands lay crossed in front of her face, the black stone of the floor vivid between her splayed fingers. Danielle saw a long wound across the back of one, and blood welled onto her skin as she watched, mesmerized.

A hand in a leather glove gripped her wrist, and a voice yelled her name. Danielle tried to respond but could not, and then suddenly the hand withdrew. Danielle pushed onto her elbows and slowly drew one knee under her as pain screamed from a thousand new sources. There was a wall in front of her, and she reached and pressed a hand against it as she dragged her other foot under her. The wall shook under her hand as another violent concussion roared across the chamber, and somewhere far away she heard stone shatter.

Strong arms lifted her to her feet. One arm wrapped around her waist, and a shoulder wedged under her arm to support her.

Wyn's face was right next to hers. Blood plastered her hair to her face but her green eyes were fierce and determined as she dragged Danielle through the doorway.

The throne room shook with emerald fire. In the center of the room stood Lord Bradon, his hammer a blaze against the black power of the magus. He whirled the hammer around him in ferocious arcs as he stalked his enemy, and he unleashed it to crash against the vile, black sword. The magus screamed in fury, an inhuman screech that drove daggers of pain through Danielle's head. Threads of cold darkness swirled around the magus, and its sword lashed out in sweeping blows that cut through Bradon's fiery aura, causing it to pale and flicker.

But again Bradon fought back as he drew on deep reserves of strength. His hammer fell again, and the impact shook the floor and made enormous stone blocks tumble from the ceiling in a shower of dirt and rocks. A statue wrenched from its plinth and crashed to the ground, long spines breaking free and scattering across the floor.

"Come on, your Ladyship, time to get back into it," Wyn urged. "He needs you."

Danielle knew that she was right. Dark tendrils swirled around the Templar and he cried out at their touch. He lashed out defensively and momentarily drove the magus back a step, but Danielle saw that their touch had weakened him and the magus could sense it too. It shrieked in hunger and moved forward again, and its cruel, black sword rained heavy blows onto Bradon's hammer, driving him off the altar, each strike shaking the room with its force.

Danielle shook her head and desperately tried to clear the fog that clung to her mind. She ripped open the buckle of her sword belt and released the strap around her chest. The hilt of the Martyr's Blade slid into her hand as she pulled it from its sheath. The long blade came free easily. Deep whorls in the metal of the blade caught and held the light of Bradon's fire and sent shimmers cascading across its surface.

The magus turned to her then, and its foul, black mouth gaped wide in rage. It took a step towards her, then Bradon's hammer slammed into its back and splashed fire across it. The magus shrieked and turned on the Templar, lashing out with its sword to knock his hammer aside and drive him to his knees.

Danielle desperately focused on the Word she had been taught so many years ago. It slipped and squirmed in her mind, a structure so intricate and fragile it seemed impossible to hold.

Wyn shouted a warning and suddenly moved from her side in a blur. Danielle caught a glimpse of a pale shape that rushed towards them from the shadows and a long blade reached for them. Wyn fell upon it.

A quick glance behind showed Danielle that there would be no help from Killock or Cormac. Husks surged up the steps, their withered hands clutching swords and axes and spears. More came from the ledge above, every crypt they had passed on their way disgorging its contents in one overwhelming wave. Killock moved through them like rushing water and his long sword arced as he downed husk after husk. Cormac stood in the center of the doorway and turned aside all that approached him. But it could not last, so many kept coming.

The Word formed in her mind and she clutched at its shape. She let it flow into the Blade, but it twisted and unspooled as it went and the sword lay dormant. Again she focused on the Word, trying to hold all of its complexities perfectly in place, but desperation tore it apart before she could even try to say it.

A groan escaped through her clenched teeth. Then calm flowed over her like the warm swell of a gentle sea. Determination clamped down over the rising panic that boiled within her. She began again, this time methodically piecing the Word together one tiny element at a time, as if she were studying it safe within the archives, not deep within the lair of a Crunorix magus. The pieces of the Word were exquisitely fashioned, each one simple and precise. It was how they fit together that made the Word so complex, as if they were shattered crystal that had to be re-made into an elegant chandelier. Danielle took each shard, held it in her mind, and carefully placed it next to the others until the pattern began to build, solid and clear.

But it was slow. Danielle heard Wyn cry out somewhere nearby, a shout of rage and pain and fear that stabbed her heart cruelly, but she forced herself to remain focused.

The magus again brought its foul sword down onto Bradon. The Templar managed to block it to the side with his hammer, then wrapped emerald fire around the corrupted creature in a twisting vortex. Black armor burst into flame and was ripped from the magus as it shrieked in pain. Its skin cracked open and boiled as the emerald flames twisted and curled around its foul shape. It struck out wildly, its sword sweeping high through the air as it recoiled from the Templar's power. The blade impacted with the twisted arm of a statue and the stone shattered and ripped from its base. It toppled heavily to the ground and smashed into the side of Bradon's leg.

Bradon roared in pain and his fire went out as his leg twisted beneath the statue's weight. He heaved the stone to the side and faced the magus, but the moment had given the creature time to recover and it attacked, its blackened form smoking as its cold darkness rushed forth to cover the Templar.

More of the Word's fragments clicked into place within Danielle's mind. Deep layers of intertwined structure that had seemed so impossible to grasp now acted as the roots of an ancient tree and anchored the shape and gave it foundation.

The magus descended on Bradon, who met it from one knee, his wounded leg unable to support him. Darkness rushed from every shadow to swirl around the magus, a torrent of coldness that congealed about the thing's sword in an emptiness that throbbed painfully in Danielle's mind. It brought its sword down onto the Templar in a terrible blow. Bradon raised his hammer in defiance and caught the blade on its head. The hammer shattered under the blade's impact, and a great burst of emerald light was unleashed that ripped across the altar. Stone shattered and convulsed from the shock. Huge slabs cracked asunder and fell from the ceiling in a remorseless rush of rock and dirt that obliterated the altar and the room around it. In an instant the light was gone, replaced by swirling dust and darkness.

A scream of pain and denial tore from Danielle, and she stepped towards the chaos as if in a trance. She could see nothing but dirt and dust and shadow that boiled into obscuring clouds, and massive shards of stone that tumbled across the floor.

"Bradon!" she called his name frantically, then again in fear. "Bradon!"

The floor trembled under her feet as the echoes of the crash continued to resound through the room.

Then slowly, horribly, a shape emerged from the chaos in front of her. Skeletal limbs moved under torn, black skin. Red eyes stared lidlessly within swirling dust. Tendrils of dark shadow rose from the shattered stones behind it and twisted through the air to be absorbed into its flesh as it moved relentlessly towards the woman before it.

The sword's Word hung in her mind like a glowing constellation of lights, almost complete. Only two small fragments remained. They slotted into place as Danielle watched the magus rise up before her. Cold and hunger reached out for her and she saw again the abyss of emptiness within it.

Then she let the Word flow into the Blade. Danielle cried out as energy poured from the Weapon to flood her and the sword. Fiery red and gold patterns swirled across her skin. Brighter and brighter they blazed until she appeared as a naked figure of pure white light wreathed only in flames. In her hand, her Blade shone brighter still, the silver light of a sun forged into steel, so brilliant it could not be gazed upon. Slowly and gracefully she ascended the steps and her feet left footprints of fire on the stone.

Danielle held the Blade defiantly above her, and drove the magus back, away from where Bradon had fallen.

The magus recoiled from her and shrieked in agony as the light burned away its shadow. Darkness streamed from it as if it were smoke from a fearsome inferno. Danielle plunged the sword into the magus, and the silver blade sank into it as if it pierced only water. Flames erupted from the terrible wound and flowed across its skin, leaving destruction in their wake. Silver light blazed forth from cracks that split and gaped across the magus as it twisted and shrieked, but it could not pull free. The storm of light built to a crescendo, and an immense vortex of wind sucked in all of the cold hunger and all of the darkness of the abyss and consumed it as the blaze burned brighter and brighter.

Danielle stood alone at the top of the altar steps, a being of light and fire. The magus was gone, the shadows were gone, the hunger was gone. *Bradon is gone.*

She let the power return to the Blade and it rushed from her with an exquisite burn that made her gasp.

She fell to her knees in front of the wall of shattered stone. She reached to touch a towering slab in front of her and brushed it with her fingertips. It felt as solid and unyielding as a mountain, and a cold hand of fear clutched her heart. Her eyes sought in anguish for some sign of movement, any sign that Bradon had escaped, but found none.

People surrounded her and gentle hands helped her stand, and hushed voices said her name. But she could not look away from the stones piled before her. They rose up in an unbearable tower, implacable in their weight.

A cry rose from deep within her, a wail of denial and pain and grief that shattered her as it tore forth to echo endlessly from the cold stones.

Part Two

Wyn

"No!" Danielle sobbed. "We cannot just leave him here."

Killock knelt beside her and gently wiped a tear from her cheek.

"I know," he said softly.

Danielle met Killock's gaze. Wyn saw that the knight's face was stricken, his eyes hollow. She had never seen him like this. *Like a broken blade.* It scared her.

Danielle nodded to Killock and took a deep, shuddering breath, and Killock helped her to her feet. Tears ran silently down her cheeks as she kissed her fingertips, and placed them softly on the immense stone block before her.

"Goodbye," Danielle whispered, and then turned away.

"Wyn?" asked Killock.

"Yes?" Wyn heard herself answer from far away.

"We need to go," said Killock, and he held out his hand to her.

"Yes," she said, still distant, and she took his hand although she did not know why. But at the touch the world became real once more. The long wound down her cheek throbbed, and the cold, wet smell of the cave sank into her chest. It was a loathsome place, empty, silent, and full of shadows.

Small rocks skittered and shifted in the pile and she listened intently, but they soon subsided. *Stupid girl, he's not going to crawl out from under that.*

She gripped Killock's hand and pulled him to a stop.

"Wait," she said firmly, with a finger raised.

He did not question, just stood and watched as she turned to face the pile of rock that filled the room behind them. Images raced across her mind and tumbled over each other; a deep rumbling voice that carried across a campfire; a bristling black beard, crusted with snow, split by a flashing smile; a look of disappointment and sadness in a dark, stone chamber that made her heart quail with shame; a huge presence beside her, massive and constant as the sun.

You said you failed me, Bradon's last words to her echoed sadly in her mind. *You said you didn't protect me, but that's not right. I was going to tell you. I felt safe with you.*

One last image flooded her mind and she held on to it. His tall shape riding next to her, so big it blocked out the sky. And a booming laugh, head thrown back, eyes twinkling in joy from a joke well played, and the deep happiness that came as she realized that she just might be this man's friend.

She wanted to carve it on the cold stones, to somehow let others know what was lost here, but saying it would have to do.

"Lord Bradon was a funny man," she said quietly but firmly, then took Killock's hand again to lead him away from their friend.

***

Killock guided them through the tunnels, his eyes strangely vacant as if he was seeing far into the future, and he barely responded when spoken to. *He knows what is happening*, Wyn decided, *but he doesn't care.*

They passed through more natural caverns, each one empty, the only sounds the echoes of their own footsteps. They passed chambers lined with crypts, but the occupants remained still. Whatever power had animated the husks and wights of the catacombs had passed with their master. The husks in the throne room had dropped to the floor at the moment Danielle destroyed the magus, once again becoming desiccated and still.

They crossed a deep chasm across a stone bridge, and passed through a towering archway into dank tunnels of black stone. Killock turned decisively at every intersection, although how he knew which path to follow, Wyn could not tell.

Mairi was exhausted, so Wyn took her hand and whispered with her as they walked to take her mind off the trek.

Wyn gave Mairi's hand a squeeze. "I can show you how to use that knife, if you'd like."

"Yes, please," Mairi nodded her head.

"It's a deal then." Wyn shot the passage a foul look. "As soon as we are out of this horrible place."

"I'm glad we're leaving," Mairi agreed.

***

Wyn's stomach and ribs ached with deep pain on every step, and sparks of agony flared across her forehead and cheek. She gritted her teeth against the pain and pressed on. *I haven't taken a beating like that in years, not since Quinn's boys caught me.*

The memory was still vivid for Wyn, despite the fact that it was now almost eight years old. She remembered a beautiful summer night, the warm sun lasting long hours past the evening bells. She had watched the sun finally set from the top of the old broken tower before climbing down to start her nightly search for food.

They had waited for her on the narrow path between the town wall and the drover's yard. She had thought that they were going to kill her, but instead they left her bleeding and broken in the foul mud. She had lain there for hours, overwhelmed by pain and despair, waiting for help from a life that had not existed since her mother had died. Then she had dragged herself to her feet and staggered to her nest in the broken tower, too angry to stay on the ground and die. She never gave up again.

And where's Quinn now? Killed by his own knife alone in a locked room. Piss on him and that asshole Brok, I got them both.

Worse than the pain of her wounds, Wyn felt a cruel hollow in her chest that she could not ignore, a terrible emptiness that grew whenever she thought of Bradon. But her grief did not muffle the world, it sharpened it. She was surprised by how alert she felt, as if her senses had become fully alive. She saw that Danielle was deeply in shock as she walked silently and without any awareness of the world around her, and Wyn wondered why she did not feel the same. Every drop of water into a puddle, every scuffle of a boot on stone, every creak of a leather strap was sharp and clear and distinct. The dank odor of the slippery walls that seeped into every breath, the chill air that crept to touch every piece of exposed skin, all etched themselves vividly into her mind.

So different from when Mum died. Her heart shrank from the thought, and she locked it deep inside her, behind doors forged long ago from the bitterest of hardships. Harrowing memories lurked behind those doors, of a young girl in the darkest of despair who had lost everything, lain down in the dirt and prayed for death to end the pain of a broken heart and a broken life. But Wyn had fashioned the doors of cold, unyielding steel, and only faint echoes ever whispered through them.

The narrow passageways twisted and turned. Torches hissed and flickered as they passed under the low arches that supported the ceiling, and dark shadows jumped behind each pillar as they passed. Wyn kept a knife drawn even though they had seen no enemy since the magus was destroyed. The passageways were too full of blind corners for her to feel comfortable without a blade in her hand.

The sound of water was everywhere again. A stream trickled down the center of the passageway, collected in the gaps between the stones, spilled and ran to the next puddle. The walls glistened moistly in the light of the torches. Drops pattered onto hoods and shoulders from the low ceiling as they passed.

Killock carried Aileen. She clung to the knight, overwhelmed by pain, exhaustion and suffering.

Mairi stayed close to Wyn. The young girl stepped around the puddles diligently, but her bare feet slipped on the black lichen that grew out of the water. *She's not complaining either.* Wyn felt a fierce surge of pride for the girl who had endured so much.

Killock came to a junction, and for the first time halted the group with a raised hand. He gently placed Aileen on her feet, and turned to the others.

"Wait here, I will return," he said, and was gone without waiting for a reply. His boots splashed softly in the stream as he moved away.

"You doing alright?" Wyn asked Mairi.

"Yes, I'm fine," Mairi replied, but Wyn could see her shivering miserably.

"Here, you can have my cloak. Not sure what we can do about your toes though."

Wyn wrapped Mairi up in her cloak, and Mairi held it tight around herself.

"Wyn, do you think my da knows I'm alive?" Mairi asked in a hushed voice.

"I'm sure he hopes it. We'll get you home soon, no problem."

"I know," Mairi sounded worried. "But what if he came looking for me and he's here in the caves somewhere? Or maybe he got back to the camp and heard what happened and left?"

"Is he a good da?"

"Yes."

"Then he won't leave you." Wyn tried to sound certain, but she was not at all sure if this was true. She did not remember anything about her own father, who had abandoned his wife and infant daughter, never to return.

A good da would be the opposite of mine. He wouldn't leave you. You would always know he was coming back, no matter what. He'd make you feel safe, like Lord Bradon did, always ready to protect you. He'd let you boo-hoo all over him when he hugs you and he would pretend not to notice. And he'd come and find you at the bottom of a dungeon and rescue you.

"Did you know that Sir Killock saved me from a dungeon, just like he did you?" Wyn asked Mairi, and smiled when she was rewarded with an astonished look on the girl's face. "It's true. Just when I thought I was done for, there he was."

"Me too," Mairi nodded.

"Your mum, where is she?"

"I don't know," Mairi whispered, and Wyn saw tears glint on her cheeks. "Reverend Crassus took her when she said he couldn't take me. Then he took me the next day anyway."

"And your da was away trapping?"

"Yes. He thought Reverend Crassus was gone finally. He hadn't come back in so long and Da had to set traps or he would have nothing to sell. So he went out, but that was the day Reverend Crassus came back."

"I'm sorry, Mairi, I am." Wyn pulled the girl close. She missed her own mother too, but it had been a relief when she had finally passed, the sickness had been so painful and cruel. *So different from today. The hole where Bradon used to be is just, there, like a big gaping emptiness that hurts around the edges. Like he's more than just missing, it's like a wound.*

"But that's just it," Mairi replied miserably. "Why wouldn't Da think I was gone just like Mum?"

"Well, because he's your da," said Wyn. "That's what fathers do." *I hope.*

Mairi nodded silently, and relaxed against Wyn, deep in thought. Wyn glanced around and caught Danielle's eye. The noblewoman stood a few paces down the passageway, and quietly watched Wyn with a small smile on her face. She nodded to Wyn and Wyn smiled back, not sure what she had done but glad Danielle had something to smile about, whatever it was.

A few more moments passed before Wyn heard the faint echo of familiar footsteps splash towards them, and soon Killock returned. His face was more rigid than usual, and Wyn saw that his eyes were hollow with pain.

"We go the other way," was all he said. He scooped up Aileen again, and led them down the right-hand passageway.

The path twisted and turned like a snake, and the endless drip of water and the tight confines of the tunnel made it seem as if they burrowed ever deeper into the mountain.

Then Killock stopped. Ahead, a short flight of steps descended into a pool of dark water, the passage flooded nearly half-way up the walls.

"Maybe the other way after all?" Wyn ventured, but Killock shook his head and plunged into the water. It rose to his waist and he held Aileen curled to his chest, careful to keep her as dry as possible.

"Oh. My. Shit." Wyn gasped as she entered the pool. The freezing water drove aching fingers deep into her bones. The water came up to her ribs, and her skin contracted painfully as it tried to escape the liquid's touch. Mairi stood uncertainly on the steps, and Wyn scooped her onto her hip, as high out of the water as she could manage. Killock forged ahead and Wyn was forced to follow. Each step drove small waves farther and farther up her torso.

Fortunately, the pool did not extend for long. After a short distance, more steps rose from the water. Wyn gratefully sloshed up the stairs and clutched her hands together in front of her face as she shivered uncontrollably.

"Killock, we have to stop, we are exhausted," Danielle pleaded with the Templar, but he shook his head.

"We are almost there, I think. We can stop when we reach the exit." Then, without further word, he turned and moved on.

Killock was right. After one more turn the passageway entered a larger space. The torches revealed tall stone figures on either side of them that towered into the dark recesses of the ceiling. The walls curved away beyond the reach of the torchlight, although Wyn could see wide steps between two towering pillars that loomed from the shadows ahead of them. The room was a hushed place, and their movement caused echoes to reflect from the distant stone walls.

Killock led them up the steps and past the pillars, twin figures of stone with claws for fingers and cowls that hid their faces. On the far side of the pillars was another wide space, with balconies high on the walls overlooking it and two wide doorways leading out.

One door opened directly onto stairs that ascended beyond the reach of the torches. The doorway on the left drove straight as far as the light could reveal, wide and empty.

Killock indicated the doorway that led to the stairs.

"That leads up to the surface. I am not sure exactly where it will come out, but that is the way to go."

"Where does that go?" Wyn asked as she peered down the left-hand passage. It suddenly seemed darker than before, and colder, and its wet stone glistened far into the shadow.

"I don't know," replied Killock. He moved to stand at the entrance to the tunnel and quietly considered it for a moment. "But wherever it leads, that is where our enemy came from."

Wyn felt the touch of a noose tighten around her neck, and her eyes suddenly stung. There was something about the way Killock was standing, or in his voice. She knew what he was thinking. *He's going to leave me.*

"You can't go!" The words came out shrilly, far louder than she had expected. She swallowed heavily and tried to dislodge the pressure she felt in her throat.

Killock turned to face her, a startled look on his face. "I didn't say that I was."

"You're going to." Wyn's breath suddenly caught, and she could not continue. She felt strangely dizzy, as if a merciless pressure swelled in her mind, and the world shrank into a tunnel so focused that everything else faded away. *Is this what fainting feels like? I'm not going to faint.* She tried to swallow and keep steady, but her throat was closing, and the sensation grew worse.

"Surely not," Danielle frowned. "Not now, not when we are so hurt, so weary."

Killock shook his head slightly, bewildered. "I agree. But someone must go, and soon, to discover what we can about our enemy."

Prickles of sweat suddenly broke out all over her body, and beads ran down Wyn's back as she fought against the dizziness. Her breath just would not seem to come. "No!" she begged. "You can't leave me."

Her mouth opened in shock as she realized what she had said, and she covered it with both hands as pain and fear and embarrassment overwhelmed her. "I'm sorry," she whispered. "I'm sorry I didn't mean that."

Killock stepped close and rested a hand on her shoulder, and she saw his mask drop for the first time since the throne room, concern etched deeply into the weathered creases of his face.

"I'm not leaving you, Lady Shadow." Killock gave her shoulder a gentle squeeze and held her gaze, his grey eyes soft. "I promise."

Wyn stared at him, and as she did the terrible dizziness started to fade. She felt her awareness widen, and she took a deep breath of the chill, dank air.

"I'm just being ridiculous." Wyn tried a smile but could not hold it. "I'm fine."

"You're not being ridiculous," Killock said softly. "Far from it. But you don't need to worry. Wyn, you can count on me."

"Alright." Wyn's voice was so faint she was not sure if he had heard her, but he must have because he nodded and patted her shoulder again.

He turned, took Cormac aside, and spoke with him in a low voice while the young soldier nodded his head in agreement. Then he hoisted Aileen onto his hip and carried her up the stairs as the rest followed.

Mairi glanced at Wyn with a puzzled expression on her face as they climbed after him.

"Yes, sweetheart?" Wyn asked.

"Is he your da?" asked Mairi.

Danielle covered her mouth and tried to conceal a smile, but Wyn merely grinned and looked at the weathered knight ahead of them. *So serious and gruff all the time, but always looking out for me. And I believe him when he says I can count on him.*

"He'd be a good one, wouldn't he?"

***

Killock left the catacombs with all of his winter clothing save his cloak, and with his small shelter and pack of gear. None of the rest had a bedroll, let alone a tent. All their supplies had been lost with their saddlebags. Danielle had cut up most of their blankets for bandages and she had thrown away her gloves. Wyn's coat and leggings were slashed and torn, and were not thick to begin with.

Mairi and Aileen were the unluckiest. The girls had only their light dresses and blouses, and no boots, gloves, or cloaks. Cormac fashioned clothes for them from their last blanket, with wraps for their feet and hands, and a shawl for their heads and shoulders. The adults took turns carrying the girls and sheltering them with their bodies and their cloaks.

Their only good fortune was the calm weather. Grey clouds made the sun a vague brightness in the southern sky and the snow lay thick under the dense pine forest. But the wind stayed calm and the clouds held their load of snow. A blizzard would have killed them as surely as a troll.

But the only tracks they crossed were those of deer and small creatures. Mairi declared one set a rabbit, another a fox, as she displayed the skills learned at the side of her father.

Despite their thin luck, Wyn knew that Mairi and Aileen would not survive the night with no food, no warm clothes, and no shelter. They stopped frequently to let Killock light a small fire to thaw their hands and feet, but it was not enough. Wyn had long since lost feeling in her toes and shivered constantly, and she noticed that Danielle's lips were a striking blue against her dark skin.

They found the cabin as evening descended. It was small but sturdy, likely a trapper's lodge. Built of thick, rough logs daubed with mud and straw, and a sturdy sod roof, the cabin had a single small room with a wide stone fireplace built of fitted river stones.

The cabin's sudden appearance was miraculous. It stood next to a small, frozen stream on the steep side of a narrow valley. Tall pines surrounded the cabin and gave it shelter, and it was built on the southern face of the hill to protect it from the worst of the mountain winds and absorb the most of the weak, winter sun.

Inside, they found a large cedar chest stocked with blankets, spare clothing, and materials for making traps. Cormac discovered a small stack of cut wood under a hutch, and quickly built a blazing fire for them to huddle around and watch the steam rise from their boots and leggings. The cabin was well-caulked and the fire quickly warmed the small room. Mairi donned boots and a cloak she found in a chest and went with Killock to set enough of the snares to bring in a healthy brace of rabbits the next morning. They slept, then ate, then slept again, and slowly restored some of the life they had lost under the mountain.

The next morning Killock went to scout. Mairi taught Wyn how to set a snare while Danielle and Aileen watched, and Cormac repaired torn clothes with a deft stitch. Laughter filled the cabin as Wyn expertly snared her own finger, and Wyn saw Danielle smile joyfully for the first time in days. *Since we were kidding around on the stairs, I suppose. When she was so nice about my wet clothes. Seems like years ago now.*

Danielle finished brushing out Aileen's wild tangle of hair, tied it in a simple braid, and sat back with a contented smile.

"Bradon loved to tell stories," Danielle said softly. "Do you remember, Cormac?"

"I do, m'lady," Cormac nodded. "Always ready for a tale was his Lordship. Not the greatest of stories, I'd say, but they surely did well from him doing the telling."

"No, you are right, the bards did not need to fear for their livelihood," Danielle laughed.

"Do you remember the one about the bear, m'lady?" Cormac grinned. "I think his Lordship must have told that one a hundred times."

"Oh, the bear!" Danielle clapped her hands. "The bear who wanted to be a man, I do. I heard that one the first time I visited Irongate Castle, almost four years ago now, I suppose."

"Is that where he lived?" asked Wyn. "In a big castle?"

"Yes, Irongate is his family's home, for ages and ages," Danielle explained. "It is a terribly foreboding place. I arrived by boat, and from the docks the castle looks like a mountain, all sheer cliff walls and tall peaks, made of black stone, and covered in scars. I almost turned around and got right back on the boat to go home. But Bradon was waiting for me with a carriage to take us up the hill, and he pointed out all of the different gates and towers and keeps and he was so proud of them all, and I remember thinking I was ready to push him off the battlements if I had to hear about one more flanking tower or postern gate."

"His Lordship did like a well-made flanking tower," agreed Cormac.

"He really did, the dear man." Danielle smiled at the memory. "So there I was, bored to tears and wondering why on earth I had thought going to Irongate to help defend villages from the clans was a good idea. And then we went to the great hall for dinner." Danielle turned to Wyn. "Irongate has a vast great hall, and Bradon had it filled with tables so that all of the household could dine together. There were six wide hearths to keep it warm, and everyone came, hundreds of people, families of soldiers, servants, and of course all of his cousins and their families. It felt as if it were a festival, with bards playing merry tunes and everyone shouting and laughing."

"Is that when he told the story about the bear?" asked Aileen. "Did the bear get to be a man?"

"Yes, it was," Danielle nodded her head. "Lord Bradon stood up, and the room hushed very quiet, and they even turned down the lanterns. I thought he was going to give a toast, but then he walked down amongst the tables and told his story to everyone. It was marvelous. All of the children gathered around close, and they helped him tell it. They rode on his back when the bear rescues the children from the river, and they piled all over him when the children hide the bear from the sheriff's hunters. He said 'Can they see me? Can they see me?' from under the pile, and all the children were pointing out bits of him that were still sticking out, and squirming around to cover the gaps."

Danielle's gaze grew lost in the fire for a moment, the flames shining on tears that filled her golden eyes, a tender smile on her lips.

Wyn felt an ache unwind deep within her as she imagined the scene, and heard Bradon's booming laugh and saw his broad smile. It made her eyes burn as it passed through her, but it also made her smile.

"What happened to the bear?" asked Aileen.

"Oh, let me see." Danielle wiped her cheeks and pulled the girl close. "He decides he much prefers to live in the forest as a bear. I seem to remember there were many issues with wearing pants, and a terrible fuss at a tea party. But the village loved him for all of the things he had done to help them, so they visited him in his cave and he was not lonely anymore."

"Oh," said Aileen, so clearly disappointed in the telling that Wyn and Danielle burst into laughter, and even Cormac had to hide a smile by feigning interest in the tunic he was mending.

Killock returned late that day and announced that he knew where they were. He had followed the valley south until it widened and joined a much larger valley. From high on the ridgeline Killock had observed the ruins of an old water mill on the banks of the small stream below, and recognized the crumbled finger of stone that was all that remained of the mill's tower.

They were far to the east of where they had gone underground, only a few day's walk from Dolieb.

"Thank God," sighed Danielle blissfully. "How lovely to think of an inn, and hot water for a bath. I feel I am completely covered with dirt."

"And if there's an inn, there's a tavern," smiled Wyn. "I think I know just the one. You'll like it, your Ladyness. The owner plays a mean fiddle."

"That sounds… wonderful," said Danielle half-heartedly.

"Maybe not then," giggled Wyn. "Cormac, how about you? You up for a drinks and a fiddle?"

Cormac smiled and nodded his head. "I'm always up for a drink, even if I have to listen to a fiddle."

That night Cormac pillaged the cabin for gear and gathered bedrolls, packs, and small tarpaulins that could be set up for shelter if necessary. He filled a large cauldron with snow and heated it over the fire until it melted and their canteens were filled.

At noon the next day they departed the cabin.

Danielle

They entered the gates of Dolieb as wind began to blow in earnest from the north, hissing across the deep-packed snow that covered the countryside.

They hurried through the twisting lanes as strong gusts chased the townspeople indoors, banged loose shutters and stung exposed skin with flakes of driven ice.

A little different than last time, Danielle reflected as she held her hood in place. *Horses, a retinue, warm fingers. All traded for gear made of twine and blankets, and torn clothes that look like we stole them from a scarecrow.*

"Oh, leave off!" Wyn cursed as the wind pulled her hood from her fingers and whipped ice into her face. "It's doing it on purpose now!"

Danielle had to agree. The gusts were spiteful, as if frustrated that they had reached the small town before the gale could bring its full strength against them in the open wilderness.

It had been a close thing.

Their first day of travel from the small lodge had been idyllic. They had meandered down the valley, sometimes chattering, sometimes moving in contented silence, absorbed in each other's company. The thick, powdery snow creaked and shoofed under their boots. Wyn recounted tales of her greatest snowball victories in the streets of her youth, brought to mind by the cheerful childhood noise of softly scrunching snow. Many of the memories involved the utter destruction of blustering shopkeepers or delivering icy humiliation to aloof gentry. "High-muckities" Wyn called them, and she delighted in retelling their comeuppances.

They passed the night in the ruins of the old mill house that Killock had spotted the previous day. Killock lit a small fire, and as its orange light flickered over the ruined stones, they enjoyed a dinner of rabbit and licked the grease from their fingers in a delightfully rustic way.

In the morning they awoke and crawled from their blankets to discover a layer of fine snow had fallen over them while they slept. The low, grey clouds were moving from the north, stirred by some vast pressure as yet unfelt in the lowlands.

They hurriedly packed their gear and moved down the fading trail, glancing behind them as they went. They eschewed stopping at midday and decided instead to eat the remains of their dinner as they walked. The trees sighed and shifted, and the first tug of wind on their cloaks caught them as they crested a small ridge. Dolieb squatted at the foot of the valley before them, grey smoke rising from dozens of chimneys behind its tall, wooden palisades. Killock led them to the gates, then detoured to the nearby Temple army encampment to report their return while the rest of them hurried into town to find an inn.

The gale moaned across the rooftops as they scurried through the twisted streets. They ducked through a low, pointed archway and crossed a small courtyard, their boots slipping in the icy mud of the lane. On the far side of the courtyard, a lantern swayed on a hook beside a sturdy wooden door. Above it swung a plank with a faded painting of a large bird carrying an arrow in its beak.

Wyn yanked the door open and they tumbled inside as the wind slammed the door behind them.

The tavern was almost empty. Three farmers played dice at a table near the fire. On the far side sat a group of trappers, talking quietly. A fire burned under a cauldron in the center of the room and filled the space with a damp heat and the smell of a bubbling broth.

Cormac took Mairi and Aileen and went to arrange for rooms. Danielle hesitated, but Wyn led her to the fire and plunked her pack onto a table, nodding greetings to the room as she held her hands towards the warm blaze. Danielle sat next to her. Drops of melted ice ran down her face, and dripped from the end of her nose, but she was too exhausted to care.

Wyn obtained two bowls of broth from the tavern keeper. The broth tasted scalding hot with a bit of brown mixed in, but Danielle sipped it gratefully, relishing the warmth that oozed into her stomach with each swallow. Patterns of grease shimmered across the surface of the broth and Danielle found them mesmerizing as they broke apart and then rejoined as she stirred them.

"Just arrived?" one of the locals seated nearby asked, a thin man with a ragged beard and an old sheepskin jacket.

"Yeah," agreed Wyn. "Barely in time, I think."

"A dangerous road for two young women, especially this time of year." He scratched his chin and took a deep swallow from his mug, his eyes flickering over the wrapped sword that Danielle wore across her back. She had bundled it in old canvas sacking as best as she could, but there was no mistaking the long shape.

Wyn laughed. "You don't know the half of it."

"Is that right, miss?" The thin man took another deep swallow.

"That's right," said Wyn, and she stretched her long legs in front of her and crossed her boots on the bricks surrounding the fire pit. "For starters, in every tavern there's some shit-stained idiot wearing a jacket made from his last fuck trying to tell us how dangerous the road is. It's that hard for a girl to have a quiet drink."

The fire popped and crackled in the silence that followed. Then a deep chuckle from one of the men, and then another. The thin man nodded and raised his mug to Wyn.

"Fuck you, too," he said pleasantly.

Wyn smiled and raised her mug in return, then drained it in satisfaction.

Danielle quietly let out her breath, suddenly aware that she had been holding it. *Scared by a tavern? It is amazing how brave I was, with Bradon beside me.*

Cormac returned with the girls and they ate and drank amidst a hushed murmur of conversation. The wind moaned past the shuttered windows and made the bowed roof beams groan as the storm enveloped the town, but inside, the locals paid it no mind. It was just winter.

Aileen barely finished her broth before she fell asleep, her head resting comfortably on Danielle's lap. Danielle stroked her hair and let her thoughts roam to another time, many years ago, when she would stroke her sister's hair as she fell asleep cuddled in Danielle's lap. Danielle had been only nine, and her sister seven, the two inseparable as they cared for each other after their mother died. Danielle remembered the feeling of gentle breathing and soft hair under her fingertips as welcome warmth in an empty, echoing home.

Their rooms were at the top of a short flight of stairs. Wyn carried Aileen up the steps, the sleeping girl's arms and legs wrapped around her. Wyn grinned at Danielle over Aileen's shoulder, a delighted smile that melted Danielle's heart.

She cares for others so selflessly and so easily. A sister, a friend. Especially for those who need the most help. Danielle could feel her heart throbbing powerfully as she watched Wyn carefully lower Aileen onto one of the narrow beds in the girls' room. *I love her.*

The thought felt strong and right. It was still bewildering, but Danielle was sure of her love now, and every moment confirmed it over and over again. The feeling had surprised her the first time she realized what it was, as she held Wyn in her arms in the cavern by the waterfall, but even then she knew it was true. Once she named the feeling, and recognized its true identity, it was with her at all times. Sometimes subtle, sometimes overwhelming, but always there.

I love her, she thought it again and enjoyed the pulse of happiness from her heart. *But I do not know what I should do about it.*

Danielle and Wyn took the room farthest from the stairs. They had been given two candles made of yellow tallow to light their way, and the flickering light showed them a cramped space with a low, sloped ceiling. A small window of warped glass set low in the wall, heavily shuttered, leaked freezing air into the room. In the candlelight, frost glistened on the thick wooden beams of the outer wall. A small iron stove stood against the inner wall, radiating a dull heat from the glowing coals. A bucket contained their coal allowance for the night.

A bed took up the rest of the inner wall, crudely built but solid, and atop it, a clean palette of straw that smelled fairly fresh.

"Well, the door has a latch," said Wyn. "And it will be warm enough next to the stove. Sorry about the rest, your Ladyness."

Danielle turned to her in puzzlement. "It is fine Wyn. In fact, thank God for it on a night like tonight."

Wyn nodded and glanced around the room again. "It's just, well I wasn't sure if it would be alright for you. Honestly I can't believe I brought you to a place like this, it's so small and bare and rough."

"Oh, do not worry about me," Danielle smiled. "I may be a high-muckity but I am well-used to sleeping in odd places. Maybe not without an armed escort, but I have you with me now."

Wyn laughed at that, obviously relieved. "I'm just glad I didn't have to sneak in the back when no one was looking to find an empty room."

"Do you do that?" Danielle asked.

"On a cold night, it's that or a barn. The barn is usually the better idea if there is one, although you end up smelling of cow and the farmers arrive awful early in the morning to chase you off. Stables are best. Horses smell nice and no one comes to milk them so you can get some proper sleep before buggering off."

"Even I have slept in a stable," Danielle laughed. "Although they were my own stables. I was disappointed that there was no fiddler downstairs."

"I guess he wasn't in the mood, what with there being only a few customers."

Danielle leaned the Blade against the wall, and gratefully sat on the bed. She barely had time to think about unpacking the blankets from her pack when a quiet knock sounded on the door.

"Yes?" Danielle called out. Wyn eased her pack off and placed her hands on her knives, listening carefully.

"It's Killock."

The Templar stamped snow from his boots and shook out his cloak in the hall before he and Cormac entered the room and filled what little space there was.

"Did you make it to the encampment?" Danielle asked.

"Yes, it's just south of town, on the road."

"Was Torbhin there? Or the Captain?" Wyn asked in a quiet voice, so full of hope it was painful to hear, and Danielle's heart beat heavily as she waited for Killock's reply.

"No," Killock said flatly, and Wyn's face fell. Danielle felt her breath catch and she swallowed heavily to loosen the tightness in her throat. *That does not mean anything, they might have gone anywhere*, she told herself. But she feared that was not true.

Killock pulled a small leather bag from inside his coat and passed it to Danielle. "There were messages from Benno for you there."

Wyn closed the door and latched it as Danielle sat on the edge of the bed and poured the contents of the bag into her lap. There were five containers, each one sealed by the Bishop's Word. She pulled on the silver chain she wore around her neck until the small ring that hung from it came free from her tunic. It was a simple band to look upon, but a careful examination revealed symbols etched into its inner surface. Danielle touched it to the message containers one after the other, each time softly whispering the Word that opened them. Small sheets of parchment unrolled from inside each one, dozens of pages covered in small, cramped script. Danielle smiled as she imagined Benno hunched over the desk in his scriptorium, scratching the tiny letters with his finest quill.

Danielle was not sure in which order to read them as Benno had neglected to date any of them. Some were obvious responses to her messages to him, while others could have been written at any time.

Wyn sat on the bed next to her and held a candle for better light. "What do they say?"

"Many things," said Danielle, reading while she spoke. "This one says to be careful, the dear. This one says that Reverend Whitebrooke thinks the rituals are from a book called the *Sanguinarium*, whatever that is, and to search for it at Reverend Ezekiel's temple or see if Reverend Crassus has it. Not by name of course, he simply says 'in the possession of those responsible for the atrocities'. Too late for that I am afraid."

"Who is Reverend Whitebrooke?"

"He is the Archivist in Bandirma. A big, loud man, not at all what you would expect from a scholar. Have you not met him?"

"I've only been to Bandirma once, when Sir Killock first took me there," Wyn frowned at the knight. "And you kept me hidden in the cellars the whole time. I didn't meet very many people before we had to leave."

Killock smiled slightly, unperturbed.

"Well, it looks as if we are going there now," continued Danielle. "This one says to return as soon as we have 'dealt with the perpetrators of this heinous Crunorix magic'. Martyr's tears, no wonder he had to write so small. And he says to take care not to encounter any patrols from the royal army. That is troubling."

"Should be no problem," Wyn laughed. "I've been avoiding them for years."

"'Make all speed' he writes. We will have to see if there are any horses we can use at the encampment," Danielle mused.

"And maybe some warmer clothes," said Wyn. The building trembled as the storm blasted it with fresh ferocity.

"Danielle, what shall we do with Mairi and Aileen?" Killock's voice was quiet. "I had planned to take them home once we were safe."

"Of course they must be taken home," Danielle smiled. "Bishop Benno would surely agree. You will just have to ride quickly to catch us."

"Thank you," Killock nodded his head.

Danielle laughed. "Killock, you do not need my permission. You may do as you wish. I will just tell you when you are wrong."

"I wished to ask," Killock said simply.

Danielle hesitated, not sure what to say.

"I would like to go to Twin Pines as well, m'lady," Cormac ventured. "My brother's sword lies somewhere in the high meadow, and I would like to search for it. Your pack as well, m'lady. Lord Bradon promised you we'd look for it."

"Yes, Cormac, please do so." Danielle felt a strange disquiet. *These are not my servants, they are my friends.*

"Thank you, your Ladyship," Cormac nodded.

"Good." Killock turned to the door and rested his hand on the latch. "The storm should blow itself out in a few hours, so we can depart at first light."

The men left for their room, and Wyn set the latch on the door behind them.

The room was quiet save for the moan of the wind across the roof and the creak of the shutters over the windows. Danielle removed her boots and coat and quickly crawled under the blankets as Wyn carefully banked the coals in the stove.

"Wyn, it is fine, come to bed," Danielle urged from beneath the blankets.

"Are you sure?" Wyn sat on the edge of the bed. "I'm fine with the floor."

"Do not be ridiculous," Danielle laughed. "Climb into bed before you freeze to death."

Wyn smiled, kicked off her boots and cloak, and slipped under the covers. Danielle pulled her close and they curled into each other, their legs and feet intertwined.

"Ohhh, feels so nice to be warm," Wyn sighed with pleasure.

"It does feel nice," Danielle agreed. "I think I might have toes again."

"Made me laugh watching the boys ask your permission," Wyn giggled. "Glad they figured out who's boss."

"Me?" Danielle laughed. "I cannot tell a Templar and a Temple soldier what to do. I do not have any kind of real rank in the Temple at all. They were just being polite."

"Titles and rank don't make someone the boss," Wyn said firmly. "Trust me on that."

"I do," Danielle replied, but she still felt it was more likely the men were simply being gentlemen, which was a relief. *I would be a terrible leader, anyway. I have no idea what a soldier or a Templar should do.*

The room grew quiet, but the silence was comfortable and Danielle felt herself grow drowsy. Wyn's breathing became soft and Danielle lost herself in the gentle movement of Wyn's back against her chest. *I love you*, she told her with each breath. *I love you.*

***

The Temple encampment was nestled amongst thick pine trees on a rise that overlooked the road. Soldiers dug from under the fresh snow as smoke from cooking fires wafted through the trees. Trails blazed by patrols connected the encampment with the road, and Danielle was grateful that she would not have to clumsily wade through the deep snow. *My boots have only just dried out.*

Mairi and Aileen looked about themselves in wonder. Circles of tents were strung under the trees, and soldiers moved about in all directions. Squads were already at drill in a small clearing, and long lines formed at every cook fire. A smith pounded dents from a breastplate as they passed, and laughter carried from the ice cutters in the nearby stream as a soldier slipped and fell on the ice.

Many of the soldiers stopped to smile and wave at the young girls as they passed, tough faces suddenly turned playful and friendly.

A buzz spread through the encampment as they were noticed, and more soldiers gathered to watch them pass. Smiles and respectful greetings met Sir Killock, but Danielle knew that most of the men were there to see her.

Danielle was aware of the effect she had on men, ever since she turned fourteen and, much to her relief, sprouted long legs and full breasts. The attention was usually a source of pride and sometimes laughter, depending on the antics and immaturity exhibited by the viewer. This time it made her feel a little sad, and it did not take Danielle long to realize what had changed. *I want Wyn to look at me like that*, Danielle sighed longingly to herself. *I wonder if she ever will. If only I dared to ask her about what she said…*

Danielle turned to watch Wyn. Wyn laughed and joked with Mairi as they walked, a steady stream of cheerful chatter which brought smiles to both their faces. Wyn twisted to look over her shoulder at something Mairi pointed out. Her long, blonde ponytail curled around her slender neck and shone in the weak winter sun as it swung through the air, and Danielle drank in her high cheeks, sparkling green eyes, and beautiful mouth. Wyn laughed and stuck out her tongue at Mairi as the girl giggled.

If she notices me looking at her, I will ask her, Danielle decided. *I will whisper in her ear and we will laugh and she will smile and say 'Of course'.* Danielle laughed at herself. *Apparently I have become fifteen again, and am still writing secret letters that are never sent.*

They reached a large tent in the center of the encampment before Danielle's promise could be put to the test. A knight stood in front of the tent, resplendent in freshly-polished armor and a magnificent fur-lined cloak. He was not a large man, but stood tall and easy in his armor. His hair was mostly grey, although a trace of its original auburn streaked through it, and he wore a trim beard.

The knight bowed to Danielle as they approached, and then to Killock, and swept aside the flaps to invite them into the tent.

Two more knights awaited within, younger copies of the first. They stood awkwardly as the knight offered wine to his guests.

"Lady Danielle, I am glad to see you safely returned," the knight said as he passed her a cup. "Sir Killock has told me of some of the hardships you have endured."

"Thank you, Sir Lochlan." The knight's name popped into her mind just in time.

"Sir Killock mentioned last night that you might need some horses, and perhaps some winter clothing?"

"Four horses, tents, and gear," Killock confirmed.

"It is my pleasure. And supplies too, of course," Sir Lochlan smiled graciously.

"Sir Lochlan, might I ask for news of what has occurred since we departed?" Danielle wondered. "Have there been any of the attacks we feared? Or new ritual sites discovered?"

"No, my lady, fortunately not," Sir Lochlan replied. "Nothing since you and Lord Bradon left, and I have heard similar reports from the other groups."

"Those are good tidings," Danielle agreed. *Thank God we accomplished that much.*

"Yes, Sir Killock related that you caught the man responsible for the rituals, and destroyed his master as well," Sir Lochlan smiled thinly. "Remarkable news, and I only wish the cost was not so high."

"Yes," Danielle agreed softly. Sir Lochlan turned to Killock, but Danielle continued. "Might I ask, what are your plans, Sir Lochlan?"

The knight turned to her, a small frown of confusion on his brow. "My plans, your Ladyship? I plan on staying here and guarding Dolieb, as I was ordered by Lord Bradon."

"I see." Danielle met his eye and held it. "You have hundreds of men in this camp, do you not?"

"Two hundred and eleven, my lady," Sir Lochlan agreed.

"And, as you said, it seems the attacks you are guarding against have stopped, have they not?" Danielle continued without waiting for a reply. "Is this the best place to attack an enemy that might appear from the High Fells?"

"No, my lady," Sir Lochlan smiled easily. "We are much too far away. They would have all the time they needed to assemble, and could flank us at their leisure. This is where we would fall back to if necessary, to stop a victorious enemy from using the road."

"Oh." Danielle looked around the tent to see if anyone else thought the situation was strange. But no one spoke. Killock seemed content to listen, and Cormac held the carefully neutral expression that soldiers learned to wear around officers. Only Wyn smiled at her and nodded encouragement. *Alright, I suppose the worst thing is that I could make a fool of myself, and I am sure Bradon would not be content with letting Sir Lochlan remain here.*

"I am sorry, Sir Lochlan," Danielle flashed him her brightest smile. "But perhaps I do not understand? Since we know where our enemy came from, and we know their nature, can we not devise a plan better suited for defending against them?"

"I think you understand very well, my lady," answered Sir Lochlan. "If you asked me what we should be doing, then I would say we should gather our forces and move to a position where we can actively scout the catacombs you discovered. A closer position would allow us to move in force against any enemy and destroy them in detail as they emerged."

"That sounds like a good idea," Danielle agreed. "Do you not think you should do that instead of staying here?"

"Well, yes, my lady, except I was given orders to stay here," Sir Lochlan was apologetic. "Until I can get a message to Bandirma to receive new orders, or they send a new commander."

"I think you have just been given new orders, Sir Lochlan." Killock's voice was matter-of-fact.

"I'm sorry, your Ladyship, Sir Killock, but I'm not sure you can do that," Sir Lochlan frowned.

"Of course not," Danielle told him. "But you can. You are the senior commander after Captain Alistair, are you not?"

"And I think we all know what Alistair and Knight Commander Maeglin would say about senior field commanders not taking action while they waited for orders," Killock added.

Sir Lochlan tapped his lip as he considered. Then he smiled. "I take your point, my lady. I believe I have a new plan."

"I am very pleased to hear it," smiled Danielle.

***

Soldiers quickly gathered horses and supplies for them and they readied themselves as the encampment uprooted itself around them.

"He's not wasting any time, is he?" Wyn laughed.

"No, he is not." Danielle pushed down an urge to run into Lochlan's tent and tell him she had changed her mind. *I have no idea what I just told him to do. What if that was a terrible idea!*

"You were grand, by the way." Wyn absentmindedly carved patterns into the snow with her toe as she spoke. "Oh, Sir Littlelamb, I was just wondering why you are hiding over here in your pretty little tent instead of fighting? Do you not think you should move your ass?" Wyn giggled.

"It did seem strange," Danielle agreed. "And I do not sound anything like that. I do not have an accent."

"No accent?" Wyn laughed. "Your Ladyness, I wish I had your accent! Everything you say sounds fancy."

"I am glad you like it, but I am quite sure that I am the only one here without an accent," Danielle insisted.

Cormac and Killock arrived with the horses and they quickly packed their borrowed gear into saddlebags, and donned their new winter clothes. Sir Lochlan provided them with warm woolen cloaks and coats, lined with fleece, and leather boots and gloves that fit as well as could be managed. Wyn laughed at the heavy soldier's boots she was presented, and stomped a flat circle in the snow with them before discarding them in favor of a fistful of thick, woolen socks. She managed to pull on three pairs and still fit into her old boots.

"Perhaps you should take extra food?" Killock suggested to Danielle and Wyn as he checked their supplies.

"What makes you think we can't catch our own food?" Wyn asked indignantly. "Got some practice, I did. Mairi can tell you. I'm an expert in catching little pink fingers now."

"Perhaps you should take all the food," Killock mused. Danielle laughed, grateful for the easy comradeship.

They led the horses down the track to the road, and Killock turned to Danielle.

"Follow this road south to the crossroads at Tuireadh Cnoc. At the crossroads, head south until you reach the Rathad an Thuaidh and that will lead you straight to Bandirma," Killock instructed. "There won't be many settlements until you pass the crossroads, so you will likely have to camp at night until then."

"We will be fine," Danielle assured him. "We will see you in Bandirma."

Killock nodded, and they made their farewells. Aileen cried when Danielle hugged her goodbye, and Mairi beamed when Wyn presented her with a dagger, although Danielle was not at all sure where Wyn had procured it.

Killock approached Wyn, and Danielle saw the faint traces of a proud smile cross his face for an instant. He placed a hand on Wyn's shoulder and looked quietly at her for a moment.

"I am so very proud of you, Wyn," Killock began roughly, and cleared his throat. "Thank you."

Wyn stood with her hands held in front of her, a hesitant smile breaking through the attention. "Yes, sir."

"I want you to take care of Lady Danielle for me," Killock said softly. "She needs you now."

"Of course I will," Wyn nodded her head, trying to hide her confusion as she glanced at Danielle, then at Killock. "We'll be safe, I promise."

Killock nodded and gripped her shoulder awkwardly. Then he turned and hoisted Aileen behind Cormac where he sat on his dappled grey mare, then mounted his own horse and helped Mairi settle in behind him.

They waved one final time as they paused on the last curve of the road before it plunged into the forest. Danielle saw Killock raise a hand in response.

And suddenly they were alone on the road.

The horses plodded steadily through the quiet forest. Danielle relaxed into the sway of her horse and reveled in the simple grace of not having to walk in wet boots.

This is lovely, she thought as she listened to the gentle sigh of the trees in the breeze and Wyn's soft humming beside her.

"What is that tune you are singing?" Danielle asked. "It sounds very joyful."

"Hmmm? Oh that? It's a céilí," Wyn grinned. "We didn't get a fiddler in Dolieb, but maybe we can find a tavern somewhere on the road that has a proper céilí."

"One can only hope we are so lucky," Danielle replied dryly.

***

Wyn spotted the lodge as they crossed a narrow stream an hour before dusk, and they decided it was unlikely that they would find a better place to spend the night. The cabin was a long way off the road and Danielle doubted they would have seen it at all if Wyn had not noticed the overgrown trail leading in that direction.

The cabin was clearly the hunting lodge of a local noble or wealthy merchant. The door was fastened and the windows shuttered, but Wyn easily opened the lock and they were soon inside.

The lodge had a single, large room with a stone fireplace in the middle and a collection of comfortable hand-made chairs and tables. Danielle got the horses settled under a shelter behind the lodge. She discovered a hutch stacked with cut wood, and they eventually managed to light a fire amongst much laughter.

They ate a dinner of a cold meat pie washed down with a spiced wine that Danielle heated over the fire. The fiery taste was delicious, and the warmth crept into her fingers and toes.

Then Danielle moved a cauldron over the fire and melted snow until the water steamed.

"It will feel so good to get some of this filth off," Danielle sighed gratefully. "If only we had a proper tub to soak in. Would you like to go first?"

"I don't think so," Wyn laughed. "If you cleaned the dirt off me there would be nothing left."

"No arguing. I cannot go to a tavern with someone so dirty," Danielle teased.

"A tavern? So that's the deal, is it? I wash and you'll come with me to a tavern? And pay?"

"A wash now, a full bath when we get to an inn. Then you may escort me to hear your céilí, and yes I will pay."

"A quick tops and tails would do me wonders," Wyn conceded as she examined the caked dirt under her fingernails. "I don't think I've ever been so disgusting, and if you'd seen me when I was… well, you'd know that was saying something. But you need to go first, your Ladyship. There'll not be much clean water left once I'm done."

"I do not mind," Danielle protested, but Wyn would not hear of it.

"It's not right that I should get the water all mucky. No one will notice if I'm a bit filthy, but it's near a crime not to have you looking your best." Wyn crossed her arms and glared until Danielle accepted.

Danielle took a lump of hard soap and rubbed it in the hot water until it softened, and sacrificed a blanket for a towel.

She hesitated with her fingers on the laces of her shirt, flustered and excited as she wondered what removing her clothes in front of Wyn would be like. *Will she stay and chatter and not care in the slightest? Will she take notice of me? And what will I do when it is her turn?*

But in the end Wyn sat on one of the bunks and busied herself with trying to mend her clothes, and Danielle cursed herself softly. *Why do I wait? Why can I not tell her how I feel, or ask her how she feels?*

Danielle stepped out of her leggings, knelt on the blanket and slipped her shirt free. She slowly washed out her hair and sponged her skin until they returned to their normal color, the warm water sliding soothingly across her skin. The cabin was quiet save for the trickle of water, the pop of the fire, and a soft stream of curses from Wyn as she struggled with her leggings.

When Danielle finished she could not bear the thought of putting on her own filthy clothes, and instead donned woolen breeches and tunic borrowed from the Temple camp. Danielle wondered what soldier had donated them. They were darned with a tight stitch that showed care and attention, and were made with a soft thread, clearly not someone's cast-off, even if they were a bit threadbare and thin. They fitted Danielle reasonably, although whomever the soldier was, she was not as tall as Danielle, and the tunic was very snug around Danielle's chest.

But they were clean, and Danielle swept her wet hair back from her face with both hands and relished the glorious feeling of fresh skin under soft cloth.

Then she turned to Wyn. "Now it is your turn."

Wyn swung out of the bunk, still angrily tugging on the laces of her leggings. She stopped as she caught sight of Danielle, and stared.

"Maker, you clean up well, your Ladyness," Wyn smiled. "I wish I could wear a shirt like you do."

Danielle blushed in delight. For just a moment she imagined she had seen more in Wyn's gaze than friendly appreciation. She had seen desire so many times from so many people that mattered nothing to her, it was startling how powerful it was, even for an instant, from the girl she wanted to see it from the most.

"Thank you, Wyn." Danielle tried to cover her pleasure.

"Now it's time to earn myself a céilí," Wyn announced, and straightened her shoulders as if she readied herself for battle.

Wyn strode purposefully towards the cauldron of steaming water, and Danielle hesitated, convinced that there must be some innocuous excuse that would allow her to stay with Wyn without causing embarrassment, but unable to think of what it might be.

Wyn stamped angrily on the legs of her pants until they came off and kicked them aside. Danielle caught a glimpse of long, pale legs, lined with the soft shadows of lithe muscles, before she glanced away. No matter how much she yearned to gaze, she would not take advantage of her hidden feelings.

Instead she collected Wyn's leather leggings from the floor and took them to the bunk where Wyn had waited. "Shall I see if I can fix these?" she asked. "I have stitched enough wounds I ought to be able to mend a rip."

"Never mind the tears," Wyn called from the center of the room. "The damn laces won't, well, lace. I've been running about with my pants falling off."

Violent splashing noises filled the cabin as Wyn attacked the bath, while Danielle straightened Wyn's leggings on the bunk in front of her. The black leather had worn through over the knees, and the seams had split. There were rips as well, several that had clearly started life as clean cuts before tearing wide.

Danielle saw that the laces had been torn out, leaving behind ripped leather where there should have been eyelets for the ties.

Wyn had knotted the laces together to create a belt of sorts, using the only remaining intact hole to secure it. Danielle passed a finger over the torn fabric, and tears welled in her eyes as she realized with sad certainty how and when the damage must have happened. *She was this close to tragedy. Maker, please take care of our friend Corlath, who gave his life to avert that fate.*

"So, what do you think?" Wyn's voice made Danielle jump. She had not heard Wyn cross the room, and she stood leaning over Danielle's shoulder, wrapped in a blanket, water dripping from her tangled hair. "Any hope for them?"

Danielle wiped her eyes with the back of her hand and tried to hide her face. "No…" Danielle scrunched the leggings into a tight ball. She could not stand the thought of Wyn wearing them again.

Wyn was silent for a moment, and Danielle waited, still refusing to turn her head. "Burn them," Wyn said flatly.

Danielle nodded and swung from the bunk without meeting Wyn's gaze. She hurried to the fireplace and dropped the wadded leather ball onto the flames as quickly as she could. The thin leather smoldered and smoke burst from it. Danielle watched until flames danced over their surface and they were consumed. Only then was she able to breathe slowly as the tightness left her throat.

Wyn was quiet for a moment as well, and then walked to their bags and rummaged through them to find fresh clothes to wear, clutching her blanket closed with one hand. But soon Wyn was laughing to herself as she pulled on her borrowed clothing. Danielle crossed the room and joined her, and smiled as well. Wyn's tunic fit well enough. Its previous owner was nearly as long and fit as she was. But the breeches came from someone very different. They were far too short, and so baggy as to be shapeless.

"I think they packed a spare tent by accident!" Wyn bent double with laughter, and Danielle joined her, giddy with the release of days of pain and loss.

The laughter gradually passed, leaving them happy and breathless. Danielle spread a blanket next to the fire, sat cross-legged on it and ran her fingers through her hair until the worst of the tangles were gone.

"My poor hands," sighed Danielle glumly. Her knuckles were scraped and bloody, and her fingernails ragged and torn. "It will be weeks before they look normal again."

Wyn pulled the waistband of her breeches tight and knotted it, still giggling. Then she tugged morosely on the wet tangle the dunking had made of her hair. "I bet I look like a drowned cat," she said. "I think it's time this all came off."

Wyn produced one of her long knives and gathered a handful of her damp hair, ready to slice the tangles away.

Danielle spoke quickly to rescue Wyn's blonde tresses. "Would you like me to braid it for you?" Danielle asked. "I would be glad to, and then perhaps you will not need to cut it all off. It would be a shame to lose."

"Like the one you did for Beardy-Bradon? Oooo, yes please," laughed Wyn. "Can you make it all fancy and tra-la-la?"

"Of course, tra-la-la is my most famous style of braiding," Danielle smiled through a pang of sorrow. *I will miss braiding your beard, you old bear. I always thought I would still be combing it for you when it was grey. How regal you would have looked.* She pushed the thought away and patted the blanket in front of her. "Come and sit in front of me here so we can keep warm while we do it."

Wyn slid into place in front of her and wrapped her arms around her knees. Danielle scooted close behind, one leg on either side, so that she could feel the warmth from Wyn's body against her thighs.

Danielle carefully spread Wyn's hair across her back and stroked it softly, gently untangling the knots as she went.

The fire popped and crackled, but otherwise there was a deep, comfortable silence with the rise and fall of Wyn's back under her hands, the silky pass of her hair across her fingertips.

This is the moment to ask, Danielle realized. *But I am too nervous to do so. I have not stopped thinking about it since she said it. Maker, am I really so incapable of asking for something that I want?* She took a deep breath. *And what if there is no tomorrow? So many things I wish I had said to Bradon.* She risked a small prayer for God to give her the strength to get the words out of her mouth. She had practiced them in her thoughts countless times so that they would sound merely curious, but they still stuck in her throat and were awkward when she finally uttered them.

"Wyn, I was wondering if I could ask you. What you said before. About… well, when you said, about how you like... About shafts and nice… well, that you like them both." Danielle quailed inside. It had come out worse than she could have imagined.

"Oh yes?" Wyn asked, and Danielle could hear the grin in her voice.

Danielle felt the heat rise to her face. *Please let her think it just the idle curiosity of an insulated Lady.*

Wyn giggled and sent delightful shivers through Danielle's fingers and against her thighs. "Your Ladyness, I can hear you blushing."

Danielle carefully tied another braid, furious with herself for having made such a mess of things. *I am up to my elbows in it now though, so I may as well continue.*

Danielle tried to pitch her voice nonchalantly. "It is just that I was curious. I am not sure how such things are in the north. I am sorry to pry if I have embarrassed you."

"Not likely," Wyn laughed. "I don't mind at all. And yeah I guess I meant it, although it's not like I know a lot about it."

"No? It was a joke only?"

"Not a joke, no." Wyn sighed contentedly and relaxed to lean on Danielle.

Danielle closed her eyes and relished the feeling of Wyn's weight pressed against her chest. Then she placed her hands on Wyn's hips and guided her upright again so that she could continue braiding. She let her fingers linger for a moment on the smooth curve of Wyn's waist, the thin cloth of her shirt almost unnoticeable, before forcing them to return to work.

Danielle watched her fingers slip through Wyn's hair and remained quiet, although she was desperate to ask more questions. Did she dare hope that Wyn's nature might allow the fiery girl to feel something for her? The possibility had haunted her, more with every day that passed. But now long moments stretched with nothing but the sound of gentle breath and the hot noises of the fire. Still, Danielle stayed silent and trusted Wyn to continue when, if, she wanted. She felt Wyn take another deep, contented breath and exhale with a satisfied sigh.

"There was a girl in Littleford named Kenna," Wyn's voice was soft and low as she continued. "An actual milkmaid if you can believe that. Such a sweet thing. Curly red hair and the biggest ditties, or I mean boobs, your Ladyness, or whatever the proper word is."

Danielle laughed. "I like the sound of 'ditties.' It feels wonderful to say. But I would say breasts, or perhaps just chest to be polite."

Wyn giggled gleefully. "I'd pay coin to hear you say that again. It sounds so proper or something when you say it."

"I promise I will say 'ditties' to you later, but right now you must tell your story."

"Right, so her 'breasts' then," Wyn continued. "I was working with some bards, dancing and singing all over Albyn, and I guess I caught her eye with my dancing because it sure wasn't my singing."

"You are a dancer? I should like to see you dance."

"Love to dance. It's like fighting, only a bit less bloody." Wyn waved her hands in circles as she conducted. "We would do these whirling dances with jumping and leaping, or these slow dances to grab all the eyes while the rest of the group, um, worked the room."

"Kenna comes up to me all shy and asks me politely. She was so sweet about asking, and I suppose I wondered about what she would feel like, and what she would do. But it was more than that, you know? I really wanted it, not just curious or whatever. It was strange to feel that way about a girl, that's for sure, but it felt right at the same time." Wyn laughed softly. "You probably noticed I don't really think too hard about stuff before I jump. So we found a spot and…"

Danielle controlled her breath and forced her fingers to continue to fold and tuck and hold and tie. An ache pulsed deep within her abdomen and rose into her chest as Danielle pushed back images of Wyn, long and lean next to the voluptuous shape of the mysterious Kenna.

"And was it nice?" Danielle asked, pleading for the answer she had practiced in her mind so many times, dreading the answer she had resigned herself to.

"Oh yes," Wyn's voice was low. Wyn shifted against her, her back warm against Danielle's stomach through their shirts. "She was really nice and, uh, really knew what she was doing."

Wyn squirmed against Danielle and then giggled. "Ha, my nips got all crinkly just thinking about it. Or maybe that was too much? I never know when to stop, I'm sorry."

"No, of course not. Why would I be offended? It sounds lovely," said Danielle calmly, although she felt a wonderful tremble pass through her thighs. She concentrated on Wyn's hair as she laced the soft strands over and around into an elaborate weave. *I have no idea what to say next. If only I had any sort of practice speaking of such matters. What do people say to each other about intimate things?*

The silence stretched but it was not strained. Wyn felt warm and relaxed against her, breathing slowly and contentedly as Danielle stroked and smoothed her hair. Danielle wondered what she was thinking. The braid had almost reached the end, which meant she had little time to continue the conversation.

Then Wyn broke the silence, her voice soft and far away.

"It was just so different from romping with the boys. I guess that's why it sticks in my mind." She laughed and returned to herself. "You know how it is usually."

"No, I am afraid I do not know."

There was a pause as Wyn digested that.

"You mean you've never?" Wyn's voice was incredulous, and she twisted around to catch Danielle's eye.

"No, I have never been with someone in that way. Hold still." Danielle positioned Wyn back in front of her.

"Maker's breath, what a waste," mused Wyn. "But how? They must be crawling after you."

"I have had suitors, of course," answered Daniele matter-of-factly. "But my family is an old and proud one so it is expected that I marry someone equally old and proud, which, as you can imagine, is not a pleasing thought. I cannot bear to think of some sweaty, hairy baron touching me. Why should I allow that?"

"Ewww, not likely," giggled Wyn. "But you could have anyone you wanted in the meantime, couldn't you?"

"I wish that were true," said Danielle sadly. She tied the braid with leather thongs to finish the job. She was quite pleased with the result. Wyn's hair swept from her forehead into soft twisted strands that came together at the back of her head to create a five-strand braid that laid beautifully down her back like a golden crown and veil. The leather ties bound it at intervals a hand's-width apart to create bright blonde segments outlined by the dark leather of the ties. The end she left free, a soft tuft that Danielle brushed lightly against her cheek as she savored its gentle touch. She left the bangs loose to frame Wyn's pointed chin, but made sure to securely weave the annoying strands that needed to be constantly tucked behind her ears into the braid.

Danielle smoothed the braid into place, leaned forward and hugged Wyn close. She breathed a sigh of contentment as she felt Wyn's strong, warm back press against her chest, and Wyn relaxed against her to share the comfort of the moment.

Danielle dropped her gaze to where their legs stretched out next to each other by the fire, and watched Wyn's bare toes wave happily back and forth. *She has such small feet, but strong.*

Danielle was sad that the braid was complete before she finished her imagined conversation, but she realized that she likely would not have followed through with it anyway. *It was difficult enough just asking her if she liked being with women, imagine how I would have ruined telling her that I have feelings for her. Perhaps it is best that it ended like this, a lovely memory to take with me to my dreams.*

"So, your Ladyness," Wyn turned slightly so that she could see Danielle's face, the firelight casting a soft glow across the girl's neck and cheek, "why is that?"

"Why is what?" Danielle suddenly feared that Wyn had read her mind.

"That you can't have anyone you want. Why is that true?"

"Oh, that. It is quite ridiculous. My potential marriage has political power that would vanish if they knew of any liaison. I cannot risk it. Not for a dalliance."

Wyn stayed silent, clearly unconvinced, and Danielle suddenly felt angry with herself. She had said the same words to herself so many times they had become rote. Somehow she had convinced herself that it was the right thing to do. Or she had been convinced. But normal people would surely react like Wyn, perplexed by such a bald statement.

"So instead I will shun all of my suitors and keep them all hoping for their turn at the trough," Danielle continued with the story she had spun for herself over many years.

"They can't all be ancient and shriveled and horrible, the ones sniffing around after you I mean," Wyn laughed. "You never know. One of them might be prince wonderful with talented fingers and a huge cock. Or, uh, not sure what high muckities call those."

"It does not come up at court as often as you would think," Danielle laughed. "But it would not matter."

"Why?" Wyn wrinkled her nose in concentration. "Because then you could be happy. Because what you just said sounds really lonely and miserable. This stuff is too important to mess around with. You have to be happy, right?"

Danielle felt her heart pound against Wyn's back and knew that she must be able to feel it too. But Danielle suddenly did not care. *I am terrified, but I do not care because she is right, it is too important not to tell her, whatever the result. Of course it was Wyn who brought me to this moment, of course it was.* Danielle could feel heat start to rise up her neck as she readied herself. *Maker, please let me do this right.*

"You are right, Wyn." Danielle was pleased her voice was soft and steady. "But it does not matter because I have never liked men in that way, so I would not ever marry one."

Wyn's eyes went wide and her mouth formed a perfect "O", then a deep smile spread across her face. Danielle forced herself to keep her gaze steady, although she wanted desperately to look away. "Oh my goodness, is her Ladyness tricksy? Does she dream of a delicious duchess or a bouncy handmaiden? But why is that a problem? Do they care about that in the south?"

"Not normally, no, but when it comes to politics and family power it is anything but normal," answered Danielle. "For what family would seek to marry their son to me if it were known that I would not bear his children?"

"What about their daughters?"

"If it were just about love, then yes," Daniele replied. "But politics is about inheritance. They want their own blood to inherit, and that means children born from wedlock. So my marriage is only tempting if they think that is a possibility. As soon as it is not, my family loses its political power, which is why I have never told anyone, and it is why I have never risked a dalliance."

"I'd tell them all and be happy. You're already all rich and powerful, right? So that way you can have your cake and eat it too," Wyn settled against Danielle's chest again and rested her head on Danielle's shoulder. "If she's named Cake, that is," Wyn giggled.

Danielle caught her breath as the heat rose all the way to her cheeks.

"I know you are right, Wyn, but I have such difficulty asking for what I want," said Danielle. "Especially when important things like my family are at risk."

"If it was just messing about for fun then sure, I get it, it's nice and all but if it hurts your whole family, then no way," Wyn said thoughtfully. "But if it was more than that, something serious that could make you happy, then what if you missed that?"

"I have never cared about that before," said Danielle softly. "But I do now."

"Oh! So there is someone, is there?" said Wyn, and she sighed contentedly. "Well, if we make it home from this, don't forget what I said. It's too important to mess around with, so you need to tell her and don't worry about all that other stuff."

"I think you are right," Danielle smiled.

"Good," replied Wyn. "But why tell me? I'm awful at secrets."

"I asked you because I wanted to know how you felt. It was selfish of me." Danielle cursed herself again, even now hesitating long after she had jumped from the cliff.

"I don't mind. I got to lie in the arms of a beautiful lady while she played with my hair, and I even got a little shiver thinking about Kenna, so it's not been a bad day. But I still don't understand. Why tell me?"

"Someone once told me that these things were too important to mess around with. You were right, Wyn. How can I continue to live such a lonely life? I must risk making a mistake or I could miss that which will fill my heart with happiness," Danielle said as her heart pounded in her chest. "I told you this because I hoped perhaps you might have interest, and now I am asking you if you might feel the same for me as I do for you."

"For me? You're not serious."

"Yes, Wyn, of course you."

Danielle felt Wyn's body tense against her. Wyn drew in a deep breath and let it out slowly. Then she turned and faced Danielle on her knees and met her gaze intently. "You can't want me. I'm all boney. And rude. And you could do better with your eyes closed."

Danielle reached out and took Wyn's hands in hers and moved to settle on her knees before she replied. "Wyn, you are a beautiful, strong woman, and I dream of the touch of your strength under my fingers, and to feel your fire. But please… I agree this is important so please understand that I mean this with all my soul. Your beauty is not the reason I love you." Wyn's eyes grew almost black, so wide were her pupils as she gazed at Danielle.

"Wyn, you are the most beautiful spirit. You have so much passion, so much fire and compassion and kindness. You care for what is right and you stand up for it, no matter the odds. I fell for you when you stood against Lord Lucious, and I fell in love with you when you refused to let that camp sacrifice that poor girl Meghan. Your spirit blazes so brightly, so purely.

"I did not understand at first because I have never felt a passion like this before, but each moment I have spent with you has made it more clear, until it has shouted at me with thunderous words at every heartbeat.

"I love you, Wyn. That is why I have told you these things and have done such a terrible job of doing it."

Wyn was quiet for a moment, her breathing deep and her eyes wide, before she spoke.

"Danielle, you're crazy… how can you…?" Wyn took another deep breath and collected herself. "Listen, I'd have a romp with you in a heartbeat, if that was what you were asking. You're gorgeous and you're sweet, if you don't mind my saying so. And I think if I'm honest I wanted that even before now, although I never really properly thought about it like that.

"But feelings and love and such? I've never felt that way about *anyone.* Maybe I never will. Maybe I can't. And it has nothing to do with you being a Lady, or a girl neither." Wyn gazed at her with a fierce intensity. "I won't lie to you and say I feel something when I don't, just for a bounce or two. I won't play games with that."

Danielle laughed, tension suddenly rushing from her. *It feels good, so good it must be right.* "Wyn, I know that you may not have these same feelings for me. How could you when I only realized a short time ago myself, and I have been thinking about you for days and days? But this is so important that I will take that risk for this chance of finding happiness. And maybe you will feel the same one day, but I know that may not happen. All I am asking you is to be with me and see what happens, and that will fill me with such joy."

"But you know me, I'll blow it. Everyone'll know." Wyn's eyebrows arched in concern. "I don't want you to risk your family for me!"

"I do not care if they know," whispered Danielle, gazing straight and clear into Wyn's bright eyes, and she raised a tentative hand to glide softly across Wyn's cheek, suddenly nervous to touch her now that it carried a far deeper intimacy. "I told you, you are right… this is too important. So I will give my sister the damn title and may it make her happy."

"What?" Wyn's voice was barely a whisper.

"My sister can be the Marquessa."

Wyn sat quietly, stunned. A single tear ran unimpeded across her cheek, and Danielle reached to catch it gently with her thumb.

"You'd give up your title?" Wyn asked, her voice catching. "For me?"

"Of course I will," Danielle smiled. "Wyn, have you not been listening? I love you, I want to be with you. Who would care about a title compared to that?"

"Oh, I don't know," Wyn gave a small smile, "how about everyone in the world."

"And do you care what they think?" Danielle asked. "Because I do not."

Wyn gave a proper smile then, and wiped her eyes roughly. "Nope, me neither."

"Then could you give this a chance, and be with me, and know that I love you, and that you are not taking advantage of me. I want this, with all of my heart." Danielle dropped her gaze, too nervous to watch Wyn's response. "Please think about that…"

Wyn moved closer so that their knees touched, then raised a gentle hand to lift Danielle's chin until Danielle found herself gazing into Wyn's green eyes.

"Please?" Danielle asked softly, and hope dared to let her smile.

"Oh, yes." Wyn slowly leaned forward, a sultry movement that reminded Danielle of a cat, and Wyn slid into place against her, body pressed against body, and her lips brushed against Danielle's ear.

"You said you thought about me for days and days." Wyn's voice was a breath against her neck.

"Yes," Danielle whispered, and she breathed in Wyn's warm scent, and felt the soft touch of her hair against her cheek.

"Did you think of us together?"

"Yes." The word barely came out, but Wyn must have heard.

"Good," Wyn sighed in pleasure. "Because that's what I want."

***

Danielle woke with a start, and for a moment could not remember where she was. Her heart pounded, and she wondered if she had cried out in reality as she had in her dream.

The lodge was quiet. The fire had subsided to a pile of glowing embers and the remains of the largest logs, now popping occasionally as their ends pulsed with glowing webs of warmth. The room was softly dark, the fire the only illumination. There was no wind to creak the trees outside or scratch branches on the roof, just the fire and the deep quiet of the mountains.

Only the soft breath of the girl next to her.

Wyn lay snuggled against her, deeply asleep, her head resting on Danielle's shoulder. Danielle felt Wyn's warm hand curled across her hip, and Wyn's chest gently rose and fell against her arm.

I am glad I did not wake her.

Danielle slowly eased from under Wyn and the thick blankets they had spread on the floor next to the fire. Despite the heat from the glowing embers, the air felt chill against her bare skin, so she wrapped a blanket around her shoulders as she stood at the window. She took her ring on its silver chain from where it nestled in the cleft between her breasts and turned it absent-mindedly as she looked through the glass.

The forest was hushed and dark under the trees, just a few patches of weak moonlight visible as it shone on the thick snow. *Deep and dark and quiet and still.*

She traced shapes into the condensation that coated the window, wavy lines of nonsense that somehow felt deeply satisfying to draw. Her finger squeaked against the glass and she let it rest there to enjoy the cold touch. It drew her further from her dream and returned her to their cabin in the woods.

"Dani?" Wyn's sleepy voice whispered behind her.

"I am here." She turned to the room. Wyn watched her from the blankets, raised on one elbow. The glow from the fire traced one side of her face, neck, and shoulder in a long, curved line and shone golden off her hair. A smile flashed in the velvet darkness.

"Come back to bed, it's cold." The blankets shifted as Wyn moved to make room.

Danielle smiled and nodded. She padded across the room to the bed and let her blanket fall to the floor in a rustle of cloth. Wyn pulled back the covers and she quickly crawled under and curled inside Wyn's arms.

"Want to talk about it?" Wyn asked.

Danielle breathed deeply. "It was just a dream. Did I wake you?"

"Not likely. I'm knackered," Wyn stifled a deep yawn. "But something got you out of bed."

Danielle nodded, and rolled over to face Wyn, their faces just a hand's breadth apart. Wyn was her whole world from here. Green eyes reflected the firelight as she gazed back, and the long sweep of hair that, somehow, impossibly, had escaped its braid to lie across Wyn's cheek. Danielle reached out and smoothed the hair back behind Wyn's ear, then sought out her hand and held it tight between them.

"You do not mind if I tell you?"

Wyn gently shook her head.

"I was home, I think," Danielle began. "I was swimming in the ocean and diving under the waves, and it was lovely." In her dream the turquoise water was so clear she could see every detail of the sandy bottom far below her. Gentle waves slowly pushed her backwards and forwards as she hung suspended above the rocks and reefs, and the warm water slipped over her bare skin with hardly a ripple. Danielle had spent countless hours in the bay beneath her family's home swimming in just such water, diving and exploring the coral on the bottom.

"I did not need to breathe, you see, so I could swim all the way to the bottom where the coral grows and steal pearls from the oysters." Danielle reached out and stroked Wyn's hair and the side of her cheek, the soft skin warm under her fingertips.

When Danielle last visited her home she had returned to the ocean and even coaxed a painfully embarrassed Bradon to join her, although the Templar swam more like a bear than a porpoise, thrashing and slinging water from his shaggy hair on every stroke. She had not been able to convince him to dive with her, so he clung to the side of one of the rock pillars that pierced the surface while she slid into the depths. She had brought him back a beautiful sea urchin, purple and black and red. He looked as if she held a troll in her hands.

It was one of her fondest memories, full of laughter and the warm swell and surge of her favorite place in the world.

Danielle felt a tear leak from her eye and run down her cheek into the blanket beneath her. She took a deep breath.

"There was a cave under the coral, and the water pulled me into it."

The memory of that cold, dark place as it loomed beneath her sent fear through her even now, safe and warm in the blankets with Wyn holding her hand. The cave felt like a wound, raw and sucking. In her thoughts Bradon's laughter rang hollow as her dream memory of the cave beneath their feet invaded her real memory.

In her dream she had known who was waiting for her in the cave. She fought frantically against its pull and strained for the surface with all of her strength. But the abyss claimed her and drew her down until the light faded and all she could feel was the cold presence waiting for her in the dark. It hurt to think of it now, and the words fled long before she could utter them. *Saying them will not make them true,* she told herself desperately, but that was little comfort. The truth was no better.

She took another deep breath, then another, then forced the words out.

"And he was there, waiting for me. I tried to pull him out, but I could not, and then I could not breathe under the water anymore and I was trapped in that cave with him." Danielle took a shuddering breath and tried to wipe the tears away, but she could not stop them.

Wyn pulled her close and held her tightly and stroked her hair, and gradually the tears passed and with them a small part of the pain, enough to let her breathe again.

Killock

The horses plodded into the camp on the Gylden Beck as a light snow dusted the cloaks of the riders and settled on the manes of the horses. The camp was peaceful, the distant thump of an axe on wood the only sound.

Killock walked his horse to the small clearing in the center of the camp and swung to the ground. He helped Mairi down as voices called out, the settlers suddenly aware of their presence. Doors on cabins opened, flaps on tents hurled back, and those in the nearby forest were called to return to the camp.

Killock stood beside Mairi and rested a protective arm around her shoulder as the settlers pressed close, and exultant praises and shouts grew overwhelming. Shrieks of happiness accompanied Aileen's family's arrival, and she was swept into her mother's embrace, tears flooding both their faces.

Mairi shifted back and forth as she strained to find her father in the crowd. And then he was there, pushing forward and calling her name, and Mairi gave a joyous shout and ran to him. He hugged her, kissed her brow and stroked her hair, and thanked Killock with tumbled words.

Then Killock strode to the tall, wooden post that stood grimly in the center of the clearing, its iron manacles still hanging black and ominous from their nail. Killock borrowed an axe from a settler as he passed and stood before the post. The crowd pulled back and waited, quiet with anticipation. Killock swung the axe powerfully into the base of the post. The blade sunk deep and the wood splintered. Killock hewed at it methodically, and passed the axe to willing hands once the cut was started, so that all could strike its hateful shape.

"Then Crassus is truly gone?" a woman asked, and Killock nodded his head.

"Brought to justice," Killock announced, and there were cheers and shouts of happiness.

The settlement celebrated that evening, and burned the post in the center of a roaring bonfire as a fiddle and pipes played and people danced and drank. Killock and Cormac were seated in a place of honor near the fire, although Cormac had little opportunity to enjoy it as he was kept dancing through the evening by an endless series of requests.

Many approached Killock and asked after loved ones taken by Crassus, and Killock's heart grew heavy as he watched them turn away with their hopes dashed over and again.

Mairi brought her father to Killock and she related their story, and her father wept in gratitude for his daughter's life.

"It was my pleasure," Killock replied, and he realized that was the truth even as he said it. He remembered with a smile the deep feeling of dread that had filled him when he first understood that he was to be responsible for leading two girls from the depths of Highward Tor. *And now I find that I regret we have reached the end of our journey. I will miss Aileen's endless, cheerful chatter, and Mairi's quiet interest in the forests and hills we crossed. Perhaps Bradon was right after all, that I might not be the lone wolf I once was. Strange to think.*

Killock knew there was something not quite right with that thought. He would miss the two girls, but mostly he was pleased that they were once again safe with their families.

But as he watched Mairi merrily terrify her father with her retelling of their encounter with the wight, her eyes big and her fingers spread wide into claws above her head, Killock understood a much deeper feeling that had lurked within him. It sometimes rose as anxious concern, sometimes as extraordinary pride, sometimes as simple happiness. But it was always accompanied by a feeling of loss, a piece of himself missing. And it always drove his thoughts to Wyn.

Bradon, I am glad you are not here to know that, once again, you were right, Killock thought wryly. *How did you see it so clearly, so long ago? I am indeed old enough for Wyn to be my daughter.*

***

The horses slowly moved through the thick snow of the high meadow until they reached the tall cliff of black rock that loomed over it to the north. There they stopped, and the two riders dropped from their saddles into the snow.

Killock held his horse by its bridle and stroked its nose as he gazed around. The ground against the cliff face was littered with bodies, dozens of men and horses scattered in front of him. The snow hid some of the corpses under the soft shape of gentle mounds, but many more jutted from the pristine surface, black, jagged shapes frozen in an attempt to escape from the ground.

Killock saw that many of the corpses were the withered remains of husks, their shrunken flesh and parched features marking them as the tormented victims of fuil crunor. But he could also see the bodies of the Temple soldiers who had fallen here, many still surrounded by the foes that had brought them down.

"It's a miracle that any of you survived." Killock shook his head in wonder.

"Not a miracle," Cormac disagreed. "It was Lord Bradon. He held them off until Lady Danielle could find a way out of here."

Killock nodded, then frowned at the low clouds to the south where a dim glow betrayed the location of the afternoon sun.

"Let's find what we need before it gets too dark to search."

They hobbled the horses a short distance away and moved through the battlefield.

Killock found the pack less than two dozen steps from the cleft in the cliff wall that led to the black tower, still attached to the body of Danielle's horse where it had fallen. He unstrapped the pack from the saddle, and carefully checked the contents.

The hunt for Corlath's sword proved to be much more arduous. Cormac tried to trace the path that he and his brother had followed that night, but he was soon forced to concede that there was no way now of telling where that path might lie. So they started a more methodical search, starting at the body of Corlath's horse and slowly moving toward the gap that led up through the cliff, the only landmarks they had to work with.

Every lump needed investigating. Rusted axes, broken spears, shattered shields, and endless bodies, twisted and stiff under the snow.

A withered body along the cliff base caused Killock to pause in his search. Two long arrows were buried in its skull, the grey feathers of their fletching standing like small pennants over the grisly remains. Killock glanced up and looked over the corpses scattered around him. Dozens of arrows protruded from the snow, a forest of quills in an arc centered on a small recess in the cliff wall.

Killock stood quietly as Cormac approached.

"Torbhin?" the soldier asked. "And look, there is the Captain's horse. Maker's breath, Sir Killock, they're not here."

"They fought their way free." Killock pointed to the signs of the tale. "They climbed the cliff wall here, along with a third man, and escaped. After that they must have made their way along the top of the cliff and followed you into the tower."

"Into the tower?" Cormac involuntarily glanced up, although the sheer rock cliff blocked any view. "We never saw any sign of them. Do you think they could have followed us the entire way through?"

"No," Killock said with sad certainty. "They will not be coming back."

Cormac began to question, but stopped himself after seeing Killock's face, and Killock could not bring himself to say any more. He wanted to remember Torbhin by the eager smile the young ranger had tried so unsuccessfully to conceal as he rode from the army encampment at the head of Lord Bradon's party, the last time Killock had seen him alive. Or Alistair by his strong hand and reassuring grip as they had parted ways that same morning, and the promise the Captain had quietly murmured to Killock, that he would 'watch over the lad'.

But it was hard. His thoughts too easily turned to a dark passageway filled with the signs of struggle and pain and fear. And death. *They fought together until the end, at least there is some small comfort in that. They did not face the end alone.*

Killock turned away from the corpses. "We have gone too far. Your brother's sword will be somewhere closer to where we found the pack."

They had lit a lantern to push back the evening gloom by the time they found the sword. Cormac shouted in triumph as he raised it high. Its long steel blade flashed brightly in the lantern's light, the silver badge of the Queen prominent on its hilt.

Killock watched Cormac buckle the sword around his waist, and turned to walk to the horses.

He stopped after only a dozen steps. His skin crawled and his shoulders hunched as he felt an icy chill pass over him and he was suddenly certain that they were being watched.

The Templar scanned the cliff face, seeking any telltale sign of a watcher, any small movement, but found none. The black rocks were still and silent.

"What do you see?" Cormac asked in a hushed tone.

"Nothing," Killock admitted. "But someone watches us nonetheless."

Killock launched into a run, and they sprinted across the ground to the narrow gap in the cliff that Danielle had discovered on the night of the battle. Killock pressed between the jagged rocks that guarded the entrance, and leapt up the uneven steps on the far side, Cormac close behind him. As he reached the high ledge at the top of the stairs he stopped between the weathered pillars that marked the exit. Bare rock and ice met his gaze, but he could sense a baleful presence here that lurked beyond his sight, intense as it glowered at him from somewhere on the ledge before him.

Killock quickly sank to one knee and pulled a soft leather wallet from his pack. His gloved fingers fumbled with the hoops of his Diviner as he raced to assemble it. One after another the hoops slotted together until all of them were aligned. A gust of wind shifted his cloak and scattered ice fragments across the stone and Killock felt the cold eyes intensify their gaze upon him.

The Word pulsed through his mind and into the hoops, and they filled with light. Killock watched it settle and grow clear, then raised the hoops to meet the watcher.

Now he could see the black tower that clung to the ledge. Its jagged horns twisted upwards and gashed the belly of the low clouds as they shifted and roiled above it.

At the base of the tower a shadow flickered and danced like a flame in a high wind. At one moment the shadow was a tall man wearing a crown set with black gems, and in the next moment, he appeared to be no more than a ragged pennant of smoke. But the shadow was the source of the frozen gaze, and in it Killock saw two eyes that never wavered as they stared at him.

Behind the shadow were other figures, translucent and indistinct. Killock saw them gather around the shadow figure, and as they passed, he recognized the burning red eyes and blackened skin and felt cold fingers clutch at his heart.

Killock leapt to his feet, and cried a warning to Cormac. But as he did he saw the shadow figure fade, and the dreadful shapes around it went with it. Killock felt its cold gaze finally disperse.

The knight counted one hundred heartbeats before he forced himself to relax and let the energy drain from the device's hoops. Cormac waited patiently next to him, his brother's sword held ready in his hand, a questioning frown on his face.

"Something has come forth," Killock told him, searching for words to describe the shadow figure. "A shadow against which the magus seems like mere smoke."

"It was here?" Cormac glanced uneasily around the ledge.

"Its attention was here, although it was not, I think." Killock hoped that was true. "But it saw us, and it was accompanied by magi that seemed to be its servants."

Cormac turned towards the emptiness that hid the black tower. "You said that the portal under the tower was still open. The one that led beyond the tower, to wherever the magus came from."

"Yes." Killock wanted nothing to do with that long, dark passageway, but it had lingered in his thoughts ever since. *I knew it was in my future.*

"If that passage still lies open…" Cormac began.

"I had hoped to never again enter those black tunnels," Killock sighed wearily. "But I suppose that was foolish."

"We will need food and water," said Cormac, "and better lanterns."

"No, *we* won't," Killock decided. He passed Danielle's pack to Cormac and held the soldier's eye. "You are going to take this to Danielle and tell her what we found here."

"There's no chance I am letting you go in there alone," Cormac laughed bitterly.

"Cormac, I wish you could come with me. I am not trying to be a hero," Killock assured the soldier. "But it will be easier for me to pass undetected if I am alone, and staying hidden is the only chance I have of returning."

Cormac looked unconvinced, but Killock did not give him a chance to argue.

"Ride as fast as you can, and promise me you will take care of Wyn and Danielle until I return." Killock waited until Cormac nodded his acceptance before he turned towards the hidden tower. "And tell Sir Lochlan to get his army here soon."

He took a deep breath. Then Killock strode across the ledge as the black tower slowly emerged from the gloom to welcome him.

Karsha Hali

The great raven flew high above the world, searching for something interesting.

He left the grey stone hill with all of its people tunnels and thin smoke trailing from dozens of chimneys. He ignored the docks for today and flew to the north and west, cawing loudly to show the boat people that he had not forgotten them. The docks were always interesting, but today he was looking for something new.

He passed over frost-touched farmlands. The fields lay as fallow patchworks of dark earth and grey stone. Rotten snow lurked in the shadows along the low walls that bordered the fields. A few cows lowed in their barns, but the sound hardly carried to the raven, and cows were not interesting.

Forested hills passed beneath the raven. Dark pines covered them like a thick pelt, swaying and bending in swathes that rippled as wind passed over them. The raven spread his wings wide and rode the wind when it came, or powerfully beat his wings to drive ahead once the wind passed. Wind was also not interesting.

An eagle soared above the hills, turning lazy circles as it arrogantly cried its presence to the world. The raven beat his wings harder and darted towards the eagle, who cried out and swerved to meet him. But the raven was far too nimble, and the eagle far too slow. The raven cawed in delight as he flew on, watching the eagle ponderously flap away, trying to regain the height it had lost. Eagles were interesting, if only because they were so easy to taunt. But only for a moment, so the raven flew on.

Grey clouds hung low enough to obscure the higher hills ahead, and the raven flew through their icy mist, his keen eyes searching for dangers looming ahead. The tallest pines brushed at the raven's claws as he dipped and swooped through the trees, then the ground fell away and the raven went with it, dropping from the clouds over a narrow valley. Bits of snow and ice swirled around the raven and left a thin white crust on the ground below, making it harder to see interesting things. A lone leafless tree stood in the middle of the valley, and the raven perched amongst its highest branches. The wind caused the branch to sway and rock and blew snow at the raven, but the bird paid it no mind, staying warm within his thick, ruffled feathers.

Something interesting was coming towards him.

Two riders approached along the twisting road that ran beneath the raven's tree. They huddled inside their cloaks to fend off the wind and snow. One of the riders carried something very powerful strapped on the saddle in front of her, and that was more than interesting. That was exciting.

The raven cawed loudly in happiness, and swooped low to land on the piled rock wall that ran alongside the path.

He cawed at the riders again as they approached, and regarded them with a sharp eye. The rider with the exciting thing passed close by. The raven saw she had hair the same color as his feathers. He cawed loudly in amusement to have seen a raven person.

"He's laughing at us," the other rider said, and the raven saw that she had golden hair. That was very interesting indeed.

"I do not blame him at all," the first rider said, and then they passed him by.

The raven waited until the riders disappeared into the grey mist, and launched into the air again, flying in a wide circle as he continued his search.

***

Karsha blinked as the soft glow of the candles in his room slowly came into focus. Flying with Bran was always grueling, the bird's mischievous thoughts difficult to unwind from his own. Karsha usually liked to wait until the bird returned so that he could talk with him, but this time he had needed to see with his own eyes.

The spirits were right. Lady Danielle brings the Blade to Bandirma.

Karsha rose from the cluttered table that stood in his small room. A gust of freezing air rattled the window and seemed to swirl directly through the pane, completely overwhelming the weak heat generated by the small fire that smoked in the fireplace. A very nice young acolyte named Auraleigh had come that morning to set the fireplace with a lovely coal fire, and she had left him a bucket of coal to keep it going. But Karsha had let it die down due to inattention, and now the tiny room was far too cold.

He wrapped another blanket around his shoulders and tried to rescue the fire, poking at it with an iron to see if there was any hidden heat left in the coals. A few glowed weakly and Karsha tutted in disappointment. *That will never do*, he decided, and dumped the remaining coal on top.

He then found some parchment and a quill and quickly scrawled a few lines. He tried to blot the worst of the blobs of black ink he spilled with another piece of parchment, and rolled the message into a small ivory tube that he pocketed deep within his robes. *When Bran gets back he can take this to Boone, and then I will have to do without my scout for a few days.*

The fire was producing even less heat than before, so Karsha abandoned his room and ambled into the Temple itself. He had no particular destination in mind, but Bandirma fascinated him and he enjoyed wandering through it. He reasoned that he had an hour or two to kill.

He found himself in the kitchens first, lured by the smell of meat sizzling for dinner. Huge iron spits hung above the row of blazing fires, and slabs of venison and beef turned and dripped under the supervision of several kitchen stewards. The bakers were also busily at work, their ovens full of thick, brown bread to be used as trenchers, and cauldrons of winter stew bubbled heartily against the back wall.

Karsha let the heat blast over him as he stepped through the doorway, savoring the warmth and the smell. It felt a bit like home, although too dry. Regardless, he craved the heat, a welcome relief from the endless cold of his adopted home.

He was greeted by name and he laughed and shared a joke with those he passed. He had made it his first business to become an accepted part of the kitchens upon his arrival, and now it paid off as samples were pressed on him as he went. He sipped and munched, and tucked small packages into pockets for later.

Once through the kitchens he found himself in the Sanctuary, high on the upper balcony. He leaned on the railing, surveyed the bustle on the lower floor and examined the top of Saint Taliesin's stone head. The sculptor had taken the time to carefully carve all of the great man's great hair on the top of his great head, which could only be viewed from the highest balcony.

Karsha liked the Sanctuary. Its majestic, open space felt comfortable, and it embodied Bandirma in all the right ways. Big and imposing, yet full of small, caring details and a very human energy. Karsha had seen many marvels of human engineering in his travels, but Bandirma was unique. In the boundless desert he had seen sandstone walls so mighty that they kept the sands from swamping a city larger than any here in the cold north. In the steaming jungle he had witnessed towers that rose high above the trees, clad in shining stone and metal of every color in the rainbow, a forest of spears that pierced the sky.

But never had he seen a city built underground, and at such a scale. The hallways were wide, open and beautifully finished with inlays and statues. There were colossal rooms such as the

Sanctuary and the Cathedral itself, open and airy for no reason other than to provide a sense of space underneath the pressing rock. From where he stood he could see down to the floor of the Sanctuary where dozens of tiny figures strode back and forth like ants. The founders could have built normal structures behind a wall, or even on the top of this very hill, for a fraction of the effort. But they had not. They had built a marvel instead.

"Good afternoon, my lord," a voice said in Karsha's ear, and he turned, puzzled. A tall man in splendid robes stood near him on the balcony, handsome with iron-streaked hair and a thin, trimmed mustache. Karsha recognized him as one of the high priests that had greeted them on their arrival, but the name eluded him.

"Ha!" Karsha replied pleasantly. "Many years since anyone has mistaken me for a lord. You do not seem to be that foolish, so you must be very polite." *Reverend Ail,* he remembered suddenly.

"Well, I thought it was better than 'hey you'," Reverend Ail said with a friendly smile, and he joined Karsha at the railing. "Do you enjoy the Sanctuary? The hubbub is very soothing for me."

"Like the chatter of geese as they tell stories to each other," Karsha agreed. "A man could listen for hours."

"Is it?" Reverend Ail asked. "I have never listened to geese, I must confess. Eaten them, yes, but not listened to them, which suddenly strikes me as very rude. Mostly they honk, do they not?"

"Oh yes." Karsha cupped his hands and produced a loud noise utterly unlike a goose. He frowned. "I thought I could do that."

"No, I'm sorry, that was awful," Reverend Ail shook his head in consolation. "If you enjoy the wildlife I could show you the gardens, or perhaps arrange a trip outside the walls?"

"It is too cold for such things." Karsha shivered at the idea. "Ice and rain fit to freeze a man to death. No. I will remain inside where I can listen to the crowd and wonder if the geese could understand what is being said."

"A wise choice, I'm sure," agreed Ail.

"The tall lady with the chain, the statue by the Martyr, who is she?" Karsha asked, pointing downwards into the Atrium.

"That is Saint Rowenna," answered Ail. "She freed the slaves of Setisthor and cast down their snake god-king, I believe by strangling him with chains she tore from the posts in the slave market beneath his palace walls, if I remember my history correctly. She then spared all of the masters of the city and they joined her in razing the place. I believe I would have buried them under the bricks instead."

"Did she have red hair?" Karsha wondered.

"Now, that little bit of history I am afraid I do not know," admitted Ail without any sign of embarrassment. "I'm afraid you will need to ask Reverend Whitebrooke, our Archivist."

"She reminds me of a red-haired spirit I once spoke to, a spirit of flame," said Karsha. "Also a lady I saw in a brothel on the Summer Coast. She had some chains too, I remember."

"But surely not a sainthood," said Ail reasonably.

The two men chatted comfortably until Ail was called away by other duties. Karsha left the balcony and followed the curved passageway that encircled the Sanctuary until he found himself in the maze of small tunnels in the cliff overlooking the outer bailey. Most of the chambers here were designed to defend the Temple if it were ever attacked, although to his knowledge that had not happened in all of its centuries of existence, and the chambers bore out that tale. A few were still used as watch posts, but most were filled with crates or stacks of old furniture. Many had broken windows that no one had bothered to replace, and cold rain and hot sun had leaked through the wooden shutters to ruin the rooms' contents.

Karsha found one chamber that still boasted unbroken glass and settled on a box that gave him a good view through the window. He kicked his heels against the wooden crate as he munched on his plunder from the kitchens and watched the life of the bailey outside.

Rain still fell in misty clouds and people crossing the courtyard covered themselves with hoods and cloaks. Karsha knew the rain would turn to ice and snow by the evening, thanks to his flight with Bran, and the thought made him shiver. Ice he hated more than rain, although snow still filled him with a delighted fascination, even after all these years. It seemed so improbable.

***

Two riders appeared at the end of the River Gate tunnel, and their horses moved wearily through the snow-filled gloom as the evening bells rang. They crossed the bailey to the stables, and Karsha watched them dismount, unload their saddle-bags, and walk toward the Temple. They brushed against each other as they walked, as if drawn together if they took more than a few steps apart.

Karsha recognized the darker rider the moment she rode through the tunnel. There was no mistaking the Queen's sister. Even road-weary and travel-stained, her exquisite beauty radiated from her. The blonde rider, on the other hand, he could not place, although there was something familiar about her that tickled the back of his mind. She was lively, even though she must be exhausted from her journey. She hopped from her horse at the stables and did a small pirouette on her toes as she stretched out her legs and back. Karsha saw her smiling and laughing as the two walked towards him, and again he felt a tickle of familiarity.

They were met half-way across the bailey by acolytes who sprinted to them, followed closely by Bishop Benno, striding into the swirling snow to embrace Lady Danielle. He greeted the blonde rider more formally. The acolytes took their bags and the whole entourage moved up the steps and out of sight as they entered the temple.

Karsha scrambled from his box and brushed crumbs from his blankets. The Queen would want to know immediately that her sister had arrived, and that she had brought the Martyr's Blade with her. Karsha would wait and see what was revealed about the blonde girl. She might actually be the most interesting thing Bran had found that day.

Karsha started towards the Queen's apartments in the Inner Temple. His bare feet scuffled across the stone floor as he hurried, suddenly remembering the bucket of coal he had dumped in the fireplace so many hours before. *The place is made of stone… how bad could it be?* But he went as fast as he could anyway.

Wyn

The long tunnel of the Tùr Abhainn echoed with the slow hoof beats of their horses as evening's gloom descended. Torches guttered and snapped as wind rushed through the tunnel, bringing with it the swirling shards of ice that had plagued Wyn and Danielle for most of the day.

Hooded forms hurried about them as if they were rocks to be avoided, and even the half-glimpsed soldiers in the guard room waved them past, more concerned with their steaming stove than who might be entering the Temple.

Wyn was road-weary and cold, but she was excited for her return to Bandirma. The heavy battlements of the outer wall soared into the gloom as they rode across the stone bridge. Rows of lanterns on poles made patches of warm yellow against the smooth stones. Light spilled from the wide Temple doors into the bailey, glinted off the thin crust of snow, and cast golden light up the thick pillars of the portico roof.

Wyn had been to Bandirma only once before, immediately after Killock had brought her from Kuray, and her stay had been brief. She had worked with Killock for three months as she learned the hidden signs and special language of the Temple spies.

Upon departing Bandirma, Wyn had been tasked with one assignment after the next as she received instructions from cunningly passed notes or whispers from messengers, and she had never returned.

Life as a Temple agent had not been much different from her life before the Temple. Always moving, always staying out of sight, never leaving a trace. Usually the assignments involved doing something thiefy and fun. She rifled through a noble's private messages in his study in the middle of the night, lifted a key from an unsuspecting mercenary in a tavern, or made sure the right person discovered the wrong letter exactly when he needed to.

But for all of the similarities to her life before Bandirma, the last two years had also been different. She had a purpose, a place, a position, and it all began in Bandirma. Here, she had started to understand that she could always turn to someone. She felt like she was part of a larger purpose. *Perhaps even the start of a family*, she realized, suddenly missing Killock's quiet presence. The massive stone hill with its endless walls and tunnels, filled with people and their energy, made her new life real.

She never met any other recruits and it had been strictly forbidden to meet with the acolytes and squires in the Temple schools. Their work had nothing in common, and Wyn would have been in real jeopardy if she had encountered a familiar face on a mission. She had stayed out of sight when she was not with Killock, and the few people she met during the training had never been introduced, nor seen again. The point was to be herself, the same Wyn that she had always been as far as anyone could tell, freshly released from the dungeons of Kuray and ready to cause more trouble. Until Killock returned from escorting the girls home, it was likely she knew no one here, and, most importantly, no one knew her

Wyn's eyes roamed the towers and battlements of the bailey and found familiar shapes everywhere. The long, low storehouse against the northern wall had a small, locked room in the back and hosted the best dice game in Bandirma that no one was supposed to know about. The soaring spire of Bird Shit Tower, which she had not climbed, tempted her still. *Maybe this time,* she thought playfully.

They rode slowly to the stables through the busy courtyard. Wyn hopped off her horse, stretched her back, and hefted her bags over her shoulder as the stable boys collected the reins. Danielle smiled at her and began to speak, but Wyn jumped in first.

"I remember, I remember." Wyn drew a serious expression across her face and raised a warning finger. "No snogging until you tell your sister."

"Snogging?" Danielle frowned in puzzlement.

"A snog…" Wyn explained. "A kiss, but dirty." She ran her tongue across her lips. "As in, 'Let's have a quick snog and a grope while no one is looking'."

"I do not wish a grope, thank you very much," teased Danielle. "Perhaps a caress."

"It's the same thing," laughed Wyn.

"We shall see," smiled Danielle. "But yes, I wish to be the one to tell my sister, not some overheard rumor, and there are too many people here for us to have any chance of privacy."

"I'll be good, I promise," Wyn assured her.

They walked close together towards the Temple, lugging their packs and the wrapped Blade.

Before they had travelled even half-way Wyn heard Danielle's name being called, and a pack of acolytes swarmed around them and offered to carry their bags. An older priest with a jolly face and grey hair that floated around his head in the chill breeze embraced Danielle and patted her shoulder warmly, beaming affection.

"I am so very pleased to see you safely returned, my lady." Concern and sorrow filled his face. "I received your bird from Dolieb. I grieve with you for our loss. Lord Bradon will never be forgotten, and I fear we will never see his like again."

"I cannot seem to remember that he is gone." Danielle smiled forlornly. "I turn to speak with him, and I am surprised he is not there."

"The Council has granted Lord Bradon a cenotaph in the Cathedral itself, and a full Requiem Mass."

"He would be very pleased," Danielle decided. "He always enjoyed being the center of pomp and fuss. But have you heard of any other survivors from our party making it back? Captain Alistair, or any of the men with him?"

"There was a scout named Torbhin," Wyn ventured. "He's a ranger, like Sir Killock."

"I am sorry, there have been no other messages aside from yours." The priest shook his head slowly, and then breathed deeply and smiled. "But there is always hope, and we must remind ourselves to think of joyful memories to honor our friends as they deserve."

Wyn was not sure she could do that. Try as she might, all she could think of was the sight of Alistair and Torbhin disappearing into the swirling snow, and the silent bulk of grey stone where Bradon had stood.

Danielle introduced the priest as the Bishop, and he turned to Wyn with a friendly smile.

"Ah, the Bronwyn I have heard so much about." He took one of her hands in both of his and pressed it warmly. "Sir Killock spoke of you with such high regard, and so has Lady Danielle in her letters. I am, well we all are, so grateful to you for your efforts."

"Thanks, your Holiness, but it's just Wyn." Wyn gave him her brightest smile. "I hate being called 'Bronwyn'. It sounds like people are praying to me."

"Then 'Wyn' it shall be, of course." Benno nodded his head agreeably. "And you may call me Bishop Benno, or Reverend Benno, if you prefer. I discover I hate being called 'your holiness'. It sounds like people are making fun of me."

Wyn laughed and nodded. *He seems alright, especially for a high-muckity Bishop. Doesn't mind me taking the piss anyway.*

Benno led them up the wide stone steps and through the towering doors into the Temple. In the Sanctuary, bright light blazed from hundreds of candles in chandeliers and from lanterns hung on ornate hooks on every wall. Wyn gazed at the high, vaulted roof and the tall statue of Taliesin in the center. She had forgotten how tall and wide the space was, although she remembered very well how high the top of Taliesin's head was. *I wonder if anyone else has climbed him since?*

Benno ambled through the Sanctuary and down the wide hallway that led to the Inner Temple.

"I fear your bird generated more questions than answers," Benno mentioned to Danielle as they walked.

"I understand," replied Danielle. "Much of what we found defies encapsulation, so I did not try."

"It started a debate that I fear may lead to bloodshed amongst the Council, regarding how some of the more obscure passages in the *Necronix* might be supported by your observations. But what troubles me most is the role of this priest, Crassus. That he was responsible for the rituals seems certain, but how did he learn fuil crunor? None of the archivists can find more than a vague mention of any ritual in all of our records. Yet a hinterlands priest not only finds the rituals, he manages to teach them to himself, and perform them?"

"Lord Bradon and Sir Killock discussed that very concern. We could think of no solution save that perhaps Crassus found the magus, and was either corrupted or willingly became its slave."

"Hmmm. And do you think that is likely?"

"It is possible, I suppose. The magus could have concealed itself from High King Ruric and been hidden in the Sliabh Log all this time. But that is just conjecture. Has the Council not discovered anything to shed light on this?"

"Perhaps. One of the archivists tells us of a book called the *Sanguinarium*. Apparently this book contains the knowledge of the rituals, but as to how Crassus could have possibly gotten his hands on it, or been able to decipher it if he did, there are no explanations. There is no real proof that the book even existed. In any case, when you have refreshed yourself from your journey, perhaps you could tell us the details that could not be entrusted to parchment, and we might together solve this vexing problem."

"Happily," Danielle sighed in exhaustion, "but not until I have had a bath and a sleep, please. I find I am deeply knackered."

Wyn burst into laughter. Danielle looked at her in puzzlement as Wyn tried unsuccessfully to stifle herself. Wyn noticed that several of the acolytes with them were also in a deep struggle to keep their composure.

"What have I said?" laughed Danielle.

"I'm sorry!" Wyn giggled. "Sorry! It's just hearing you say that was fantastic."

"I am pleased to hear it of course, but what thing did I say?"

Wyn glanced around the group. None of the acolytes would meet her eye, and Benno offered no more than an interested smile on his face.

"Really?" Wyn asked. "Alright, well it was just that you said 'knackered'."

"Why is 'knackered' funny?" Danielle asked. "I heard you say it. It means 'tired' does it not?"

"Um," Wyn giggled again, caught between a promise of good behavior and a deep need for mischief.

"I seem to remember that when I was an acolyte it meant exhausted from having sex," Benno observed flatly. "I am fairly sure about that," he added.

"Oh!" Danielle laughed. "Well, that is not… I did not realize."

"Well, regardless of the cause of your fatigue, you should, of course, rest before we meet," Benno carried on, seemingly unruffled. "One additional thing. I am sure you will be pleased to know that your sister is here in Bandirma. She awaits you, impatiently."

Danielle stopped and Wyn saw a delighted smile light up her face.

"She is here? Right now?"

"Yes," Benno answered. "I dare say she would love to see you as soon as possible."

"Of course." Danielle suddenly faltered and quickly glanced at Wyn. "But it will have to wait until tomorrow. I am too tired and too filthy to think right now."

"I am sure she will understand." Benno nodded his head and a small smile flickered at the corners of his mouth.

He turned to the hovering acolytes around them. "You lot, take Lady Danielle's bags to her rooms."

Then Benno turned to Wyn.

"And, Wyn, I was not sure if you had quarters when you were here last?"

Wyn was taken aback. She had not thought of her room in Bandirma in forever. It was a small cell deep in a corner of the acolyte's area of the temple, unremarkable except that it was the first time since she had left her home that she had a place that she could call 'mine'.

"I did, but it was just a room down in the acolyte's dormitories somewhere," Wyn answered. "I don't even remember where it was."

"Could she not take one of the extra rooms in my apartments?" Danielle asked quickly. "It would be no problem at all."

"Of course," Benno answered easily, but there was an appraising expression on his face that made Wyn worry that he knew they had something to hide. She did her best to smile pleasantly.

Benno said nothing further, and led them briskly through the corridors to a quiet section of the temple far from the main hallways, where only a few well-spaced doors indicated the accommodations of the highest echelons of the Temple. Danielle's was tucked at the end of a short passage. Benno said his farewells and left them 'To recover from your journey.'

The polished wood door opened into an enormous main room, larger than Wyn's entire childhood home. A freshly laid fire roared and snapped in a massive fireplace in the far wall, and deep, comfortable chairs surrounded it. Small candelabra were placed on the mantle and on little tables against the walls and provided a bright, cheery glow to the room. Wyn's boots trod softly on thick, woven carpets that lay across the floor, and she saw that an enormous bear-skin was laid in front of the fire for the comfort of any feet being warmed there.

Paintings and tapestries covered the stone walls, and glass and crystal winked at Wyn from all around – bottles in a cabinet, charms on a side table, crystal pendants under the candelabra.

She gazed around the room, and moved along the wall, gently touching the frame of a painting, the bangle of a candelabra and the soft fabric of a chair as she passed to make sure they were solid and real.

"I am looking forward to a soft bed and some new clothes." Danielle sighed euphorically as she moved to the fireplace.

"So we're going to get to meet your sis? That's sweet. What's her name?"

"Gabrielle, and yes she can be very sweet, and she can also be very annoying."

"Gabrielle, like the Queen?"

"Well, yes like the Queen. Wyn, she *is* the Queen."

"Who's the what now?"

"My sister, Gabrielle. She is the Queen. She married King Arian five years ago, and now she is the Queen. I thought you knew."

"Oh… shit."

"Are you alright?"

"Well, luv, you see I've met the Queen before. And she was none too happy with me. Threw me in the dungeon, actually."

"What? She threw you in the dungeon?"

"She did indeed. If Sir Killock hadn't talked them into letting me out I would likely still be there. All because of a bit of fun. No sense of humor, your sis."

"What on earth did you do? Perhaps she will not remember you."

"I think she might. Um, I sort of took some of her things. From her room. Her panties, actually."

"Oh my Lord, that was you."

"Told you did she? Yeah, it was sort of a lark. More to see if it could be done, although I got quite the pretty penny for them."

"You sold my sister's panties."

"Well, most of them. Kept one pair for myself. Don't usually wear knickers at all, but I do like the feel of those royal undies on my tushie every now and then. Quite the racy pair, actually."

"I think you are right. I think she will remember you."

***

Wyn hurried from Danielle's apartments, a gleeful grin on her face. She was supposedly on her way to the kitchens to find some food, but she had a short errand to run first. *Assuming I can remember where my stupid room was.* It was strange that she had not thought about it for almost two years, and now all of a sudden she was in a rush to remember, but Wyn did not dwell on that. She just wanted to find the room, and more importantly, the box she had stored there.

She passed endless rooms, each one filled with people she did not know engaged in tasks she did not care about. The passageways were busy, and Wyn twisted and turned smoothly through the crowds as she searched for a landmark she recognized.

She rounded a corner and almost collided with an acolyte hurrying the other way. Wyn stepped gracefully aside, but the acolyte was not so fortunate. She staggered as she flinched away from the impact, and Wyn caught her and broke her fall.

"Shit, sorry," Wyn apologized. She helped the acolyte to her feet, a willowy girl about her own age with a tangle of red, curly hair and a nice smile. "Are you alright?"

The girl smiled uncertainly, but brushed her hands off on her woolen robe. "I think so, you just startled me."

"That's me, loud and scary," smiled Wyn. "What's your name?"

"Aine," the acolyte answered, her accent placing her firmly in the far north of Albyn.

"Hi Aine," smiled Wyn. "I'm Wyn. Listen, do you think you could help me? I am trying to find my room, but it's been a while and I am not sure where it was."

"We could ask the stewards, they should know," Aine replied.

"Sure thing," Wyn agreed. "Who are they?"

"Come with me," Aine laughed.

The stewards turned out to be the hundreds of craftsmen who tended to the temple. Chambermaids, carpenters, masons, cooks, stable boys. Aine tracked down a steward in a small, cramped office overflowing with stacks of leather-bound books, each one filled with endless lists of names in small, exquisite handwriting. After some ponderous searching he located Wyn's name in one of the books, and Aine led her deep into the winding passageways that made up the acolyte's dormitory.

"Here it is," Aine said, and stopped at a small, wooden door. It was on a featureless hallway that led through the acolyte's wing, isolated and hidden. There were only two other doors in the short hall, and both rooms had been used for storage when Wyn had last been there. Aine fumbled with the latch for a moment before she stepped back.

"Oh, it's locked," she said, clearly confused. "I wonder why?"

"Why don't I give it a try?" asked Wyn. The simple iron lock released with a snap after a quick twist with a metal pick. "There we go, it was just stiff."

Aine gave the door a shove and it reluctantly opened. The room beyond was very small, just large enough for a cot with a trunk at its foot and a small basin on a stand near the door. The walls were bare stone except for a small niche carved above the basin. Most of the floor was taken up by a stack of wooden benches set on their ends against the wall.

"Why are those in here?" Aine wondered. "I'm sorry about that. I'll ask a steward to take care of them."

"Don't worry about it," said Wyn as she looked around the room. It smelled musty, and there was dust thick on the floor. The cot had no mattress or blankets on it, just a wooden frame with a few frayed fringes of rope twisted across its width, and it had been tipped on its side and shoved against the wall to make room for the benches. The room felt so much smaller and meaner than the one she remembered. In her memory it had been snug but not oppressively so, and at the time having her own bed and a door to close were luxuries unheard of. *Still, I've been in worse, that's for sure.*

Aine stood in the hallway, clearly embarrassed as she waited to see if there was anything she could do.

Wyn peered under the basin and found the stone she had carefully loosened from the wall. She slipped the end of her knife into the small crack and popped the stone free. Behind was a narrow hole with a small box.

Wyn took the box and peered inside. A few knick-knacks filled it. A keepsake from her mother and a couple of mementos from her life before the Temple, including one that made her smile as it caught her eye with a flash of bright red cloth.

She closed the box with a snap.

"Thank you, Aine," said Wyn. "I was missing these."

"No problem." The acolyte flashed a smile. "Listen, I was just going to go to the kitchens to get dinner with some friends. Would you like to come too?"

"I can't right this moment, but tomorrow? Do you like a good céilí?" asked Wyn.

"There's one in town tomorrow," Aine nodded her head.

"Perfect." Wyn was very pleased with herself. *I've got my things, I made a friend, and now I have a place to take Dani dancing tomorrow.*

They returned to the main level together, then Aine departed for the meal hall and Wyn headed off, confident she could find her way to the apartments.

She found herself in the Atrium at the foot of the tall statue of the Martyr that stood at its end. Wyn did not care for it. Her face was too serene, too noble. She stood as if she were dead already and untroubled by it, instead of fighting and raging as Wyn liked to think of her. Wyn looked at the long sword the statue held, and giggled as she noticed how wrong the sculptor had been. *Can you believe I've actually seen your sword? I know, right? Dani has it.* Wyn closed her eyes and remembered the shadow-filled cave and the golden figure who blazed so beautifully. *She was so lovely, and so scary, like a goddess. Was that how you were?*

Wyn patted the statue's foot and then moved on through the busy hallways. *And then she said she loved me.* She felt a warm throb deep between her hips at the thought, and she surprised a soldier by twirling around him, and laughed merrily at the look on his face.

I'm acting like a lunatic, but I don't care. It felt as if joy was fizzing all through her body, and there was too much of it to contain. *I'm glad Dani is going to talk with her sister tomorrow, because otherwise I just might burst!*

She was still surprised when she awoke each morning to discover that it had not been a dream. *Because it feels like a dream, it's that bizarre.*

Danielle had taken her completely off-guard that night in the hunting lodge. Wyn's heart beat faster as she remembered Danielle's lovely, passionate, hope-filled profession of love. And she still felt a wonderful deep ache of pleasure whenever she remembered the night of tender passion that had followed, as they had discovered each other. *I never thought I was tricksy, not even after having that bounce with Kenna. That was exciting and new and sweet, but I hadn't thought to ever repeat it.* But her body had wanted Danielle's so intensely, and it happened so fast and felt so right and good that Wyn wondered if she had desired Danielle for much longer without realizing it.

Wyn had awoken before dawn the next morning worried about what the cold light of day would expose. She had waited on edge for the first awkward silence, or hesitation in a touch.

As they led their horses down the snow-covered hillside below the lodge, Danielle had taken her hand and held it as they strolled through the forest to the road. The touch had sent a rush of warmth through Wyn, and happiness had bubbled from her in a joyful torrent of words that lasted the rest of the day.

Wyn laughed now as she thought back. She had been so nervous that first night as they prepared their camp. *Should I try to kiss her? Did I want to kiss her? And Dani pulled our bedrolls together when I didn't know what to do.* Doubts vanished as they snuggled together for warmth under the blankets and held each other tenderly, their low voices talking and giggling far into the night.

The next morning Danielle told Wyn that she loved her again. *I told that stupid story about the time we got that goat back for old Yorik, and Mellon lost his pants and had to talk to the sheriff, and she laughed and said 'Wyn, I love you' just like that.* It made Wyn's heart flutter, and there was something about how simple and easy it was said that made it more real.

They had shared their first kiss not long after that. *Well, not our* first *first, but the first one in the real world.* Wyn had agonized over what her body was feeling since the morning in the cabin, nervous about touching, about sleeping together, about any intimacy. But as time passed, worry turned into desire. Simply holding hands felt so right and so comfortable. And there had been touches as they traveled. A finger's touch on an arm, a hip that swayed against a hip, a hand that rested on a shoulder. Each one intimate and treasured.

And Wyn had realized that she wanted more. She found herself watching Danielle as they rode. The way her hips swayed with the gait of the horse, the way her tunic shifted as she leaned, the way she looked when she smiled, or frowned, or laughed. Wyn had always admired Danielle's beauty, but now there was a deeper, more urgent ache, driven by the memory of what could be hers again.

There had come a night when she lay awake long after Danielle's breathing became a deep, soft movement against her back and wished that their thick traveling clothes would vanish and she could feel the smooth warmth of Danielle's skin against hers again. She had not dared to do more than lie chastely alongside her that night, but the next morning she had vowed to do something about it.

I was so nervous all day, Dani must have thought I was crazy. Hours had passed and the moment never felt right. Then all of a sudden it was. They had walked their horses across a field of winter stubble to a nearby stream to let them drink, and climbed a stile across the path. Wyn caught Danielle as she hopped down, but she landed slightly off-balance in the thick tufts of grass and fell fully into Wyn's arms. Danielle laughed and held Wyn close for a moment, and Wyn gazed into her golden eyes and desire overwhelmed her. Their lips brushed together tentatively and Danielle's eyes widened with joy. Then Wyn kissed her long and passionately, and they held each other tight as urgency slowly became tenderness. *It felt so good, too, it felt right with Dani.*

Each day had been more blissful than the previous, their companionship closer, their affection and intimacy deeper, and Wyn shook her head in amazement as she wondered how it could be possible that two such different people could fit so well together.

It feels wonderful, she thought, and she stopped to lean on the rail of the high Sanctuary balcony for a moment. *Tomorrow Dani can talk with her sis, and then nothing to worry about.*

But the thought stirred an uncomfortable pressure in the back of her throat and an ache of loneliness in her chest. She had not had that feeling in years. *Not since Mum got sick.*

Stupid girl, all happy and you have to spoil it, she breathed in deeply. *Dani hasn't said anything to make you think she's changed her mind.* But other things had changed. They were here in Bandirma, surrounded by the real world instead of the fantasy of two girls on a trail with just themselves for company. *Is it really so hard to think that she might change her mind? I've not told her I love her or anything.*

The thought made her a little queasy. *Of course not, because I don't, and I won't say that just to be greedy. If she changes her mind, then fair enough. I can't expect her to throw away her life for someone like me.* But Wyn could ignore neither the deep avalanche of unhappiness that cascaded through her with the thought of losing Danielle, nor the nauseating echo to the thought that resonated through the locked door in her mind.

She drew in a deep breath and quickly pushed the thought down. *Stop it! I'm not in love with her, so just stop it! I won't go through the pain of losing someone I love again, I just can't. It was too hard, it hurt too much.*

The door in her mind closed with practiced ease, and the echo died away. Wyn took in another deep breath. *I'm just being stupid. She doesn't want to leave me. She's not said anything like that at all, in fact the opposite.*

Wyn let her breathing settle. She watched the people move across the stone floor far below and forced her thoughts to memories of the road and her heart lifted again. And then she laughed. *I'm being silly again. Why am I mooning about trying to cheer myself up when the real thing is somewhere close by?*

Wyn giggled at the thought and hurried towards Danielle's apartments.

***

"Dani?" Wyn called as she entered the main room of Danielle's apartment.

"Wyn, is that you? I am here," Danielle's voice called from a doorway on the far side of the room.

Wyn stepped through into a bedroom as luxurious as the main room. The ceiling arched more than three times her height in the center. Lanterns hanging from iron braces around the walls gave the room a soft, warm glow. A fireplace warmed the room. Elegant chairs and a small table stood in one corner, and carved wooden wardrobes lined the walls. Heavy drapes covered one wall, a promise of wide windows or perhaps a balcony. The bed stood on the far side of the room, with a wide mattress covered in pillows and a thick goose-down duvet that created a soft mountain of clouds, beneath a high canopy supported by four beautifully carved wooden posts.

Danielle crossed the room towards her, her fingers busy as they replaced an earring. She wore only a long, silk robe tied with a sash, and her bare feet padded on the thick carpets scattered about the floor. Her hair was wet and hung down the back of her robe in a heavy, shining wave. Danielle paused to kiss Wyn as she passed, a warm, soft touch of full lips that moved on before Wyn could press against them.

"Do you want a bath?" Danielle asked as she moved to sit at the small table, still adjusting her earrings. "The water is lovely and hot."

"Um, alright," said Wyn. She felt very much out of her depth, lost in this massive set of rooms with their luxurious appointments and the notion of a hot bath waiting somewhere nearby. She looked for it, expecting there to be an iron tub sitting in the corner, but did not see one.

Then she noticed another door that led from the bedroom. Wyn opened it. Inside was a room entirely dedicated to having a bath. In the center of the room, a deep pool held tiled benches and a steady stream of water steamed as it poured from a fountain shaped like a sea serpent wound around a water jug. The floor was tiled as well, and a mosaic on the bottom of the pool depicted a golden sun shining on a blue ocean.

On the far side of the pool stood a flawless three-fold mirror, taller than Wyn, made of silver and glass. A small bench and a chest filled with towels and robes rested above a bed of warming coals. Candelabras on stands at the four corners of the pool and another two on either side of the mirror bathed the room in the warm, gold light of dozens of candles.

Wyn was astonished. The only bath house she had ever seen was in Kuray, but that had been a public building where the inhabitants went to lounge in the hot springs that bubbled from beneath the city. It had been larger, but much less elegant, and she had not actually done anything like take a bath while she was there. She had been much too busy investigating the clothing of the patrons.

Is this what Danielle is used to? What can her house look like if these are her 'rooms' here in Bandirma? Martyr's tears, I took her to the Lucky Duck and she didn't say a word!

Wyn closed the door behind her and slowly walked to the pool. Steam wafted from the surface of the water, and she crouched, dipped a hand, and was amazed by its heat.

Wyn continued around the pool and approached the mirrors. The last time she had seen her reflection in anything other than a puddle or a warped pane of glass in a window had been before her mother had died. Her mother had owned a small hand-mirror that she would use for brushing her hair, and Wyn would sneak it from the small cedar chest in which it was kept and play with it when no one was watching, using it to peer around corners and under tables. Until she had broken it. Her mother had been very sick by then, and Wyn concealed the crime from her in the fear it would have broken her heart.

She was curious, and somewhat fearful, to see what she really looked like now, so many years later. She had felt desperately self-conscious that night in the hunting lodge as she had removed her clothes to kneel naked before Danielle, a feeling that was horribly strange and unsettling to Wyn. But she could not help it. The deep glow from the fire had revealed Danielle's body to be a vision that surpassed anything she had thought possible, a beauty that could not be enhanced by any jewel or expensive clothing. And although Danielle had told Wyn that she was beautiful, that hope felt faint and weak next to the fear that emotion had blinded Danielle to facts that would become very apparent the next time they were together in that way. It just seemed horribly unfair if Wyn could not bring more than being loud and rude to the table. *She's gorgeous, and I'm a boney stick. It must be terribly disappointing for her.*

A pang of worry pulled on her stomach as Wyn stepped in front of the mirror. *Get it over with and look*, Wyn scolded herself. *I've done scarier things than look at myself, I'm sure. I just can't think of any right at this moment.* With a deep breath she raised her head high and looked at her reflection.

A stranger looked back at her.

Where she remembered a round face with a small nose, thin lips and wide cheeks, she now saw high cheekbones, a strong jaw with a pointed chin, a wide mouth with curved, smiling lips, and wide-spaced eyes, slightly turned up at the corners under thin eyebrows so faint that they were more an impression than a feature. The wound across her cheek was no more than a pink line from cheekbone to jawline, although there was now a gap in her eyebrow with a small scar running through it.

I've got freckles! she realized, staring intently. There they were, a pale smattering across her cheeks and nose and her forehead as well. *I wonder where they came from?*

Dirt streaked her face, long lines that leaked from the corners of her eyes where tears had been forced out by the cold wind, and wide smudges on her cheeks and forehead.

Her hair fell across her face in long strands that curved over her eye to end above her chin. She carefully stroked it into place above her ear, and ran her fingers over her face, exploring the shapes she could see in the mirror.

Is this what Dani sees? she wondered. *It must be… this is not the girl I thought I was. I wonder… am I pretty? Dani told me I was beautiful, but I never really thought she meant what I looked like.*

Her fingers ran down the curve of her jaw, then traced over her lips, surprised by the difference between how they looked and felt. They were pale, and chapped by the cold, but she no longer saw the stupid pouty mouth of the young girl she remembered. Her upper lip curved gently above a full lower lip that looked nice and soft, and when she thought of that her reflection dazzled her with a lovely smile with flashing teeth. *Oh!* She smiled at herself again, amazed by the way her face transformed.

Encouraged, she knelt and unbuckled her boots and kicked them off to the side, then stood upright before the mirror again. A quick glance over her shoulder showed her that the door was still closed. She considered what she would say if Danielle came in during the next few moments and laughed at the thought. Her hand reached for the ties of her shirt, and she slowly unlaced them until it hung open. Then she unlaced her leggings until they hung loose from her hips. She bent and eased them down her legs and kicked them into a pile next to her boots. Then she slowly slipped her shirt off and let it fall to the floor behind her.

Alright, let's see.

Wyn turned slightly one way, then the next as she watched her image. The golden light from the candles glowed softly across her skin as she examined herself from every angle.

Her body had changed along with her face since the last time she had really seen it. She remembered a skinny body with no waist or hips, knobbly knees on long, gawky legs, and a chest that looked like a boy's with a couple of small bumps on it. The only time she had seen herself naked since then was when changing clothes or hopping in a river for a swim, and she had not realized how dramatically she had changed.

Scrawny had matured into lithe, and definite curves had appeared as well. She had a narrow waist and a gentle curve over her hips, and a long curve from her hips all the way down her thighs.

Her legs were longer too. They were still thin, but lean muscles ran their length and created soft shadows and curves that moved under her supple skin, and when she turned and pointed her toes the muscles on her calves and thighs stood in sharp relief, long, strong and smooth.

Wyn checked the door again and made sure it was still firmly shut, then returned to her reflection.

She reached up and ran gentle fingertips across her breast to feel the curve. They were still small, there was no denying that. But now they curved out from her chest instead of just being little pink bumps, and they were smooth, high and firm. To her delight there was even a visible curve underneath. Her nipples crinkled into tiny, pink nubs from the touch of her fingers, and Wyn smiled as she felt a dart of pleasure.

Above her breasts her chest had long, smooth muscles under her collar bone and across her shoulders, making beautiful curves and valleys as they went. Her neck was long and thin and there was a deep, gentle shadow in its hollow. She ran her hand down her neck, between her breasts and across her abdomen, tracing the shapes of the firm muscles that lined her flat stomach. When she twisted, she saw them shifting beneath her smooth skin, their long shapes strong under her fingertips.

Wyn sighed in satisfaction and let her fingers trace idly along the long, gentle curve from the shallow indentation of her bellybutton to the small patch of golden curls, almost invisible in the glow of the candles.

Better than I ever hoped, she reflected as she shifted her weight back and forth to watch the shadows move across her skin. *Still a bit hard and boney, but I actually look like a girl. Better than most I'd say.* The idea made her feel warm inside, delighted and relieved.

Wyn's fears rapidly drained away, and she sang softly to herself as she moved to the tub and slowly lowered herself into the water, feeling its heat soak deep into her tired muscles. *I'm pretty, I actually am pretty, she was telling me the truth. I'm really not a bad catch, in maybe a tough kind of way I guess. Strong and beautiful, like she said.*

A small basket sat next to the pool and she peered in. A soft-bristled brush and some soap nestled amongst jars filled with powder. She had no idea what the powder was for, but she thanked the Maker for the other two. The soap and some vigorous scrubbing with the brush made short work of the days of travel that caked her skin, and she dunked her head to wash her hair as well.

She sat on the bench and stretched her arms on the tiled lip so that the water just covered her breasts and lapped at her throat, and she kicked lazily with pointed toes and made small ripples in the pool.

She relaxed and let all of the aches and pains recede. The sound of the water trickling into the pool was soothing, and she fought off a yawn as she found her mind drifting along with her body. She remembered the dream Danielle had told her about in the cabin, at least the part of it about swimming in the ocean. Wyn wondered what that would feel like, to drift high above the bottom, and let the waves splash you back and forth. She had never been a marvelous swimmer, although she could dive with the best of them, but there was something about Danielle's description that had stuck with her. *I want to see that,* she decided. *I want to go there and swim and have Dani show me where she used to play.*

She closed her eyes and imagined it as best as she could. Diving from tall rocks, splashing in warm water, playing in the gentle waves. She could almost hear Danielle's laughter and see her smile, and Wyn floated blissfully and enjoyed the vision as her toes plished happily in the warm water.

Her daydream soon moved on to other things. Danielle's graceful form swimming effortlessly through the waves to rise from the ocean, the water glistening on her dark skin. Wyn squirmed deliciously in the pool, then sat up and opened her eyes. Her daydream was pushed firmly away by the need that had been in the back of her mind for days.

Dripping, she left the pool, draped a robe around herself, and crossed the tiles to the bedroom door.

There she paused.

Is this what I want? Because going out there now, here in the real world, that makes this real. Not just a romp on the road. Can't say 'that was sweet, but…' afterwards. This'll mean I want something more, and I'm her girl until she realizes I'm broken and can't ever give her what she wants, and she leaves me. It's going to break her heart when it happens, and she doesn't deserve that.

But it feels so right to be with her, and it hurts just to think of losing her. Is it not possible that there's a chance I might love her some day? Just a chance that this might be it? I told her that it was worth risking anything for that chance, and I meant it, too. Am I not being absolutely stupid for not taking my own advice?

Don't be stupid, she admonished herself, and she took a deep breath to try to calm her nerves.

Am I ready for this? She dropped a hand to the sash of the robe and deliberately pulled it loose. The robe hung open and Wyn shivered as air passed over the drops of water beading on her skin. *I am. I want it so much.* She opened the door and entered the bedroom. Danielle was seated at the table as she brushed her hair in a small mirror, and she looked up as Wyn opened the door. Wyn saw Danielle's eyes moving over her, and then Danielle put down the mirror and stood to face her.

Wyn was breathing deeply now, and she could feel her heart pounding. She padded slowly across the floor to Danielle and gazed at her face as Danielle's eyes moved across her body.

"I'm clean now," Wyn said softly. "But I'm very wet."

Danielle's golden eyes widened and her mouth opened slightly as a small gasp whispered from her. Danielle reached a hand out and slipped it inside Wyn's robe at the waist, and her fingers slid gently over Wyn's hip.

Wyn slowly raised her hand and ran her fingers across the back of Danielle's neck and into the thick locks of her hair. Then she kissed her, deeply and passionately, and her tongue pushed urgently into Danielle's mouth to taste her, then pulled back and opened for Danielle as she responded in kind. Wyn's arms went around Danielle's shoulders and she ran her fingers through Danielle's hair, and Danielle embraced Wyn around the waist and pulled her close. Their kisses grew until Danielle pulled back with a gasp and held Wyn at arm's length.

"You promised you would be good," whispered Danielle.

"I plan on being good," smiled Wyn innocently.

Danielle's eyes roamed across Wyn's face and lingered on eyes, lips, cheeks. Then Wyn saw Danielle's gaze drop to run the length of the long gap in Wyn's robes. Wyn quivered in excitement as she enjoyed the feeling of being looked at with desire, and held still as best as she could. Then Danielle's eyes re-focused on Wyn's, and she slowly ran her tongue across her lips and swallowed heavily.

"Now I am all wet too," Danielle breathed.

Wyn laughed in delight, and her eyes sparkled in the candlelight.

"Good, because I've been dreaming about this for days now," Wyn said.

Wyn felt Danielle's hands tighten on her hips, and she pushed Wyn backward to the bed and threw her upon it. Wyn gasped and grinned with pleasure and waited as she allowed Danielle to do as she pleased.

Danielle dropped one hand to the sash of her robe, and slowly pulled it free. She let the robe hang open and pull from her shoulders. It sighed to the floor behind her in a rustle of silk and she stood glowing in the candlelight.

The light traced Danielle's beautiful, high cheekbones and the smooth curve of her cheek. Her exquisite mouth was slightly open to reveal white teeth and the tip of her tongue as she moistened her full lips. Her shining black hair had become disheveled to hang over one side of her face in long curves, but she made no move to push it back, instead keeping her gaze locked on Wyn's face.

Wyn's eyes hungrily roamed across Danielle's body and took in every detail of the glorious vision in front of her.

Danielle's dark skin glowed in the candlelight and was traced in gold. Her body curved in sensual arcs that made Wyn ache to feel the smooth length of Danielle's long thighs, her hips, and her narrow waist slide beneath her fingers.

Danielle breathed deeply as she felt Wyn's eyes devour her, her full breasts rising and falling, firm and soft and curving to deep velvet shadow underneath. Wyn let her eyes fall lower to trace Danielle's long, firm stomach as it sloped downward into deep shadow, the soft skin smooth over taut muscles as she breathed.

Wyn knelt on the bed to come face-to-face with Danielle. Wyn slowly eased her own robe from her shoulders and held her head high as she bared herself for her lover's gaze. She watched Danielle's golden eyes as they dropped to Wyn's body and moved across it, her pupils dark with excitement, and Wyn felt a fierce pride swell within her, a confidence she had never felt about her body before. Wyn arched her back and lifted her chin and let Danielle look her fill.

Then Danielle stepped forward and ran her fingers through Wyn's hair, and stroked it tenderly, before she gently lowered her lips to Wyn's. Wyn closed her eyes and let the kiss fill her, stirring flames of passion and need deep within her.

Danielle moved her mouth next to Wyn's ear. "Is this what you dreamed about?" Danielle whispered, and her lips brushed against Wyn's skin.

"Mmmm-hmmm," Wyn moaned contentedly, and she took Danielle's hands and drew her down on top of her.

Ránnach

Long after the middle of the night the dogs began to bark and howl against the door. Angry snarls rumbled in their throats whenever they paused from their chorus, anxious to be set free into the night.

The room was lit by the soft glow of the embers in the fireplace, the dogs no more than shadows as they prowled back and forth in front of the door. Bowed wooden beams supported a low roof that was black with years of smoke, and the stone floor was bare save for an old, scarred table and a raised platform for a bed covered in thick furs. A row of iron pots and pans hung from an ancient mantle above the fireplace, blackened and split by age and heat.

A figure stood against the front wall of the room. A short, thick beard, wiry and untamed, caught the light of the fire as the figure turned. Powerful muscles covered his bare chest and arms. Blue eyes, cold and pale, narrowed under a strong brow, and a strong hand gripped an axe with a beautifully engraved, hooked blade.

Ránnach snapped his fingers and the dogs hurried to circle his feet. A low symphony of growls throbbed around him as they all moved to the door. A quick twist of the simple iron latch and the door swung open. They moved into the cold night air, the dogs clustered around him, held in check only by his command.

The clearing around the stone hut was quiet and bathed in the cold light of a silver moon, bright after the warm, dim interior of the hut. The thick forest stood silently at the edge of the clearing, the shadows pitch black under the trees. A gentle sigh rustled the tall pines and stirred the shadows as faint shafts of moonlight penetrated to the forest floor.

Behind Ránnach rose the jagged, black shape of the Warden tower, its ruined peak a crumbling, empty silhouette against the spread of stars. The black stone walls cast an impenetrable shadow across the north side of the clearing and over the forest, but Ránnach saw that the wooden doors into the tower were still closed. Whatever had disturbed the dogs lay elsewhere.

Beyond the tower rose the western range of barrier mountains that bordered the wide valley of Tír an Síoraí. Sheer faces rose, rank upon rank, and their endless snowfields shone white in the moon's light. At their highest points, so high that they appeared on the verge of tipping over him, their razor sharp peaks trailed shimmering mist to the south as unfelt winds tore across them.

Ránnach warily crossed the clearing, his axe balanced in his hand. The dogs led him to the southern edge where the forest lay thickest.

The wolf watched him from the shadows with unblinking eyes that reflected the moonlight. Ránnach could see that the wolf was a big one, larger than he had seen in many years. Its tongue lolled wetly as it sat behind the rotten trunk of a fallen tree, its fur a shaggy black with streaks of grey around the muzzle.

The dogs growled and barked ferociously at the sight of the intruder, but Ránnach did not release them.

"Hush now." Ránnach's voice was low and calm, and the dogs obeyed instantly, their chorus dying to a few half-hearted whines and heavy panting. Ránnach crouched to watch the wolf and matched its gaze. The wolf sat on its haunches, its ears cocked forward, turning its head slightly as it followed the movements of the dogs as they paced around Ránnach.

Then, apparently satisfied, the wolf loped between the trees and quickly disappeared.

Ránnach rose and slapped the axe against his calf a few times as he peered into the forest. Then he turned to the hut and called the dogs to him.

***

The sun painted the western mountains in bands of pink and orange as Ránnach left the hut the next morning. Before leaving, he donned a jerkin of dark brown leather with a web of grey steel rings woven into it, and a faded, black, hooded cloak. He carried his axe in his hand, and added a short, broad-bladed sword sheathed at his belt and a long, yew bow slung across his shoulders. He chose two dogs to accompany him, seasoned veterans of many hunts. The first was a grey mastiff the size of a pony, with a drooping, black muzzle and sad eyes. The other was more wolf than dog, with shaggy, red fur and a long, white nose. The rest of the pack he left in the clearing, commanded to guard.

Ránnach moved through the forest easily. He followed game trails when he found them, but did not hesitate to venture between the trees as well. Ránnach found the tracks of the wolf from the previous night, along with signs of other animals, but nothing raised his concern. The wolf's trail headed south and showed no interest in returning to the tower. As he climbed up a steep ridge the sun rose over the eastern peaks and bathed the forest floor in dappled shadows. The air was cool under the trees, but the day would quickly warm in the meadows.

At midday, Ránnach reached a deep gorge where the river churned between rocks far below the edge of the cliff. He stood on a wide boulder that jutted from the lip and watched the river below. Chill mist from the water swirled from the shadows to meet him while warm sun soaked into his cloak. He pushed his hood back and let the sun warm his head and the shaggy crop of long, dark blonde hair he had pulled into a thick queue that hung down his back.

The roar of the river thundered far below him, in full flood as always this far into winter. Every mountain bordering the valley wept torrents of snowmelt as the snowpack on their highest shoulders gradually pushed downward into the warmer air below. Otherwise the forest was hushed and peaceful.

He called the dogs to heel and began the trek north towards home.

***

The sun perched a finger's-breadth above the western mountains as he returned to the clearing. Ecstatic barks and a forest of wagging tails beating on his legs greeted him as the pack frisked around him. He leaned his bow and quiver against the wall of the hut, and took the dogs to the well to draw buckets of ice-cold water for them. He doused his head and shook the water from his shaggy hair before a chorus of snarls from the pack alerted Ránnach that he was not alone. A figure stood in the shadows of the trees, camouflaged by the dappled sunlight that shifted and played across him.

Ránnach brought the dogs to heel with a command. The shadowy visitor stepped from the trees and approached him across the small compound. He was dressed in a worn, grey cloak and brown, threadbare leggings and tunic so faded by the sun that they also appeared grey. His shaggy hair was iron with grey streaked through it, and he wore a scraggly beard that was almost all grey. Yet the man did not appear old or frail. Weathered, perhaps, but he moved easily and wiry muscles corded on his forearms and neck. At his side hung a long blade with a worn and stained hilt, but the man's hands did not come near it as he approached.

Ránnach re-assessed the man with every step. At first he looked like no more than a vagabond, some huntsman or wood cutter. But ten steps later he appeared more likely to be a soldier or perhaps a bandit, someone well-used to a sword. By the time they drew within speaking distance, Ránnach felt that the stranger was more dangerous than that. He looked severe and sharp, like the steel blade of a knife.

"What do you want?" Ránnach's voice was easy but there was metal under its surface.

The stranger watched him stoically for a moment, then glanced around the clearing and above the surrounding trees to the high, white-capped peaks beyond.

"What is this place?" the stranger replied. The man's voice was thickly accented, and Ránnach had to strain to understand him.

Ránnach glanced at the tower and the open clearing behind him, and returned his gaze to the stranger. A small smile stirred at the corner of his mouth but it did not touch his pale eyes.

"This is my tower," said Ránnach, "which makes me the warden. Who are you?"

"A warden?" The stranger ignored his question. "You catch poachers?"

Ránnach shook his head slightly and his smile widened but still did not touch his eyes. He settled his stance slightly wider and let the axe slide through his hand until he could tap it against his boot.

"No, not poachers."

"Easy." The stranger held up both hands with palms facing Ránnach. The stranger spoke slowly and as clearly as possible, his eyes locked on Ránnach's hand. "I am from the Temple."

"What temple?" asked Ránnach.

"*The* Temple?" The stranger shrugged. "It doesn't matter. I am from the south. My name is Killock. I have come from across the Fellgate."

"The Fellgate?" Ránnach laughed mockingly, and his eyes turned to the massive peaks that rose hazy and distant to the south. "Perhaps you should go." Ránnach raised his axe to his shoulder.

"You don't want to do that, lad," Killock said softly.

"No?" asked Ránnach, and he stepped forward.

Killock's blade traced a silver blur in the air, faster than Ránnach could follow, and a tremendous blow sang up his arm from his axe. The haft twisted and was wrenched from his stinging fingers.

Ránnach was stunned for a heartbeat. Then a real smile crept across his lips and his pale eyes narrowed.

Ránnach's short blade came into his hand as he leapt forward. Killock twisted to the side and his sword swept out, but Ránnach was ready. He took the blade on his own sword and drove past it. His shoulder came up into Killock's chest in a bull rush that drove the breath from Killock's lungs and lifted his body into the air from the brutal impact. As Killock staggered back, Ránnach's fist lashed out and caught the stranger under his jaw and spun him around, and a kick sprawled him into the dirt.

The dogs greeted his victory with a storm of barks and howls. Ránnach collected his axe as he watched the stranger slowly crawl onto his hands and knees, then turn over to lie on his back, breathing deeply.

"Maker, what was that?" Killock groaned.

"That is how a warden goes easy," said Ránnach. "Now, Temple, are you done?"

"Easy?" Killock sat up and dusted off his hands. He glanced around and found his sword, then slowly and painfully rose to his feet and stepped to retrieve it. Blade in hand, he turned to face Ránnach.

"Now, let's see you try that again." Killock's voice was calm, but Ránnach felt a small chill of excitement run through him.

Ránnach smiled and obliged. He came at the stranger fast, knowing that Killock would expect him to use his strength again. But this time he used his speed and slid to the side at the last moment. His axe whipped out and took Killock's legs from under him.

But the stranger was not there. He slipped to the side, smoother than ice and faster than thought, and his blade struck twice, each time connecting with Ránnach's head. The first blow stunned him, the second knocked him to his knees.

Then a weight hit him in the chest and drove him to the ground. Killock landed on top of him, a knee rammed painfully into his diaphragm, and a hand locked around his thumb and palm and twisted it in such a way that Ránnach was forced to thrash and bend until he lay helpless under Killock's boot. A cold, sharp pain slid into place against the pulse in Ránnach's neck.

"Are you ready to talk now?" Killock's calm voice washed over him. The dogs howled in rage, but still Ránnach did not release them.

"Not bad for an old guy," Ránnach managed to snarl through the pain. Killock laughed and released him, and Ránnach crawled into a sitting position and shook his aching hand.

"I like the way you fight, Temple," Ránnach grinned. "We will have to finish this one day."

"Not any day soon, I hope," Killock replied.

"We will see." Ránnach hopped to his feet and retrieved his weapons from the dirt. He called his dogs to him and crossed the clearing to the hut.

"There's a jug of ale in the well tied to a rope," Ránnach called over his shoulder. "Bring it with you, Temple."

The dogs contentedly gnawed on old bones as the stranger cautiously stepped through the door and into the hut, the dripping jug in his hand. Ránnach placed two mugs on the old table and gestured for Killock to fill them with the chilled ale. He sat on the splintered, wooden bench and watched the stranger pour, then swept up a mug and took a deep drink. He savored the cold, fiery taste of the liquid for a moment, then leaned forward on his elbows.

"Now I am ready to talk." Ránnach's pale eyes watched the stranger drink deeply from his mug, then slowly swallow as a satisfied smile crept onto the corners of his mouth. "Good?"

"Very good," replied Killock.

"So tell me, what would you like to talk about?" Ránnach asked.

"You said that you were a warden." Killock took another long sip. "That this was your tower. What do you protect against? What is the tower?"

Ránnach watched the stranger's face as he tried to decide if he was mocking him, but he found no clues there.

"I meant that I am a Gravewarden, I guard the Grave. And this is my tower because I tend to its Seal."

"The Grave… do you mean the Black Grave?" Ránnach saw a gleam of excitement break through his guest's mask.

"Yes, the Black Grave," Ránnach agreed. "Now your turn to talk. You said you came from across the Fellgate, but it is closed."

"True, the Fellgate is closed, but I found another path." Killock studied the ale in his mug. "It led me through the mountains to here… to Tír an Síoraí. I have always dreamed of seeing Tír an Síoraí."

"You have come to the ass-end of it, nothing but forest and old barrows for leagues," Ránnach laughed. "But you said another path? There is no other path. For hundreds of years people have searched."

"I think this one is new," Killock frowned. "Which is the problem."

"Explain yourself, Temple. You make no sense."

"There's a lot I don't know," said Killock. "We found a fuil crunor ritual site. It was used to open a portal into the lair of a magus that was feeding on the rituals. We destroyed the magus, but the portal remained open. I followed it."

"There were many branches along the way," Killock's voice grew quiet and distant as he remembered. "I avoided the paths that passed into shadow. The way I followed led me here."

"Why should I believe you?" Ránnach's eyes narrowed. *Could it be possible? When the Grave was sealed it did not destroy the lich priests. That is why the Gravewardens exist, to stand guard over them.* "The Grave has been sealed for a thousand years, the Fellgate closed for hundreds."

"Believe what you want," Killock shrugged, unconcerned, "but if you would like, I can show you. Seems like an actual Gravewarden would want to know for himself."

"You think so?" Ránnach swirled his ale. "Perhaps. Perhaps you wish to show me a place where bandits are waiting to kill me? Who can say?"

"You're scared of bandits? I had my sword at your throat," said Killock reasonably. "If I had wanted to kill you, I could have."

"True," Ránnach agreed. "But as you said, there is a lot you do not know. Perhaps you need my help?"

Killock nodded. "I do, but not for robbing a barrow. Tell me about your tower. You say that it has a Seal? Is that how the Grave is closed?"

Ránnach sat back and considered the stranger. He was not sure what to make of him. *I like him, with his stone face and his crazy story, and he fights well. And if what he says is true…*

"Come," said Ránnach, and rose from the bench and made for the door. He strode across the clearing to the tower.

Ránnach led the way inside the tower through a small wicket gate, the doors long ago rusted into immobility. The tower's interior was cold, the thick stone walls that blocked out the sun trapping the chill night air. Bright sunbeams cut shafts across the stone floor from gaps in the gate, filled with shining motes of dust that hung suspended in the air as if trapped by the light. Far above them a bird flapped clumsily to a perch, the echoes of its wings the only sound in the tower.

Ránnach led the way up some stairs to the upper floor. At the top of the stairs was another room the width of the tower. Two towering arches cut through the outer wall let in sunlight and a gentle breeze. One looked over dark green forest, the other faced the nearby foothills of the imposing barrier peaks.

The upper floor was the heart of the tower, the great Seal, and in its center the Wardstone itself. Around the walls, wide pillars rose up and arched to form a high ceiling with a pinnacle directly above the Wardstone. The stone ceiling was cracked and a chunk was missing, and through it Ránnach could see the jagged spire of the ruined tower.

Killock stood near the top of the stairs and took in the Seal, then moved to the eastern archway to look over the forest. From that vantage point, densely forested hills rolled away eastward, each one lower and gentler as they fled the rocky foothills to the west, until finally at the end of visibility a dark line of shadow outlined the river canyon.

Between the tower and the canyon another Warden tower raised its jagged, black shape from the forest like the broken shaft of some tremendous spear. Killock glanced at the Wardstone, then at the other tower.

"The stones can see each other," Ránnach confirmed for the stranger. "Each one joined to the next." Ránnach locked his hands together to demonstrate.

"How many towers?" Killock asked.

"Seventeen, all the way across the valley," answered Ránnach.

"Each one with a Gravewarden?"

"Of course."

Killock nodded, then turned from the view and regarded the Seal itself.

Circular rings of precious metals were inlaid into the floor, each one a different width and a different spacing from its neighbors. Each band was engraved with a long orbit of runes that surrounded elaborate, geometrical shapes and patterns, and there were threads of metal that formed similar patterns across the stone between the rings.

In the center stood the Wardstone. A dome of obsidian, black as night but so polished that it blazed with reflected light from the open archways. A path lined with metal threads crossed the rings and allowed the Gravewarden to approach it without treading on the surface of the Seal.

Ránnach watched Killock's reaction carefully. The stranger was impressed, that much was clear, but there was a familiarity and a comfort in his posture as he crouched near the rings that made Ránnach think that he had seen something like it before. *He knows what is important*, he thought, *and he is not afraid of it, or overawed. Excited, yes, although he hides it well.*

"Have you ever seen something like this?" Ránnach asked.

"Only once," the stranger answered in a hushed voice. He stood and turned to face the Gravewarden. "Not the same, but similar."

Ránnach nodded and let the silence return. Killock slowly circled the room. He stopped to examine the Seal in places, then returned to the open archway to look over the forest once more. Ránnach joined him there.

"So, Temple, why are you here?" Ránnach watched the stranger's profile, his weathered skin and deep-set grey eyes.

"I was not sure at first," Killock replied. "I didn't even know where I was. Some forest with an old, ruined tower on a hill."

Killock turned from the view and faced the Gravewarden. "But now I wonder if fate might have brought me here."

"Fate?"

"Luck then," Killock shrugged, "whatever you believe in."

"Neither of those. I don't need luck and I won't bow to fate."

"Fair enough," Killock continued. "But I am glad I am here, whatever the reason. I told you that fuil crunor was being used in my land. The rituals created husks and wights and killed many people, and worse, summoned a magus. We managed to destroy it, but it cost us, dearly."

Killock paused for a moment before he continued. "I thought only to discover where the magus came from, but instead I found you, a Gravewarden, an order of warriors who have guarded against this foe for a thousand years, when we have desperate need for aid in doing exactly that. Do you see why I might call that luck?"

Ránnach laughed. "If the magi are finding a way out, then the Gravewardens will be very interested in meeting the man responsible."

"That was my hope," agreed Killock. "How can I convince you my story is true?"

"You cannot," Ránnach shrugged. "In a thousand years the Seal has never failed. Other barrows have been opened, or people have gone in to search for fame and glory, but no magus has ever come out."

"You are not worried that someone may have found a way?"

Ránnach's face grew somber, and his eyes narrowed fiercely. "Of course. This is why tomorrow you will show me how you got here. Once I have seen it with my own eyes, then I will know."

"That will be my pleasure," Killock smiled. "It was a dusty little crypt, about a half-day south of here, but I can find it again."

"Then we will leave at first light," Ránnach led the way down the stairs, "and if it is as you say, then we will visit the other Gravewardens and convince them of the truth."

"I don't want to know what will happen if I am lying, do I?" asked Killock.

Ránnach laughed, a harsh sound with no humor in it. "You know already."

***

The broken stone door lay innocuously in the middle of a meadow filled with small, yellow flowers. Fat bumblebees meandered from flower to flower and filled the air with the heavy sound of their droning buzz. Golden sun shone from the south, strong enough to bring warmth to the day after a chill night.

In the center of the meadow was a small hill, no higher than a house. On the north side it had been dug away many centuries ago to create a barrow under its flower-covered surface, and the stone door placed there to seal it so that its occupants' rest would not be disturbed.

Long centuries of weather had worn away the soft sides of the hill as well as the door, until the door collapsed to the side and cracked through the middle as it fell, and now it lay half-concealed in the bright yellow carpet. The barrow gaped open and Ránnach saw rough stone steps leading into its dim interior.

Ránnach squatted next to the door as his two dogs ran back and forth across the meadow and snapped at the bumblebees.

"Open a few months, no more," Ránnach decided. "Was it empty?"

"No, they are still in there," answered Killock.

"More of your luck, Temple," Ránnach stood. "Very few barrows this close to the Grave are untouched by the Crunorix."

"I thought you didn't believe in luck?"

"I just don't need it," Ránnach replied. He whistled his dogs to him and set them to stand guard at the entrance. "In case something comes out that isn't us," he explained.

Killock led the way into the barrow. They descended a short distance through a tight passageway that ended in a small, circular room. Pale roots of the weeds and grasses that covered the hill creeped between the flat stone blocks that formed the low ceiling. In the walls were four crypts, simple, stone coffins placed in shallow alcoves. No carvings adorned the coffins or the walls themselves.

At the far end of the room, a wide crack ran through the floor where it had subsided, taking loose stones from the wall and one of the coffins into the chasm with it. They lit small lanterns, and, using the coffin as a ledge, Killock carefully lowered himself into the earth. The drop was no more than the height of a man, and led to a dark tunnel made of black, roughly-fitted stone.

Ránnach joined him in the tunnel and paused to examine the walls.

"You may be right," Ránnach said as he ran his fingers across the black stone. "This is not part of the barrow."

Down they went, Killock ahead with his lantern held high. The tunnel twisted, curved and grew colder with every step. Soon the warm sun was a distant memory.

The tunnel opened into a wide, shadowy space with a line of pillars carved into twisted shapes with long limbs raised in supplication to the stone weight of the ceiling above. Water dripped from between the cracks in the vault and ran down the cowled faces as if they wept.

Ránnach approached the nearest pillar and tapped it with his axe. The short, sharp ting of metal on stone echoed from the walls.

"This is their work, for certain. The Grave is filled with this sort of hideous shit," Ránnach said. He looked around the room.

Five exits opened in the walls, each one a dark tunnel that curved from sight. "Which way did you come from?"

"This one," Killock said. Cold air slowly oozed from it, dead and wet.

"You first." Ránnach pointed the way with his axe.

At the far end of the tunnel stood a pair of stone doors set between heavy blocks of black rock. Iron torch stands were driven into the stone on either side but both were empty. Ránnach raised his lantern and peered around the room. Shadows flickered across the tunnel as light played over the statues on either side.

Ránnach approached the door. "This leads to the Grave," he said and shone his lantern on the black stone. "The stone here reeks of them."

"Can you sense them?" Killock asked. "There was an emptiness, like a black shadow except with nothing there. But it's everywhere, I cannot tell where it is coming from."

"It *is* coming from everywhere." Ránnach passed his axe in a wide circle. "The Grave was built with fuil crunor rituals, every stone is bathed in it."

"Have you ever been inside?"

Ránnach stared at him for a moment before letting a smile twist one corner of his mouth. "Yes, we all have. To become a Gravewarden you must."

"Why?"

"This is where the wights are," said Ránnach with the half-smile that never touched his eyes. The Gravewarden reached into the neck of his tunic and pulled out the leather cord he wore around his neck. Dozens of long, white teeth hung from it in a fan, each one as sharp and thin as the blade of a stiletto. "To become a warden we must enter the Black Grave and kill a wight. Many fail."

Images of a stone chamber, deep underground, flashed in Ránnach's thoughts. He remembered torches that guttered in the chill air as the ring of wardens spread around the room. Then inhuman shrieks in the darkness beyond the torchlight. Shouts of warning as steel flashed around the perimeter, and then the black gleam of dead eyes as the ring parted to let a pale form enter.

Ránnach tapped a gloved finger against the longest of the fangs and felt the sharp pressure of it through the leather.

"You did this alone?" asked Killock.

"Other wardens come with you, but you must make the kill or the ritual will not work." Ránnach tucked the necklace back under his jacket of steel rings. He had been confident as he had descended into the Grave with the other wardens, but the wight had shown him his error in just a few dozen heartbeats. His shield shattered, his axe wrenched from his hand, he had been driven to the ground by the creature's ferocity. He had thought himself dead in that moment.

But instead of despair he had found cold rage, and with that rage the strength to fight off one more attack, and then another, and another. Of the five initiates in Ránnach's group, only he had survived the trial. The other four perished under the pale blades in that darkened crypt, their bodies dragged to the surface and burned on a pyre during the final ritual that made Ránnach a Gravewarden.

"There is a ritual?" asked Killock. "What does it do?"

"It makes you a Gravewarden," said Ránnach shortly.

Killock watched him for a moment, and turned away stoically. "Do you wish to see farther?"

Ránnach pulled the door open in answer and led the way into the Grave.

The halls were narrow and twisted, the chambers small and mean. Rough-hewn stones lined them, and low arches forced the two men to duck as they passed.

Killock knew where he was going. He chose without hesitation at each intersection, every time turning from the cold, dead presence Ránnach could sense sleeping in the heart of the Grave far away.

Then the path plunged deep into the earth and entered an area where the shadow lay thickly in the stone. The tunnel opened into a vast space. Spiked pillars erupted from the walls and climbed into the darkness, covered in black iron bands that wept rust. Deep pits opened in the center of the space and the path arched above them on a bridge of thin stone held by iron braces that descended from the shadows.

They slowly crossed the bridge as thick, chill air swirled around them. In the center stood a tall tower hewn from a pinnacle of stone that rose from the deep pit. The bridge connected to the top level where a temple had been carved, four thick pillars that held a stone slab over a black altar. A narrow stair wound around the exterior of the tower, and Ránnach saw balconies and other bridges below.

Three shallow steps led from the top of the tower to the altar, and Ránnach ascended carefully, axe in hand. His boots crunched softly on small rocks that littered the ancient stone, and there was a distant echo of some far-off sound, so remote as to be unrecognizable. Otherwise, the vast, open space was eerily quiet.

The top of the altar was shaped to take the body of a man, with wide channels carved to hold torso, limbs, and head. Thick iron bands were held in place by long spikes driven into the stone, rotten with rust. The black stone was stained deep brown where blood had pooled and flowed across it countless times, and the surface looked strangely warped, as if it had melted slightly and then re-formed.

The channels flowed down the sides of the altar and across the floor, bent and twisted to form the corrupted markings of fuil crunor. From there they connected with gutters that drained down the sides of the tower in all four corners.

Killock stepped to join him and Ránnach held a warning hand against his chest.

"I know what this place is," Ránnach said in a low voice as he turned to Killock. "The blood pits. The magi would sacrifice their human priests and use their blood to turn their followers into creatures filled with lust for death and violence, forced to revel in that which they abhorred the most."

"The priest's blood did that?"

"Yes. Our lore says that the priest's blood would mark the victim and cause him to burn with a thirst for killing that could not be satisfied." Ránnach glanced around at the blood-stained stones of the altar. "Touch nothing."

Killock followed his gaze and nodded silently. Then he pointed into the gloom where Ránnach could just discern the vague shape of another bridge at the edges of the lantern's light. "That is where I came through."

Ránnach stayed silent as he considered his options. So far the Grave had been quiet, more so than he had ever known it to be, but he knew the silence would not last, and it could change in a heartbeat. The pits were disquieting. He never expected to come this far into the Grave, and it had surprised him greatly when he realized where they must be.

Yet he had not seen anything that would confirm the story that Killock had told him. They had encountered no distance-spanning portals to allow the magi to pass the Seal.

"How much farther to reach this portal?"

Killock considered his answer in silence. "I really don't know," he eventually admitted. "You cannot tell when you reach one. There's no sense of a Word, it is far more subtle. Bradon said that they descended a stair for hours before realizing that they hadn't made any progress whatsoever."

"Then we must go farther," Ránnach decided with a shrug. Killock nodded his head quietly, felt the weight of his sword in his hand, and indicated the stairs with it.

They descended the narrow steps together, their lanterns small glows against the sheer rock walls. The outer edge of the stairs had crumbled away in places and gaped open to reveal an endless fall into the depths. As they descended the air grew colder until their breath hung in chill clouds of icy mist around their heads.

They reached the level of the bridge Killock had indicated. A thick mist swirled from the depths and coated the stones so that they glistened in the lantern light. The bridge extended out of sight and they continued until they seemed to walk on stone suspended in the mist. Killock paused and turned to face the way they had come as Ránnach waited silently. When the knight turned back he shrugged.

Ránnach tapped his axe against his leg, and headed farther into the mist. *No sense in turning back now. They could be behind us as easily as in front.*

Slowly the mist became darker, and black stone walls loomed ahead. The bridge ended in a pair of colossal stone gates.

"Those were open last time," Killock said.

Ránnach did not respond. He stood indecisively in the center of the bridge and turned to stare back the way they had come, then faced the gates again. *Something is not right,* he thought, *what has changed?* The Grave still loomed on all sides, the chill air still drifted endlessly around them.

But it felt different at the same time, as if there were an echo of it, faintly heard from far away.

"Are you alright?" Killock asked.

"I think we entered one of your portals," Ránnach said. He strode purposefully to the stone gates. "Quickly, help me open these."

The massive stone slab moved slowly even with both of them straining against it. It rumbled and shook against its iron hinges as it opened, and shuddered to a stop with a deep boom that echoed into the emptiness around them.

Beyond the gates, ancient steps, shattered and crumbling, led into a vast, natural cavern. Its floor was covered in a forest of stalagmites of all sizes, and a black pool wound around their bases and mirrored them in perfect stillness. Vague shapes loomed above, beyond the reach of the lanterns.

On the far side of the cavern, Ránnach saw another tunnel, but he had come far enough. He now knew that Killock's story was true. With every step he could feel the echoes of the Grave becoming more and more clear. Somehow he was both in the Grave and also far away, and there was a cold shadow that linked the two that chilled him deep inside.

"How much farther is the path to your side?" Ránnach asked.

Killock thought quietly for a moment. "Two days at least. Does that mean you believe me now?"

"Yes." Ránnach turned to look up the stairs to the open gates. "The path is open. If they were called from their slumber there is nothing to stop them."

"So will you help close the path? Can the Gravewardens help us?"

"Let us go and ask."

They quickly retraced their steps to the long bridge and hurried across it, once again swallowed by the thick mist. But long before they could see the tall pillar of stone at the far end they suddenly stopped. There was a movement in the mist as it swirled around something on the bridge. A pale form watched them with dead eyes.

Then it screamed. Its piercing shriek echoed again and again against the distant walls of the chamber, and was answered by a dreadful, rasping sigh that came from every direction at once.

"Ruric's balls," Ránnach cursed. "It summons the husks. Quickly, we must pass the bridge before they climb up to us."

Ránnach raised his axe and bounded towards the figure blocking their path. The wight screeched its rage and leapt to meet him.

Its pale blade rent the mist in a long arc and Ránnach blocked it with his axe. The impact swept him from his feet and threw him into the ancient rail that bordered the bridge. Ránnach felt the stones crack and give under the impact, but they held. He scrambled to the side and the wight's blade collided with the stones, showering long splinters of cold stone across the bridge.

There was a blur of silver and grey as Killock attacked. The sharp crack of steel against hardened skin rang out twice as Killock's sword slammed into the wight's head and neck, but the weapon rebounded as if it had struck stone and left only the shallowest of wounds. Killock grunted and dove to the side as the wight responded, its sword scraping sparks from the stones as it sought the knight.

Ránnach regained his balance and fell on the wight from behind with a ferocious, two-handed blow. The axe sliced skin and shattered bone as the blade struck violently and tore a terrible wound through the wight's neck and jaw and smashed it to the floor.

Killock stood amazed as Ránnach wrenched the axe free.

"How..." he began, but Ránnach pulled him into a run.

"I will tell you if we survive," Ránnach promised with a laugh.

Their boots pounded on the bridge as they sprinted through the mist. Ránnach could hear shrieks echo through the darkness as the wights called to each other. They reached the narrow ledge on the tall stone tower as the first husks spilled from the stairs ahead of them. His axe swept four from the ledge as he whirled it left and then right, and Killock's blade danced in a silver blur that carved through the rest. They raced for the stairs then and made the first flight heartbeats before more husks surged from the depths and pursued them.

Ránnach flew up the stairs with Killock right behind him. They reached the altar at the peak of the tower and started across the high bridge, but skidded to a stop when the pale form of another wight appeared before them. Ránnach risked a look down the tower. They had only moments before the husks reached them. Before he could move Killock darted towards the wight.

A long thrust of his sword caught the wight under its chin and drove it back a step, then Killock followed with a vicious cut that ripped across the pale flesh from hip to shoulder. The wight screamed in rage and fell upon Killock. The knight stumbled backwards towards the edge of the bridge and the wight pursued.

Its pale blade plunged towards Killock, who at the last moment slid to the side. Killock twisted underneath the wight, grabbed it and lifted with shoulder and hip and back, and suddenly the wight was gone, a shriek that disappeared into the yawning gulf below the bridge.

Ránnach laughed with delight, then pulled Killock to his feet and urged him along the bridge as the husks boiled from the stairs in pursuit.

They passed through the stone doors at the end of the bridge and into the twisting brick passageways. Ránnach followed Killock as he guided them without hesitation through the maze.

A glimmer of daylight shone ahead and shortly they were at the collapsed ceiling. They ran through the ancient barrow and burst into the sun-drenched field.

Ránnach sank to the ground and blithely endured the slobbering welcome of his dogs as he let the sun's rays warm his skin. A shadow fell across him and he opened one eye. Killock stood with a hand extended, and he took it and was helped to his feet.

"Not bad for someone still wet behind the ears," Killock smiled slightly, his face cracking into a strange mosaic of lines.

"I think they are going to like you, Temple." Ránnach tucked his axe securely into its loop on his belt.

"Who are?"

"The other Gravewardens." Ránnach began walking towards the north. "They love old shit."

"Are they all as funny as you are?"

"No, I am afraid they are quite dour."

The two men reached the shade of the trees and moved into the shadow of the forest.

"So, about that axe," Killock ventured. "Can I get one?"

Benno

Weak sunlight shone down the length of the long passageway that led from the Temple to the gardens on top of the great hill. The snow had stopped falling, the clouds had thinned enough to expose a few small patches of pale blue sky and, for a brief moment, a misty sun low on the horizon.

In summer months the winding garden paths meandered around carefully tended beds of flowers, shrubberies, and trees. A stream burbled from one small pool to the next, and the path arced over the brook across small wooden bridges. People young and old wandered or took their rest on benches and small lawns, reading, laughing, and enjoying sunlight and shifting leaves after a day within Bandirma's stone hallways.

In the winter months the gardens were less popular. The plants were trimmed to bare stalks, fallow beds were covered with leaves and protected from the winter freezes, and the rain, wind and cold forced the benches and lawns to keep an empty vigil.

Beyond the gardens lay a small lake and farms that extended all the way to the edge of the cliff. From the gardens, none were visible, although there was a well-worn path that followed the stream towards the lake.

Now, snow lay thickly over the garden and smoothed all shapes into gentle curves. Trees wore snow on the top of every bare limb and the stream had frozen across its surface. Surprised ducks slipped and pecked at the ice, then returned to the small lake whose deeper waters remained open.

The calm day enticed a few others to the gardens. Tracks in the powdery snow followed the path, and one of the small lawns proudly featured a rotund snowman with a priest's headdress perched rakishly on its head.

Benno led Danielle through the tunnel to emerge blinking in the low, winter sunshine. Two acolytes walked hand-in-hand on the far side of a small pool, wrapped in thick robes, boots and woolen mittens, but otherwise no one was visible, and Benno was pleased to have a moment's solitude.

Benno watched his companion take in the low sun. Danielle closed her eyes as the feeble warmth stroked her face and she smiled at the touch. Then she exhaled deeply in contentment, breath steaming into the air as she looked around the snowy garden.

"It is a pleasure to see you so radiant, my lady. A tremendous weight is gone from your shoulders. You fairly glow."

"Thank you, Reverend. I am happy. It is strange to say because I would have sworn I was happy before, but I think underneath I knew I would be lonely for the rest of my life."

"I know solitude was a struggle for you. Have you told your sister yet?"

"I have not. I would like to tell her face-to-face. We are to meet at the evening bells, and I will tell her then."

"How do you think her Majesty will take the news?"

"I hope she will be delighted for me. I never told her why I have never taken a husband, so that will be a surprise, but I am sure she will be pleased to hear that I finally have found someone I love."

"Your sister is a very compassionate woman."

"She can be. At other times she throws people into dungeons for stealing clothes."

"For stealing clothes?"

"Yes. Oh, it does not matter."

"As you wish. And will you inform her Majesty that she is to be the new Marquessa?"

Danielle stopped dead in her tracks and stared at Benno.

"How did you know I was going to tell her that?"

"You could not hope to maintain your family's position if it were known that you were partnered to a commoner, and a known thief at that," Benno replied. "I am assuming you do intend on marrying the girl."

Danielle nodded quietly. "I have not thought that far, nor do I have any idea what Wyn would think of such a notion. But I know that I wish to spend my life with her, if she will have me."

"Well then, as I said."

Danielle gently rubbed a line of snow off the branch of a small tree on the side of the path.

"Yes, I will renounce the title," she said softly, and she smiled consolingly. "It is best for everyone."

"I hope that is so."

"Do you think it would not be?" Danielle asked in surprise.

"I do have a concern, I am afraid, although you could not have known of this complication." Benno pondered his next words carefully. "I am sure it will surprise you to learn that the Queen has been demanding we give her the Martyr's Blade. It is the purpose of her visit, in fact. She was very disappointed when she learned you were not here and she would have to wait."

"Give her the Blade? But why?"

"Her wizard, Karsha Hali, has convinced her of its importance. He knows of the fuil crunor rituals, and has sensed the power behind them as we have. And he has correctly determined the Blade's critical role in the struggle, and wishes for the Queen to have the Weapon serve her, not the Temple." Benno spread his hands apologetically. "Of course I reminded her Majesty that the Blade serves you, not the Temple, but I fear I have only moved the burden of defying her onto your shoulders."

"And when she becomes the Marquessa, she will not have to ask any more." Danielle sighed in frustration. "But I must give up the title, and I am not sure what we can do about Gabrielle's insistence on taking the Blade."

"There is likely nothing we could do about it," Benno gathered his robes around himself more closely, "if she were to become the Marquessa."

Danielle glanced over at him, puzzled. "What do you mean?"

"You don't have to abdicate the title," Benno's voice was casual.

Danielle's eyes went cold. "Is that your advice?"

"It is not my advice, it is merely an option that must be mentioned, however distasteful. Many people have sacrificed their own lives for a cause before now."

"Sacrifice? Yes, I know about sacrifice." Danielle's voice was ice, and Benno knew that he had made a mistake. "I have seen it, I know its cost, and I was willing to pay it too. But until that time comes and my life must be sacrificed, it is mine to live."

Benno bowed his head before her gaze. "My lady, I am sorry. It was an ill-thought phrase, and I regret it deeply."

Danielle nodded her acceptance, but he could tell she was seething, no matter how expressionless she kept her face. *Perhaps I should abandon this conversation? She is unlikely to be persuaded now that I have made such a pig's breakfast of the thing. No, that accomplishes nothing. This must be done and it must be done now.*

They walked in silence for a spell and followed the path as it meandered down one side of the stream, then crossed over a small, wooden bridge and continued on the other side. Benno saw Danielle slowly bringing her anger back under control as they walked. Finally, she stopped beneath a holly bush and turned to face him.

"This is not a cause, it is about who gets to carry a sword," Danielle said dismissively.

"True, although that decision may have lasting consequences."

"You do not know that is true." Danielle walked again, more quickly now.

"You do not know that it isn't." Benno moved with her as the soft snow scrunched under their boots. "How many people could actually wield it? Do you think your sister could wield it?"

Danielle did not answer him and they walked in silence for a short time. Benno waited patiently, taking special interest in every tree and bush they passed as he looked everywhere but at the noblewoman. He hated the necessity of this conversation and the pain he would have to cause Danielle, but it had to be done. His heart went out to this lovely, lonely woman, but he could not let one person's happiness outweigh the needs of the Temple. So many depended on him making that choice every time.

Danielle stopped on one of the small bridges across the stream and turned to Benno.

"Have you asked Him about this? Is this His advice as well?" she asked.

"I have not, but I think you know as well as I do what His answer would be. He would say 'follow your heart, do what you know is right'."

"Yes, exactly. This is what I am doing."

"But what is your heart really telling you?"

"What do you mean? It tells me that I love this woman, and I should do everything I can to be with her, forever."

"Wonderful. I am glad to hear it. I was concerned that there might be a chance, just a chance, of course, that two young, beautiful people, who endured hardships and conquered challenges together, and who faced death and survived together, isolated and alone, might find comfort in each other when comfort was so desperately needed, and that the comfort might feel like more than it really was."

"A trail romance? You think I am infatuated and need to come to my senses?" Anger settled deeply within Danielle's eyes again.

"No, I am merely asking you the question." Benno met her gaze unflinchingly. "Have you asked it of yourself? Have you looked deep inside and asked yourself, 'what is my heart telling me?' Is this fresh romance, so quickly joined, is it really love?"

"I did not come to this realization frivolously or carelessly," Danielle replied. "My heart knows she is worth everything to me. Reverend, do you really take me for a person who would become besotted over a pretty smile? Many have offered themselves to me before, and all have been rebuffed."

"Of course I think it is possible, my lady." Benno shrugged his shoulders. "She is everything that is strange and exotic to you. It would not be the first time someone fell for a person who is new and exciting."

"Wyn's past may have been what made her into the woman she is today, but it is *her* that I love, not her past."

"Very well, then I am happy for you and I hope that young Bronwyn brings you continued joy." Benno held her eye a moment longer, then resumed his stroll around the path. They walked quietly, each deep in their own thoughts.

Love… why did it have to be love instead of lust? Benno was unsure of his next move. Danielle seemed determined enough that continuing to push her to deny her feelings would only send her running to the Queen to put her declaration into action. *And once that is done, well, it is done.*

Benno had hoped to convince her to push Bronwyn aside and sacrifice herself to duty to her family and the Temple once again, but that hope was fading.

But that was not the only option which would solve all of Benno's problems.

"Once Gabrielle is the Marquessa as well as the Queen, your family's political power will be almost unmatched," Benno mused, almost to himself. "Her children will inherit your family estates in Lavandou as well as the throne of Albyn."

Danielle nodded, and quietly waited for Benno to continue.

"As I consider it further, your union with Bronwyn would actually be of considerable advantage, since there could never be any children who might stake a claim to your family through you, the older sister and rightful heir." Benno paused and leaned on the railing of one of the small bridges to examine the frozen stream as he spoke. "Good for you, and good for your family."

"Yes, your Grace, you see why I think this is the right thing to do." Danielle joined him at the rail. "I have considered this carefully."

"Then please, also consider this." Benno kept his gaze firmly on the icy surface beneath them. "The only negative is the urgency with which you are proceeding. Simply keep your relationship with Wyn a secret until we no longer need the Blade, or we know that the Queen has a wielder to take your place. Almost everyone would be satisfied with such an arrangement. The Temple keeps its Paragon and her Blade, your family keeps its standing at court, and you keep Bronwyn. I suppose the Queen will be disappointed, but I have at least given her an acceptable compromise with the promise of an alliance, and she will get the Blade and your title in the end."

"You ask me to tell Wyn she must be hidden away, never to be acknowledged, never to be accepted, our relationship illicit." Danielle's face remained calm but Benno could see the strain in her shoulders and in the way she folded her arms defensively over her chest. "To tell her she is not good enough to be seen with me."

"I doubt Bronwyn's feelings will be hurt to be kept on the side," Benno offered. "She seems to be more of a realist than that."

"The one has nothing to do with the other," Danielle snapped. "Just because you expect the world to discard you does not make it easier when you are thrown away. Hope must make it worse. It would surely break her heart, and I know it would break mine to tell her that I do not love her enough to be seen with her."

"It is not so black and white as that," Benno kept irritation from his voice as well as he could. "I am not suggesting forever! A short time, balanced against the dreadful threat we all face right now. What is a little time, compared with raising the Blade against the Crunorix when they return?"

"It does not have to be me!" Danielle's calm broke and she spat her words in fury.

"You make an extremely risky wager," Benno shot back. "Who will wield the Blade if not you? There may be no one else, and there is certainly no one in the Queen's service. Why take such a risk over such a trivial thing as a few months? And not even a few months apart from each other, just a few months in secret?"

"It is *not* just a few months." Danielle raised her hands in exasperation. "It is a lifetime of her knowing I wanted to hide her, and me knowing that I asked her to hide."

Benno took in a deep breath and forced calm into his voice.

"My lady, I do understand that this is not an easy choice." Benno rested a hand on her arm to comfort her. But Danielle did not uncross her arms, and he could feel muscles rigid with strain beneath his fingers. "You know I love you dearly, and I hate the idea of hurting you in any way, but I had to because of the stakes, and I know you understand that."

Benno dropped his arm and tucked his hand into the pocket of his robes again.

"I ask you to do the same," Benno sighed regretfully. "Consider what is at stake, and if you do not wish for my counsel, then ask Bronwyn what she would do."

He returned down the long hallway and left Danielle alone in the winter garden amongst the bare trees, stark in the pale snow.

***

Benno hurried straight for his apartments through the hushed hallways of the Inner Temple.

The Bishop's quarters were tucked deep inside Bandirma, almost underneath the Cathedral. They were extensive and comfortable, with public rooms for greeting distinguished guests, a spacious bedroom, a scriptorium filled with deep leather reading chairs and shelves of heavy books, and a drawing room with a wide fireplace and enough room for a dozen people to relax in comfort.

Once inside Benno threw his cloak onto a chair in frustration. His stomach churned from the conversation in the gardens, hatred for his part in trying to deny happiness to someone for whom he cared deeply roiled next to guilt for having failed to accomplish his purpose. He poured himself a glass of wine and stood staring into the drawing room fire. *I managed to hurt Danielle deeply while not actually securing the Blade for the Temple… a shameful display.*

Benno drained his glass and then filled it again. *As long as she doesn't give the title to the Queen.*

Nor did he wish to speak to God about it. The situation was a shameful one, and he was embarrassed by his role, however justified he felt it was. The last thing he wanted to do was to talk with Him about it. In any case, what he had said to Danielle was truthful… Benno felt sure he knew what He would say to him, and it would likely be the same message as the one He would give Danielle. *'Do what you know is right'. But I do not have Danielle's certainty. All I can say for certain is that I know what is right for the Temple.*

Benno took a sip of his wine and savored the rich taste. *Perhaps I should join Danielle and renounce my position as well. I could become a country parish priest and live out my life drinking too much wine, milking cows, and delivering long-winded sermons to napping farmers.*

A knock on the door broke his bucolic reverie. He opened it to find Reverend Whitebrooke outside and quickly invited him in. Whitebrooke accepted a glass of wine from the Bishop but only took a sip before he broke the silence.

"How did Danielle take it?" Whitebrooke asked.

"As we suspected she would, not well," sighed Benno wearily. "I do not think I persuaded her."

"She is intent on the Queen assuming her title?"

"Danielle was quite angry with me," replied Benno. "I hope she will consider better options."

Whitebrooke sipped his wine, a frown deep across his face.

"What will you do if Danielle does not consider your options?" pondered Whitebrooke. "And the Queen claims the Blade?"

"If that happens we can do nothing," Benno replied shortly. "I have tried to convince the Queen and that damn Karsha Hali that the sword is better off with Danielle, or with us. I have tried to convince Danielle that she should put the needs of the Temple before her own needs. If Danielle ignores the Temple, if she refuses to compromise her feelings, it's over. All we can do in that case is hope that the Queen knows what she is doing."

Whitebrooke slowly nodded his head. "Yes, I was afraid you would say that. Well, if there is truly nothing to be done…"

Benno was surprised that the Archivist did not sound more upset by the news. Whitebrooke had never struck Benno as the most stoic of men, but he was pleased to not have this argument.

"I may have some welcome news for us," Whitebrooke continued in a deep rumble, and he swished his wine around his glass. "We have uncovered something very interesting about the fuil crunor rituals that Lady Danielle discovered inside the catacombs, as well as some clues as to the missing *Sanguinarium*."

"Oh, yes?" Benno asked hopefully.

"Yes, although it has raised a question." Whitebrooke pondered his wine for a moment, lost in thought. "I wished to ask you, as I know my own judgment in this area has not always been sound."

"Of course, please ask." Benno perched on the edge of a chair. Benno knew that the clashes between himself and Whitebrooke after Benno took the Bishop's ring had left many scars. Working with the Archivist in the years since had never been easy because of those wounds, but that had changed as they allied more closely in the matters of rituals and sacrifices and ancient magic, the secrecy and the dire nature of their work forcing them together at first, then perhaps healing those scars.

"As I am sure you will recall, after my wife… died," Whitebrooke hesitated, and Benno was surprised at the pain he heard in the Archivist's voice, even after so many years. Whitebrooke did not speak of his wife any more, and had not for years, and Benno had hoped that time might have healed some of the pain of her death. *It does not sound like time has helped. The pain sounds as fresh as if she had passed only recently.*

"After she died," Whitebrooke began again, "I searched for a way that might allow me to bring her back. I even went so far as to seek out treatises on fuil crunor, as I grew convinced that the magi's control over death might contain an answer."

"Yes, I do remember," said Benno.

"Of course." Whitebrooke finished his wine in a gulp. "The last time we spoke of this, I told you of a rumor, or perhaps a myth, of a Word that the Crunorix used to bring back the dead. Do you remember that?"

Benno nodded, but remained silent and let the Archivist continue.

"You called it dangerous, and an obsession, and you were right on both counts." Whitebrooke's voice grew strong and certain. "Their knowledge was lost, and more importantly, corrupt. I did not see that at the time, but it has become clear to me since."

"I am glad to hear it." Benno leaned forward and set his glass on the end table.

"The events of these last few weeks and months have made me consider." Whitebrooke caught Benno's eye and held it. "The rituals have returned, which means someone has deciphered them. And we have learned of this book, this *Sanguinarium*, which contains all of their knowledge. Perhaps this mythical Word is not so mythical. Perhaps it is in this book. I find myself wondering, would it be possible… could you conceive of a way in which you, or the Temple, could ever consider using such a Word, for even the best of reasons?"

"You know that cannot be." Benno shook his head sadly. "If anything, this has shown us that the corruption of fuil crunor is just as powerful as we had ever feared, not less. Surely you can see that?"

"I can, you are right." Whitebrooke stood and drew a deep breath. "I merely ask because we have found some references that might allow us, if we so desired, to use a fuil crunor ritual. Just to find our enemy, of course, and only with our own blood. No real sacrifice would be needed."

"And you think we should do this?" Benno held his breath as he waited for the answer.

"No, I do not," Whitebrooke frowned, angry at the thought, "but some of the archivists do, and I wanted to ensure that you and I were aligned against this."

"We are," Benno nodded anxiously. "And does this have something to do with what you have discovered?"

"No… well, partly I suppose, although it will be easier to just show you." Whitebrooke placed his glass on the mantle. "The archivists are exceedingly eager to show off."

"It's not Reverend Turlough again, is it?" Benno knew he could not take another audience with that withered old stick right now.

"No, not this time," Whitebrooke laughed. "In fact, it was his assistant, Reverend Meara, who made the discovery. We may want to think about retiring Turlough in the near future and elevating Meara."

"Sounds like an excellent idea," Benno replied, as he followed Whitebrooke out the door. "I think Turlough has crossed the line where the wind from his ass means more than the wind from his mouth."

Once again Benno hurried to match the long strides of the Archivist as they headed for the archives. Whitebrooke was intent on speed, and met any attempts at conversation with the briefest of replies.

The archive doors were closed, and Whitebrooke took an iron key from his pocket and unlocked them, then locked the doors behind them.

"I don't want to risk anyone seeing this," the Archivist explained when Benno gave him a questioning look. "You will understand when we get there."

Whitebrooke took a candelabra from a table, lit the candles with a taper left smoldering on the room's mantle, and led Benno into the stacks.

Benno had not been deep into the archives for years, not since he was an acolyte and had spent a year transcribing copies of ancient books that were on the verge of becoming unreadable.

Some of the books had been interesting and gave Benno a view into forgotten lore or new philosophies, but most had been spitefully boring. Long treatises on fungi, or memoires so biased and sycophantic Benno frequently considered misplacing them in the Abhainn Fuar rather than copying them. The year had crawled by in a haze of ink-stains and hand cramps, and Benno had avoided the archives as much as possible since.

Whitebrooke led them through the upper stacks to a heavy iron door that blocked the way. He paused to produce another ancient key. Benno felt the small pulse of power as the Archivist's Word unlocked the mystical locks on the door, and Whitebrooke turned the key to unlock the rest.

Behind that door lay the real treasures of the archives, artifacts and knowledge so powerful, or so dangerous, that their very existence was often a secret.

Whitebrooke passed level after level as they went deeper and deeper down a long narrow staircase, until finally he stepped off the stairs long after Benno had lost count.

The room Whitebrooke led them to had only one door in it. This one, unlike all of the others, made of stone instead of iron.

"What place is this?" Benno wondered.

"This room is veiled by the most powerful Devices in all of the archives," Whitebrooke explained as he produced a simple stone key on a steel chain. The key was no more than a finger-thin cylinder with a flat head, but Benno saw carvings on its surface. "It is for artifacts that no one must ever know exist, let alone that we possess."

The key slid into the lock smoothly and Whitebrooke focused on it, his eyes closed. Benno felt the Word pulse strongly and the door shuddered as hidden mechanisms slid open within it. Beyond lay a small room, featureless, and on the far side a door the twin of the first. Whitebrooke sealed the outer door, strode to the inner, and unsealed it with the stone key.

A sudden coldness flooded the room and penetrated cloth and skin and flesh. Benno felt shadows twist in the cold, and his breath caught as Whitebrooke pushed the door open.

"Whitebrooke, what…" began Benno, but then words failed him as he stared, stunned, into the room beyond the door and a dreadful understanding twisted in his stomach like a knife.

A cold and congealed stench oozed from the room. The bodies of nine archivists had been laid in a circle, their feet pointing outwards, their arms and legs spread wide. Benno recognized priests and priestesses, old and young, now all staring with dead eyes at the ceiling. Black markings squirmed across their naked skin in the dim light of a lantern, and more markings painted with blood covered the floor. A body, torn apart beyond recognition, lay in the center.

The cold shadows twisted and swirled around Benno, and the world went dim as he felt their icy touch burn into his skin. He staggered to a knee, his body overwhelmed by the pain. His shocked mind flailed helplessly, trapped in pain and disbelief. Black shadows clouded his vision.

No. The thought whispered from deep inside, no more than an instinct.

No! He clung to it, and its intensity burned away his confusion. Long years of study and practice showed him the pathway to follow, and the ornate patterns of a great Word formed in his thoughts.

"NO!" He shouted the thought and with it, the Word. Bindings within his amulet released, light flowed through the labyrinth of runes engraved into its silver surface, and immense energies exploded forth. Fire, golden and pure, raged through the room in a blazing inferno.

Benno felt the pressure of the shadows against his flame, pushing like a tree-root through stone. He shaped and re-shaped his Word, meeting each incursion with brilliant light that forced it back.

He felt a Word of power slap at him from behind and pain ripped across his mind. He bared his teeth in rage and turned his fire on the man behind him. In an instant Whitebrooke was bathed in an inferno of golden flames that sought a way through to the Archivist's flesh. Benno could feel Whitebrooke's Wardpact weaken under his assault and re-doubled his power. He shaped his Word more precisely and his flames turned white hot as they licked over the Archivist.

Then Benno hissed in pain as more tendrils of shadow forced their way through his aura. He realized he could not let his focus slip for even an instant. Sweat poured from him as he unleashed Word after Word with all of his skill and might against the shadows. A vast, dark wave loomed high above him, an ocean of weight he had to hold at bay. The pressure grew stronger, and his body sang with the icy touch of the shadow as it slipped past his flames. His light was now surrounded by shadow and it encroached on all sides.

Then Whitebrooke's powerful voice bellowed forth. Strange words tore from his throat, each one filled with malice and hunger. Benno felt a void yawn wide beneath him, an abyss that hungered to be filled with a craving so strong that Benno felt his heart labor and his breath grow short. A black ache filled the room from where Whitebrooke stood, and Benno saw an ancient iron-bound book, open in Whitebrooke's hands as he read from it.

Benno shouted defiance and fire sizzled across the room. It struck Whitebrooke with a deep concussion that threw the larger man violently against the far wall of the room. Benno struck again, and flames danced across Whitebrooke's torso, leaving smoke and smoldering cloth in their wake as the Archivist heaved and buckled under the impact. Whitebrooke shouted in pain and Benno felt the hunger of the abyss recede.

But Whitebrooke was not done. He lurched to his feet, powerful legs spread wide, mouth locked in a snarl of rage. Another Wardpact locked into place around him and then his chant began anew.

Benno's fire whipped across the room again and danced over Whitebrooke's Ward. It pulsed a deep purple and trembled under the impact but held.

Whitebrooke's words reverberated through the shadows and the emptiness of the abyss, and Benno felt the world shrink as his light was pressed on all sides. It blazed brightly in defiance, but the swirling forces brought against it slipped past again and again, each time wracking Benno with pain and numbing coldness. His light flickered, a small star at the bottom of a vast ocean as it pulsed and flared against the cold pressure that bore relentlessly upon it.

Then his strength failed. He collapsed to the floor. Agony blazed through him and his throat locked in a scream that would not end. His back arched and his hands spasmed open to grasp helplessly on the unyielding stone floor.

Whitebrooke's voice soared triumphantly as he crossed the room to stand over the Bishop.

"God damn you," Benno spat through clenched teeth.

Whitebrooke paused in his chant and laughed, his voice harsh and cracked with the strain of the foul words he had uttered. "Perhaps He will."

Whitebrooke cradled the book close to his chest and knelt beside the Bishop. Benno felt the touch of light cobwebs drag across his mind, a whisper of a thought gone before he could understand it. Whitebrooke nodded approval.

"You can hear him, can't you?" Whitebrooke's mouth twisted into a cold smile. "It took me weeks, but he was chained, imprisoned deep in the Abyss. Now he is almost free."

"I am sorry we could not be allies in this grand endeavor." Whitebrooke shook his head sadly. "But you turned your back on the truth. You called it an obsession, you told me to abandon it, to abandon her. And you chose to follow a lie. I don't blame you for that, for it took me years to realize that we had all been deceived, but I wish it had been otherwise."

"Grand endeavor?" Benno spat the words. "Death and corruption, damn you."

"Unfortunate means to an end," Whitebrooke rose to his feet. "Soon they will call me a savior."

"Unfortunate?" Benno's laugh was a sob. "Once you would have cared. Can you not see how much you have been changed?" He struggled to focus his mind past the pain and the cold that was draining him. His hand lay curled on the stone in front of his face, the dim light of the lanterns reflected on his silver ring. *If I can just unlock it, just for an instant.* But it was so difficult. Tears squeezed from his eyes as he held desperately on, praying for time in the hope of a chance.

Whitebrooke bowed his head and stepped back and Benno saw a shape pass across the reflection on his ring. A figure stepped around Benno and stood next to Whitebrooke. He appeared as smoke, or a shape seen through thick glass, solid yet shifting and distorted. The figure's face drifted into solidity and Benno saw a regal visage, the gaze stern and yet understanding, then the form shifted and became vague again.

"Goodbye, your Grace. I hope it can give you some small comfort to know that I will take care of your flock once you are gone, and I will tell them you died bravely." Whitebrooke closed the deep wrongness that was shaped as a book and carefully locked the ancient iron clasps into place.

Then Whitebrooke strode from the room. The dark shade drew nearer and shadow streamed from it and joined with those that clung to Benno. Benno strained helplessly against the terrible coldness that wrapped around every limb as cobwebs again brushed across his mind, and this time they did not pass but grew thick, and tendrils spread throughout his body, enveloping his heart. A sound grew from the webs, a whisper of threads rubbing against threads that became clearer with every moment.

Benno, the shade's whisper called to him, a gentle surge of water across a stone beach. *Join with me and do not despair, but know eternity.*

A great Word echoed in the Bishop's mind, searching for the silver ring that lay so close in front of him, but the endless abyss swallowed it, and then there was nothing.

Danielle

The hallways of the Inner Temple were more quiet than usual as Danielle strode toward her apartments, deep in thought.

Anger gave way to a hot determination to cast her decision and let it harden to steel. Most of the anger had been directed inwards at her own temporizing. *Always delaying that final step, when it would be so easy to commit. And every time I delay, there is another reason to change my decision, another complication to run from rather than face. And now I have done it again. Delayed and equivocated when I might have shouted my decision to the world, and Benno takes advantage, and tempts me to change my mind.*

Danielle was tired of it. Tired of being in a position where she even had to think about such things. Benno was one of her dearest friends and mentors, the man who had brought her to the Temple many years ago. And yet he was willing to hurt her, just to use her. *Not even that. Just to use my sword.* Yes, he had couched his intentions in polite questions and reasoned arguments, but to teach by asking had always been his way.

Danielle felt very alone. Her family was shrinking. *Bradon gone, Benno hidden behind the mask of his title, even my sister…*

Danielle sighed sadly as she thought of her sister. They had been inseparable, from the time they could both walk and talk, always together. They planned their lives together, they played together. They combined to wreak mischief, and united to conceal it. They opened their hearts to one another, they reveled in triumphs, they consoled in defeats. Their parents' deaths merely strengthened their ties.

Even distance did not weaken their bond. When Gabrielle left their home to join her husband in the north, letters wore out their poor birds with their frequency and weight.

Not until the devastating end to Gabrielle's marriage did they start to separate. The grief and despair Gabrielle suffered, and the new responsibilities she inherited, combined to harden her in ways that still were not clear to Danielle.

Danielle found herself outside the Cathedral, the magnificent chamber in which the priests and priestesses gathered to worship and hear God's messages. She opened one of the tall, wooden doors and it swung easily on its massive hinges.

Inside, she walked the long aisle to the high altar, the room quiet except for her echoing footsteps.

The Cathedral was, to Danielle's eyes, the most beautiful room in Bandirma. Its ceiling soared high above the floor, higher than the tallest trees. Majestic pillars flared against the ceiling into myriad arches that formed stars radiating from the highest points.

The walls were deeply recessed with colored glass windows that filled the length of the Cathedral. Light was channeled through cunningly carved passages to fall behind each of the windows, and filled the Cathedral with a warm, multi-hued glow. The Cathedral was buried in the heart of the Temple, yet it always felt as if it stood atop the hill.

Four figures entered the Cathedral, three garbed in the ornate robes of the highest orders of the priesthood. Danielle recognized them all.

And now the Council takes its turn? I should not be surprised.

Reverend Ail and Reverend Hayley walked with their heads together as Hayley whispered something of immense importance, to judge from the look of attention on Ail's face. Danielle liked

Reverend Hayley in small doses, as her intensity and sharp wit became quickly overwhelming, and she found Reverend Ail to be always charming.

Reverend Dougal, on the other hand, was tiring from the first. Decades older than the other three, Dougal was harsh and unforgiving in all things regarding the Temple, and since it had filled every moment of his life it made the short, white-haired priest a horrendous curmudgeon.

Last of the group was Reverend Nesta. She walked near Reverend Dougal but made every effort to ignore the man. Of the three she was the only one wearing simple, brown robes instead of heavy finery, and her jolly, round face and pink cheeks caused her to be mistaken for a cook any number of times. But Danielle knew that she was perhaps the most formidable of the four. Under the loose bun of brown hair and behind the twinkling eyes lay a fierce intellect and a will of steel.

Danielle's fears of another intervention in her love life and the dispensation of the Blade were misplaced. The four Council members gathered around her and greeted her warmly, then asked after her health and her recent mission. Reverend Nesta held Danielle's hand within her soft grasp and mourned the loss of Lord Bradon, tears unashamedly running down her cheeks, while Reverend Dougal lambasted the decision to send only two Templars on the mission, when in years past the Temple surely would have sent twelve.

"Dougal, dear, there are only seven Templars now, and there are many demands on their time," admonished Nesta.

"Well, we should have sent seven then." Dougal glared at the group. "What could be more important than this?"

"I do seem to remember discussing exactly who to send when we decided to send Lord Bradon and Sir Killock," Reverend Ail mused. "Dougal, I thought you made a very compelling case that *one* Templar should be enough for a vague rumor far off in the hinterlands."

"Well, now we are down to five. That's half the number we should have!" Dougal fussed. "The Circle is empty!"

"Six, dear, not five," Nesta corrected him. "Sir Killock did not perish."

"Killock? I don't count mac tíre as a Templar," Dougal sniffed. "Wouldn't be one in my day."

"Sir Killock brought us out of Sliabh Log when no one else could. If not for him we would all have perished in that place," said Danielle fiercely. It felt good to let her anger out, and Dougal made for a deserving recipient. "And he discovered the secret of the magi's portals, as well as being the first man in centuries to reach Highward Tor."

"Noble accomplishments to rank with any Templar," Reverend Hayley agreed. "All merely the latest of his long list of such deeds. Speaking of recent accomplishments, Reverend Dougal, how is your treatise on the works of Cian coming along? Have you finished your first draft yet, or is it still appallingly difficult to locate your references in the archives?"

"Mock all you wish, but Cian's efforts to catalog the clans of the western mountains were vital to the success of King Otho," spluttered Dougal.

"I am sure Cian was an historical giant," soothed Hayley.

"Wasn't he long dead by the time Otho allied with the King of Albyn?" pondered Ail helpfully. "I suppose Otho must have had better luck finding Cian's journals that you seem to be having, Dougal."

"We will leave you be," said Nesta quietly to Danielle as the others continued to bicker. "I am glad to see you returned to us."

Danielle thanked her, grateful that they were leaving. She needed time and silence to consider all of the demands and desires that had swarmed through her mind and heart since the night she decided to throw caution to the wind and declare her feelings for Wyn. More and more consequences of her confession to Wyn pressed upon her. But the pressure did not bring clarity. The same thoughts circled now as they had days ago, carving a deep rut in her mind, no clearer despite time and repetition.

The voices of the four Council members faded as they left and Danielle approached the high altar.

The high altar was a marvel. Its rich, black color stood out against the pale marble that covered the rest of the floor. The altar was bathed in light from a window that depicted a golden tree that grew in a chamber within the earth.

Behind the altar rose the great Seal, a magnificent, obsidian stone laced with thousands of threads of precious metal that formed patterns of extraordinary beauty. The Seal had been placed there upon the founding of Bandirma, some said by God himself. Only the Bishop knew the Word for the Seal, a Device of such power that Danielle wondered if any other Device could be compared to it.

Danielle found tremendous comfort in gazing at the Seal. She could trace the lines of it forever, following them as they crossed and re-crossed, always discovering herself unexpectedly back where she started.

She did that now, letting her finger run slowly along the shining metal as her thoughts calmed and she regained her purpose.

Time passed. She was not sure how much, but her mind was ordered and her will was resolved.

***

"How did it go with the Bishop?" Wyn asked when Danielle reached her apartments.

"It went well."

"That good, huh?" Wyn grinned wryly. "So, have you come to your senses yet?"

"I have, but not as you think. Wyn, are you ready to meet the Queen?"

"You're sure?" Wyn looked at her intently. "I mean, we're here, right? Not out there. And there are Queens and Bishops everywhere, Martyr love us. But I'm still me, you see?"

"Wyn, what are you talking about?"

"Oooo," Wyn stomped in frustration. "I'm so bad at this! It's hard to say what I mean, but you just say stuff like it's easy."

"Do you mean talking about my feelings towards you? It was very difficult the first time, because I was afraid of what you might say. But now it is easy. I love you."

"See? You can talk about this kind of stuff." Wyn shook her head in bewilderment. "I was trying to say, to ask, just I wanted to make sure, that now that we're here and I'm still me, that you still wanted to do what you said. Because that's big, that is. That's changing your life, and how can you know? And I'm just me is all."

"Oh, I am sure of it." Danielle gazed fiercely into Wyn's eyes. "So sure that it hurts because I cannot tell you how much I am sure, I cannot find words to do it. And as you told me in our cabin, it is too important to mess around with."

Wyn smiled, a soft, happy smile. "Well. Alright then, your Craziness."

"Now, go and get cleaned up and put on your best clothes."

"My best what? Dani, you are looking at my best, my only, clothes."

"Oh." Danielle shook her head in disapproval, glancing over the threadbare tunic and shapeless pants Wyn was wearing. "Well, go and bathe, and you can borrow something of mine."

"Sure, I bet you have a lot of stuff laying around just perfect for girls my shape."

"We will make do," Danielle soothed. "Go clean yourself up; I will take care of the clothes."

"Maybe you should talk with your sis without me."

"Why would I do that?" Danielle asked, astonished.

"I'll just embarrass you, that's why," said Wyn sadly. "No matter what I do there is no hiding the fact that I am a rat from the streets. One that's been scrubbed until it squeaked, true, but a rat, and a scruffy one. I'll just make you look bad in front of your sis."

"Do you think I care about where you are from?"

"No! No, it's not that at all," Wyn shook her head, "but I know how others will think and no, I don't give two shits about what they think about me. But I *do* care what they think about you *because* of me. They'll think you're crazy, and I don't want them thinking that about you. Look, this is your moment with your sister, and I don't want to screw it up."

"Wyn, I am proud of you and I want others to see what I see."

"What, me starkers?" giggled Wyn. "Well, that would be an audience the Queen wouldn't soon forget."

"No, that is just for me," Danielle admonished her. "No, I meant the woman I am proud of, that I love, and as it happens, she acts like you!"

"I suppose so," smiled Wyn. "I guess there's no accounting for taste, yeah?"

"Exactly," agreed Danielle. "However, even a scruffy rat would not wear those pants."

"You're not getting me into a frilly dress." Wyn frowned in disgust.

"It will be fine, you will see. Gabrielle is getting everything she wants, and that makes Queens very happy, especially when the Queen in question is the little sister."

***

Wyn returned from the bath clean and pink, and stood awkwardly in a silk robe as she awaited review.

"Beautiful," Danielle pronounced. "Now, clothes."

The most likely outfits were laid on the bed, rich fabrics in black to catch others' eyes, and in green to match hers. Creamy leather leggings, soft tunics, patterned stockings, slim dresses, and not a frill or flounce to be found on any of them. A lady's maid with two chambermaids as reinforcements waited nearby, ready to assist.

"Pants!" Wyn exclaimed joyfully. "Oooo, they're so soft."

"I thought you might like to stay in leggings," Danielle smiled. "Try them on."

"What, right here?" Wyn glanced at the maids and lowered her voice. "In front of them?"

"No, you stand behind the screen," Danielle pointed, "over there."

But the leggings were a failure. As were the tunics. The dresses were the worst. No matter how many pins were used or how much padding was stuffed, cloth sagged where it should have stretched, flapped where it should have draped, or dragged where it should have trailed elegantly. An attempt with a corset ended with cursing and threats of spilled blood. Danielle covered her mouth and tried to stifle her laughter, but joyful noises bubbled between her fingers uncontrollably.

Wyn stood with arms crossed and glared at Danielle. "Keep laughing, Giggles. I'll get my revenge later."

But once the laughter had calmed, even Danielle had to concede that her clothes would not do for Wyn.

"I'm sorry, m'lady," the lady's maid tutted. "It will never do. Not unless a seamstress can re-stitch them. You are very different shapes."

"Yeah, no kidding," Wyn snorted in amusement as she peered down the loose neck of the dress she was wearing. "I think one of my boobs got lost in here."

"We have until the evening bells," Danielle sighed in frustration. "That is when the Queen is expecting us."

"We need something much closer," the maid shook her head, "or something less fitted."

"Then we need to get something new," Danielle decided.

"Dani, I look ridiculous in these nice clothes." Wyn tugged glumly at the long sleeve of the dress.

"I meant, why not get you some clothes that you like?"

"Well, fine, sounds easy, but I don't really know anything about that. I've never owned more than one pair of pants. Do they come in colors other than black or brown?" Wyn asked, eyes big and innocent.

"Come with me. I know just the shop."

***

The town of Bandirma bustled that afternoon under its coat of fresh snow. The wind held its breath and the clouds were not pouring snow or rain, so the people of the town flooded the streets to take care of business before the winter weather returned.

Young boys brushed piles of snow from the stoop of one store to the stoop of the next and received a silver penny from each shopkeeper in turn to clear their steps. Wagons filled with cut firewood parked in the main square, and the woodcutters did good business resupplying the townsfolk. A ship had arrived from across Loughliath and was now being unloaded. Stevedores rolled huge barrels of wine, ale and cider down the streets from the docks to the taverns and inns that welcomed the libations.

The town was wealthy. Most of the buildings were made of stone, with wide windows, high gateways, and open rooms. The Temple across the river ensured a steady stream of money as the town served its needs: food, carpentry, masonry, fuel, blacksmithing, husbandry… or clothing.

The acolytes and stewards of the Temple dealt with tasks such as stitching robes and patching rips, but the town supplied the vast army of stewards, acolytes, and soldiers with their simple but sturdy clothing. And when it came to proper tailoring suitable for the highest echelons of the Temple and their noble guests, some of the best tailors in the north worked in Bandirma. Only Kuray could rival their styles and exotic cloths. The beautiful raiment of the clergy, knightly surcoats, the luxurious suits and dresses of the town burghers. All could be found in the town.

Those who needed the best of the best visited the shop of Cillan. The dresses that Danielle had purchased from Cillan were her most prized. The seamstress brought in beautiful fabric from across the world and created the most marvelous designs, exotic and original.

But Cillan's special talent was that she did not just create clothes for a royal ball. She created clothes for all occasions. Uniforms for soldiers, coats for cold winter days, riding outfits, clothes for simple times, or clothes for elegant times. She made them with no preference or disdain for any request.

If anyone had a chance to create something "perfect" for Wyn, it was Cillan. Of course, there was not time for a new creation. They would have to find something that could be altered on the spot, but Danielle had faith in Cillan's proven abilities, even for Wyn's long, lithe frame.

A brief, whispered conversation and Cillan was eagerly added to their conspiracy, and she quickly cleared her shop of other customers, each a tongue well-used to spreading gossip and intrigue. Cillan guided Wyn into the fitting rooms, and Danielle sat in the front room of the shop and waited as Cillan worked her magic. It would take time, of course, but Danielle did not mind. She was content to occupy herself with exquisite, wonderful memories of the previous night.

It had been an experience beyond what she could have imagined, and she laughed inwardly as she realized that she was, very correctly this time, knackered. The long ride to Bandirma gave their first night of passion time to simmer in their memories and stir stronger desire. And the days of easy companionship had removed any feelings of reserve.

Even the simple touch of her skin against mine was almost overwhelming. It was sensual in a way I never imagined.

Danielle sighed contentedly and smoothed her dress across her lap, and the silky fabric slid across her thighs in a pale reminder of Wyn's touch. Danielle wondered how long one should wait before initiating another such night.

The door opened and Wyn stepped onto the fitting dais. Her image was reflected in a series of large mirrors and Danielle caught her breath in delight.

Wyn wore a long-sleeved tunic of dark green with silver thread woven into swirling patterns across it. The tunic descended from a high collar that fit snugly around her long neck, and was split in a narrow V that was held together between her breasts with a silver brooch shaped like an open torc. The tunic hugged her lithe form to her waist, where a beautiful, triple strung belt fashioned of twined leather braids hung. Below the belt the tunic clung to her hips and the curve of her leg and ended a hand's-breadth below indecency.

Long boots wrapped her legs in supple leather dyed a deep black, worn over tight leggings of soft, black leather that traced the curve of her legs until they disappeared beneath the tunic.

"What do you think?" Wyn asked as she twirled on the dais and admired her own stunning reflection.

Danielle rose to her feet, her heart pounding. Before her stood a beautiful young woman, tall, strong and proud.

"Wyn, you look amazing."

"I know, right? My first dress, can you believe it?" Wyn smiled merrily.

"I am not sure you can actually call that a dress, but it suits you very much," said Danielle.

"Look what it does." Wyn twirled again and the tunic flared to reveal a flash of smooth leather that curved into mystery. Wyn laughed in delight at the look on Danielle's face. "That's what I thought too! Shall I do it again?"

"No!" Danielle whispered, and she blushed furiously. "Not here, not now."

"Awww, it's sweet that you're shy," Wyn smiled. "Is it alright to wear? I'm pretty sure you shouldn't be having thoughts that make you blush while you're meeting a queen, right?"

"Perhaps not," laughed Danielle. "But it is very much you, much more than the boring old clothes you had. You should wear it."

"All right then, I'm good to go."

They donned their cloaks to return to the Temple, and meandered through the town square and across the bridge.

"Now I need to get dressed," Danielle told Wyn as they returned to their rooms.

"Aren't you already?" Wyn asked. "You look really nice."

"This?" Danielle glanced down. "No, this is just a dress. When you meet with a Queen, even a Queen that is your sister, you need to wear a *dress*."

Danielle chose her wardrobe carefully, inspecting and discarding her way through the clothes she kept in her apartments. She did not have her favorites here. They were far too light for the cold north so she had left them at home in Venaissin, but over the years there had been enough formal visitors of grand-enough status that she had assembled a decent set of choices. In the end she picked a long dress of a deep, wine-dark red.

A simple knot secured it around her neck, the strings held together at the base of her neck by a silver brooch shaped like a porpoise. The dress was cinched just beneath her breasts by a cord that tied behind her back, and fell straight to her hips. The fabric of the dress hugged her hips and draped elegantly to the floor. Her shoulders were bare, as was her back as the dress plunged to the gentle curve below her waist. Danielle shook her hair out so that it cascaded down her back in waves of black fire that shone darkly in the light.

Over the dress was fastened a heavy belt of silver buckles that curved around Danielle's back, over her hips, and rested low under her abdomen.

Danielle eschewed all but the simplest of jewelry. She chose silver bands that circled her upper arms and a silver circlet that shone from her brow, and she wore her ring on its silver chain. It hung heavily between her breasts as if all of the weight of her decision to let it pass to her sister now lived within it.

"Oh, Dani, you look like a goddess." Wyn sighed in deep adoration.

Danielle smiled radiantly. She turned to a small box on her dressing table and took some shining objects from it.

"I have something for you," Danielle said. She moved to Wyn and carefully fastened on her a pair of silver ear cuffs that formed a spiral of glimmering silver thread from the tip of Wyn's ear to the lobe, with small silver pendants that dangled, flashed and sparkled as she moved her head. Then she took a gold thread and wrapped it around Wyn's long, thick braid until it glimmered along its entire length.

She stepped back and surveyed her work. Wyn's green eyes shone in the lantern's light, and an exhilarated smile showed a flash of white teeth between her lips. "Beautiful," Danielle pronounced. "I know you do not like jewelry, or at least you never wear it, but for today I think you should."

"Well, I can't wear stuff like this while I'm working, even if I could afford it, but it feels nice. But, Dani, how much did you spend on all of this? Too much I'd bet. Can we sell it afterwards?"

"No, we cannot," said Danielle firmly. "These are for you, and I will not have someone else wearing them. You look wonderful in them, which makes them more valuable to me."

"Lady-like?" Wyn asked in a tone she usually reserved to imitate the high-muckities.

"In no way."

"Perfect."

Danielle turned to the door. "Are you ready?"

"One last thing I almost forgot. I'll be right out," said Wyn.

"It is not your knives, is it?" Danielle asked pointedly.

Wyn laughed. "I'd not likely forget those, would I?"

"That is not a 'no'," Danielle noted.

"It's really not, is it?" Wyn grinned, then disappeared behind the dressing screen.

"Do you need help?" Danielle asked.

"Well, how much time do we have?" Wyn's voice asked from behind the screen.

"Very little," guessed Danielle.

"No help then," answered Wyn. "Trust me, we don't have time for proper helping right now."

Danielle paused, puzzled, then closed the door and waited in the main room as she had been told.

She did not have to wait long. Only a few moments passed before Wyn joined her, a wicked smile on her face.

"Alright, ready when you are," Wyn grinned.

Danielle linked her arm through Wyn's, filled with a strong desire for some physical contact with the fiery spirit next to her, and they passed through the temple to the Queen's apartments.

The evening bells sounded through the temple as they approached the knight standing guard in full armor outside the door. Danielle was glad it was Sir Ceredor, whom she had met several times in the years since Gabrielle became the Queen. He looked very imposing with his scarred face and his hawk-shaped helm with wings soaring on either side of his visor, but she knew him to be a fair and even-tempered man, and devoted to her sister. He made Danielle feel safe.

Sir Ceredor nodded respectfully, then opened the door and stepped through to announce them.

"Are you going to tell me what it was you almost forgot?" Danielle whispered as they waited.

"Oh yes," Wyn's eyes sparkled mischievously. "Look."

Wyn glanced down and behind herself, and Danielle followed her gaze. Wyn turned her hips, and casually flipped up the hem of her tunic. Her leggings were cut low beneath her hips and laced up the side. In the gap between the leather ties Danielle could clearly see bright red lace snug against Wyn's skin. Wyn hooked a finger through the lace and showed it to Danielle.

"*The* panties?" Danielle whispered.

"Oh yes they are," giggled Wyn.

"What if she sees?" Danielle felt a huge smile spread across her face, and her anxiety vanished for a moment.

"And what exactly would the Queen be doing in my pants to see them?" Wyn asked, eyes innocent and wide. "Honestly, you can hardly see them even with my pants off. I'll show you later if you want."

"I suppose you are right, how could she know?" Danielle agreed. *I need some levity right now*, she realized, *this mischief feels very good, and good to share now, when we are about to stand beside each other for more important things.*

"I think I like this," Danielle told Wyn in a conspiratorial whisper. "Being naughty. But whatever made you think to do it?"

"Mmmm," murmured Wyn sensually. "I guess I'm just getting used to having something beautiful between my legs. Spoiled really."

Danielle caught her breath in astonishment as pleasure washed through her, and she smiled in delight as Wyn winked and let her tunic fall into place as Sir Ceredor summoned them inside the room. Then Danielle saw her sister greet her with open arms and Danielle embraced her tightly, grateful that her smile would not seem out of place because she could not have stopped beaming if she had tried.

Gabrielle looked radiant. Danielle was surprised by how much her sister had matured. She had grown from a stunning girl into a beautiful young woman, full of confidence.

This evening the Queen wore a white dress, brilliant against her dusky skin, with a long train that swept behind her. The dress was worn off the shoulders to reveal her lovely neck and collar bones, and draped open down the back to leave her shoulder blades bare. A large diamond necklace lay at the base of her throat and sparkled against her skin.

Then Danielle had to greet her sister's wizard, a much less pleasant experience. Karsha Hali hopped forward, swept up her hand, kissed her lightly on her knuckles and favored her with a smile with more gaps than teeth. Danielle was gracious and returned the smile, but she had never warmed to the man. He always appeared to be harboring secrets and smiling about them, which might make him a good advisor but it also made him an extremely unsettling companion.

Her sister swore he was loyal and indispensable. *And Gabrielle was always a very good judge of character.*

"Gabrielle, may I present to you, Bronwyn, my consort." Danielle watched her sister closely as Wyn curtsied gracefully.

Gabrielle's face changed from an interested smile to slight confusion, then to a real smile of pleasure. Danielle felt a warm flush of appreciation for her sister. *I had not expected anything else really, but I have kept this secret from her for so long.*

"Bronwyn, I am so very glad to meet you. It pleases me to see Danielle so joyous."

"Me too, your Majesty. I mean, it's very nice to meet you too, and it's also nice to see your sister happy."

"Happiness is a treacherous, cruel thing," mused Karsha. "Thank the gods, or else there would be no great stories."

Gabrielle took Wyn's hands in her own and held them. "Tell me, Bronwyn, where is your family from?"

"Well, I was born in, uh, the north, but I grew up in Glen Walden. That's near the road to Irongate."

"Glen Walden? The name rings a bell. I think I must have been there."

"Yes, your Majesty, you and King Arian came one summer a few years ago. We all lined up and watched your carriage go by. You had white horses and they had golden feathers on their head thingies."

"A grand hunt that day," said Karsha. "Baron Arledge wished to conquer the king of the boars whom he said lived in the deep woods, to bring honor to his King and to his own house. But the dogs could not track him, and they settled for a fine deer which did nothing to lessen the Baron's shame."

"Oh yes, now I remember. We stayed with Baron Arledge and he was so angry after that hunt. The King thought it was very amusing." The Queen turned to Wyn. "Perhaps we met while I was there?"

Wyn laughed. "No, your Majesty, I'd remember that."

"Well, you seem very familiar. We must have met. What is your family name?"

"Um." Wyn looked to Danielle for help.

"Gabrielle, Bronwyn's family is not landed," interjected Danielle.

"They are common?" the Queen asked.

"Ha!" Karsha shook his head in mirth. "Most uncommon if she has snared your sister's heart."

The Queen ignored her wizard. The news of Wyn's family origins did not seem to shock Gabrielle. It would be impossible for Wyn to pretend to be anything else. Her accent alone told the tale as if it were written in black ink on parchment. The Queen clearly just wanted to hear them say it.

"Well, we can easily do something about that, since you are the love of my sister's life." The Queen held Wyn's gaze. "A Knight of the Tower perhaps?"

"Oh, no thank you, ma'am," Wyn laughed at the thought. "I wouldn't know what to do with something like that."

"A Knight of the Garter," Karsha sucked on one of his teeth.

"A what?" Wyn glanced at the wizard in surprise.

"It is just the name of another order, that is all," explained Danielle quickly.

"She is very striking," Gabrielle said to Danielle without taking her eyes off Wyn. Then she sighed regretfully and a sad smile appeared on her full lips.

"Danielle, I am sorry, but you know it cannot be. You have to tell her."

"I know nothing of the sort," Danielle snapped back. The hurt in Wyn's eyes made her want to lash out, but she bit off the rest of what she wanted to say.

"Of course you do." The Queen continued to gaze at Wyn. "I am sorry, Bronwyn, I am sure you are quite wonderful, but you have to understand that Danielle is not free to choose just any partner."

"I think she's pretty good at choosing for herself, actually," retorted Wyn.

"But that is just it," the Queen's voice soothed like honey. "She is not really choosing for herself. She needs to choose for our family and our family's future."

"Must always be careful." Karsha shook his head sorrowfully. "So many try to bed their way to the top."

"Is that right," said Wyn coldly, and pulled her hands from the Queen's grasp. Wyn looked as though she had been slapped. Her eyes narrowed dangerously and her face paled except for two bright pink spots over her cheeks, and the newly-healed wound down her cheek flamed red against her skin.

"How dare you?" Danielle fought to keep her voice low as she accosted the southern wizard. "You presume to know our feelings, you patronizing bastard?"

Karsha shrugged, unperturbed by the ire unleashed against him. "Don't need to know. Seen plenty of love, plenty of greed. They often look the same, and sometimes one becomes the other. And sometimes it's just a big cock or some pretty teats. A house cannot rise or fall because of any of those things."

"I don't want anything to do with your stupid titles," Wyn spat out. "If I can make her happy, then grand, and if you lot who call yourselves her family don't care about that then you can kiss my pucker. If I don't make her happy then she can tell me to fuck clean off, but that's up to her, not you."

"Of course we are glad she is happy," Gabrielle moved to a side table where she carefully poured herself a glass of wine, "but it is more than just her happiness at stake here, and she knows it. And she should have told you, too."

"I did," Danielle stood with fists braced on her hips, "and do you know what she said? She said I was crazy and I should not do this. That is what kind of person Wyn is."

"She is right," the Queen answered. "You should not do this. You cannot do this."

"Yes, I can." Danielle suddenly felt full of energy and her fingertips began to tingle. "Because I am not the Marquessa. Here, take the damn thing." Danielle yanked her ring from around her neck and dropped it with a clatter onto the small wooden table.

There was silence as the ring bounced and rolled to a stop in the center of the table. *I cannot believe I did it. I actually went through with it!*

"That does make a difference." Karsha peered at the ring. "A ring is often given to represent love, although not usually like this."

The Queen moved to the table and placed a single finger beside the ring and turned it slightly as she gazed down.

Then, without picking it up, she turned to Wyn.

"And what of you, Bronwyn? Much as I desire this ring I will not take it if I think my sister is deceived. We have seen the strength of Danielle's love for you. The proof lies here on this table to start. But I am not as convinced it is returned in kind."

Danielle's stomach churned. Gabrielle had surprised her, although Danielle was not sure why she had thought her sister would place her desire for the title above her concern for her sister. *I am so grateful for her love, but not right now, please!*

"Well, she's wonderful, right?" stammered Wyn, completely flustered. "I mean, I wasn't sure when she first told me about, well, about the feelings she had. Feelings are important, yeah?"

Wyn looked to Danielle for help. "She does not need to explain how she feels, it does not matter," Danielle insisted. "All that matters is that I am sure."

"Of course it matters, Danielle." Gabrielle shot a look of annoyance at her sister. "We promised to take care of each other, and that is what I am doing, even if you cannot see that."

"I do see that, but this is not fair to Wyn. This is private, something for us, just for us." Danielle felt a tear burn her eye and blinked it away.

"Seems fair to me," Karsha answered. "There's a ring sitting on that table that says the same. Time to know, one way or the other, then you can decide what to do."

But I do not want to know, I am just happy right now. But part of her did want to know, the part that hoped.

Wyn looked stricken, eyes wide as she looked to Danielle for help.

"Just tell them the truth, Wyn," was all Danielle could think to say. "That is what you have always told me."

Danielle saw Wyn's mouth set into a severe line, and her eyes narrowed.

"Fine, alright, although this has nothing to do with this lot. When you told me that you had feelings for me, in the cabin..."

"I said I loved you."

"Yes, loved me." Wyn took a deep breath. "Listen, I'm talking and this is hard enough to say, what with the Queen and that withered numpty standing there and all. Anyway, I told you that I don't mess around with that kind of stuff, feelings for each other and so on, because it's too important, right? It matters. Not like just screwing about, that doesn't mean shit."

"Yes, you told me," said Danielle.

"And I told you that I didn't know if I would ever feel that way about you, that it might just be a romp. I never lied to you about that."

"Yes, you said that," said Danielle from far away.

"Dani, I'm going to say this badly, I know it, but you're right. I need to tell you the truth. I know I've been fooling myself about my feelings for a little while now, but I guess I didn't want to admit it because it makes my stomach hurt to think about."

"We cannot have that," whispered Danielle. Dismay pushed against her throat, and she could not swallow.

"Well then, we've only known each other for a flash more than a biscuit really, if you think about it. And I think you are one of the most wonderful people I've ever met, even though you're all rich and powerful, and you scare the shit out of me all the time with your magic. You're wonderful. And brave. And kind… anyway, you know what I'm saying."

Wyn took another deep breath, and steeled herself. Danielle closed her eyes.

"That night in the cabin, you told me you thought I was beautiful," Wyn said, "but that wasn't why you loved me."

"Danielle, I think you are incredibly, amazingly gorgeous, and you make my knees weak just thinking about, um, stuff, but that's not why I love you either." Wyn paused, and took her hand, and Danielle's eyes opened wide. "It's because of what I said just now, about how amazing you are, and kind, and brave, and strong. But most of all it's because I need you, so much it makes my heart tremble, because the truth is that I was broken before you found me. And now… not broken."

"And I know you need me for stuff, like to show you how to take what's important to you," Wyn's voice was certain and strong as the words tumbled out, and Danielle gazed into Wyn's eyes as her heart pounded. "But I need you to show me how to do things too, like how to be with someone, and how to need someone. I've never needed anyone before, and it feels really scary and what if something happens to you? But it also feels so good, so it's tough to talk about. Anyway, I just love you and it feels really good and I want it to go on, so please can it just keep going?"

Wyn turned to the Queen. "I love her. Martyr protect her, that's the truth."

"Thank you, Bronwyn." Gabrielle nodded her head and a smile crossed her lips. "Thank you for bringing happiness to my sister. She deserves it."

"Please, Gabrielle, take the ring," Danielle asked.

The Queen nodded with a warm smile, and wiped tears from her own eyes. She raised the ring off the table and held it for a long moment, a look of astonishment on her face, before slipping it on her finger.

Danielle suddenly felt immense relief surge through her body and she felt dizzy. She still was not sure that she had actually heard what she had just heard, or seen what she had just seen. She looked at Wyn. "Really?" she mouthed silently, and Wyn nodded her head happily as a smile lit up her face.

Karsha intruded, another hideous smile cracking his face. "Wonderful," he croaked elatedly. "Wonderful. The gods will be so pleased to hear this story. Unless one of them is in love with one of you already, in which case they will likely do something dreadful to you."

"Um, yeah, well, let's hope not then," giggled Wyn.

Karsha produced two glasses of wine and thrust them at the two women, then ushered them to the half-circle of deep chairs next to the fireplace. Gabrielle reclined elegantly next to Danielle and smoothed the fabric of her dress across her lap. Danielle caught Wyn adopting the same posture on the other side of her and suppressed a laugh, afraid it might sound a bit hysterical with all of the emotions that coursed through her at that moment.

"So now we really do need to find a new title, but for you this time," said Gabrielle. "I am afraid it cannot be too grand or the old families will grumble, but something that will at least give you some standing at court."

"You do not need to," Danielle replied. "It does not matter to me."

"It matters to me." The Queen wiped away any objection with her hand. "Karsha, what did you suggest earlier?"

"Don't remember," Karsha said around a mouthful of wine, but Danielle saw him glance at Wyn with a sharp look.

"You said Knight of the Garter, but that does not make any sense. The other Lords would complain bitterly, and these two will not want to spend their lives at court as the Order demands." Gabrielle looked puzzled by the poor advice.

"Something else then," Karsha said. "A baronetcy."

"Hmmm," the Queen replied, clearly distracted. She turned to Wyn. "Bronwyn is such a beautiful name, but I heard Danielle call you Wyn. Is that a pet name, or do you prefer it?"

"Well, she likes it is all," lied Wyn, "like I call her Dani, in private."

"I have rarely heard it shortened like that," the Queen persisted. "Almost never, in fact."

"Thanks, your Majesty, it's a little odd but she likes it I guess." Wyn took a deep drink from her cup.

"I used to call her Dani, when we were little. And she called me Gabi. A long time ago," Gabrielle said thoughtfully, then her expression softened and she sipped from her glass. "A baronetcy then. We will have to look at the lists when we return to Kuray."

"Thank you, Gabrielle. Not just for the title, although that is generous. For everything, for taking the ring, for being my sister." Danielle gripped Gabrielle's hand in gratitude.

"Do not be silly. You took care of me for years and years, and you have never let me do a thing for you. Now I am the Queen, so if I can finally help you, I will."

Danielle gratefully settled in the chair. Tension was leaving her in waves. *It is done, I did it, and she said she loved me.* Her only regret was that she could not tell Bradon about it.

The Queen laughed at something Wyn said, but Danielle was not really paying attention. She only listened to the voices as noise as she let relief fill her.

"Danielle. You see, she is lost," her sister's laugh sparkled through her thoughts.

"I am sorry, I was just thinking this was the first time I have felt completely relaxed in years," Danielle said.

Wyn snorted with laughter and choked on her wine. "Nothing!" she apologized. "Sorry, it's nothing."

Gabrielle laughed again. "My sister, blushing. I never believed I would see the day. I thought her corset was made of steel."

"Gabrielle!" Danielle was shocked.

"What?" the Queen protested. "You two clearly do not need to be told anything about each other's undergarments, and if sisters cannot share some intimacies, who can? And do not worry about Karsha, I doubt we can tell him anything new about intimacies, whether or not they involve corsets."

Karsha nodded introspectively. "True."

Gabrielle leaned forward and rested her elbow on her crossed legs, then placed a hand on Danielle's knee as Karsha and Wyn continued to trade jokes and laughter.

"Danielle, listen," she said softly. "I am overjoyed for you, and I am glad to take the ring, if only to let you have what you want. I know the sacrifices you have made for us over the years. But you know that there is one thing that I want, that I must now ask. I hope that you will not begrudge me that."

"You mean the Martyr's Blade," Danielle replied.

"Yes." Gabrielle squeezed her knee. "I know Bishop Benno does not agree, and I know you place great stock in him, so I, too, respect his thoughts. But I must know if you will accept my decisions on the matter… regardless of your own wishes."

"I will." Danielle leaned towards her sister, so close that their heads were almost touching. "But please understand. Benno is right. I have seen it with my own eyes. The Blade cannot be squandered, not now, not when it should be our mightiest Weapon in a time of dire need."

"It is truly the Crunorix returned?"

Danielle lowered her voice even further to a whisper. "I have seen one, a magus. It fell beneath the Blade, but not without dreadful cost."

"I heard the terrible news that Lord Bradon had fallen." Gabrielle took Danielle's hands in hers and gripped them tightly. "General Boone has told me how much Lord Bradon has done for the realm, and I know you were very close, I am so sorry."

"He was a dear man, and a wonderful friend," said Danielle. "You have met him, did you know?"

"Have I?"

"Yes, at your wedding." Danielle smiled fondly at the memory. "That is where I met him, too."

That night was still vivid in Danielle's memory, not just because of the gala and pageantry of the wedding, or the strange sights of the cold, northern country her sister had chosen as her new home. More than all of that, Danielle remembered the quiet certainty of a priest who spoke of a life of purpose and meaning. But Danielle knew that she would have never followed Benno to Bandirma, save for the deep rumble of the lord who promised her safety by his side.

"Of course, all of the Templars were there, were they not? But I hardly knew what was happening. Which one was he?" Gabrielle frowned in concentration.

"Very tall, with an enormous beard, always laughing," Danielle replied. "You told him he looked as if he were the Lord of the Mountains. He was very pleased. I cannot tell you how many times he has repeated that story."

"I do remember him now." Gabrielle smiled at the memory. "He seemed caring, despite his size and strength. It is hard to think that he has passed."

"It is hard for me, as well." Danielle gripped Gabrielle's hands in return. "But it happened nonetheless. He could not stand against the magus, nor could I. None of us could. Only the Blade was its match."

Gabrielle patted Danielle's knee and bit her lip as she had done as a girl when her thoughts became intense. Then she caught Danielle's eye again.

"I believe you, Dani, I do, and Karsha has told me the same. Which is why I want you to keep the Blade. You are the best to wield it, no one can take your place. But I want you to wield it for *me*. Benno wants what is best for his Temple. I want what is best for my people. Perhaps we are close enough to ally in this, but our causes will not always be the same, and I wish to know that my people will always come before his Temple."

"Gabrielle, I belong here."

"I know," replied the Queen. "But now I am asking you to wield our sword for me. In all else I know your loyalty will be given to the Temple. I do not expect you to answer now. Talk with Benno, take his counsel. But do it soon. I must leave within the week, and if you will not wield the Blade for me, then it will go with me to seek another wielder elsewhere."

Danielle sat back in her chair and took a deep sip of wine from her glass. Things were moving so fast. A moment before she considered herself done with Blades and titles and responsibilities. A moment before that she feared she may lose Wyn. Now she had it all back again. Her head spun as she listened to Karsha tell a story about a wizard who climbed a mountain to speak with, if she heard it right, a goat who could reveal the moment of your death. Karsha even hopped up to demonstrate how the goat would perform to answer the questions, and Wyn laughed and clapped her hands in glee. Even Gabrielle was laughing.

Then Karsha stopped in mid-sentence and was suddenly still. He held up his hand as the Queen started to ask him a question, his eyes half-closed.

The room grew hushed, and Danielle could feel her sister tense beside her. *This is not usual,* she thought.

Karsha suddenly rummaged in his robes as he dug through his pockets and chains with urgency. Danielle heard him mutter in a guttural language under his breath. He produced a small charm in the shape of a tiny cage made of straw woven into a lattice and tied in knots to keep the shape. Karsha said a few more words, then untwisted a knot and let the charm fall open.

Something barely seen swirled through the room and disappeared in an instant, something fast and primal. Danielle leapt to her feet in shock, but it was gone before she could catch her balance. Wyn yelled in surprise and vaulted backwards over her chair, landing in a crouch, ready to move in any direction.

Karsha paid them no attention. Instead he scurried to the door and opened it to shout to Sir Ceredor. "Bring Sir Osythe and the guard. Quickly!"

Then he turned to the room.

"Your Majesty, we must go. You are in danger."

"In danger? Here?"

"Yes." Karsha bobbed his head vigorously. "Take only what you need. The rest we leave."

"The Blade," Gabrielle turned to Danielle, "where is it?"

"In my room, warded and veiled."

"No time for that now," Karsha said urgently. "We must go."

The door opened and Sir Ceredor entered, sword drawn, closed the door and dropped the latch behind him. "The guard is assembling in the hallway. What are our orders, your Majesty?" Ceredor's voice sounded like a steel blade on the whet stone.

Gabrielle paused for a moment to consider.

"Hold the passageway for as long as you can. Send an escort with Danielle. She is going to retrieve something from her chamber. Make sure she gets there and back again."

"Your Majesty, your guard protects you." Sir Ceredor was adamant.

"Do it," the Queen commanded.

Then she turned to Danielle. "Dani, please hurry. I do not know what is going on, but Karsha is not wrong about these things."

"I will, but I must sound the alarm. If there are enemies in the Temple…"

"Yes, but go now. Hurry!"

"Dani, come on!" Wyn called urgently from the door.

Danielle ran to the door and Sir Ceredor opened it for them to leave. Two soldiers from the Queen's escort were ordered to go with them.

They rushed through wide passageways towards Danielle's chamber. The hallway remained quiet, lanterns glowing cheerfully. It felt unreal. Everything was normal, yet there was so much dread in Danielle's heart.

Danielle looked for anyone to help her sound the alarm, but the passageway was empty. She led them to the Inner Temple doors, where knights always stood guard. Beyond them, Danielle could hear the distant sounds of the outer temple as they drifted to her, a welcome sign of normality. The knights were there, as expected, dressed in full armor as they watched those who entered and exited the Inner Temple.

"Alert the guard," she wasted no time. "Something has invaded the Temple. I am not sure what it is, so alert everyone."

The knights exchanged a glance and hesitated. Danielle did not.

"Now!" she commanded.

"Yes, my lady," the senior knight responded, and he immediately turned and headed for the barracks.

"You stay here," Danielle ordered the other knight. Then she headed towards her rooms as quickly as possible. It was not far from the Inner Temple doors. Most of the larger apartments reserved for the Temple elite were in a single wing, intentionally close for the convenience of their occupants.

Danielle's rooms were farthest from the main hallway, far from the sounds of the temple, a fact that she very much regretted at this moment. She led the group through the twists and turns of the passageways as quickly as possible, until at last she saw the heavy, wooden door at the end of the small hallway that gave entrance to her rooms.

Danielle pushed the door open and strode across the room towards the bedroom, avoiding half-seen furniture in the dim room by instinct more than sight. The lanterns had been turned so low that they barely illuminated the wall where they hung, and the only real light came into the room from the hallway through the open door.

"Wait!" Wyn hissed, and grabbed Danielle's arm.

"What…" started one of the soldiers, but Wyn silently shushed him by putting a finger over his lips. She held still as ice, her head cocked slightly to one side. Danielle held her breath, not wanting to distract.

Wyn slowly stepped to the door, retrieved her knife belt from its hook, and belted it around her waist, her eyes on the room the entire time. Steel whispered as the knives came into her hands. Then she moved next to Danielle, quiet as a shadow.

"What is it, Wyn?" Danielle whispered. The room seemed deathly silent to her. The fire was mere embers, and the only sounds she could hear were the careful thud of the soldiers' boots as they eased into the room, and the thump of her own heartbeat as it beat loudly in her ears.

"I heard something," Wyn said softly, and moved a few more steps into the dark room. "Something… I'm not sure what."

Danielle stepped behind Wyn and followed her as they moved to the bedroom door. The two soldiers took their cue from Wyn and drew steel, their blades singing softly as they came to hand, and then the soldiers spread out on either side as they felt their way into the dark room.

Wyn moved to the doorway and pressed against the wall. She peeked around the corner, and pulled back.

"Pitch black." She shook her head. "Hold a lantern for me."

Danielle took down a lantern from its hook and raised the flame so that a pale glow illuminated the nearby walls, then moved to shine it into the bedroom.

"Stay with me," Wyn instructed, and slipped through the door.

Danielle followed, the lantern held high. The bedroom shifted and jumped in the light as shadows stretched and circled as the lantern moved. Strange shapes loomed at them from the dark. An upended table, its broken legs probing into the air like shattered teeth. A rug flung to the side, piled into twisted ridges and folds. A chest destroyed, its contents strewn and smashed.

Wyn glanced at Danielle questioningly, uncertain where to go, and Danielle indicated the far side of the bed where an old iron chest rested against the wall.

Wyn stole in that direction, moving sure-footedly around the chaos on the floor, eyes never still as she scanned the darkened room. Danielle crept after her. They came upon an oaken wardrobe that lay on its side, its door gaping open, and Danielle said a quick prayer of thanks. Her pack should be in there, with her lance inside, if she were lucky. *First the Blade*, she told herself, and she trailed after Wyn. She heard the soldiers enter the room behind them. One had taken another lantern, and its light brightened the room enough that they could see the walls loom in the shadows around them.

Nothing in the room had survived the destruction that had washed through the space. The wide canopy above the bed had been shredded and now hung in a curtain of tatters. Chairs had been smashed against the walls and lay in splinters.

Danielle could hear the water trickling into the pool in the bath, but otherwise the room lay utterly still. Her heart continued to pound in her ears, louder than she thought possible.

Ahead of them stood the iron chest, a powerful artifact of the Temple, laced with Wardpacts and Veils that protected and concealed anything within. Danielle had carefully placed the Blade in it upon arrival, and had felt the magical locks slide into place under her own Word.

But now the latches hung open.

Danielle raised the lid by the corner and held the lantern to chase the shadows away as she stared inside. But it remained empty. The Blade was gone.

Danielle left the lid open and turned to leave, but Wyn placed a hand on her arm and held her still.

"There's something here," Wyn whispered. "I don't know what, but it's watching us." She turned her head slightly as she listened. "The water… something about the water."

A gust of wind wafted through the torn canopy, and a wet noise crunched, as if rotten ice had broken under a hammer. Danielle turned to the sound.

The soldier with the lantern stared back at her in surprise. Blood poured from a terrible wound across his chest and neck, the grey steel scales of his armor ripped and torn open. He staggered forward a step, and shadows swung wildly across the room as the lantern fell. Then his legs gave way and he crashed to the floor.

"No no no," Wyn hissed under her breath, and she pushed Danielle towards the wall, staying between her and the rest of the room.

A shadow moved and there was the sigh of a faint rasp, then a clatter as something small was knocked to the floor.

The other soldier backed against the opposite wall, his sword poised in front of him. Wyn motioned with her knife, pointing towards the main room, and the soldier nodded.

Wyn moved in that direction and she kept between Danielle and the room as Danielle hugged the wall at her back.

Then Wyn stopped, frozen as she tilted her head to listen. She slowly raised her head to peer into the darkness above them.

Danielle raised the lantern and followed Wyn's stare as the high ceiling slowly emerged from the gloom. Something moved as the shadows retreated. Danielle stared upwards as a nightmare unfolded above her. Long, black scythes gleamed wetly in the lantern light, an armored shell twisted and slid, and a ghastly rasp echoed from the shadow.

Then it leaped from its perch, too fast for Danielle to do more than flinch. It landed on the soldier, with barbed limbs that impaled him cruelly. He screamed in agony and his fingers scrabbled against the unyielding, black armor. Then the creature whirled and the soldier tore, and blood sprayed across the walls and floor as he shrieked and kicked wildly.

"Dani, get back!" Wyn crouched low between Danielle and the creature, her knives ready.

It left the body of the soldier behind and slid across the floor. The creature moved like an insect, its limbs a chaotic blur, but so fast. Then it suddenly rushed towards them and Wyn leapt to meet it.

A whirlwind of scything blades and diving, twisting bodies exploded across the floor, too fast for Danielle to tell what was happening. Sparks flashed as steel clashed with armored skin dozens of times in the space of a heartbeat, Wyn's blades seemingly in a thousand places at the same time as they blurred through the air around her. Then she twisted away, pursued by a rush of half-glimpsed limbs and black, chitinous armor that followed her every move.

Wyn arched over the creature and leapt clear of the razor-clad limbs that reached for her. She tucked and landed on its back and drove her blades down with all of her force. Barbed points thrust at her and she tore her knives free and sprang away, leaving behind a spray of dark blood that showered across the floor.

The creature shrieked and lashed at her with writhing limbs, and its scythes left long scars in the stone wall. Wyn twisted desperately to avoid them as they tore the air around her. Backwards and forwards she ducked and weaved, deflecting the attacks with her blades as she twisted and rolled through the deadly assault.

A half-dozen quick steps brought Danielle to the smashed wardrobe. Inside was chaos, clothes torn and strewn into ragged piles. Danielle ripped them from the wardrobe as she frantically searched for her pack.

She had hung it from a small hook inside the door, but that side of the wardrobe was now on the bottom, underneath everything else. Her fingers pushed through soft fabric as they searched for the leather strap.

Danielle heard Wyn curse in anger, then the singing of steel drawn across armor in a flurry of blows. Wood splintered and fabric tore, and something heavy crashed to the floor.

Danielle did not stop her search. *It has to be in here!*

"Danielle!" Wyn called urgently.

Then Danielle's fingers touched soft, bulging leather. She grabbed it and pulled, ripping the pack free from the debris of the wardrobe. Her fingers scrabbled at the cinch knot and tore it open. The long metal shape of her lance came into her hand and she whirled to face the room.

Danielle cleared her mind to let her Word form. Layers of complexity took shape within the Word as it folded around itself. It built methodically, each shape in the sequence precisely and perfectly formed. She let it flow into the lance and felt the bindings release to funnel the power of the Weapon into the pattern she had created.

Then she looked up to find her foe.

Wyn faced it, her long legs braced wide as her blades blurred around her in an endless steel stream that deflected the writhing black nightmare of limbs that slashed, thrust, and whipped at her.

Danielle let the power of the lance boil forth, but not all of it, not all at once. A shaft of golden sun pierced the gloom and reached to touch the black, armored shell. The creature whirled and moved, too fast to see, but not before the lance carved across it, leaving an orange scar in its flesh that steamed and sizzled.

Danielle chased it with the lance, letting another pulse of energy sear through the air. The creature twisted and cut back under the beam, faster than Danielle could react, and stone boiled in a long streak across the wall.

Then Wyn fell upon it from behind, and her knives scored two long trails through its flailing limbs before she leaped away again. The creature hissed in rage and turned after her.

Danielle caught it with the third pulse. The golden beam of light walked destruction across the creature's back, and black armor cracked and steam erupted from cooked flesh wherever it touched. Limbs thrashed as it swarmed away from the light, and launched itself through the air at Danielle, its long scythes slicing towards her faster than an eye could blink.

Wyn sprang into the air above it and landed heavily on its back. Her knives drove into the gaping, steaming wound. They cut deeply through vulnerable flesh as the creature shrieked and beat its limbs wildly on the ground. Wyn rolled through the storm and came to her feet, knives poised, facing it.

It was shattered, its armor torn, savage wounds in its limbs, but still it surged towards Wyn, seeking her with its talons.

Danielle speared it with her lance, and she held it there as she let the remaining power drain into the creature. It boiled, its armor cracked, and its flesh melted into glowing, orange droplets that splattered and hissed onto the floor.

It shrieked and writhed but it could no longer escape, and as the beam finally dimmed and flickered all that was left of the creature was a foul odor and the scrape of its limbs on the ground as it twitched convulsively.

Wyn stood bent over with her hands on her knees and watched it subside. "That's the same awful thing that was watching us in the tower, I swear it."

"When you went down the ropes?" Danielle was surprised. "But you said you did not see it."

"Yeah, but I know it is." Wyn stood upright and pointed at the remains with a jab of her knife. "Sounds the same, acts the same. Quacks like a nasty death monster, you know?"

"Someone has summoned those creatures here into the Temple," Danielle realized. "It must be what Karsha sensed."

"Well I wish he would have warned us a bit more," Wyn complained. "There's 'we're in danger' and then there's 'we're in *danger*'. It would have been nice to know that Spikey here was waiting in my bedroom. Your bedroom."

Danielle nodded as she considered.

"If there is someone here performing fuil crunor rituals, this will not be the only threat. Husks for certain, since the rituals seem to create those, but perhaps wights too." She gestured to the empty iron chest. "And they have my Blade now, somehow. We need to find Reverend Benno."

"What about your sis?"

"The best thing we can do to help her is to help the Temple destroy these things."

Danielle glanced about the room. "Let me just get rid of this dress." Leggings made of supple, black leather and a pair of fleece-lined boots came to hand, then a black, long-sleeved tunic, simple and sturdy. Lastly she donned her silver steel jerkin, and a sword belt taken from one of the unfortunate soldiers. Danielle slipped her pack onto the belt, nestled it into the small of her back, and was ready.

Danielle led the way. They moved quickly through the main room and out the door, but they stopped in surprise in the hallway as they encountered a group of three Temple soldiers led by a knight. The soldiers had weapons drawn, and were as startled as Danielle was to encounter them there.

"Lady Danielle?" the knight asked.

"Thank goodness you are here, sir knight," Danielle answered. She did not know the young woman, nor did she recognize any of the three soldiers, but that was not surprising. There were so many stationed in Bandirma there was little chance she would. "You must take us to the Bishop as fast as you can. There are fuil crunor rituals being worked in the Temple."

"To the Bishop?" The knight frowned. "Lady Danielle, I'm afraid I have orders from the Council to arrest you and bring you before them."

"Arrest me?" Danielle almost laughed. *It is ludicrous, some sort of joke perhaps*. "Why?"

"For the murder of Bishop Benno."

The words made no sense to Danielle. She heard them and understood them, but she could not conceive of why the knight would say them to her. *Reverend Benno has not been murdered*, was all that she could think. *Why would she say such a thing?*

"What?" Danielle asked.

"Come on, your Ladyship," the knight said, and Danielle realized that there were no kind eyes in the group facing her. Swords were still held in hand, and the knight reached to take ahold of her arm.

Then he is actually gone?

Danielle felt her breath leave her as if she had been struck a blow. She could not seem to focus her thoughts. *It is not possible!* screamed in her mind, over and over. She saw the knight speaking to her, but no words came out, just unintelligible noises. The knight was clearly angry, but Danielle did not care.

Danielle's legs did not want to support her any more. She took a step back and leaned against the wall, then slid into a crouch. *I was just talking to him,* she remembered. *How could he be dead between then and now?*

She realized Wyn was urgently calling her name, and glanced up. Wyn leaned over her, anxiety written in every part of her body. But there was more than just concern for Danielle, she thought. *What is she saying?*

"Dani, come on, you need to listen," said Wyn. "She says they're arresting us for what happened to Reverend Benno."

Wyn's words were like an icy blast of wind through her mind. Grief and confusion were pushed down and suddenly she could think again. "Why arrest us?"

"She's not really, um, in the mood to talk," Wyn replied, tilting her head towards the knight. Danielle saw that Wyn was right. The Knight had not put away her sword, and she wore a frown of fixed purpose. *She looks very angry, which I understand if she thinks we did what she says we did.*

Danielle took a weary breath and slowly stood up and leaned heavily on Wyn's arm. As she did their heads came close together, and she was able to whisper in Wyn's ear. Wyn pulled back slightly, surprise followed closely by a slight nod of her head.

Danielle turned to face the knight. "Of course we will come with you, we have nothing to fear." Danielle made her voice sound tired and defeated, an extremely easy task under the circumstances. "But who ordered our arrest? Who claims we did this?"

"The order came from the Council," the knight replied as she sheathed her sword. The soldiers relaxed as it appeared the arrest would go smoothly.

Wyn approached the knight and held her hands out together towards her.

"Do you need to tie me up?" Wyn asked, her eyes big and frightened.

"Not if you swear to…" the knight managed before Wyn's fist smacked into the knight's throat and knocked her staggering backwards to the ground. Wyn quickly pounced on her and knelt on her neck and chest.

Danielle moved at the same time, and her hand dove into her pack and came out holding her lance. She brandished it at the stunned soldiers before they could draw their swords.

"Draw steel and die," she told them, slowly traversing across the group with the elegant Weapon. At least two of them knew her reputation, for they immediately raised their hands and stepped back, and the third, suddenly alone, followed their lead.

The knight thrashed under Wyn's weight, but only for a moment before she passed out. Her arms fell limply to the floor, and her legs stopped twitching. Wyn rose, checked to make sure the knight was breathing now that her hold was loose, and dragged her unconscious form into the apartment.

It worked! Danielle thought. *Well of course it did. How on earth would they be able to tell if a Device was empowered or not.*

Danielle herded the soldiers after Wyn and made them stand in the bathroom while she closed and blocked the door with a heavy table.

"What now?" Wyn asked.

Danielle was not sure. *Why on earth would the Council think we murdered Reverend Benno?* Her thoughts trailed off in confusion.

"I think Karsha was right," Danielle said to Wyn. "I think we need to leave, right away."

"Alright, but what's going on? Dani, you have to tell me." Wyn sounded confused, and Danielle could not blame her.

"I do not know, Wyn, I am sorry," said Danielle, a trace of desperation edging into her voice. She tried to push it down but there was too much grief and fear and it lodged in her throat. "But we arc in *danger*, I know that. Fuil crunor rituals here in the Temple, and Reverend Benno killed. And they want to blame us for it all, you heard her. We need to be somewhere safe until it can all be worked out."

"Let's find Killock," Wyn stated firmly, and Danielle suddenly realized what she needed to do.

"No, Wyn, Killock is too far away, but there is someone else. We need to go to God."

Whitebrooke

Even with the help of Reverend Ezekiel and both acolytes the summer sun shone high in the sky over Nóinín Cnoc by the time the beans were harvested. Baskets strained to hold the crop, the beans a deep green against the bleached wicker.

Ezekiel stood and stretched his back as he reached the end of his row, and mopped his face and head with a small rag before replacing his wide-brimmed straw hat. His dirt-stained robes were tied into a knot like a peasant's dress, and his bare feet were stained as dark as the earth, but he did not care in the slightest. If his knees had allowed, he would stay in the fields all day.

The temple's wagon waited half-filled with the harvest, and Ezekiel watched the farmers load the last few baskets from the field as he sat on the stone wall that surrounded the fields. Beyond the wall were the temple pastures, covered as always at this time of year by a blanket of the small, white flowers that gave Nóinín Cnoc its name.

A movement on the worn path that led to the temple caught Ezekiel's eye. A lone rider emerged from the forest and passed along the meandering trail towards the temple. Ezekiel watched the rider for a moment, and began the walk up the hill to meet him.

The rider already stood in the temple yard by the time Ezekiel arrived.

"Hello, Ezekiel," the new Archivist greeted the old.

"Whitebrooke." Ezekiel smiled and wiped his hands on his rag before gripping the larger man's in welcome. "It is good to see you again."

Whitebrooke nodded. He had not been to see Ezekiel since before the winter snows, but it felt much longer than that.

"Come inside and help me find something cold to drink," Ezekiel offered, and Whitebrooke gratefully accepted. The road from Bandirma had been hot and dusty.

The temple kitchen was small and homey, filled with hanging pots and scarred cutting tables. Its pantry lay deep beneath the stone floor, and had a large icebox. Ezekiel retrieved a jug of mead from it that was quickly covered with drops of condensation. He poured a mug for his guest, one for himself, and savored the first sip with eyes closed.

Whitebrooke took a deep draught and the cold liquid sent chills into his skull.

"You look tired," Ezekiel sounded concerned. "I was sorry to hear about the election. You would have made a good Bishop."

"Apparently not many agreed with you," Whitebrooke growled. "The truth is I didn't have time. My research was more important, and the others refused to understand that."

"I voted for you, anyway." Ezekiel sipped his mead. "Benno will do alright, I suppose. He is a fine priest, and a very good politician. But it would have been nice to have a Bishop who appreciated the history of the Temple a bit more."

Whitebrooke nodded, frustration swirling in his chest. He had been so confident that the election was his and he would no longer have to deal with the Council interfering and trivializing his work. He knew he had only himself to blame.

"You mentioned your research?" Ezekiel ventured hopefully.

"Yes." Whitebrooke gathered his thoughts. "I found a reference that I think might be the key."

"The key to what?" Ezekiel asked, and a frown settled across his face.

"You know to what," Whitebrooke answered shortly. "No other research is more important."

Ezekiel remained silent for a moment, rose from his stool, and faced the kitchen window. A soft breeze wafted through the lace curtains and brought with it the sound of bees busy in the flowers beneath the sill.

Ezekiel gathered his thoughts, and turned to face his former pupil.

"Whitebrooke, it has been almost two years now," Ezekiel's voice was gentle. "I hoped you had ended your search. You cannot help her now."

"Ended?" Whitebrooke scowled in confusion. "Why would I end my efforts? My work is too important to abandon. It is for *everyone*, not just for Aislin."

"It is a noble thought, and your devotion to your work does you credit." Ezekiel returned to his stool and placed a hand on Whitebrooke's arm. "But, my dear boy, God himself told us no magic could save Aislin, no magic can cheat death, and none can provide a way to return from beyond the shroud."

"Yes, He said that," Whitebrooke agreed. He considered his next words carefully. "But I am not sure He told us the whole truth."

"Why would you think that?" Ezekiel was shocked, and pressed his hands on the table in front of him, as if he were about to push himself up.

But it was Whitebrooke who stood, and he paced in the narrow gap between the wall and the kitchen table, ducking to avoid the iron pots that endangered his head.

"Do you recall the scrolls of Duibhir?" Whitebrooke asked.

"The Hooded Knight?" Ezekiel nodded. "Yes I do. I believe he has the best description of the events of the Conclave after Ruric's death."

"I agree." Whitebrooke stopped his pacing and turned to face the table. "Which is why it is such a shame that so many of his scrolls are missing."

"We don't know how many are missing," Ezekiel cautioned. "A break in thought doesn't necessarily indicate an entire missing scroll."

Whitebrooke dismissed the argument with a sweep of his arm. "We know some are missing. And I believe I have found one."

"Where?"

"In a transcription made by Beledain."

"Beledain never transcribed Duibhir's work." Ezekiel shook his head.

"Not knowingly, and he assembled the scroll incorrectly, but he clearly found one of the scrolls," Whitebrooke's words gained speed and volume in his excitement.

"But, even if it was one of Duibhir's scrolls, what is the import?"

"He writes of a book discussed at the Conclave. The book contains a description of a Word completely unknown to me. Duibhir names it the Word of Life," Whitebrooke's voice rumbled powerfully in the small kitchen.

Ezekiel's face became rigidly blank.

"You have heard of the Word of Life before?" Whitebrooke challenged him.

"I have," Ezekiel's voice was grim, "and it is *not* what you seek."

"You know this Word?" Whitebrooke insisted. "You know what it does?"

"No, but I know which book Duibhir refers to." Ezekiel met Whitebrooke's eye and held it. "There is only one book that speaks of such a Word. The *Sanguinarium*."

"The Crunorix book?" Whitebrooke could not contain his eagerness. "The Word is explained in there?"

"I will tell you what I know, but only so that you may see that this Word will not help you." Ezekiel stabbed at the table with a boney finger to emphasize his words.

Whitebrooke nodded acceptance.

"No one has read the *Sanguinarium*, not since the time of the Conclave," Ezekiel explained. "We are told that the Nameless

King created the Word of Life, the terrible secret he kept that allowed him and his priests to command the dead and pervert life into undeath. All of his followers strove to master the Word, his magi and his priests."

"So He did lie to me." Whitebrooke closed his eyes. "A Word to control life. A Word to control death."

"In a way, yes," Ezekiel spoke harshly. "But look at what they did with the Word. They did not create life, they did not preserve it, they corrupted and perverted it."

"A Word is a tool." Whitebrooke met Ezekiel's gaze in a challenge. "You taught me that. It is how the Word is used that makes the action good or evil."

"You must not read the *Sanguinarium*," Ezekiel pleaded. "No one can, and this Word of Life cannot give you what you want." Ezekiel continued more gently. "Let her rest beyond the shroud."

Whitebrooke kept his gaze locked on Ezekiel's for a moment, then sighed despondently and nodded his acceptance.

"You are right," Whitebrooke agreed. "But it is a bitter disappointment to swallow."

Ezekiel watched him for a moment more, then his gaze softened and he moved to comfort his former student with a gentle touch on his arm.

"You have labored so diligently for her," Ezekiel consoled. "No one could have done more."

***

Whitebrooke stood on the small balcony attached to his rooms and let the cold wind from the lake curl around him. In the distance the faint tone of the evening bells sounded and he took a deep breath, the freezing air a welcome stimulant. He held the Bishop's ring in his hand and turned it slowly, gently rubbing the smooth metal with his thumb.

Behind him his rooms stood dark in the evening gloom. Dim shapes cluttered them, tables and desks heavy with bulky tomes, leather chairs long ago sacrificed to hold more books.

Whitebrooke let the wind rifle his hair for another moment, then returned to the room.

The heavy curtain swayed slowly in the open balcony door and Whitebrooke stood in the doorway to wait. Shadows shifted against the wall, and then he was there. A movement within the shadow suddenly separate, a silhouette of a man.

The dark shape was clearer than Whitebrooke had ever seen him, no longer a shade. The dim light revealed elegant features, dark eyes, and a handsome smile. He wore a long, deep grey tunic embroidered with patterns of silver thread, and his thick, silver hair swept back in shining waves from a high forehead which bore a circlet with seven gleaming stones set in it.

He placed a hand on Whitebrooke's arm and gripped it firmly, white teeth gleaming in the low light as a pleased smile flashed across his face. Whitebrooke could feel the warmth of the hand on his arm, and the touch brought a strength that filled Whitebrooke's massive frame.

"Well done. Well done indeed," he congratulated Whitebrooke, his voice rich and resonant. A faint echo laced the sound, as if the man stood at a distance. The first time he had called to Whitebrooke his faint whisper was as fleeting as the touch of a snowflake, gone before it could truly be perceived. But the whispers had accumulated and grown in strength.

"Thank you, my lord." Whitebrooke held the Bishop's ring between thumb and finger. "The ring is ours."

The regal figure nodded and stepped between the stacks of books. He ran a finger across the cover of an ancient, leather-bound tome and paused to consider the gilded title.

"Are you ready to continue?" he asked Whitebrooke.

"I am." Whitebrooke's voice rumbled in counterpoint to the man's smooth tone. "Danielle will soon be with her sister."

The figure nodded, satisfied.

"My lord," Whitebrooke continued. "Before you go, may I see her?"

The man smiled and nodded. "Of course. You have given me so much, I gladly return the kindness." He indicated the shadows against the wall with a subtle gesture of his fingers, and

Whitebrooke saw another shape appear and move toward him. She glided between the books and as she neared, Whitebrooke saw that she, too, was clearer than he had ever seen her. She extended her hands, and Whitebrooke took them gratefully.

"Aislin," Whitebrooke murmured.

She smiled and stroked his cheek with gentle fingers, and he felt the warmth of their touch.

"I will leave you, then," the man said. "You have given me the strength to thin the shroud more than ever before, but only for a short time. Soon, however, you will free the Word from its prison with the Blade, and then we will tear the shroud. Aislin will pass through with me and return to you."

"Not just her," Whitebrooke emphasized. "All who pledge to us will be ever free from the curse of mortality. This was never just to assuage my own grief."

"It is your nobility of purpose that will cause others to hail you as their savior," the man assured Whitebrooke. "Let that thought fill you with the strength to finish your tasks. I know they are arduous."

Whitebrooke nodded and felt the man's presence fade, but he did not look away from her eyes, not until they returned to the shadow once more.

***

The Council awaited him in their chamber, as did Sir Maeglin. The Knight Commander stood against the wall of the chamber with arms folded, conspicuous in his distance from the others.

Sir Maeglin was a tall man, almost as tall as the Archivist, but lean and strong instead of broad and powerful, with shoulders and arms chorded with long muscles like steel. His eyes were deep-set under a strong brow with thick eyebrows, and he had a mouth that seemed permanently set into a thin-lipped scowl.

Maeglin wore a breastplate made of dull grey steel, unadorned save for a beautiful pattern of scales that flared across his chest. A black cloak was draped over his armor, fastened to his breastplate by a small gold pin in the shape of a ferocious sea serpent, his one concession to extravagance.

Five of the Council were there, all but Sebastian, unlooked for in his distant tower. Nesta's wide face wore a mask of grim anger that painted bright red spots on her cheeks, but the others seemed stunned with sorrow.

"What have you found?" Nesta wasted no time. "Is he truly gone?"

"Yes," Whitebrooke answered. "Murdered. There is no longer any doubt."

"Was there ever?" Dougal muttered.

"And the ritual?" Nesta continued. "You feared it was fuil crunor."

"There is no way to know, but yes, I believe it to be a fuil crunor ritual," Whitebrooke let anger resonate in his growl. "I have asked Meara to continue to examine it, but it matches the rituals discovered in the hinterlands in many ways."

"Meara?" Nesta frowned. "Surely something of this import…"

"What choice do I have?" Whitebrooke snapped. "Ten of my best, murdered along with the Bishop to fuel this foul ritual." He drew a deep breath to collect himself. It was difficult to control his anger and impatience. *You are the fools who have brought death and pain upon us, all so that you can protect a lie.* Fury twisted in his stomach and became sorrow, a fresh pain for the lives that he had been forced to take. *They will be remembered as martyrs, I will make sure of it*, he reminded himself, thankful that anger and grief were to be expected. Indeed, the Council showed only concern and shared pain as they waited respectfully for him to continue, and even Nesta's appraising glance revealed no suspicion that she might be the target of Whitebrooke's rage.

Whitebrooke pulled calm resolve across his face. "I would have chosen Meara regardless."

Nesta nodded her acceptance. "How long until we can see the murder site?"

“Not until Meara finishes her research,” Whitebrooke forced concern into his voice. “It is far too dangerous until we are sure the fuil crunor ritual has been contained.”

“Have you found anything to help us?” Hayley wondered.

“Yes, I have,” Whitebrooke nodded. “Karsha Hali performed the ritual that killed Bishop Benno.”

“The Queen’s wizard?” Liadán was aghast. “But why?”

“We will have to ask him that.” Whitebrooke was pleased that the first question was to Karsha’s motive, not his guilt. It was all too easy to think the worst of the strange southerner. He knew the next lie would not be so easily believed. “But there are worse tidings than that. I am afraid that Lady Danielle aided Karsha Hali.”

“That is not possible,” insisted Haley. “Danielle would never turn against us, and she certainly would not harm Bishop Benno. It is ridiculous to even consider such a thing.”

“I agree,” Whitebrooke soothed. “Which is why I believe she must be in thrall to Karsha Hali, forced to act against her will. But the fact remains that it was Danielle who requested that I send the archivists to meet her, and it was Danielle who asked Benno to join them. He told me himself after he finished speaking with Danielle. It was simple luck that I was delayed or I would have been there too.”

“That is not proof she was involved,” Nesta noted.

“No, but do you not agree it is more than enough for us to be cautious?” Whitebrooke appealed to them with arms wide. “Should we not at least arrest her and question her? If this is but coincidence, then we shall quickly determine the truth.”

“Alright then,” Nesta concurred, “arrest, but no more.”

“I’m sorry to raise a sticky point, but what about the Queen?” Ail asked hesitantly. “She is hardly likely to agree to us simply marching in and grabbing her counselor.”

“Then she shouldn’t have a counselor who is a magus,” scoffed Dougal.

“Well, no, obviously, but she may not believe us.” Ail looked around the group for help.

"What in God's name is the matter with you people?" Sir Maeglin's voice cut across the chamber like steel. "Our Bishop is murdered, our priests and priestesses killed. We know who is responsible, and yet you mutter and debate."

Maeglin shook his head angrily and strode to the door.

"Sir Maeglin, where are you going?" Nesta challenged him.

Maeglin stopped with his hand on the latch and turned to Nesta.

"I'm going to arrest Karsha Hali. I'm going to arrest Lady Danielle," he stated, "and then we can discuss the niceties."

"And if the Queen objects?" asked Liadán.

"Let her," said Maeglin. "I'm sure you can appease her… and she won't complain for long once she knows she was the one that brought the snake into our home."

"There must not be bloodshed," Nesta cautioned the Knight Commander.

"We will overwhelm them," Maeglin smiled grimly. "It will be over so quickly they won't have time to fight back. But if one of her guards decides to draw steel against my men…"

"You will need my help against the wizard," Whitebrooke spoke up. "I am the only one of us who has studied the fuil crunor rituals. If he decides to fight, I can protect us."

Maeglin considered for a moment, then nodded his head brusquely. "Let's go, Reverend."

Outside the Council chamber Sir Maeglin gave quick orders to his knights to clear the passageways around the Queen's apartments, and to assemble unobserved in a more distant section of the Temple.

"Are you ready?" Maeglin asked the Archivist.

"I am ready for the wizard, but there is something we must do before we make our move," Whitebrooke told the knight.

"And what is that?"

"We must retrieve a Weapon from Lady Danielle's rooms."

"Why?" Maeglin frowned. "She is with Karsha Hali and the Queen, is she not? Whatever is in her room can wait."

"Who knows what other servants Karsha Hali commands, and if one were to take up the Weapon while we are occupied with its master…" Whitebrooke's voice echoed ominously from the stone walls.

Maeglin's eyes narrowed to slits as he watched the Archivist. Whitebrooke let him think.

"Very well." Maeglin shook his head in frustration. "You have until the men are assembled. Then we go."

"That is more than enough time," Whitebrooke smiled at the Knight Commander.

***

The Martyr's Blade lay exactly where he expected it would be, carefully secured inside the iron chest that he had placed in Lady Danielle's rooms the day before by request of the Bishop.

The iron chest opened gladly to his Word and revealed the Blade, carefully wrapped in a linen shroud. Whitebrooke wasted no time taking it, although he dearly wished to savor the moment.

He paused at the door to the bedroom to leave a gift for anyone who should come seeking the Blade. Words of the fuil crunor rose painfully from his mouth in a chant as he summoned forth more of the power he had drained from his archivists earlier. The chant tore a rift in the air of the chamber, and cold shadow leaked through the hole to congeal on the floor. His chant gave the shadow substance and form and he continued until it moved and became aware.

Sir Maeglin waited for Reverend Whitebrooke in the hallway outside.

"It was there, as I thought," Whitebrooke told the Knight Commander, and watched his response as he showed him the wrapped Blade. Maeglin nodded, his face impassive.

"Is she still with her sister?" Whitebrooke asked.

"Yes. Is it time then? Do you finally have everything you need?" Sir Maeglin's voice carried an undertone.

"It is time." Whitebrooke met the Knight Commander's gaze. Sir Maeglin fell in step with Whitebrooke, the leather straps of the knight's heavy steel cuirass creaking with every stride.

The two entered the larger hallway that led towards the Inner Temple. Soldiers and knights awaiting orders were gathered there in full armor.

"Clear the halls and tell Sir Hollis that his men will be advancing shortly," Sir Maeglin told his captains, and the knights bowed and moved quickly to obey.

Then Maeglin gathered the soldiers and led them through the back hallways of the Temple, until they joined with a second force standing ready near the Queen's chambers. They numbered ten knights and over forty soldiers, and double that number taking positions to seal off this section of the Temple.

A fierce smile settled deeply on the Archivist's face as he watched the soldiers prepare. His prey was trapped, he had the Blade, he had the Bishop's seal. Whitebrooke had most of the tools he needed. The last was almost in his hands. Then he could turn his attention to his true task.

Whitebrooke listened as Sir Maeglin spoke with Sir Hollis, a veteran captain who had distinguished himself time and again fighting in the Ironbacks under Lord Bradon. Maeglin had chosen only his best captains for the task of bringing justice to the Bishop's murderers.

But even the best of men, or perhaps especially the best of men, would question the orders that Maeglin issued. It was no simple thing to arrest the Queen's counselor. They knew this action could easily lead to war, and the Queen was beloved by those in the Temple as well as by her subjects. Many of the priests, acolytes, and soldiers of the Temple came from lands that swore fealty to the Queen, and allegiance was not easily forgotten just because a priest's robe or a knight's surcoat was donned.

"We are sure then?" Sir Hollis asked the Knight Commander. "The wizard is responsible for the murder?"

"Yes," Whitebrooke answered, continuing the tale he had fashioned for Sir Maeglin and the Council. "He is the one who has brought the Crunorix into our lands again, brought their rituals into our halls to murder Bishop Benno, and we fear that Lady Danielle is in his thrall. She may resist us, but we must capture her without harm. Only then do we have a chance of breaking his control."

Sir Hollis nodded, his thin face set with purpose.

"Then you are clear?" Sir Maeglin pressed the point and held his captain's eye. "Capture Lady Danielle if you can, but above all else you must apprehend Karsha Hali. He ends today in a cell or on a pyre."

"Yes, sir," Hollis replied.

"Tell the men," Maeglin commanded.

Whitebrooke listened as Sir Hollis gave out his orders. The soldiers were grim-faced and focused. They grieved for their Bishop, for he had been well-liked and respected, and the nature of the murder, here in their own home, had wounded them all to their souls. They were ready to prove their worth, even more passionately because it was too late.

"Are you ready?" Sir Maeglin asked Whitebrooke. "We will break through the Queen's guard, but the wizard, he's yours."

"Don't worry about me, Maeglin," Whitebrooke rumbled. "Karsha Hali will not be a problem."

***

As they approached the Queen's apartments the sounds of combat echoed off the stone walls of the passageway, steel on steel, steel on stone, steel on flesh, and cries of rage and pain. Whitebrooke saw the hall filled with struggling forms, the soldiers of the Queen's guard clashing with those of Sir Hollis.

"So much for overwhelming them," Whitebrooke accosted Sir Maeglin, although he cared little whether blood was shed or not. *As long as Danielle is taken alive.*

"They were ready for us," Maeglin rasped, eyes fierce with anger. "They knew we were coming. How?"

"We can ask them," Whitebrooke replied. "Once they have been subdued."

Whitebrooke knew that Maeglin's men would eventually overwhelm the smaller force of the Queen's, but it would take time to grind them into submission, and buying time for their Queen was all that they desired.

In the center of the defenders stood a tall knight, her silver armor splashed red with blood. The soldiers of the Queen's guard clustered around her and used her as the center of their resistance, and she would not break or fall back. Sir Hollis faced her, his shield held warily on guard as he circled to her left. Her sword whirled in blinding arcs as she drove back a Temple soldier to her right, then reversed to smash aside Sir Hollis' shield.

Sir Hollis attacked, and his blade struck expertly against her guard. She parried his attack, then twisted to strike across his exposed side. Her heavy blade tore through steel rings and thick leather and sent him staggering to his knees.

She roared triumphantly and shouted the Queen's name, and her soldiers took up the call defiantly.

Sir Maeglin grunted in displeasure and dropped his visor into place. He summoned a squad of soldiers to follow him and advanced to battle.

The Queen's knight saw them coming and shouted a warning and a challenge as she stepped forward to confront him.

Maeglin did not hesitate. His sword flashed out quick as a snake's tongue to knock aside her blade, then rang heavily as it struck her shoulder and bit deeply into her armor.

She struck back, sword whirling through the air. Maeglin stepped backwards to avoid the first blow, then knocked the second aside with his own blade, again giving ground. She lunged, and the point of her sword struck sparks from his armor as it passed beneath his arm.

Then Sir Maeglin clamped his arm down onto the sword and trapped it against his breastplate. Before she could pull back he twisted into the blade and it tore from her grasp. His turn continued and his own sword extended in a gleaming arc that sang death as it passed between her helm and her gorget, trailing a thick spray of blood from the tip as it tore through the soft fabric and flesh beneath.

Maeglin had already targeted his next opponent by the time she crashed to the floor, hands at her throat as blood drenched her breastplate. He passed through the Queen's soldiers coldly and precisely, a deadly scalpel. As he broke their line the squad of soldiers that followed him cheered as one and crashed into the breach. The defenders' line was split, and they were forced to fall back.

Whitebrooke held forth a heavy gold amulet that hung on a steel chain around his neck. The Device was ancient, a treasured artifact of the Temple taken from deep within the archives, a Wardpact of immense power. On its face, six curling waves formed a ring that surrounded the amulet. At Whitebrooke's touch the waves swirled and revealed a ruby that flashed in the light of the lanterns.

Whitebrooke assembled the amulet's intricate Word with practiced ease, and the Wardpact responded to his whispered command. The waves spun around the ruby as the bindings within released, and Whitebrooke's Word shaped the energy into a protective shell around him.

As reinforcements surged forward he went with them until he reached the door defended by the Queen's soldiers. He ordered men to smash the door and it shook under the assault of hammers and maces.

Whitebrooke waited impatiently. Beyond the door he could feel Words of power flaring into life without concern for concealment. And something else, something he could not identify, primal and strange.

The door's heavy wood splintered and ripped from its iron hinges, and the soldiers shoved the door inwards through a hastily made barricade of furniture.

Inside the room, the defenders' reserves fell upon the Temple soldiers. A powerful knight led them, his helm the shape of a screaming hawk, and he wielded a mighty cavalry sword that carved destruction through the invaders' ranks.

One defender dared to attack Whitebrooke. He let the soldier's blade impact with his Ward and watched as the sword shone a deep orange and then shattered in the man's grip. The soldier screamed in agony and dropped to his knees, his hand a smoking ruin. Whitebrooke left him there.

A half-seen form rushed at Whitebrooke from the side. Black wings spread above him, somehow wider than the room itself, and pitch black eyes gleamed behind a wicked beak that croaked a terrible cry of rage. Black talons wrapped themselves around Whitebrooke, and his Ward pulsed bright white and then shuddered to sickly ochre under the assault.

Whitebrooke wrenched the Blade from its sheath and lashed out at the creature, but it turned to wisps of smoke even as the sword passed through it.

The priest turned to seek the source of the immense bird, and saw the southern wizard, Karsha Hali. The man stood against a small door in the corner of the room, a ragged ball of faded black cloth with wiry legs planted defiantly. As Whitebrooke watched, Karsha dropped a small object into a pocket in his robes, then held forth another. He sang in a guttural voice, and the object sprang open.

Black smoke poured from the object and washed across the floor towards Whitebrooke. It wound around bodies and furniture and other obstacles like water over stones in a stream. A low, eerie hum filled the room as the smoke drew closer, and Whitebrooke saw shapes congeal from it, thousands of flying insects that swarmed towards him. Behind them emerged a creature of impossible size, a wasp longer than his arm, its segmented body a purple so dark it looked almost black.

The insects swarmed across Whitebrooke's Ward. Already weakened, the Ward faded from orange to carnelian, and Whitebrooke knew he had little time to react.

It is my turn for a trick, little man.

Whitebrooke chanted the fuil crunor, and the words scored his throat and mouth as he uttered them. The last of the power he had taken from the archivists now drew cold shadows from the air in front of him. He wrapped the shadows around himself like a cloak and saw the insect spirit recoil from its cold. Then he turned on the wizard.

Darkness rushed across the room and surrounded Karsha. Whitebrooke felt the little man's light flicker and dim under the immense pressure of the shadow as dark consumed the light.

Whitebrooke raised his chant to a crescendo and tore open an entrance to the endless Abyss, and it gaped wide to consume all, uncaring of loyalty. Soldiers screamed and dropped to convulse on the floor as their life flowed into the Abyss.

There was a surge as the wizard's light twisted and changed. The darkness roiled and filled the space where the light had been.

Whitebrooke ended his chant and let the power return into the Abyss. All around him the room was still, the bodies of those he had slain twisted and consumed. He strode to the door that Karsha had guarded and flung it open. Beyond were the magnificent private chambers of the Queen. Elegant windows allowed the dim evening light to cast grey shadows through the open space. Curtains billowed in front of the wide doors that Whitebrooke knew led to a balcony, and a chill wind swirled against his face and rippled his robes as he entered the room.

A quick glance showed no other movement in the room. Immaculate, still, and silent, the room revealed no signs of the chaos and destruction that had taken place just outside its door. The Queen's personal items were laid on the table just as her maid had left them. Her gown for the evening was carefully readied on the dressing stand. The massive bed was made with deep pillows and perfectly arranged goose-feather covers.

Where are they? A tug of doubt pulled from deep within, but Whitebrooke pushed it down. He moved to the open door and swept back the curtains to reveal the wide, stone balcony beyond. A crust of snow covered the stone railings that framed the long view to the south over the gentle farmlands that served Bandirma.

Whitebrooke cursed inwardly. *Danielle is not here! Nor the Queen. Where can they be?*

A movement on the balcony caught his eye. A raven perched on the railing, its glossy black feathers ruffled in the chill wind. It cawed at the priest, a harsh, accusatory sound, then spread its wings and flew away. Whitebrooke could hear it cawing as it disappeared into the gloomy evening clouds.

Whitebrooke closed and latched the door, and returned to the main room. Temple soldiers were entering it now, swords drawn and ready for a fight. They stared in horror at the bodies lying in the room, the twisted forms unnatural and obscene.

Sir Maeglin approached the priest. "What happened here, Reverend?"

"A fuil crunor trick of the southern wizard, Karsha Hali," Whitebrooke let revulsion drip from his words. "I was lucky to survive, even forewarned."

The knight nodded understanding, his face grim.

"Is the wizard dead?"

Whitebrooke was not sure. The way the light had twisted away, right on the brink of the Abyss, made him wonder. *It doesn't matter either way. I need him to be the enemy, not a conquered foe.*

"He escaped," Whitebrooke told Maeglin. "And there is no sign of the Queen, or Lady Danielle. We must find them quickly."

"I will start the search," responded Sir Maeglin, and he wiped his sword clean and sheathed it with a snap. "Every man not already on guard will sweep the Temple, room by room. And I will send out the rangers as well. If Lady Danielle and the Queen somehow make it past the walls, their tracks will be easy enough to find."

"Danielle cannot be allowed to escape," Whitebrooke could not keep the anger from his voice. "And after this massacre, we would be best served by making sure the Queen remains our guest as well. At least until she can be persuaded we acted justly."

"We shall see," Maeglin said calmly. "They should not have been able to escape from these rooms either. I would like to know how they accomplished that bit of magic and I will make sure it doesn't happen again. Perhaps your priests can tell us how they vanished from under our noses?"

"'My priests'?" Whitebrooke asked, his voice rumbling low. He did not care for the implication in the knight's voice. "Yes, *my priests* will do their job. You make sure your men do the same. I am sure the Council will not want to hear of another failure like this one."

Maeglin turned to Whitebrooke at the slight. Maeglin's eyes narrowed dangerously, and the priest fought down the urge to take a step away from the smaller man. But when the knight spoke his voice was calm. "If the Council wants my sword they can ask for it."

"There's no need for that," Whitebrooke dismissed the Commander's defiance. "I am sure you will satisfy the Council's wishes."

"They can satisfy themselves for all I care," said Maeglin coldly. "In case you have forgotten there's me, then the Bishop, then God. I don't answer to the Council, and I certainly don't answer to archivists."

"The Council can revoke your title," Whitebrooke replied, his voice a low threat. "And there will be a new Bishop soon."

"As I said, if they want my sword they can have it." Maeglin met the priest's eyes without blinking. "For the other, I know which way the wind blows in the Council chamber. That is why you are getting my full support. But that's the last I want to hear about what I *have* to do until you are actually wearing that ring. Until then I'll do my job, you go and take care of yours, and I'll let you know what I need from your priests when I need it."

"Very well," agreed Whitebrooke, a slow smile crossing his face. "I see we understand one another then."

Sir Maeglin nodded and turned to depart, but as he did a soldier appeared with a message. Maeglin listened, and turned to Whitebrooke.

"While we were busy here, Lady Danielle has been strolling around the Temple with some of the Queen's soldiers telling every knight she met to raise the alarm."

"What?" Whitebrooke was amazed. "How is that possible?"

"She must have walked out just before we sealed the area. She was last seen at the Inner Temple gate. The knights there said that she was going to her rooms."

"We walked right past her," Whitebrooke scowled.

"They sent a knight with some soldiers to arrest her." Maeglin headed for the door. "We should go and see how that went."

***

By the time that Whitebrooke and Maeglin arrived outside Lady Danielle's rooms, the hallway was already crowded with Temple soldiers and priests. Whitebrooke pushed past them. In the bedroom were the remains of his shadow demon, cut to pieces and emanating a vile stench. Two dead soldiers of the Queen's Guard lay torn apart.

"I'm sorry, sir," a young knight with a simple face tried to apologize to Sir Maeglin. "We found her and another woman leaving her rooms and tried to arrest her as instructed. But she was armed with a Weapon, so we had little chance."

"Are you a Knight of the Temple or a chambermaid?" Whitebrooke demanded, furious. *They had her, right here, and let her walk away!*

"A Knight, your Reverence," she answered, her face red.

"And yet the four of you could not overcome two little girls." Whitebrooke dismissed her with a wave of his hand, disgusted. "You may go."

Whitebrooke stood and surveyed the carnage in the room, deep in thought. He had accomplished the hardest part of his plan, but the critical last piece was slipping through his fingers. *It's not over yet,* he reminded himself.

"How long have they been gone?" Whitebrooke turned to question Maeglin.

"Half hour, no more. Do you think the woman with her was the Queen?" asked Maeglin.

"Even your chambermaid over there would recognize the Queen," Whitebrooke sneered. "I imagine it was that vagrant girl Danielle is so infatuated with."

"Is that right?" Maeglin asked, and his eyes narrowed slightly. "Well, that will mean multiple trails then, even easier." Then he strode away, shouting orders as he went.

Whitebrooke remained to survey the room once more. An acolyte hovered annoyingly on the edge of his vision but Whitebrooke ignored him. He knew that it was a message from the Council. *They can wait,* he decided.

At first the shambles around him told no story. Clothing, bedding and furniture lay scattered in every direction, torn and spoiled. Some pieces still smoldered, likely from whatever Weapon had slain the demon from the Abyss, and blood congealed in thick puddles underneath the bodies of the two slain soldiers.

A few details attracted his attention. Nowhere did he see weapons, nor packs. Beautiful, thick cloaks and warm, soft jackets lay scattered about the floor, but what Whitebrooke did not see was winter traveling gear. *So they took the time to ready themselves for a winter journey. They won't get far.* Whitebrooke had never known the rangers to fail on a hunt, and he doubted that two noblewomen, a ruffian pulled from a jail cell, and an ancient wizard from the far south would be the first to foil them.

Wyn

Fresh snow fell across the rolling farmlands that bordered Bandirma to the south and west, an icy snow that swirled on chill gusts of northern wind from across Loughliath. Thick clouds blotted out the moon and turned the farmlands into a dim landscape of dark shadows and grey patches with few discernible landmarks.

A vague movement to the north was whitecaps on the endless surface of Loughliath. Waves rushed onto the rocky beach at the foot of the grey cliffs of Bandirma, clunking and chattering as the smooth stones banged against each other in the froth.

Two figures emerged from the deep shadows under the cliff and scrambled across the beach. Spray wafted in the air as larger waves struck massive boulders off-shore, and Wyn felt its icy touch burn against her cheeks as they stumbled off the beach.

Away from the shore, the land was flat and covered in brittle winter grass that poked through the thin crust of snow. In the daylight, Wyn knew that she would be able to see for leagues in every direction, but darkness concealed them now, and the susurration of the waves on the nearby rocks covered any noise they might make.

Bitter wind gusted off Loughliath and hissed through the bent grass. Wyn and Danielle walked with their faces turned away from the wind, their breath long streamers of mist in the dark air, and slowly the colossal bulk of Bandirma receded behind them until it became simply a tall mound far to the west.

The night sky gradually turned from black to grey and the women pressed on with new urgency until they reached a thick band of trees. Small streams trickled from Loughliath into a wide marsh that blocked any approach from that direction. The farmers drained the water into their fields during growing season, but in the winter they closed the dykes and turned the land beyond into icy mud. Near the lake the ground was firmer, although cut by the numerous tiny streams that fed the marsh. Wyn led the way under the trees, and felt the pressure between her shoulder blades fade as their thick trunks blocked the distant black presence of Bandirma from view.

Danielle stopped against the thick trunk of an old oak and leaned against it to rest. "Can we stop, please? Wyn, I am exhausted."

Wyn moved close to Danielle, and they sat together and watched the broad surface of Loughliath surge against the shore through the trees. It appeared endless, a wide, flat horizon that stretched from east to west without break.

Wyn tucked her hair behind her ear and held her gloved fingers over the tip of her frozen nose. "Do you think your sis got away?"

"I hope so," Danielle replied softly. "Karsha seemed to know what he was doing. As long as she did not wait too long for us to return."

"Is she always so scary?" Wyn asked. "I mean, I didn't actually end up in the dungeons this time, but I thought I might for a moment there."

"I am sorry, Wyn." Danielle shook her head softly. "It was unfair of her to put you through that. I know she was trying to look out for me, but good intentions aside she had no right to force you to speak about such private things."

Wyn nodded, but realized she was not actually angry any more. True, she had thought about spitting in someone's wine glass at the time, but now there was a warm feeling in her chest and stomach, a comfortable pressure that soothed away the feelings of need and emptiness that had lodged there for so long. The change had occurred during the Queen's questioning, and Wyn quietly gave thanks that the Queen had insisted she expose her feelings.

I said 'love' and it felt all strange. Like it was hot or something and it was all across my skin when I said it. And I didn't even know I was going to say it, really, not until right that moment. But that's when the feeling started, right then.

Wyn closed her eyes and drifted through her memories, savoring the beautiful smile on Danielle's face as Wyn's words flowed across her.

"It's alright," Wyn said softly. She rearranged her hood and pulled it lower down over her face to try to keep more of the wind off. "It ended up better than last time, anyway. No cells."

Danielle nodded thoughtfully.

"I do not think she recognized you, although she will, given a bit more time." said Danielle. "Karsha knew who you were, even though he did not divulge his knowledge."

"Yeah, I got that. About shit myself when he started going on about garters."

"Hopefully it will all come up when we are carefree and safe and we can laugh about it. Really, you should be the one holding a grudge. You were the one thrown in the dungeon, not her," Danielle said indignantly.

"Well," said Wyn thoughtfully, "I did get a nice pair of knickers out of it, so it's pretty fair all things considered."

"True," Danielle laughed softly.

Wyn waited for the wind to subside again before asking Danielle the question that had been on the tip of her tongue since they started their escape.

"Did you really mean it when you said we were going to talk to God?"

"Yes, absolutely," answered Danielle. "He is not far away as I said, and I know that He will help us."

"Can you not just pray to Him?"

"No, I am afraid not. Only the Bishop can speak directly to God, or at least, the person holding the Bishop's ring. It was crafted for just that purpose."

"But what about all that chanting and praying in the temples?"

"He told me that was more like a feeling. He can sense it, but not to hear individual thoughts."

"Oh." Wyn replied. "Lord Bradon said He was nice."

"He is, very kind and very nice," Danielle turned slightly to face Wyn. "Wyn, are you nervous? Because you do not need to be."

"Why would I be nervous? I'm going to meet God is all. I haven't exactly been the best person, you know? I may have done a few things that weren't, well, right."

"You have also done many things that *are* right, and your heart is so very compassionate and caring. He knows we are human, that is why He loves us and cares for us, so it will not offend Him that you may have broken some laws, because it is the real you He will treasure."

"The fact that He can see inside me is not really making me feel any better," Wyn grumbled.

"It should," said Danielle. "What is in your deepest heart, that which makes you the person you really are, is what made me love you."

"Alright, well, remember all that deep person stuff if He starts talking about what happened in Lady Muirne's house."

"I will," said Danielle. She was quiet a moment. "What happened in Lady Muirne's house?"

"That's a tale for another time." Wyn threw pine cones at a distant tree until she ran out of ammunition within easy reach.

"Listen, Dani, I've been trying to work it all out," Wyn finally said hesitantly.

"What have you worked out?" Danielle shifted closer to Wyn and rested her head on Wyn's shoulder.

"Well, none of this really makes any sense to me. The rituals, and magi, and wights, and Spikey, and Reverend Asses. But what doesn't make sense to *anyone* is how a piece of shit like Reverend Asses could learn to be a proper Crunorix, like how you and Bishop Benno were saying."

"Did we? That is right, but I do not remember talking with the Bishop about it."

"It was when we arrived. You were sleepy." Wyn idly twisted pine needles together, making strange, jagged shapes. "Anyway, last night someone snuck into our bedroom, summoned up Spikey for us and took your Blade. And we know it wasn't Asses, because he's smeared all over the floor back in the catacombs," Wyn explained.

"That is so, but we always knew there could be more than one Crunorix priest."

"Well, there's no more 'could be' about it. There *is* another Crunorix priest, and he's in Bandirma. Two things we didn't know before, right?"

"I suppose that is true. But how does that help us? It could be anyone."

"Oh, well, see, I don't think that's right." Wyn spread the spines of her needle creation until it bristled in all directions like a hedgehog. "He's been very sneaky, but nowhere near sneaky enough. We can catch him now."

"We can?" Danielle held out her hand and Wyn deposited the needle ball into it for review. "How do we do that?"

"We use Reverend Asses," Wyn grinned. "Whoever he is, he must have known Asses. He didn't just bump into him at a tavern and say 'I've got this book of Soggywhatsitsname, would you like a go?' No, he knew the fucker, and he would've gone to see him sometime just before the rituals started."

"*Sanguinarium*," Danielle offered. "The book."

"That's the one," Wyn agreed.

"How does this help us find out who this other Crunorix priest is? Even if he did know Reverend Asses?"

"That's all I need, that is." Wyn sighed happily. "People will have noticed him, and they'll have noticed Asses. People talk. Trust me, I've found more hidden stuff from talking with tipsy drovers and servants in taverns than you would believe."

"Is this what you do for Sir Killock?" Danielle began to add needles to the ball, weaving a long stem. "I did not know."

"Yeah, mostly." Wyn watched Danielle's fingers as they wove. "Find secrets, find out what people are up to. Why, what did you think I did? Something naughty, I expect."

"I am not sure, but this sounds so exciting." Danielle closed her eyes for a moment and sighed in contentment. "Finding out secrets, playing at being someone. Do you wear a disguise?"

"What? No," Wyn laughed. "Mostly it's just talking and putting pieces together. It's like opening a lock. All the pieces are there, you just have to line them up right. But that's the easy part, really. It's amazing what people will tell you, especially when they're drunk and they think they've got a shot at getting in your pants. The hard part is once you've found what you're looking for, and you need to go and get it."

"I am sure." Danielle offered the completed needle flower to Wyn. "A beautiful flower for my love. Very prickly though."

"That's the one for me." Wyn smiled and took the creation, slowly twirling the stem between her thumb and fingers.

"Will it really be that simple?" Danielle tucked her hands into her cloak.

"Should be," Wyn replied. "Might take a return trip to the hinterlands, but I'll find him. Just as soon as I'm not running for my life. Speaking of…" Wyn clambered to her feet and brushed dirt and leaves from her cloak.

"Is it time to go already?" Danielle took a deep breath and stood also.

"Well, it *is* an escape," Wyn laughed.

"Fine," acquiesced Danielle as she squared her shoulders. "If I die from fatigue I would like my epitaph to mention the fact that I died bravely, without complaint. How much farther?"

Wyn could not keep a straight face. "We're here." She smiled in the grey light. "We've made it."

"We are?" Danielle looked around in puzzlement. "You said there was a boat."

Wyn pointed toward the lake shore through the nearby trees.

Danielle peered through the dim light, and turned to Wyn, confused.

"I'm pointing right at it," Wyn laughed. "Come on, I'll show you."

A stone water break had been constructed along the lake front, and covered in dirt and plants to conceal it. Behind it was a trench lined with flat stone slabs under a low roof, similarly concealed. The trench was kept dry by a lock at one end, but could be flooded if the gate was raised.

Wyn cleared away the branches and leaves that had fallen over the entrance, and pulled back the roof to reveal a long, low shape.

It had the name *Èan Mear* painted in black across the stern, and it was narrow enough that Wyn could reach across it from side to side if she stretched out both of her arms. It was very long, and streamlined. It had a small shelter in the center and a single mast that could be raised and lowered by manipulating the dozens of lines and pulleys that lay along its roof, and a simple rudder at the stern was affixed to the rail of a small cockpit fitted with a bench.

Killock had shown it to Wyn. The boat was maintained to allow clandestine trips across Loughliath when they needed to avoid the busy town docks to come and go. Killock had sailed them far across the lake and showed her how the mast could be lowered to slip under trees and bridges, and how the rudder could be raised to traverse shallows. Wyn loved that day. She had ridden on the bow of the boat as it had knifed through the water, leaning as far forward as she could as the water rushed beneath her, and felt the wind fill the sails and heel the boat far over onto its rail. It had made her hoot with delight.

But then she took the tiller, and it had all gone wrong. Terms like 'luff' and 'about' were yelled without any apparent cause or meaning, and no matter what she did the boat just pointed the same direction and stayed still, its sails quivering in the wind but not catching any of its power.

Killock ended up lying on the shelter roof and laughing, even after she had sprayed him with a handful of water.

Wyn and Danielle needed the boat now. Loughliath stretched far beyond the horizon to the north. A colossal out-thrust of the High Fells came south to meet it, jagged teeth that formed the north-eastern border of Albyn. *That's where Danielle said the Mountain was, the one where God lives. Sliabh Mór.*

Only one road traversed the western side of Loughliath, the Rathad an Thuaidh. It was heavily traveled until it forked. The main road curved towards Kuray, and a much smaller trail clung to the lake shore. This was the Rathad an Sliabh, which often disappeared under a carpet of moss and leaves as it passed through the forest. But the Rathad an Sliabh led the way to Sliabh Mór, and the road was well-watched.

Danielle stood next to Wyn as they looked at the boat nestled on its cradle. Its sleek, wooden sides were smooth and polished, and the long thrust of its prow narrowed to a cutting point. Wyn liked its shape. *It looks fast.*

"So." Wyn turned to Danielle. "You said you knew how to sail one of these, right?"

"Oh yes." Danielle smiled and nodded. "It is not as big as some of the ones we use at home, but this will do very nicely."

The wind whipped the surface of the lake into grey waves and whitecaps streamed into spray under the wind's assault. Wyn's fingers were numb by the time they raised the mast, and as she looked over the turbulent water a slight pang of concern twisted in her stomach.

"Can there be too much wind?" Wyn asked casually as waves crashed on the rocky shore a few paces away.

Danielle caught her look. "This is just a little gale, and you cannot get big waves on a lake. We will be fine once we get away from the shore."

"Wonderful," Wyn said to herself.

They pushed the boat from the shelter and through the opening until it floated free behind the water break.

"Ready?" Danielle asked.

Wyn hopped onto the boat in front of the mast. Danielle walked the boat the last few steps, then stepped gracefully into the cockpit and took the tiller.

Wyn pulled the lines she was told to pull and the sail rose up the mast. Excitement coursed through her and quelled her concerns. She felt the power of the wind as it thrummed in the rigging, and the boat rocked and bobbed as if eager to taste the waves.

Danielle pointed to a line that ran from the end of the boom and Wyn braced her feet against the wall of the cockpit, as Danielle had shown her, and pulled. The boom swung towards the stern of the boat and as it did the sail caught the wind and suddenly filled, a beautiful curve of taut canvas. Wyn felt the strain come to her through the pulleys and held firm, and suddenly the boat slid forward, faster and faster. The prow cleared the breakwater and Danielle eased the rudder, calling out for Wyn to pull the boom even closer. The boat responded and leapt ahead, and the prow knifed through the water to leave a frothing wake behind them. Wyn whooped with joy as the boat trembled and bucked and carved through the waves in a long, smooth arc as Danielle guided it from the shore. It heeled until the grey water boiled under the rail and icy spray showered the length of the boat and drenched them both.

Wyn could not believe the speed. The surface of the lake rushed by as if they were on a galloping horse, and the small woods that had concealed the boat were soon a mere smudge behind them. Danielle held their northwesterly course and they sped across Loughliath until the horizon was an unbroken sweep of water, unchanging as the dull winter light slowly faded into the west.

When at long last the western shore came into view its deeply forested hills rose until they vanished in the low, scudding clouds.

"I cannot see the mountains," Danielle called to Wyn. "I do not know where we are."

"What do we do?"

"I have to use my guide," Danielle replied.

"Alright!" Wyn yelled back, but Danielle was motioning for her to move to the tiller.

"You have to steer, I cannot focus on it and steer at the same time." Danielle shifted to make room on the pilot's bench.

"Oh, that's not a good idea." Wyn shook her head emphatically. "I couldn't steer when it wasn't a storm."

"Just hold it like this," Danielle demonstrated. "I will be fast, I promise."

"Promise you won't be mad at me when we're all drowned and nasty." Wyn settled onto the pilot's bench and placed her hand on the long tiller. The polished wood thrummed with the passage of water over the rudder, and surged with each wave as the boat tried to yaw to match the wave's thrust. Danielle held it with her for a moment to guide her. She pushed against the surge of a wave, and slipped into the trough to ready for the next wave. Slowly she let go, and Wyn piloted the ship.

She felt the current sing to her through the wood of the tiller and felt the pull of the sails through the lines. The rudder flexed and strained and the prow rose and fell, and the wind hummed through the rigging and the water surged along the keel, and Wyn thrilled to the sense of riding that limitless power.

Danielle returned to the bench and braced against Wyn, the pilot's seat barely big enough for both of them. The tiny guide shone brightly and Danielle pointed ahead and to the left. Wyn started to move out of the way but Danielle simply wrapped her hands around the tiller next to Wyn's. The wood pulsed and trembled in their hands as the water ripped past. Then Danielle eased the tiller slightly away and the boat turned into the next wave. Wyn felt the sudden surge of pressure against the rudder and the tiller vibrated as it held the boat true. The prow climbed high, then knifed down the back side in a rush as Danielle pulled the tiller close again.

They held it there for as long as possible, braced with their boots a mere handbreadth from the white wake that boiled under them, until finally they ran under the shelter of a long spit of land that curled into the lake, their destination achieved.

Danielle guided the boat in a long curve towards the shore. Wyn lowered the sail, and the boat drifted swiftly until it closed with the pebbled beach. Danielle swung the tiller to bleed off its speed in a tight turn, and left it bobbing a few paces from shore.

Wyn vaulted ashore with ropes, secured the boat to an old tree that grew on the edge of the lake and helped Danielle lower the mast onto the roof of the boat.

They hid the boat as well as they could, and took shelter under a tall boulder that blocked most of the wind. A small fire warmed their fingers and faces as they huddled under blankets, and they ate some stale, dried biscuits they found in the boat's storage bins. Wyn stared contentedly over Loughliath as she munched on the dry, crumbling, tasteless bread.

"I like sailing," she decided. "Can we do it again?"

"Yes," smiled Danielle. "As long as I do not freeze to death." Danielle shuddered under the blanket.

"Oh, listen to you complain about being cold with your lovely fur-lined jacket and your lovely fur hood and your fur hat. Honestly, you southerners are soft." Wyn considered that for a moment. "Actually, I can vouch for that last bit."

"Ha ha, yes I am cold and weak because I am from the south," Danielle teased. "And you forgot my fur-lined boots. But I can feel you shivering right this very instant."

"Maybe just a bit," admitted Wyn, then she laughed. "Because it's bloody cold."

"Yes, exactly. Please, next time can we go to my home to go sailing? It is so much warmer, and we can sail across the bay and swim and dive, and we will not need any fur-lined clothes to survive."

Wyn was quiet for a moment as she let Danielle's words soak in. *Well, I probably shouldn't push it, but when has that ever stopped me?*

"Do you mean 'we', as in me, too?" Wyn asked. "You don't really want to take me there, I don't think."

"Of course I meant 'we' as in you, too," said Danielle, her eyebrows arched in surprise. "It will be wonderful. I cannot wait to show you the cliffs and the groves, and the bay of course. You will think you have found paradise!"

"Do you not think it'll be a bit awkward when we meet your friends, me being so rude and loud?" Wyn's voice lilted as she imitated Danielle's accent. "Oh, Wyn, wipe your mucky trotters and come meet Her Ladybits the Empress of La-di-dah. "

"I am not concerned," said Danielle firmly. "Besides, the Empress of La-di-dah is a bitch and she is not invited to my home."

"Well then," Wyn laughed, and a deep happiness settled inside her. "I think I'd like to learn more about that beautiful southern tongue you were telling me about."

Maeglin

The wind had built steadily since sunrise and slashed him with a mixture of ice and rain, thin and stinging, as he stood on the edge of the precipice. Far below him the grey waters of Loughliath crashed against the cliffs at the base of Bandirma. From this height, he could see far across the white-flecked water until it disappeared into an indistinct haze that obscured the northern horizon. The low farmlands to the east were a flat plain smudged with shades of white and grey.

His men fanned out from the base of the cliff. Small black dots crawled across the ground so slowly that at times he wondered if they were actually standing still. As he watched, they spread into a line that stretched across the beach and the frosted ground inland, and began to creep to the east. They had reached a small inlet by the time Maeglin finally heard voices approach from the plateau.

The knight turned from the view and watched the Archivist's approach. Whitebrooke dressed in thick robes and gloves, but he left his head bare, unconcerned by the ice that frosted his shaggy beard and hair. His breath steamed from him as if he were powered by bellows as he strode across the fields, his massive form impervious to the wind that swirled around him.

"Why am I here?" Whitebrooke accosted the Knight Commander as he approached. "I hope you have found something worth my troubles."

Sir Maeglin waited silently as the priest stomped to a stop next to him, his hands on his hips as he stared across the eastern landscape.

"Cold and windy," Whitebrooke decided. "I saw the same earlier from my privy window."

Maeglin let the remark pass. "We have found their trail."

"About time," Whitebrooke replied, and he stared intently eastwards. "Down there?"

"Right here," Maeglin pointed to an old farm building perched on the lip of the cliff a stone's throw away.

Whitebrooke looked at the building and a deep frown settled on his face. "Explain yourself, Maeglin."

"Do you not know where we are?" Maeglin enjoyed the look of confusion that crossed Whitebrooke's face.

"In the middle of a field. What are you driving at?"

"That is the Geata Thoir." Maeglin pointed at the farm building.

Whitebrooke followed the knight's finger. "That building right there? I have heard of the East Gate of course, read about it. It's still open? I thought it long gone."

"It's still open, although we don't talk about it."

Whitebrooke turned to the knight. "Very interesting, but if I had wanted a history lesson I could have stayed in the archives."

"I'm sure," Sir Maeglin walked towards the building, "but if you want a lesson in what we found this morning, you'll have to come with me instead."

Maeglin did not wait to see if the priest followed. He moved to the farm building and pushed through the door. The guards stood back as he passed, not wanting to catch his eye. He had put them on double shift, standing guard for another four hours while hoping that Maeglin would be satisfied with their punishment. *We'll see what we learn about last night.*

Whitebrooke caught up as Maeglin descended the steps to the heavy iron gate under the building. It was unlocked and creaked open at his touch. The two men strode rapidly down the path until it passed inside the cliff face, and stopped before a massive metal door. Maeglin approached the door as Whitebrooke gazed in interest around the tunnel.

"It's so much smaller, and shabbier, than I had imagined it," Whitebrooke's voice boomed in the confined space. "Still, the door lives up to its history."

"When the watch changes, the new guard checks the gate." Maeglin indicated the ornately carved door, its steel bars retracted, its three immense locks opened. "This morning they discovered that someone passed through the gate last night."

"And you think it was who? The Queen?" Whitebrooke peered into the gears of the locks, then turned to hold Sir Maeglin's gaze. "Danielle?"

"It was Lady Danielle." Maeglin had no doubt. "The rangers found the tracks of two people who approached the gate last night. Both small, both women."

"How on earth do they know that?" Whitebrooke asked.

"It is obvious to a good tracker. The angle, depth, size of the tracks, the length of the stride. They are rarely wrong."

"And where are the women now?"

"They passed through here sometime between two and eight hours ago. My trackers are following their trail from the exit as we speak. Since they do not have horses I have also ordered scouts to stand by. Once the trackers know their heading, the scouts will overtake them."

"So we will have them soon?" Whitebrooke asked. "You are sure this time?"

"We thought we had them last night, but they simply walked past us." Maeglin watched the priest carefully. "How did they know of this gate? How did they breach it? The gate isn't a well-known landmark, and there are only three keys. All are accounted for."

"Likely it was the girl, Bronwyn," said Whitebrooke thoughtfully. "Killock would have shown her, would he not?"

"Killock?" Maeglin's eyes narrowed. "What does Killock have to do with her?"

"He trained her," said Whitebrooke, as if this was common knowledge.

"Why in God's name did you keep that to yourself?" Maeglin was stunned.

"What difference does it make?" Whitebrooke demanded loudly.

"All the difference in the world," Maeglin held his voice rigid. "We're not just chasing some pickpocket through the wilderness. Killock's people are trained to escape, to move without being seen. It couldn't be *more* important."

"Now you know," said Whitebrooke shortly. "So no more excuses. Do your duty, Commander, and quickly."

Maeglin kept his hands still, although they ached to answer the priest's disrespectful tone.

"Was there anything else to see?" Whitebrooke glanced around the room, seemingly unaware of Maeglin's furious gaze. "The Council is very busy this morning. The funeral must be planned, and the priests summoned home for the Convocation. Sebastian tells me it will take him days just to write the messages."

"I am through with you, you may go," Maeglin dismissed the Archivist.

Whitebrooke glared angrily at him, then collected himself.

"I will tell the Council that we can expect success very soon," Whitebrooke informed the knight, and he started back up the trail.

Maeglin let him walk a few more steps before calling to halt the priest. "Whitebrooke, something you said last night?"

The Archivist paused at the entrance of the tunnel and turned back as the wind flapped his robe and tugged at his beard. "Yes?" Whitebrooke answered shortly.

"This girl, Bronwyn. You said that Danielle was infatuated with her?"

"That is what Benno told me," Whitebrooke said impatiently. "What of it."

"I just wanted to make sure I had heard you correctly." Maeglin turned from the priest and began the trek down the tunnel to join his men, deep in thought.

Something doesn't make sense in all of this. Lady Danielle is controlled by her sister's wizard, then recruits her new lover to the cause? A lover who happens to be one of Killock's people, and Killock doesn't notice? Maeglin shook his head. It was not in the least bit believable. *Almost as unbelievable as someone under the control of a magus suddenly falling into a trail romance and bringing her new love home to Bandirma to meet her master. So perhaps Danielle was not controlled until after her return, the magus controls Bronwyn as well, and they immediately assassinate the Bishop. Then go shopping for clothes?*

It was obvious Whitebrooke was withholding knowledge from him. The story had too many problems. Some facts were clear. Bishop Benno had been assassinated with fuil crunor, and Whitebrooke wanted Lady Danielle to stand for the crime.

I will learn more when we catch them. Maeglin pushed his questions away for the moment. *And now I know Bronwyn guides them, and her relationship with Killock is clear, catching them suddenly becomes easier. Killock's people don't flee. They conceal themselves, then use the hidden paths to move unseen. Which means we should be looking in some very specific places.*

The Knight Commander knew the secrets of Bandirma as well as anyone. He also had trained with Killock, so he knew exactly what the Templar taught his students. If the two women escaped the surrounds of Bandirma he would have little chance of finding them, but right here, right now, he could practically predict their movements.

Sir Maeglin reached the base of the tunnel and joined his captain on the beach. His horse had been brought from the stables, and he mounted in one smooth movement and settled into the saddle without thought or effort.

Maeglin walked his horse forward and up the small embankment to follow his men. *East… nothing that direction but the marshes. That leaves Loughliath.*

"Tell the scouts to ride ahead to the forest. They should search for a concealed boat on the lake shore, just within the trees."

"Yes, m'lord," his captain answered, and spurred forward to carry out his orders.

If the boat is still there, then the trail is a feint and we should turn south, or even re-search the Temple. If it's gone, then where are they headed? They could not risk the river… they would be spotted trying to run under the bridge. So, either the eastern shore and the villages there, or somewhere far along the Rathad an Thuaidh to the west. Or the Mountain.

Sir Maeglin smiled as the wind flung icy mist into his face and flattened the long grass around his horse's feet. For the first time he felt he knew his prey, and could almost hear the cry of the hounds.

Danielle

The road wound endlessly through the Cnoic Bán, the steep hills that crouched at the foot of the Sliabh Mór. Moss covered the ground and crept into the sides of the road, and only the center, where travelers passed in enough numbers to wear it away, remained clear. The tangled branches of maples and ash stood bare and stark against the sky, while giant fir trees speared the low clouds.

Stone figures watched the road from the forest, their grand forms smoothed into shapeless lumps by rain and moss. Danielle always found them to be mournful under their green blankets, and longed to know who they were. The statues had guarded the forest long before the Temple had made Bandirma its home, and now no one living had the knowledge, not even Killock, who usually knew every excruciating detail of the history of a place.

Far to the north, thunder rolled across the lake, and ebbed and echoed amongst the hills. As if in response, the wind strengthened, and ice and rain splattered the road around them.

Danielle and Wyn had been walking for hours, and Danielle was certain that the imposing doors to the Mountain could not be much farther. Danielle could feel the bulk of Sliabh Mór concealed beyond the clouds. The great mountain's presence made the clouds flow around it and added a touch of deep cold to the air that smelled like stone and ice that never melted.

The short winter day neared its end, and the weak glow of the sun had long since passed behind the unseen mountains to the west. The hills of Cnoic Bán rapidly grew dim in the oncoming twilight.

The women were exhausted and cold, the rush of their race across the lake long since faded under the heavy fatigue of a sleepless night, a steep climb and fear for their lives and the lives of those they loved. Wyn had stopped asking questions, a sure sign that she was on the verge of collapse. *We must be nearly there… the switchbacks were always the sign that the journey was over.* She usually traveled this route on horseback, but as Danielle's weary feet could attest, walking took much longer.

They reached the clouds as the Rathad an Sliabh wound higher. Mist streamed past them, cold and grey, and covered their damp cloaks with droplets of chilling water. Dark shapes loomed at them as the wind made the clouds thicken and thin. At times their view was limited to just a few paces around them, other times they were allowed to see some distance ahead. Danielle remembered a deep ravine that led to a sheer cliff, the final stretch of road that ended at the gate. *We are almost there.*

"Wyn… in a few more moments we will be able to see the door," Danielle spoke loudly to be heard over the wind.

"That's too bad. It was just starting to get really lovely out here," replied Wyn.

"Who is the southern hothouse flower now?" Danielle teased, although the attempt was ruined somewhat by the deep shivers that made her teeth chatter with cold.

"Me, I am. Please can we be pretty southern flowers! I'll even wear a frock and frills or whatever silly things you wear down there," Wyn begged.

"There is always a splendid fire going in God's hall, roaring hot," said Danielle as she thought of the deep room with its comfortable shadows.

"Good, that's good," shivered Wyn. Then she stopped and put a hand on Danielle's arm. "Is that it?"

Danielle looked ahead. The thick mist streamed in front of her, but through it she saw a darker mass rear high into the sky, sheer and solid. As the mist ebbed she made out more details. Immense stone doors carved into the cliff face, high enough that one could ride through the doorway and still not be able to touch the top. On either side stone pillars supported wide bowls that rested on top. Danielle had expected them to blaze with fire to welcome the weary pilgrims, but today, they remained dark and cold.

The doors themselves stood closed, their grey bulk impervious to the gusting wind. Heavy iron rings that served as door knockers bore detailed carvings which depicted the founding of Bandirma centuries ago.

"Yes, we are here, thank the Maker." Danielle breathed a sigh of relief.

They trudged across the last few steps. The wind redoubled its efforts, angry that they were almost beyond its grasp. It swirled to blow their cloaks from them and tugged at their hoods, driving icy fingers into every gap in their clothing.

Danielle stepped to the doors and grasped one of the iron rings with both hands. She slammed it against the stone once, then again, each time producing a heavy thud that boomed hollowly.

"You have to knock?" Wyn asked.

"I do not know… in the past the doors would be open, the fires lit," Danielle drew her cloak about her shoulders more securely. "But those times I had been summoned."

"I hope He's not in the privy then," mused Wyn. "That would be awkward."

Danielle waited impatiently for a few more gusts of wind, and banged the ring again.

Finally, the doors split apart with a thunderous crack of sound, and slowly eased inwards with a deep rumble beneath their feet as hidden mechanisms took the strain of the doors' massive weight. A shaft of light bathed the two travelers in a warm, yellow glow.

As the doors swung wide they revealed a figure waiting within, tall, lean and shining. The light reflected off her silver mail, the silver wings on her tall helm, the blade of the long, heavy spear that she held easily in one hand, and the round shield of silver she held in the other.

Danielle stepped through the doorway, a smile of relief and greeting on her face. "Rúreth, it is good to see you again."

But her smile faded as the warrior lowered her spear to block Danielle's path.

"You are not welcome here, Lady Danielle," said Rúreth coldly, her face grim within her helm. "The Council seeks your arrest on grave charges."

"That is a false accusation," Danielle replied angrily. "How could you think that I had anything to do with that terrible crime? The Council are fools to believe it, as are you."

"I did not say I believed it," replied Rúreth. "But nevertheless I will not allow you to enter. Return to Bandirma and face your accusers."

"That's a laugh," said Wyn. "Just chuck ourselves into the fire, is that it? Not a chance."

"Then remain fugitives," Rúreth shifted slightly and the tip of her spear slowly traveled across the width of the doorway until it was poised, its broad-bladed tip ready to sweep forwards. "Run and hide with your sister or feed the wolves. I care not. But you will not enter so long as I am guarding Him."

"For how long have the Templars been slaves to the Council?" Danielle demanded.

"Never," Rúreth replied. "It is my privilege to guard Him against all threats. I opened the door because of your past service to Him, Lady Danielle, but that is far as I will allow."

"They are welcome," the Voice rumbled through the very stone of the hallway and echoed through the space. Rúreth hesitated only a moment, then stepped aside and raised her spear upright to allow them to pass.

"Sorry, would love to chat," said Wyn, a friendly smile beaming across her face as she mocked the Templar. "But we have to go. Wanted, you see. We'll let you know if we need any doors opened."

They crossed the hall and entered a wide passage that led deep into the Mountain. Danielle waited until the passage took them out of sight, and then moved close to Wyn.

"That was a Templar you were taunting," whispered Danielle. "How do you do it? I have never seen you intimidated."

"If I learned anything about Templars, traveling with Lord Bradon and knowing Sir Killock, and you, too, your Ladyness, if you don't mind my saying, is that there's usually a person under all the high-muckity titles and shiny hats. They may not know it themselves anymore, but they're in there somewhere. So the bitch can kiss my pucker just like anyone else."

Danielle laughed softly. "Yes, we are all people. And that one has a well-deserved reputation for a ferocious temper and a love of battle."

"Oh…" said Wyn, and she risked a glance over her shoulder. "Good to know, that is."

Danielle nodded agreement, and they moved deeper into Sliabh Mór. The walls of the passageway flickered bright orange from a fire that roared in a far room, and long shadows danced and shifted across the floor. Danielle quickened her step, anxious to enter. The weariness and tension that filled her melted away in the heat that emanated from the room, and her step and heart lightened as she strode from the passageway.

She stopped and closed her eyes to savor the sounds and scents of this deep sanctuary. The fire hissed and cracked and roared, banked high to flood the room with heat and push back the deep chill of the stone.

Danielle was aware of Wyn close beside her, shifting nervously as she peered around the room. *Poor thing, so anxious. I remember the first time I came here. I was frightened out of my wits as well.*

"My Lord," Danielle opened her eyes and addressed Him. "This is Wyn, the amazing, wonderful woman I love and have the privilege to call my friend."

"Um, pleased to meet You, your Holiness," said Wyn as she peered into the shadows. She curtsied hesitantly, not sure which way to face.

"Wyn," the Voice rolled, and the sound trembled in the stone and reverberated in Danielle's chest. "You have brought such happiness to someone I love deeply. Thank you."

"Oh!" Wyn said, eyes wide as the voice washed through her. "Yes your, uh, Godliness, well, she's lovely, and I mean, she makes me happy too."

"I am glad," the Voice rumbled across the room. "Come now and sit. You are weary in body and spirit."

Danielle did as she was bid. She gratefully removed her sodden cloak and coat, hung them on a hook by the fire and collapsed onto a deep couch. Wine stood ready for them in two goblets near the chair, and food, a thick, crusty bread, hot broth and a soft cheese. Danielle had never seen a servant in the Mountain, but a traveler's needs were known and met. She was too weary to eat, although she was hungry, but she sipped the wine thankfully. Its warm glow thawed her insides as the fire warmed her skin from the outside.

"My Lord," said Danielle as she stared, mesmerized, into the fire. "You are right, I am weary. There has been so much grief since last we spoke. Lord Bradon, he fell…" The words caught in her throat and Danielle had to stop.

"I grieve that we shall not see him again," He replied, slow and thoughtful. "Yet perhaps even now he stands with the Maker on the other side of the Shroud, or feasts with his ancestors in their golden hall."

"I know," said Danielle softly. "I just miss him."

There were no words for a moment and the fire filled the room with its hot noises.

"He made me laugh," Wyn said, her voice firm. "And he took care of me."

"He did the same for me," the Voice rumbled in the shadows like thunder across distant hills.

Danielle watched the surface of her wine reflect the fire as she remembered his strong, bearded face and his smile, although it was difficult not to see cold, grey stone and feel the weight of a mountain pressing down instead. She breathed deeply and pushed the thought away as firmly as she could. *More than grief drove us here.*

"The evil that Bradon gave himself to destroy followed us home, my Lord," said Danielle sadly. "Is Reverend Benno truly slain?"

"Yes," He replied. "The shadow took him."

"I had hoped it was not true," said Danielle. "But I feared it would be. A creature of shadow came to kill us in our room, and the Blade was stolen."

Silence fell across the room once more and Danielle waited patiently as she sipped her wine. Wyn shifted against her on the couch, nervous at the silence, but Danielle squeezed her hand in reassurance. He sometimes retreated into quiet as His attention was elsewhere, sometimes for a very long time. It had unnerved Danielle the first time, but now it simply felt comfortable to wait.

Time passed easily. The warmth of the room and the soft sofa drew worry from her. Wyn closed her eyes and her head grew heavy on Danielle's shoulder.

"The loss of the Blade is ill news," His voice rumbled across the room, and Danielle felt Wyn startle next to her. "It must be recovered."

"Who took it?" Danielle asked. "Who was responsible for the fuil crunor ritual in the Temple?"

"The Council sends messages that say it was the wizard, Karsha Hali."

Danielle wondered if that were true. *The man was irritating, that is for certain, but a Crunorix priest?*

"I do not believe it," Danielle said out loud. "We were with him when he first sensed it. It was not his doing. He was frightened for the Queen. And the Queen had the Blade, so there was no need for him to steal it."

"You gave your sister the Blade?" Danielle was not sure if it was laughter or concern that rumbled in His voice.

"I did," confessed Danielle. "I promised it to her. I am sorry, for I know how important it was to You and to the Temple, but I had to."

"It doesn't matter," Wyn rose to her defense. "The Blade was nicked while we were talking to them anyway, so it wasn't them."

"I understand," His voice echoed across the room. "It does not diminish the joy I feel for your happiness. Instead the joy grows, knowing the depth your love must have, for you to have given up so much for it."

The Voice changed then, and grew more powerful. "But that does not alter the dark tidings of the Blade's loss."

"I know," Danielle said softly. "I believed it safe, but I should never have left it, no matter how well I thought it guarded."

"We just need to go and get it back, right?" Wyn asked. "Then no worries and all the doom and gloom goes away, yeah?"

"If we could find it," replied Danielle.

"Well, yeah, but we can do that," Wyn jumped to her feet in excitement. "We do stuff like that all the time. Find some precious shiny and nick it, easy as wishing!"

"But, Wyn, this is not some noble's secret letters in a desk drawer," said Danielle. "Whoever took it will likely conceal it with Veils, if he has not already spirited it away."

"Oh, not likely I don't think," Wyn grinned. "If he scarpers then everyone will know who he is, and he's not going to just chuck it into a wagon or something. Not with all the soldiers searching everything that moves."

Danielle felt a faint stir of hope. She had not thought through how few choices their enemy might actually have. "We escaped though."

"We had me!" Wyn laughed. "No, I know, he could avoid the searchers, maybe, but why would he send it away? It's too shiny, right? No, I bet it's bunged under a mattress somewhere right now, and he's sitting on it sweating through his knickers, terrified someone will come looking and the gig will be up."

Danielle laughed at the thought. *I want it to be true. Why should it not be as she described?*

"Then our only concern is that everyone in the Temple is busy looking for us so that we can be put on trial."

"Yeah, well I bet S*omeone* in this room could do something about that," said Wyn and she looked significantly towards the shadows.

"Perhaps I could," the Voice replied, amused. "Wyn, your passion is inspiring. Thank you."

"My pleasure, your Godliness," Wyn beamed.

"Now, you must take your rest while I make preparations for the morrow," the Voice said gently.

"Gladly," said Danielle, for she could barely think through the fog of weariness that encompassed her. She rose, gathered her cloak and coat from their hooks and led Wyn from the sanctuary. The visitor rooms waited nearby, comfortable if utilitarian, and Danielle had used them many times. A bed, a fire, a wash-stand. Everything she desired right now.

Danielle led them to the closest one, not concerned with the minor differences between them, and they gratefully hung their cloaks and stood their boots next to the hearth, then pulled the mattresses from the cots and laid them together in front of the fire.

Danielle sank onto the palette and Wyn curled against her and rested her head on Danielle's chest. Danielle held Wyn close and drifted into a deep, lazy contentment as she lost herself in the feel of Wyn's soft hair against her cheek and the warmth of Wyn's long fingers around her arm.

"What did you think of Him?" Danielle asked Wyn as they watched the orange flames leap and pop and glow against the stone.

"His voice is yummy," replied Wyn dreamily. "It's like when you have a soft, fat cat all curled up on your chest and he's purring away."

Danielle smiled fondly. "Yes, just like that."

"So, you're sort of a Temple-y type of person," Wyn said.

"Yes, that is right," said Danielle. "There is a very fancy title, but all it means is that I have pledged myself to serve the Temple. But I am not a priestess. I have not been anointed."

"No," Wyn laughed. "I was pretty sure you weren't a priestess."

"Wyn! You will make me blush again," teased Danielle. "Besides, there are many priestesses in the Temple who are beautiful, passionate people."

"You wouldn't say that if you'd seen the old biddies from the temple in Glen Walden," said Wyn, her face scrunched in distaste. "Ewww… I just thought about them naked."

"It is true that many of the priests and priestesses are older. It takes time to complete the studies."

"I think Reverend Crawa must have started her studies before the Cataclysm."

Danielle laughed joyfully, and they sat in silence for a while as the fire quietly crackled next to them. Danielle saw that Wyn was lost deep in her own thoughts, a small crease of concentration between her eyebrows visible in the fire's yellow glow. Danielle gave her time, content to watch Wyn's fingers trace idly over the embroidery on Danielle's shirt.

"But," Wyn started again, and glanced up to catch Danielle's gaze. "You do know Temple stuff though. I mean, you've talked to God a bunch and you know all the high-muckities, right?"

"Yes, of course."

Wyn held her gaze for a moment before looking away. "Fine… well… good," she said.

"Wyn, was there something you wanted to ask me?"

"It's stupid," Wyn sighed ruefully.

"Wyn, you can ask me," said Danielle. "Something is clearly troubling you."

"Alright, but it's sad, so I didn't really want to say." Wyn took a deep breath before she continued. "It's just I can't stop thinking about what happens, you know, *after*. Ever since Bradon… it just keeps sneaking up on me. I've never really thought about it before, not even when Mum died. I was just glad she didn't have to stay here. So I was wondering if you might, you know, *know*."

"I do not think anyone knows for certain."

"Not even God? You're serious."

Danielle stretched out her legs towards the fire, and remembered a day long past in the deep chamber under the Mountain and the soothing rumble of the Voice surrounding her.

"I can tell you what He told me if you would like."

"Yeah, go on."

"He said that there is a shroud over our sight that divides the world we can see from the world of the spirit, which is called Annwn, the Unseen Realm. It shines silver like a thousand stars, but is not distant or cold. Beyond the shroud lies paradise, which my people call Cieux. In the north I have heard it named Tìr na nog. It is a land of golden fields and gentle hills, and warm sun upon sparkling waters. We travel there when our journey in this world is at its end and pass through the shroud to dwell in its golden light." Danielle felt Wyn sigh against her, and she pulled her tight.

"Are the others there too?" Wyn asked.

"Yes, all whom you have loved, and all who love you."

"Does everyone go there?"

"No, sadly not. Those who are damned, who have corrupted their spirits in this world, cannot pass through the shroud."

"Good," said Wyn firmly.

"It is not so sad, you see." Danielle smiled softly to herself. "It is just that we miss those that have gone before us."

"Yeah," said Wyn. "Except, are you all sort of, spirit-y and just float around? Or can you touch and laugh and hold hands, or kiss or climb things? I mean, are you *you*?"

"I believe you can do all of those things, that you are *you*," said Danielle. "You can feel the sun on your skin, and the wind on your face, and touch the grass. And yes, also hold hands and laugh."

"Because otherwise it would be really boring," decided Wyn. "Is that what He meant when He said Bradon was on the other side with the Maker?"

"Yes," said Danielle.

"What was the part about the golden hall?"

"That is what the clans of the Ironback Mountains believe. That your spirit passes under the mountain to be judged by Ddraighnall, the white dragon. If Ddraighnall judges you worthy you get to live in a magnificent golden hall with all of your ancestors and the other great warriors, forever and ever." Danielle smiled in the dark. "It also seems like there is a lot of ale involved."

"Is that Bradon's people then? All beardy and wild?" Wyn giggled in approval.

"Yes, his family comes from one of their legendary kings, and he always claimed he could feel their spirits in him."

"I think he'd like that. A golden hall filled with huge beards and girls that look like Rúreth I bet, all tall and grrr!"

"I think he would too," Danielle laughed.

"So, what happens if the dragon doesn't like you?"

"He eats you."

"Awww, poor little beardys." Wyn stretched her toes into points and yawned. "That must be a shock."

"True," said Danielle. She waited quietly for a moment, but Wyn seemed to have run out of questions. "Does that make you feel any better?"

"I guess so. It beats lying under a cold stone in the dark." Wyn shivered slightly at the thought. "I hope you're right."

"So do I," said Danielle softly.

***

All night the storm roared and thundered against the Mountain. Rain turned to sleet that lashed the forest, but deep within the Mountain there was no sign of the tempest. The stone halls and rooms remained hushed, still, undisturbed.

The storm moved south with the morning and dragged colder air from the mountains in its wake. Ice sheathed the bare branches of the trees and coated the dark places amongst the stones, and flakes of snow swirled in the grey mist.

Long after dawn, Danielle and Wyn broke their fast by the fire in the sanctuary room with thick bread that steamed as they cut it open. They smeared it with honey, golden and warm, and ate winter pears, yellow and tart.

With their needs for food and sleep satisfied, they explored the Mountain. Their footsteps echoed in the vast silence as

Danielle led Wyn through its long passageways and rooms. Grand chambers that could have contained hundreds of people, and dormitories that could have provided beds for them all. Stables ran the length of one of the outer walls with stalls of empty stone, all save one which housed a beautiful stallion, tall and proud, with a glossy, black coat and a white blaze on his face.

A shrine stood in the center with passageways that radiated from it like spokes on a wagon wheel. The altar was bare except for a single tall candle that burned with a steady flame. Beyond the sanctuary a massive door remained closed as always. It led deeper into the Mountain, but Danielle had never seen what lay on the far side.

Rúreth stood guard outside the door, silent and watchful. Danielle wondered if the Templar ever slept, or if her zeal kept her awake.

Then the Voice rolled through Sliabh Mór and summoned them to the sanctuary.

"The Council has been informed of their mistake in blaming you for Reverend Benno's death and are instructed to aid you in your search," His voice rumbled from the shadows. "And the Templars have been called home to aid in the search as well."

"Thank you, Lord." Danielle felt relief wash through her, the strain of her brief exile fully erased.

"I ask you once again to take up a task for me," the shadows stirred as the deep Voice echoed through the room. "To retrieve the Blade from our enemies so that once more we might bring it against them."

"Gladly," replied Danielle.

"Then I wish you safe travels, and my thoughts remain with you. May they comfort you and bring you strength of heart and soundness of purpose," the Voice reverberated through them.

"Thank you, my Lord," said Danielle, and she curtsied gracefully.

"Goodbye, your Godliness," said Wyn cheerfully, and she copied Danielle's curtsey. "It was nice meeting you!"

"Farewell, my lady, farewell, Wyn. Remember the joy and love in your hearts, even when times seem dark. It will sustain you. It will empower you. It will drive away the shadows."

Then the room was still, and Danielle knew He directed His attention elsewhere. They gathered their packs, donned their thick winter garb, and stuffed the bread and pears from their breakfast into their packs for the journey.

"So," said Wyn as they stood ready to depart. "Are we walking back to Bandirma?"

"I suppose, although it is a long way to walk. We could return to the boat and sail back."

"Or we could ride," said Wyn, a wide smile creeping across her face.

"But there is only one horse, and that is surely Rúreth's mount."

"Yes, but what if God said we could take it?" Wyn said mischievously.

"But He did not."

"I'm sure He meant to. Likely He just forgot." Wyn's smile grew broader. "We just got dry we can't go straight back into the lake."

"I cannot tell Rúreth that He said that, she will know I am lying immediately," Danielle was certain.

"No she won't, luv, trust me, because I'm going to be the one to tell her," laughed Wyn. "You just back me up. I'm telling you, if we wanted her shiny, pointy hat we could have that too, no problem."

Danielle hesitated a moment longer before she realized that giggling and mischievous chaos was now a part of her life.

"Alright, let us go before I can reconsider."

***

The stallion made short work of the road, even bearing two riders and their gear. He moved smoothly and tirelessly down the switchbacks and into the forest. He held his head high as his hooves pounded steadily against the stone pavers.

It feels so good to be riding again, Danielle reflected, *watching these hateful, endless turns roll by.* The wind was chill but she did not mind, and she pulled her hood back so that she could feel the wind blow through her hair. Wyn was warm against Danielle's back. She held Danielle tightly around the waist and moved deliciously against her with the rhythm of the horse. Danielle laughed with joy as she urged the stallion to greater speed. *How different from yesterday.*

They entered the low forest along the shore of Loughliath and left the paved road behind them. The stallion's hoofs thudded on earth thick with leaves and pine needles, muted enough so that they could hear the rush of the wind in the tops of the tall fir trees.

"Stop! Stop! Stop!" Wyn cried, and Danielle felt Wyn suddenly tense behind her.

Danielle hauled sharply on the reins and brought the stallion to a skidding halt as his hooves slipped in the leaves and mud of the road.

"What is it?" Danielle whispered.

"Something's wrong up ahead." Wyn shifted back and forth as she peered into the forest on all sides. "We need to get out of here, Dani. Back up the road, fast."

Danielle turned the horse, but even as she did, cloaked figures swarmed around them from the thick underbrush on either side of the road and grabbed at her legs and the stallion's bridle. She put her heels to the stallion's flanks and he reared and lashed out at the men with his hooves, and Danielle saw figures scramble to get out of the way.

Wyn shouted and struck at the men at their sides as Danielle urged on the stallion. He leapt into motion, but hands ripped at her legs and cloak, and suddenly Danielle was wrenched from the saddle.

She struck the ground violently and her head slammed against the thick root of a tree. Danielle felt blood burst into her mouth and stars exploded across her vision as the impact drove her into darkness.

***

Danielle floated in an unknown ocean so lightless that she could not see her own hand. Shards of silver stabbed across her vision, strange metal fish that painfully struck her in the head over and over again.

She flailed at the fish and tried to drive them away, but they were relentless, and transformed into pulses of red pain that throbbed against a cold, rigid surface. Danielle tried to make sense of the feelings, but they faded into obscurity as she focused on them, or spun into dizzying circles around her.

Light crept into the darkness, a pale glow that floated above her. She watched it, mesmerized, as it grew brighter. Soon the glow revealed rough bricks on a wall, then the silhouette of black bars across a small window. Danielle's world settled as she made sense of what she was seeing. *A cell, deep underground.* The clank of metal on stone revealed manacles around her wrists fastened to a thick chain. She pushed herself off the stone floor and sat against the wall as the room spun dizzyingly. The throbbing pain in her head flared with the movement, and nausea swirled in the back of her throat.

Footsteps approached the window, heavy and purposeful. Iron creaked as a lock was turned, and then a door opened, flooding the cell with torchlight bright enough that Danielle had to shield her eyes.

A towering form holding the torch filled the small doorway, and had to duck under the lintel as he entered. The torchlight revealed a mane of brown hair that flowed in untamed waves from his high forehead, and the ornate robes of a high priest dragged across the filthy floor.

"Reverend Whitebrooke?" Danielle's voice was a dry croak, her mouth parched.

Whitebrooke knelt beside her and offered a small flask, and she drank gratefully. He held a finger across his lips and she nodded understanding.

"I am glad you are awake," Whitebrooke spoke quietly, his deep voice a muffled rumble. "Can you walk?"

"I think so," Danielle whispered. "What has happened?"

Whitebrooke produced a small iron key and unlocked Danielle's manacles. "You have been accused of being a Crunorix, my lady, and a murderer."

"But, there was a message," Danielle protested in a hiss of breath. "God sent a message."

Whitebrooke pocketed the key and scooped up the torch from the floor. "There was," he agreed, and he held his hand before the torchlight so that Danielle could see the silver flash of the ring he wore. "His voice came to me, as I safeguard the Bishop's ring until the Convocation, and I told the Council of His wishes. Yet men were sent to abduct you and hide you away in the deepest cells, far from any eyes. Whoever is truly behind the murders and the fuil crunor rituals that have been used in our home, they are making sure that your voice is never heard."

"But you believe me?" Danielle squinted at his face. The flickering torch cast deep shadows from his heavy brow and crooked nose. "You believe I had nothing to do with it?"

"I do," Whitebrooke assured her, and he rose and offered his hand. "Bishop Benno relayed to me much of what you have accomplished, to aid in my research in the archives. Enough so that I know the accusations must be a lie."

Danielle nodded, took his hand, and he helped her stand. The room wobbled and she held on to his arm for support. She was surprised to feel the unmistakable shape of a sword at his side under his robes.

"Why should I trust you?" Danielle challenged the Archivist.

"What reason have I to lie?" Whitebrooke mopped his brow with the sleeve of his robe. "But perhaps this will earn me some trust."

From within his robe he drew a small bundle, two packs tied together by a thin belt with a pair of long knives sheathed on it.

"Here." Whitebrooke offered the bundle to Danielle. "Maeglin gave these to me for safekeeping, but I think you should have them."

Danielle took the packs gratefully. A quick check showed her that they still contained her lance and guide, as well as the smaller items she had packed. Nothing was missing. She tied the belt around her waist and settled the pack against the small of her back.

"So Maeglin at least knows that I am here? And he told you?"

"No, my lady, he did not. But of course I recognized several of the Devices you carried, and so I immediately began to search for you. My Diviner led me here."

"Very well," she nodded to the Archivist. "Thank you. What about Wyn?" Danielle held out Wyn's pack and knives. "Where is she?"

"Just in the next passage, never fear." Whitebrooke gestured down the dim hallway.

Danielle nodded and let Whitebrooke lead her as she leaned heavily on his arm for support. The torch flame licked the low ceiling as the priest hurried as fast as Danielle could go. His thick hand was moist with sweat, and he nervously glanced behind them every few steps as they went.

A small door appeared from the gloom, made of heavy wood with iron bars and hinges deeply set into the stone. Whitebrooke produced a ring of keys from under his robes, fumbled with them for a moment, and opened the lock on the door with a black iron key.

"Wyn?" Danielle whispered. The cell appeared empty as she glanced inside. A shadow stirred and Wyn materialized, her manacles held ready to be used as a flail in her hands.

Sweat plastered Wyn's hair to her face and neck, and blood oozed from her nostrils and one ear to make a slick sheen across her cheek.

"Hi, luv," Wyn said brightly. Blood made her smile a hideous grin. "You look about like I feel. Are you alright? Who's this? My knives!"

"My head hurts," admitted Danielle as she handed Wyn her pack and weapons, and she touched the side of her head with tentative fingers. They found caked blood and a painful lump that sent fresh waves of pain throbbing through her. "This is Reverend Whitebrooke, the Archivist. He freed me from my cell."

"Here, take the key." Whitebrooke held it out to Danielle as if it were likely to bite him. "In case you are captured, so that they will not question how you escaped."

"Oh, very brave." Wyn rolled her eyes. "My hero."

"It will do you no good if I am locked up as well," Whitebrooke insisted, and Danielle agreed. She took the offered key and Whitebrooke quickly turned away and strode down the passageway again. "Hurry, follow me."

"Hold on a moment." Wyn refused to move. "What's your plan?"

"There is a boat waiting for you at the docks. Three of my acolytes will accompany you there, and you will be dressed as acolytes as well, in case you are questioned."

"Really? That's the plan?" Wyn spat blood on the floor. "Why don't I find us a way out instead?"

"Alright, that doesn't matter," Whitebrooke replied impatiently. "But what does matter is that I know where the Martyr's Blade is, and we are going to take it on our way out."

"You do?" Danielle was shocked. "How do you know about the Blade at all, let alone where it is now?"

"Benno told me, of course." Whitebrooke beckoned with his free hand. "Please, we have to hurry. I will explain as we walk."

They followed the passageway as Whitebrooke's low voice rumbled off the stone. "Benno told me you had taken the Blade and killed a magus with it. He also had me place a special chest in your room to keep the Blade safe, but when I went to check on it after he was found murdered, the chest was empty."

"But how do you know where it is now?" Danielle asked.

"I have been researching everything in the archives relating to the Crunorix since the first ritual markings were discovered," Whitebrooke answered. "I believe I know more than any man alive about how to detect a fuil crunor ritual, luckily for us. I guessed that whoever took the Blade would attempt to conceal it using fuil crunor, and I was right. The very spell intended to hide it from us gave its location away."

"You are sure it is where you think it is?" Danielle could not keep the skepticism from her voice.

"Yes, I am sure," Whitebrooke snapped. "I went myself earlier today, at immense risk I might add, to confirm it."

"Oh, well if you went yourself..." Wyn scoffed.

"Yes, we are very lucky," Danielle offered. "Thank the Maker your research was so timely."

"Indeed, thank the Maker," Whitebrooke replied, and moved on.

Danielle touched Wyn's arm and caught her eye. Silently she indicated Whitebrooke with a nod, and shook her head. Wyn rolled her eyes and nodded agreement, and they hurried to catch the priest.

Danielle found her guide in her pack as they walked. It glowed softly as she formed her Word and released the guide's bindings. The golden symbols pulsed and floated free of the surface, and she examined their movement as she followed Whitebrooke. *It cannot find a direction, poor thing. But all that means is that the Blade is indeed veiled.*

The Archivist stuck to dark tunnels far from the bustling core of the Temple. They left the dungeons and passed through empty, echoing storerooms. Then down another cramped passageway and Whitebrooke urged them to greater caution and silence as they approached a heavy iron door at the end.

"We are here," Whitebrooke murmured. "The chamber was empty before, but be ready."

Danielle nodded, and gripped her lance. Whitebrooke pushed open the door and it shuddered ponderously on its hinges as it swung wide.

A round chamber was revealed on the other side of the door. At one time it must have served as a cistern or reservoir, for the room was dominated by a pit as deep as a man is tall, and wide stone drains led into the room from three sides. The drains were closed by iron gates, and rust stained the stone along the drain's lip and down the side of the pit, although the water itself had long dried away.

A narrow walkway orbited the pit, and old iron ladders led into it between the drains.

But Danielle saw that the chamber was no longer abandoned.

A wide circle made up of a broad band of intricate symbols contained within long channels had been carved into the smooth stone of the pit. From the circle, spokes radiated towards a central point. The twisted symbols of fuil crunor covered each of the spokes, wriggling and scratching across the floor.

In the center of the circle lay a long shape shrouded in cloth wrappings.

Around the pit were lanterns hung from iron stands, and Danielle saw open chests against the wall packed with leather-bound tomes and scrolls.

"It is still here." Whitebrooke pointed a thick finger at the bundle on the floor. "Quickly now, before we are discovered."

Danielle made no move towards the Blade. Instead she paced slowly around the walkway above the pit and watched the Archivist.

"You are sure that is the Blade?" Danielle asked.

"Yes, of course I am sure." Whitebrooke frowned at Danielle. "What are you waiting for?"

"But how do you know?" Danielle pressed the Archivist. "Did you examine it?"

"What else could it be?" Whitebrooke demanded.

"Reverend Crawa's cane?" offered Wyn helpfully. "A small, sleepy troll? Or maybe it's a big hunk of cheese."

"Cheese?" Whitebrooke frowned. "You think it is a trap?"

"Of course it's a trap," Wyn snorted contemptuously. "We're just trying to decide if it's *your* trap."

"But, why would I free you, and give you back your weapons, only to lead you to a trap?" Whitebrooke challenged.

"I am not sure," Danielle replied thoughtfully. "My guess is that it was not safe to bring whatever that bundle is to the cells."

"If you don't want to examine it, then use your Word, activate it," Whitebrooke offered quickly.

"No, I think not," Danielle shook her head. "It does not seem wise to empower a Weapon that is not in my hand. There is no telling who might end up with it."

"This is insane," Whitebrooke pleaded. "It's right there. Pick it up so that we can leave."

"No," Danielle replied coldly, and she raised her lance to rest the tip in her left hand.

"Pick it up, damn you!" Whitebrooke bellowed.

"Dear me, little piggy, what a fuss," Wyn cooed as she slipped her knives from their sheaths.

Whitebrooke seemed to sag. "You are right, Danielle, you are right. It is a trap, but I had to. He promised me that he would bring her back if I brought you here and you picked up the sword."

"He?" Danielle snapped. "Who is he?"

"The shade." Whitebrooke glanced nervously about the chamber.

"Did you murder Bishop Benno?"

"No!" Whitebrooke answered quickly. "He did that too. I will help you, but you have to help me, too. He promised me, Danielle, he promised he would return my wife to me, and I believed him, God help me. But all he has shown me is her shade, and he keeps asking for more."

"Help you? Fuck you!" Wyn hurled back at the priest. "Do you know how many people you've killed, you stupid bastard? Little girls! Corlath! Bradon!"

"I did not know." Whitebrooke held his hands up defensively. "Crassus did all of that, all I did was give him the book. I did not know what he was doing, not until I read your messages, I swear it. But the shade was too strong by then, I couldn't do anything. But now you are here, we can stop him with the Blade."

"Perhaps so," Danielle's voice was ice. "And why do we need you alive to do that?"

"Oooo, did you hear that?" asked Wyn, her voice smooth as silk. "I'm going to enjoy this."

"Danielle, listen to me," Whitebrooke begged. "He will be here soon. I can free the Blade from the trap. It's our only chance. Otherwise start running, and pray you are not too late."

"That is the true Blade?" Danielle asked.

"Yes, veiled and trapped, but real." Whitebrooke mopped his face with his sleeve again. "I told him we couldn't chance…"

Whitebrooke's voice trailed off and he turned and stared toward one of the ancient drains that led into the room.

Danielle followed his gaze, and felt a brush of cold fingers cross her mind with the lightest of touches. Then it was gone, but a deep shiver passed through her. *At least we know that part was not a lie. Can I do this? Do I dare to try, unprepared, tired and injured? But what better chance will I have to end this, and I know the Blade's power. If that is the Blade.*

"Quickly then, free the Blade," Danielle commanded. Whitebrooke hurried to one of the iron ladders and descended into the pit. Danielle watched the priest stride to the bundle in the center of the circle, where he began a chant in a harsh, choking language. Dark shadows writhed across the markings on the stone floor, and Danielle saw the air over the bundle shift and warp.

Danielle turned to Wyn. "Wyn, you must go, before this shade reaches us and it is too late."

"Very funny," Wyn grinned fiercely. "So what's the plan, Beautiful?"

"Is there no way I can persuade you to leave?" Danielle reached out and tucked Wyn's hair behind her ear for her. "You remember the magus. There is nothing either of us can do against whatever this shade is. Either the Blade will destroy it, or we will die. It would lighten my heart to know that you were safe, no matter which occurs."

"Sure, except I promised I'd take care of you." Wyn shrugged. "Anyway, if I leave now I won't be able to correct you when we're old wrinklies sitting around telling stories."

Danielle felt a wonderful heat flash across her skin, from her neck all the way to her fingertips and toes, and her heart suddenly felt light. "Well, we cannot have that, can we?"

"There's a smile worth staying alive for," Wyn beamed. "So, what's the plan?"

"Kill it fast," Danielle replied. "I do not have any Devices to protect me, not even the smallest Ward, so it will be the Blade, or nothing. We must stay alive until I can use its Word. And then hope it is enough."

"Well, it's just a shade, whatever that is." Wyn laughed dryly. "It's not like we're fighting the Nameless King or whatever."

I hope not. Danielle tried to clear her head of pain and dizziness, and began to form the Word for the Blade. She could feel the cold presence more clearly now, as if two black eyes watched from beyond the stone walls and iron gates that led into the chamber. *Not eyes. Holes.*

Whitebrooke finished his ritual and lumbered to the walkway where Danielle stood, the Blade naked in his hand. He laid it at her feet, and glanced towards the center of the room.

"How much time do you need?" His voice sounded suddenly calm and sure.

"A lot," Danielle replied. She bent and retrieved the Blade from the ground at her feet. The heavy sword felt awkward in her two-handed grasp, but the deep whorls of its metal danced and shone beautifully in the torchlight. "The Word is… elaborate."

"Then get started," Whitebrooke grunted, and turned to the chamber. He drew a long steel sword in one hand, and held an ornate amulet in the other.

Danielle began. Once again she pulled the Word apart into its shining components and carefully re-assembled it, piece by piece. Agonizing heartbeats passed as the Word took shape in silence.

A long shriek of metal grinding against stone filled the chamber, and one of the metal sluice gates was wrenched open. Danielle saw a pale shape step through, a wight. Danielle heard a second gate burst open to the side.

Whitebrooke bellowed a challenge and a Word pulsed from him. The wights screamed as concussions filled the room.

Danielle ignored the chaos as the Word assembled in her mind amid pain and waves of nausea. Pieces flickered and shifted, but she knew its pattern now, and it grew rapidly.

The cold presence grew as well, and raced Danielle.

More thunder filled the chamber, and Danielle felt the pulse of another Word surge from Whitebrooke. "Danielle, hurry!" he shouted, and Danielle caught a glimpse of the priest as he whirled his sword against a closing circle of implacable foes.

The Word erupted from her in a silver flash. She guided it into the Blade and felt the sword's mighty bindings open wide. Once again the fire rushed over her skin, once again the exquisite pain made her gasp as the fire transformed her.

Around her the wights shrieked in agony and tried to pull away from her. She pursued them, and they disintegrated and streamed away in the fire's tempest as if they were ash.

Cold dared to touch against her mind, and she whirled to face the source. A black, writhing rift opened over the center of the floor, and within it the empty gaze of the Abyss. She strode to the rift and plunged the Blade into it. Fire seared the wound in the air, and the cold shadow was consumed, until nothing was left.

But the cold eyes that watched her still festered beyond the walls, far from the reach of the Blade's fire. Sealing the rift had done nothing to abate their power. She felt their touch draw slowly back from her mind, as if tendrils clung to her thoughts and only unwillingly slid away.

Danielle surveyed the chamber. Black stains on the stone walls were all that remained of the wights, and the rift was gone. The black markings on the floor were cleansed wherever she had walked, her fiery footprints burning away the runes like dry grass.

Then she could hold the power no longer, and she trembled as it passed from her into the Blade, and she sank gratefully to her knees.

Wyn appeared next to her, and wrapped her arms around Danielle to hold her tightly.

"You did it, Dani," Wyn told her joyfully.

"There was nothing there," Danielle whispered, and sought out Wyn's gaze in confusion. "The rift was empty. There was no shade."

"Well, that's good?" Wyn said hesitantly.

A dreadful thought began to grow in Danielle's mind. *The enemy lost nothing here. It was no more than a feint, but to what purpose?*

"I do not know," Danielle replied quietly. "But I fear that I have been a fool."

"Very well done, your Ladyship," Whitebrooke's voice echoed in the chamber, bold and strong. "Very well done indeed."

Whitebrooke

The two women huddled on the floor in front of him, and Whitebrooke withheld an urge to laugh at the rage that flashed across their faces. *Yes, you knew all along, and yet, and yet…*

The one with a saint's name and a hellion's soul acted first. She vaulted to her feet and crossed the floor between them faster than Whitebrooke could react. His sword rose uselessly as he flinched far too late to block her knife.

The curved blade touched his Wardpact and the blackened steel flashed a brilliant white an instant before it detonated. The shock threw the girl violently aside and she tumbled loosely to the floor. Whitebrooke ignored her and strode toward Danielle as the noblewoman leapt to her feet, the Martyr's Blade held ready in her hands.

Her stance was awkward, the Blade held too low for such a heavy Weapon. Whitebrooke pushed forward. His sword swept through a careful arc and Danielle swung heavily to meet it. She leapt back as the Blade's weight dragged her off-balance, and Whitebrooke pressed methodically. He had trained with the knights of the Temple since he was an acolyte, relishing the clash and spark of combat as he became a skilled yet unspectacular swordsman, and he knew his height and strength gave him an advantage over most opponents. *Much more than a match for poor Danielle with a sword far too heavy for her.*

Danielle darted back and attempted to reach into her pack. Whitebrooke quickly attacked, unwilling to give her a chance to retrieve the deadly Weapon she kept there. Whitebrooke feinted and she abandoned her pack and tried to parry, but far too late, and in the wrong direction. His blade struck and knocked her sword aside. His backhand caught her across her hands with the flat of his blade. She cried out and the Blade rang loudly as it hit the floor.

Danielle bent to grab it, but Whitebrooke slid the point of his sword against her throat. She froze, and slowly stood in response to the insistent pressure of his blade.

"That's right, my lady," Whitebrooke soothed.

"God damn you," Danielle cursed through clenched teeth.

"That is exactly what Benno said." Whitebrooke could not help but laugh.

"It does not matter what you do to me," Danielle said fiercely. "I will give you nothing. Nothing, you bastard."

Whitebrooke frowned and gestured toward one of the chests against the wall before he replied. "There are manacles in there. Chain her up, then yourself."

"Do it yourself." Danielle turned to the fallen girl.

"I cannot chain you and hold a sword to your throat at the same time," impatience crept into his voice. "So if you insist on being unhelpful I shall bludgeon you into submission, then chain you once you are unconscious. So, I will ask again, please chain Bronwyn, then yourself."

Danielle breathed deeply as she collected her anger, and did as she was told. She dragged the heavy iron chains across the floor to the crumpled form of Killock's thief. *Or is she Danielle's thief now?*

Danielle knelt and Whitebrooke allowed her to examine Bronwyn for a moment. He was surprised to see that the blonde girl still lived. *At least for now. She must have been able to dodge away from the blast at the last moment. Astonishing.*

Once they were both chained, Whitebrooke tested the manacles and stepped away.

"That's better," Whitebrooke said reasonably.

"Why are you doing this?"

"I told you the truth, I did it for her." Whitebrooke smoothed his robes down. "My wife, my Aislin."

"Your wife?" Danielle asked, confused.

"Yes. She passed many years ago, long before you came to the north." Whitebrooke glanced at the unconscious girl on the floor. "Perhaps even before she was born. And I dedicated myself to discovering a way to return her to me."

"Fuil crunor," Danielle's voice was quiet.

"Not the fuil crunor rituals you have seen," Whitebrooke scowled. "But you are right in a way. And what I found I will use to reverse the trick that God played on all of us. With your help."

"You are insane." Danielle closed her eyes wearily. "What makes you think I will help you? I should have killed you."

"You will be glad you did not." Whitebrooke waited for a response, but she remained silent. "You will be glad."

Danielle ignored him. She carefully rested Bronwyn's head on her lap, and tenderly stroked a strand of hair out of the unconscious girl's face, gently tucking it behind her ear. A memory stirred deep within him, of brown curls passing under his own fingertips. But the memory twisted and once again there was blood on his fingers, and her head heavy in his hands. Whitebrooke felt anger spark. *Why do they not understand? Benno, Danielle… are they truly so blind?*

"Listen to me," Whitebrooke commanded, and Danielle raised her head and met his gaze. Her cheeks shone with tears but her golden eyes were fierce. "Listen to me," he repeated, his voice booming in the stone chamber. "God told us that the Maker gave us each a gift. But that is a lie. It is not a gift, it is a curse! The curse of mortality. The curse of death. This is the secret I discovered, all those years ago, the trick that God played on all of us. The Word of Life can undo that curse. It brings immortality, it conquers death. Imagine it… all of the pain, all of the loss, all of the waste… I will wipe it all away. A new age of humanity, deathless, immortal. And I will bring that gift to us. Do you not see it, my lady? Is it not a glorious future? Are you not glad that you failed to stop me?"

"I see that you have forgotten your wife," Danielle's voice was soft, but it burned with cold contempt.

"I have not forgotten. She is my reward, he promised…"

"A reward?" Danielle's words slashed across him. "You murder and kill for fame and glory, and then demand a reward? You should pray that she never returns to see what her husband has become."

"Murder?" Whitebrooke forced his words through clenched teeth. "They stood against me, when they could have helped. Ezekiel hid the knowledge from me, Benno forbade my research… God told me there was nothing He could do! He lied to me!"

"Revenge, greed." Danielle shook her head. "You are a small man whose petty evil has unleashed true horror upon us all." Danielle dropped her gaze and returned her attention to Bronwyn. Fury boiled through Whitebrooke, and he trembled with the urge to smash the defiance from Danielle's lovely face with his fists, and to watch her golden eyes as he snapped the blonde girl's neck with his powerful hands. *Then she will truly understand what it means to suffer.* But even more he wanted to carve their bodies, to trace jagged marks across their skin with blood and torn flesh, and see the bitch's face as she realized that their life, their gift, would feed his power.

Not yet, not yet, but soon, and he used the thought to slowly master his anger as he silently watched the noblewoman. Danielle carefully gathered the girl's blonde braid, and arranged it to lie elegantly across Bronwyn's neck and chest. Then Danielle gently wiped blood from the girl's lips and cheek, and cleaned away the grime that had streaked from the corners of her eyes.

"I will not help you," Danielle said quietly.

"You already have," Whitebrooke said brusquely. He walked to the Blade on the floor. "I had this. I needed its Word."

He picked up the Blade and held it up to the light, and turned to stare at Danielle. "And now I have that as well. Thanks to you, my lady. You spoke it beautifully."

"Va te faire foutre," Danielle's laugh was a groan.

"You have clearly absorbed your consort's delicate mouth." Whitebrooke let it pass him by. She was beneath him, petty. *Not so haughty now, my lady, are you?*

"First we will see if this Word actually works. Then we will see if you wish to remain defiant."

Whitebrooke strode from the room and quickly mounted the stairs to a higher level where Maeglin's soldiers awaited him.

"I have caught two of the prisoners, trying to escape through the drains. Return them to their cells," he instructed the knight who led the soldiers. "But touch nothing. They were conducting ritual magic down there."

The soldiers hurried down the stairs as Whitebrooke returned to his rooms and barred the door behind him.

He held the Blade to the light from the windows and examined it reverently. The Blade was beautiful, straight for most of its length with a gradual taper to a fine point at its tip. Both edges were razor-sharp. It was far longer than an infantry sword, yet not as massive as a cavalry sword, a strange size, but one that felt comfortable in his hands. The Blade's metal was deeply whorled and made the outer surface seem translucent, as if it were an opening into a pool deeper than the Blade's actual width.

Whitebrooke watched the whorls twist in the light as he held the Word in his mind. It was like no Word he had ever encountered. It was an onerous task to hold the shining constellation all at once. As he focused on one part, the other elements became hazy and indistinct. He tried again, anchoring the Word with his will, and let it flow into the Blade, but it fragmented and tore apart as it passed from him.

A tinge of concern brushed against his throat. He had not considered that he would not be able to master the Blade's Word. His skill with Devices was unparalleled in the Temple, and the reason the Council appointed him Archivist. Yet this Word, he could not hold.

Whitebrooke breathed deeply and calmed himself. *It is a matter of practice, that's all. She has had the Blade for years, I, for mere moments.* But he did not have time for practice.

Whitebrooke encased the Word in his powerful will once again, and locked the Word in place as if it were within a steel trap. Every piece rigid, every piece welded in place. Sweat beaded across his brow as he tried to contain its complexity, and unleash it into the Blade. For the briefest of moments the Blade pulsed with silver light, but then the Word fragmented and drifted through his focus like sand.

But it was there… however briefly it was there. All I need to do is master it. Which means I do not need Danielle any more.

Whitebrooke was relieved. Keeping Danielle alive was a risk. Someone on the Council would eventually start to listen to her and ask questions that Whitebrooke could not afford to answer. The sooner she was gone the better.

***

The horse thundered along the Rathad an Sliabh as it serpentined from the thick forests toward the great mountain, and thick foam gathered around its bit. Reverend Whitebrooke sat astride the splendid, pale stallion, his ornate robes covered by a thick cloak that trailed and flapped in his wake. Grim knights rode with him, heavy in steel armor as they urged their mounts to greater speed.

The horses' hooves clattered on the stone cobbles of the road as they raced around another switchback, and Whitebrooke caught a glimpse of towering, grey cliffs that soared behind the clouds. *I am close now.*

The knights fell back at his command and he rode on alone.

Ahead, the road leveled and the cliffs pressed on all sides. Whitebrooke reined in as the entrance to the Mountain appeared before him through the mist, and the horse slid to a stop on the icy stones and crusted snow. Whitebrooke dismounted and held the Bishop's ring before him. He whispered its Word and the ring quietly pulsed in response.

The enormous doors to Sliabh Mór shook the ground as they swung open at his command. Slowly they pulled apart and bright light spilled from them onto the snow-covered ground at their base.

Whitebrooke stepped through the doors and entered Sliabh Mór. The hall was empty, bare and hushed. Whitebrooke's boots rang harshly on the stone floor and echoed down the tunnels. Tall statues framed the entrance, their serene faces watching over those who entered the Mountain, their long shadows climbing up the wall and across the vast ceiling.

He stopped in the center of the hall and waited for the guard dog.

She did not keep him long. Footsteps of metal on stone rang out, growing louder as she strode purposefully towards him. He faced the sound and took a deep breath to ready himself. He had never tested himself against such a foe, and the Templar's legend unnerved him as it loomed in the back of his mind.

Rúreth stepped into the hall, tall and silver, a stern expression on her face as she came to a halt opposite him.

"Whitebrooke?" Rúreth's voice rang from the stone walls. "Why have you entered the Mountain?"

The Martyr's Blade pulled free of its sheath with a whisper, and he raised his ornate amulet on its steel chain in his other hand.

"Stand aside, Templar," Whitebrooke challenged her. "I have no quarrel with you."

Rúreth dropped the visor on her silver helm in reply, and readied her spear. "If you seek to harm Him, you have a quarrel with me."

"So be it." Whitebrooke raised his Weapon in response.

Rúreth spoke her Word and her spear pulsed with silver fire. Whitebrooke replied with a Word of his own, and he felt the bindings within his Wardpact open and fill the air around him.

Rúreth screamed a challenge and launched herself at him, and her spear blazed a silver trail from its point. It crashed against his Ward, which rippled orange with the strain. A flash cracked like lightning from where the spear touched the Ward, and a blast knocked the Archivist from his feet and sprawled him across the floor.

Whitebrooke scrambled to his feet, and was shocked to see Rúreth advancing toward him again. Her spear oozed smoke along its length as if it came fresh from the smith's fire, but it had not shattered, and was otherwise unaffected by the power of his Ward.

He was not as fortunate. His Ward was gone, its energy spent, ripped apart by the Templar's spear.

Rúreth closed with him and struck before he could ready another Word. Her spear swept in a vicious arc across his chest and he barely brought the Blade up to parry in time. He lunged at her in riposte but she spun away from the thrust easily. Her spear knocked the Blade aside, and a thundering kick to his midriff sent him staggering backwards again.

The Templar leapt in pursuit. The spear thrust at him, quick as a snake's strike, and again his parry barely deflected it in time. The spear tip wavered in front of his face like a twisting leaf, slashed across his shoulder, ripped cloth, dug through the steel rings underneath, and scored his flesh in a long gash.

Whitebrooke bellowed and countered with the Blade. Its perfect edge cut air as Rúreth dodged back, then cleaved through the shining steel of her shield as she blocked his second swing. A thrust of the spear jammed painfully into the thick steel plate over his chest and the Templar danced away from the reach of the Blade.

Whitebrooke raised his Wardpact again, his gloved fingers fumbling in their haste as he raced desperately through its Word. Rúreth reacted quickly and plunged forward, her spear flashing out as if shot from a bow. The Word roared through his mind even as the spear streaked across the last gap toward him.

But Whitebrooke's Word did not form the Wardpact's energy into a shell. This time it channeled the Device's power away from Whitebrooke. A tremendous concussion ripped through the floor. The ground shattered explosively as the shockwave screamed outwards, filling the air with shards of splintered stone.

The power passed through the air as well, a distortion that fled the amulet as fast as thought, a blur barely seen. When it passed the spear, the Weapon twisted, shook, and splintered as if it was glass struck by a hammer. The pulse found Rúreth an instant later. Armor tore, blood sprayed, and the Templar was batted aside like a doll.

Echoes from the impact shook dust from the ceiling, and the wide face of a pillar sheared free, crashed to the floor, and shattered into countless pieces.

Whitebrooke rose to his feet. Rúreth pushed herself to a knee as a long moan of rage and pain escaped her. Blood and dirt stained her shining armor, and one leg twisted grotesquely underneath her. She discarded her mangled shield and limped to face the priest, the broken remains of her spear held like a sword in one hand.

"You cannot hope to defeat me now, Templar," Whitebrooke's voice rolled magnanimously across the destroyed floor. "Join me instead. Renounce the false god and join me. Do not sacrifice your flame for a lie."

"I'm not planning on sacrificing myself today," Rúreth's voice oozed contempt. "Least of all to a traitorous bastard like you."

"Very well," Whitebrooke ground the words between his teeth.

He approached her cautiously, Blade held ready. Her first thrust ripped his robes along his forearm, but she hissed in pain through clenched teeth and staggered from her thrust, unable to follow her attack.

Whitebrooke began a methodical, careful attack. He stayed at the full reach of the Blade, and used heavy, sweeping blows that were difficult to block with a broken bit of spear. Rúreth was forced to move, and her leg betrayed her. The Blade raked across her breastplate, then tore a twisted pauldron free. Rúreth gathered her will, lunged, and the attack slid home between two of the steel plates over Whitebrooke's ribs, but her leg buckled with the strain and she fell awkwardly.

Whitebrooke struck quickly, even as pain blossomed from his side. The Blade flashed silver in a long arc and fell onto Rúreth's arm, just below the shoulder. The heavy edge tore through the silver steel and sliced deep through muscle and bone, and Rúreth gasped in agony as her spear fell from useless fingers.

Blood poured from her shattered right arm, the mail twisted and ruined, and her leg trailed uselessly behind her. Still she strove to stand on her remaining leg, pushing with her last strength to lever herself upright.

Whitebrooke knocked her to the ground with a kick, and sheathed the Blade. Rúreth struggled to roll onto her back, and drew a long dagger with her left hand, but Whitebrooke simply stood on her wrist, and ground with his boot until her fingers spasmed open.

He knelt upon her arm, and grasped her breastplate firmly to hold her still. A small iron knife appeared in his hand, and he began to saw the leather straps from her armor. Her struggles were weak now, her strength flowing into the rapidly growing pool of blood on the floor. Whitebrooke worked quickly, and pulled her armor free.

"There will be a sacrifice, after all," he taunted her, and a grim smile of satisfaction crossed his face.

"Glory to the Maker and all the Maker's creations," she intoned, her voice strong and sure despite her pain. Her eyes opened and found his. "Do your worst. Soon I will be at the Maker's side. And I will be waiting for you."

He began his chant, the tortuous words of fuil crunor twisting and scoring his throat as he cut the ritual markings into Rúreth's abdomen. She renewed her struggle, but he continued his work, his strength too great for her weakened state.

Her cries faded to soft animal noises as his chant reached its crescendo, and he brought the knife across her throat and finished her.

A cold wind blew across him as shadows leached from her wounds and twisted around the priest. Their cold fire seethed with energy that flooded his body and mind, and he closed his eyes and let the sensation fill him.

He drank in the shadows until Rúreth's corpse was nothing but a withered husk on the floor. Then he rose to his feet and faced the long passageway into the Mountain. In that direction lay the deepest door that never opened. Whitebrooke knew He would wait there now.

The room was dim, the fire unlit, the only light from scattered lanterns around the walls.

"You disappoint me," the Voice rumbled through the room and echoed from the stone walls. "All the pain you have caused, all the suffering. So much you have corrupted. All for the sake of vainglory."

"No, not for glory, or power." Whitebrooke faced the imposing doors at the far end of the sanctuary, and hurled his words at the stone. "I asked you once to pierce the shroud, to bring back one who has crossed over. Do you remember what you told me?"

"I told you I could not."

"That's right, you told me, 'No'." Whitebrooke's mouth contorted with rage. "You lied to me!"

"You do not know of what you speak."

"I know enough!" Whitebrooke shouted defiance. The echoes faded as he glared at the stone door. "All I wanted was Aislin to return to me. You say it was glory that drove me, but it was never for glory. And you told me that no way existed."

"Her death was cruel," the Voice wrapped around Whitebrooke and pulsed in the stone. "But it would be crueler to deny her place with the Maker."

"And what of the Word of Life?" Whitebrooke challenged. "You denied me, you lied to me, and all the time you knew."

"You know only what the Lord of the Abyss has told you," the deep Voice rumbled through the Archivist. "And his words bear little resemblance to the truth."

"I know the truth about you, of what you truly are. I know his truth as well, and that you lie when you name him. I know the truth about the Word of Life." Whitebrooke let the Blade slide from its sheath. The Voice did not reply. "He said that you would fear this Blade, and I see that is also the truth."

"I do fear it, but not for the reasons you think," the Voice rolled through the room.

"Why did you conceal the Word of Life from me?" Whitebrooke shook his head in sorrow. "We could do so much good with it. Not just for Aislin, but for everyone. But instead you kept it from us!" Whitebrooke raged. "You kept it from me! You kept it from her!"

Whitebrooke let the echoes from his voice die away, and slowly he positioned the sword in front of him. "You profess to care and love us, yet leave us to wither in illness, bleed in battle and utterly, ultimately perish."

"I do, though it pains me grievously. The power of the Word of Life is eternity, that is true, but it pales next to the gift of mortality. The Nameless King is evil, do not listen to his words."

Whitebrooke shook his head. He had known what this creature who called himself a god would say. His lord had predicted it, every word. Whitebrooke had hoped to discover otherwise. He had spent so many years in service to the Temple, he did not want the service to have been a lie. *But there is no mistake, is there? No gleam of misunderstanding that could pardon your crimes.*

"Enough." Whitebrooke's voice rang flat and harsh across the room. "You know what I have come for, give it to me."

"Yes, I know what you seek. Here it is."

A tremor shook the floor as hidden mechanisms rumbled into motion, and a sharp crack echoed through the chamber as the deepest door began to open for the first time since the founding of the Mountain.

A ghostly point of light appeared beyond the door. It pulsed and waned, as if black curtains blew in an unfelt wind. The light was grey, then blue, then bright silver as it throbbed, and Whitebrooke saw that it emanated from a thick mist in the shape of a sphere no more than the size of his fist. Within the mist was a core of darkness. It pulsed to its own rhythm, surfacing as a black stain as the mist grew thin, then submerging as the light grew stronger.

The light moved. It swayed and came closer, higher than a man is tall. As it neared, Whitebrooke became aware of a massive shape behind it that moved closer with the light. The shape grew clear as it approached. It towered over the priest, twice his height and in the form of a man. Yet as it emerged from the shadows Whitebrooke could see that it was not a man.

Pale skin, light as alabaster, flawlessly beautiful yet as seemingly lifeless as a stone statue, hairless and smooth. Black eyes smoldered like hot coals. It eschewed clothing for it had no need of it. Although the shape had a man's form, it was not birthed from mortal stock.

The glowing light was imbedded in the center of the pale chest. As its misty form pulsed, ripples of energy throbbed under the white skin.

"You think you know me," the Voice boomed. "Learn that you do not. Learn that my name is Tempest, my voice is Thunder, my will is Cyclone. Know that I am Céledùn, Keeper of the Word."

The Archivist's powerful mind roared out and flooded into his Wardpact. The Device blurred into motion and golden light shone forth to surround the priest.

Inhuman words thundered and rolled through the room, crashed against stone, and impacted with incredible force against Whitebrooke's Ward. The world grew dim and muffled, and the golden light pulsed a sickly red.

Whitebrooke felt sweat pour from his body. He had never dreamed of such a force, such an elemental power. His Ward bent and tore under the assault as if it were gossamer cobwebs.

Whitebrooke began to chant the fuil crunor, the words glass in his throat, and they sounded weak and indecisive against the thunder of Céledùn. But the power he had taken from Rúreth rushed forth eagerly, and emerged as shadows that swirled around his fingertips, their frozen touch a chill caress. He altered his chant and the shadows tore open a path to the Abyss, a rift that twisted and writhed in the air of the chamber. A dreadful hunger throbbed from the rift, an emptiness that craved the life that Whitebrooke had ripped from the Templar, and it sucked the power from him in tendrils of shadow that streamed through the rift and into the Abyss.

Whitebrooke let it pass from him gladly.

Gaping cracks radiated across his Ward, and his mind twisted under the pressure as he tried to reinforce his Word to hold for one more moment of searing agony. White pain burned between his eyes, and a cry burst from him as he clung to the last shreds of his Ward.

As his foe descended upon him, a presence entered the chamber from the Abyss. Tall and thin, it shifted as if seen through a flickering fire as it passed through the rift, then became solid as it stepped forth. It no longer appeared as a shade. A man stood before the massive form of Céledùn, and the life he had absorbed from the Bishop and the Templar gave strength and flesh and power to his form. He wore armor of black and gold, and a sable cape embroidered with seven stars. A golden crown set with seven shining gems rested on his brow.

Whitebrooke crawled to his knees, unaware that he had fallen. *My king.*

He wielded a magnificent silver sword, so like the Martyr's Blade that it could be its twin, and it blurred through the dim light of the chamber as he closed with the Keeper.

They strove against one another and the chamber shuddered. Pale fire licked from the silver sword and was answered by thunder. Again they clashed, and stone cracked and fell, shattered, to the floor.

A terrible storm filled the chamber, driving the priest to the floor. Tongues of flame leapt into the air, clouds of smoke billowed from the battle, and thunder smote the stone. The King's fire engulfed Céledùn, and the Keeper was burned, but his words tore the flame into ragged streams and Céledùn threw his enemy back. The King cried out in ringing command and dark shadows entwined Céledùn and stained his skin as if a foul plague had infested his flesh.

But the Keeper's voice was greater, and answered. Shadow streamed from the King as if strong wind tore snow from a high mountain ridge, and his fire fluttered and was extinguished.

Whitebrooke held the Blade before him. Its Word gleamed in his mind. He brought his will to bear on it, and his mind burned as he branded the Word into place. It shifted and blurred but he would not be denied. His mind shrieked in agony as he held the Word together by will, and forced it into the Blade.

Power blazed within the metal. Brilliant white light coursed along its length and burned through his arms and he cried out in pain and shock. Whorls of flame cascaded across his skin as the power filled him. Whitebrooke strode forward and struck Céledùn, and flames encircled the Keeper in a vortex of fire that licked across his burned and shadow-blackened skin. Céledùn fell to a knee, a groan of agony shaking the very mountain, and collapsed beneath the flames.

The shade stood nearby, once again gossamer in the Blade's light, its power consumed. Whitebrooke could still see its eyes, strong and demanding, and there was movement as it beckoned him closer.

"There is the Word you seek," the shade's voice was soothing. "Free it."

The Blade's light fell upon Céledùn's face and he closed his black eyes and lay back, as if content. Then Whitebrooke swung the Blade high above his head and plunged it into the swirling light in the Keeper's chest.

The Blade tore the mist apart. Smoky strands curled around the Blade and disappeared as the fire consumed them. The dark heart within was revealed. Its surface shimmered like oil in the Blade's light and ripples crossed its surface as the heat of the Blade drew near it. Whitebrooke pulled the Blade back, as he had been instructed, and waited.

The heart pulsed and contorted, free of its misty shell, and burst into a thousand half-glimpsed shapes that whirled into the air. As they rose from Céledùn they clung to his skin like drops of water, only to reluctantly pull away as they streamed into the air. With their passing, a vast sigh filled the room, a rush of ancient breath that escaped the slain god.

The swarm fled the light of the Blade and coursed through the chamber as they sought the Abyss. Whitebrooke watched them go and listened as the shade whispered welcome to them.

Then the Blade's fire flickered and expired, and Whitebrooke collapsed to his knees, unable to hold its power any longer. Pain throbbed cruelly through his mind as every thought seared a burning trail behind it. He sat, unable to move, as the rift he had created slowly collapsed into itself. The shade called to him from its depths with promises and praise.

Eventually he found the strength to rise to his feet and leave the room. He could not look at the still form of the great guardian he had called God that lay broken on the floor. The pain in his mind would not recede, but he pushed it aside as he staggered down the long passageways.

Frozen air blew through the open doors and scattered snow across the floor. The chill wind revived his seared body and he leaned on one of the enormous doors as he took deep breaths to steady himself.

From where he stood he could see Loughliath spread out under him to the southeast, its grey waters dull and flat under the heavy clouds. The forested hills of Cnoic Bán rolled southward, each ripple lower and gentler as they drew farther from the towering peak above him. Somewhere far out of sight beyond them the grey hill of Bandirma awaited his return to lead the Temple into a new age. They would mourn the passing of their false God, but he would show them a new God, one that truly loved them.

He pressed his forehead against the cold stone as he looked out at the world, and tried to numb the pain.

Tuireadh Cnoc

The steep, craggy hill stood covered in short grasses and bare rock where the winds had scoured the thin soil. Its crown was a bald dome, long weathered to smoothness by rain and snow, but deep gullies with sharp ridges covered its sides, torn by hundreds of tiny streams that wept from the summit. Goats occasionally roamed the lower gullies in their search for thistles, but none made the long climb to the top and its meager fare.

No villages or farmsteads lay in the valley beneath the hill. It loomed over a broad curve in a wide stream that would suit fields or a mill, but only open meadows and small clumps of oak and ash trees spread before it, frosted white by snow and ice. No one lived within sight of the hill.

Four trails passed beneath the flanks of the hill, a crossroads dictated by geography rather than desire. The trails were no more than simple tracks, deeply rutted and filled with icy mud in the winter wet, and marked by small cairns to stop travelers from wandering into the meadows by accident. At the crossroads, rock walls had been built, the loose stones framing the intersection. A signpost stood lonely and bare, its tines pointing mutely down each trail, its boards long since rotted into pulp in the tangled blackberry bushes at its feet.

An ancient oak tree also stood at the crossroads, its gnarled limbs bare and black against the winter sky. Dozens of ravens perched in the tree and watched the trails, croaking and cawing as the chill wind ruffled their feathers and knocked the branches together.

As midday approached the ravens spied a rider on the western trail and greeted him with a chorus of harsh calls. The rider's magnificent black warhorse jogged easily along the track, its head high, its long tail and mane shining like black fire in the grey winter light. The rider was clad in unadorned, black enameled armor that creaked against its leather straps as he moved, and underneath he wore a thick, black tunic lined with sable against the cold. A black cloak lined on the inside with a shocking white ermine draped across his shoulders and across his horse's flanks. A heavy blade was sheathed at his side.

He rode with his hood pushed back and his head bare. His hair was a pale blonde, cut crudely short, and he had a strong face with wide cheekbones and narrowed eyes that sent fierce crows' feet spidering from their corners, and a mouth that rested naturally in a stern line. He was clean-shaven, his pale skin red across the cheeks in the chill air.

The knight guided his horse through the crossroads and past the chorus of ravens to head toward the hill. Up the steep flanks he rode until the horse could no longer find a path, and he dismounted and led the stallion up the final ridge to the crest.

Wind wafted his pale hair and swept his cloak to the south as he surveyed the top of the hill. It was called Tuireadh Cnoc in the old tongue, named after the henge of standing stones that encircled the top. No one knew who had placed the stones there, but they had stood since long before any of the kingdoms or peoples who now called Albyn home. Their massive shapes were smooth and bulbous, as if wax had melted across their tops to leave strange pits and divots in their surface. Some had eroded until they were nubs, while others stood taller than a man.

Seventy-one stones completed the outer circle, while another seventeen stood close together in the inner circle.

The knight in black approached one of the largest stones of the outer ring and settled there to wait. His horse cropped the short grass as the knight watched the trails. At dusk he covered the horse with a thick blanket and filled a feedbag with oats, then settled against the stone and wrapped himself in his bedroll against the freezing wind. No fire would burn on the top of Tuireadh Cnoc even if he had the wood to attempt one.

At dawn he resumed his vigil, crouched at the edge of the hill as he carefully shaved his face clean with a small steel razor. As the last of the pale whiskers were scraped away a figure appeared on the trail from the west, a rider who followed the same path that the knight had taken the day before.

The newcomer was powerfully built through the chest, shoulders, and arms, and heavy in the stomach and face. His hair was long and black and flowed across his shoulders from under his thick steel helm. Dark eyes stared from within, wide and penetrating, as if the rider could see far past the outer skin and deep into the inner thoughts and spirit. Heavy lips surrounded a wide mouth that showed little emotion as he led his grey stallion onto the top of the hill to join the knight. He wore grey armor, elaborately engraved across the breastplate and shoulders with dragon symbols patterned after the gods of the Ironback clans, and a thick-bladed sword was sheathed at his side.

The two men greeted each other and clasped hands, but said little else. The rider in grey removed his helm and let his hair stream with the wind as he joined watch with the rider in black.

Before midday two more riders appeared together on the trail from the south. They too made the long, winding trek up the hill and joined the two waiting men.

The first of the pair was a slender, beautiful woman with exquisite features and an oval face, large, dark eyes and deep red lips. Her hair was as black as a raven's breast, and silver beads shone from its depths.

She wore a long dress of a deep, muted red, accented with swirls of a richer red. Golden lace hemmed it, and a heavy amulet of a dark green metal rested against her skin beneath the hollow of her neck. An embroidered cloak hung from her shoulders, black with patterns of red woven across it.

The fourth rider was a tall man, elegant in a long, green tunic. He had a handsome face, with a strong jaw and cheekbones carved as if from marble, and a patrician nose with an arrogant slope to it. His hair was short and dark and precisely groomed with a feathering of grey around the temples, and he wore a trim mustache and goatee. Soft leather boots and leggings covered his legs, and a warm fur cloak was fastened around his shoulders.

They too greeted the previous riders and clasped hands, and now conversation filled the air as they waited, comfortable and familiar, but muted, as if all four riders bore a heavy weight on their shoulders.

The final rider appeared near dusk and from the north. Mud splashed under the hooves of his chestnut stallion as it galloped down the trail. A worn grey cloak streamed behind him, and his wiry frame was encased in a threadbare grey tunic and coat. His iron-colored hair was cut short and he wore several weeks' worth of scraggly beard on a face whose deep lines seemed permanently set into a squint against wind and sun.

He quickly reached the top of the hill and greeted the others who waited for him.

"Killock," the knight in black said curtly as he grasped him by the arm. "I was sorry to hear of Bradon."

"He will be missed," agreed the lady, and she brushed her lips against Killock's wind-burned cheeks and held his gaze for a moment as a sad smile played across her mouth.

The man in green greeted Killock warmly as well, with an embrace and a sincere "I am glad to see you."

The large man in grey armor simply nodded his head in greeting, his face a mask as his eyes probed Killock's.

"We all felt the summons, Killock, and now nothing for many days," the man's voice was deep and sonorous. "Rumors of your quest with Lord Bradon have also reached me, and it seems the tidings are grim."

"You are right, Faron, they are," agreed Killock. He scuffed the toe of his boot into the tough grass, then raised his eyes to meet each of the other four as he continued. "As grim as can be. A portal has opened under the High Fells, and deep within it we encountered a magus and its undead minions. Lady Danielle was able to defeat it, but not before Lord Bradon fell to its shadow."

"This threat, does it continue?" the knight in black asked, his voice steel sliding across steel. He rested his hands on the pommel of his sword as if his foe might appear before him at any moment. "Is this why we Templars are summoned?"

"The threat is far from passed." Killock shook his head. "I fear we have only felt its opening move."

"And the news from Bandirma?" the lady asked, her eyes wide with concern as she glanced around the group.

"I am sorry, Lady Rowenna, I haven't been near a temple in many days," Killock replied, and it was clear that of the group only the man in the green tunic knew of what she was referring.

"We stopped at the temple in Littleford, and there was a bird." She glanced at her companion. "The message said that there was a battle with a magus in Bandirma, and that Bishop Benno was killed."

"That cannot be true," said the knight in black angrily. "A magus in Bandirma?"

"The messages were very clear, Roland," the tall man in the green tunic replied smoothly, unperturbed by the knight's ire. "Both Sir Maeglin and Reverend Whitebrooke confirmed it. Apparently it was that strange man from the royal court, Hali, I think his name is."

"Then Benno is truly dead?" Killock looked stunned.

"I'm afraid it seems so," the tall man replied.

Silence overwhelmed the group as each considered the news. Killock stared southward across the long valley, his eyes unseeing as his mind turned inward. Roland stood with jaw clenched and coldness in his glare, while Rowenna and the man in the green tunic stood close, patient in their grief.

Faron observed them all, his deep, brown eyes calm as his gaze moved over them. He raised his hands outwards to include them all. "Come, my friends," he said, his voice honey poured over thunder. "It is not seemly for us to let sadness tear at our hearts, not when our brother stands beside the Maker. Let our grief instead fill our hearts with a thirst for vengeance against those who dishonored him and took him from us too soon."

"Yes, you are right, Faron." Roland nodded his head.

"Vengeance, and justice, and perhaps some retribution as well, absolutely," the man in the green tunic said, and his mouth curled into something far from a smile. "His black heart torn from his chest and fed to the pigs, poor creatures. I'm sure Bishop Benno would laugh in joy at the thought."

"Gwydion, don't be so cruel," said Rowenna, annoyed. "Of course Benno would not want any of this, but he wouldn't hesitate to do what needed to be done, even if it was hard."

"No of course he wouldn't, my dear," said Gwydion. "'Kill 'em all!' he'd cry."

"Gwydion!" anger flared in Rowenna's voice and she stomped her foot. "Don't be such an ass."

"Would you have us do nothing against this Hali then?" Roland asked Gwydion, incredulously.

"Not at all." Gwydion bared his teeth in another humorless smile. "I *crave* the chance to kill him. I *relish* the thought of watching him burn on a pyre for what he did. But I am not *simple* enough to think that will lighten my heart or return a murdered friend."

"Let that feed your fire." Faron clenched his fist and held it up fiercely. "Let it forge you anew into a tool for justice."

"Don't worry about me, Faron," Gwydion laughed and nodded his head. "I'll be standing right beside you."

"Good." Faron nodded his head, satisfied.

Roland's voice was steel. "How could one man have triumphed over so many great and powerful minds?"

"Well," answered Gwydion, "the message also said that Lady Danielle was to be captured on sight, and returned to Bandirma to face charges of murder for her part in Reverend Benno's death."

Killock turned to the others, shock written clearly across his face for an instant before his expression went absolutely blank.

"I... see," was all he said.

"I thought you might find that interesting," said Gwydion.

"Gwydion, are you saying that Lady Danielle aided in the murder of the Bishop?" Roland's face grew dark.

"I am saying that Whitebrooke's message said that." Gwydion shrugged his shoulders eloquently. "I think it's bullshit."

"But you believe the rest of the message," Faron's deep voice was a statement.

"I do, actually," Gwydion conceded with a sigh. "I believe Maeglin, as much as I despise that tiresome man."

"A disaster," Roland stated. "The Crunorix returned, the Bishop murdered, and a member of the Queen's court accused. Bandirma needs us there now."

"What say you, Killock?" Faron asked.

Killock stared over the valley below them for another moment before he turned to face the others.

"I don't believe it," said Killock, his voice icy resolve. "I don't believe the story we are told."

"Yes," Faron agreed, and a small smile flickered across his lips.

"The magus we encountered," continued Killock as he worked his way through his thoughts. "Very powerful, yes, but it was hidden. The rituals, its lair, all secret, all concealed in the shadows, as far away as possible. Everything crafted for it to stay hidden and grow ever more powerful. And now we are to believe that the Crunorix priest responsible decided to walk into Bandirma and confront us in our seat of power?"

"Who is to say how the Crunorix might think?" said Roland. "Perhaps he was desperate? Perhaps he was insane?"

"Both are certainly true," said Gwydion, and a wry grin flashed across his perfect, white teeth. "But I see what Killock is saying. The Crunorix takes the greatest of pains to remain in the shadows, and then throws all of that away just to murder one man?"

"And as for desperate, why?" Killock frowned as a new thought came to him. "We had no idea who he was, so why reveal himself at all?"

"If he was discovered, or for some reason we cannot discern," Rowenna ventured. "Perhaps he just sought to cause strife amongst ourselves, or to distract us as he licks his own wounds."

"True," agreed Killock. "Yet those aims he could have achieved just as well at any time. The timing of the attack, so soon after Danielle's return to Bandirma, speaks loudest to me. Perhaps she learned the truth, or some knowledge she brought with her revealed him."

"*That* would be a reason to act desperately," agreed Faron. "*That* is a story that is believable."

"But if it was not Karsha Hali, then who?" Rowenna asked.

"When we find Danielle, we can ask her," Killock replied.

"When we find… what makes you think she hasn't been captured already?" Roland scowled. "Or that we could find her if the rangers could not?"

"I asked someone to take care of Danielle, and I know she would not fail," Killock spoke quietly, but there was steel in his voice. "But she needs my help, and I must not fail her. I will find them."

"We need to go to Bandirma," Gwydion pointed out. "To find out what actually happened, who is actually alive, who may or may not be a Crunorix. As well as the start of Danielle's trail."

"Yes," agreed Killock. "And we must be cautious or else we risk ending up like Benno and Bradon."

"Let's not do that," agreed Gwydion.

"Someone should go to the Mountain," Rowenna suggested. "Surely He must have advice for us, and Rúreth is there as well. We could use her help."

"I do not think any of us should travel alone," said Roland. "Not if what Killock has said is in any way true."

"We can go then," Gwydion indicated Rowenna and himself.

"Good," agreed Roland. "Join us in Bandirma as soon as you can. I cannot stand to have this murderous bastard alive for one more day than is necessary."

The other Templars nodded grimly, quickly readied their mounts, and descended the hill. They broke into a gallop as they reached the eastern trail and flew across the valley to disappear into the thick forest that bordered it.

Epilogue

Bran perched high atop the tall, thin tower. Cold wind ruffled his feathers and he preened them into place with his sharp bill as he watched the endless stream of pigeons flapping frantically to and from the tower. The raven had spent the morning tormenting the pigeons, but it was no longer interesting.

He tilted his head back and forth as he directed his gleaming eye across the massive hill that reared above the tower, the frosted buildings that spread along the foaming river at the base of the tower, and the wide, wind-whipped surface of the lake.

It was too early for fish to be unloaded at the docks, nor was there any corn being sold in the market. For a time it had been interesting to watch all of the people scurry about the walls and courtyards, in such numbers that Bran cawed to them in excitement, but that was no longer interesting either, and the raven sought new things to catch his eye.

An image of tall towers perched on the side of a snow-covered mountain tickled the raven's thoughts, but he shook out his wings and cawed angrily, and the image faded. The towers were far away, he knew, and he wanted to see something closer.

Bran launched from his perch and swooped close to a small person in a brown robe who was trying to feed the pigeons. The person squawked and dropped his bowl of grain, and the raven gobbled as much as he could before more people came to wave at him with long, bushy sticks. The raven cawed in triumph and soared from the tower, his wings slapping the cold air as he climbed into the sky.

He was soon high above the grey stone hill and its towers, and the raven threw out his wings and cawed loudly as the wind caught him. He circled ever higher, until he reached the underbelly of the icy clouds. He followed the wind at first, too lazy after his climb to fight with the spirits of the air.

The river twisted beneath him, a grey snake that reflected the clouds as it curved around the dark hills. The raven disdained to follow the river's course, preferring to let the wind carry him across crest and valley uncaring of the undulations of the land beneath him.

Bran spotted something interesting on one of the river's meanders, and swooped lower. There upon the river the raven saw a small boat that spread its brown sail and flew through the water as if it dared to race the wind. The raven cried a challenge to the boat and sped past it, but the person steering the boat paid the raven no attention. The raven was disappointed, but as he soared away from the river he knew that he should not be surprised, for the boat was guided by a raven person, with hair as dark as his own feathers, and such a person would not be easy to torment.

Find us more, the tickle in the raven's thoughts asked, and Bran cawed in agreement and left the boat behind.

Northwards he flew then, swooping and beating his wings as he slipped through the wind. Thick forest darkened the hills he flew over, the trees heavy and dripping in the chill mist. The forest tried to conceal its secrets from the raven as he passed over it, but the raven was not fooled. He saw hunter and prey, ancient trees and new saplings, creatures and people. None of them interesting.

The hills began to grow taller, and steeper, and the trees on the ridges were dusted with white. To the east the raven could once again see the grey stone hill and its towers and walls, barely visible in the far distance through the chill mist.

A rider on a dappled grey mare raced through the forest along frost-rimed paths, urging the horse to ever greater speed as he crossed the last leagues towards the stone hill. Bran laughed at the rider, for the raven knew that the people the rider sought were no longer there. But Bran would not tell the rider the secret of where they were now, and he cawed loudly as he flew away.

More, the tickle whispered, and the raven flew on. Now he flew beside vast grey water, and the hills became sharp ridges rising towards towering mountain peaks covered in snow and ice. People clung to a small, twisting trail that wound its way into the clouds. One was injured, and the others clustered around him and helped him to his horse. Bran perched on a stone to watch the injured person suffer, which pleased the raven, and he hoped that the person would die so that the raven could feast on his juicy flesh, for the raven detested the person.

The person did not die, and rode down the trail with most of the people in attendance.

But some of the people rode higher, and the raven followed them to a door that he had never seen beyond, no matter how hard he had tried. Now the door stood open, but Bran did not want to go inside. He screamed angrily and hopped from one foot to the other in frustration, but he could not bring himself to enter the dark shadows beyond the wide portal.

The raven flew spitefully at the faces of the people who had come to the door, and felt some satisfaction as the people cursed and ducked.

Never mind, the tickle told the raven. *There is more to find.*

Bran was weary now, and the lure of the white towers began to pull more strongly on his thoughts. He turned his tail on the dark mountain, the endless water and the grey stone hill and flew towards the northwest, day after day, resting only when the world was too dark for him to find anything interesting.

The raven crossed rolling hills and twisting streams. Now Bran saw a long, undulating river of spears winding its way towards him on a road, thousands of shafts held skyward on the shoulders of people wearing heavy metal as they tramped the trail into mud. They bore pennants of brilliant white with thick, black markings crossed on them, and at their head rode a person as hard as steel.

The raven cawed a raucous salute to the steel person and pressed onwards.

He passed a bare hill standing in a wide valley, with dozens of ancient spirits standing upon it, frozen into stone thousands of years ago. Riders stood upon the hill as the raven passed over, and he swerved towards them and flew close to them so that he could see them clearly, for each and every one of them was interesting.

Then at last came a day when Bran saw ahead of him the white castle perched high on its mountain above a deep, forested valley. Buildings spread around the base of the castle's mountain and down the valley, with stone walls and stone roofs and stone paths between them. Snow fell thickly over the valley and the raven pushed through it, the wet flakes clinging to his feathers. Higher and higher the raven soared above the valley, until at last he reached the height of the white castle.

Long pennants swirled from the towers and the walls of the castle, brilliant white with black markings. Bran flapped wearily to the largest of the towers. He passed a wide balcony on which another raven person stood, pensively gazing southward as the snow made a white crown in her raven hair. The raven was too tired to land on the balcony and speak with the person, even though she sometimes gave him treats, and instead swerved to a small window in a turret that stuck from the side of the castle like a crooked finger. The window was open, and warm, yellow light spilled from it onto the window sill.

Bran landed on the sill heavily, his claws sinking into deep ruts in the wood that matched his grip perfectly.

Well done, the tickle praised him. Bran croaked indignantly in reply.

Of course, the tickle agreed, and held out a hand filled with corn. The raven croaked happily and gobbled the corn, for he knew there was plenty more.

"Very well done," the tickle said, and scratched the raven's breast. "Now, you will be very interested to hear what I have seen since last we spoke. Would you like to hear that story?"

***

No Coward Path

The story continues in Book 2, *No Coward Path.*
Coming soon…

About the Author

Joel Manners has created epic worlds and memorable characters in video games for more than 30 years. He brings his talent for storytelling to the epic fantasy genre in his debut novel, The Martyr's Blade. He lives in Austin, TX with his wife and two boys. And this dog his wife made them get, but honestly, she's pretty sweet. The dog. His wife too. Although he suspects that might change if she sees this.

Connect with Me
www.JoelManners.com

Made in the USA
Lexington, KY
13 September 2016